E. V. THOMPSON OMNIBUS

Ben Retallick

Chase the Wind

Also by E. V. Thompson

THE MUSIC MAKERS
THE DREAM TRADERS
CRY ONCE ALONE
BECKY
GOD'S HIGHLANDER
CASSIE
WYCHWOOD
BLUE DRESS GIRL
TOLPUDDLE WOMAN
LEWIN'S MEAD
MOONTIDE
CAST NO SHADOWS
SOMEWHERE A BIRD IS SINGING
WINDS OF FORTUNE
SEEK A NEW DAWN

The Retallick Saga

BEN RETALLICK
CHASE THE WIND
HARVEST OF THE SUN
SINGING SPEARS
THE STRICKEN LAND
LOTTIE TRAGO
RUDDLEMOOR
FIRES OF EVENING

The Jagos of Cornwall

THE RESTLESS SEA
POLRUDDEN
MISTRESS OF POLRUDDEN

As James Munro

HOMELAND

E. V. THOMPSON OMNIBUS

Ben Retallick
Chase the Wind

E. V. THOMPSON

timewarner paperbacks

A *Time Warner* Paperback

This omnibus edition first published in Great Britain by
Time Warner Paperbacks in 2002

Previously published separately:
Ben Retallick first published in Great Britain in 1980 by
Macmillan London Ltd
First paperbacked in 1982 by Pan Books Ltd
Published by Warner Books in 1998
Reprinted 2001

Chase the Wind first published in Great Britain in 1977 by
Macmillan London Ltd
First paperbacked in 1979 by Pan Books Ltd
Published by Warner Books in 1998
Reprinted 1999

A CIP catalogue record for this book is available from the British Library.

ISBN 0 7515 3300 9

Printed and bound in Great Britain by
Mackays of Chatham plc, Chatham, Kent

Time Warner Paperbacks
An imprint of
Time Warner Books UK
Brettenham House
Lancaster Place
London WC2E 7EN

www.TimeWarnerBooks.co.uk

Ben Retallick

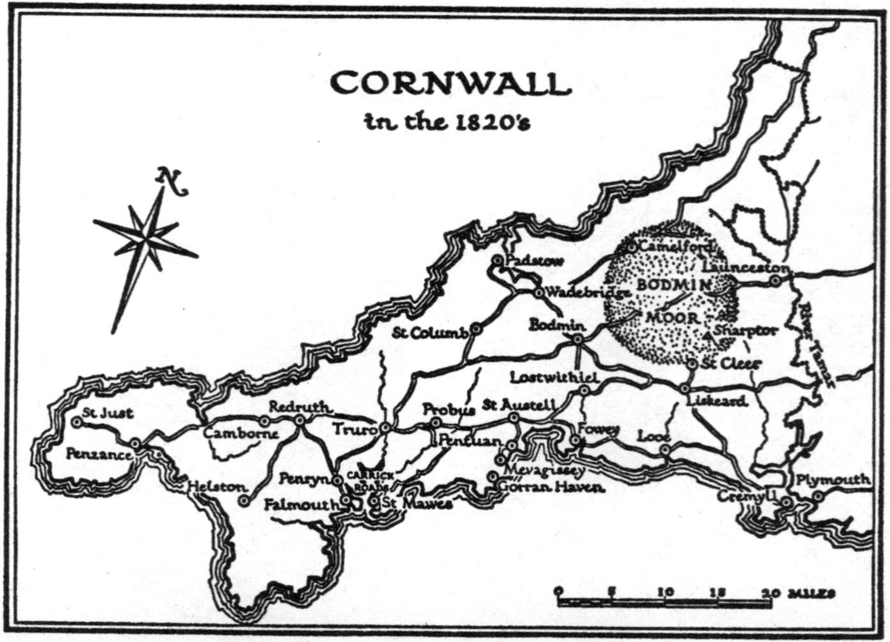
CORNWALL
in the 1820's
N
St Just
Penzance
Helston
Camborne
Redruth
Penryn
Falmouth
Truro
CARRICK ROADS
St Mawes
Probus
Pentuan
St Austell
Mevagissey
Gorran Haven
St Columb
Padstow
Wadebridge
Bodmin
Lostwithiel
Fowey
Looe
Liskeard
St Cleer
Sharptor
BODMIN
MOOR
Camelford
Launceston
River Tamar
Cremyll
Plymouth
0 5 10 15 20 MILES

Chapter One

It was bitterly cold at the surface of the cliff-edge Money Box mine. The night wind blew from the sea with an icy ferocity, and the waiting miners about the shaft huddled closer together, cursing those ahead of them for their tardiness in descending the creaking ladders to the underground levels.

The wind carried spray from the rocks at the foot of the cliff, and young Ben Retallick tasted salt on his lips as he stood shivering in a threadbare thin shirt and cheap serge trousers.

'How's your dad, boy?'

The question came from one of the men pressing close behind him. Ben could not see his face in the poor light.

'Not so good, but he says he'll be back to work as soon as he can breathe easier.'

'He'll not be working underground again. I've yet to know a man with tin dust in his lungs get better. Tell your ma to take him right away from the mines if she wants him with her for a few more years. There's many a place in Cornwall where he'll be able to breathe air as pure as the Lord made it. Hereabouts, the dust clings like a disease.'

Ben frowned in the darkness. His mother had been saying the same thing to his father for as long as he could remember.

Martha Retallick came from the south coast fishing-village of Mevagissey and desperately wanted to return there. Pearson Retallick would have none of it. He was a tinner, at home only amongst the engine-houses and mountains of mine waste in the far west of Cornwall.

All the same, Pearson Retallick's health had been deteriorating rapidly of late, and the time would soon be at hand when he would have to do what he was told. This latest bout of lung sickness could hardly have come at a worse time. Working a poor tin lode on a high rate of tribute – or commission – Pearson Retallick and his partner had unexpectedly struck it rich: the poor-quality lode had suddenly opened out into a wide seam of ore. The two men needed to take out as much of it as they could before the next bidding-day. At that time the pitch they were working would be reassessed by the mine captain and auctioned off to the miner who was prepared to work it at the lowest rate of tribute.

The fire-doors in the engine-house of the nearby Botallack mine opened momentarily, throwing a red glow to the sky. In the unnatural light Ben saw the empty shaft of the Money Box mine yawning below him. Swinging on to the wooden-runged ladder, he began the climb down.

It was warmer in here, heat rising up the shaft from the lowest levels of the mine a hundred fathoms below, the cold night wind cut off by the rough-hewn walls.

Ben had only to descend to the thirty-fathom level. The tunnel where he worked sloped gently away from the shaft, extending beneath the rocks at the foot of the cliffs and under the bed of the Atlantic Ocean. It was here that Pearson Retallick and his partner mined the most ancient of all metals – tin.

Pausing at the mouth of the narrow tunnel, Ben lit a candle from the spitting, jumping flame of the half-inch butt he found wedged in a crevice there. He stuck the newly lit candle on his hard-brimmed hat and entered the tunnel. He had gone only a few yards when he heard the protesting squeal of an ungreased wheelbarrow, and a flickering light advanced along the tunnel towards him.

A short broad-shouldered youth, stripped to the waist, brought the heavily laden wooden wheelbarrow to a halt. Flexing the fingers of his hands, he rubbed the back of one of them across his glistening dirt-streaked face.

'Your pa still bad?'

Dick Hooper spoke with the thick soft accent of Cornwall's far west.

Ben nodded wordlessly.

'Josiah ain't going to take kindly to that. If he had his way, we'd all be working non-stop until bidding-day.'

Josiah Clamp was Pearson Retallick's partner. The brunt of the additional work caused by the illness of Ben's father was falling on his shoulders.

'Pa says if he's no better tomorrow he'll get someone to come in and work for him.'

'You'd best get along and tell the bad news to Josiah. I've got to get down to the sixty-fathom level. My brother should be down there working but he's sick, too. I've promised to help out for half a shift.'

Ben looked at the older boy in sympathy. At sixteen years of age, Dick Hooper was the head of his family, and its only permanent breadwinner. His father had died of lung sickness a year before, leaving Dick to support a mother crippled with rheumatism, and a consumptive brother. He would now work a half-shift at the lower level of the mine, then go home for a couple of hours' sleep. Returning to the mine at dawn, he would work a full day shift with the energetic Josiah Clamp.

'Leave everything just as it is, Dick. I'll tip the barrow after I've spoken to Josiah.'

'Thanks. I'll do the same for you some day.'

Dick Hooper lifted his crumpled shirt from the wheelbarrow. Tying the sleeves about his waist as he went, he hurried off in the direction of the main shaft.

In less of a hurry, Ben set off to find Josiah Clamp. Walking along the narrow rough-walled tunnel, Ben could hear the rumble of the storm on the sea-bed above him as hundreds of tons of shingle moved with the waves. The sound of stones grating one upon the other was a nerve-racking din in the confined space of the tunnel. Occasionally, an extra-powerful undersea current would dislodge a giant boulder and send it bouncing along the sea-bed in a terrifying game of underwater bowls. Echoing through the thirty-fathom level, the noise set every nerve in Ben's young body tingling. It gave him a feeling of raw exhilaration he had never experienced above grass. Ben was a natural miner. He had an instinct for his work, bred into him by countless centuries of Cornish tinners.

Josiah Clamp lay full length in a narrow fissure between two masses of granite, checking on the lode that opened out again beyond the rock.

Ben had to tap the miner's boot-clad foot three times before he wriggled his way backwards towards him.

When Josiah Clamp's head came into sight, he turned and glared at Ben, then looked beyond him.

'Where's your pa?'

'He's still sick. He'll get someone else in tomorrow.'

'That's no help to me tonight,' Josiah Clamp snapped.

'Damn! Why couldn't your pa have hung on for another week? Well, there's nothing else for it; I'll have to use black powder to bring this lot down. That should give you enough ore to carry away tonight. We'll have to take tomorrow as it comes.'

Josiah Clamp's statement dismayed Ben. His father would never allow gunpowder to be used on this level. He said that the sea-bed was too close above them – proof of which was the salt water oozing down the walls of the tunnel. When Ben reminded Josiah Clamp of this, the miner turned on him angrily.

'Do you think I don't know it for myself? But your pa isn't here to give us the benefit of his opinion, so I must do what I think is best. That means I'll blast. That idler Dick Hooper has left plenty of ore lying about here. You get to moving it while I set the powder and prepare the fuse.'

Ben's father was often saying that Josiah Clamp took too many chances in his eagerness to make money, but there was little that Ben could do to prevent him tonight. He could even understand the miner's reasoning. With one man trying to do the work of two, there was need for desperate measures. All the same, Ben felt a deep uneasiness about this operation.

Ben emptied the wheelbarrow left behind by Dick Hooper, then trundled it back to the work-face to pick up more ore. The Money Box was a small mine. It was a single shaft, used by the men to reach their working levels and also for hoisting ore to the surface. A horse-whim raised the ore. The same source of power operated the rag-and-chain pumps bringing up water from the lower levels of the mine.

Because of the limited means available for raising ore, each pair of miners was allocated a very short period of 'lifting-time'. In order that this should not be wasted, Ben needed to have enough ore at the shaft to fill the huge iron buckets or 'kibbles'.

He had been working for an hour and was trundling an overloaded wheelbarrow towards the shaft when Josiah Clamp overtook him.

'Quick! The fuse is lit. Take cover.'

Hurriedly dropping the wheelbarrow to the ground, Ben followed the older miner and flung himself down behind a stacked pile of waste rock. Putting his hands over his ears, he remained tensed for almost two minutes, anticipating the explosion.

Nothing happened.

Ben uncovered his ears as Josiah Clamp cursed and scrambled to his feet.

'I thought the powder felt damp. It must have gone out. It's that bloody storeman at the Botallack mine. I pay him with good money and he palms me off with old powder that won't light.'

Ben grinned knowingly. Josiah Clamp had not paid over the counter of the Botallack mine store, of that he was quite sure. The storeman there was one of Josiah's cousins. He would have stolen the gunpowder and passed it on to Josiah in a gin-parlour for no more than the price of a drink or two.

As Josiah Clamp hurried back along the tunnel, Ben took up the shafts of the wheelbarrow again, leaning against the weight of the load.

He had taken no more than five unsteady paces when it seemed that the whole tunnel erupted about him with a terrifying roar. Ben was thrown forward over the top of the overturned wheelbarrow, an agonising pain in his head. It felt as though his brain had been crushed.

Josiah Clamp had been only partially correct about the gunpowder. It *was* old – but not damp. The straw-and-gunpowder fuse had merely been reluctant to burn. Spluttering and spitting, it burned a spasmodic course towards the gunpowder packed in a deep hole at the end of the tunnel. Not until Josiah was examining its burned-out trail did the powder suddenly flare up and take a leap forward. It had less than a foot to travel. Before the horrified miner could turn and run, he was blown into eternity.

Josiah Clamp was not to die alone on this stormy March night. As Ben picked himself up, gasping for the oxygen that had been burned up by the explosion, the ground beneath his feet began to tremble. Ben reeled about the tunnel for what seemed an age. In fact, it was seconds only before he realised that the thunderous roaring was not in his tormented head. It came from the tunnel behind him – and Ben knew what it was.

The explosion had blown a hole in the sea-bed!

The level was in darkness, every candle blown out by the force of the explosion, but Ben ran for his life, oblivious of the jagged edges of rock that grazed his head and outstretched hands. In his panic-driven flight he would have plunged to his death down the mine shaft had he not fallen headlong over the pile of tin ore waiting at the mouth of the tunnel.

Ben scrambled over the ore and his hands located the ladder leading to the surface – and safety. He climbed on to the ladder just as tons of sea-water and dislodged rock spewed from the tunnel mouth and thundered into the shaft.

The ladder began to vibrate dangerously and, although Ben was now above the level of the tunnel, the water soaked the lower part of his legs. He had begun to climb higher when his ankle was grasped from below and a hoarse scream for help reached him above the deafening roar of the water.

For a long terrifying moment Ben imagined that Josiah Clamp was trying to drag him down with him to a watery grave. He kicked out violently in an effort to break free. Then, as quickly as it had left him, reason returned. Ben realised that the hand holding his ankle belonged to another human, trying to escape from the tunnel that led inland from the thirty-fathom level.

The ladder was shaking in a frightening fashion as tons of water pounded at its lower sections. All the ladders were linked together, and it would not be long before the steel pins attaching it to the wall of the shaft were wrenched free.

This was not the moment to be thinking about what *might* happen. Gingerly, Ben lowered himself until he could reach down and grip the hand of the unknown miner below him.

As Ben secured his grip, the fingers released his ankle and closed about his wrist. With his legs twisted securely about the ladder, Ben heaved with all the desperate strength that was in him. Slowly, the unseen miner struggled clear of the thundering water pouring unceasingly from the ruptured tunnel – and then he was crouched, panting, on the rung below Ben's feet.

Disentangling his legs from the wildly juddering ladder, Ben shouted, 'Climb! The ladder will go at any moment.'

With these words, Ben began climbing as fast as his shaking legs would allow. He had made ten rungs when the ladder swung wildly to one side, with a suddenness that nearly dislodged him. He knew that the ladders below him had been swept away, leaving the one on which he was standing hanging by only one pin.

Slowly and fearfully, he climbed the last few feet to the ladder above. Behind him, the man he had rescued did the same.

Now they were both safe, Ben had to rest for a few seconds. His legs felt weak and were trembling so violently that he was afraid they would take him no farther.

'Are you all right?' The voice from the ladder below him was not that of a man, but of a boy, like himself.

'Yes. At least, I think so. And you?'

'Yes, but I have lost my boots. The water must have torn them off while I clung to the ladder. They were new only last week!'

It was such a ridiculous thing to worry about after coming so close to death that Ben felt an overpowering urge to giggle. The sound caught in his throat and came out as a choked sob. Ben gulped in air noisily until he knew he had control of himself once more.

'We had better get up top and tell them what has happened.'

Ben resumed the upward climb. This time he did not stop until he stepped off the ladder on to the ground at the top of the shaft.

Immediately, he was surrounded by the men who worked the whim, and off-duty miners brought from their beds in nearby houses when the water burst into the Money Box mine with a boom that was heard for a mile around.

'What's happening down there? What level are you from?' Questions came at Ben from all sides.

'Thirty fathoms.'

No one worked above this level. The played-out tunnels of the ten- and twenty-fathom levels were now utilised as draining-adits.

'How many of you got out?'

A lamp was held up to Ben's face and in its light he saw the mine captain. Fresh from his bed, he tucked a nightshirt inside his trousers as he spoke.

'Two of us.'

Looking about him for his companion from the shaft, Ben saw only the faces of the anxious miners.

'Get a rescue team together. We'll go down to see what can be done.'

'Nothing can be done now.' The choking feeling in Ben's throat had returned. 'Josiah Clamp blew the top off the thirty-fathom level. The sea is in, the ladders swept away. You can't get down there – and no one will ever get out.'

For long moments the only sounds were the booming of the sea emptying into the mine and the mournful dirge of the wind as it plucked at the taut ropes of the shafthead whim.

'There are more than thirty men down there!' one of the miners whispered in horror.

'Thirty-four, and every one of them as dead as the Money Box mine,' corrected the mine captain grimly. To Ben, he asked, 'What is your name, boy?'

'Ben. Ben Retallick.'

'You will remember this day, Ben Retallick. It is the day the Lord has seen fit to take the lives of thirty-four men – and hand yours back to you. Make sure it is not wasted.'

The mine captain rested a hand heavily on Ben's shoulder, then turned away before any man could see his face.

Ben was left shivering in the darkness. Then he, too, turned and headed for home. Wednesday, 18 March 1818, was barely half an hour old. It was Ben Retallick's fifteenth birthday.

Chapter Two

In the cold grey light of early dawn, the last piece of furniture was carried from the Retallick cottage by a surly wagoner and dumped unceremoniously on the farm-wagon that stood outside the door.

'That's the lot. If you don't hurry up and climb on the wagon, we'll still be on the road when night falls.'

'If we are, then you'll need to find Mevagissey in the dark,' declared Martha Retallick. 'You'll not get paid for another day. You've been given your guinea. How long it takes you to earn it is your own business. Now, save your breath for helping with my husband.'

Pearson Retallick looked ill and frail as Ben and the wagoner helped him from the house and lifted him carefully on to the back of the wagon. He sat on a straw mattress, propped against the high driving-box seat. There was little meat on him, and he would never again earn his living digging tin beneath the ground in a mine.

Ben knew it, and so did his mother. Armed with this

knowledge she had been able to get her way after many years of trying in vain to win her husband and son from the mines.

Martha Retallick hated mines and everything that went with them as deeply as her son loved them. The dust; the noise of the stamp-hammers and machinery; the ugly tall chimneys – even the miners themselves. Once above ground they had little interest in anything but brawling and drinking – and raising new generations of miners and bal-maidens to follow their unhappy example.

Martha Retallick's brothers and cousins were fishermen. Her father and his father before him had been fishermen, too. It was a permanent way of life, a healthy living. In Mevagissey old men might be seen standing on the jetty at dusk, sucking contentedly on their pipes as they talked and waited for the fishing-boats to return to harbour.

There were no old men in the mining areas. Those who miraculously survived the ladders, the roof falls and the hundred other daily hazards to be found below ground ended up like Pearson Retallick, dying of lung sickness, with half of their allotted lifespan unfulfilled. Few miners found contentment in their work – and Martha Retallick firmly believed they never would. They attacked and violated the land, taking what they wanted and discarding the remainder, leaving deep scars for all to see. She was convinced this was the reason they were paid back a hundredfold by the land. It took from them their health and happiness – even life itself.

Such was Martha Retallick's deep-rooted belief. Because of it, she used the disaster at the Money Box mine to force her husband to abandon mining once and for all. The mine would never be worked again, and Pearson Retallick's career came to an end with it. He would never again be able to find employment as a miner. The family's future now depended upon what she and Ben were able to earn. Ben was still classed as a boy. He might earn twenty shillings a month – if he were lucky enough to find a generous and sympathetic mine captain. For the surface work she was able to do, Martha Retallick would bring in another twelve shillings. Neither job would provide them with a house.

Martha Retallick argued that, if they returned to Mevagissey, Ben could go fishing with her family while she worked in the family's fish-cellar. Together they would earn twice as much and could live in the house occupied by Ben's grandfather and grandmother until they found somewhere of their own.

Supported by Ben, Pearson Retallick held out for as long as he could, but had finally been forced to give way to the logic of his wife's argument. He had agreed to leave the St Just mining area and move to Mevagissey.

Ben protested in vain that *he* was a miner and not a fisherman. His mother would not be thwarted now. She told Ben he was lucky to be alive. He should accept the disaster at the mine as a warning and turn to something else. To go down a mine and risk his life again would be flying in the face of providence.

As Martha Retallick closed the door of the tiny mining-cottage for the last time, she had not a single twinge of regret. She had arrived at this cottage as a young bride. Ben, her only son, had been born here. But that was the only good thing to which she would admit during the whole of her life at the Money Box mine.

Climbing up to the high wagon-seat, she nodded to the wagoner. Flicking the reins, he shouted unintelligible orders to the horse. The beast leaned into its padded collar, and the Retallick family was on its way.

There was no one to see them leave the Money Box mine. No friends to wave, or wish them well in their new lives.

The out-of-work miners had already moved away to seek work elsewhere. Only the families of the men who had died remained. There was nowhere for them to go. They would stay on at the derelict mine until hunger and desperation drove them out to join the scores of beggars and discharged veterans of Wellington's great and victorious army, roaming the lanes of Cornwall.

The journey along half the length of Cornwall passed without incident, although Pearson Retallick was shaken up badly by the pot-holed road. By the time they began the steep descent of the hill leading down to Mevagissey village he was in a state of exhaustion.

The horse, too, was tired. Head hanging low, it slipped and slid on a road wet and muddy after the storms of recent weeks. Halfway down the hill, on a sharp and narrow bend, they overtook a young girl. Across one of her shoulders was balanced a long pole, at each end of which was a large and cumbersome basket.

As the wagon passed, the tired horse slipped – recovered – then slipped again. The wagoner was so busy braking the wagon and cursing the horse that he hardly noticed the girl.

She stood as far back from the road as was possible, balancing on the very edge of a short but steep bank that fell away to a half-filled ditch. Unfortunately, there was little room at this particular spot, and as the wagon slid to one side it clipped one of the baskets.

Ben watched in awed fascination as the baskets and pole swung lazily in a wide arc, twisting the girl around. She lost her footing, stepped backwards and tumbled down the bank, the baskets falling with her. As the girl landed in the ditch they crashed to the ground and burst open, releasing a number of indignant, noisy and wildly flapping ducks.

Martha Retallick had not seen the accident occur, and she was startled when Ben leaped from the wagon to the ground. He slid down the bank to the unfortunate girl's aid while the wagoner continued to curse his horse, working all the time to keep the wagon on the road.

When Ben reached her the girl lay half-submerged in mud, her thin legs protruding from a froth of petticoats and dress. Reaching down he grasped the neck of her dress and pulled her to her feet.

She came out of the mud like a cork from a bottle, but she showed very little gratitude to her rescuer. Flailing wildly, her fists caught Ben two substantial blows in the face. He immediately released his grip on her dress, and she slipped on the wet grass and fell back into the ditch.

This time Ben made no attempt to help her. Looking up at the road he saw the wagon disappearing around the next bend. His father waved to him, a wide grin on his pale face.

'Well! Don't just stand there. Help me!'

The girl was on her hands and knees in the ditch, glaring up at Ben.

'Why? So you can hit me again?'

Clamping her mouth tight shut, the girl hoisted her skirt above her knees with one hand and used the other to pull herself from the ditch.

'It was your cart that knocked me off the road. Look at my ducks! They are everywhere.'

She grabbed at one of the birds, which was head down in the ditch, worrying at the mud. The duck complained vociferously, but she unceremoniously dumped it in one of the baskets and went in pursuit of another at the edge of the water.

Ben helped her to recapture the remainder of the ducks. It was not an easy task, and by the time the last one was safely back in its basket he was almost as wet and muddy as she was.

'Look at the time!' complained the girl, glancing up at the sky. 'The boats will have been in for ages. The best of the fish will be gone long before I get to the quay.'

'I'll help you carry the baskets.'

'No, you won't! You've caused me enough trouble.'

The girl's dark eyes warned Ben off as she shouldered the pole and baskets, but she did allow him to help her up the steep bank to the road.

As he walked beside her down the hill, he said, 'I'm sorry you've got all muddied up. The wagoner has never been to Mevagissey before. He didn't know how steep the hill is.'

The girl snorted derisively and they walked together in silence for a while. Then her mouth twitched in a sudden mischievous smile, and she gave him a sidelong glance.

'I don't suppose it was your fault really. Besides, you are as muddy as me now. I haven't seen you before. Do you come from Mevagissey?'

'No, from St Just.'

'Isn't that where all the mines are?'

'Yes, I'm a miner.'

Seeing her incredulous look, Ben's chin went up. 'Well . . . my pa was a miner. I worked with him. Now we've come to live in Mevagissey.'

'Why? There are no mines here – none worth mentioning, anyway. A good thing, too. Miners are digging farmers' graves, that's what my dad used to say. What are you going to do here?'

'My pa is ill. He can't work any more. So, when the mine flooded, Ma said we should come here for me to learn fishing with her folks.'

Ben lapsed into a deep silence as he remembered the Money Box mine.

The girl looked at him with sudden renewed interest. 'The mine you worked in . . . was that the one where all the men were drowned?'

'Yes.'

Ben clenched his fists tightly, and she could see the tension in him.

'I heard that only one miner, a boy, escaped. Was that you?'

'There were two of us, but I don't know what happened to the other one.'

'That must have been an awful experience.' She looked at him with a new respect. 'What's your name?'

'Ben Retallick.'

'I'm Jesse Henna. Me and my ma have a small farm up the hill at Pengrugla. Just a couple of fields really. But we get by.'

They had almost reached the small harbour now. Ben stopped at the entrance to a lane that was so narrow that the upper storeys of the houses on either side were only inches away from each other.

'This is where my grandpa lives.'

She nodded. 'Then you had better go. They will be wondering what has happened to you.'

Ben had turned to walk away when Jesse Henna called out to him.

'What is the name of your mother's kin?'

'Dunn.'

'I know them. They are good fishermen. I'll look out for you when I next come to Mevagissey and trade for any fish you've caught.'

Ben raised his hand in acknowledgement and made his way to Grandpa Dunn's house.

The little fishing-cottage had always fascinated him on his infrequent visits here as a small boy. Cosy and lacking light it tucked tight into the hillside. The back door actually opened out of the roof on to a narrow terrace that descended in a series of elongated cobble steps to the harbour.

Ben let himself in through the front entrance and walked into an atmosphere that was as chilly as winter rain. Grandpa Dunn was leaning well back in his rocking-chair, watching the smoke from his clay pipe drift upwards towards the low beamed ceiling of the kitchen. In front of the fire Grandma Dunn busied herself with pots and skillets, arranging them noisily on the black foundry-made range. The old lady's bristling disapproval was held in check only by the smug satisfaction of being proved right – after sixteen years of waiting.

Grandma Dunn had never approved of her daughter Martha's marriage to a miner. She had given it her reluctant blessing in a moment of uncharacteristic weakness, upon learning that Pearson was a Methodist – as were the Dunn family. But she had warned her daughter that no good would come from such a union. Mining, she had declared, was the Devil's work. The Prince of Darkness had his kingdom in the bowels of the earth. Men who invaded his domain either paid tribute to him or suffered the consequences. As a small girl, Grandma Dunn had listened to the fire-and-brimstone sermons of the aged John Wesley. His words had burned into her soul, allowing of no argument. Hell was in the darkness beneath the ground. Heaven was above; it came down to meet at the sea where a fisherman earned his living. It stood to reason, therefore, that a fisherman was closer to the Good Lord than any other man alive.

Grandma Dunn did not hear Ben arrive, so busy was she with her own thoughts. When she turned round and saw him for the first time, her hands found her hips and she glared at him in disapproval.

'Goodness gracious, boy! What *have* you been doing to get yourself in such a state? Whatever will the neighbours think? Away with you. Get out of those clothes before you dirty up my kitchen. You'll not sit down at this table in filthy trousers like those.'

'These are my best clothes! I've only got my working-trousers—'

'Don't argue with your grandmother, Ben,' Martha Retallick interrupted quickly. She wanted to avoid an argument at all costs. 'Your working-trousers are clean; they will do fine. You'll find them in the old trunk, upstairs in the back bed-room. Go on, now.'

When Ben left the room, Martha Retallick tried to explain why Ben was in such a mess.

'Hah!' The lines about Grandma Dunn's mouth deepened and her mouth clamped shut for a moment. 'There is no need for any boy to get into such a state. You are my daughter, Martha, and are welcome to stay here, but I'll have no miner's ways in this house.'

Still grumbling, the old lady turned back to her cooking, and Martha Retallick breathed a sigh of relief. Family dissension had been averted – for a while. She would need to talk to Ben. To tell him to tread lightly in this house. Martha had succeeded in bringing her family to Mevagissey after many years of trying. She wanted nothing to go wrong now.

When Ben returned to the kitchen, an appetising meal of fish and potatoes was placed upon the table in front of him. Grandma Dunn, her feelings aired, was in a better mood.

Martha Retallick asked why places were not being set for her three brothers and received a look of surprise from her mother.

'Why, bless you, girl, I keep forgetting how long it is since you were last here. Your brother Mark has been married these four years, and Billy for three. Between the two of them they have given me five grandchildren.'

'And Walter? Is he not married yet?'

Grandma Dunn's jaw snapped shut as fiercely as a gintrap. 'There is more than one girl's mother with reason enough to wish Walter had married years ago; but you had best be asking your father about Walter and his goings-on.'

'He is off at a parliamentary reform meeting,' said Samuel Dunn. He spoke through his fingers as he dislodged a fish bone, caught between two of his remaining teeth. 'Very strong for reform is our Walter.'

'Does Walter think we should all have the vote?' asked Pearson Retallick, speaking for the first time since Ben had entered the house.

'Walter thinks all manner of nonsense,' interjected Grandma Dunn. 'Unless he can learn to hold his tongue about some of it he will find himself in serious trouble. Sir John Vincent up at Lamorrack House has already warned him about preaching sedition to the estate workers. He told Walter that Parliament in London intends bringing in laws aimed at those who put foolish ideas into other folks' heads. Walter ought to listen to him. I've told him many times that no fisherman will benefit from all this "reform". It is a squabble between gentlemen. It won't put more fish into the nets, or sail a boat home at the end of the day. Instead of tramping around the countryside talking about things that don't concern him, Walter should spend more time down on the quay, repairing his nets.'

Pearson Retallick would have pursued the subject, but his wife silenced him with a look. For a while the meal continued in silence. Then Samuel Dunn spoke to Ben.

'I hear you want to become a fisherman?'

'No . . . but Ma wants me to become one.'

Spoons stopped scraping on plates as everyone looked at Ben. For a moment he wished he had thought before speaking out, then his grandfather laughed.

'That's the same thing. We'll send you out with Walter tomorrow. He'll teach you all you need to know about fishing. Whatever your grandma might think, there is no better fisherman along this part of the coast. This time next year you'll be catching as many fish as a Mevagissey-born boy, you wait and see.'

Ben doubted whether he would ever fulfil his grandfather's hopes, but he said nothing of his thoughts.

As soon as the meal was over, Ben went to bed in the small dark back-bedroom he would share with his mother and father. That night he dreamed of fishing-boats being washed through flooded mine tunnels by wild sea currents, while a dark-eyed girl with black hair called for him to come with her and rescue some ducks.

Chapter Three

Early the following morning, Ben was shaken into wakefulness before the sun had risen. Bleary-eyed, he made his way downstairs to the kitchen. A tall bearded young man was dipping his head repeatedly into an iron-banded bucket that stood on a slate-topped table in a corner.

Raising his head and blowing hard, Walter Dunn grinned at Ben. 'Come on, youngster. Mevagissey fish don't wait around for those who lie in bed all day. Here, wake yourself up with this.'

Shaking water from his hair, he reached for a rough towel and rubbed the excess water from his face as he backed away from the bucket.

Ben was more cautious than his exuberant uncle. Cupping his hands, he brought the water up to his face. It was breathtakingly cold. Had Walter not been watching him, Ben would have forgone the unnecessary luxury of this early-morning wash altogether.

Breakfast became a hectic affair as the rest of the household rose and crowded into the tiny kitchen. Ben was glad when it was over and he was able to set off with Walter, followed by the good wishes of the family.

As he strode briskly beside Walter Dunn, men nodded to them. One or two called out to Walter, asking him about the previous evening's reform meeting. It was a subject about which Ben knew nothing, and he listened carefully as Walter spoke about 'rotten boroughs', 'purchased votes' and 'potboiling franchises'. It did not take him long to realise that Walter Dunn believed passionately in parliamentary reform, and the right of every man to vote for a Member of Parliament to represent him in the House of Commons in London.

But Ben's main interest was in the work that lay ahead of him. As he and Walter made their way along the edge of the quay, he asked Walter about the day's fishing.

'Are we going after pilchards?'

'We are going out after any fish that might be about,' declared Walter. 'If we catch pilchards, then so much the better, but I doubt if we will find any at this time of the year.'

Walter stopped suddenly, and Ben looked up at him questioningly.

'Look, Ben, times are not good for anyone – fishermen in particular. We have to make a living any way we can. Some of the things we do have very little to do with fishing. Ask no questions and keep your mouth shut about anything you see and hear. You do that and no Mevagissey man will be able to fault you. Is that clear?'

It was not, but Ben expected he would find out soon enough. He nodded.

'Good! Now, come and meet the fishermen you'll be working with.'

Walter led the way down a flight of green-stained stone steps that disappeared into the water of the harbour. Bumping against them were two twenty-foot-long wooden boats into which five men were loading nets and baskets.

Walter's introduction was brief. 'This is Ben, my sister Martha's son. He's been mining down-country until now, but the mine has closed and his father is sick. He'll be fishing with us in future. Mark . . . Billy, Ma says she expects you up at the house to meet Martha when we get back tonight.'

Mark, the eldest of Samuel Dunn's sons, was not happy with Ben's presence.

'I'm sorry to hear about Pearson, but do you think it's wise to bring the boy out with us? The Frenchie is expected any day now . . .'

'I have told Ben there's more to earning a living at sea than shooting a net and tucking fish. He'll learn, the same as we had to.'

Mark Dunn shrugged and turned back to his work. Walter told Ben to take his place in the bow of the boat crewed by Walter and two other fishermen. It was not long before they were ready to put to sea, and they left the small harbour in company with the other boat, in which were Mark, Billy and a third fisherman.

It was the first time Ben had been in a boat. He did not enjoy the novel experience. Although it was by no means a stormy day, there was a fresh south-easterly wind blowing, and a fairly heavy swell. Within minutes of leaving harbour Ben began to feel ill. He kept his queasiness to himself for as long as he was able. Then, without warning, he was forced to make a dive for the gunwale. Hanging with his head only inches above the undulating water, Ben lost his breakfast.

His discomfiture brought a cheer from the following boat. When Ben raised his head miserably, he saw Walter and the two fishermen in his own boat grinning at him, greatly amused.

'Never mind, Ben.' Walter leaned back on an oar, sending the boat sliding over the crest of a long round-topped roller and tilting into the trough beyond. 'You'll feel better when we give you some work to do. Mevagissey has never yet lost a man or boy from seasickness. I doubt if you will be the first.'

Huddled in the bow of the boat, Ben could only nod miserably. He wished his stomach would keep time with the rise and fall of the vessel.

About a mile from the shore, the men in the two Dunn boats began casting their long seine-nets. Fastened at each end to one of the boats, the net was cast in a wide circle. When both ends were brought together the net was tightened until the fish were trapped inside its diminished circle and the fishermen were able to scoop the fish into their boats. Ben found this movement of the boat even more upsetting than being under way, but Walter set him to tucking fish and kept him busy.

The shooting out and drawing in of the net was repeated many times during the day. In between, Ben continued to suffer seasickness. By the time the day's work was over and the boats returned to Mevagissey, he was close to exhaustion.

It did not help his misery when he saw Jesse Henna waiting at the quayside. Clean and cheerful, she was the last person Ben wished to meet in his present dejected and sick state.

'Hello, Ben. How did your first day's fishing go?'

The pale and drawn face he turned to her told his story better than any words.

'Oh! You were seasick, then?'

'You might say that, missie,' one of the grinning fishermen answered her question. 'Young Ben was hung over the side for so long we might have mistook him for a long-line if he hadn't twitched once in a while.'

The laughter of the men in the boat was echoed by the

fishermen standing on the quay. Brought up to feel equally at home on sea or land, few of them had ever suffered from seasickness. It was an amusing affliction from which only landsmen suffered.

Ben felt too wretched to take offence at the laughter of the fishermen. He had been longing desperately for his return to the land. Now, standing on the steps of the quay, it seemed the land, too, was swimming about him. He reached out to steady himself against the stone wall.

Jesse was highly indignant at the jeers of the fishermen. 'Being ill is nothing to laugh about. I would like to see your faces if you were to stand at the top of a deep mine shaft. The thought of climbing down in the dark would set your knees knocking so hard you wouldn't stay on the ladder for two minutes. It wouldn't worry Ben.'

'You'm probably right, missie. That's why fishermen go out in boats and miners should stay at their diggings.'

Jesse had done Ben no favour by reminding the listeners that he had worked in a mine. Miners and fishermen were different breeds of men, each scornful of the other's way of life.

But Jesse used the fisherman's retort to come to the main reason for her visit to the quayside. 'As a fisherman you'll likely have caught something worth trading for three dozen eggs. They were laid this very day.'

From the basket resting on the ground at her feet she took a clean brown egg.

All differences were forgotten, and swift bartering began. When the eggs and a dozen and a half fat mackerel had changed hands, Jesse asked Ben, 'Are you going home now? I'll walk a way with you.'

Ben wanted desperately to turn his back on the boat and the harbour, but he knew there was more work to be done.

'I have to help bring the fish ashore before I go.'

Jesse shrugged, putting on an air of indifference to hide the unexpected disappointment she felt. 'It doesn't matter. Here, have these . . . I saved them for you. They are to thank you for helping me with the ducks last night.'

She reached a hand into a pocket of the apron she wore. Pulling out two eggs, she thrust them at Ben. When he had taken them she turned away abruptly, ignoring the thanks he called after her.

'Well, I don't know!' exclaimed Walter, scratching his thick black beard. 'You've been in Mevagissey for hardly a day and already you've found yourself a pretty young maid. Tell me, Ben. How come you know young Jesse Henna?'

Ben told Walter the story of the wagon and the ducks. By the time he ended every one of the fishermen was chuckling.

'You got off lightly, young Ben,' commented Walter Dunn. 'Had I been a wagon that upset her I would have legged it away from there as fast as I could go. Jesse Henna was as likely to have hit you with the pole she carried, as look at you. She is a wild one, and no mistake.'

Ben remembered how Jesse had come out of the ditch swinging at him with her fists, but he kept the memory to himself. As they worked he asked Walter what he knew of Jesse Henna.

'Not much more than I have told you already. She and her mother have a place up at the head of the valley, at Pengrugla. They keep some livestock and mind their own business. What more is there to say?'

'What happened to her father?'

'Ah! Now, that's a question that might have more than one answer. Jesse's mother used to work up at the big house, at Lamorrack. She's a handsome woman – and was an even prettier maid. She married Tom Henna in something of a hurry. Folk said Jesse's birth came as more of a surprise to poor Tom than it did to Sir John's son, Colman. Whatever the truth of it, the Vincent family allowed Tom to get away with a great many things that might have hanged another man.'

Ben was intrigued. 'What sort of things?'

As they talked, they stood in line with the other fishermen, passing baskets of fish from the boats to the quay. Walter called down to one of his brothers, who was in a boat.

'Billy! You knew Tom Henna well enough. What would you say about him?'

'Tom Henna? He was a clever poacher and no respecter of other folks' livestock or property. There was talk of him taking part in more than one highway robbery on the old toll road. Such talk apart, he was a likeable enough chap – if you didn't fall foul of his quick temper.'

'What happened to him?'

'He fled the county and joined the Army after almost killing a man in a fight at Pentuan. It seemed he was as good at fighting Frenchmen as Cornishmen, and he died a hero's death at Waterloo. Sir John Vincent let Jesse and her mother stay on at Pengrugla – "in recognition of Tom's sacrifice for King and country", so 'twas said.'

'Does Jesse know about the talk?'

'Who knows? I certainly wouldn't ask her. If you have any intentions towards her, then neither will you,' Walter said. 'That's the last basket, Ben. We'll finish off here now. You get on home and tell your grandma we'll be there within the hour. Don't forget to take your present with you. I would lay you a wager that young Jesse came to Mevagissey especially to give them to you. Bringing the other eggs was no more than an excuse. She's a nice young maid, Ben. You could do a lot worse . . . But away with you now.'

Slipping the eggs into separate pockets, Ben set out for his grandmother's house, wishing the world would stop swinging about him.

It was almost dark now, the tangle of fishermen's cottages effectively blocking the last light of the setting sun from the narrow streets of the village. Ben was so deep in thought about Jesse, and of what Walter and the others had said, that he did not see the faint glow of a pipe in the shadows beside the door of the Dunn cottage.

'Is that you, Ben?' It was Pearson Retallick.

'Yes, Pa. You shouldn't be sitting outside now. It's coming in cold.'

'I've been waiting for you to get home. They've had you working a long shift out there today. How did you enjoy the fishing?'

'It was all right. A bit new to me, that was all.'

Ben was glad it was dark, he had never been able to lie to his father.

Pearson Retallick was not taken in by Ben's words.

'You are bound to find the work difficult at first, Ben. It's very different to working below ground – but a sight healthier! I wish I had taken to fishing. I could have been out there with you today. A father likes to teach his own son to make his way in life. All I seem to have done is to lead you along a short path to nowhere.'

'You taught me mining, Pa – and you taught me well. That's what you know about – and what I enjoy doing. I always will. Fishing might be healthier, but I am no fisherman. I know it, and so do those I have been out with today. Sooner or later Ma will have to know it, too . . .'

'And what is it I am to know?'

Martha Retallick had gone upstairs to shut the windows of the bedrooms against the cool night air. She had heard Ben's last few words.

Looking up, Ben could just see the white of her face against the dark shadow of the window. 'We are talking about fishing, Ma. I am no more a fisherman than Walter is a miner. He'll tell you the same thing when he comes home. I spent most of the day being sick over the side of the boat. I was no help to him at all.'

'Then you'll need to keep going back to sea until you *stop* being sick, won't you? You are as much a Dunn as a Retallick, and the Dunns have been fishermen for as far back as anyone in Mevagissey can remember. There is no reason in the world why you shouldn't be one if you set your mind to it.'

Martha Retallick's face disappeared, and the window was slammed shut with a crash that set the small glass panes shivering.

'Your ma is right, Ben.' Pearson Retallick's quiet voice pricked the bubble of Ben's anger. 'Give fishing a chance – just to please her. She's had little enough pleasure from life so far. I'll have a chat with Walter in a week or so. If he agrees with you that you'll never become a fisherman, I will take the matter up with your ma then.'

Ben dreaded the thought of going to sea for another few weeks, but he knew his father would keep his word. For his part, Ben would do what was expected of him until then.

As it happened, Pearson Retallick's intercession would not be necessary. The stage was already set for a drama that would shake Martha Retallick's faith in the permanency and respectability of fishing.

Chapter Four

Ben's second day at sea began in much the same way as had the first. No sooner had the two Dunn boats nosed out of the smooth waters of the harbour into St Austell Bay than Ben's stomach began rebelling against the alien combination of wind and sea.

True, his nausea subsided to some extent when they began working the nets, but towards mid-afternoon the wind freshened from the east and the feeling returned. The boat bounced and lurched beneath him, and when Ben was not helping with the catch he stayed huddled miserably in the bow of the boat. He did his best to keep out of the way of the fishermen, but they cursed him soundly when the unpredictable movement of the sea caused them to stumble against him.

Then the dark-blue sails of a three-masted barquentine appeared on the horizon, and the three men in the boat forgot all about Ben. They called to the fishermen in the second boat, and they, too, became inexplicably excited. From that moment, they fished in a desultory manner, seeming not to care whether or not they caught any fish.

By now, Ben was thoroughly ill and miserable. He wanted only to return to harbour. He was relieved when, one by one, the other Mevagissey boats stowed their fishing-gear and headed for home. Soon the two Dunn boats were the only ones still fishing. Ben looked eagerly towards Walter, waiting for him to give the order to stow their fishing-gear and return to Mevagissey.

The order never came. The fishermen sat at their oars, smoking their foul-smelling clay pipes and giving an occasional half-hearted pull on their oars to bring the bow of the boat into the sea.

They stayed out until the sun was sinking beneath the horizon into a fiery sea and Mevagissey was no more than a distant sprinkling of lighted windows. Only then did Walter give his order. It had the fishermen in the two boats moving with an alacrity that astonished Ben. The long net was hauled onboard, and the men strained on their oars with a vigour that made light of the long day's work behind them.

But they did not head for Mevagissey. Instead the two fishing-boats headed out into the waters of the English Channel. They were going to meet the barquentine, now bearing down upon them with every inch of her blue sails spread to catch the wind.

Minutes later the two fishing-boats bumped against the heavy timbers of the barquentine and a voice carrying a strong French accent called for Mark and Walter to come on board.

His indisposition temporarily forgotten, Ben watched with great interest as the two Dunn brothers swarmed up ropes let down from the sailing craft. His excitement quickened when, seconds later, a cargo that had little to do with fishing was handed down to the waiting fishermen. Casks and barrels were stowed in the boats beneath the day's catch. Others were lowered into the water and secured to the stern of the fishing-boats by long stout lines.

The operation was carried out with well-practised efficiency. By the time Walter and Mark returned to their respective boats the oars were already being run out. Moments later the two boats were heading for the distant harbour of Mevagissey.

The clandestine operation had taken less than ten minutes. Looking back into the Channel, Ben saw the shadow of the French barquentine heeling over under full sail. Turning westward, she headed along the Cornish coast to another illicit rendezvous.

In that short time, Ben had become a 'freebooter'. A smuggler.

Walter had brought a bottle of fine-quality brandy with him from the French ship and it now passed from man to man as they pulled for the shore. The bottle was handed to Ben, but the first whiff of the pungent brandy fumes made his stomach rebel again. He gave it back to the nearest oarsman, untasted.

As the fishermen laughed and joked amongst themselves, Ben looked ahead over the bow of the boat. He hoped that if he took huge gulps of the cold air blowing on his face his stomach might settle down again.

Sliding through the water, side by side, the two boats were no more than two hundred yards from the sea-wall of Mevagissey harbour when Ben saw an indistinct movement between the fishing-boats and the cottage lights, visible through the harbour entrance.

'There's a boat ahead of us!' he called to Walter.

At his words, the fishermen stopped rowing instantly. Leaning on their oars, they listened, straining their ears into the darkness. The only sound was of the incoming waves rushing through the crevices of the nearby rocks, and the squeaking of oars in the rowlocks of the other Dunn boat as it forged ahead.

Walter sent a long low whistle across the water in an attempt to attract the attention of his brothers. It was doubtful if they heard him – and it was already too late.

A flame spluttered hesitantly to life ahead of them. It was joined by another. Suddenly there were half a dozen torches flaring, the flames from them blowing in long irregular streamers.

'It's the Revenue men!' whispered one of the fishermen in Walter's boat. Walter waved the man into silence. A large Revenue boat was heading towards Mark and Billy Dunn's boat, driven through the water by eight of the King's men, one to an oar. More of them crowded in the stern, eager for the action to come.

'Mark and Billy will need help . . .' Even as Walter made the observation, the Revenue boat went alongside the other fishing-boat with a splintering of oars and a great cheer from the King's men. Then the dull crack of a musket-shot echoed across the water.

One of the men in the boat with Ben uttered a startled oath. 'I'm not tackling armed Revenue men, Walter. Pull for the harbour – and be damned quick about it!'

'But . . . Mark and Billy . . . ?'

'It's too late to help them. Unless you want the Revenue men to take all your father's sons, we'll need to get in fast as we can. Hurry, man! You're helping no one by dithering out here.'

Crouched in the bow of the fishing-boat, Ben's heart beat as fast as a sparrow's wing. Peering over the gunwale he saw the other two vessels locked together as their occupants fought out an unequal battle.

Common sense prevailed over family loyalty. There were at least fifteen men on board the Revenue boat, most of them armed.

Walter said, 'Ben, get back here to the tiller. I'll tell you what to do as we go along.'

Ben scrambled to the stern of the boat. He had only the vaguest idea about steering a boat, but it needed only a couple of experimental pressures on the tiller to give him the knowledge he would need. By this time the fishing-boat was cutting through the water, the sea slapping heavily against the bow.

Their desperate attempt to escape the attentions of the Revenue men was noisy. As they passed around the fringe of the light cast from the torches they were spotted. A cry went up from one of the King's men, and seconds later a musket-ball sped angrily above Ben's head. Fortunately for himself and his companions, the captured fishermen realised what was happening. They created such a disturbance that the Revenue men were hard pressed to hold them and quickly lost interest in Walter's boat.

Ben guided the boat through the wide gap in the harbour wall. Once inside, Walter shipped his oar and came back to take the tiller himself.

'Good work, Ben. I'll take her now. We'll need to get alongside and clear the boat before the Revenue men follow us in.'

'What will happen to the others?'

'It will be time to think about that when the Revenue men bring them in. We've men enough in Mevagissey to prevent them being taken off to gaol. If we fail . . . ? We'll worry about that when the time comes. Here, take this rope and stand by to jump the moment we touch the steps.'

Although it was dark in the harbour, Walter brought the

fishing-boat in skilfully and swiftly, guided by his knowledge of the lamp-lit windows of the houses around the harbour. Soon the boat scraped along the stone wall of the quay and Ben could make out the deeper shadow of the steps. Leaping ashore, he secured the rope to a huge iron ring.

He had hardly finished tying the knot when a number of men appeared from the shadows about him. At first he thought they must be Revenue men, but when one of them greeted Walter in a low voice Ben realised that smuggling in Mevagissey involved more men than were in the Dunn family.

In quick low monosyllables Walter explained what had happened out beyond the harbour. The Mevagissey men immediately set to clearing the boat of fish and contraband. Not ten minutes after entering the small harbour the boat had been emptied and pulled clear of the steps. Once it was moored amidst a jumble of other fishing-boats there was no way of connecting Walter with the events of the evening.

There was still work for the fishermen to do. With the boat safely tucked away they turned their thoughts to those who had been taken by the Revenue men. Surrounding Walter, they listened as he laid plans for an elaborate rescue attempt.

Ben was given no part in this promised action. Walter Dunn sent his nephew on his way with an order for him to go straight home. Ben was a boy – and this would be a night for men.

Ben made his way to his grandparents' house, not knowing whether he was disappointed or relieved to have no part in what was certain to be a desperate and dangerous exploit. Along the way many men passed him, all hurrying to the harbour. It seemed every fisherman in Mevagissey intended being on the quay to provide a reception committee for the Revenue men and their prisoners.

When he entered the Dunn house, Ben gave his news to the

stunned occupants. Grandfather Dunn immediately reached for his coat and rushed from the house without a word. Grandma Dunn sank down on a chair, convinced that her two sons would be hanged. Not until much later did Ben learn that there was very good reason for her concern. It was less than a year since a fisherman from a nearby village had been convicted of smuggling and publicly hanged for his misdeeds. The government of the land was determined to stamp out smuggling in Cornwall – and was prepared to adopt harsh measures to achieve its ends.

Ben's mother listened in white-faced consternation as Pearson Retallick questioned his son about the events leading up to the Revenue men's ambuscade.

When Ben told him the whole story, the sick miner rounded on his wife, who was now trying to comfort her mother.

'Do you realise how close Ben has been to getting himself arrested for smuggling?'

Martha Retallick looked up, startled. She was unaccustomed to angry outbursts from her even-tempered husband.

'They wouldn't have done anything to Ben. He didn't know what was going on. He just happened to be in the boat, that was all . . .'

Her argument died away, defeated by its own weakness.

'There's not a judge in the land who would have believed him – and you know it well. Is this your idea of a better life for our son?'

'I am sure nothing like this will ever happen again . . .'

'So am I.'

Pearson Retallick was overwhelmed by a violent spasm of coughing. When it subsided, he spoke more quietly. 'I may not be much use to you any more, Martha, but I can still think like a man. Ben is a miner and not a fisherman. He doesn't belong in this house. Neither do I.'

Turning, Pearson Retallick saw Ben watching him, wide-eyed.

'You have seen and heard enough for one day. Off to bed with you now.'

'I want to wait until Walter comes home.'

'What he is doing could keep him from the house all night – or for ever. Go to bed now, Ben. I need to talk with your mother.'

Reluctantly, Ben left the room and climbed the stairs to their bedroom. At the top of the stairs he opened the window and leaned far out, looking into the darkness towards the harbour. He could see nothing, and no sounds carried to him on the night air.

Ben slid between the rough blankets and began to think about the events of the last two days – especially of what had happened after the meeting between the two Dunn boats and the French barquentine. He now knew why the fishermen had expressed their misgivings about having a stranger go out with them. Smuggling was as much a part of their lives as fishing.

Ben had no objection to becoming involved in such activities, but he wished Walter had trusted him enough to tell him what was likely to happen. He wondered what the fishermen did with the contraband when it came ashore. He would prefer to help with this side of the operation. Ben knew he was no sailor and would never become one, no matter how hard he tried. Even thinking about boats and the movement of the sea made him feel ill.

From the room downstairs, the sound of voices came to Ben as a low monotonous drone. He could make out nothing of what was being said and eventually he dozed off.

He woke up with a start as the door was pushed open on ungreased hinges. Pearson Retallick entered the room and prepared for bed. There were many more people downstairs now; Ben could hear their voices raised in heated conversation.

'What's happening, Pa?' Ben whispered. 'Is Walter home yet?'

'Yes.'

Ben waited for his father to say more. When nothing was forthcoming, he said, 'What of the others – Mark and Billy?'

'Rumour has it they have been taken to Plymouth to be put on board one of the warships there. If it is true, they will be sailing for the Mediterranean before the week is out.'

Ben gasped. 'The Revenue men can't do that! Mark and Billy have families—'

'That should concern you no more than your future worried them. Think yourself lucky that you are safe in bed and not being pressed into the Navy, leaving your mother behind to weep for you.'

Ben lay quietly in the darkness for a long time before he asked his father quietly, 'Will Walter be going fishing in the morning?'

'He might – but you won't be going with him.'

'Why? What am I going to do?' Ben sat up on his mattress, a great surge of relief going through him.

'We will all need to leave this house, Ben. Someone will have to take in Mark and Billy's wives and children if they are not to be thrown on parish charity. Your grandma wasted no time in pointing that out to me. This is the obvious place for them to come. There will be no room for us.'

'Where will we go?' The news filled Ben with excitement. He hoped they might return to the mining district of Cornwall's far west where he could go back to work that was familiar to him. His hopes were dashed by Pearson Retallick's next words.

'The Vincent family up at Lamorrack House want a woman to work in their kitchens. Your ma and me are going up there to see them in the morning. I am hoping they might find a house for us if I do odd jobs in the grounds for them.'

'What about me?'

'I would like you to bide your time for a while, Ben. Likely I will need you to help me out for a while. Just until my strength returns, that's all.'

Ben understood. His father's pride was too great for him to admit that he was incapable of holding down a job of work without his son to help him. The knowledge brought a lump to Ben's throat, and he said no more of his own hopes.

Chapter Five

The following morning, Walter and the two men who fished with him put to sea about their normal business. By so doing they would stay clear of any questioning Revenue men who might search the village for the companions of the captured men. Ben saw Walter before he left the house and was shocked by his tired and haggard appearance. Walter was taking the blame upon himself for not having done more to rescue his two brothers. Nothing Ben said could convince him otherwise.

Pearson and Martha Retallick left the village to walk to Lamorrack House immediately after breakfast. They had not been gone many minutes before the families of Mark and Billy Dunn descended upon the small cottage. Soon it was filled with the noise of wailing women and the crying of bewildered children.

Ben beat a hasty retreat. For an hour or two he wandered the narrow streets of Mevagissey, unused to having so much time on his hands. He looked on without any great interest as a new boat was launched from the small boat-building yard in a corner of the harbour. Ten minutes later he was looking in through the door of the mill, watching huge granite grinding-stones rumbling one upon the other in powerful unison, driven by a creaking timber water-wheel revolving on an outside wall.

There was little else to interest Ben in Mevagissey. Eventually, he decided to set off to meet his mother and father. They should be on their way back from Lamorrack House by now.

Ben made his way along a rough track through the valley to the north-west of the village. Within minutes he was in a new world. Rounding a low hill, the track cut through a small wood and left all sight and sounds of Mevagissey behind. Only the bird-calls and the sound of a stream flowing swiftly over a shallow bed of stones disturbed the deep peace.

Ben was unused to such countryside. In St Just every tree had long since been cut down and burned as fuel for home and mine-engine boiler; the song-birds driven far away to undisturbed countryside where they could build their nests. The trees had been replaced by tall stone-built engine-house chimneys, bird-song by the clank and clatter of whim and stamp-hammer.

Ben stopped once to watch a crimson-crowned woodpecker scale a tree, tapping at a hundred crevices in search of insects. Next, he searched the skies for a bird that was sending out plaintive cries, like those of a lost kitten. It was a buzzard with blunt tip-tilted wings, circling high above a nearby field.

So intent was Ben on watching the hunting bird that he walked along totally oblivious to his surroundings, his head high, eyes following the progress of the buzzard.

The bird changed its flight-pattern, banking in a long gliding dive. Ben turned around, walking backwards as he followed the bird's flight.

Suddenly he bumped against something – something that moved and shoved him hard in the back, sending him sprawling full length on the path.

Ben looked up from the ground to see two boys of about his own age looking down at him. One was grinning, the other scowling. Ben was certain thay had not been ahead of him before he turned around. They must have been hiding among the trees.

'You want to watch where you're going,' said the scowling boy, the larger of the two. 'You nearly knocked us down.'

The second boy's grin widened, and Ben stood up slowly and carefully brushed himself off. Not until this was done to his satisfaction did he meet the larger boy's eyes.

'You're quite right. I *should* have been looking where I was walking. But I am not going to apologise. You could have stepped out of the way. There was no need to push me over.'

'Move out of the way for a fisherman?' The big boy's look was scornful. He nudged his companion with his elbow. 'Do you suppose all fishermen walk backwards? Perhaps it's because they row their boats that way. They get used to it, I suppose. Makes you wonder how they get on when they go to bed with their women, don't it?'

Ben waited quietly until the two boys had finished laughing.

'You could wet yourself, laughing like that,' he said, addressing the larger of the two boys once more. 'I'm sorry to spoil your joke, but I'm not a fisherman. I'm a miner. Now, if you move aside, I'll be on my way.'

'Miners are no better than fishermen,' said the boy aggressively, the scowl once more on his face. 'And what is a miner doing along here, eh? We've got no mines in this valley. We don't want none, neither.'

'What I'm doing here is my own business.' Ben moved to step around the scowling boy. Quickly side-stepping, the boy blocked his path once more.

Ben's heart began to beat a little faster. He knew he was in for a fight. The thought did not trouble him unduly. He had been in many fights before. Among miners, fighting and wrestling were favourite pastimes. But Ben had two opponents here. He would need to land the first punch. He moved to one side as if to try to pass the boy in front of him again. Waiting until the other boy did the same, Ben quickly shifted his feet and put his shoulder behind a punch aimed at the larger boy's groin.

Ben had been working underground in a mine from the age of ten, and during the last year at the Money Box mine had been pushing heavy wooden wheelbarrows loaded with up to three hundredweight of ore. He had muscles that were the envy of grown men.

The scowling boy let out a cry of agony and slumped to his knees as Ben turned to meet the rush of the second boy.

He took him in a 'bear hug' and both boys crashed heavily to the ground, rolling over and over until they were brought up short by a tangle of briars.

Ben released one of his arms and aimed a blow at his adversary's face, but the other boy was quick and wiry. He got home with a couple of punches of his own before Ben's heavy fist landed.

By this time the first boy had recovered sufficiently to launch himself at Ben. For a while, Ben was hard put to hold his own against the two country boys. Then unexpected help arrived in the form of a shrill-voiced girl who pulled off one of the boys and held him by the collar of his shirt while she laid about him with a stick.

It was Jesse Henna, and she and her flailing stick proved too much for Ben's assailants. They fled along the path past a startled brown cow. Jesse's voice followed them until they were out of sight.

'You should be ashamed of yourself, Joe Teague. You too, Billy Rowe. Neither of you would dare start a fight on your own – nor stay when it's two against two . . . even though one's a girl. You're bullies and cowards, the pair of you.'

Turning back to Ben, Jesse's mood underwent a swift change.

'Are you all right? Have they hurt you? Here, let me look at your eye; there's a nasty graze just beneath it. Come over to the stream and let me bathe it for you.'

Ben allowed her to lead him to the stream. After washing his face, he brushed down his clothes as best he could while Jesse inspected his eye and 'tut-tutted' at him for not keeping still.

'It's all right,' he said at last. He felt she was making far too much of the graze. It only hurt when he blinked his left eye.

'It's not all right,' retorted Jesse. 'But it's better than it was before.'

Wiping a fragment of dirt away with a flourish of her pinafore, she asked, 'What started the fight?'

Ben shrugged, disconcerted by the closeness of this slim and dark-eyed girl whose whole being vibrated with life and energy. 'They just wanted a fight. But what are you doing here? I thought you lived up there.'

He waved a hand in the general direction of the head of the valley.

'I do, but our cow has been down at the valley farm – where Joe Teague lives. We use their bull. I'm taking her home now. Where are you going?'

Ben told Jesse about the interview his parents were having with Sir John Vincent and informed her he was on his way to meet them.

'Oh! I thought you might have been coming to Pengrugla.'

She sounded disappointed. Puzzled, Ben asked, 'Why should I be going there?'

Jesse coloured up and said quickly, 'It doesn't matter. Where will you live if your mother gets a job at the house? Perhaps Sir John will offer you Tregassick. It's empty at the moment. That would be nice. You would be close to our place there. But I thought you were going to become a fisherman. Why aren't you out with the boats today?'

'I doubt if I will go fishing again. There was some trouble last night . . .'

Jesse stared at him uncomprehendingly, but at that moment a horsedrawn farm-cart came into view along the track and Jesse had to shoo her cow out of its path. As they stood back to allow the cart to pass, Ben saw his parents seated in the back. They called for the wagoner to stop, and Ben's mother beckoned to him.

'What on earth have you been up to?'

Martha Retallick's hands went up to straighten Ben's hair and she peered closely at his grazed eye.

Jesse had driven her cow further along the track and now she returned to stand near the wagon. Feeling awkward and tongue-tied, Ben introduced Jesse to his parents, adding that she was the girl who had been knocked into the ditch by the wagon from St Just.

'Humph!' Martha Retallick began vigorously slapping the dust from Ben's jacket. 'It looks to me as though she has had her own back on you today.'

'It wasn't me who got him dirty,' explained Jesse cheerfully. 'He got in a fight with Joe Teague and Billy Rowe. That's how he hurt his eye. But you should see them. Ben gave them what for, even before I arrived to help him.'

'Did he, now? I'm sure I should be pleased to hear that, but I doubt whether Sir John Vincent will be interested to know how well Ben can use his fists. All he will see is a scruffy boy with a grazed face and dirt on his clothes. That's not the sort of lad he'll want working for him.'

'Work for Sir John Vincent? Doing what?' Ben looked apprehensive. 'Does that mean I'll have to work up at his house?'

'No, Ben,' Pearson Retallick answered his son. 'It seems Sir John owns the Happy Union mine down at Pentuan. It's tin-streaming – no underground work – but it's a mine. Sir John has given me a job, too. Counting the wagonloads of ore going on the ships down at the harbour. But you had better get up to the house. Sir John wants to see you, to learn what you are capable of doing.'

Martha Retallick sniffed. 'You needn't look so pleased, my son. It doesn't mean that I suddenly approve of mining. I don't. If this had been underground work, I wouldn't have let you take the job, even if it meant losing my own. Working above ground is different.'

Ben remembered that his mother had said much the same thing about fishing, but he did not want to remind her of the previous night. He felt happier than he had for a long time. He was going back to mining – and his father would be working, too. The future suddenly seemed much brighter for both of them.

'Did Sir John give you a place to live, Mrs Retallick?'

'Yes, he says there is a house and barn at Tregassick where we'll be comfortable enough. Why?'

Jesse gave Ben a brief triumphant glance. 'I thought it might be Tregassick. We'll be near-neighbours.'

'Not if we don't get a move on, you won't,' said the driver

of the farm-cart. 'Stay here talking for much longer and my cart will take root. We'll never get your bits and pieces up to Tregassick at this rate.'

'Then what are you waiting for?' snapped Martha Retallick. 'Get your horse moving. I intend being in by nightfall.'

The driver shook his head in despair and cracked his whip above the flank of his startled horse. As they moved off, Martha Retallick called to Ben, 'You go straight up to Lamorrack House and see Sir John Vincent now – and brush the dirt from your clothes before you get there.'

Waving his hand in acknowledgement, Ben turned his back on the trundling farm-cart. When they caught up with the cow Jesse gave it a sharp smack across the rump with her stick and the beast trotted along the track ahead of them, its udder swinging awkwardly from side to side. Jesse fell into step beside Ben, and when they cleared the trees and came out into a long meadow she pointed ahead of them. 'There's Lamorrack House.'

In the distance Ben saw a gigantic mansion set among tall trees. It was the largest house he had ever seen. It must have contained at least forty, or even fifty, rooms.

'What is Sir John Vincent like?'

Jesse shrugged her shoulders. 'He's rather nice, really. A bit strict – but I expect that's because he's a magistrate. His son is a magistrate too – and a Member of Parliament – but I don't like Colman very much. Sir John owns all the land about here, and the fishing tithes at Mevagissey. He's always been very kind to me and my ma.'

She suddenly looked serious. 'You'd better not let him find out that Walter Dunn is your uncle. Sir John believes all reformers should be horse-whipped, then hung, drawn and quartered as traitors.'

'I know nothing of "reform", and before these last couple of days I hardly knew Walter.'

'All the same, make certain Sir John doesn't learn you are related. If he finds out, you won't be at Tregassick for very long.'

The track became steeper as they left the valley and began the climb up the hillside towards the house. At close quarters Lamorrack House looked even larger than before. The sheer size of it completely overawed Ben. Seeing this, Jesse decided to accompany him to the house. She gave the cow a sharp slap on its rump and it went swinging on its way along the track. It would find its own way to Pengrugla from here.

Ben was grateful for her offer. Ahead of them were at least three paths through the wooded gardens of Lamorrack House. He was terrified of ending up in the wrong place and incurring the wrath of the titled and all-powerful landowner.

Jesse led Ben along a track that kept to the trees. As they approached the house, hemmed in on either side by tall flowering rhododendrons, Ben saw a tall man of about thirty-five standing on the path ahead of them.

Jesse saw him, too. 'That's Reuben Holyoak, Sir John's gamekeeper.'

She greeted the gamekeeper as they drew closer, but Reuben Holyoak was scowling at Ben, and it was to him he spoke.

'What are you doing here? These are private woods.'

Ben was taken aback by the undisguised hostility of Reuben Holyoak to a complete stranger but he replied politely enough.

'I've come to see Sir John Vincent.'

'What for?'

Ben had no intention of telling his business to this man. 'You'd better ask Sir John Vincent. He wants to see me.'

'That's right,' agreed Jesse. 'Ben and his parents are moving in to Tregassick.'

Reuben Holyoak's scowl shifted to her. 'What has it to do with you? Why are you here with him?'

'Oh, Reuben! Ben is going to be a neighbour and he's new in these parts. He needs all the help we can give him.'

'Is that so?'

The surly gamekeeper gave Ben his attention once more.

'Then I'll give you some neighbourly advice. Keep out of Sir John Vincent's woods if you don't want to fall foul of me. I'll give you some, too, Jesse. Don't latch on to every stranger you meet. Walking with them in such out-of-the-way places can lead you into trouble.'

Jesse's mouth dropped open in astonishment. Then colour rushed to her face and surprise turned to anger.

'What I do is none of your business, Reuben Holyoak – and I don't "latch on" to every stranger who comes to Lamorrack. You'll do well to bridle your tongue – or I'll loose mine. It was no stranger who tried to get me into trouble in these very woods when I was thirteen years old. Sir John doesn't treat such matters lightly.'

Now Reuben Holyoak's face glowed a fiery red, and without another word he strode off along the path.

Jesse gave Ben an embarrassed grin. 'You mustn't take any of that too seriously, Ben. I don't think Reuben meant anything he said to you.'

'What about . . . the thing you reminded him of? When you were thirteen?'

Jesse laughed shakily. 'It was nothing. Reuben was feeling fatherly towards me and went too far. That's all.'

Jesse was being less than honest with Ben – and he was aware she was not telling the whole truth. Reuben Holyoak was old enough to be Jesse's father, but there was nothing paternal in the way he looked at her. He had been filled with jealousy when he spoke to Ben. Reuben Holyoak wanted Jesse.

Ben did not doubt that he would do everything within his power to ensure she went to no one else.

The path they were on led to the servants' quarters, at the rear of the great house. Before reaching the back door, Jesse gave Ben a final brush down with her hand and inspected him in a manner that reminded him of his mother. Then she wished him luck and left him to knock on the door.

After passing through a huge kitchen, occupied by at least half a dozen servants, Ben was led along numerous dim passageways and then made to wait in a small stone-flagged hall.

It was almost an hour before the summons came from Sir John Vincent. During that time many servants passed to and fro through the hallway, but not one of them paused to speak to Ben. He became so nervous that he would have left the house had he thought he could find his way back to the kitchen door.

Then a stony-faced butler came to fetch him. Looking at Ben's heavy miner's boots, he sniffed loudly and told him to avoid walking on the carpets. Ben was taken to a large walnut-panelled study where the thick-piled carpet had him walking on tiptoe, wishing he owned a pair of shoes.

Sir John Vincent was seated at a desk in front of the study window, writing on a long sheet of paper. The quill pen scratched across the page with bold swift strokes and occasionally Sir John jabbed at the wide-rimmed ink-jar with unerring accuracy.

After a couple of minutes, he put down the quill and looked up at Ben. His eyes took him in from head to toe and lingered briefly on his face.

'How did you come by that graze?'

Ben fingered his eye quickly, 'I . . . I was watching a bird as I came through the woods . . . I walked into a tree.'

'Ha!' Ben could see that Sir John Vincent did not believe him. 'I want no troublemakers working for me, Retallick. No one is going to disrupt my mine by fighting. Do you understand me?'

'Yes, sir,' Ben gulped.

'You came towards the house a while ago with young Jesse Henna. How long have you known her?'

'Only a few days. She fell into a ditch. I helped her out and caught some of her ducks . . . sir.'

He added the 'sir' quickly because he sensed that Sir John was waiting to hear it.

The baronet frowned at Ben's disjointed explanation, but he did not pursue the matter.

'I see. Well, you will be neighbours, so it is as well that you get along. Now, tell me of your mining experience.' Sir John Vincent leaned back in his chair.

Happy to be talking of something he understood, Ben told the baronet of his five years spent working underground with his father, and of the things he had learned from him.

It was not long before Sir John held up his hand to silence Ben.

'All right, Retallick. It is clear you have not wasted your time so far. Keep up your interest in mining and you will one day become a much-sought-after miner. Get down to the Happy Union stream-workings in the morning. Tell Captain Ustick I have taken you on. He will put you to work. You will be on boy's wages until you have proved yourself. With shoulders like yours it should not take you too long.'

Sir John Vincent tugged at a bell-cord beside the desk, and a few moments later the butler arrived to show Ben out. He had reached the door when the baronet called to him.

'Retallick?'

Ben turned around.

'Don't fall into bad company at the Happy Union. I am told some of the men have been heard talking about parliamentary reform. Any man reported to me for involving himself in such matters will be instantly dismissed. Remember that.'

The baronet returned to his letter, and Ben was ushered from the room. He was now the latest employee of Sir John Vincent, eighth baronet. Champion of the 'rotten' boroughs of Cornwall.

Chapter Six

Ben and his father set off for work together at dawn the following day. The diminutive harbour at Pentuan, where Pearson Retallick was to work, was less than a mile away. The Happy Union mine was half a mile further on.

The way was downhill. Even so, Pearson Retallick was forced to rest when they were no more than halfway to Pentuan. His impaired lungs were incapable of supporting him for any sustained effort – even walking.

'I think Ma likes the new house, don't you, Pa?'

Ben made conversation so the enforced delay would not seem any longer than it was.

'I'm sure she does . . . nothing to dislike about it. Roomy . . . no one overlooking us. It might be a bit lonely for a while . . . but that isn't a bad fault.' Pearson Retallick summoned up a faint smile when he was able to breathe more easily. 'Your young maid had no trouble finding us there.'

Jesse Henna had called at Tregassick within minutes of their arrival there. She brought with her milk, eggs and a pair of willing hands to help Martha Retallick scrub floors and tidy up the house. It had lain empty for many months, and there was much that needed doing.

'Jesse is nobody's maid,' Ben retorted with such indignation that Pearson Retallick's smile widened. 'She goes her own way. She felt like helping Ma, so she did. That was all.'

In spite of his own words, Ben knew there was the beginning of an understanding between Jesse and himself. After Martha Retallick had persuaded her that she had done enough work for one day, Ben had walked Jesse to her home. Not many words were spoken by either of them along the way, each content to be in the company of the other. The walk in the warm spring evening had passed all too quickly.

'We're not going to be much use to Sir John Vincent sitting up here talking of other things. We'll need to be on our way or the day will be half over before we get to work.'

Pearson Retallick had recovered sufficiently to go on. Pushing himself up from the grassy bank where he had been resting, he set off down the hill at a determined pace. Ben followed, wishing there was a way to tell his father to walk more slowly, without reminding him he was a sick man.

At the foot of the hill a small river met the sea on a beach of smooth sand. Here Ben parted company with his father, Pearson Retallick going to the loading-jetty, close to the beach, Ben making his way up-river to the tin-streamings.

The Happy Union 'mine' proved to be very different from those in which Ben had worked, farther west in Cornwall. The 'levels' were not tunnels deep in the ground, but trenches dug in the hillside to form an intricate interconnecting pattern. Water was pumped to the highest level and used to wash the ore-carrying gravel down to the lowest. Here it was picked out and crushed to extract the tin.

The captain in charge of the Happy Union mine was a huge

bearded Cornishman who weighed at least three hundred and fifty pounds. His name was Loveday Ustick and he made Ben repeat the details of his mining experience.

Captain Ustick's shrewd eyes never left Ben's face during the whole time he was talking. When Ben finished, the big miner hooked his thumbs into the wide leather belt over which his stomach overflowed. His bushy eyebrows almost hid his eyes as he said, 'You think underground miners are God's chosen people, don't you, boy?'

Ben was surprised. 'Far from it, Cap'n Ustick. If they were, God would make life a whole lot easier for them. I know more about underground mining than I do about anything else. I have never stopped to wonder whether a miner was any different from a streamer.'

Captain Ustick's eyebrows returned to their normal position, and Ben saw that the tin-streaming captain had very blue eyes. 'Don't start thinking about it now, Retallick, and you'll get along fine at the Happy Union. I'm the best damn tin-miner you'll ever meet, but I've never found it necessary to try to squeeze this body of mine into any miserable little mole-run. Now, get to work in that bottom level over there and show me that you know what raw tin looks like.'

The task Ben had been given was children's work. He smarted at Captain Ustick's way of letting him know that his experience in deep mining counted for nothing here. But he said nothing and settled down to the fast rhythm of picking out the ore-bearing gravel from among the waste. He had been working steadily for a couple of hours when a shadow fell upon the trench. Looking up from his back-aching task, he saw the mine captain.

'All right, Retallick, you've had yourself an easy morning. Now we'll see how you manage a wheelbarrow. Someone is needed to take ore to the crusher farther along the level. Hurry up, now.'

That was the second of five different tasks given to Ben that day. At the end of it Captain Ustick declared himself satisfied with Ben's progress. He allocated him to a permanent team with the task of winning ore from the rich lower level of the valley. Ben had been accepted as a tin-streamer.

There was another boy of Ben's age working with the team and Ben looked up on more than one occasion on the second day to see the boy watching him, a frown on his face.

Not until they took their noonday break did the other boy approach Ben. He waited until Ben had moved away from the other tin-streamers to inspect the water-wheel that produced power for the stamps to crush the ore.

'You're Ben Retallick from the Money Box mine?'

'What if I am?'

There was such a natural belligerence about the other boy that Ben sensed trouble. Nevertheless, this boy's voice was familiar. Ben tried to remember where they had met before.

'I owe you my hand, Ben Retallick. I am Moses Trago. You pulled me up the ladder, the night the sea came into the Money Box mine.'

The hand that gripped Ben's was strong and firm. 'But for you I'd be down the mine now, along with all the others. I couldn't have held on in that torrent for long.'

Ben was delighted to meet someone who had also been an underground miner – and he was relieved he was not going to be called upon to fight this tough-looking dark-visaged boy.

'What happened to you when we reached the top of the shaft? I looked around and you had gone. No one could tell me who you were.'

'I had my reasons for not staying.' Moses Trago looked embarrassed. He felt he owed Ben an explanation.

'I . . . I ran away from home, such as it was. I heard my father was trying to find me. To get me to go back. If word got around that I'd been saved from the Money Box mine, it might have led him to me. So I just upped and left. It's not bad here. Some of the streamers are a bit nosey, but loosen a tooth or two in their heads and they soon learn to mind their own business.'

Ben looked at the other boy's large hands and the wide spread of his shoulders. Moses Trago would have no problem holding his own against any man.

'Where are you living?' Ben asked.

Moses Trago waved his hand vaguely towards the valley, up-stream from where they were standing. 'Along there a way. A few of us have built places for ourselves in the woods. And you?'

Ben told Moses Trago about the house at Tregassick and of the work his mother and father were doing. He invited Moses to come and see them. The serious secretive boy said he would, but Ben was left with the feeling that social visits were foreign to Moses Trago's nature.

When the time came for them to resume working, Ben and Moses Trago took up their tools and worked side by side. They talked about mutual acquaintances in the mines of the far west, and Moses told Ben what the area around Pentuan had to offer. During their conversation, Ben learned a little more about the parliamentary reform movement. In spite of Sir John Vincent's opposition it seemed that the movement had a strong following among the tin-streamers of the Happy Union and the miners from the huge underground mines only a few miles away at the head of the valley.

There was an urgent need for reform. Votes were sold and bought like so many shares in a mine, yet the vast majority of the men in the country were unrepresented in the House of Commons.

The same cry for suffrage was going up from many of the new industrial centres in the Midlands. It was a voice that was determined to be heard. Most miners, together with the men, women and children of the Midlands, lived and worked in appalling conditions – but nobody cared. Those who sat in Parliament were too busy keeping the country's ever-increasing wealth in the hands of the few powerful landowners who had made them Members of Parliament.

Ben learned from Moses that Walter Dunn was one of the most active local reformers, with a large personal following.

At the end of that day, Ben went home from work well satisfied with life. He was once again among miners – men who spoke the mining language, using mining words and sharing jokes that made no sense at all to anyone who was not a miner. Ben was almost back where he belonged.

During the next few weeks, Ben's happiness was marred only by the knowledge that his father's attempts to reestablish himself were not succeeding as well as his own. Pearson Retallick's problem lay in the distance they lived from the small harbour at Pentuan. The walk was too much for his dust-laden lungs. Once there, he was fine – the work was neither hard nor demanding – but he had to walk home up a steep hill at the end of the day.

At first, Pearson Retallick waited for Ben to finish work, and they would go home together. But, as the weeks went by he was obliged to rest more and more frequently along the way. Reluctant to allow Ben to witness his constant battle for breath, he began making excuses to walk home alone. Most nights he would remain at Pentuan, waiting until Ben had gone, before beginning his journey. Always he arrived home in a state of near-collapse.

It was a situation that could not last indefinitely. Pearson Retallick would soon have to give up working. Ben became desperately worried at the effect it would have on his father. He was not a man to spend his days happily at home, doing nothing but watch the seasonal changes in the fields and woods about the house.

One evening, when Martha Retallick was working late at Lamorrack House, Ben and his father were alone at Tregassick, and Ben tried to broach the subject.

He found his father excessively touchy.

'There's nothing wrong with me that I can't cope with. I can manage as well as the next man. You begin worrying about me when I ask for your help, not before.'

He spoke so sharply that Ben turned away, hurt. He went to leave the house, but before he reached the doorway his father called him back.

'I'm sorry, Ben. I shouldn't have spoken to you in that way. I know you mean well. I know you care. But this is something I must work out for myself. If I give up, or pass the problem on to you, I'm finished. I become a burden to everyone I love. I don't think I could live with myself if that were to happen, Ben.'

Ben wanted to argue with his father, to tell him that becoming a burden was not important. The only thing that mattered was for Pearson Retallick to stay alive and remain with his family for as many years as possible.

Ben could not bring himself to speak the words. His father had just said more to him about his illness than he ever would to anyone else. The subject was closed, and Ben left the house filled with unhappiness.

Then, in June of that year, an event occurred that, terrible though it was, gave Pearson Retallick a temporary respite.

For days a south-easterly gale had pounded Cornwall.

It was particularly severe along the stretch of coast about Pentuan and Mevagissey. In Mevagissey the sea-wall was breached and heavy seas sank many of those boats that could not be quickly drawn up to the safety of the narrow water-washed streets.

At Pentuan things were even more serious, but the danger was not appreciated until it was too late.

The village was little more than a cluster of houses huddled in the lee of a hill, protected from the sea by a wide bar of sand that stretched across a gap between the cliffs. This sand also prevented the sea from running up the wide valley to where the Happy Union tin-streaming mine was situated.

During the days of the storm, this natural barrier took an unprecedented battering. Driven by winds of near-hurricane force, the waves from the bay roared up the beach, attacking the protective ridge. Each wave, as it made a grumbling retreat, took with it tons of irreplaceable sand. Not until the highest tide of the year was expected, and the storm showed no sign of abating, did the residents of Pentuan suddenly realise the very real danger they were in. By now, only a thin strip of sand stood between the village and the sea.

With every villager helping, the men from the Happy Union mine toiled all night to reinforce the inadequate barrier, using rocks and trees carried from the woods behind the valley. They were still working when the final dawn broke and the tide threw its great weight behind the raging storm.

News of the fight to keep back the sea had spread around the countryside. It was a Sunday, and the cliffs and slopes on both sides of the beach were soon crowded with sightseers. Some, more brave – or more foolhardy – than the others, lined the road behind the sand. They were mostly young men and girls. The former, outdoing each other in a bid to impress their companions, ventured ever closer to the inadequate breakwater. The girls, in their turn, gasped and screamed as waves hit against the reinforced sand-ridge and threw spray thirty feet in the air, drenching those young men daring enough to stand their ground.

'Damned young fools!' muttered Captain Ustick as he returned from ordering a group of the young men away from the makeshift breakwater. Wielding a broad pointed shovel, the captain of the Happy Union mine was working as hard as any of his miners – and perspiring more than any two of them. 'If they have so much energy to spare, they should come and help us, instead of showing off before the maids like stupid young fighting cocks.'

Although he had warned them off, Loveday Ustick never thought the young men were in any real danger, although the tide was already encroaching farther inland than anyone in the small coastal village could ever remember – and it still wanted half an hour before high tide.

The situation changed suddenly and dramatically at the very moment Sir John Vincent arrived on the scene to see for himself how the coastal barricade was withstanding the storm.

Driving a pony and trap, Sir John turned from the road on to the flat waste ground behind the barrier just as a series of huge waves broke against it. The waves had been building up across almost two hundred miles of English Channel. The first one roared up the beach, flinging hundreds of tons of sea-water against the hastily constructed barricade. As it subsided, it could be seen that a gap, fifty feet across, had been torn in the breakwater. Captain Ustick knew there would be no holding back the sea now. He bellowed for his men to run for their lives.

Even as they ran, a second wave, larger than the first, thundered in from the sea. It smashed through the gap, crumbling the sea-wall on either side as though it were a biscuit, and a ten-foot-high wall of water surged into the valley beyond.

The foolhardy young men and screaming girls were overwhelmed by the rushing water and carried away, struggling and shouting as sea-water poured into the valley. Driven by wind and tide, it swept away everything in its path.

The wave had rushed past Sir John Vincent, but his pony and trap were on low-lying ground. Within seconds, water was swirling about him, higher than the floor of the trap. The pony, chest-deep in water, was thrown into a panic. It reared and plunged in terror as Sir John fought to keep it under control.

Bowled off his feet by the sea-water, Ben regained his footing no more than two arms' length away from Sir John Vincent's terrified pony. Floundering towards the animal, Ben caught hold of the harness just as the baronet slipped and fell in the trap.

'Whoa! Whoa!' Ben's experience with horses had been limited to patting the rump of the old blindfolded beast plodding a never-ending circle on the whim of the Money Box mine, but he had no fear of them. Calming the animal quickly, he led pony and trap to the safety of higher ground.

Dishevelled and wet, Sir John Vincent regained his footing and began berating the animal. Ben turned away as screams rose from the throats of nearby spectators.

'Boy? Retallick?'

Ben turned as Sir John Vincent called to him.

'Thank you, boy. You kept your head and saved me from a thorough soaking – at the very least! Come and see me at Lamorrack. Do you hear me?'

Ben nodded; then, as the screams of the crowd of young girls and women rose in a crescendo, he turned to watch the drama being enacted across the flooded valley, where a river of water, now a hundred yards wide, poured in from the sea.

Some of the miners had formed a human chain in a vain attempt to reach three young girls in the centre of the torrent. Swept along by the force of the water, their dresses floating around them, they were as colourful as flowers in a stream – and equally as fragile.

When the men farthest from shore were out of their depth and floundering helplessly against the pull of the tide, a couple of them broke away and attempted to swim to the girls. Even as they did so, the girls disappeared, pulling each other down as they sank. For a brief second one of them rose to the surface, choking violently. She disappeared again and there was only the swirling water spreading ever wider across the valley.

Then Ben saw Jesse. Pale-faced, she stood at the edge of the flood, her hands up to her mouth, watching the spot where the three girls had disappeared.

As Ben reached her, she looked up at him, her eyes wide and frightened with the horror of the scene she had just witnessed.

'Did you see them?' she whispered hoarsely in disbelief. 'They just sank and disappeared . . . drowned!'

It was the first time Jesse had been a witness to such a tragedy. It came as a shock to Ben to learn that others had not witnessed violent deaths. He had lived all his young life in a mining community where death was commonplace and arrived in many guises. He knew that the three girls they had just been watching were not the only ones to lose their lives in this disaster. When the water subsided many more bodies would be recovered.

Reaching Jesse's side, he put a hand on her arm. 'You'd better go home now, Jesse.'

She stood as though she were in a trance, looking out across the flooded valley. 'I know one of those girls, Ben. Her name is Kathie. She sat next to me in church this morning . . .'

Jesse was in a state of shock and Ben put an arm about her shoulders. 'I'll take you home.'

As though in a dream, Jesse allowed Ben to turn her away from the water and lead her slowly up the hill towards Pengrugla. Not until they were well away from the sounds of the pounding sea and the cries of the crowd waiting ghoulishly for more excitement did Jesse emerge from her shocked state.

A sob came from her, racking her body from head to toe. She turned to Ben, and he held her while she cried as though she would never stop.

It was the first time Ben had ever held a girl in his arms. It made him feel older than his fifteen years, and more of a man than working a hard day underground among miners ever had.

He held her until she was able to control all but the occasional ragged sob. Then he pushed her gently away from him.

'Are you all right now?'

Her eyes and nose red from crying, Jesse bit her lip and nodded vigorously. 'I think so. Thank you, Ben.'

When they reached the junction in the path where they would go in different directions, Jesse stopped and caught Ben's arm.

'You've been very kind to me, Ben.'

Ben smiled at her. The memory of her warm body in his arms was still with him. It was a very pleasant feeling.

'You were upset, that was all. Anyone would have been . . . after what happened.'

'I'm glad you were there to look after me, Ben.'

Before he realised her intention, Jesse stood on tiptoe and

kissed him on the lips. Then she turned away and ran off along the path to Pengrugla. Ben watched her go, his face as fiery as an autumn sunset and his chest puffed out with all the importance of his newly discovered manhood.

Chapter Seven

Moses Trago paid his first visit to Tregassick that afternoon. He came to tell Ben and his father that the flood had devastated the Happy Union workings. Choking the pumps, it had caused the engine to seize up. The giant water-wheel had been washed away and the main drain culvert from the mine was blocked for all its length. The deep levels of the stream-workings were under sixty feet of water.

There would be work for Ben, Moses and the other tin-streamers, helping to bring the mine back to production, but no ore would be mined for many weeks. It meant that Pearson Retallick would not have to make the daily return walk to Pentuan harbour for a while.

Moses Trago's makeshift home in the valley beyond the mine had also been swept away. Martha Retallick, pleased that her son had found himself a friend, tried to persuade Moses to stay at Tregassick for a few days. Moses declined the offer, accepting only the meal that she laid before him.

The truth was that Moses Trago did not feel comfortable

inside a house. His makeshift home in the woods would have appalled Martha Retallick, but the home from which he had run away was little better. It was a rough cromlech, formed from huge slabs of rock set into a hillside, high on Bodmin Moor. It had once housed the bones and worldly possessions of a Bronze Age chieftain, but these had been removed long before Moses Trago's father and his young family took up residence.

Another visitor to Tregassick that evening was Walter Dunn. He was on his way to a reform meeting at the Crinnis mine, a couple of miles away. Learning of the disaster at Pentuan, he called in to check that his brother-in-law and Ben were safe.

'I hear that seven bodies have already been recovered in the valley, with as many more still missing,' he said. 'Half the houses in the village have been washed away. Mother says it's the Lord's way of wiping out sin, Pearson. First your mine in St Just, and now the Pentuan stream-works. She says nothing good ever came from burrowing so deep in the earth.'

'Is that so?' snorted Martha Retallick. 'I don't see that our Mark and Billy have much to thank fishing for! I don't like mining myself – but only because it kills far more than it will ever make rich. That doesn't mean that men who work beneath the ground are any less godly than those who earn their living on the sea. How many of those who died today were from the mine? Tell me that, if you can.'

'There's no call for you to get your dander up with me, our Martha. I am only repeating what Mother said.'

Walter Dunn stood up and grinned ruefully at Pearson Retallick. 'I came out of my own house to get away from women with tongues like fish-hooks. There are two of them down at Mevagissey who spend half their days weeping for their menfolk, and the other half blaming me for letting them go smuggling. I don't like to remind them that I'm the youngest brother. It was Mark and Billy who taught *me* about free-trading!'

'You were quick enough to learn,' retorted Martha Retallick. 'But what they are really blaming you for is not getting yourself caught along with Mark and Billy. It's as well for them that someone in the Dunn family was born lucky. They would be in a sore plight now without you at home to fish for them.'

'Thank you, sister. I'm glad someone is on my side. But I must leave now for Crinnis. We have an important meeting there today. With any luck we'll make some progress towards ridding ourselves of Members of Parliament elected to office by men like your Sir John Vincent.'

'I don't want to hear a word against Sir John Vincent in this house,' snapped Martha Retallick. 'He gave us work and a home when we needed both. Don't you forget that.'

'Moses and I will walk along with you a way,' said Ben hurriedly to Walter, hoping to avert an argument. 'I want to see how they are getting on with cleaning up at Pentuan.'

Pearson Retallick cast a glance out of the window and said, 'Well! Today is a great day for visitors. Here comes young Jesse Henna.'

Jesse was still looking pale after the events of the morning, but she produced a wan smile for Ben. It was the first time she and Moses Trago had met, and Ben was surprised at the surliness of Moses when Jesse said she would accompany them to Pentuan. It was apparent that Moses Trago had little time for girls, and his sullen silence had an effect upon them all as they walked down the hill to Pentuan.

It was as much to provoke conversation as anything else that Ben asked his uncle exactly what was meant by 'parliamentary reform'.

'It is just what it says,' replied the fisherman seriously.

'We are trying to reform a corrupt voting system – one that allows men like Sir John Vincent to buy votes and send his son to the House of Commons in London. He doesn't do it to help the people of Cornwall, but to protect his own selfish interests. Farmers, fishermen and miners have no say at all in the running of the country. Forty-four men are sent to Parliament from Cornwall, some of them with no more than ten votes behind them. Yet, up-country, there are whole towns with thousands of people and no Member of Parliament at all. That's why things in this country are so bad for the likes of us. Farmers' men are fed by the parish, and seven-year-old children work ten hours a day on the mines for threepence because their fathers can't find work. You've seen for yourself that good fishermen need to turn to smuggling to feed their families because their earnings are paid out on unfair taxes and tithes. When we speak up for ourselves we are branded as agitators by Sir John Vincent and his land-owning friends. The day will soon come when they'll need to change their tune. Many gentlemen elsewhere are beginning to think as we do and support our cause.'

Walter Dunn spoke with great feeling, and Ben realised how deeply he felt about the reform cause.

'You don't need to take my word for anything, young Ben. Come along to the meeting with me and hear what others have to say.'

Remembering Sir John Vincent's warning, Ben was about to decline the invitation, when Walter added, 'You'll enjoy seeing Crinnis. We are holding our meeting close by the new engine-house at the mine there – and what a mine it is, too! None of your tin-streaming. It's a deep copper mine, giving work to nigh on a thousand men.'

There was a hunger in Ben for the sight of an underground

mine and, looking at Moses Trago, Ben saw his own eagerness reflected on the other boy's face.

'Sir John wouldn't like it if he knew you had been to a reform meeting, Ben,' Jesse warned.

Moses Trago rounded on her. 'What's it got to do with Sir John Vincent – or with anyone else? Come on, Ben. Let's go to Crinnis. We'll see again what a *real* mine looks like.'

'Will you come, too, Jesse?' asked Ben. 'You'll enjoy looking round a mine.'

Jesse shrugged. She knew she would not be able to prevent Ben from going now. 'I don't mind – but I'm coming with you to see the mine, not to listen to a lot of foolish talk.'

She looked at Walter Dunn defiantly as she spoke the words, but he only grinned at her.

Moses Trago lost much of his enthusiasm when Jesse agreed to accompany them, but he kept his thoughts to himself.

'How long will it take us to get there?' queried Ben.

'If we step out when we reach the top of Pentuan Hill, we'll be there inside an hour.'

Pentuan village was cleaning up in the wake of the great storm and flood. The water had subsided with the tide, and the villagers were hunting among the ruins of their collapsed houses for lost belongings.

As they passed through the village, Jesse fell silent, and Ben knew she was thinking of the girls she had seen drown. He would have liked to say something to make her feel better, but could think of no words that would not sound foolish in front of the others.

When they reached the top of the hill beyond the village, Walter Dunn pointed out the chimney and tall engine-house of the Crinnis mine. The mine was perched on the cliff-top just round the curve of the bay, and Ben imagined he could hear the clatter of stamp-hammers carried to them on the wind.

It was not long before they met up with others on their way to the meeting. Walter was known to most of them, and Ben fretted as their pace slowed to talk of reform and a preview of the evening meeting.

Eventually, Ben, Moses and Jesse hurried on ahead and left Walter to come on more slowly with his friends.

There was never any danger of losing their way. It seemed that all the men and boys, and a fair number of women, from the surrounding countryside were going to the reform meeting.

There were already at least five thousand people crowded into the flat piece of open ground between mine and cliff, but it was to the engine-house that the three made their way. As it was a Sunday, there were no men working underground on the mine, but the engineer kept the big engine at work pumping out water from the foot of the fifty-fathom-deep shaft. The huge cast-iron beam rocked easily on its greased pivot, with only the hiss of steam from the cylinder and the creak of chain and giant pump-rod to hint at its power.

This was a big mine, with far more equipment than they had possessed at the Money Box mine, but Ben and Moses moved from building to building, examining each piece of machinery minutely. Listening to their comments, Jesse thought a stranger could have been forgiven for thinking that the mine equipment had been made by the gods and not by Man.

The workings of the Crinnis mine extended far under the sea, and gradually the memories of the last minutes of the Money Box mine replaced the novelty of being on a deep-working mine. Ben and Moses allowed themselves to be drawn by the applause to the field where the reform meeting was being held.

The organisers had built a platform at one end of the field. On this stood the campaign officials and speakers. Ben saw that Walter Dunn was one of them. But, when they arrived, it was a thick-set grey-haired man who was drawing the crowd's applause. Ben and his companions pushed their way forward until they could hear his words more clearly.

'. . . all over the country, men – aye, and women, too – are rising in support of parliamentary reform and the cause of universal suffrage.'

'What does "universal suffrage" mean?' Jesse whispered loudly.

'Shh!' Ben understood it no more than Jesse, but there could be no misunderstanding the grey-haired man's next words.

'When are you people of Cornwall going to do something about the rotten boroughs within your own borders? When will you make your feelings known to those who spend a few guineas to buy votes for their own candidates, then sit back and grow fat on your labours? Not six months since, the people of London moved to seize the Tower of London! They would have succeeded had others come in from outside the capital to help them. Then, hardly a week ago, the workers of Derby fought against mounted soldiers for the right to be heard. Will you be left behind while other men fight for *your* rights? Will you do nothing here in Cornwall while the country continues to be ruled by a corrupt Parliament – and while a mad King sits upon the throne of England?'

The speaker's words stirred a feeling of excitement within Ben, but the roar of a concerted '*No!*' burst forth from five thousand throats startled him and Ben looked about him in alarm.

Inexperienced in the ways of mass meetings, and unaware of the transient nature of a crowd's enthusiasm, Ben believed he was in the midst of an imminent uprising against King and country.

Jesse felt the same way. Tugging at his sleeve, she whispered, 'Let's get away from here, Ben. I don't want to stay any longer.'

Ben would have liked to hear more of the speaker's words, but Jesse was already edging away.

'All right.' Ben looked about him for Moses Trago, but he was lost in the crowd. It did not matter. Moses Trago was quite capable of looking after himself.

As the speaker continued to shout abuse and pile insults upon the names of the infirm King George III and his Ministers, Ben and Jesse pushed their way through the noisy and enthusiastic crowd.

They were almost clear of the noisy throng when Ben looked up – and saw Reuben Holyoak standing not twenty paces from them. The gamekeeper was looking in their direction, but Jesse was not yet clear of the crowd. If Reuben Holyoak did not see her, there was a good chance Ben would go unrecognised. Turning hurriedly, Ben bundled Jesse back towards the heart of the meeting, doing his best to silence her puzzled protests.

When they had been swallowed up by the crowd, Ben told her the reason for his actions.

'Are you certain, Ben? Reuben Holyoak would not get involved in parliamentary reform. You must have been mistaken. You've only seen him once . . .'

Ben shook his head vigorously. 'It was him.'

'Then he must have been sent here by Sir John to take the names of any Lamorrack workers at the meeting. Did he see you?'

Jesse's face was pale. Sir John Vincent had an unreasonable hatred of 'reformers'. He would dismiss any of his servants who showed an interest in their cause.

'I'm not certain – but we'll need to go a long way round if we're to be sure of missing him.'

They went through the Crinnis mine and over the nearby fields, circling around the noisy meeting before they were on the Pentuan road.

The roars of the crowd at the meeting pursued them halfway to Pentuan. If Reuben Holyoak was there to take names, he would be kept busy searching among the thousands of reformers for a familiar face.

Ben and Jesse hurried homewards as fast as they could go, but they lost their race with darkness when they were still in the Pentuan valley. With the lights of the battered village behind them, they could have been the only two people in the dark silent night. It was a warm and companionable feeling, and the problems of the morrow receded rapidly.

'How did you and Moses come to be friends?'

The question from Jesse came suddenly, as though she had been thinking about it for some time.

'We both worked on the Money Box mine.'

After an initial hesitation, Ben told Jesse the story of the night the sea burst in upon the Money Box mine. It was the first time he had talked about it in detail since then. When he reached the point where he and Moses were clinging to the ladder while water poured down the shaft, trapping every miner in the mine, Ben's voice became hoarse and he found it impossible to continue.

In the darkness Jesse reached for Ben's hand and squeezed it sympathetically. 'I think you were very brave, Ben.'

'I was lucky, that's all.'

'Yet at the Crinnis mine you and Moses talked as though you looked upon a mine as being the most wonderful place in the whole world! Why, Ben?'

Ben thought about it as they walked along the path together. Here in the clean air of the night, with a sky full of stars above them and not the slightest hint of danger in the surrounding countryside, the need of a born miner to wrest a living deep underground was not easy to put into words.

After thinking about it for a long while, he said, 'Mining is the only thing I know how to do well, Jesse. I feel at home on a mine. I was ten years of age when I first began working an underground shift with my pa. He was the same age when he went below grass – and so was his pa. The Retallicks have been miners for as far back as anyone can remember. My pa felt bad about making me go down there with him, but I can remember that I'd never felt so happy in all my life. Working underground is not easy to describe, Jesse, because it's like nothing else I know. When you begin digging out a new level, following a lode, you know you're going where no other man has ever been before. It's not just digging out earth and stones. Everything down there has its own meaning and its own colour – colours you don't see above ground . . .'

Ben faltered, unused to making such a long speech and laying his feelings bare in such a manner.

'I'm a miner, Jesse. One day I'll be as good as my pa. There's many a man would be proud to be able to say that.'

Jesse did not doubt him for one moment. She knew Ben had just shared a very important part of himself with her.

They walked in silence for a while, and Ben was very much aware of the fact that he was still holding Jesse's hand, but he made no move to do anything about it.

'I don't think I like Moses Trago,' Jesse said unexpectedly.

'You met him today for the first time. How can you say that?'

She shrugged. 'It's a feeling I have. There's something in his eyes when he looks at me. I find it frightening,' she shuddered. 'Let's talk of something else.'

Pushing aside all thoughts of Moses Trago, mines – and Sir John Vincent – they chatted about their houses, the livestock on the Henna 'farm' and the people who farmed the land in the area. Born and raised on the Lamorrack estate, Jesse knew everyone for miles around.

In no time at all they arrived at Jesse's house. Reluctantly, Ben released her hand. Somewhat gruffly, he announced that it was time he went home. But he made no immediate move to leave her.

'Thank you for taking me to see the Crinnis mine, Ben. I have often wondered what a mine was like – especially since you came here.'

Jesse, too, was reluctant to have Ben go, yet she was unable to think of words that might make him stay a while longer.

'It was good to see a proper working mine again.'

They stood in awkward silence, the familiarity of a few moments before gradually slipping away.

Suddenly, the door of the house, only a few yards away, opened wide and Jesse's mother was silhouetted in the doorway, the yellow light of a lamp behind her.

'Jesse? Jesse, are you out there?'

'I'm here, Ma.'

'Then you come in this minute. I've been worried sick about you.'

Maude Henna took a step outside the house and peered into the moonlit night. 'Who is that with you?'

'Ben Retallick.'

'Then it's time he was home where he belongs. You come straight indoors now, or I'll come out and fetch you.'

The door swung shut, and Jesse grinned at Ben. 'I think my ma wants me to go in.'

She leaned forward and kissed him quickly. Backing away

from him, she said softly, 'I like you, Ben Retallick. I like you a lot.' Then she was gone.

Ben walked home with his hands in his pockets, whistling loudly. It was a song he had heard in the miners' inns around St Just – a man's song.

Chapter Eight

Ben felt less like a man the following day. After spending his working-hours fruitlessly searching for lost equipment at the flooded Happy Union mine, he arrived home to find his mother waiting for him in a state of some agitation.

'Hurry up and wash and get into your best clothes. They are upstairs laid out for you. Sir John wants to see you up at the big house.'

'Why does he want to see me?'

Although he asked the question, Ben was certain he knew the answer and his heart beat faster. All day long he had been thinking of the unfortunate meeting with Reuben Holyoak at the Crinnis mine, wondering if the gamekeeper had seen him. Now he knew, and it seemed Reuben Holyoak had wasted no time in informing his employer.

'How should I know what's in Sir John's mind? All I know is that the butler told me you were to come to Lamorrack House the minute you arrived home from work.'

'Sir John Vincent can wait until I've had something to eat.

I've been working all day without a break to get his mine cleared up and I'm hungry.' Ben needed time to think.

'You can eat when you get back from seeing Sir John. So the faster you get up to the big house, the better for yourself. Hurry up, now. I have your father to tend to when you get off.'

Ben had looked for his father when he first entered the house. Not seeing him, he had assumed he was out somewhere.

'Tend to Pa . . . ? What's wrong with him?'

'He's not feeling so good. He's gone upstairs to bed.'

In spite of Martha Retallick's repeated demand that Ben hurry off to Lamorrack House, Ben's immediate concern was for his father, and he went upstairs to the bedroom to speak to him.

Pearson Retallick was propped up in the sparsely furnished main bedroom, looking wistfully out of the window at the sun-soaked fields and the blue sea in the distance.

Turning his head as Ben entered the room, Pearson Retallick gave him a tired smile, 'Hello, Ben. I wish we'd found this place a few years ago. Perhaps I should have listened to your mother after all. The three of us could have made a good life here together.'

'Doing what, Pa? You trundling a wheelbarrow in a streamworking and me sitting in a boat off Mevagissey, waiting for a French smuggler . . . or an English press-gang? No, it's nice enough out there but I would rather be following a lode along an underground level – so would you.'

Pearson Retallick coughed quietly, drawing shallow breaths of air into his dust-filled lungs. When he could speak again, he said, 'I've spent too many years following tin lodes, Ben. I carry a part of every one of them inside me now. I am thirty-seven – and I'm finished. I'll never work another pitch again. But what am I doing talking to you like this? Take no notice, Ben. I'm just feeling sorry for myself for being a-bed on a fine day. Didn't I hear your mother say that Sir John wants you up at Lamorrack House? You'd better get on your way. Likely as not he wants to make you captain of the Happy Union . . .'

Pearson Retallick's laugh brought on another bout of coughing, this one more serious than before.

It hurt Ben very deeply to see his father in this condition and he turned away. 'I'll go up to Lamorrack House now. You try and get some rest while I'm gone.'

'Ben . . . ?' The word was forced out as Pearson Retallick fought hard for breath. Ben turned back to his father as he gasped out what he wanted to say. 'Whatever it is – whatever Sir John wants of you – go along with him, Ben. We depend on Sir John's goodwill . . . and your mother is happy here.'

Ben nodded unhappily. 'She'll not have to leave here because of me, I'll see to that.'

As Ben put on his best clothes, he wondered what he ought to say to the baronet. Then he put all the ideas from his mind. No doubt Sir John had already decided what he was going to do with Ben. If that was so, the only course of action left to him was to say he was leaving, going away somewhere. Then perhaps Sir John would allow Martha Retallick to remain at Tregassick.

When he went downstairs, Ben's mother fussed at his appearance. Brushing off the shoulders of his jacket, she tried to pull the too-short sleeves down over his exposed wrists.

'You be certain to call him "Sir John" when you speak. And listen to what he has to say to you. Don't say anything unless he asks you a direct question. Do you hear me, now?'

'I hear you, Ma,' Ben said irritably. 'I'll be polite to him, but Sir John is only a man, the same as any other.'

Martha Retallick stopped her fussing. Taking a step back from Ben, she wagged a finger only inches from his nose.

'That's just the kind of thinking to land you in trouble, my lad. Sir John Vincent is *not* just another man. The Almighty may rule the hereafter, but on this part of God's earth Sir John Vincent rules for Him. Upset him and you'll need to go a very long way to make a new start. I know; I work in his house. I see what goes on. You heed my words or we'll all suffer. Your father is ill upstairs, and it won't be long before you are the breadwinner for this family.'

'All right, Ma. I'll try not to upset Sir John.'

Secretly, Ben thought Sir John Vincent was probably already angry with him, but it would be no comfort to his mother if he told her the truth. She was worried enough already about his father's illness. A widow's lot was not an easy one in the unenlightened days of the early nineteenth century.

Ben set off from Tregassick displaying far more confidence than he felt, and it was fast seeping away by the time he reached the Hennas' small farm. There he saw Jesse turning out the Hennas' two milking-cows into a field.

She commented gaily on his smart appearance, but her mood changed abruptly when he told here where he was going.

'So Reuben did see us! He's wasted no time doing something about it. What will you say to Sir John?'

Ben shrugged. 'I'll think of something.'

'Wait a minute. I'll come to the house with you.' Jesse reached the decision suddenly.

'This has nothing to do with you,' said Ben in alarm. 'Keep out of it, Jesse. There's little sense in both of us finding trouble.'

'You needn't worry about me. I get on well with Sir John –

you ask anyone. He won't do anything to me, and I may be able to help you.'

'Haven't you got work to do? What about the cows . . . ?'

'I've already milked them. The rest of my work can wait. This is far more important.'

The expression on Jesse's face allowed of no argument. Jesse Henna was a very determined young woman – as anyone who opposed her quickly discovered.

Ten minutes later they were walking through the trees surrounding Lamorrack House. Ben nursed a vain hope that Sir John might have forgotten he was coming and have gone out somewhere.

But there was to be no evading this issue. Sir John Vincent was at home. Furthermore, Ben was informed that the baronet was annoyed because Ben had not come to the house very much earlier.

The servant who took Ben to the library was not at all sure about allowing Jesse to accompany him. But Jesse thrust out her chin and told the servant that Sir John would wish to see her, too.

He did not. When she and Ben entered the room together, Sir John Vincent's grey eyebrows met in a heavy line across the bridge of his nose and he snapped at her, 'What the devil are you doing here? I did not send for *you*. Only for this whippersnapper.'

'If it's about yesterday, then you'll want to see me, too, because I was with Ben,' Jesse retorted, looking at the baronet defiantly.

Ben held his breath in dismay. It was just such an angry confrontation as this he had been so anxious to avoid.

'You were at this – this – meeting of rabblerousers?'

'We were both at Crinnis – but not at the meeting. Ben took me there to see the mine. After we looked all over it we had to pass through a crowd who had gathered for some meeting. That was when Reuben Holyoak saw us – and I know it must have been him who told you he saw us there. Though I don't suppose he explained what he was doing there himself?'

'Reuben Holyoak was there on my instructions. But he made no mention of seeing you, only Retallick.'

'I don't suppose he mentioned the other boy who was with us, either. The one whose life Ben saved when they were both working on a mine, farther west?'

Sir John Vincent looked perplexed. He shifted his gaze from Jesse to Ben and back again . . . Then he threw back his head and laughed. 'By God, girl! You are snapping at me for all the world like a vixen defending one of her cubs. I swear you've got more guts than any man or woman on the whole of my estate. Now, the pair of you sit down and tell me what this is all about. No, you keep quiet for a few minutes, Jesse. You have said enough already. Let me hear what you have to say, Retallick.'

Taking his cue from Jesse's explanation, Ben told the baronet that, as it was a Sunday, he had decided to take Jesse to Crinnis and show her over the big mine there. When they left the mine they had found themselves caught up in the meeting of reformers.

Sir John Vincent asked Ben a number of technical questions about the lay-out of the Crinnis mine and the surface machinery they had there. He displayed a surprising knowledge of the cliff-top workings, but when Ben began answering his questions in detail Sir John Vincent threw up his hands to stop Ben's flow of words.

'Enough! You have no need to air your knowledge of mines in here. You said you went to Crinnis to look over the mine workings. Now I believe you. But what is all this about saving the life of some lad . . . ?'

Ben gave a very brief version of his first meeting with Moses Trago. As Sir John Vincent listened, he studied Ben's face.

'You seem to make a habit of rescuing people, Retallick. I have not forgotten your assistance to me yesterday.'

He put a finger and thumb inside a pocket of his waistcoat and pulled out two dull golden guineas. Holding them out towards Ben, he said, 'Here, take these. I am told your father is not too well. I have no doubt you will find a use for them.'

Delighted with the sudden turn the interview had taken, Ben took the coins and thanked the baronet.

'I always reward those who do me favours, Retallick. I also deal harshly with those who do me ill. Remember that. As for this "reform" nonsense, I will have none of it on this estate. Neither will I tolerate such revolutionary ideas within my magisterial district.'

'What is revolutionary about a man wanting a say in his own future, Sir John?'

Jesse asked the question in apparent innocence, but Ben saw Sir John Vincent's expression harden and he was glad he had not asked the same question.

'Coming from anyone else that would be crass impudence, Jesse. I and the other landowners of this country have looked after our tenants and workers for centuries. I will continue to protect them – against themselves, if need be. The man in the field, or in the mine, knows only what food is short today, or what commodity costs more than it did yesterday. He knows nothing of the cause – or of the efforts being made on his behalf to set things to rights. There is no reason why he *should* know. Such things are better left to those who possess all the facts. Were he to be given power to act on his own behalf, or even to vote, England would go the same way as France. The mobs would take over and terror would stalk the countryside. Eventually, some blackguard like Bonaparte would come along, take over the country and lead it to total ruin.'

Sir John Vincent glared belligerently at Jesse for a few moments, then his face softened.

'Why am I telling you of such matters? They do not concern you, Jesse. Run along to the kitchen, now, and see if Cook can find you a cake, or something. I want to have a word with this young man. Oh! You need have no fear. It has nothing at all to do with your visit to Crinnis.'

In spite of Sir John's assurance, Jesse left the room with obvious reluctance, but she knew better than to disobey a direct order from him.

When the door had closed behind her, the baronet eyed Ben in a speculative manner for so long that Ben began to feel uneasy. Suddenly, Sir John spoke to him.

'That girl is fond of you, Retallick.'

Ben did not know what he was expected to say, and so he said nothing.

'Well? Don't just sit there like a simpleton, boy. I said Jesse is fond of you. What are your feelings towards her, eh?'

'I am fond of her, too, Sir John.'

To Ben's great relief, the baronet beamed. 'Good! Good! But there is more to life than being fond of someone. What ambitions do you have for the future?'

Ben had no hesitation in answering this question. 'I want to work as a miner . . . in an underground mine. Perhaps one day become shift captain – or even a mine captain.'

'H'm! I can think of better ways of earning a living, but it so happens I will be opening a deep mine just outside Mevagissey before long. That should keep you in the area long enough for me to keep an eye on the pair of you. All right, young Retallick. You can go now.'

Ben left Sir John Vincent's library thoroughly bewildered,

not at all sure of the reason for the last private session of questioning. He decided that Sir John Vincent must be taking a special interest in him because he had led his pony and trap from the flood waters of Pentuan. That was what he told Jesse when they were on their way home.

In Sir John Vincent's library the door swung open and a tall pale-faced man in his early forties entered the room.

'Good evening, Father. Did I see a couple of estate brats leaving the house just now? What had they been up to?'

'Estate brats, Colman?' The look Sir John Vincent gave to his only son was decidedly cold. 'The girl was Jesse . . . Jesse Henna.'

'Was it, now! I *have* been away from Lamorrack for a long time. She has reached an interesting age.'

Sir John Vincent looked at his son in disgust, 'Jesse is almost fifteen, Colman – an age when many young girls are wedded off. As a matter of fact, that was partly why I had her and the lad in here. They make a good couple. I am thinking of settling the farmhouse at Pengrugla on them.'

Colman Vincent lost his air of indifference. 'Is that wise? Such a generous gesture is certain to set tongues wagging . . .'

'Damn the wagging tongues! It is a little late in the day for you to care what people say, or think, about the Vincent family.'

Colman Vincent shrugged. 'You must do what you think best, Father. But I trust you realise that marrying Jesse off to someone else is going to upset your faithful servant, Reuben Holyoak?'

'Holyoak? He is old enough to be Jesse's father!'

'Perhaps. But, of course, he is *not* her father. Reuben has told me more than once that he would like to wed Jesse.'

'You would not go along with such an indecent arrangement?'

'Why not? The girl would be gaining a respectable husband and a certain status in life. After all, Reuben Holyoak is a *head* gamekeeper. I don't suppose he would be too demanding, either. If the girl wanted an extra-marital romp in the hayfield with her young swain, I am sure the old stag would be only too happy to have someone blunt the edge of her appetite, so to speak.'

'I will thank you to keep your crude talk for your London friends, Colman. It is out of place in this house. Young Retallick will wed Jesse as soon as he is old enough to support her – and they will have Pengrugla. I will make my wishes known to her mother tomorrow. Now, you may leave me. I have work to do.'

Sir John Vincent turned his back on his son, leaving Colman Vincent to seek the amorous gamekeeper and inform him of the decision that had been made about Jesse's future.

Chapter Nine

Maude Henna called on the Retallick family late the following evening, bringing with her an unusually quiet Jesse. Pearson Retallick saw them coming along the path towards the house. He was feeling a little better today and occupied a wooden rocking-chair in the kitchen, looking out through the open doorway.

'Martha! We have company – and all dressed up in their Sunday frills, too. It must be something of importance.'

He looked across the room at Ben. 'Have you been up to anything I should know about?'

Ben's face turned a deep red, but he shook his head vigorously, hoping his guilty thoughts did not show. On the way home from Lamorrack House the previous evening, he and Jesse had followed the course of a stream through the woods surrounding the big house. They were still in the woods when dusk fell.

In the dark seclusion it had seemed perfectly natural for him to kiss Jesse. She had responded with inexperienced but enthusiastic ardour, and his hands had begun an exploratory journey of her body. Jesse stopped him before he was able to answer all the questions that had long plagued him, but not until he had made a number of discoveries to stir his own body physically and thrill him with their future promise.

Last night, their newly awakened passions had been an exciting experience for both of them, but if Jesse's mother had found out . . .

By the time Jesse and her mother entered the house, Ben's cheeks wore a fiery glow, fanned by his guilty and imaginative thoughts.

His sense of foreboding increased when Jesse entered the room without looking at him. Behind her, dressed in her church-going clothes, Maude Henna was tight-faced and serious. This was no informal neighbourly call. Martha Retallick responded to the mood of her visitors by bringing out the tea she kept for special occasions. Until it was made, they all sat or stood about the small room, making stilted comments about the weather and the ever-rising cost of foodstuffs.

Not until she had sampled her hostess's tea did Maude Henna broach the matter she had come to discuss.

'Sir John sent for me this morning. He wanted to speak to me about my Jesse . . . and young Ben.'

As Pearson Retallick flashed his son a 'What haven't you told me?' look, Martha Retallick threw up her head defensively.

'I don't believe my son has done anything to which Sir John can take exception.'

Maude Henna looked startled. 'Oh, no! Neither of them has done anything wrong. No, that's a long way from the truth of the matter. Sir John wants there to be an understanding between our two families. When Ben is old enough, Sir John wants him to wed Jesse. He said that on the day they are married he will settle our little farm at Pengrugla on the two of them.'

Jesse looked at Ben for the first time since she had entered the house. It was a look that contained both happiness and apprehension. Ben's answering smile contained a great deal of relief. But no one was paying any attention to them. While Pearson Retallick listened to Maude Henna's words in slack-jawed astonishment, Martha Retallick groped blindly behind her for a heavy wooden chair. Grasping it, she sat down quickly.

'Ben to wed Jesse . . . ? But they are both no more than children?'

Maude Henna snorted. 'Children? Jesse has been putting in a full day's work since she was big enough to hold a stick and drive a cow to pasture. From what I hear of your boy, he has led a similar life. They don't remain children for long these days, Mrs Retallick. There are maids a-plenty hereabouts who are wedded and bedded by the time they reach Jesse's age. Ben is a bit too young to take on the responsibility of a wife just yet, but he's a big boy. In a year or two he'll be able to call up a man's wage. Leastways, he would if he worked on the land, or on a fishing-boat.'

'But why should Sir John concern himself with who our Ben marries . . . and give him and Jesse land as a wedding gift?'

Pearson Retallick had heard none of the rumours concerning Jesse Henna's parentage.

'Sir John has always taken an interest in Jesse,' replied Maude Henna, meeting and holding Martha Retallick's eyes. 'My family have worked for the Vincents for as long as anyone can remember, and Sir John has always been a generous man. Mind you, I am not saying that I entirely approve of this arrangement and, if it were not Sir John's express wish, I might have more to say about it. I had hoped to see my Jesse married to a man with more of a future than a miner.'

Martha Retallick bristled. 'My family are fisherfolk with their own boats at Mevagissey, Mrs Henna. I had no thought of lowering my station in life when I married Pearson.'

'No, of course not. Besides, Ben won't be a miner when he has his own land.'

Martha Retallick did not share Maude Henna's confidence. She could not have wished for more for Ben . . . if he were able to settle to working on the land. She knew how much mining meant to Ben and was fully aware of the hold that mining took on a man. There was also her own future to consider. If Ben took over the farm at Pengrugla, he would have a wife and mother-in-law to support there. Little money would be left over to help his own mother and a sick father.

'Did you know anything about this, Ben?' Pearson Retallick questioned his son.

'No. Well . . . not exactly. Sir John asked me what my feelings were for Jesse, and I told him. That was all.'

'H'm! You must have left him in no doubt about them.' Pearson Retallick smiled happily. 'I am pleased for you, Ben. Pleased for you both.'

Martha Retallick said nothing. She was still thinking of what being related to the Henna family by marriage was going to mean. Jesse was a good girl, even if she did have a disconcerting habit of speaking her mind at times when most other girls would remain silent. She would be welcome in the family. But Maude Henna . . . ? She believed herself to be a sight too good for other working folk. Martha Retallick expected trouble with her.

Then Maude Henna began talking about the future wedding and, seizing their opportunity, Ben and Jesse slipped from the house.

As they walked through the wood behind Tregassick, Jesse took Ben's hand. 'So we are to be married, Ben? What did you really tell Sir John when he asked you about your feelings for me?'

'I can't remember now.'

'Oh, Ben! You can't have forgotten something of such importance so quickly.'

'All right, what would you have said to him had he asked you?'

Jesse was quiet for a few minutes. Then, softly, she said, 'I would have told him I love you very much.'

There was such sincerity in her voice that Ben knew she meant every word.

'Now tell me what *you* said.'

'I told him . . . I am very fond of you.'

'Honestly, Ben?' Jesse's face glowed with happiness. 'I'm glad, Ben. Very, very glad.' She hugged him excitedly in her happiness.

Ben grinned in embarrassment. 'Not so fast! I didn't tell Sir John I would marry you . . .'

'That doesn't matter. You will. You just wait and see.'

Ben held Jesse to him, but as the heat of the previous evening returned to both of them the voice of Maude Henna rang out, calling for her daughter to return home with her to Pengrugla.

The summer of 1818 passed faster than any season Ben could remember, and with it passed Jesse's fifteenth birthday.

Ben spent the hot summer days toiling, shirtless, in the reopened Pentuan stream-workings, enjoying the unaccustomed luxury of sunshine on his skin, and he developed a healthy tan. Most evenings he went to Pengrugla to help Jesse with the chores. Afterwards, if they finished early enough, they would stroll through the woods to Mevagissey and there watch the return of the fishing-boats with their own daily harvest.

These were good days for Ben and Jesse, but there were many in Cornwall who shared little of their happiness. For the farmworkers and tenant farmers in particular, it was a difficult year. Prices, rents and taxes were cripplingly high – but wages remained low. Many more farmworkers were forced to rely upon parish relief to keep themselves alive. Others literally fought each other for work. Often it was no more than gathering seaweed to manure the fields, or wedding crops for the paltry sum of threepence a day. Given such a situation, it was not surprising that the reform meetings were increasingly well attended. At the meetings, desperate men with families close to starvation listened as speaker after speaker blamed all the ills of the country upon a government that did not represent the vast majority of the British people. It did nothing to help, but they gained comfort from the knowledge that *someone* was aware of their plight.

There was a great deal of truth in the arguments of the reform speakers. The country *was* run for the benefit of a privileged few. The distribution of parliamentary seats, in Cornwall in particular, was a disgrace. Cornwall held tenaciously to forty-four seats. The whole of Scotland could boast of only one more; Wales had only twenty-four; and the huge industrial cities of the Midlands – none!

But such facts were lost in the extravagant claims of those who spoke in favour of immediate parliamentary reform. They told their listeners whatever they wanted to hear. Reform would bring down the price of goods. Reform would give a living wage to the impoverished farmworkers, freeing them from the spectre of the dreaded workhouse. Reform would cure all ills.

Few men paused to ask how such a desirable state of affairs would be achieved – and no one attempted to tell them. Embracing parliamentary reform, universal suffrage, abolishment of tithes and taxes – and general freedom from want – the reform movement attracted anyone with a grievance against the established order in the land.

Ben met his uncle, Walter Dunn, frequently and the talk always turned to reform. In spite of his own reservations, Ben found his interest in the movement quickening and he asked many questions – for which Walter Dunn was always ready to provide answers.

But Ben was working hard at the Happy Union, determined to make the most of the opportunity Sir John Vincent had given him and Jesse. He would not allow himself to be drawn into the parliamentary reform movement. As it grew in strength throughout the country, it attracted to it the type of man about whom Sir John had warned Ben.

The new reformers used the general unrest to sow seeds of the revolution that had borne such bloody fruit in France. In the Midlands, workers wrecked the new machines that had taken the places of so many of their fellow-workers. In Manchester, troops were called to put down riots. Scores of protesters were arrested.

In a desperate attempt to quell the unrest the administration of Lord Liverpool hanged many of the ringleaders and sent others to the penal colonies of Australia. Yet still the people of the land clamoured for 'reform'.

Even the most innocent of meetings needed little provocation to make it erupt into violence, as Ben and Jesse learned for themselves, later in the year.

One of the Pengrugla sows had produced a fine litter of fourteen piglets and, as soon as they were weaned, Ben and Jesse took them to a Saturday market in Mevagissey.

By late afternoon the last of the piglets had changed hands for a very satisfactory price. Ben and Jesse were thinking of returning to Pengrugla when suddenly a sullen-faced Cornish farmworker entered the square where the market was being held, only yards away from them. At the end of a halter he led a drab and none-too-clean young woman.

'Hear me! Hear me!' the man called in a loud voice. As men gathered about him, he shouted, 'I've come to auction off my wife to the highest bidder. She's not too clever, and her looks aren't of the best, but she's a willing worker and has a still tongue in her head. What am I bid now? Do I have an offer of a shilling?'

'You do! I'll bid a shilling for her.'

The excited call came from a scrawny-bearded ancient who stood no higher than the woman's shoulder when he came forward eagerly to confirm his offer.

'Then I'll make it two . . .'

A broad-shoudered man wearing a military coat limped forward. Ben saw he had one leg cut off below the knee. In its place was a leather-topped wooden stump.

The old man glared at the newcomer, then he pulled out a worn purse. Opening it carefully, he slowly counted its contents with one bony finger.

Looking up again, he eyed the woman, then said to her husband, 'I'll give you two and fourpence – and that's my best offer.'

'Then you'll need to keep your trousers on in bed tonight if you want to stay warm,' cried the one-legged ex-soldier jubilantly. 'I have a bright half-crown here that says she'll be mine for certain.'

'Yours she is, then,' said the woman's lawful husband. Snatching the silver coin, he handed the end of the halter-rope to the ex-soldier before he changed his mind. 'You'll not regret your bargain – though she might need a good cuffing to drive her from bed on a cold winter morning.'

'I'll worry about pushing her out of bed after I've got her there,' said the one-legged man. Delivering a smart slap to the rump of his 'bargain', he gave the crowd about him a lewd wink.

Grinning at the ribald shouts of the onlookers, the ex-soldier led his purchase from the market. She, for her part, walked away behind him without so much as a backward glance at her husband. Indeed, throughout the whole transaction she had neither spoken nor shown a moment's interest in the proceedings.

Ben had been watching the auction with great amusement, but when he turned to Jesse he saw her hands were clenched to her side in a paroxysm of ill-controlled fury.

'Did you see that?' she hissed angrily. 'That . . . that man! He sold his wife as though she were a pig . . . or a cow for which he had no more use!'

'She didn't seem to mind,' replied Ben innocently. 'And I think she'll be happier with the one-legged man than with her husband.'

'What has that to do with anything?' Jesse rounded on him. 'She *chose* to marry her husband. That didn't give him the right to *sell* her in a market! If *that's* the way you think, Ben Retallick, you can forget about marrying me. I have no intention of ending up in Mevagissey market with a rope around my neck, being auctioned off for half a crown!'

Throwing up her chin, Jesse pushed her way through the amused bystanders and stalked away from Ben.

She allowed him to catch up with her at the edge of the harbour, where the crowd was thinner. He took her arm. 'Look . . . Does that please you?'

Ben pointed to an inn close to the water's edge. Seated on

a bench outside the door were the one-legged man and the woman he had just purchased. As Ben and Jesse watched, a serving-girl came from the inn and put two large tankards on the table in front of the ex-soldier and his half-a-crown woman. Raising a tankard to his lips, the ex-soldier said something to the woman and nudged her in the ribs. She responded with a smile that transformed her dull features before they were hidden behind the second tankard.

'Well . . . she may be happier,' agreed Jesse, grudgingly. 'But no man has the right to sell his wife to anyone else.'

'That needn't trouble us. You said only a few minutes ago you'd decided not to marry me.'

'No, I did not!' Her good humour restored, Jesse linked her arm through Ben's. 'I said I wasn't going to be auctioned off at some market. Neither will I. You won't want to get rid of me, Ben Retallick. Not once I am yours.'

She was still smiling at Ben when a voice called, 'Hello, you two young sweethearts. Have you come to Mevagissey to attend our meeting?'

Walter Dunn fell into step beside Jesse and winked at her. To Ben he said, 'You had better hurry up and wed this young lady. She is prettier every time I see her. Wait too long and I'll take her to church and wed her myself.'

'You don't need to go to church to get yourself a wife,' grinned Ben. 'They sell them at Mevagissey market.'

He told Walter of the incident he and Jesse had just witnessed and Jesse broke in to say, 'Can you really expect Parliament to give the vote to men who behave in such a manner?'

'They are little different in high places,' retorted Walter Dunn. 'There's not a landowner in the country who hasn't auctioned off sons and daughters to the highest bidder, in return for power or a title. The Prince Regent himself is only waiting until he is given the crown of England before he gets rid of his queen and puts another in her place. Come to the reform meeting if you want to learn more.'

Ben shook his head. 'I'll be staying clear of your reform meetings. Jesse and I have too much to lose. Besides, Sir John is opening an underground mine here in the spring. I intend working on it.'

'I doubt whether Sir John Vincent will appreciate your caution. He'll use you both in the same way he does everyone else. As and when it suits him. But I'll save my speeches for those who appreciate them. If you change your mind, you'll find us along the quay. Our main speaker today is one of the Spencean Philanthropists who marched on the Tower of London last year. Had they succeeded in taking it we would have parliamentary reform now – and everything else this country so desperately needs.'

Walter Dunn walked away, skirting the crowds attending the market.

As they watched him go, Jesse said to Ben, 'Walter will land himself in serious trouble one day if he goes around saying such things to people.'

'Trouble is as necessary to Walter as food. Without it he could not live. But it would break my grandma's heart if she lost the last of her sons. Let's forget about Walter and his reform movement. If we don't leave now, it will be dark before we get home.'

But Ben and Jesse had left it too late to avoid the trouble that suddenly flared up around them.

Mevagissey was only a few miles along the coast from the great naval port of Plymouth where three ships-of-the-line had been making ready to put to sea with a fleet setting out for the Mediterranean. The bulk of the fleet sailed along the English Channel from Portsmouth – only to learn that the Plymouth ships had been unable to find crewmen and were hopelessly undermanned.

The angry admiral ordered the three West Country vessels to break away from his fleet and make up their complements by sending press-gangs ashore along the southern coast of Cornwall. One of the Plymouth ships, the seventy-gun *Caesar*, sailed into St Austell Bay and sent two of her boats ashore at the tiny fishing-hamlet of Portmellon. When they landed, the found the village almost deserted. Most of the men were either at Walter Dunn's reform meeting, or had fled to the hills about Portmellon when they saw the boats coming inshore from the man-of-war. This coast had a long experience of press-gangs.

Aware of the admiral's anger, the young midshipman in charge of the press-gang was determined not to return to his ship empty-handed. Foolishly, he led his men over the hill to Mevagissey, a scant half-mile away. Along the road they scooped up a couple of unsuspecting fishermen who had been heading for the Portmellon boat-yard.

As they entered Mevagissey, the sailors found themselves in the midst of a thousand Cornishmen attending Walter Dunn's meeting. The two fishermen who had already been taken by the press-gang cried out for help, and the fishermen among the crowd were quick to respond.

With only twenty sailors under his command, the young midshipman had no chance of keeping the two impressed men and he let them go. His main concern was now to extricate his sailors before they were injured by the angry fishermen. There was no returning over the hill to Portmellon. He felt his only chance lay in fighting his way to the harbour in Mevagissey and commandeering a boat.

This the midshipman did with considerable skill until, when only yards from their goal, one of the sailors tripped and fell on the stone cobbles of the quay.

Had the midshipman merely stood his ground until the sailor regained his feet, all might have been well. The mob had secured a victory by rescuing the two fishermen, and they were content to drive the sailors back to their ship without any impressed fishermen. But the midshipman lacked experience. He saw only that one of his men was on the ground surrounded by angry fishermen. Drawing a pistol from his belt, he went to the aid of the downed sailor.

A young fisherman foolishly reached out and attempted to pull the pistol from the midshipman's hand. There was a noise like the crack of a packhorse driver's whip, and a puff of black smoke momentarily hid the fisherman and the young naval officer from view. When it cleared, the fisherman could be seen sitting on the ground. Clutching his stomach, he watched in disbelief as blood oozed between his widespread fingers.

A sudden shocked silence fell upon the crowd and it was far more terrible than the shouting that had gone before. Then a rumbling roar of anger broke from a thousand throats, and an avenging flood of men rushed forward. The sailors broke and ran.

The mob split twenty ways in pursuit, and it was one of these groups that engulfed Ben and Jesse. Unable to escape, they were forced to go along with the angry crowd or risk being trampled beneath the fishermen's boots.

They were still with the crowd when the sailor they were pursuing was cornered on the edge of the stone quay with no way to escape. He had a cutlass in his hand, but as the crowd advanced towards him he let it drop helplessly to the ground and opened his mouth to plead for mercy. His voice escaped as a terrified squeak, and Ben was distressed to see that the sailor was no more than a year older than himself.

Even as the boy sought for words with which to plead for his life, a cobblestone flew through the air and struck the young sailor in the face. He took an involuntary pace backwards – and stepped off the edge of the quay. As he dropped fifteen feet into the dirty water of the harbour, he struck his head against the stone wall. A cheer went up from the mob, but it died away in ragged discord as those in front moved forward and saw the motionless sailor floating face downwards amidst a stinking scum of fish offal.

'Ben! He mustn't be allowed to drown. Why doesn't someone get him out?'

There were others with similar thoughts. A big fisherman pushed his way to the edge of the quay and growled. 'Has the war with the French been over so long that we've forgotten what British sailors did for us? Has none of you got brothers or sons at sea who might be ordered to do no more than this lad did?'

Men shuffled their feet, discomfited, avoiding the fisherman's eyes.

'Someone get me an oar, or a hook. I'll pull him to the side.'

Ben ran to the harbour steps, where there were boats moored alongside the wall. A scream from Jesse stopped him.

'He's gone under!' she shouted.

When Ben looked from the fisherman to the harbour there was only the scum on the water to be seen, swirling with the falling tide.

Kicking off his heavy boots, the fisherman who had been addressing the crowd jumped into the foul water of the harbour. After some hesitation, two younger men jumped in after him. Others hurried past Ben to put out a boat.

The fishermen searched for fifteen minutes before a woman on the far side of the harbour called to them. She could see something floating beneath the surface, fifty yards away.

It was the missing sailor. He was quite dead. The fishermen

in the boat brought him to the quayside where he was lifted ashore and gently laid out by some of the women.

'There will be hell to pay because of this,' muttered the big fisherman who stood wet and shivering, looking down at the body.

'It was an accident,' said one of the other men uneasily. 'No one is to blame. We did our best.'

'I hope to God the coroner believes you, but I wouldn't think it likely.'

A grim-faced Walter Dunn pushed his way through the crowd gathered about the body. 'He's not the only one. Two more sailors have died today – and they were not drowned. There will be murder warrants sworn out before this matter is settled.'

Chapter Ten

The investigation into the death of the three sailors was carried out by Sir John Vincent in his capacity as a magistrate. For a whole month Mevagissey had a full company of marines billeted in the village. Off-shore, a frigate patrolled the bay to prevent the escape of the unknown murderers and succeeded in totally disrupting all smuggling activities.

The sailors who manned the frigate were in a vengeful mood, and more than one Mevagissey fishing-boat lost its nets, run down by the naval vessel. The fishermen could make no complaint – there was no one to whom they dared report the incidents. The occupants of the fishing-boats had to accept that they were lucky to have escaped with their lives.

Sir John Vincent learned nothing from the tightly knit little fishing community. Angrily, he banned all future meetings of the reformers, and as a punishment to the village declared they would have a Revenue prevention-boat stationed permanently at Mevagissey.

The fishermen grumbled among themselves, but they realised they could have been dealt with in a much more severe manner. Had the killers of the sailors been discovered, there would have been more than one fisherman's body hanging outside the grim grey walls of Bodmin's gaol.

The reformers still met, but only in small groups now, each man known to the others. The meetings were held in houses, where no outsider could hear what was being said.

Such secrecy soon became essential throughout the whole land. Alarmed by the gathering momentum of the reform movement, the government of Lord Liverpool increased its efforts to repress the reformers. Troops were used to disperse even the most orderly of meetings. Lord Liverpool's own agitators were sent out to stir other meetings up to such a pitch that magistrates had to be sent for to break up the meetings and order the arrest of the speakers. Many leaders of the reform movement were thrown into gaols in towns and cities all over England. Those who came to trial were quickly transported to places where survival and not reform became every man's goal.

Survival of a different kind was going on in the Retallicks' house at Tregassick. During their first long winter there, Pearson Retallick fought for life with every painful breath he took. To his family he made no complaint, assuring them he would be all right when the warmer weather arrived.

In February of 1819 work began on the long-awaited underground tin mine just outside Mevagissey, and Ben and Moses Trago both moved there from Pentuan. Ben was grateful for the opportunity it offered to earn more money. With Pearson Retallick's continued ill-health, money had become a matter of some importance to himself and his mother.

The first task facing the miners was to dig a vertical shaft through ground that was mainly clay and shale. It needed boarding up for every foot of the way. Eventually, a depth of twenty fathoms was reached. Here Moses Trago and Ben left the shaft-digging gang and teamed up with a hymn-singing miner five years Ben's senior. Together they would drive a horizontal tunnel from the shaft, in search of the tin believed to be there. Wrightwick Roberts, at twenty-one years of age, was as thick-bearded and broad-shouldered as any man working the Mevagissey mine – and he was twice as industrious. He thrived on hard work. As he swung a pick, or hammered a drill into a rock-face, he sang from the sheer joy of mining – and from his unshakeable love of God.

Once Ben asked him why he sang hymns the whole time he worked. Wrightwick Roberts wiped perspiration from his eyes and looked at Ben with great seriousness.

''Tis necessary, Ben. Up at grass there's the Lord's good air and the trees and birds to remind us of His great works. Down here in the darkness of the earth the Devil is always on the look-out for new disciples. There's nothing like a good hymn to remind him that we belong to the Lord. Shout "Allelujah!", Ben. You'll feel better for it, and the Devil will have to work his mischief elsewhere.'

Moses Trago grumbled that they had so much waste rock and shale to shift that he would welcome the Devil himself if he brought his own shovel and paid for his own candles.

Wrightwick Roberts hastily made the sign of the Cross and warned Moses Trago against calling on the Devil, even in jest.

'He has keen hearing and a mind for mischief, Moses. If you need more help than you have already, then call upon the good Lord. Pray to Him, and He'll give you the strength of ten men.'

Behind Wrightwick Roberts's back, Moses Trago signalled to Ben that he thought the religious miner was soft in the head.

But no one could dispute the strength of Wrightwick Roberts's arms. He was one of the strongest men Ben had ever known. When, after a week, they came upon a wide seam of rich tin ore, his redoubled efforts kept Ben and Moses Trago toiling harder than either of them had ever worked in their lives.

The trio were soon bringing more ore to the surface than any other team in the mine. One day, as they were cleaning up in the boiler-room of the mine, Ben asked Wrightwick Roberts what he intended to do with his share of the money they were making.

Wrightwick Roberts's face glowed with the fervour of his thoughts. 'I intend using it to become a preacher, Ben. To follow in the footsteps of the great John Wesley. I want a circuit of my own and a chance to carry the Word to those less fortunate than myself.'

Ben had learned something of Wrightwick Roberts's upbringing during the time they had been working together. Now he looked at him in amazement.

'To those *less* fortunate than yourself, Wrightwick? You were an orphan, brought up by the parish and sent out to work as soon as you could tell ore from rock. You look upon yourself as being *fortunate*?'

'Above all men, Ben. The good Lord chose me, and from the day I accepted Him I have known true happiness. Yes, I am a *most* fortunate man.'

Such simple faith made a deep impression on Ben, but Moses Trago was more convinced than ever that the big black-bearded miner was a simpleton.

Since they had been working at the Mevagissey mine, Ben and Moses had become close friends. Ben had managed to overcome Moses and Jesse's mutual dislike for each other to such an extent that Moses now lodged at Pengrugla. He slept in their barn, but ate his food with the Henna family.

His contribution to the family's income would be a great help during the winter months when the farm was producing little that could be sold.

Once the rich seam of ore had been found, Ben saw little of Jesse. He and his partners needed to mine as much ore as possible before settling-day and they worked as many hours as was physically possible. Because of this, Moses Trago saw things that escaped Ben's notice.

Late one evening, as they walked home from the mine in the darkness, Moses said to Ben, 'You haven't been to Pengrugla for a few days.'

'No,' agreed Ben. 'It's been a busy time for us all. When I last went to Pengrugla, Jesse spent all her time fussing over a cow that's due to calf at any time.'

'The cow had twin calves two nights ago, Ben.'

Moses Trago's words made Ben feel guilty, although he knew Jesse understood how hard he was working. In two days' time it would be Sunday. He would spend the whole day with Jesse then.

They walked in silence for a while, then Moses said, 'Look, Ben, I don't want to cause any trouble, but . . . do you know Sir John Vincent's head gamekeeper?'

'Reuben Holyoak? Only too well. Why?'

'It's probably nothing . . .' Moses Trago already wished he had kept quiet. 'But he's been hanging around Pengrugla a lot lately. Last night when Jesse went out late to shut up the pigs I heard her arguing with someone. I thought it must be you at first, until I heard a man's voice. It was an older man. I got up to go and find out what it was all about, but before I'd got my boots on I heard Jesse run into the house and bang the door.'

Ben went cold at the thought of Reuben Holyoak molesting Jesse again.

'I'll come up to the house with you and see Jesse tonight.'

'Good . . .'

Suddenly Ben put a restraining hand on Moses Trago's arm and brought him to a halt.

'What is it, Ben?'

'Shh! I saw a light across the far side of the pigs' field – there!'

It was the small dancing light of a flame being put to a pipe.

'That must be Holyoak waiting for Jesse now. He'll meet up with me instead.'

Ben was slow to anger – but he was angry now. His aching limbs forgotten, he was grateful for the hours of hard physical labour he had performed in recent weeks. It had given him rock-hard muscles and a strength that went far beyond his years.

'If you intend tackling a gamekeeper at night, I'd better come with you,' declared Moses Trago. 'Otherwise he'll go to Sir John Vincent and swear you and he fought because he caught you poaching.'

Ben knew Moses Trago was right. Men who protected game were powerful enemies. The distant colonies were peopled with a great many young men whose only crime had been to fall foul of a vindictive gamekeeper. The game laws were among the harshest on the statute-books. But Ben did not want Moses involved in what he had to do.

'I don't intend fighting Reuben Holyoak unless I have to. I'll wait until Jesse comes and see if I can learn what this is about. You go home – and take the long way. Don't disturb Holyoak.'

Moses Trago hesitated, but before he could argue Ben had gone, slipping away into the shadows of the high earth-covered wall surrounding the Hennas' pig-field.

Ben knew where the wall was at its lowest. Climbing over carefully, he dropped to the ground in the field and stealthily made his way to the side of the building that housed the pigs. Inside, the pigs snored, twitched and squeaked in sheer bad temper as they huddled together in restless sleep.

Ben was no more than fifteen yards away from the gate here, and the aromatic smell of tobacco smoke was carried to him on the night air.

For almost half an hour Ben waited in the darkness. He began to think that Jesse might already have completed her chores. The same thought must have come to Reuben Holyoak.

Ben heard the gate creak open as Reuben Holyoak came into the field to check that the pigs were not already locked away.

Ben held his breath and pushed back into the shadows as Reuben Holyoak passed only a few feet from him. The game-keeper reached the door of the pig-sty just as one of the pigs squealed and began to snort and snuffle noisily.

Reuben Holyoak drew a small fire-pistol from his pocket and struck sparks from it. A feeble flame flickered in the doorway, and he leaned in to look at the restless pigs.

It was an opportunity too good to be missed. A few hurried steps took Ben to the doorway and, before Reuben Holyoak could turn, Ben's shoulder hit him in the back. The game-keeper was knocked to his knees inside the pig-sty, the extinguished fire-pistol flying from his grasp.

As Ben slid the heavy wooden bolt into place on the outside of the door, the pigs complained vociferously from within as Reuben Holyoak stumbled clumsily amongst them.

Ben stood back and grinned wickedly. The door had been made to withstand the combined weight of ten hefty pigs. It would not budge beneath Reuben Holyoak's fists.

'Let me out! Do you hear me? Let me out! I'll have you for this, whoever you are. Let me out!'

Ben walked away from the pigs' house to the gate of the field. Passing out on to the path, he closed the gate behind him and met Jesse hurrying towards the field.

'Ben! What are you doing here? And what's that noise from the pigs' house? What's going on?'

Ben took Jesse's arm. Turning her around, he began to walk her away from the gate. 'Everything is all right. The pigs are locked away for the night – but they have company. Ask Moses to come down and let them out tomorrow morning.'

Jesse pulled against Ben and stopped.

'Is Reuben Holyoak in there with them?'

'Yes.'

'But Napoleon is in there, Ben! He's the most evil-tempered pig in Cornwall. He'll have Reuben's leg off.'

'Not if Reuben climbs up on one of the beams and sits there all night.' Ben smiled at Jesse, and she saw his teeth gleam in the darkness. 'Reuben won't get any sleep, but he'll be safe enough.'

He chuckled, and a moment later Jesse was giggling with him.

'Reuben won't forgive you for this, Ben.'

'He can never be certain it was me – and, if all I've heard is true, he is too vain to complain to anyone. He would become a laughing-stock.'

'How did you know Reuben has been bothering me, Ben?'

'Moses told me. Did Reuben try anything with you, Jesse?'

'No.' Jesse shook her head, but much of the lightheartedness had gone from her. 'He only wanted to talk.'

'About what?'

As they walked, they had swung away from Pengrugla,

taking a path that led to a grassy bank above a stream. It was one of their favourite spots.

Jesse said nothing until she and Ben were seated on the grassy bank and he had his arm about her.

'Reuben asked me to marry him, Ben.'

Her answer took Ben by surprise. He knew the gamekeeper wanted Jesse. He had seen the way he looked at her. But Ben had not expected Holyoak to declare himself now. He must know how things were between Ben and Jesse – that their understanding had Sir John Vincent's blessing. He expressed his thoughts to Jesse.

'I think that's why he is so persistent now, Ben. He knows about Pengrugla and is trying to make me change my mind before it's too late. Reuben has big plans for his own future and he told me I could be a part of them.'

'What sort of plans. He's a gamekeeper. He'll never be anything more.'

'Don't be too sure of that, Ben. Reuben is well thought of by Colman Vincent – and Lamorrack will be his one day. But Colman prefers to live on his Devon estate, and Reuben hinted that *he* will be given the job of running Lamorrack when that day comes.'

Ben had to admit that Reuben Holyoak had made an offer that would impress many girls – and most mothers. If Reuben had been speaking the truth, he and his wife would live like the lord and lady of the manor during Colman Vincent's long absences.

'What did you tell him, Jesse?'

She looked up into his face quickly. 'Do you *really* need to ask me that question, Ben? I told Reuben that I love you and would marry you in preference to him if you were a beggar.'

Ben kissed her and Jesse snuggled against him.

'But, if you made it so clear to Reuben Holyoak that you want nothing to do with him, why is he still bothering you?'

'Reuben just can't accept that I won't one day change my mind. Perhaps I am partly to blame for that, Ben. When my pa was killed I leaned on Reuben a lot. He was kind to me; but then he wanted to be more than just "kind", and I stopped seeing so much of him.'

After a brief pause, Jesse said unhappily, 'Reuben would think twice about bothering me if my pa were still here.'

She sounded so miserable that Ben's arm tightened about her.

'What was he like, Jesse . . . your pa?'

'He was fun. He never let anything or anyone trouble him. He had a temper, though. No one would take any liberties with him. He was brave, too. Sir John had a letter from one of the officers who was at Waterloo with him. It said that my pa was one of the bravest soldiers in the regiment . . .'

She was silent for a long time; then she whispered, 'Sometimes I wish he hadn't been so brave. He might still have been here with me and Ma . . .'

Ben kissed her again. This time he tasted the tears on her cheek and held her to him until she wriggled in his arms.

'I'm all right now, Ben.' Her voice was muffled and she rubbed her face against his shirt. Then she looked up at him in the darkness. 'I wish Pa could have met you, Ben. He would like you.'

'Would he?' As Jesse disentangled herself from him to tie her hair behind her neck, Ben lay back on the soft turf with his hands beneath his head. 'Perhaps he would prefer you to marry someone with Reuben's prospects.'

He half rolled over, towards Jesse. 'I sometimes worry about myself, Jesse. I listen to Walter talking about his reform movement and wonder what it is inside him that drives him on all the time. He believes wholeheartedly in what he is doing. There is no doubting voice inside him to tell him that perhaps he might be wrong. That reform might not achieve all he claims it will. I wish I had such unquestioning faith in something – anything!'

'I'm glad you haven't, Ben. Walter has no time for anything but "reform". I suspect that's why he has never married. No girl is going to take second place to parliamentary reform.'

'All right, then, take Wrightwick Roberts – he's the miner who works with Moses and me. He believes so strongly in religion that he is determined to become a preacher. He works like two men because he's after something special – an ambition. Even Reuben Holyoak has that – but I don't, Jesse! I dig in the ground. I'm excited when we find good ore and I enjoy digging it out. If we haven't found the ore, I'm just as happy to be underground looking for it. I don't want any more. I'm happy with my work – and I'm happy with you. But when I look around me I feel I should be after something more in life.'

'Ben Retallick, just so long as you're happy with me, I don't care if you never have an ambitious thought in your head. One day you'll be the best miner in the country, and everyone will want you to work for them. Don't feel ashamed of enjoying your work. There are many people so busy trying to get somewhere that they never have time to enjoy what they have. I'm *glad* you're not like that, Ben. I love you just as you are. I wouldn't want you to be like Reuben Holyoak – or even Walter Dunn.'

Ben reached out for her, and she went to him. Jesse had realised, as had Martha Retallick before her, that Ben might one day own Pengrugla, but it would never make him a farmer. Ben was a miner – and a miner he would remain.

* * *

Much later that night, Jesse let herself quietly into the darkened house and slipped into her bed with a sigh of relief. Her mother had not heard her come in. Jesse lay awake for a long time, remembering. Occasionally she ran her hands down the body that had been brought to life tonight and given a whole new meaning.

Jesse had given Ben peace of mind about his love of mining to the exclusion of all ambition. She had also come to an understanding with her own tangled emotions.

She had realised tonight that she belonged to Ben Retallick – and he to her. She determined that she would hold nothing back from him – ever. Mining was a dangerous occupation, and Ben might be taken from her at any time. She dreaded the thought of such an end to her happiness, but, if it happened, she knew she would regret nothing they had done together – only the things they had *not* done.

Now she would never have the greatest regret of all.

In the darkness of the night, with only the stars to bear witness, Ben and Jesse had consummated their love, and Jesse had crossed the threshold of womanhood.

Chapter Eleven

During that year of 1819, Jesse and Ben's relationship became one of deep love and understanding. It was a time of constant discovery for them both. They laid their plans for the future, for themselves and for the family they would have and raise at Pengrugla.

They agreed that Ben should continue to work at the Mevagissey mine. The money he earned would be used to build up the stock on the small farm. When Jesse and Ben had a son he would have a choice – to follow in Ben's footsteps, or to become his own master. A yeoman farmer, working his own land.

They decided the wedding would take place late in 1820, when both of them were seventeen. By then, with the aid of the industrious Wrightwick Roberts, Ben hoped to have saved enough to ensure the success of both Pengrugla and his marriage.

During these happy summer months, Mark and Billy Dunn returned from their enforced voyage to the Mediterranean.

England's problems there had been temporarily solved and half the huge fleet ordered back to their home ports.

The two men returned to Mevagissey as heroes, and accepted the new status as their due. But Mark, at least, had served his country with something less than distinction. Ben learned of this when he went to Mevagissey one day and unexpectedly walked into the backyard of the Dunn home when Mark was stripped to the waist, washing.

The whole of the fisherman's back was crisscrossed with scars, grim evidence of a brutal lashing.

Mark Dunn slipped his shirt over his head hastily and scowled at Ben. 'No other man in Mevagissey will see me without my shirt on, boy. You hold your tongue about what you've seen today. Do you understand me?'

'I carry no tales of things that are none of my business,' retorted Ben. 'I have other things to think about.'

'I wish I could forget as easily.'

Mark Dunn fastened his shirt and tucked it inside his trousers. 'I'll carry the memory of two hundred lashes with me to the grave.'

Ben winced, it was a beating to sear the mind of the strongest man, 'Why . . . ?' he began; then stopped. As he had declared earlier, it was none of his business.

However, as his secret was now shared with Ben, Mark Dunn seemed not to mind telling him the details.

'You were going to ask why I was tied to the mast and humiliated before the whole ship's company, right? Well, I'll tell you, Ben. It was because I know more about sailing than some of the fools they put in charge of King George's ships – and because I wasn't above telling them so.'

Mark Dunn's eyes glittered angrily at the memory. 'We were off the coast of Greece when we were caught in as fierce a storm as any I've seen anywhere. The fool captain ordered more sail shaken out in a bid to outsail it. I said we stood in danger of foundering if we did as he told us. Some of the other men agreed with me, and the captain had us secured in irons. The ship lost a mast and five good seamen – but I was still in the wrong for having spoken my mind. I took two hundred lashes and the others a hundred apiece. That's your fine navy for you, Ben boy.'

Ben murmured sympathetically about the wrong that had been done to Mark.

'Aye, it were wrong, boy. But as every one of those lashes bit down on my back I swore it would be another nail in the coffins of the Revenue men who put me on that ship.'

Ben looked at his uncle in alarm. 'You know there's a Revenue boat stationed here now?'

'I know. I also know it's manned by some of the men who took Billy and me. I'll have 'em, Ben boy. I promise you that. It may not be this week, or even this year, but I'm a patient man. I'll have 'em.'

Ben was to remember Mark Dunn's words. Before the year was out, three of the Mevagissey Revenue men had died from unexplained 'accidents'. Two were found drowned in the harbour, having apparently fallen in when intoxicated. The third was keeping a night watch from the cliffs to the north of the village and it was believed he missed his footing and tumbled down the cliff to the rocks below. Each of the three had been a member of the crew of the boat which had taken Mark and Billy Dunn prisoner.

With the return of the two brothers, local smuggling activities immediately increased, despite the presence of the Revenue men. Contraband was landed in various coves around Mevagissey and packed on ponies for carriage up the hill past Tregassick. Pearson Retallick, kept awake by the pain in his chest and his difficulty in breathing, heard the muffled hoofs of the ponies passing by almost nightly.

So regular were the illegal night journeys, Pearson learned to tell how many ponies were being used and even how heavily laden they were. He felt a great deal of sympathy for their lead pony. Its breathing was almost as noisy as his own.

One night, earlier than usual, Pearson Retallick heard a new sound in the quiet night. It was the furtive movement of men, betrayed by a whispered order, a stifled cough, and the careless rattle of a powder-horn against a musket lock.

Fighting against his own coughing, Pearson Retallick struggled from the bed and made his painful way to Ben's bedroom.

'Ben! Ben, wake up!'

Disturbed from a deep sleep, Ben was momentarily confused. 'What is it? What's happened?'

'Shh! Keep your voice down. Get dressed and go to Mevagissey. Find Walter, or one of the others. Tell them the Revenue men are out and about. It sounds as though they are setting a trap up by the wood. Go quickly – and take care, Ben.'

Ben asked no more questions. Swinging his feet to the floor, he dressed swiftly.

'Remember, go with caution, Ben.'

His father's hoarse whisper reached him as Ben let himself quietly from the house.

There was a full, smugglers' moon hanging bloated above the tallest trees of the wood, and Ben took a detour around the deep shadows. Once clear of the wood he made good time until he reached a place where the path divided, going in three different directions. Ben paused uncertainly before choosing the middle path. It led directly to Mevagissey and was the most unlikely path for the smugglers to use, but it was the quickest way to the Dunn cottage. Grandfather Dunn would know where his three sons were carrying out their nocturnal trading.

Ben was only a hundred yards along the track when he heard the blowing of a pony somewhere to his right. It had to be the smugglers, already well on their way along one of the other paths. The moon chose that moment to slide behind a large silver-fringed cloud. Cursing beneath his breath, Ben stumbled blindly back the way he had come.

Reaching the junction, he collided bodily with the unseen man leading the first of the smugglers' ponies.

'Who's there? Speak up or be shot!'

The demand came as a hoarse whisper, but Ben recognised the voice of Ned Hunkin, one of the two men who fished with Walter.

'Keep your voice down and speak no names, or we'll all be shot. There are Revenue men up ahead. They're hiding close to the wood, waiting for you.'

'Are they, be damned!' This was Walter's voice. 'Do you know how many there are?'

'No.' Ben repeated everything his father had told him.

'Good boy! Get along home now and leave us to attend to this.'

'What will you do?'

'Ask no questions. The less you know, the better it will be for you. Hurry now.'

Ben did as he was told, smarting at his curt dismissal. However, when he reached home and repeated what had been said, his father agreed with Walter.

'Walter is no fool, Ben. He'll have made plans for just such an occurrence as this. It's best that there's no one else around to see what happens.'

Martha Retallick had been woken by the comings and goings in her home and she said, 'I hope Walter has planned well. The family have just got Mark and Billy home. It will be the end of your grandpa and grandma if they are taken again, Ben.'

Martha Retallick need not have worried. This was a night for smugglers.

Led by only a few men, the laden ponies headed inland along a lesser-known path. Walter took the remainder of the smugglers in a wide circle around the Revenue men's ambush. He waited for the moon to show him the position of every one of the Revenue men, then he mounted a swift but brief attack.

Coming as it did from such an unexpected direction, the assault took the Revenue men completely by surprise. In the ensuing confusion they shot two of their own number and were still fighting each other long after the Mevagissey men had faded into the night.

It was a notable victory in the age-old battle between smugglers and the authorities. For weeks the Revenue men had to endure the jokes of small boys, warning them to 'Look out! There may be another Revenue man creeping up on 'ee.'

At Tregassick, they woke on the morning after the fight to find a keg of best French brandy on the doorstep. For many nights afterwards it served to dull the constant pain of Pearson Retallick's clogged lungs and he slept in a welcome drunken stupor.

But Pearson Retallick's relief from pain lasted only as long as the brandy. Afterwards, the deterioration in his health caused Ben more concern than ever. Now the sick man was able to leave the house only to sit for hours in a chair set outside the door. This was pleasant enough during the long fine summer days, but when the deep mists of November rolled in from the sea the door had to be kept tight shut, and Pearson Retallick was forced to spend long hours alone in the house.

Ben knew the pain in his father's chest increased with the cold weather. More and more often, when Ben looked at him, there was an expression of resigned weariness on Pearson Retallick's face. Gradually, the sick man became increasingly withdrawn and morose. Ben worried about him every time he left for work. One morning, when his mother had already left to go to Lamorrack House, Ben went to his parents' bedroom and, to his consternation, found his father seated on the edge of the bed, dressing with painful difficulty.

'What do you think you're doing, Pa?'

Pearson Retallick turned his face towards his son and gave him a weary grin that reminded Ben of better days, when such a look regularly passed between them.

The memory struck deep – and it hurt.

'I'm getting out of bed and going downstairs, Ben. If I don't, I'll lie up here and rot away. That's no life for a man, or for his wife and son, is it, now?'

'You'd be better staying in bed until the days warm up a bit. There's a frost outside this morning. If you insist on getting up, I'll light a fire for you before I leave. In an hour it will have warmed the house. Stay in bed until then.'

'Cold mornings don't trouble me, Ben. Do you remember some of the winter mornings when we were at the Money Box mine? We'd go outside the house together and break the ice on the barrel to get water to wash with. You were no more than seven or eight when we began doing that together, Ben. At times it tore the very guts out of me to see your poor little body shivering in the cold, knowing you had to go off and spend a full day breaking ore in the cold wind without enough warm clothing on your back.'

Pearson Retallick screwed up his face, fighting the tears that threatened to expose his extreme weakness. He eventually managed a laugh which was quickly chased away by a bout of coughing.

'It's funny how life turns about, Ben. Now it's your turn to stand over me like some young giant, looking at my poor thin body and feeling pity for *me*.'

Pearson Retallick looked up at his son, and the muscles in his face twitched with the emotion he was feeling.

'You're a good boy, Ben. We've had some grand times together, you and me. We've never been overburdened with goods and chattels, but there has always been more than enough love in the house for all of us.'

'There still is, Pa – and there are many more good times yet to come. It's not pity I feel for you, it's pride. Pride that you've always worked so hard for Ma and me. Pride that you kept going long after most other men would have given up.'

Pearson Retallick was unable to control his tears now. They ran unchecked down his cheeks, and his voice came out as a whisper. 'Thank you, Ben. But I've always been an honest man – to myself and to you. I know how much of a burden I am. No, Ben, don't try to hide behind kind words. You know it's the truth, just as I do.'

Fiercely, Pearson Retallick cuffed his eyes with the back of his hand. 'Now, go down and light that fire, then get yourself off to work. Don't let a good pitch of tin lie idle because you're back here, humouring your foolish old pa.'

Ben had never seen his father in such a melancholy mood. He set off for work more worried about him than he had ever been before.

All that morning, as Ben swung a heavy hammer, driving a borer into a narrowing tin lode, he kept seeing the tortured face of his father, fighting for control of himself.

By mid-afternoon, the unsettling nagging at his mind was so strong that he could bear it no longer. Telling his two workmates that he was worried about his father, he announced that he was returning home early.

Moses Trago grumbled that he would never be able to keep up with Wrightwick Roberts on his own, but the religious miner sympathised with Ben.

'It's written that you should "Honour thy father and thy mother, that thy days may be long in the land which the Lord has given". Go and obey the Lord, Ben. I only wish I had known a father about whom I might concern myself.'

Leaving the mine behind him, Ben felt suddenly foolish about going home so unexpectedly. What would he tell his father? That he could not work for thinking about him? Pearson Retallick would give his son a gentle smile and send him back to the mine. Perhaps Ben should say they had lost the lode and stopped work early.

Then, as he drew close to the house at Tregassick, Ben's earlier anxiety returned a hundredfold. There was no smoke coming from the fire he had lit that morning, although the day was still very cold. He had left a pile of logs, ready cut, beside the fireplace. His father needed only to place them upon the fire. Ben's first thought was that his father had been taken ill before he finished dressing and had not made it downstairs. He broke into a trot.

When he reached the house a quick glance in the kitchen confirmed that the logs had not been touched. The fire had died an early death. Running up the stairs, Ben called to his father and flung open the bedroom door. The room was empty. Ben checked his own bedroom; then every room in the house.

Pearson Retallick was not there.

By now Ben was thoroughly alarmed. His father had not

left the house for weeks. He was far too weak to go off on his own.

He went outside and looked about him wondering where to begin his search. Then he saw the door of the old barn standing half-open. It had been closed when Ben set off for work. There was no reason why Pearson Retallick – or any one else – should have gone inside. The barn held only a broken-down farm-cart and a miscellany of rubbish that needed sorting and throwing out.

The door protested noisily as Ben pulled it wide open.

'Pa? Are you in here?'

For a moment Ben saw nothing. Then, in the light from the evening sun shining through a broken window, he saw an exaggerated distorted shadow cast on the wall beside him. His eyes widened in horror. Shielding his eyes against the sun's rays, Ben took two unsteady paces into the barn.

His agonised cry sent a cluster of roosting birds fluttering in panic from a crevice high up in the wall.

Ben had found his father.

Pearson Retallick was dangling at the end of an old length of rope, secured to a wooden beam. His head was laid side-ways on his shoulder, the toes of his heavy mining-boots swinging only inches above the dusty barn-floor.

Weary of life after years of constant ill-health and bouts of excruciating pain, Pearson Retallick had relieved his family of the burden of nursing him during his last years of total incapacity. It was the final act of a caring and courageous man. Pearson Retallick was buried on a wet and stormy night, at a spot where the path from Tregiskey to St Ewe crossed the track from Mevagissey to St Austell.

By taking his own life he had put himself beyond the absolution of the Church. In spite of the pleas of Ben and his mother, the vicar of Mevagissey was adamant. Pearson

Retallick could not be laid to rest in consecrated ground. He had committed a sin that carried its stigma to the grave – and beyond.

The funeral took place, as tradition decreed it should, at an hour as dark as the deed itself. Pearson Retallick's mortal remains were laid to rest where two paths met – and passed on. This was the only cross he would ever have to mark his grave, a diluted balm to soothe the unhallowed soul that was doomed to haunt this place until men's memories grew dim and unreliable.

All ordinated clergy were forbidden to officiate at such an internment, but after helping Ben and Moses Trago to dig the grave to a respectable depth Wrightwick Roberts pleaded Pearson Retallick's case to the Lord with a powerful prayer. He reminded Him of the pain the miner had been given to bear during his lifetime and begged pardon for the deed that had hastened God's own mercy.

The mumbled 'Amen' went up from only a few throats. Ben, Martha Retallick, Moses Trago, Jesse and Walter Dunn were the only mourners to brave the cold night and risk the displeasure of the Church.

Afterwards, Ben and his two miner companions used their long-handled shovels to fill in the grave and cover up their work as well as they could. Body-snatchers were active, even in this remote part of the country.

It was as well that none of those who trudged homeward from the unmarked grave could see into the future. Pearson Retallick's suicide was only the first incident in a winter that was destined to change the life of each one of them.

Chapter Twelve

Standing at the cold damp graveside and sharing in a small way the grief of Ben and his mother, Moses Trago had inexplicably felt himself to be a part of a family again. It was an uncomfortable disturbing feeling – but one that would not be shaken off.

For the first time since running away from home, Moses began to think about those he had left behind at Sharptor, high on Bodmin's moor. Most of all he remembered his mother. A colourless beaten women, she had given birth to five sons and seen three of them laid in the ground before they were old enough to know her. The two who survived were brought up in abject poverty in the cave home on the moor.

Matthew Trago, Moses' father, spent much of his time and all of his money in moorland gin-houses. He found his amusement in beating his wife and whichever of the two sons was not quick enough to run from the house when he staggered home roaring drunk.

John was the younger of the two brothers. Moses remembered him as a quiet, almost simple boy who rarely spoke his own thoughts. John had a stoicism that stood him in good stead when he fell foul of his father's fists. Because he neither showed pain nor defended himself, his beatings became brief perfunctory affairs.

With Moses, it had always been different. He had fought back from the very beginning, his rage increasing with every blow his father rained upon him.

It was Moses Trago's memories of his father that he had tried hardest to forget. His earliest recollections were of the terror he brought with him into the makeshift house. The first sounds Moses could recollect were his mother's screams as his father pummelled her from corner to corner of the home. Moses grew up hating his father and the cromlech home on the tor.

His very few happy memories began when, at the age of six, he was old enough to accompany his mother to the mine and help her to sort the ore. There, for the first time in his life, he heard voices raised in conversation or laughter, and not in anger or terror.

As he grew older, it became evident to everyone who knew him that Moses had inherited his father's dark temper. It flared up repeatedly at Matthew Trago, bringing Moses some severe beatings. The worst of them on the occasions when he tried to protect his mother.

Eventually, life at home became unbearable for Moses. One night he stole away and headed for the deep tin mines of St Just.

Now, after four years, the sharp edge of his hatred had dulled. When he stood looking down at Pearson Retallick's lonely grave, Moses Trago remembered a few long-forgotten things: the feel of his mother's hand holding his as they set out for work before dawn on a winter morning; the sympathy in his brother's eyes as he looked at Moses' face, bruised and battered by yet another beating.

There was still nothing but hatred for his father in Moses Trago's heart, but now Matthew Trago was no more than a dark shadow. He loomed large behind the others, but no longer carried the menace he had once possessed.

Moses realised he wanted to see his family again – alive. He did not wish to return to Sharptor to stand at a meaningless graveside and think of them as they had once been.

Moses Trago grappled with his new and unwanted sentiments for many days before giving Ben and Wrightwick Roberts the surprising news that he was leaving the Mevagissey mine and returning home to Sharptor. Wrightwick Roberts accepted the news in silence. After mulling it over for many minutes, he said generously, 'You could not have chosen a better time to leave, Moses. We have lost the lode and it might be many weeks before we find it again. Go now, and you will have money in your pocket to take with you. Stay, and you will spend it before there is more to take its place. Set off now, before you change your mind.'

Ben received the news with mixed feelings. He was sorry to be losing his friend, and he said so, but he understood why Moses had to go.

Moses was relieved that his two colleagues had accepted his decisions so readily. He smiled at Ben's words.

'Given a week or two you will need to stop and think if my name is mentioned, Ben. Besides, you will have other things to think about soon. A wedding to arrange. But if ever you feel the need to work in a big mine again, one going deep enough for copper as well as tin, come to Sharptor. You will be able to choose from a dozen mines, many of them already down to the two-hundred-fathom level.'

'I would like to see them, Moses. But I intend staying here. I might even become a farmer one day, when Jesse and I are married.'

Moses Trago shook his head. 'You are a miner, Ben. A good miner. Mining is in your blood. You'll never settle down to milking cows and feeding pigs and chickens. That's women's work.'

That evening, Moses Trago treated Ben and Wrightwick Roberts to a couple of ales in a Mevagissey inn. The next morning he set off for Sharptor, and home.

It was little more than twenty miles distant. Moses Trago knew he would make the journey fairly comfortably in one day. On the way he passed the great Crinnis mine. The size of the working made him more eager than ever to return to an area where mining was a serious business. Sir John Vincent had opened the Mevagissey mine to satisfy a whim. He would not make a fortune, and the mine would never amount to much. The ore was not there in sufficient quantities.

At Lostwithiel, Moses Trago paused to view the great round castle of Restormel and marvel at the ancient workmanship of the Norman fortress. From here, the road began to rise steadily, and he caught occasional glimpses of Caradon Hill rising above the edge of Bodmin Moor. It was no more than a stone's throw from Sharptor. Then he saw Sharptor itself, its granite heights perched on the slope above Henwood village.

As Moses drew closer and felt the springy turf of the moor beneath his feet once more, the first doubts about the wisdom of returning stirred within him. He had been away a long time and had left without a word to anyone. He had never thought what his going would mean to his mother or brother John.

Moses slowed, reluctant to cover the final mile. By the time he arrived at the heights above the strange dwelling it was dark. He moved forward ever more slowly until he could have pitched a stone in through one of the high window-openings.

There was a flickering orange glow inside the home, and Moses knew it came from a cooking-fire in the centre of the cromlech.

Moses Trago squared his shoulders and strode to the door. Pushing it open, the foul smell from inside rushed out, threatening to overwhelm him. He stopped inside the entrance, shocked at the chaos he saw there. It looked as though no attempt had been made to tidy the place for many months.

Before the open fire, a boy of about fourteen years of age squatted, stirring a pot that was perched at a crazy angle on sagging iron bars above the flames. There was no sign of his mother.

Moses stood inside the door waiting for the boy to turn and look at him. When nothing happened, Moses said quietly, 'Hello, John.'

For a few long seconds, the figure crouched at the fireside with the ladle poised in his hand. Then John Trago rose to his feet and slowly turned to face his brother, an expression of sheer joy spreading across his face.

'Moses! Moses . . . it really is you?'

Suddenly the two brothers were clasping each other, both laughing stupidly. Finally, holding his brother away from him at arm's length, Moses said shakily, 'Well, it's nice to know someone is pleased to see me – but where's our ma?'

The happiness slipped away from John Trago's face, and the shoulders beneath Moses' hands rose and fell in a shrug.

'I don't know.'

'You don't know? What do you mean?'

John Trago shrugged again. 'She left us, about a year after you went – and took the baby with her. Yes, that's right, she had another child. A boy again. I came home from the mine one day and they were both gone. I searched for weeks, but no one had seen them go. She must have gone off over the moor . . . somewhere.'

John Trago made a helpless gesture in the direction of the moors that extended for ten empty miles to the north-west.

Moses gnawed at his lower lip as he looked at the boy standing before him. Almost as broad-shouldered as himself, brother John yet looked very vulnerable and helpless dressed in clothes that had obviously been handed down from their father. They were neither clean nor in good repair. Where they hung too far from his body they were tied in with string.

'How have you managed without her?'

Another shrug. 'We get by. Sometimes Pa brings a woman home with him. She stays until he beats her too hard. The rest of the time I do whatever needs to be done.'

Pity welled in Moses for his younger brother. 'And Pa? How is he?'

'He doesn't change, Moses. He works, he drinks and he fights. Sometimes he does more of one than of the others, that's all.'

Moses Trago's spirits sank within him. He had secretly hoped a miracle might have occurred to change his father's ways. He should have known better. Miracles happened only in the pages of the book Wrightwick Roberts carried about with him – and already Mevagissey could have been a million miles away.

Moses accepted some of the weak and foul-smelling stew cooking in the pot on the fire, then he sorted out some of his own clothes for his brother. They were old working-clothes, but John Trago's delight was such that Moses might have presented him with a suit of velvet.

The two brothers talked together well into the night. They were still talking when they heard the noise made by someone staggering along the path towards the house. Moses rose to his feet slowly, his heart pounding at the thought of the encounter to come. Moments later the door crashed open and Matthew Trago stumbled drunkenly into the stone house.

Moses was shocked at his father's appearance. John had declared that their father had not changed. He was wrong. Years of dissipated living had taken a heavy toll on Matthew Trago. There was less weight on his bones, and his face was bloated and stained. He had the look of a wild animal about him, and an expression approaching madness in his eyes.

Matthew Trago opened his mouth to release his habitual roar of anger at John, then realised he was looking at his eldest son. For a brief moment something akin to pleasure showed on his face, but it went before Moses could be certain.

'Oh, it's you! Decided to come home again, have you?'

Moses nodded.

Matthew Trago belched noisily. 'If you've eaten my supper, I'll knock you back outside again. D'you hear me?'

'I hear you.'

Something in the quiet way Moses spoke the words caused Matthew Trago to look at him again. This time it was not the look of a drunken man, but the shrewd assessment of a fighter. He saw the wide shoulders and hard muscles that filled out the shirt his son wore.

'You think you've grown big enough to take your father now, do you?'

'I *know* I have.'

Moses whispered the words and tensed himself for what was to come.

Father and son stared at each other for what seemed an age to the anxiously watching John. Then Matthew Trago grunted.

'H'm! Happen you could be right.'

Turning to his other son, he roared, 'What are you standing there like an idiot for? Give me my supper.'

Moses Trago had returned to Sharptor – and he was now a man.

Chapter Thirteen

As the spring of 1820 neared, Ben found himself working longer hours than ever before. Wrightwick Roberts had once more found the tin lode. It was wide enough now for two men to work at it standing side by side. They brought in two boys to help, but at the end of each shift they all had to lend a hand to clear the ore that had been mined in the rich working.

Nevertheless, when he left the mine each evening, Ben went to Pengrugla to help Jesse complete her day's chores. Jesse's mother had fallen ill. A doctor had been called in and, after muttering vaguely of 'palpitations' and 'heart flutters', he ordered her straight to bed. At first, Maude Henna scorned his instructions, but when she fainted whilst carrying food to the pigs Jesse insisted that she go to bed immediately and remain there for a while.

Contrary to Moses Trago's gloomy predictions, Ben enjoyed working at Pengrugla. Without the constant presence of Maude Henna, it was almost as though he and Jesse were already married.

Then the second blow of the winter fell.

Ben arrived home from Pengrugla one night to find Tregassick in darkness. There was no sign of his mother, and for one panic-stricken moment Ben thought it was a tragic repeat of the day he had returned home and discovered his father's body hanging in the barn.

The barn was empty and, sagging with relief, Ben realised that his mother must still be at Lamorrack House. She had said nothing about there being any social function for which she would need to work late, so Ben set off to the big house seeking her. He had gone no more than a hundred yards when he heard someone hurrying towards him in the darkness.

'Is that you, Ma?'

'Ben! Thank goodness! I thought I would never get home. It's been a terrible day.'

Reaching Ben, his mother clung to him, breathing heavily.

'What's happened? Why are you so late?'

'Sir John was thrown from his horse this evening,' Martha Retallick began to cry. 'At his age he should have known better than to go riding alone.'

'Is he badly hurt?' Ben felt genuine concern for the aged baronet.

'Hurt? He's dead, Ben. He died not an hour since, with only his sister at his bedside, poor man.'

When Martha Retallick had brought her tears under control, she said, 'There'll be changes at Lamorrack House now, Ben. Colman is not the man his father was. I'll never get used to calling him "Sir" Colman. They can make him a duke, he'll still have all his father's faults and none of his virtues. Sir John's servants are shedding tears tonight – but as much for themselves as for poor Sir John.'

* * *

Sir John Vincent's funeral was held a week later. Every servant and all his employees were given time off to attend. The Mevagissey mine was closed for the day, as was the Happy Union stream-working. All the miners attended the service. Wearing their Sunday clothes, they stood awkwardly at the back of the church. In the main they were chapelgoers, followers of John Wesley. Unused to the pomp and medieval symbolism of the Church.

Sir John Vincent had been a well-known and respected county figure, and most of the pews in the church were filled by Cornwall's gentry. The Carews, Boscawens, Edgcumbes and St Aubyns were all there. Outside the church their carriages filled the narrow lane for a hundred yards, the footmen in unfamiliar livery subjected to many sidelong glances from the young servant girls from Lamorrack House.

Once the funeral was over, the tenants and workers on the late Sir John Vincent's estate waited for their new landlord to declare his intentions. No one had any doubt that he would bring about changes. They were inevitable. Sir John's life had been filled with a great many interests, but they all revolved around his estate at Lamorrack. It had been the hub of his whole life.

Not so Sir Colman Vincent. He had been born at Lamorrack House and was the Member of Parliament for nearby Pengony, but he had spent very little time in the county. His time was divided between the estates he owned in Devon, and his London business commitments. His visits to Lamorrack House had been infrequent when his father lived. There was little reason to believe they would increase now.

Over the next week, things gradually returned to normal as the tenants of Lamorrack went about their familiar daily tasks. They began to relax. Perhaps things would not change after all.

Then came the day when Ben's whole world collapsed about him.

He came up to grass after the day's shift to find Jesse waiting for him. This itself was unusual enough. She should have been busy at Pengrugla. But one look at her face told Ben that something was very seriously wrong.

'Jesse . . . what is it? Your mother . . . ?'

'No, Mother is the same. Let's get away from here, Ben. I must talk to you.'

Ben's immediate thought was that Jesse had learned she was expecting a child. It was a matter that was bound to concern her, but to Ben it mattered very little. It meant only that they would need to marry earlier than they had intended. More than half the marriages in Cornwall were advanced for the same reason. The tongues of the village gossips would wag only until the next couple came in for their attentions.

Ben said as much to Jesse – but she was not with child. This problem would not be solved in such a simple manner.

They had climbed the hill from the mine now, and Jesse was unable to keep the news to herself any longer. Turning to Ben, she blurted out, 'Ben, Sir Colman Vincent is taking Pengrugla away from us!'

Ben looked at her in disbelief. 'He can't do that. It was promised to us by Sir John.'

'*We* know that, but Sir John must have forgotten to put it in writing. Sir Colman claims he knows nothing about any such promise. What's worse – he's given Pengrugla to Reuben Holyoak!'

Ben was stunned. This must be a bad dream.

'I don't believe it. Why should he do this to us?'

'I don't know. It was Reuben Holyoak who came to the house to tell me. Sir Colman has made him his agent, as we knew he would. He's leaving Reuben to run the whole estate. But I never dreamed he would take Pengrugla from us . . .'

Jesse choked on the words. Desperate with worry, she had been turning the same questions over and over in her mind since Reuben Holyoak had come to the house. Unable to say anything to her sick mother, she had brought the insurmountable problem to Ben. Now she broke down. 'I don't know what to do, Ben. We can't leave Pengrugla. Ma is so ill the move would kill her.'

'We'll marry right away, Jesse. Then as soon as your ma is well enough we'll take her to Tregassick with us.'

Ben was mentally groping for a solution – any solution.

'It wouldn't work, Ben. Tregassick is part of the Lamorrack estate. Reuben Holyoak would have us out in no time. Besides, things are not that simple.'

Ben was angry and confused. Turning all the possible alternatives over in his mind, he was not listening to what Jesse was saying.

'We can go to the far west of Cornwall, back to St Just. Yes, that's the answer. I'll find work tributing on one of the deep mines. I can earn enough to keep us all. You, me and your ma. I expect my ma will want to stay at Mevagissey – or even Tregassick. Reuben Holyoak will have no cause to turn her out with us gone—'

'Ben, stop! Listen to me, please! You don't understand. When we first moved to Pengrugla, Pa borrowed a lot of money from Sir John. It was never repaid; Sir John never asked for it, but the debt is still there. When Reuben came to the house today he told me that, if we try to go away anywhere, Sir Colman will demand full settlement of the debt. He'll commit Ma to a debtor's prison, if necessary. Oh, Ben! What can we do?'

Ben suddenly realised the full extent of Reuben Holyoak's scheming.

'Reuben Holyoak is moving into Pengrugla – but he wants you to stay there with him?'

'Yes. He says that, if I marry him, Sir Colman won't press for the money Ma owes him.'

A sob prevented Jesse from saying more. Ben held her to him until she stopped trembling and had regained control of herself. He knew now what he had to do.

'Reuben Holyoak may be lying. I'll go and see Sir Colman first thing in the morning, Jesse. He probably knows nothing of what's happening – or of Sir John's promise to us.'

Ben was wrong. Sir Colman Vincent knew very well what was going on.

It was almost noon before Ben was shown into the room where Sir John Vincent had first questioned him about his feelings for Jesse. In spite of the late hour, Sir Colman had the appearance of a man who had not been out of bed long enough for good humour to have caught up with him.

For Ben, the matter he had come to discuss was of the utmost importance. The whole future of Jesse and himself hinged upon its outcome. Slowly and carefully he began to explain the purpose of his visit, determined not to leave out anything that might be important.

He had scarcely begun when the new baronet cut short his well-thought-out appeal.

'Yes, yes! I know very well why you are here, Retallick. Before you say any more you should know that I took all this into consideration before reaching my decision. Nothing you have to say will persuade me to change my mind, I assure you. Reuben Holyoak is to manage the Lamorrack estate and he wishes to move into Pengrugla at the earliest opportunity.'

'Sir John promised Pengrugla would come to Jesse and me when we married—'

'I have only *your* word for that. Even if it *were* true, I would not consider myself bound by such an extravagant promise. My father was a generous man – far too generous. I am surprised there are any Lamorrack lands left.'

'But . . . Mrs Henna and Jesse? What will they do?'

'I understand Reuben intends asking Jesse – Miss Henna – to marry him. It is a good match. I support it wholeheartedly. So there would seem to be no problem. Was there anything else, Retallick?'

Ben was able to contain his anger and frustration no longer. 'You are going back on Sir John's word – and forcing Jesse into a marriage with a man she detests. It's wrong—'

'Hold your tongue, Retallick! To give you Pengrugla would make me the laughing-stock of the county, whatever my father's intentions. As for the Hennas, I am forcing them to do nothing. Jesse is free to make up her own mind. She can marry Reuben Holyoak and stay – or she can wed you and move out. I will not influence either decision.'

'What of the debt Mrs Henna owed your father? Are you willing to forgo that?'

'No, I am not. But it does not concern you – unless, of course, you intend paying it off?'

Sir Colman Vincent gave Ben an amused smile, then signalled his dismissal as though he were a dog.

'Get out, Retallick. Oh! . . . One thing more. Tell your mother I intend pulling down Tregassick and rebuilding a house for my aunt there. You will both need to move out as soon as possible. Shall we say . . . by the end of the month?'

It was now the twenty-first day of March. Ben and his mother had ten days in which to find somewhere else to live.

Ben held his hands tightly to his sides, resisting the almost overwhelming urge to step forward and knock Sir Colman Vincent to the floor.

Instead, he said, 'There's a strong move in this country for parliamentary reform, Sir Colman. I've never fully understood it before. Now I do. It's to rid ourselves of men like you.'

'Damn your insolence, Retallick! Come back here . . .'

Ben stormed out of the house, forcing startled servants from his path, leaving Sir Colman Vincent mouthing threats to an empty room. Ben knew he had just thrown away his job at the Mevagissey mine, along with everything else. It did not matter now. Nothing mattered. He had lost Pengrugla for himself and Jesse – Jesse herself was no longer his. For her mother's sake she would be forced to bow to Sir Colman's pressure and marry Reuben Holyoak. Ben did not know how he was going to tell her . . .

It would have been wiser for Reuben Holyoak to have stayed well away from Ben that day. He had seen Ben go to Lamorrack House – and it was not hard to guess the reason for his visit. Reuben Holyoak knew Sir Colman would give Ben short shrift. He waited at the edge of the wood for Ben to make his way home, prepared to gloat over his downfall.

Reuben Holyoak stepped into Ben's path confidently, a long-barrelled flintlock fowling-piece cradled in the crook of his arm.

'Has Sir Colman told you you'll need to move from Tregassick by the end of the month?'

'Out of my way, Reuben.'

Ben's cold anger fooled the older man. He believed Ben was returning from Lamorrack House a thoroughly defeated young man.

'Keep away from Pengrugla between now and then. I'll

be moving my things into the house and I don't want you hanging around Jesse—'

Ben swung his fist with all the force of the pent-up anger that was in him behind it. The blow knocked Reuben Holyoak backwards, the long flintlock flying from his grasp. Ben stooped to pick it up, and as Reuben Holyoak struggled to one knee Ben swung the gun, clubbing him to the ground again.

Suddenly, all Ben's anger and desperation broke free. The man lying on the ground shielding his head with an arm was responsible for the disaster that had fallen upon the Henna and Retallick families. Without Reuben Holyoak, he and Jesse would still have had a future with each other. Ben raised the gun again and again, each time bringing it crashing down on the other man's head and face.

Ben did not come to his senses until he realised he was holding only the long chiselled barrel in his hand. The stock was lying broken and splintered upon the ground.

There was blood everywhere. It was on Reuben Holyoak's face and head – and even on Ben's trembling hands.

Ben looked down at them in horror. He had no doubt that he had killed the gamekeeper. He had *meant* to kill him. Sir Colman Vincent would know immediately who was responsible for the death of his new estate manager. He would issue a warrant for Ben's arrest – and Ben would surely hang for what he had done today.

Ben let out an agonised cry and began running. He did not stop until he reached the house at Tregassick and stumbled in through the door.

He called out, but there was no answer. His mother was not at home. Panting hard, Ben ran up the stairs and sat down heavily on the edge of the bed in his room, his head in his hands.

He had gone to Lamorrack House to try to persuade Sir

Colman to honour the promise made by his father, to make everything all right again for Jesse and himself. His efforts had gone disastrously wrong. Nothing would ever be the same again now. Ben was a fugitive. A hue-and-cry would be raised for him. Someone might already have discovered Reuben Holyoak's body and be hurrying to Lamorrack House to tell Sir Colman at this very moment . . .

Ben sprang to his feet and began bundling a few items of clothing together. He had to get well away from Mevagissey. He desperately wanted to go to Pengrugla, to explain to Jesse what had happened – but he knew he dared not. If Ben were taken at the Henna house, Jesse might become implicated in Reuben Holyoak's death. No, Jesse would understand. She would know why he had been forced to leave so hurriedly.

At least there was no question of Jesse being forced to marry Reuben Holyoak now. He had resolved that problem, at least.

As he left the house, Ben's anguish increased as he thought about his mother – but she would make out. Mark and Billy Dunn had taken their families from Grandpa Dunn's house. There would be room for her there.

The sudden combination of unforeseen circumstances had shattered the thin shell of manhood Ben had built up around himself. He had been doing a man's work, and his relationship and future marriage with Jesse had given him the status of a man. Now all that was gone.

Ben left Tregassick close to tears, desperately aware of his scant experience of life. Confused and afraid, he could think only of getting as far from Tregassick as was possible.

Chapter Fourteen

Fleeing from Mevagissey and the expected wrath of the law, Ben headed eastward. He was deeply unhappy and totally bewildered by the sudden change in his fortunes, aware that he had failed Jesse when she most needed him. He tried to think where he had gone wrong. What other approach he might have made to Sir Colman Vincent for things to have turned out differently. If only Sir Colman had been prepared to give him a hearing . . .

It had been the sheer frustration and hopelessness of the situation that had caused Ben's anger to explode into such violence when confronted by Reuben Holyoak. Now he was a fugitive and acutely aware of the dangers he faced. More than once on the road eastwards he heard the sound of a horse and rider coming along the road behind him and he hid in a ditch or hedgerow until they had passed by. As soon as he was able, Ben left the road and struck out through woodland, away from the eyes of man. But always he headed towards the east.

Not until he reached the busy mines along the wide valley

of the River Tamar did Ben begin to breathe more easily. Here he was once more in a mining community. The call 'One and All' meant something to these people. When a miner was in trouble the others closed ranks to protect him. Ben was as safe here as he would be anywhere.

He found work in the mines, but was unable to settle down to enjoy mining. As a precaution against being traced, he changed his place of employment again and again. Before long Ben had vanished in the tide of miners who ebbed and flowed from mine to mine along the length of the Tamar valley.

The parliamentary reform movement was strong here but, although his sympathies were with them, Ben avoided their meetings. There was always the chance that someone in the huge crowds might have been a magistrate's agent.

Gradually, though, Ben's nervousness decreased. He was able to walk the roads without the urge to hide whenever a horseman rode by. One day, Ben met up with an old miner who was on his way to the stream-works at Pentuan. He was sick with lung disease. To him Ben entrusted a guarded verbal message for Jesse. Afterwards, Ben worried for a month lest it be overheard by someone who would pass news of his whereabouts to Sir Colman Vincent. But no constables arrived to arrest Ben, and there was no reply from Jesse.

Ben moved from mine to mine in the Tamar valley for a full year and then felt the need for some permanence in his life. He had cut all ties with his earlier existence and could never return to take them up again, but neither was he able to settle here.

His eyes turned to the dark hills of Bodmin Moor, not very many miles to the westward. Moses Trago lived there. He was a link with the life Ben had once known. It was as close as Ben would ever come to finding it again – yet far enough removed to be safe.

When Ben arrived in the shadow of Sharptor's rocky crags and made enquiries, he learned that Moses was working at Stowe's Hill mine, with his father and brother John. On a fine summer evening, Ben waited at grass for Moses Trago to come up from his shift. Moses now sported a fine curly black beard, and Ben would have allowed him to pass unrecognised had his friend not seen him and let out a loud howl of greeting.

Excitedly, Moses introduced Ben to his brother as the man who had saved his life in the Money Box mine disaster before insisting that Ben accompany them to the ale-house in Henwood village.

It was apparent as soon as they walked through the door of the dingy miners' inn that Moses was well known here. He was hailed by the landlord and many of the miners already inside, but Ben wondered whether it was his imagination, or whether there was a lack of warmth in the greetings. They were given in a manner suggesting that the inn's customers were fearful of offending the broad-shouldered miner, rather than pleased to see him.

Moses Trago was more garrulous than Ben could ever remember. He spoke expansively of all the mines in the district, of the rich ore they were bringing to grass, and their bright hopes for the future. Not until the third mug of gin was on the table in front of him did he think of asking Ben what he was doing in the village.

Ben took a hasty look about him before replying, but nobody else in the ale-house was paying him any attention. He told Moses only that Sir Colman Vincent had forced him from his home, that he had taken back Pengrugla – and that Jesse had been unable to leave. He added that Reuben Holyoak had been at the root of all their troubles.

Moses slammed his mug down on the rough wood of the

table in front of him and let out a bellow that turned every head towards him.

'I knew it, Ben! After I let him out of that stinking pigs' house I said you should have made sure he was unconscious before you put him in. There would have been nothing left of him in twenty-four hours. He would simply have disappeared and nobody would have been any wiser. You are too soft by half, Ben Retallick.'

Every man in the room was staring at him, and Moses glared back at those who were not quick enough to avoid his eyes. 'But I'm not – and I know what to do to anyone in this cheap ale-house who doesn't mind his own business.'

Suddenly everyone found something to occupy him. The young black-bearded miner was a powerful man, his shoulders wide enough to seat a man on each of them. It was a feat he had performed more than once in this very room. He was also a man with an uncertain temper. That, too, was equally well known.

'But to hell with Reuben . . . whatever his name is. To hell with Sir Colman Vincent, too. Let either of them come here, if they dare. We are all miners in this place, Ben. We bend to no man. "One and All" is the cry, and one and all it is. If someone from outside takes on one, he takes on every man of us.'

Moses Trago clapped a hand heavily on Ben's shoulder, 'You'll be all right with us, Ben. You stay here and learn how we look after our own.'

Ben's senses gradually faded away in a sea of cheap gin. He remembered Moses saying he must come with him to his home on Sharptor, but later in the night he had a hazy recollection of stumbling through tangled fern and needle-sharp gorse. Then Ben remembered no more until he felt drops of water splashing on his face.

At first he thought it must be raining. But when he opened

his eyes he looked into a sky so bright and blue it was painful to behold. With a groan of self-pity, Ben screwed his eyes tight-shut once more.

This time a deluge of water hit him in the face, and a young female voice said, 'If you think I've nothing better than to stand here trying to bring you out of a drunken stupor, then you'd best be thinking again, mister. I've got work to go to.'

The sky was still excruciatingly bright when Ben opened his eyes again. Not until he turned his head sideways did the clanging in his skull settle down to a brain-crushing pounding.

Ben found himself looking at a pair of none-too-clean feet, peeping from beneath a long and equally grubby dress. He raised his eyes slowly and carefully. No more than five feet above him was a sharp-featured young face, looking down at him with an expression of intense scorn.

Ben struggled to sit up, and the whole nauseous world swung about him. He groaned again, putting finger-tips to his painful forehead.

'Jesus! You must have had yourself a time last night. What were you celebrating?'

Ben had never before heard an Irish accent. It sounded strange to his ears.

'I wasn't celebrating anything.'

His tongue felt three times its normal thickness.

'Are you telling me you got into this state for no reason at all? Holy Mother! I've found myself a looney. Here, looney. Get this down you.'

She had a jug in her hands. Stirring its contents vigorously with a wooden spoon, she handed the jug to Ben. He put it to his mouth, only to recoil violently when he got a whiff of the mixture.

'Ugh! It smells terrible. What is it?'

'Herbs to clear your head. The smell doesn't matter. You're meant to drink it, not sniff at it.'

Ben threw back his head and downed the drink as quickly as he could. For a long time he sat on the ground gagging and spluttering. The mixture was spicy and attacked his throat every inch of the way down.

'My, but you're a baby! What's your name?'

'Ben . . . Ben Retallick. Who are you?'

'Aileen Brenahan – but what am I doing standing here talking to you? I'll need to be getting to work or they'll find someone else to take my place. Are you working?'

'Not yet. I arrived here only yesterday.'

'Then you'll not have a place to stay, either. Speak to my father. That's him over there by the stream. I'll be away now.'

Ben discovered he could now turn his head without fear of it falling off. As Aileen Brenahan hurried away, he looked to where she had pointed. He saw a wizened dark-skinned little man squatting at the edge of a fast-running stream. He was soaking grasses in the water and weaving them into the framework of a basket with incredible speed.

Climbing carefully to his feet, Ben staggered to the stream.

'Good morning to you!'

The little man had the same accent as Aileen Brenahan and spoke without looking up from his work.

Ben mumbled an inaudible reply before dipping his head in the water of the stream. It was icy cold and he came up gasping for breath. He plunged his head under the water again and held it there until his ears sang. Shaking much of the water from his hair, Ben unwrapped the kerchief from his throat and wiped his face. When he stood up he had a magnificent view over the wide Tamar valley to the high hills of Dartmoor, more than fifteen miles away.

Bringing his attention back to his immediate surroundings Ben saw that Aileen Brenahan and her father were not the only ones living on this moorland slope. Clustered about the ruins of an early and long-abandoned Newcomen engine-house were a number of makeshift dwellings. Built from turf and tree-branches, they were supported here and there by a dry stone wall. There were many babies in evidence. They crawled loose-legged across the space between the shanties and squatted in full-bellied satisfaction, enjoying the early-morning sun. Not one of them wore a stitch of clothing.

Ben had stumbled upon an encampment of the Irish peasants who came to England seasonally to work on the land. For the last couple of seasons they had learned that employment here was as scarce as in their own country, but still they returned, taking work wherever it was to be found. Undercutting the already-low wages of the English workers, they earned for themselves the bitter resentment of miner and farmworker alike.

'You'll be a mining man, I'm thinking? Leastways, you drink like one. If my Aileen hadn't found you last night, you'd most likely be at the bottom of a shaft by now. There are two of them not fifty paces from where you're standing at this very moment. Ah, but she's one for helping helpless creatures, is my girl. Back home in dear old Ireland we always have a house full of poor injured creatures of the wild. Although I say it, who shouldn't, there's not another girl in the whole world with more kindness in her heart than Aileen Brenahan. She takes after her dear departed mother – may the blessings of our Holy Mother be upon her soul. She has the same beauty of looks, too. Yes, you'd go far to find another girl like my Aileen.'

Dowal Brenahan looked up at Ben with dark bright little eyes that made Ben think of a weasel he had once snared.

'Would you be from around these parts, young sir?'

'No, but I'll be staying . . . if I can find work.'

'Is it work you're after? Well, now, you're talking to the right person.'

The Irishman put down the half-completed basket. Rising to his feet, he advanced upon Ben with outstretched hand. 'My name is Dowal. I'm happy to make your acquaintance. If you are looking for work, then you'll do no better than to hurry down to the Wheal Slade.'

Dowal Brenahan pointed to the floor of the valley, where an untidy jumble of mine-buildings and heaped ore-waste was dominated by a round-chimneyed engine-house throwing out dark coal-smoke. 'Aileen works there as a bal-maiden. She was telling me only last night that a ladder slipped and three men were killed yesterday – may God rest their souls.' Dowal Brenahan crossed himself piously. 'They'll be looking for strong young Cornishmen like yourself. Get on down there now, before they find someone else.'

Ben hesitated. 'I'll need somewhere to leave this.' He picked up the bundle of belongings he had somehow managed to keep with him throughout the previous night's drinking.

'You needn't fret yourself about that. Give it to me. It will be here when you finish work tonight. I'll do more. As my Aileen has taken you under her wing, I'll have a couple of the women put up a shanty for you. Nothing grand, you understand? No more than a place to sleep and keep your things dry. Away with you, now.'

Ben hurriedly changed into his underground working-clothes and set off down the hill to the Wheal Slade.

When he reached the mine, Ben saw it was even more of a mess than it had seemed from the hillside. Wires supporting the shaft-head lifting gear were loose, roads were half-buried in mine-waste, and there was a general air of slackness and apathy about the place.

Ben had seen such mines before, but he had never before worked on one. It was typical of a mine that was being run by a lazy and inefficient mine captain. When Ben entered the mine office, he understood why. It was early in the morning, but there was a strong smell of gin hanging on the breath of the mine captain.

'Bad news travels fast in these parts,' grunted the captain, when Ben told him why he was there. 'Yes, I *am* in need of men. If you have the experience, you'll do. One of the men who died was a tributer, the others tut-workers. Which would you prefer to be?'

Ben said promptly that he preferred to work as a tributer. He did not fancy the idea of working for this man on a fixed wage.

'Please yourself,' shrugged the captain. 'Most of the tut-workers are Irish anyway – and there is no shortage of them. The tribute team needing a man is on the forty-fathom level. Tell Tom Shovell I sent you.'

As Ben closed the door behind him, he heard the clink of a bottle against a pewter mug. The mine captain was fortifying himself against the problems of the coming day.

Ben had reached the top of the shaft when a young girl left the nearby dressing-floor and ran to speak to him. It was Aileen Brenahan.

'Are you coming to work here?'

'Yes, down at the forty-fathom level.'

'I'm glad you were able to find work so quickly.'

Aileen Brenahan smiled, and Ben noticed the way the dark skin crinkled at the corner of her pale-green eyes. 'Where will you be staying?' she asked.

'Your father said some of your women will build a place for me up on the hill.'

'I thought he might do that. I'm glad, Ben.'

For some sudden inexplicable reason, as Ben looked at Aileen Brenahan standing loose-limbed and happy before him, he thought of Jesse. It was as though he had been dealt a severe body-blow. Although he had tried not to think about her since leaving Tregassick, there had been many times like this, when memories flooded back and he knew he was not succeeding.

Abruptly, he swung on to the ladder in the shaft.

'Wait a moment.'

Aileen Brenahan drew a cloth from a large pocket beneath her apron and unfolded it to reveal a huge pastie. Breaking it in two, she handed one piece to Ben.

'Take this. You'll have had nothing to eat for a while, I'm thinking. It will keep you going.'

She was right. Ben had eaten nothing since noon the previous day.

Taking the food from her, he pushed it inside his shirt. He intended eating it on his way down the ladders, but he found such a feat quite impossible. The ladders were flimsier than any he had ever trodden. It needed no feat of imagination to realise why three men had fallen to their deaths on these ladders. Most mines had a man, or a team of men, constantly checking and repairing all ladders. It seemed that the captain of the Wheal Slade gave the safety of his miners scant attention.

At the forty-fathom level, Ben realised he had no candles with him. Taking a lighted one from a niche in the tunnel wall, he made his way along the level. Suddenly there was a rush of feet from somewhere ahead, and a collision of bodies. Ben's candle was knocked from his hand and he was grabbed and dragged to the ground behind a pile of granite rock. Moments later there was a roar in the level that hurt Ben's ears and momentarily deafened him. The explosion was followed along the tunnel by a dense rolling cloud of dust and fumes that caught at Ben's throat and set him coughing, along with the unseen men about him.

It was some minutes before the air cleared enough for one of the men to scrape a light for a candle. It spat and spluttered indecisively, but in its dim yellow light Ben saw the faces of two men, dirt-caked and red-eyed from the dust that still hung in the air.

One of the miners looked at him angrily. 'What are you doing on this level? You could have got yourself killed – and us along with you!'

'The captain sent me down here. He said you were short of a man.'

'The Wheal Slade might well have been short of three more. Didn't Captain Clymo tell you we were using explosives?'

'He told me only that I would find you at the forty-fathom level.'

The two miners exchanged glances.

'If Captain Clymo didn't live on the mine, he would forget where he had to go to work each day,' said the younger of the two miners. 'I'm Tom Shovell. This is Ezra Hooper. He's on night shift but stayed on to help me out.'

'You have only two men working at a time? No boy to carry the ore, or shift the waste?'

Ezra Hooper snorted. 'This is the Wheal Slade, not one of your big St Just mines. Captain Clymo keeps the rate of tribute screwed so low that after paying for powder and candles we're lucky to break even on settling-day. We're working for a shilling in the pound, and all we have to show for our efforts so far are heaps of waste rock. Unless we find tin soon we'll end the month owing money to the mine!'

'Then perhaps we should be looking for tin now and not sitting here talking about it.'

Tom Shovell and Ezra Hooper looked at each other; then both men grinned at Ben's words.

'He's right,' agreed Ezra Hooper. 'I think he'll keep you working, Tom. I'll go home to my bed and see you both tonight.'

He clapped Ben on the shoulder and walked away with the weary step of a man who had spent too many years working below ground for a living.

Tom Shovell was perhaps five years older than Ben, and tall and lean. Wiping some of the dust from his face, he said, 'Since you're so eager to be working we'll make a beginning. You can use Ned Rodda's tools. He was killed on the ladder yesterday. If we make any money, you can pay his widow for them. She'll have need of every penny she can get with three young maids to bring up.'

Ben said nothing as he followed Tom Shovell along the level. He would pay Ned Rodda's widow for the tools – but he would buy new tools at the earliest opportunity. Ben was as superstitious as any other miner. He would not be happy working with a dead man's equipment.

Ezra Hooper had not been wrong about the amount of tin to be found in the forty-fathom level. The tributers were following a seam no more than inches wide. It was hardly worth the effort they were putting into the work.

During the morning, Ben helped Tom Shovell to drill holes for more gunpowder. He also stacked the waste rock and carted away what little ore they had won. During his journeys to and fro along the tunnel he stopped many times to examine the walls. By the time they stopped for a midday break he was so thoughtful that Tom Shovell commented upon his silence.

'I've been looking along the level. I think you're following the wrong lode.'

Ben expressed his opinion with a certain amount of hesitation. He had been working underground at the Wheal Slade for no more than a few hours. He knew nothing of the ground they were working. Yet here he was implying that the men he had joined did not know their jobs.

He saw by Tom Shovell's expression that the same thoughts were going through the mind of the other man. He hastened to explain his audacious remark. 'I think the main lode was thrown off course about thirty yards back. Am I right?'

Tom Shovell nodded. He was not unduly impressed. Such an observation proved nothing. A young lad in his first year below ground could usually see where a lode had suddenly ended and a search made to find it again.

'We lost it right enough, but Ezra found it again.'

Ben shook his head. He was committing himself fully now. 'No. He found what he *thought* was the lode. It was a "whisker" – a breakaway lode. I remember my pa showing me a similar mistake in the Money Box mine. Nobody believed him then, but he persuaded his partners to go out a few feet, and the main lode was there. He could tell by looking at the rock. Come with me; I'll show you.'

Tom Shovell was sceptical, but he followed Ben along the tunnel. Ben led him unerringly to the place where the original lode had been lost.

'Here you can see where the old lode was. Now look at the ground on this side of it – where the new "whisker" was found. It's different.'

Tom Shovell took the candle from his hard hat and held it up to the rough-hewn wall of the level. It would have taken a very keen eye indeed to discern any difference in the composition of the ground, and yet . . .

Ben moved to the far wall of the tunnel. 'Now look here.'

Once again it would have taken a keen and expert eye to

notice a difference, but on close examination it could be seen that the grain of the rock here was similar to that which had been worked along the level as far as this spot.

'If we went out from here, we would find the main lode again. I'm certain of it.'

Tom Shovell rubbed the stubble about his chin and wondered just how experienced Ben was in tin mining. He knew nothing about this young man. For all he knew, he might have been thrown out of mine after mine for making similar rash assertions. Ezra Hooper was a miner with years of experience behind him. It had been his decision to follow the present lode. On the other hand, Tom Shovell knew that after so many years of underground work a man became tired, liable to make simple, yet costly, mistakes.

'How far off the lode do you think we might be?'

Ben shook his head. 'I don't know. I doubt if it will be more than six feet.'

Tom Shovell frowned. 'We will need to use powder. A charge here will block the tunnel. If you're wrong we'll have lost half a shift's work.'

Tom Shovell looked at Ben again and made up his mind.

'If you are right, we'll take home a sight more money than we can look forward to at the moment. All right, Ben. I'll go up and get some more gunpowder from Captain Clymo. You begin boring the holes to take it – and, Ben, I hope you're right.'

Ben tried not to think about the possibility of being wrong. He hammered at the long spade-tipped drill as though his life depended upon the hole he was making in the tunnel wall.

When Tom Shovell returned they both worked hard. For a long time the only sound in the confines of the tunnel was the clang of steel upon steel. Neither man felt like talking.

When the holes were deep enough, the gunpowder was

carefully tamped home and the fuse, made from gunpowder-filled straws, carefully inserted in the holes. Finally, when all was ready, a candle was set at the end of the fuse and both men ran to safety.

After the fumes from the explosion had cleared, Tom Shovell and Ben returned to the spot and examined the newly exposed rock face eagerly. They found nothing but more rock.

Ben tried not to look at Tom Shovell's face as he said, 'I think we should drill and set the powder again.'

'Of course,' Tom Shovell realised how Ben was feeling and he tried to sound cheerful. 'We've hardly put a dent in this rock yet.'

Picking up his drill and hammer, he began to chisel out another hole in the wall of the level. Ben followed his example.

They had been hammering without rest for twenty minutes when Tom Shovell let out a whoop and pounced upon the waste he had just scooped for the hole he was drilling. He picked up a piece no larger than a pea and held it out to Ben. It was cassiterite – tin ore!

'You were right, Ben. It *is* here.'

Ben tried unsuccessfully to hide his relief. 'We'd better wait until I've brought down the rock and seen how much ore is there before we get too excited.'

After the second explosion they could not wait until the smoke and dust had cleared completely. Coughing and choking, they made their way back to the scene of the explosion.

Starved of oxygen, their candles were slow to light and burned unevenly. But the feeble light was sufficient to show them they had uncovered an unmistakable lode of tin ore. With a pick, Ben worked at the lode to test its richness. Tom Shovell joined in, and by the time they had cleared a fair-sized area neither man could hide his delight. The lode was at least three feet wide, and it was rich ore.

'You were right, Ben. You were absolutely right.'

Tom Shovell was known as a quiet undemonstrative man, but now he wrung Ben's hand enthusiastically and both men grinned at each other like two foolish boys.

When they had recovered from their initial enthusiasm they began breaking out the ore. By the time the two men of the night shift came down to relieve them they had an impressive heap of ore ready to be hauled to the surface.

Ezra Hooper was quick to admit his error, and he praised Ben's mining skill ungrudgingly. When Ben tried to shrug it off as mere luck, the older miner said, 'No, Ben. There is little luck to this. You've a keen eye and a feel for mining. Looking at you now I am not so tired, I can see why. You're Pearson Retallick's boy, aren't you?'

Ben looked at Ezra Hooper in pleased surprise. 'Yes. You knew him?'

'Aye, I knew him.' Ezra Hooper had not missed Ben's use of the past tense. 'We were tributing together in the far west, for a while. I've never worked with a finer partner. If you turn out to be half the man he was, there won't be a better miner on the Wheal Slade – and you've made a good start. Away you go, now, the pair of you. The longer you wait about down here, the quicker the morning will arrive.'

Chapter Fifteen

When Ben and Tom Shovell climbed wearily from the shaft, the sun had already gone down below the ridge of the moor and long shadows lay across the valley. With the satisfaction of a good day's work behind him, Ben felt happier than he had for many months, but his throat felt as though he had swallowed a spadeful of dry ore. As he and Tom Shovell washed in the boiler-house, Ben announced he was going to the ale-house in the village and invited Tom Shovell to join him.

Tom Shovell shook his head. 'Richard Hampton is preaching in the chapel at St Cleer tonight. I shall be there to hear him. You'll be more than welcome if you care to come, Ben.'

Ben shook his head. He should have realised from his companion's quiet and serious manner that he was a staunch follower of John Wesley. There were a great many of them in the mines of Cornwall.

'No, thank you, Tom. I've heard your Richard Hampton preaching on the mines of St Just. Folk there call him "Foolish Dick", but there's little foolishness in Richard Hampton. He'll have you stamping your feet for the Lord and emptying your pockets to pay for a new chapel before the night is over. I haven't the throat for shouting "Hallelujah!" I'll see you in the morning.'

After parting from his companion, Ben was no more than a dozen paces along the path to Henwood when a slim figure rose from the tall fern of the moor and fell in beside him.

'Hello, Ben Retallick. Are you on your way up the hill now?'

'No, I'm going to Henwood village to wash some of the tin dust from my throat.'

'Oh!' Aileen Brenahan sounded disappointed. 'I suppose that means you'll not be back up the hill until late.'

'And if it does?'

Aileen Brenahan shrugged unhappily. 'Nothing. You can do as you please . . . but father caught a rabbit in one of his snares today. It made a fine stew. I saved some for you.'

Ben felt ashamed of his churlishness. Aileen Brenahan and her father had been very kind to him.

'I couldn't eat a bite of food until a couple of pints of ale have washed away this dust. When that's done I'll come up there for some of your stew.'

'Is that a promise?'

Aileen Brenahan sounded happy again, and Ben was reminded that she was still a very young girl.

'It's a promise. What's more, I'll bring a jug of gin with me for your father.'

In spite of his good intentions, Ben was at the ale-house for much longer than he had intended. Moses Trago was there when Ben arrived. He declared that Ben's success in finding work was a good excuse for a celebration.

It was almost three hours later when Ben made his way up the hill to the moor in the darkness. He went carefully, lifting his feet high to clear imagined obstacles as he nursed a flagon of gin to him.

When he reached the Irish encampment the fires were burning low. At first he thought everyone was a-bed, and he was relieved. Then a voice from the shadows beside one of the fires said softly, 'Is this how you keep your promises, Ben Retallick?'

'Ah! There you are, Aileen. I met a friend, Moses Trago, in the ale-house. He insisted I have a drink with him.' Ben's tongue felt lazy, and he heard the distortion of his words, 'But I've brought the gin for your father.'

'He's sleeping – and so is everyone else who has any sense. I've kept this stew on the fire for you. Will you eat it now?'

'I've thought of nothing else all evening,' Ben lied.

'Ha! You have the blarney of an Irishman. I know that Moses Trago. If you've been with him, you'll have thought of little else but drinking and finding trouble. I'm surprised you haven't got a few bruises for me to tend to. Here, take your food and pass that gin over.'

As Ben began eating, Aileen Brenahan pushed two mugs forward into the dim firelight. Filling them both from the flagon of gin, she pushed one towards Ben. When he protested he had drunk enough already, she interrupted him curtly.

'I've been sitting around here waiting for you since sunset. Now you've finally arrived you can sit awhile and talk to me while I catch up with some of your drinking. Like most men, I've no doubt you talk better with a drink in front of you.'

Ben watched in disbelief as Aileen Brenahan lifted one of the mugs to her lips and drank the contents as though it were spring water.

The moorland gin sold to miners was reputed to be capable of dissolving a guinea of the realm within five minutes, and it brought hot tears to Aileen Brenahan's eyes. When she trusted herself to speak, she croaked, 'Well . . . ? What's happened to all the talking you've been doing down at the ale-house? Have you nothing left to say to me now?'

'Yes. I suggest you go easy on that gin. I've known a grown man fall flat on his face from less than you've drunk already.'

'I was weaned on the stuff,' replied Aileen Brenahan defiantly as she splashed more into her mug. 'Tell me something about yourself, Ben Retallick. Have you got a girl somewhere?'

'No.'

It came out so quickly that Aileen Brenahan knew it was a lie. But it mattered little. Whoever the girl was, she was not here. Aileen Brenahan was. She watched Ben take a swig of his gin and sipped her own more circumspectly now. The world was beginning to sway uncomfortably. She had no intention of allowing it to fall flat on its face.

'Where were you before you came to Sharptor?'

Ben told her about his life in the mines of St Just and of the last year spent moving from mine to mine in the Tamar valley. He made no mention of Mevagissey.

If Aileen Brenahan was aware that there was an unexplained gap in his life story, she made no mention of it. She kept Ben's mug topped up until, with his stomach full of food and a sense of well-being brought about by gin and the nearness of the fire, Ben announced that he was going to get some sleep.

Aileen Brenahan was immediately full of concern.

'I'm sorry, Ben. Here I've been keeping you talking and you haven't even seen the place that Father had built for you. Come along, I'll show you now.'

She thrust a dry twig in the embers of the dying fire. When it was well alight she drew it out and shielded it with her hand as she led the way through the gorse.

The lean-to built by Dowal Brenahan for Ben was no more substantial than any of the others occupied by the Irish families. A loose stone wall stood four feet high at one end. Leaning against it, a wooden-framed turf roof sloped away to the ground, and the open ends had been filled in with stacked turf.

Aileen Brenahan stooped to enter the lean-to through the low doorway and put the lighted twig to a candle stub.

Ben followed Aileen inside, going down on his knees to inspect his new 'home'. His belongings had been taken out of their bundle, the clothes folded neatly and placed upon a large dry flat stone. A wooden bucket filled with water stood in a corner, and a bed of sweet-smelling ferns filled half of the limited floor-space. On the bed was a blanket, apparently donated by the Brenahans.

'Do you like it, Ben?'

It was cramped inside the sod lean-to, and as Aileen Brenahan kneeled beside him her animal smell increased his awareness of her. He gave her a sidelong glance and saw she waited for his answer.

'It's grand.'

This was an exaggeration. The makeshift home would keep out the rain and much of the wind. No more.

'I knew you'd be pleased.' Aileen turned in the cramped space and brushed against the candle which stood on a piece of stone protruding from the wall.

Ben saw it falling and reached across her to catch it. He was too late. The candle fell wick downwards to the floor and the lean-to was plunged into darkness.

'Damn!' As Ben drew back, Aileen's hair brushed against his face and the smell of her was in his nostrils again.

In the darkness he reached for her. As his mouth sought hers, her two hands found his shoulders. She swayed against him as his arms went about her. He mouthed her hungrily and his body leaped into urgent life against hers.

'Wait a minute, Ben.'

Her voice was a hoarse whisper as she wriggled free of his hands. When she came back to him once more he felt her nakedness. Then they were lying body to body on the bed of fern, straining to each other.

Her hands coaxed him as she gasped for him to love her, and Ben was swallowed up by the eager ferocity of her body as he took her.

He had no recollection of falling into a deep exhausted sleep. When he awoke the sunlight was streaming in through the door-space. Ben sat up, his first thought that he must be late for work. Then memories of the previous night flooded back to him . . .

Ben sank back on the bed with a groan. It had been a long time since he had left Mevagissey, but he felt the betrayal of Jesse very deeply. He tried to tell himself such a feeling was absurd. He had been away for more than a year. During that time much must have happened.

For a long time now Ben had begun to doubt whether Reuben Holyoak was dead when he left him. Had he died, Ben was sure there would have been a determined hue-and-cry for him and he would have heard something of it by now – and, if Reuben Holyoak lived, he would be married to Jesse. Ben did not wish to dwell upon that thought. One day he would return to Mevagissey and face the truth. Now was still too soon. Ben had always known that one day another girl would come into his life, but he had never imagined it would be someone like Aileen Brenahan. He wondered what would happen when Dowal Brenahan learned of their relationship – and there was no doubt that he *would* soon find out. It surprised Ben that he had ever been accepted by these people in the first place. They were a strange, tightly knit community who seldom welcomed outsiders.

Ben groaned. He foresaw nothing but trouble as a result of his involvement with this Irish gipsy girl.

He wondered when she had left him. Last night, when he had fallen asleep? Or had she lain beside him all night, until the sun had woken her – and everyone else on this Irish-occupied hillside?

Ben sat up quickly. What was he doing lying here thinking about his romantic involvements? There was work to be done at Wheal Slade.

When Ben emerged from the hut he saw it was not as late as he had thought. The lean-to hut was so positioned that the first rays of the rising sun shone in through the doorway from across the wide valley.

Aileen Brenahan was crouched before a fire on which a pot bubbled and stewed. She had her skirt drawn above her knees to keep it clear of the earth. There was a raw primitiveness about her that made him remember the abandoned way she had come to him the previous night. As though his thoughts had reached out to her she slowly turned and smiled at him.

'Hello, Ben. I'm cooking some eggs, and we have bread. It's not fresh, but it's eatable. Would you like some tea, too? We don't usually have tea in the morning, but I made it specially for you.'

Ben looked about him. His lean-to was a little distance from the others. Surrounded as it was by yellow-flowering gorse, it might have been the only dwelling on the whole hillside.

'Where is your father?'

Aileen shrugged. 'He's probably just thinking of rising. He doesn't believe in fighting the sun to be first up.'

Hesitantly, Ben asked her the question that was troubling him. 'Does he know you were with me last night?'

'What does that matter? Will you leave Sharptor and move to another place because a tinker knows you shared a bed with his daughter? Is that why you left the last place, Ben? Because you slept with someone's daughter?'

Ben looked at her sharply, then turned away.

'I'm sorry, Ben. Really I am. What you've done in the past is none of my business. Please don't go.'

Aileen clung to his arm. 'Ben, I wanted you last night. I need you this morning . . . now!'

She saw his expression change and knew he would not be going away from her today. Perhaps not any day.

'Ben! Ben Retallick, I'm hot for you now.' She took his hand and held it to her body. 'Come with me, Ben. Come . . .'

He allowed himself to be led back to the lean-to shack. No sooner were they inside the entrance than she drew him down to the bed, breathing like a bitch that had just coursed a hare.

The sun had climbed clear of the distant hills when they emerged from the lean-to. Dowal Brenahan was squatting beside their fire.

'I took the eggs off. The water was almost boiled away. It seemed a pity to let a good pot burn through.'

He looked from one to the other of them with an expressionless face and Ben was embarrassed. No one who looked at either of them could be in any doubt about what they had been doing this morning. Aileen Brenahan's eyes had the mauve thumbprint of lovemaking beneath them, and Ben knew his own were the same.

'I . . . I'd best be getting to the mine,' he said awkwardly.

'Then take these eggs and this bread with you.'

Aileen tied them quickly and expertly inside a cloth and handed them to Ben, her hand lingering on his as he took the food from her.

'I'll walk down the hill with you a way.' Dowal Brenahan stood up, and Ben's hopes of making a quick escape were dashed.

The two men walked together in silence until they were well down the hillside.

'Is the shanty to your liking?'

'Yes, it's fine. Thank you for putting it up for me.'

'It's no more than a place to sleep, but there are many in Ireland with less. Aileen's mother and me had no more when we were first married.'

Ben made no comment. He felt sure the Irish tinker had more to say. He was right.

'Ah! but she was a good woman. Since she died it's been just Aileen and me, but we've got along well enough. You'll not be a Catholic, Ben?'

Ben shook his head.

'No, I wouldn't expect you to be. I'm not a religious man myself, but Aileen takes after her dear mother. Every Sunday she walks all the way to Liskeard to renew her faith. She goes to church twice every Sunday when we're home in Ireland. She's a good girl, Ben. Wilful, yes, but she'll make a good wife for a man.'

Still Ben remained silent. They were almost at the foot of the slope when Dowal Brenahan announced that he would come no farther.

Turning to Ben, he said, 'We are simple folk, Ben. We live by few rules. What a man takes or a woman gives is of no concern to anyone else. Mind you, if anything should happen to bring shame upon the girl's family, then the man is expected to do the right thing by her. You understand me, Ben?'

Ben nodded, his face flaming red. He knew exactly what Dowal Brenahan was telling him. The bastardy laws of the kingdom were harsh in the extreme. An unmarried girl who had a baby was likely to languish in prison for many years unless she could bring a man to court and prove beyond doubt that he was the father of her bastard child.

'Good! I knew you for a man of honour the first time I clapped eyes on you. I'll be away about my own business now with a greatly relieved mind. I have a feeling there'll be a pheasant in the pot when you reach home tonight, Ben. I should try not to be late for it, if I were you.'

With a broad wink the little man swaggered away, and Ben realised Dowal Brenahan had just given his blessing to the irregular relationship between his daughter and Ben. He had given it without rancour and with a total lack of emotion. He could have been giving Ben an unwanted cooking-pot. Somehow, it made Ben feel more ashamed of himself than he had been before.

Chapter Sixteen

That summer saw a brief upsurge in the parliamentary reform movements. It was, perhaps, inevitable. The country was being governed by some of the most hated Ministers of all time, supported by an unpopular king. King George IV had earned the contempt of his subjects by his dissolute life and the hypocritical way in which he had treated Caroline, his foolish but likeable Queen.

When Queen Caroline died in August 1821, the discontented elements in the land took to the streets in a noisy demonstration of their sympathy for her. Raising the banner of parliamentary reform, they used the occasion to reiterate their ever-growing grievances.

They resurrected all their old demands – among them the removal of Members from the 'rotten' boroughs. The demonstrators wanted these seats to be reallocated to the new industrial towns of the Midlands. The call for universal suffrage, too, was now much louder. Events in Europe had called the attention of the world to the real power held in the hands of the peasants, the artisans and all those who, until now, had been considered beneath the notice of their 'betters'. Now the ordinary people of England were clamouring for recognition. At the moment they were *asking*. But, by taking to the streets and market-squares in ever-increasing numbers, they were demonstrating their willingness to wrest power from the landowners if they had to.

These were disturbing and perplexing times for the country's gentry. They had been brought up to believe they were superior in every way to those they employed, and accepted without question their right to make decisions for the untaught masses.

Now they were being called upon to change their way of life, to reassess their traditional values and dismantle the barriers separating them from those who laboured without responsibility.

Some landowners paused to consider the new order of things. The more astute among them were prepared to give way to a number of the popular demands. They realised it was possible to harness the new mood and gain maximum advantage from minimum change.

Others vowed they would yield nothing. Among their ranks was Robert Jenkinson, 2nd Earl of Liverpool, Prime Minister of Great Britain. Backed by his Cabinet, the full weight of the law was thrown against radical reform. By introducing harsh new laws, Lord Liverpool tried not only to clear the rabble from the streets, but also to gag the writers and speakers who protested so vehemently against the Government's actions. For the first time since Cromwell's Commonwealth, the country was ruled by naked oppression.

In that hot and sultry August of 1821, the people of England let it be known they *would* be heard. They left their houses and gathered in their tens of thousands. In such numbers they could not all be arrested, and the army of the land was hard put to contain them.

In the face of such overwhelming civil disobedience, and aware of his personal unpopularity, the Home Secretary resigned. With him went many of the repressions brought in during his term of office. The reformers hailed it as a great victory for their movement and howled for the most outrageous new concessions. Workers met in the big cities of the Midlands and burned effigies of Lord Liverpool – and even of the King himself.

In Cornwall, too, the reform movement thought the end of their long campaign was at hand. The residents of the county needed good news. It had been a bad year for the deep tin mines in the west. A drop in the world price of tin had caused a number of the smaller mines to close, putting hundreds of men out of work. The miners drifted eastwards, tramping from mine to mine, seeking work.

They swelled the numbers at local reform meetings. With nowhere else to go, the miners welcomed such meetings. They offered an opportunity to air grievances and express the anger they felt at not being able to find work. But there were some who needed more than shouted words to express their dissatisfaction.

Late one pay-out evening, a meeting organised by a local reform speaker was held in the valley below Sharptor. Halfway through an unusually dull meeting, the inevitable question was raised, 'When are things going to improve in the tin industry in Cornwall?'

'I'll tell you when they'll improve,' replied the speaker, emphasising his words with a clenched fist. 'They'll improve when shareholders stop demanding an excessive return for their money.' He was giving the stock answer to a regular question. 'When tin prices drop the mine captain has to cut his costs, too. If he didn't, he would be looking for work himself. If the men who represent Cornwall in Parliament were put there by us and not by the landowners, we would have the system changed. No man would be thrown out of work just to put an extra few pence on the dividend of a man who might never have seen a mine. This is the reason we demand a change in the way Members are elected to the House of Commons.'

'If we have to wait for that to happen, we'll none of us have any families left alive to support,' shouted a miner from the back of the crowd. 'We need work to live – and we need it *now*.'

There was a loud roar of approval from the crowd. The man who had shouted the remark, a big red-bearded miner, pushed his way through the crowd and jumped upon the heap of granite waste to stand beside the meeting's speaker.

His voice boomed out above the swelling applause. 'There *is* something we can do about our jobs right away. It has nothing to do with reform, and nothing to do with landowners or shareholders.'

The applause of the miners died away and a puzzled murmur took its place.

'What happened to our jobs in the west of Cornwall I can't tell you, but I *do* know why there is no work for us here. Every man in this crowd with eyes to see must know the reason, too. We can lay the blame on the Irish. They come here in their thousands and take work that's rightly ours.'

The meeting organiser tried to regain control. 'We're not here to discuss Irish workers. They, too, have wives and children to support—'

'Then let them stay in Ireland and support them there.'

The red-bearded miner was dangerously belligerent. He had been drinking with more fortunate colleagues who had drawn wages that day.

'The Irish are no friends of the Cornish miner. They come here and take our work for half-pay. *That's* why we can't get work. *That's* why our families are starving.'

His words brought a mighty roar of agreement from the crowd. There were farmworkers present who had seen the same thing happening on the farms. An Irishman would take on any task for a wage that put himself and his family barely above starvation level. It had been a source of anger among Englishmen for many years.

'So what are we going to do about it?'

The red-bearded miner glared at those about him.

'Will you wait for God knows how many years to be given the vote and elect someone to Parliament who *might* send the Irish back to the country where they belong?'

There were a few shouts of 'No! No!' but most of his listeners waited to hear what he had to say next.

'The Irish are living here among us right now. They're up there on the moor, living in hovels fit only for pigs. Will you let them stay and take over all your jobs? Or will you come up there with me and throw them out? Tell them to clear off and go back to their own country?'

There was a tremendous roar of approval from the crowd. The red-bearded miner had given them a target for their anger and frustration: something positive to achieve *now*. They knew they could throw the Irish out of their temporary homes with no fear of retribution. The Irish were as unpopular with the authorities as they were with the people of the country as a whole. With their own language and ritualistic Papal religion, they formed an alien community wherever they went. They were bitterly resented by the conservative Cornish.

The meeting organiser tried desperately to recapture the attention of his fast-disappearing audience. His voice was lost in the uproar as the miners and farmworkers turned their backs on him and surged away up the slope to the moor.

Ben was seated across the fire from Dowal Brenahan and Aileen when he heard the first great roar from the crowd in the valley below.

'It sounds as though they are having a good meeting down there,' Ben said cheerfully. 'The reformers haven't stopped applauding themselves since the Home Secretary resigned.'

'You call *that* a good meeting?' said Dowal Brenahan, scornfully. 'How many men would you say were there – five hundred? Why, I've been to some of Daniel O'Connell's meetings where his stewards got cramp in their fingers and had to stop counting when they reached twenty thousand! Ha! A meeting, you call it? In Dublin that would be no more than a small family gathering.'

'Well, whatever it is, there are many things I would rather be doing on a fine evening such as this.'

Ben smiled at Aileen, but she looked hot and tired and did not respond to his smile. She had been in an ill-humour for some days now.

Ben lapsed into a gloomy silence; then the noise from the valley attracted his attention once more. 'Dowal, that may not be much of a crowd, but it sounds to me as though it's moving this way.'

'I would not be calling you a liar, Ben. It *is* coming closer.'

Dowal Brenahan rose to his feet and walked clear of the gorse-bushes around the camp. Ben followed.

The slope up to the high moor was steep, and the men from the meeting were strung out on the hillside. They were quieter now. Hurling threats and insults came easier when a man stood still.

'What would you think they are after, Ben?' Dowal Brenahan spoke uneasily. 'There's nothing for them up here.'

Ahead of the mob, two young Irish boys scrambled up the hillside as though their lives depended upon reaching the camp before the Cornishmen.

When the first of the two boys stumbled into the untidy Irish encampment, he gasped, 'We've got to get out . . . They are after killing every one of us.'

This dramatic information was given in Gaelic, but there was no mistaking the meaning, even before Dowal Brenahan translated the boy's message for Ben's benefit.

Ben wanted to ask the boy what had happened to make the miners turn upon the Irish, but this was no time for explanations. He did not doubt the boy's statement. There was no other reason for the men from the reform meeting to be swarming up the hill towards them.

'Get the women and children together and keep them well out of the way,' Ben ordered Dowal Brenahan. 'If they panic and run across the moor in this light, you'll lose half of them down old mine shafts.'

The warning was a necessary one. The moor had been mined for tin for centuries and was pock-marked with pits and shafts, many of them hidden by gorse and fern.

Dowal Brenahan passed on Ben's instruction and the Irish women ran from their pathetic homes. Dragging bewildered and frightened children, they took with them whatever belongings they were able to snatch on the way.

As the women and children fled to the tangled safety of the moor, the Irishmen came to join Ben and Dowal Brenahan. Each of them carried either a pick-handle, or a long pointed shovel. Without a word, they formed a long line on either side of Ben. There were not more than two dozen of them, but they were prepared to fight hard for what little they had up here on the moor. Famine and poverty had defeated them on many occasions – but famine and poverty were intangibles. The enemies advancing up the hillside were men. Men had brittle bones. Men would bleed. None of the Irishmen questioned Ben's right to be with them as they nursed their weapons and waited for the first of the Cornish miners to reach them.

Toiling up the hillside, the men from the meeting saw the line of silent Irishmen above them. Those in front slowed, waiting for more of their companions to catch up with them. When they felt they were in sufficient strength, they began to advance again, more cautiously.

'That's far enough,' Ben shouted his message when the advancing men were fifty yards away. 'What's your business up here?'

'You're a Cornishman. This doesn't concern you.'

The red-bearded miner was still the spokesman for the men from the meeting.

'I'm making it my business. You . . . Moses. What are you doing here?'

Ben had spotted his friend in the front ranks of the advancing crowd.

'We're here to drive out the Irish, Ben. There's no place for them in Cornwall. They are forcing good men out of jobs by accepting lower rates for doing the same work. Taking food from the mouths of our wives and children.'

'You have neither wife nor child,' retorted Ben. 'And how many local men have been put out of work by Irishmen? The men here work for as much as they can get – the same as any one of us. You all know the truth of that. You also know it's not the Irish who hang around a mine waiting for an accident to happen, then fight each other to take work from an injured man. Cornishmen do that without help from anyone.'

Ben was reminding Moses and the other miners of a recent incident in the Wheal Slade when a miner blew off two fingers in an underground blasting accident. By the time he was carried to grass, news of the accident had reached a group of men newly arrived from west Cornwall. The injured miner had to fight his way through a huge crowd of men outside the mine office, each of them shouting to be given his job.

'That still doesn't make this any of your business . . .'

'Neither is it yours, John Carne.' Ben had recognised the red-bearded miner. 'You've never lost a single day's work because of an Irishman – but many a man has lost his job because of your troublemaking. How many mines in the west sent you packing? I can name three for you: Wheal Stennack, Boswedden and the Balleswidden. There's not a mine left in west Cornwall where you would be employed. Is that why you've come here, Carne? If it is, I suggest you keep moving. You are not wanted.'

John Carne's face was the colour of his beard.

'I don't know who you are, lad, but if you don't move out of the way you'll go down with your Irish friends. We came up here to burn them out, and that's what we are going to do.'

The cheer of support that greeted his words came from no more than a dozen throats. Ben was quick to take advantage of the sudden lack of support for John Carne.

'There are women and children up here who have done no harm to anyone. If you are spoiling for a fight, you can have one – but it will be you and me, Carne. No one else.'

John Carne stood a head taller than Ben and he had been involved in many ale-house brawls. Eagerly stripping off his coat, he handed it to a nearby miner and began to roll up his sleeves as he stepped forward, 'I'll deal with you first – whoever you are. Then we'll come up there and clean those Irish rabbits out of their burrows.'

His words brought a great shout from the miners. They surged forward again, this time to form a large open square about Ben and John Carne. Above them, on the ridge, the Irishmen, who enjoyed a fight as much as any other men, leaned on their spades and pick-handles and looked down upon the sloping arena.

Ben and John Carne circled warily, each waiting for the other to make the first move. All round them the men forming the square shouted impatient encouragement.

John Carne was the first to take the initiative. He rushed forward open-armed in an attempt to carry Ben to the ground in a rib-crushing embrace. Instead, Ben ducked low to his left and brought his right fist up into the bearded face. Carne stumbled to his knees at the edge of the jeering crowd. When he stood up and turned to face Ben again, there was blood spreading across his beard from his nose.

Three times more the bearded miner repeated his initial mistake. Each time Ben evaded his grasp and staggered the bigger man with a well-aimed punch.

Then Carne changed his tactics. He rushed in, as before, but at the last moment launched himself feet first at his adversary. Ben dodged aside quickly, but not soon enough to prevent a flailing boot from catching him on the shin. Then the other man's legs tangled with his own and brought Ben crashing to the ground.

John Carne was a wrestling man and now he fell upon Ben, wrapping his strong arms about him. Locked together, the two men rolled through a low gorse-bush and Ben felt the needle-sharp foliage scrape against the side of his face.

When they crashed to a halt, the bigger man was uppermost.

Ben grimaced in pain and struggled to free himself as John Carne's grip tightened and his face came down within inches of his own. Ben smelled the gin-laden breath as Carne panted, 'I'm going to break your back now . . . and you can do nothing about it. Feel that?'

Carne jerked his shoulders back to increase the pressure, forcing out what little breath Ben had left in his lungs.

Ben was not defeated yet. Allowing his head to drop back as far as it would go, he suddenly brought it forward with all the strength he could muster. His forehead cracked against the bridge of Carne's nose, and the big man's grip slackened for a second. Flinging his shoulders wide, Ben broke the killing grip and threw Carne from him.

Ben stumbled to his feet in time to see the red-bearded miner's fist close around a broken piece of granite. He jumped forward, his heavy boots landing on the other man's wrist.

John Carne shouted with pain and jumped to his feet, nursing his wrist. It was the end for him. Two heavy punches sent him reeling backwards on legs as unsteady as a newborn foal's. Two more punches knocked him towards the excited crowd, and it parted to allow him to fall to the ground. He remained there, unmoving.

Ben pushed his way through the men who had followed John Carne up the slope from the meeting. With shoulders heaving, he turned to face them.

'You all know why I fought with John Carne. I'll fight any other man with the same ideas.'

He glared about him, hoping there would be no takers. His heart sank when there was a movement in the crowd and Moses Trago stepped forward.

But Moses Trago walked to his side and turned to face the crowd. 'You'll need to fight me, too. I stand with Ben Retallick.'

A silent figure moved to join them. It was John Trago. More men stepped out from the crowd, and Ben recognised each of them as a miner from Wheal Slade.

The danger to the Irish families on Sharptor was over. It was not only Ben's decisive victory over John Carne that had dissuaded the miners from pursuing their aims. Attacking the Irish had seemed right when they were at the reform meeting. Now they had seen frightened Irish women with children clinging to their skirts the enthusiasm had gone.

Looking sheepish, the men began drifting away down the hill, two of them dragging the semi-conscious John Carne between them.

'I'm obliged to you for your support,' Ben thanked the men who still stood about him as he nursed a knuckle swollen to twice its normal size.

'You needed little support from us,' grinned Moses Trago. 'You'd have taken that crowd on, one by one, and beaten every man of them. You pack a mighty punch, Ben. A fist like yours is wasted wrapped about a shovel-handle. You should be earning your living as a prizefighter.'

'I'll stick to mining – and there are many others hereabouts who would be wise to do the same. There will be jobs a-plenty if the militia are called in to break up meetings such as the one you held this evening. Lord Liverpool has transported men for less.'

'There will be no repeat of tonight's happenings. We'll not be stirred up by the likes of John Carne again. We'll be on our way now. Your friends are coming to see you aren't hurt. You'll not need us . . .'

Moses Trago turned abruptly and strode off down the hill. Looking up towards the Irish encampment, Ben saw Aileen Brenahan running down the slope towards him.

She arrived in such a hurry that she stumbled and fell at

his feet. As he helped her up, she cried, 'Ben . . . Are you all right? Oh, your poor face!'

Ben put a hand to his cheek and it came away wet with blood.

'Come up to the fire and let me tend to that.'

Aileen took him by the hand and led him up the slope. When they reached their own fire, she sat him down and bathed his face, picking out gorse-needles and making sympathetic noises the whole time.

'My poor Ben. It's fortunate the gorse missed your eye. You might have been blinded.'

'"Poor Ben", indeed! Did you see the other fellow? They had to carry him away. He'll be lucky if he has enough teeth left in his head to hold a pipe!' Dowal Brenahan poured gin into a mug until it flowed over the brim. Handing it across the fire to Ben, he said, 'I'm proud of you, me boy. You fight well enough to be an Irishman.'

'Is that all you can think of – fighting? Away with you, Father – and the rest of you standing here gawping. When I've cleared up my man he'll be wanting something to eat. Go on with you. Ben and I have things to talk about.'

Aileen spoke the last sentence in Gaelic. It was a special message for her father. He and the other men backed away from the firelight grinning, leaving Ben and Aileen together.

'What was all that about? You didn't need to be rude to them. They meant no harm.'

'I don't care about them, Ben. I wanted us to be left alone. There's something I need to say to you.'

'Keep it until the morning. All I want to do now is go to bed.'

'That's all you've wanted to do since we first met, Ben Retallick. Now it's time for us to have a talk. If we don't have it very soon, you'll find others doing the talking for me. I won't be able to hide it for very much longer.'

'Hide . . . ? What are you talking about, Aileen?' Ben looked at her in alarm.

'Ah! I knew you wouldn't have to think about it for too long. Yes, Ben, I'm having a baby. You are going to have to marry me.'

Chapter Seventeen

For the next two months Ben lived out a nightmare. He had agreed to marry Aileen Brenahan, for the sake of the baby, but he did his best to delay the date of the wedding for as long as possible.

His reluctance to stand beside her in church did not please Aileen Brenahan. She accused Ben of having used her and now wanting to cast her aside. She stopped cooking for him and made a narrow bed for herself against the far wall of their tiny lean-to hut. Finally, in October, when cold night winds began to blow across the wide valley of the Tamar and heavy moorland mists closed in upon the tors of Bodmin Moor, Aileen refused to get up from her bed and go to work. She said that the other bal-maidens were beginning to talk about her. It was certainly true that she had put on a great deal of weight about her waist, and it would not have been missed by the sharp-eyed Cornishwomen who worked with her.

When Ben remonstrated with her, saying they would need all the money they could both earn, she bluntly announced that he would have to provide for her when they were married and he might as well get used to doing it right away.

Each night Ben dreaded the thought of going home to the miserable lean-to on the moor and the sharp-tongued Irish girl. He took to meeting Moses Trago at the Henwood ale-house once more. There, he and Moses would drink until the landlord closed his establishment and pushed them out through the door.

Occasionally the two young men went farther afield to do their drinking. There were a number of small ramshackle gin-houses dotted about the moor, selling alcohol of doubtful origins. It was strongly rumoured among the miners that drinking such spirits would send a man blind, or mad, but the gin-houses were never empty. Their custom came from sick and ageing miners, with legs too feeble to carry them to authorised drinking-houses, from beggars and tinkers – and young men out to gain new drinking experiences. They were also frequented by old hags, eager to take advantage of any man too drunk to be fussy. All but the hags and aged miners were transient drinkers. Few retraced their drunken foot-steps.

One memorable Saturday night, Ben and Moses made their way to Liskeard, a fair-sized market-town only a few miles distant. Their visit coincided with the autumn fair and the settling-day for almost every tin mine in the district. The town was crowded beyond capacity. There was such a crush of bodies in every tavern and ale-house that a serving girl risked all but her dubious honour attempting to satisfy the prodigious thirst of the mining men.

Ben and Moses made for one such establishment. After pitching two drunken townsmen from a seat beside a window, they settled down to an evening of heavy drinking. The drinking was accompanied by the singing of bawdy songs, familiar to every tinner.

By midnight, with the thirst of the hard-drinking miners still unquenched, the landlord announced he was closing his tavern. Amid loud protests, he called for the miners to leave.

Not a miner moved from the premises. As their tankards were emptied they began to beat upon the tables in a steady and increasing rhythm, shouting 'Drink! Drink! Drink!' in a continuous chorus.

One giant of a miner, bolder and thirstier than his fellows, carried his tankard personally to the landlord, who stood guarding the huge ale-barrel in a corner of the room.

'I'll have this filled again, if you please, Landlord.'

'Not here, you won't. I am closed. If you want serving, you'll need to go elsewhere.'

The miner leaned closer and looked into the landlord's eyes from a distance of no more than four inches. 'You've taken my money and served me ale all evening to suit yourself. Now you'll serve some more to please me.'

Taking the landlord's hand, the miner opened his clenched fist as though it were a child's and dropped a couple of pence into his palm.

'There. Now, be good enough to serve me with a pint of ale, Landlord.'

The landlord allowed the coins to drop to the floor. 'You'll pick up your money and get out of here – now.'

'Will I, indeed?' said the displeased miner. 'I have a feeling that when I leave your tavern you'll be outside to greet me, Landlord.'

With that, the big miner cuffed the landlord on the side of his head, the blow spinning the unfortunate man around. With one hand grasping the landlord's collar and the other gripping the belt of his trousers, the miner propelled him through the cheering customers until he reached the table at which Ben and Moses were seated. With a mighty heave, the miner threw the landlord bodily over the table and through the window. The unfortunate man landed heavily on the pavement outside, surrounded by broken glass and splintered woodwork.

'Since the landlord isn't here to serve us it seems we'll need to help ourselves,' shouted the big miner. 'The first pint from the barrel is mine.'

For fifteen minutes the uproar in the tavern continued unabated. Then the landlord reappeared at the door, accompanied by half a dozen constables, taken on by the mayor for fair-day.

The landlord pointed out the big miner who had tossed him so unceremoniously from the tavern. Laying about them with heavy wooden staves, the constables forced their way to the offender. After a brief exchange of blows, they beat him to the ground and dragged him outside. Two miners who pressed the constables too closely were dealt with in a similar manner. The mêlée spilled out into the street, and immediately the age-old rallying cry of the Cornish miner echoed through the streets of the market-town.

'One and all!' 'One and all!'

The constables were surrounded on three sides by drunken miners in a fighting mood. Their lives were in very real danger. Hammering at the door of the dwelling-house at their backs, they forced their way in past the startled occupant, taking their prisoners with them.

They had hoped to make their escape through the back door of the house, but the miners had foreseen the move. Scores of men ran to the lane behind the house, shouting angrily when the constables showed their faces at the back door.

The constables ducked back into the house, and the miners began howling for the release of their colleagues. When there was no reply to their demands, stones were prised from the roadway and thrown at the windows. As breaking glass showered inside the rooms, the unfortunate tenant pleaded with the constables to release their prisoners.

Not until the miners began using a heavy stool from the inn as a battering-ram did the constables concede that they had no hope of reaching the lock-up with their prisoners. Shouting for the angry crowd to stand back from the battered door, the constables threw it open and pushed the captured miners out into the street. A great cheer went up from the besiegers, and the three rescued miners were carried away on the shoulders of their colleagues. The miners had won the night.

As they made their unsteady way homewards in the early hours of Sunday morning, Ben and Moses Trago agreed it had been one of the finest nights' drinking they had enjoyed.

That Sunday was the day the new circuit preacher came to the Methodist chapel in Henwood village for the first time.

The occasion was of no interest to Ben. It had been many years since he last attended a service in church or chapel, but it drew a larger congregation than had been seen in the tiny village for a very long time.

They were all leaving the small chapel as Ben made his bleary-eyed way towards the ale-house that evening.

'Ben! Ben Retallick, surely it is you? Allelujah, boy, but it's good to see you.'

Not until the preacher stood toe to toe with him did Ben recognise the face beneath the wide-brimmed hat. It was Wrightwick Roberts, the Bible-reading miner from the Mevagissey mine.

Looking at Wrightwick's heavy black serge suit and spotless white shirt, Ben was acutely aware of his own disreputable appearance. He was wearing the same clothes he had worn to Liskeard the previous evening. He had not taken them off when he fell upon his bed of fern in the moorland lean-to.

Involuntarily, Ben's hand went to his face and scraped against the stubble that had not been challenged by a razor for a full week.

'Wrightwick . . . What are you doing here? You were a miner when last I saw you.'

'The call finally came, Ben.' Wrightwick Roberts's face was flushed with joy. 'After wrestling with my soul for far too long, I bowed to the Lord's will. In His infinite wisdom He sent me to preach His word here, on the edge of the moor where John Wesley himself spent many waking-hours. But you . . . ? Why did you leave Mevagissey so suddenly? One day you were at the mine working, the next you were gone. No one was able to tell me the why, or wherefore.'

Ben looked at Wrightwick Roberts sharply. So there had *not* been a hue-and-cry. Had the magistrates' men searched for him they would have been certain to question Wrightwick Roberts. Ben shook his head wearily: this was not a day for thinking.

Wrightwick Roberts looked to where a group of neatly dressed villagers were patiently waiting for their new preacher to finish his conversation with this disreputable young miner.

'Where are you living, Ben? I will come visiting.'

'No!' It came out more sharply than Ben had intended. 'I . . . I'm living up there at the moment.'

Ben waved a hand vaguely in the direction of the great rock mass of Sharptor, poised above the village. 'I'm only there for a while . . . I'll be moving soon. I'll come to see you.'

Wrightwick Roberts smiled. 'That will be even more difficult. I have nowhere of my own. I stay with whoever is kind enough to offer me lodgings for the night.'

The well-dressed chapel-goers were showing signs of impatience. Wrightwick Roberts did not want to begin his new ministry by offending them. Grasping Ben's hand warmly between both of his own, he said, 'When I'm back around this way I'll look for you and we'll have a long chat about old times and old friends. God bless you and keep you well.'

When Wrightwick Roberts left him, Ben stood staring after the preacher until he passed from view behind a row of cottages. Once, Wrightwick Roberts's companions looked back at Ben, and he knew the ex-miner was telling them about him. It made Ben uneasy. He did not like to be noticed. He did not wish to think about the implications of Wrightwick Roberts's news. If he was not a wanted man . . . ! But it did not matter now – it could not matter. He would marry Aileen Brenahan and move on somewhere – anywhere.

This latest thought did nothing to cheer him. For the next few hours Moses Trago had a very morose drinking companion: one who had to be helped home to his rough bed at the end of the evening.

Wrightwick Roberts was a very observant man. He had not missed Ben's reluctance to have the preacher pay him a call. Neither had Ben's unkempt appearance passed unnoticed. When Ben was working at the Mevagissey mine he had always been exceptionally clean and tidy for a mining man. Now he had joined the ranks of those miners who neither washed nor changed when they came to grass at the end of a shift. Wrightwick Roberts wanted to know why there had been such a dramatic change in Ben, and he wasted no time in finding out.

Ben was on night shift that next week. One morning he made his way up the hill to the lean-to and found Wrightwick Roberts seated beside the fire waiting for him. The preacher explained his presence by telling Ben he was staying at a house only a mile away. He had thought this would be a worthwhile dawn stroll.

When he first saw Wrightwick Roberts, Ben tried to think of a story to excuse the circumstances in which the preacher found him – and for the presence of Aileen. Then he shrugged off any idea of lying. The whole situation was quite clear. Wrightwick Roberts was no fool.

Aileen was no less surly than she had been of late, but at Ben's insistence she reluctantly produced some moderately fresh bread and scalding-hot tea.

For weeks Aileen Brenahan had been telling Ben he must go with her to see the Catholic priest in Liskeard and make arrangements for their marriage. She thought Wrightwick Roberts's presence here now had something to do with the wedding and she was deeply disturbed. She was determined to marry Ben, but she would have nothing to do with a Reformed Church ceremony, whether the reformer was Henry VIII or John Wesley.

As soon as she could get away, Aileen went in search of her father. Wrightwick Roberts watched her disappear into the moorland mist as he sipped hot tea.

'You are blessed with few of life's comforts up here, Ben.'

Ben grunted. It had been a hard night shift, helped along by a pitcher of gin he had taken with him in lieu of food. 'It's a place to sleep.'

'I always took you to be a man who expected more from life, Ben. What went wrong? What has happened to you since you left Mevagissey? And the girl you were going to marry there – Jesse, I think her name was – where is she?'

Ben was as reluctant as ever to talk, but he was tired and unhappy. Gradually, coaxed by Wrightwick Roberts, the story of all that had happened to him came out. Ben told of Sir John Vincent's promise, his son's subsequent refusal to honour that promise, and of the fight with Reuben Holyoak. Of Jesse he said little. Here, in this place, he did not wish to think of her.

After telling Wrightwick Roberts of the things he had done since leaving Mevagissey, Ben explained to his friend about Aileen Brenahan and of the way she and her father had be-friended him. The result of that 'friendship' Wrightwick Roberts could see for himself.

'Do you love this Irish girl, Ben?' Wrightwick Roberts asked the question after a lengthy silence.

'I don't think I ever have, Wrightwick. Oh, I fooled myself for a while. I enjoyed playing at being married. But that doesn't matter now. Aileen is having my child. I'm *obliged* to marry her.'

'That's just what I thought,' said Wrightwick Roberts. 'As a preacher, I am bound to say that you are reaping the harvest of your sinful ways. As a friend, I will ask whether you are quite certain the child is yours?'

Ben looked at the preacher in surprise. 'Of course it's mine. We've been living together since I first came to Sharptor.'

'When was that?'

'At the end of June. What are you suggesting?'

'I am suggesting nothing, Ben. I don't doubt that the lump in Aileen Brenahan's belly will one day be a noisy smelly brat. However, I am curious to know how soon that day will be. If the baby is yours, it should not arrive in God's world until next March, at the earliest. I am not experienced in such matters, but I will be very surprised if Aileen Brenahan is not suckling a child before the new year is a week or two old.'

'No. You're wrong, Wrightwick. You must be wrong. Aileen knew about the child only two months ago. It is mine. It *must* be.'

As the initial shock of Wrightwick Roberts's suggestion wore off, Ben remembered the eagerness with which Aileen had come to him that first night in the lean-to. She had displayed an experience that outweighed his own. He rememebered, too, her father's unexpected acceptance of their relationship when Aileen moved into the lean-to Dowal Brenahan himself had built for him. Ben had asked no questions of Aileen's way of life before he came upon the scene. He had accepted her as a warm-hearted young girl who made exciting demands on him during the darkness of the night. Even after she had soured towards him he had thought it no more than a temporary state of mind, brought about by her condition and their difficult situation.

Ben had been a gullible fool, but it was too late now to do anything to right the situation. He had been living openly with Aileen since his arrival at Sharptor. No court in the land would declare for him in a bastardy hearing. But Ben knew it would never come to court. He could not spend the whole of his life running away from difficult situations.

He would marry Aileen Brenahan.

Chapter Eighteen

When Ben told Moses Trago for the first time about the baby, Moses treated the matter as a huge joke – until Ben said he intended to marry Aileen Brenahan.

'You're not serious, Ben?' Moses Trago looked at him aghast.

'Of course I am. What else can I do?'

Moses saw the determined set of Ben's jaw and he expressed his bewilderment. 'But you must know about Aileen? How she was before you came to Sharptor?'

'I know nothing of Aileen Brenahan before the morning I woke up to find her throwing water over me.'

Moses Trago gulped unhappily. 'Ben . . . Aileen would take any man up on the moor for a shilling. I know. I took her there myself, more than once. I thought you knew all about that.'

Ben shook his head angrily. He had been a stupid young idiot. He had been led into a carefully arranged trap by Aileen Brenahan and her father. Or had he? Ben would never be certain.

'She's not been doing the same thing while we have been living together?'

'No, she gave all that up when you came along. But you won't be marrying her now you know the truth about her, Ben?'

'I don't know the truth, Moses. Can't you see that? Aileen has told me she's expecting *my* child. It may well be a lie, but I have no way of proving it beyond all doubt. If I don't marry her, I'll be haunted all my life by the thought that somewhere in the world a child that may be mine is growing up without its father. Taunted by other children because he, or she, is a bastard. I'll not have that on my conscience, Moses. I'll go through with this wedding, even if she does insist on some Papist priest doing the marrying.'

Moses Trago tried hard to argue Ben out of his decision. Ben, for his part, did his best to drink himself into forgetfulness. But he had made his decision and it was not going to go away.

That night, Ben arrived on time for the night shift at Wheal Slade, in spite of the amount he had drunk. Soon he was working hard, doing his best to keep his semi-drunken state from Tom Shovell. If the older miner realised that Ben had been drinking heavily, he said nothing, and by the time the shift was half over Ben had succeeded in sweating most of the alcohol out of his system.

There was little more than an hour of the shift left to work when, from somewhere deep in the heart of the mine, Ben heard a dull thump and the ground began to tremble beneath his feet.

'It's a bit late in the shift to be using explosives,' he said to Tom Shovell.

'Shh! Listen . . .'

Ben was hammering a drill into the rock-face. He stopped and lowered the heavy hammer to the floor of the level.

He could hear a distant rumbling that continued for many seconds before a rush of displaced air swept through the level, extinguishing their candles.

'It's a run!' cried Ben. This was an occurrence feared by every underground miner. It sometimes happened when an explosive charge was badly sited, or made up of too much gunpowder. The roof of a level would come down in a run that could outpace the fastest man.

Tom Shovell scraped a light to his candle, and both men hurried along the level to the main shaft. As they drew near they ran into clouds of choking dust billowing upwards from the lower levels of the mine. Not until it began to clear were they able to clamber down the ladders.

Twenty fathoms below their own workings, they found a number of men huddled together at the entrance to the level from which the dust was still pouring out. The men were choking and gasping for breath.

'How long is the run?' Tom Shovell shouted at one of the crouching miners.

'We don't know yet.' The miner who coughed out the reply had only his eyes and mouth showing through a mask of dust that clung to his face. 'The roof is still falling in parts.'

'That's no more than loose stones,' said Tom Shovell contemptuously. 'Come on, Ben. We'll need to go in and find out for ourselves.'

Ben groped his way after Tom Shovell through the billowing dust. An occasional trickle of earth fell, and once half a dozen pieces of rock, each the size of a man's head, crashed to the floor beside him. But Tom Shovell was right: the run had ended. They came upon it not fifty paces further along the tunnel. They could go no further.

A couple of miners had followed them, and Tom Shovell asked, 'How much farther does this level go?'

'About a hundred feet. I haven't been along here for a week or two, but it wouldn't be much farther. All the same, I doubt whether any one will come out alive, not by the time we could reach them.'

'The miners in there wouldn't have been at the far end of the level,' retorted Tom Shovell. 'They were blasting and would have come back a fair distance. There could be a man only a few feet from us – and he might still be alive. Do you know how many men were working this level?

'Yes, seven.'

The miner saw Ben's surprise and explained, 'This level is being worked by two families, one working nights, the other days. The Kelynacks have the night shift this week. I saw them coming down the ladder last night. There was Bob Kelynack, his five sons, and Ken Pardoe, his son-in-law.'

'Good God!' Ben uttered the words in a hoarse whisper. An explosion killing all the men in a particular level was nothing new in any mine. But the thought of seven men from a single family buried beneath the rubble ahead of them appalled Ben.

'We've wasted enough time talking,' said Tom Shovell to the two unknown miners. 'Go off and fetch tools and more men. As many men as you can find. While you're away we'll pull out some of this rock.'

Within an hour there were as many helpers in the level as it would hold. They all worked furiously to dig out the earth and rock that filled the narrow tunnel. It was noon before they found the body of the first of the Kelynack family. A boy of no more than twelve years of age, he must have been runing along the tunnel towards the safety of the shaft when the roof-fall overtook him. He was lying face downwards beneath ten tons of loose rock. Behind him, in a line, were thc bodies of all but one of the others. Last of all was Bob Kelynack, the father of the family. He lay over the body of the youngest of his sons, a boy of no more than eight years of age. It looked as though the father had fallen on him in a last desperate attempt to shield his small body from the stone and earth that pursued them relentlessly along the level.

Ben and Tom Shovell continued digging for another couple of hours, but the missing member of the family, Ken Pardoe, was still not found. Wearied beyond belief, the two men allowed others to relieve them and made their way up the shaft to grass.

When they emerged the sun was already sinking beyond the moor at the end of another day. A large crowd, mostly women and children, were squatting about the mine, waiting in silence for the last body to be discovered. They were not related to the missing men, but it was not mere curiosity that kept them here. This was the traditional way of paying respect to those who had died, and expressing sympathy to their families. Many of those who waited had been paid similar simple tributes.

Ben could not remember ever being wearier than he was that evening, as he trudged up the steep slope to the moor. He hoped Aileen would not be in one of her more difficult moods.

He would have gone to the ale-house in Henwood, but it would be full of men wanting to know what was happening underground at the Wheal Slade. Ben was not in the mood for talking. All he wanted was to lie down and sleep until the weariness drained from him.

He arrived at his lean-to to find the cooking-fire no more than a small heap of cold grey ashes, and his spirits sank. Aileen had stopped cooking for him long ago, but there had always been a fire upon which he could cook for himself, or make some tea.

It did not matter; he would not argue about it now. He

wanted sleep. He made his way to the lean-to hut. Just as he was about to duck inside the low entrance, he stopped. Straightening up, he looked about him.

Something had been nagging at him ever since he arrived at the camp on the moor, but he had been too tired to appreciate its significance. Now it had come to him what was different. There was an unnatural silence up here. Usually, at this time of the day, the camp was noisy with the shouting of children and the cries of the babies, all vying with the unnecessarily loud voices of the women, raised in Gaelic conversation. Today there was nothing. Not even a whisper.

At first, Ben thought they must have gone to the valley, to the Wheal Slade. He immediately dismissed the notion. He would have seen some of them there. Tired though he had been, Ben was ready to swear there was not a single Irish woman among the crowd about the head of the Wheal Slade shaft.

Uneasily, Ben made his way from his own makeshift hut to the main camp of the others. He walked on the hard-packed earth about their huts and saw that the cooking-fires were as cold as his own. Finally, he looked inside one of the huts. It was empty. Not a pot, an item of clothing, or a scrap of food was to be seen anywhere. The Irish had gone.

A thought struck Ben, and he hurried back to his own lean-to. A look inside was enough to show him it had been stripped clean. The blanket from his fern bed was gone; so, too, were all his clothes.

His tiredness forgotten, Ben ran across the moor, ignoring the gorse that snatched at him, scratching his torn and dusty arms. He ran on until he reached the rocky outcrop of Sharptor itself. Scrambling upwards, he did not stop until he reached the summit. Here he sank to the ground, his chest heaving with his efforts, perspiration running down his face and neck.

From this peak a man had an unsurpassed view for miles around. Ben scanned the four points of the compass: the trackless moor, the farmland of the valley, and the network of paths and tracks that joined the two. He saw men and horses plodding slowly across the shadowed land, homeward bound from the ploughed fields that lay behind them. Nearer at hand, long lines of panniered ponies headed for the mines along narrow paths. There were a couple of creaking wagons, a sprinkling of pigs, cows and sheep – but no Irish tinkers.

The moor itself was an emptiness patrolled by a pair of late-hunting buzzards. Nothing moved beneath them for as far as the eye could see. It was as though a hundred Irish men, women and children had been snatched from the face of the earth.

Ben made his way back to the lean-to hut because he had nowhere else to go. As he drew near he could hear someone moving in the space about the fire.

'Aileen? Is that you?'

He hurried towards the clearing. It was not Aileen Brenahan but Wrightwick Roberts.

The preacher took in Ben's state, the weariness on his face, and his bewilderment.

'You look all in, Ben. Sit down here for a while. You've had a bad time at the Wheal Slade . . .'

'What's happened *here*, Wrightwick? Everyone has gone. Aileen, her father . . . everyone!'

Wrightwick Roberts nodded his head.

'You knew? Have you had something to do with this?'

'Yes, Ben, this is my doing. Sit down and I'll tell you about it.'

Ben looked at the preacher, trying to read something from his expression. Then he sat down heavily, shaking his head.

Squatting in front of Ben, Wrightwick Roberts leaned towards him. 'When I was last here I asked you whether you really wanted to marry Aileen Brenahan. You answered me honestly, Ben. It was a marriage you did not want but felt honour-bound to see through . . .'

'But the baby . . . ?'

Wrightwick Roberts silenced Ben with a wave of his hand. 'I'm coming to that. I told you at the time I thought Aileen Brenahan was more than five months pregnant. I was right. She confessed her state to a priest weeks before you arrived here at Sharptor.'

'The priest told you this?' asked Ben in disbelief.

'Yes – albeit reluctantly. You see, I told the priest you believed the child was yours and intended bringing it up as a follower of John Wesley. The good father wrestled with his conscience for a while, then told me you were not the father. The child was conceived almost three months before your arrival here. The rest was easy, Ben. I came up here last night and told Aileen Brenahan and her father what I knew. I said you would not be marrying the girl and I suggested they would be well advised to pack up and leave as quickly as they could.'

'And they left . . . with no argument?'

'I did not say that, Ben. I was reluctantly forced to knock down Aileen's father – and a couple of his friends – but they put up no strong argument. They knew very well that once the story got out they would receive rough treatment at the hands of the miners about here.'

Ben remained silent for a long time, then he asked, 'What will happen to Aileen now?'

'Don't you fret about that young woman, Ben. From what I have learned about her, she is more than capable of taking care of herself. She'll return to Ireland with a child in her arms and wearing a black shawl. As a poor young widow she'll get all the sympathy she needs – and likely a husband as well.'

Ben hardly knew what to say. For months he had been living with the knowledge that he would one day have to marry a girl he did not love; one who wanted him only as the father of her child, to escape the stringent penalties of the law. Now he was free again.

He began to thank Wrightwick Roberts, but the big preacher brushed his thanks aside. 'I did what needed to be done and I was the only one able to approach the priest. But I haven't finished with you yet. I'll not rest until you are more like the young man with whom I worked at the Mevagissey mine. In order to bring that about we both need to know what happened in Mevagissey after you left there in such haste. I think we can take it for granted you did *not* kill Reuben Holyoak, but that still leaves a great many unanswered questions. I'll find the answers for you, Ben, but it will take time. I am a busy man these days. When your life is back to normal you can thank me by coming to chapel and falling on your knees to thank the Lord.'

Wrightwick Roberts stood up. 'I'll leave you now, Ben. I must return to a poor woman in Henwood village to whom I can give only spiritual comfort. During last night the Wheal Slade took every male member of her family. They were her past, her present . . . and her future. What have you suffered to compare with that, Ben?'

On settling-day, when other miners contributed a shilling or two to the fund for the woman so tragically widowed in the Wheal Slade roof-fall, Ben gave half his pay to Wrightwick Roberts. He asked his friend to take the money to the bereaved woman and tell her he had collected it from the parishioners on his circuit. Ben felt guilty because on the day his own immediate troubles came to an end the Kelynack family had been dealt such a terrible blow.

'I would have given the lot,' apologised Ben, 'but I need to buy a few things for myself. Aileen and her folks took everything I owned.'

'This is a generous gesture, Ben. With Christmas so near, they will have need of the money. I am on my way to visit them now. Come with me and meet the family for yourself.'

Ben would have preferred to decline Wrightwick Roberts's invitation. The Kelynack family had known much grief. In common with so many young men, Ben found other people's grief an embarrassment. Wrightwick Roberts persisted, and eventually Ben agreed to go with him. There was little else to do on this Saturday evening. Moses Trago had already left for Launceston Town with another of his friends. They had invited Ben, but he knew the jaunt would prove too expensive for him this month.

The Kelynacks had one of the larger cottages in Henwood village. Fortunately for them it was not a mine cottage, but one rented from a local landowner. At least they would not be thrown out with nowhere to go – until they were unable to pay the rent.

Mary Kelynack was a thin pale woman with prematurely grey hair and a body worn out by years of hardship and constant child-bearing. She was not yet thirty-seven, but during nineteen years of marriage had borne eleven children. Of these eight had survived – until the tragic night of the roof-fall at the Wheal Slade. Now she was left with a widowed daughter of seventeen years of age, and two younger girls, aged ten and twelve.

Dressed in brand-new trousers, shirt and jacket, bought on credit from the mine store, Ben was introduced to Mary Kelynack. As he murmured his condolences, she looked at him with dark eyes that still retained a hint of the attractive young girl she had once been.

'I have wanted to meet you, Ben Retallick. I owe you my thanks for your efforts in trying to rescue my husband and the boys. Many miners have told me that no men worked harder than you and Tom Shovell.'

'They would have done no less for us,' replied Ben gruffly. He had grown unused to such compliments.

Eager to escape, he said, 'I saw an axe and some uncut wood outside. You'll be needing some logs for that fire.'

Ben nodded towards the kitchen fire on which burned some crumbling dead wood.

He made his way outside again and hung his jacket in the shed. Rolling up his shirt-sleeves, he began chopping and stacking logs. He worked hard, finding pleasure in the physical energy expended in his voluntary task.

After a while, the axe blade began to lose its keen edge, and he was searching in the small stone-built woodshed for a whetstone when a shadow fell across the floor in front of him. Looking up, Ben saw Kate Pardoe, the widowed Kelynack daughter, standing in the doorway.

'I'm looking for a whetstone . . .' Ben began.

Without answering, the girl reached up and took down a worn whetstone from a recess between roof and wall. Ben carried the stone outside, splashed water on it from a bucket beside the door and carefully honed the axe. When he was satisfied with the edge on the axe, Kate Pardoe took the whetstone from him and replaced it in the shed, still without uttering a word.

Ben began chopping wood furiously, disconcerted by the girl's presence and irritated by her silence. As he worked, Kate Pardoe watched him. She stood leaning against the wall of the house, her hands behind her, occasionally bumping her body back against the stone wall. She was a tall, gaunt, ungainly girl, with big capable hands, but she had her mother's dark unfathomable eyes.

'Where do you live, Ben?'

She finally spoke to him as he took a brief rest.

Ben looked up at her quickly. 'Up there.' He waved in the direction of the moor and resumed his task of splitting logs.

'But Aileen Brenahan has left now.'

Ben looked at her with such a surprised expression that Kate Pardoe laughed. 'Oh, Ben! Don't tell me you believed you were living up on the moor with her in secret? I work on the Wheal Slade, too. Everyone there knew. Aileen made quite sure of that. She wanted a father for the child she was having and intended tangling you up so tightly in her little web that you would never be able to escape. How *did* you get rid of her? What made all the Irish leave Sharptor so suddeniy?'

Ben shrugged his shoulders. Swinging the axe, he struck a log with such force that the two halves flew high across the small yard and the blade of the axe bit deep into the hard wood of the chopping block.

As Ben struggled to wrench it out, Kate Pardoe walked round him. Gathering an armful of chopped logs, she carried them inside the shed. Returning for more, she asked, 'Don't you get lonely up there on the moor?'

'No.'

It was a lie. Since Aileen and the others had left, Ben was desperately lonely in the moorland lean-to. It gave him far too much time for thinking.

'I'm quite happy keeping my own company.'

'I wish I was. Since I lost Ken, Dad and the others, the house seems so quiet I sometimes want to scream.'

'I'm sorry. It must be very hard for you.'

Kate Pardoe nodded, and the capable hands tangled in

her apron. 'We had been married for only six months, Ken and me.'

With sudden understanding, Ben realised that this tall, outwardly unemotional girl wanted desperately to talk to someone. He leaned on the axe and prepared to listen.

'They never found Ken.'

'I know.'

It was believed on the Wheal Slade that a charge had failed to explode on the level where the Kelynack family were working. Ken Pardoe, Kate's husband, must have gone back along the tunnel to re-ignite the fuse and somehow caused the explosion. There would have been little of him to collect for burial. The level had been sealed off and would remain that way until a new generation of miners came along.

'He wouldn't have felt anything, you know.'

This was why Ben had not wanted to come to the Kelynack house with Wrightwick Roberts. He was expected to find words of comfort to say to members of a bereaved family and Ben had long ago learned that all such words are totally inadequate.

'It isn't that, so much . . .'

Kate Pardoe screwed the apron into a tight ball. 'We had an argument, Ken and me. Before he went to work that night. The last words I said to him were that I didn't care if I never saw him again. I didn't mean it . . . It was just a silly quarrel.'

'I expect he knew that.'

'I wish I could be certain. What if he believed I was serious? That I *didn't* want to see him again? What if . . . ?'

The apron-strings tore away as Kate's plain face distorted and she fought the anguish inside her. Quickly, Ben took her arm and led her into the shed just as she lost all control. Great shuddering sobs racked her gaunt body, and he held her to him, stroking her hair and speaking to her as though she were a small child.

Eventually the sobs became less frequent, but Kate still leaned heavily against Ben. Not until they both heard the door of the house open did she move away from him.

'Kate? Kate, where are you, girl?'

Kate Pardoe knuckled her eyes and lifted her broken apron to her face just as Mary Kelynack put her head around the door of the shed. She looked from Kate to Ben, and a suspicious frown formed on her face.

'What have you two been getting up to in here?'

Ben opened his mouth to speak, but Kate put a hand on his arm quickly.

'It's all right, Ma. Ben and me got to talking about Ken. I . . . I'm afraid I wept all over Ben's shirt-front. It will need to be dried before he goes off anywhere.'

Another sob broke from her, and Kate Pardoe fled from the shed, pushing her mother aside. She ran in through the open door of the house, and Ben heard her wooden-soled shoes clattering on uncarpeted stairs.

'Thank God for that!' Mary Kelynack said to Ben, 'You have done more today than I have been able to achieve these last few weeks, Ben Retallick. I knew the tears were there, but she wouldn't let them come out. I have been worried sick about her. Bless you, boy. You've earned your dinner. Come indoors and eat it now, before that hungry preacher has it all.'

Kate did not come downstairs to take her place at the table until the meal was half over. There was an ugly puffiness about her eyes, but she had regained control of herself and managed a weak smile for Ben's benefit.

As they ate, Mary Kelynack directed most of her conversation at Ben in an effort to learn more of his background. He was determinedly reticent, and it was Wrightwick

Roberts who provided her with much of the information she sought.

Then Kate volunteered, 'Ben is living by himself in an old hut up on the moor. Can't we persuade him to move in here, with us? We have the room – and he's very good at chopping wood.'

'Now, that's a splendid idea,' boomed Wrightwick Roberts, before Mary Kelynack could reply. 'A woman's influence would do Ben the world of good, and he could make a useful contribution towards the rent.'

Mary Kelynack was slow to answer. When she finally made her reply, she looked squarely at Ben. 'Well, Ben Retallick? You have heard what Kate and Wrightwick think. All I have to add is that I would be delighted to have you here. It's a strange house without a man or my boys about the place. I can offer you only plain food and fare, but with four women in the house I doubt if you'll ever have a loose button or unwashed shirt. You'll be as spoiled as any man in these parts. What do you say?'

In the ensuing silence, Ben's spoon scraped noisily across an almost empty plate as he thought about the offer. It would curtail his drinking habits, but Ben was honest enough to admit to himself that he did not enjoy long evenings in the false bonhomie of the ale-house. Living here would also encroach upon his independence, but there had been many nights in his Irish lean-to when independence was no more than another word for loneliness. Life had held little meaning for him since he left Mevagissey. Living here would give him the opportunity to pull himself together again; to think things out and plan a future.

Pushing away his empty plate, Ben said, 'Your cooking puts forward its own argument, Mrs Kelynack. I would love to move in here – if you really don't mind.'

Later that night, when Ben left the house with Wrightwick Roberts to collect his few belongings, the preacher said seriously, 'You'll be well looked after in the Kelynack house, Ben. You have also taken on a great responsibility. Until the family gets over the shock of the accident you will need to be brother, father and uncle to them all.'

'It's high time I took on some responsibility, Wrightwick. Since leaving Mevagissey I have drifted from one job to another with little thought for anyone but myself.'

Ben grimaced at his companion, 'Hark at me! Before you've done you will have me riding a circuit as a Methodist preacher.'

'You could do worse, Ben – and the Lord has need of good servants.'

Chapter Nineteen

Ben soon settled into the routine of the Kelynack household. It was more comfortable than anything he had known since leaving Tregassick. He had his own clean and bright bedroom, but, except when he slept, it was no more private than any other part of the house. There was always one or more of the Kelynacks in his room with him. The two younger girls seemed afraid to allow Ben out of sight in case he, too, went away from them.

Ben knew they would miss their father and brothers most of all at Christmas and he set out to make it a specially good day for them all. For Holly, the youngest Kelynack girl, he had a large peg-doll carved by the engine-man in the Wheal Slade. The engine-man's wife sewed clothes for the doll, while one of the long-suffering whim-ponies donated four inches of mane to give the doll a head of coarse black hair. Jenny Kelynack was twelve and a tall girl for her age. Consequently her clothes had always been Kate's home-made cast-offs. For her Ben bought a blue calico dress from a shop in Liskeard. It was the first shop-bought dress she had ever owned. For Mrs Kelynack, Ben bought a family present. A big plump goose from Liskeard market for the Christmas dinner.

Ben found choosing a present for Kate Pardoe the most difficult task of all. She was a good-natured, infinitely patient girl, and Ben had become very fond of her. She was all he would have wished for in a sister. But Ben realised she regarded him as something more than a brother. Because of this, he had to buy her a present of a fairly impersonal nature. He finally chose a sewing-bag, divided into many compartments, and had her name embroidered upon it by the obliging wife of the Wheal Slade engine-man.

It proved to be a much happier Christmas Day than Ben, or any member of the Kelynack family, had dared hope for. Not until the time came for them to sit around the table for their midday Christmas dinner was the loss of the male Kelynacks brought home to them all with some impact.

The kitchen table was a huge affair, large enough to seat a dozen comfortably. Today, half the places were empty. The empty seats might have meant the collapse of the carefully nurtured spirit of Christmas, had Wrightwick Roberts not called at the house.

The preacher was paying brief visits to as many of his Methodist flock as was possible between his Christmas Day chapel services. His bluff good humour and joyful acclamation of this holy day put an abrupt halt to the family's slide into painful memory. Declining a seat at the table, Wrightwick Roberts left the house after promising to return later that evening, on completion of his last evening service.

After the midday meal, Ben sat beside the fire chatting to the others until the combined effects of heat and a surfeit of food made him feel drowsy. He announced he would go to bed to rest for a while. His decision brought a chorus of protest from the two youngest Kelynack girls, but their mother quickly silenced them. She knew Ben had worked until almost midnight the previous evening – and then he had gone on to have a few drinks with his friends in the Henwood ale-house.

When Ben awoke, his bedroom was in darkness. He sat up with a start. Something had brought him out of his sleep. There was a knocking at the door of his room and a voice called, 'Ben, are you awake?'

'Yes, I'm awake. Come in.'

The door was pushed open, and weak light from a candle standing on a shelf in the passageway outside advanced halfway across the room.

'I've brought you some tea.'

Kate whispered the words, as though afraid to waken the remainder of the household. Still stupid from sleep, Ben said, 'It's dark. How long have I slept? Is everyone else a-bed?'

'No. They've gone to chapel for Wrightwick's evening service. I said I would stay at home . . . in case you woke.'

'Oh! That's a relief,' Ben leaned back against his pillow. 'For a moment I thought I must have slept Christmas Day out.'

Kate put Ben's tea on the chair at the side of his bed. After a moment's hesitation, she sat on the bed beside him.

'I thought I heard you stir. The tea was ready so I brought you a cup. I didn't mean to wake you.'

Ben stretched himself lazily. He felt warm, rested and content. 'It's as well you did, or I would have slept until morning. I wouldn't want to waste Christmas in such a way.'

'Our Christmas hasn't been wasted, Ben – thanks to you. Had you not been in the house we would all have spent the whole day weeping. I'm glad you came to stay with us.'

'So am I,' said Ben truthfully. Had he not come to live here with the Kelynacks he would have spent Christmas Day in a corner of the ale-house, until he collapsed on the floor and was pitched out into the village street. The landlord's duty towards his customers ended when they became incapable of reaching inside a pocket for coins with which to buy more drinks.

'It seems strange to see you lying here, in this bed. This was our room . . . mine and Ken's.'

In the faint light from the passageway, Ben could make out a thin line of perspiration on Kate's upper lip.

'I miss him, Ben.'

'Of course you do. He was your husband . . .'

Kate continued to speak as though she had not heard Ben; as though she were repeating something she had carefully rehearsed.

'I miss him in ways that shame me, Ben. Before we were married there were some things I thought I would never be able to do. Things that the other women on the mine joked about to us younger girls. Now . . . now I lie awake some nights and my body screams out with wanting. You know what I mean, Ben. You know what I'm saying. Please, Ben . . .'

Tears had joined the perspiration on Kate's face now, and Ben sat up in alarm as she swayed towards him.

Her hair brushed against his face . . . Then there came a hammering on the kitchen door.

Wide-eyed, Kate sprang to her feet. 'Who can that be? You'll have to answer the door, Ben. I can't.' With that she fled from the room.

Ben swung himself from the bed and hastily pulled on trousers and shirt.

In the kitchen he paused momentarily to smooth his tousled black hair, and the banging on the door was resumed with renewed vigour.

'All right! All right! Leave the door on its hinges. I'm coming.'

Ben swung the door open, and Moses Trago stumbled into the room. He wore a wide grin on his face and in his hand waved a large earthenware flagon.

'You took such an age to open the door I thought you must have gone to bed. I've brought you a present. A merry Christmas, Ben! This is none of your cheap Holland gin, either. It's good brandy, carried from France within the month – and not a farthing wasted on Excise revenue. Taste it, Ben. It's as smooth as a virgin's bosom.'

Moses Trago sat down heavily upon a chair. Ben took the proffered flagon from him and lifted it to his own lips, sceptical of Moses Trago's claim. He was pleasantly surprised. It *was* good brandy. Ben had tasted nothing to match it since leaving Mevagissey.

'This is a *real* drink. How did it come into your hands?'

Moses Trago gave Ben an exaggerated wink. 'I won it, Ben. I was sitting on the old track across the moor behind our place, when I saw a stranger riding towards me on a donkey hung with flagons and the like. He didn't seem any too pleased to see me, but that matters little. By his accent I knew him to be a Polperro man, and they are well known to be a mite surly. Anyway, he had the nerve to order me from the path, telling me it wasn't wide enough for him to pass me with his donkey. I bet him a flagon of his brandy that it was.'

Ben smiled at Moses Trago's audacity. 'And you won the bet?'

'No, I lost. But any man who uses a donkey to push another from the path deserves to lose a flagon of brandy.'

At that moment Kate came into the room, carefully avoiding looking at Ben. Moses Trago's eyes went from her to Ben . . . and back again. He stood up abruptly, upsetting his chair. 'I'm sorry, Ben. You won't want my company. I didn't know Kate was here with you.'

'Sit down, Moses.' Ben righted the chair. 'We are waiting for the others to return from the chapel.'

Ben looked quickly at Kate. She had regained her composure now, but Ben wondered what would have happened had Moses not paid them his Christmas visit. 'Fetch some cups, Kate. We'll all have a drink.'

Kate brought three cups and set them upon the table. Moses filled them clumsily from the flagon, then he called for a toast in honour of Christmas. Kate and Ben raised their cups in reply. When they drank, Ben was alarmed to see Kate's cup empty as quickly as his own.

By the time Mary Kelynack returned with her other two daughters and Wrightwick Roberts, Kate's cheeks were flushed and her laugh rang out more loudly than Ben had heard it since coming to live in the Kelynack house.

Mary Kelynack frowned at Moses Trago and his flagon of brandy, but Wrightwick Roberts came to his rescue. He declared that brandy was just what was needed to drive away the chills of the evening and the draughts of the chapel. He insisted that Mary Kelynack sample the unexcised liquor, commenting that it was better drunk in the confines of the home than in an ale-house where a man was surrounded by temptation.

The unexpected Christmas party broke up when Kate began to sway in her seat and lost the ability to focus her eyes. She tried to stand, and Ben moved around the table just in time to catch her as she fell.

He carried her upstairs, hoping that the hand stroking his hair and neck could not be seen by Kate's mother. Setting her down very gently on her bed, he broke the grip of her arms as she tried to pull him down with her. He left Mary Kelynack to undress her and mutter angrily about the evils of drink.

Wrightwick Roberts was much more philosophical about the outcome of Kate's drinking.

'It will do her no harm,' he said. 'And the drum that will be beating in her head tomorrow will give her no peace to think about her other problems. I wish I knew of some way to bring lasting happiness to her, but I fear it is beyond me. For reasons best known to Himself, the Lord makes the sun to shine on some, while others see only the clouds. I fear poor Kate was born with her back to the sun.'

Outside the house, Moses Trago stayed close to Ben until they had waved Wrightwick Roberts on his way. Then he spoke of what had been on his mind all that evening.

'Kate Kelynack – or Pardoe as she is now. She's a fine girl, Ben.'

'Yes, I am very fond of her.'

'What do you mean by that? Is there something between you?'

'Nothing at all, Moses.'

It was the truth, but Ben did not want to speculate on how long such an innocent relationship could last. 'I look on her as a sister, why?'

'No special reason.' Moses Trago's reply came too quickly. 'Like I said, she's a fine girl . . . Do you think she would mind if I came calling?'

Ben's answering smile carried relief as well as pleasure. 'I am quite sure she'll welcome you, Moses. But I suggest you delay your next visit until she has had time to forgive you for the headache she'll have tomorrow.'

Moses Trago became a frequent visitor to the house. At first Kate's mother did little to make him welcome. Because of his wild ways, Moses Trago had earned an unenviable reputation for himself. Few mothers would have been pleased to have him call on their daughters. Not until Kate's mother learned a great deal more about his family background did her manner towards him soften a little.

It was more difficult to learn Kate Pardoe's feelings. She did nothing either to encourage or to discourage Moses Trago. She still leaned heavily on Ben and looked to him for advice and assistance.

For months, Moses Trago fluctuated between hope and despair until, in the spring of 1822, an event occurred to drive away all thoughts of romance.

Matthew Trago had done nothing to curb his drinking since his son's return to Sharptor. Indeed, it was doubtful if he was capable of giving up drinking now, had he wanted to. Alcohol had as firm a grip on Matthew Trago's life as religion on Wrightwick Roberts's. But it brought him none of the preacher's love of life.

Matthew Trago had always been a man of dark moods and long brooding silences, but his capacity for work was such that mine captains were eager to have him work for them and they overlooked his many faults.

At least, that had been true when the big miner was a younger man. More recently, drink had taken a heavy toll on Matthew Trago's faculties, both mental and physical. It now needed half a bottle of gin to get him off to the mine at all on a cold morning. Once there he sought frequent support from a gin-bottle.

While Matthew Trago was working with his sons it was possible for them to cover up his mistakes, some of which would have been disastrous in a deep mine. Then, in one of his angry drunken moods, Matthew Trago fought the captain of the Stowe's Hill mine and was dismissed on the spot.

John Trago would have left the mine to follow his father, but Moses persuaded him to stay on. Their father had taken the first inevitable downward step on the path that many miners had trodden before him. For his two sons to throw away their livelihoods and follow suit would be foolish. It was far better for them to continue to earn good money. When the day came when Matthew Trago could no longer find work, they could at least supply him with enough drink to keep him reasonably happy.

Moses Trago had made the right decision. Matthew Trago moved from mine to mine in quick succession, each period of employment briefer than the one before. He was not only a nuisance; he was also a dangerous man to have working below ground. One man, trusting enough to hold a steel drill while Matthew Trago wielded a four-pound hammer, was carried screaming from the shaft with all the bones in his right hand smashed. Eventually, the head of the Trago family was reduced to the status of a piece-work labourer – a 'tut-man' – on the worst-paying mine in the district, the Wheal Slade.

After the Wheal Slade there was nowhere for Matthew Trago to go. At first he seemed to realise this. For a few days he worked hard to keep up with his fellow tut-men. If he smelled of gin and staggered a little more after the midday meal break, nobody appeared to notice. Certainly not Captain Charles Clymo. The Wheal Slade captain was never seen outside his office after midday. His affair with the gin-bottle was well known to every miner in the district.

But Matthew Trago's attempt at self-control did not last. One morning he and another tut-man, a young simpleton, had an argument about which of them was entitled to work with a brand-new wheelbarrow. The simpleton repeated many of the phrases he had heard his fellow-workers use to describe Matthew Trago. He called the older miner a useless old drunkard, a sot, and a scrounger who drank so much he could not keep a wife.

Without further ado, Matthew Trago swung his long-handled shovel. The flat of the blade hit the simpleton full in the face, bowling him over. The young man rose to his feet holding a bloody nose. Howling like an injured puppy, he ran to the mine captain's office. By the time Captain Clymo had coaxed a coherent story from the blubbering young man, Matthew Trago was seated on a heap of ore at the top of the shaft, downing the gin he usually reserved for the midday break.

'What's all this about, Trago?' demanded the mine captain. 'What's been happening?'

Moses Trago shrugged nonchalantly and jerked a dirty thumb at the bloody-faced young man. 'Ask him. He's the one who is doing all the squealing.'

'I've already heard his story. Now I'm asking for yours.'

Matthew Trago downed the last of the gin in apparent unconcern and stared up at the sky, saying nothing.

Captain Charles Clymo looked at him disdainfully. 'I should have known better than to take you on, Trago. You are trouble. A drunken troublemaker whose mining days are behind him.'

'Are you telling me you're a better man, Cap'n? What do you see when you stare at yourself in a looking-glass? The only difference 'twixt you and me is that I sit here on a heap of tin drinking from a bottle for other men to see me. You hide behind a locked door and take yours from a glass.'

Matthew Trago tossed the empty bottle down the gaping shaft in front of him. 'That's my second this morning, Cap'n Clymo. What's your count?'

Every man and woman working above grass at the Wheal Slade had moved closer to hear the exchange between the two men. At Matthew Trago's words one of the women sniggered.

The sound was hurriedly stifled, but Captain Clymo heard and he was angry.

'Damn you, Trago! I'll have none of your insults. Get off my mine – now.'

'I'll go, Cap'n, in my own good time. You owe me money. I'll take payment in drink from your office.'

Before the captain of the Wheal Slade could stop him, Matthew Trago leaped from the pile of tin ore and made for the mine office. With a bellow of rage, Captain Clymo ran after him.

The watching mine workers erupted in cheers of encouragement. It was not every day they were treated to the sight of their lazy and much disliked mine captain moving so swiftly.

Matthew Trago gained the mine office well ahead of Charles Clymo and must have located the store of liquor almost immediately. When the mine captain flung open the door, the delighted onlookers heard him shout for Matthew Trago to 'Put them down!' Then the door swung shut behind him.

The surface workers and bal-maidens crowded around the office, and from within there came the unmistakable sounds of a furious fight. Unable to see through the curtained windows, the outcome of the altercation was the matter of excited speculation.

Suddenly, all went quiet inside. Seconds later the office door was flung open. Those closest to the door pushed back against those behind as Matthew Trago staggered out. His left hand clutched the slim necks of two full bottles of gin. In his right hand he held a short-handled cobbing-hammer, raised in a threatening attitude. The head of the hammer glistened with blood, and the women about the door gasped out their horror.

As Matthew Trago advanced through the crowd of onlookers, they fell silently back before him. Once clear of the mine he began running up the hill towards Sharptor. Those nearest to the office pushed their way inside and screams escaped from the throats of the women among them.

Charles Clymo lay sprawled on his back on the stone floor in a spreading puddle of blood. His head was battered and broken, his wide-open eyes staring into eternity.

Ben was working underground when the news of Captain Clymo's violent death was brought to him. The bearer was a surface worker sent down to find him by Kate Pardoe.

Ben immediately set off for the Stowe's Hill mine, armed with the knowledge that a man was already on his way to Liskeard to inform the magistrate of Captain Clymo's violent death. Ben wanted Moses Trago to have the opportunity to find his father before the constables arrived.

By the time Moses and John Trago scrambled to grass at Stowe's Hill, a hue-and-cry had been raised. Crowds of eager miners armed with shovels, crowbars and picks were being formed into hunting parties to scour the moor.

Moses began running up the hill to the high moor with John Trago. Ben ran with them.

'Do you have any idea where he'll go?' he asked as the three men toiled up a steep section of the slope.

'Of course. He'll go home. He has always gone home, no matter what happened to him and however drunk he might be. There's nowhere else for him to go now.'

They arrived at the cave home on the moor and Moses Trago put a hand on Ben's arm. 'Stay outside until John and I have had a chance to talk with him, Ben.'

Moses Trago and his brother went inside the moorland home and there was the murmur of voices from inside as the first of the miners came into view up the narrow track.

'Is he in there, Ben?'

Flushed from their exertions and the excitement of the chase, the miners reminded Ben of a pack of baying hounds.

'I don't know – but Moses and his brother are. You'll do well to wait here until they come outside.'

The miners held a hurried consultation among themselves. There was not one of them with enough courage to go through the door of the unusual home and risk the wrath of the uncertain-tempered Trago brothers, so they waited.

It was a long time before Moses came out. He looked taut and strained.

'What do you want?' he demanded of the waiting miners.

'We've come for your father, Moses,' said a miner from the safety of the rear of the crowd. 'He killed Captain Clymo. He'll have to answer to the magistrate.'

'He'll answer to a magistrate. When he wakes he'll be taken to Liskeard by brother John and myself. Not by a mob of vengeful miners.'

There was some angry muttering in the crowd at his words, and the same miner shouted, 'He's a murderer. You won't be able to hide him.'

Moses Trago's anger flared. He took a pace towards the crowd and they fell silent. 'I said John and I will take him to the magistrate when he wakes. Does anyone here want to call me a liar?'

His challenging stare passed slowly over them. There was not a man in the crowd willing to meet his challenge. Moses Trago spat contemptuously on the ground. 'That's what I thought. You can all go home and leave us up here in peace. When we go to Liskeard we'll not need any help from you.'

The door behind Moses opened and his silent brother came out and stood beside him.

Slowly and reluctantly the crowd began to move away. Once the movement had begun it quickly gathered momentum. Many of the miners looked back at the Trago brothers as they went, but they kept moving.

'He's in there, then?' Ben asked.

'Yes, Ben, he's in there.' Moses Trago had a strained look once more. 'Something has happened to him. It's not just the drink this time. He has no recollection of doing anything wrong. John and I could get no sense from him at all. We might have been talking to a babe.'

'What are you going to do?'

'What can we do? We can't hide him up here, and he's incapable of making an escape. When he awakes, John and I will deliver him to the magistrate in Liskeard. We'll see he is properly cared for until he's brought before the court.'

Moses Trago ran a hand through his tangled hair. 'You'd better go back to the Wheal Slade now, Ben. I am obliged to you for getting word to me so quickly.'

Two constables rode to Sharptor that evening. By the time they arrived, the two Trago brothers and their father were well on the way to Liskeard, having taken the direct route across the moor.

One look at Matthew Trago's wild expression convinced the magistrate that it was in everyone's interest to have him placed in a cell away from the other prisoners. He readily acceded to Moses Trago's request that his father be given special consideration.

The next day, at a hastily convened hearing, the magistrate committed Matthew Trago for trial at the next Assizes on a charge of murdering Charles Clymo. Pending the trial he would be held in Bodmin Gaol.

Before the Assize Judge arrived, a raving Matthew Trago had been transferred to the Lunatic Asylum in Bodmin Town, palpably unfit to plead his innocence or guilt.

Moses Trago gained much sympathy among the miners for the manner in which he had handled the situation, together with his determination that his father should be properly cared for, in spite of the harsh manner in which Matthew had always treated his family.

Mary Kelynack insisted that Moses and his brother John should come to the house and get a good meal inside their bellies at least twice a week.

Yet Kate's attitude towards Moses showed no sign of changing. She still had eyes only for Ben. Life in the Kelynack house became something of a game, Kate doing her best to get Ben alone, he in his turn ensuring there was another member of the family in the house when he was with her.

In April of that year, Wrightwick Roberts went away for more than a month to introduce a new preacher to another Methodist circuit, farther west. He returned to Sharptor on a warm May evening. Although tired after a long day on his aged sway-backed nag, he rode straight to the Kelynack house.

Ben was carefully shaping a new leg for one of the family's ageing chairs when the preacher arrived. Mary Kelynack bustled about, preparing a meal, but Wrightwick Roberts was so full of news that he stomped about the room on stiff legs, unable to sit still for even a few minutes.

'I spent last night in Mevagissey,' he blurted out when he found it impossible to remain silent for a moment longer.

Looking up at the preacher, Ben slowly lowered the half-completed chair-leg to the floor.

'Yes, Ben. I have news for you.'

'My mother . . . ?'

'She is well, Ben. I spoke to her only last evening. We were seated in the house of your grandparents. Stalwarts of the Wesleyan movement, both of them . . .'

Ben made an impatient gesture and Wrightwick Roberts returned to his narrative.

'Your mother is living in Mevagissey now, Ben. She works

in the family salting-cellar. She told me to tell you she is well, but she would like you to return home, if only to pay her a brief visit. She misses you, Ben.'

'What of Reuben Holyoak?'

'Ah, yes! Reuben Holyoak. He runs Sir Colman Vincent's Lamorrack estate and distributes malevolence and injustice to those who fall foul of him. That means most of the men on the estate. He is a much hated man, Ben.'

'So he didn't die?'

Ben whispered the words to himself. He did not know whether he was relieved or angered at the news. There was a huge emptiness within him. Had he known Reuben Holyoak would live, Ben's own life would have taken a very different course.

'He lived, Ben. What is more, it seems no complaint was ever laid before a magistrate. Your disappearance came as a complete mystery to your mother at first.'

'Jesse would have told her why I left,' said Ben brokenly. 'She must have made Reuben Holyoak promise not to make a complaint against me. No doubt it was part of the marriage agreement between them.'

Wrightwick Roberts frowned thoughtfully. 'I am not sure there ever was a marriage, Ben. Leastwise, your mother mentioned that Reuben Holyoak was living alone at Pengrugla and, as a result, the farm has been allowed to run down very badly.'

'What of Jesse's mother? She was too ill to be moved from Pengrugla. That was the main reason why Jesse had to marry Reuben Holyoak – that and the money they owed to Sir Colman.' Ben was bewildered.

Wrightwick Roberts shrugged his wide shoulders. 'I'm sorry, Ben. It seems there are many questions of importance I should have asked. Unfortunately, your grandmother was in the room the whole time I was there. She insisted on telling me of the arrest and transportation of your Uncle Walter.'

'Walter transported . . . ? For what? Smuggling?'

'No, I fancy it was as a result of his involvement with the parliamentary reform movement. Whatever the reason, it seems Sir Colman Vincent and Reuben Holyoak were involved, and Jesse did her best to have Walter released.'

'Jesse and Walter . . . ?' Ben shook his head. 'There is much here beyond my understanding, Wrightwick.'

'All you need to understand is that you are not a wanted man, Ben. The rest you can learn for yourself.'

'What's all this nonsense about Ben being a wanted man?' Mary Kelynack had understood little of their conversation. 'Wanted for what?'

The Kelynack family listened in amazement as Ben gave a brief account of the events that had caused him to leave Tregassick in such a hurry.

When he ended his story, it was Kate Pardoe who put the question that was in all their minds.

'What will you do now, Ben?'

Ben had no need to think about his reply, 'I must go home. I need to know what has been happening there.'

'And to see Jesse?'

Kate spoke quietly, but from her manner Ben knew that his answer would mean a great deal to her. Nevertheless, anything less than the truth would be unfair.

'Yes, most of all to see Jesse.'

There were a few moments during which no one in the room said anything. Then Kate got to her feet abruptly and ran from the room. Her mother went after her, calling her daughter's name.

Chapter Twenty

When Reuben Holyoak was left lying battered and unconscious at the edge of the wood on that spring day in 1820, Jesse waited at Pengrugla for Ben to return from Lamorrack House. She waited to be told that Reuben Holyoak had not been telling the truth. She wanted to hear Ben say that everything was all right once more. That they would marry, continue to live at Pengrugla, and allow life to fulfil its promise to them.

But Ben did not return. By noon, Jesse knew that nothing would ever be the same again. Ben must have failed in his attempt to persuade Sir Colman Vincent to allow them to keep Pengrugla.

Bitterly, Jesse told herself she had been foolish to keep her hopes alive. Sir Colman was no different from any other land-owner in the country. Those who worked the land were no more important to him than domestic animals. That one's tenants occasionally tried to plan their own lives was a tedious burden imposed upon the rich, and no more than that. It was certainly not necessary to consider their views.

By mid-afternoon, Jesse could remain in the house no longer. She walked to Lamorrack and asked after Ben. She was told he had left the house more than three hours before . . . in a furious mood. Now Jesse knew for certain that things had gone badly for him – for both of them.

She hurried from the big house, following the same path to Tregassick taken by Ben earlier in the day.

At the edge of the wood she found Reuben Holyoak.

The gamekeeper had taken a beating which few men would have survived. Both his eyes were swollen and tightly closed. Unable to see, he was crawling about among the undergrowth, his hands scratched and torn by brambles. As he crawled, he whined and pleaded for someone to help him.

There was no need for Jesse to ask Reuben Holyoak who had given him his injuries. She knew it must have been Ben.

Jesse was in a dilemma. She wanted desperately to find Ben, to learn the outcome of his talk with Sir Colman. Yet she could not leave Reuben Holyoak here in his present state. If he was found by someone from Lamorrack House, Sir Colman would have Ben arrested.

She would have to take Reuben Holyoak to Pengrugla. Supporting him as best she could, Jesse went home by a roundabout route, being careful to keep out of sight of the big house.

At Pengrugla she half carried the injured man inside and laid him on a settle. On his stumbling way across the room, Reuben Holyoak knocked against the furniture, and a determined rapping on the bedroom floor with a stick informed Jesse that the noise had disturbed her mother.

Hurrying up to the bedroom, Jesse had first to listen to her mother's complaint that she had been knocking on the floor for almost an hour. Then Maude Henna demanded to know what was going on downstairs.

Jesse had not told her mother of the decisions reached by Sir Colman Vincent and his newly appointed estate manager, and she did not tell her now. Jesse said only that Reuben Holyoak had met with an accident and she had brought him to the house.

As soon as she had made her mother comfortable, Jesse set off for Megavissey to fetch a doctor. Reuben Holyoak's face was such a mess that only a qualified doctor could say with certainty how much damage had been done.

On her way back from the fishing-village, Jesse struck off across the fields to Tregassick, hoping to find Ben there. The house was empty, but in the kitchen she found evidence that food had been hurriedly removed from the food-cupboard. Jesse ran upstairs, calling Ben's name.

The door of Ben's room stood open, and one quick look was enough for her to see that all but his oldest working-clothes had been taken away. Then Jesse realised the truth. Ben had gone away.

She knew why. Reuben Holyoak had taken a severe beating. In his emotive and imaginative state of mind, Ben would have been convinced he had left Sir Colman's new estate manager lying dead. There, in Ben's bedroom, Jesse sat down and wept for Ben, and for the life together they had planned.

When Jesse returned to Pengrugla, she found her mother standing pale and dark-eyed beside the settle in the living-room, prodding Reuben Holyoak with the stick she kept in her bedroom.

Full of remorse and concern, Jesse said to her mother, 'What are you doing out of bed? Come, I will take you back upstairs.'

'You will do no such thing! I want to know what is going on in my own house. I lie up in bed while doctors come and go. Then this idiot . . .' She prodded Reuben Holyoak viciously in the ribs with her stick, bringing a shout of pain from him. 'This idiot falls from the settle and screams for someone to come to his aid, shouting that he is blind. What else can I do but rise from my bed and find out what is happening? Then, after I have done my best to help him, he tells me some cock-and-bull story about Pengrugla belonging to him now. He says he is taking you for his wife! What has been happening while I have been lying a-bed, girl? What *is* going on?'

'Reuben has told you the truth, Ma. Sir Colman says he has no knowledge of Sir John's promise to give Pengrugla to me and Ben. He has made Reuben his estate manager and given him this house to live in.'

'He has done what?' Maude Henna gasped painfully. Reaching for a high-backed chair, she sat down quickly. 'He . . . has . . . !' Maude Henna began panting so heavily she was unable to continue speaking.

'You must get back to bed right away.' Jesse was alarmed. The news had affected her mother exactly as she had known it would. It was for his reason she had said nothing to her.

'Bed can wait,' gasped her mother. 'There are things that need to be dealt with first. What has all this to do with the absurd notion that you must marry this . . . this . . . *thing*?' Maude Henna waved her stick dangerously close to Reuben Holyoak's face. 'You are promised to Ben Retallick.'

'How can I marry Ben now?' Jesse cried bitterly. 'You have lived at Pengrugla for most of your life and now you are ill. If we have to move, it will . . . it will make you worse. Besides, there's the debt owned to Sir John. If we try to leave without settling it, Sir Colman will have you put in prison. I won't allow that to happen.'

'Sir Colman will have me sent to prison? He told you this himself?'

'No, but Reuben did.'

'And I spoke the truth . . . Oh! Ah!'

Reuben Holyoak struggled to sit up as Maude Henna's stick whistled through the air and cracked down hard across his shoulders.

'Your idea of the truth has never been the same as other folks, Reuben Holyoak. Save your breath.'

Angrily, Reuben Holyoak squinted painfully in a vain attempt to see something through his tightly closed and swollen eyelids.

'I'll tell you something you had better believe!' he shouted. 'Jesse won't be marrying Ben Retallick. When I tell Sir Colman what that hooligan miner did to me he'll have him thrown into gaol. He'll be sent to Van Diemen's Land for the rest of his life. Ben Retallick tried to kill me – and he came damned near to succeeding.'

'It's a pity he didn't work at it a little harder,' snapped Maude Henna. 'It would have saved everyone a great deal of trouble. Now I'll tell *you* something, Reuben Holyoak. Whoever my Jesse marries it will *not* be you. I've seen the way you look at her. At times I've felt like taking a billhook to you myself.'

As Reuben Holyoak lay back on the settle muttering vague threats, Maude Henna said to Jesse, 'Help me back to my bed. Then you go to the village and find someone to take Reuben Holyoak back to his own home before nightfall. This is not his house yet – whatever Sir Colman might say. I'll not sleep with him under my roof.'

Once upstairs, Maude Henna eased herself back into bed with a deep sigh of relief. When she closed her eyes, Jesse made to leave the room. Before she reached the door, her mother called her back.

'Jesse! I appreciate what you tried to do, child. But you shouldn't have kept things from me. You might have made a terrible mistake – one you would have regretted all your life. Now, listen to me carefully. Before you go to the village I want you to go to Lamorrack House. Ask to be taken to Miss Eulaliah Vincent, old Sir John's sister. Refuse to speak to anyone else. When you see her, tell her you are the daughter of Maude Henna – who was Maude Carvinicke. She will remember me. Tell her I must see Sir Colman urgently. He is to come here. I have some papers I want him to see . . . No, Jesse, ask no questions. Just do as I say . . . please.'

Jesse left Pengrugla with her mind in a confused whirl. She wondered whether her mother had taken leave of her senses. *Ordering* Sir Colman Vincent to come to Pengrugla to see her!

There was a moment as she approached the big house when Jesse's courage almost left her and she thought of ignoring her mother's instructions. Then Jesse remembered all that had happened and she cast her doubts aside. There was nothing to be lost now. With Ben gone nothing really mattered.

Jesse found things changed at Lamorrack House. The servants appeared fearful of doing anything that might cost them their jobs. The maid who opened the door to Jesse was reluctant to allow her inside the house. Eventually, Jesse managed to convince her of the importance of her errand. After a brief wait in the servants' hall, Jesse was shown upstairs to a magnificent room with a huge window, giving a spectacular view down the valley to Mevagisey and the sea beyond.

Jesse had not seen Eulaliah Vincent for many years and she marvelled at the white-haired frailty of the late Sir John Vincent's elder sister. But, for all her years, the old lady had a keen eye and a sharp mind. Jesse had no need to explain who she was. When she entered the room, Eulaliah Vincent put down the small circular tapestry on which she was working and beckoned for Jesse to approach her.

'Closer still, girl. Ah! I thought as much.' Eulaliah Vincent reached out and took Jesse's hand, 'I would know those looks anywhere. You are Maude Carvinicke's child. I think your mother's married name is Henna?'

Jesse nodded, fascinated by the bright bird-like eyes of the old woman. 'Yes, I am Jesse Henna.'

Eulaliah Vincent snorted in gentle derision. 'Jesse, indeed! What sort of a name is that? I would hardly have expected your mother to call you Eulaliah, but I suggested many other names to her. Nice names. Alice, Harriet, Grace . . .'

'I was baptised Jesse Harriet.'

A pleased smile crossed Eulaliah Vincent's face. 'Harriet was my mother's name. Maude would have known that. She was brought up in this house and knew this room well. Did you know your mother was my personal maid from the time she could reach high enough to hang up a dress? But of course you know. Ah! Maude was more than just a maid to me. She could almost have been the child I was never fortunate enough to have myself. I – But you have not come here to hear the reminiscences of an old lady. Your mother must have sent you to me. Is she ill, child? Are you in need of help?'

Jesse passed on her mother's message and, in answer to Eulaliah Vincent's persistent questioning, she filled in many of the background details that had led to the request.

By the time Jesse ended her story, the old lady was trembling with anger.

'Colman did this? How *dare* he! That *he* of all people should make Maude suffer . . . No matter. I will attend to this immediately.'

Eulaliah Vincent tugged at a bell-pull beside her chair. When a maid answered the call, she snapped, 'Where is Sir Colman at this moment?'

The startled maid was unused to finding her mistress in

such an angry mood. 'He's downstairs, entertaining friends, ma'am.'

'Is he, indeed! Go down and tell him I want to see him in my room – this instant! And on your way down you can show this child out.'

Eulaliah Vincent patted Jesse's hands. 'You can stop worrying, child. Go off and find this young man of yours. Tell him there has been a dreadful mistake. Arrange your wedding – and don't forget to send me an invitation. Go now.'

Jesse left Lamorrack House bemused by the course events were now taking. How could her mother possibly influence Sir Colman's decision on Pengrugla? And why was Eulaliah Vincent so angry with her nephew because of his actions? But there remained one problem about which Eulaliah Vincent had been able to do nothing. Ben had gone. Unless Martha Retallick knew his whereabouts there was no way of letting him know that all would be well.

Jesse did not need to go all the way to Mevagissey to fetch help for Reuben Holyoak. She had not long left Lamorrack House when she met a party of men who knew him. They promised to go to Pengrugla and see him safely home while Jesse went on to Tregassick.

Martha Retallick was home, but she was as distraught as Jesse had been earlier. She knew no more about Ben's hurried departure than Jesse herself.

Jesse stayed for a while comforting Martha Retallick before anxiety for her own mother drove her home to Pengrugla.

Reuben Holyoak had gone, but a saddled horse stood outside the door and the sound of raised voices came from the bedroom. Jesse called up the stairs to ask her mother if all was well, then had to retreat hurriedly as Sir Colman Vincent came down. He was in such a hurry that he slipped down the last two stairs. Steadying himself, he stood tall in the narrow hall and glared down at Jesse, his face contorting in rage.

'Damn you and your mother! If you want to marry a nobody, then so be it. I have done my best to arrange a satisfactory marriage for you. I will do no more. Tell your mother you can remain at Pengrugla as non-paying tenants, but stay away from Lamorrack House. I do not want to see either of you there, ever again.'

With this final remark, Sir Colman Vincent pushed past Jesse and stormed out of the house. He slammed the door so hard behind him that a heavy piece of mortar fell from around the door-frame.

Concerned at what his anger might have done to her mother, Jesse ran upstairs and into the bedroom.

Maude Henna lay back against her straw-filled pillow, looking utterly exhausted. When she opened her eyes, Jesse was distressed to see tears trembling there.

'It's all right, Ma. Everything is all right now. We can stay at Pengrugla. I'll work hard and we'll manage.'

'Have you found Ben?'

'Not yet, but he'll be back, you'll see.'

'When he returns he'll not have to fear what Reuben Holyoak might do; I have seen to that. But I don't want to stay at Pengrugla, Jesse. I want to give it back to Sir Colman.'

'But he said . . .'

'He said many things, Jesse. Most of them hurtful. There is no debt to be paid off on Pengrugla now. We can leave and let Sir Colman have it for his new manager – but Reuben Holyoak will occupy it alone. You and I will sell off the stock and rent a small cottage in Mevagissey. You'll need to work, but there will be money set aside for bad days, and enough to pay for your wedding when Ben returns.'

'*If* he returns,' said Jesse despondently. 'Ben thinks he has killed Reuben Holyoak. He'll put as many miles between himself and Pengrugla as he can.'

'He'll be back one day, but waiting for him may call for a deal of patience. Go away and let me sleep now, Jesse. This has been a long, long day. I am tired . . . so very tired.'

Chapter Twenty-One

Maude Henna died in her sleep during the night. Distressed as she was, Jesse knew her mother had died as she would have wished – at Pengrugla.

The knowledge gave her little comfort. In the course of a single day, Jesse had lost everything she loved: Ben, her mother, and Pengrugla.

Had she wished, she might have kept Pengrugla. Eulaliah Vincent told her so on the day of Maude Henna's funeral. She came to the house to collect some letters that had been in Maude Henna's keeping. Eulaliah Vincent told Jesse she had written them to Maude Henna – or Maude Carvinicke, as she had then been – to be kept by her should she ever find herself in trouble. Now the need had passed.

Jesse found the letters in a tin by her mother's bed and handed them over without question. Unable to read, she had little interest in them, only a great curiosity about their contents. She did not doubt that the letters had been responsible for making Sir Colman change his mind about Pengrugla. But

Pengrugla held nothing but bad memories for Jesse now. She wanted no more to do with it. She would go.

A widowed mother and daughter setting up home together was one thing. A lone sixteen-year-old girl doing the same thing was very different. It was now that Ben's mother came to the rescue. Ordered to quit Tregassick, Martha Retallick returned to the home of her parents and took Jesse with her.

For a few days, Jesse found her new surroundings bewildering. She had lived all her life at Pengrugla, enjoying the freedom of an isolated farmhouse. Now she was living in a house in a village, crowded on every side by similar houses. There were people wherever she went, wherever she looked.

Walter Dunn recognised how miserable she was and one morning took Jesse with him on a fishing trip. The unique experience made her forget her misery for a few hours, and from that day she began to gather the threads of her life about her once more.

Walter wanted her to go fishing with him again, but Jesse had seen the frowns and the scarcely concealed disapproval of the other fishermen and their womenfolk. She did not want to antagonise them unnecessarily. Instead, she asked Martha Retallick to take her with her to the Dunn's fish-cellar to learn how to salt fish. She needed to earn a living until Ben returned to Mevagissey – and she was determined never to lose her faith that he *would* return.

The work in the cellar was hard on her uncalloused hands, unused to the effect of constant immersion in heavily salted water. They soon became raw and painful. She managed to hide her discomfort from the others, but Walter was more observant than the rest of the family. One evening, when they were all seated for a meal, Walter reached across the table and took one of Jesse's hands in his own. Turning it over, he looked at the raw and inflamed fingers.

'Good God! Why haven't you said something about this before now, Jesse?'

Jesse pulled her hand away. 'It's nothing. It will be all right once I am used to the work.'

'Of course it will,' declared Grandma Dunn. 'Every other girl in Mevagissey manages well enough.'

'Every other girl in Mevagissey is handling salt and fish by the time she can walk. Jesse has had to keep smooth hands for milking cows and nursing young livestock. No, salting is not for her. She can come down to the quay and gut fish, but she'll do nothing at all until her hands are better. Tomorrow I am going to Gorran Haven. Jesse can come with me.'

Grandma Dunn was not pleased, but her displeasure was not aimed solely at Jesse.

'Why do you have to go to Gorran Haven? Haven't they got enough fishermen there?'

'They have, and they'll have more tomorrow. The St Mawes men are coming. That is why I need to be there. Their tithes have been doubled. Mevagissey could be the next. I am going to see what needs to be done to prevent it happening here.'

'You'll be leaving Mark and Billy to do your share of the work, no doubt? It's a good job all the fishermen hereabouts don't just walk away from their boats and go off seeking trouble at every opportunity. If they did, the tithes would never get paid – however low they might be.'

'I did my share of Mark and Billy's work when they were off on the King's business. If someone doesn't do something to stop the tithes increasing very soon, we might as well give the landowners our boats and work for *them*. As it is, we risk our lives every day to line the pockets of men who don't know one end of a boat from the other. Sir Colman Vincent is one who wouldn't recognise a seine-net if he fell over one. But it is no use talking about it in this house.'

Walter spoke to Jesse again. 'I'll be leaving early in the morning. Be sure you are ready, young lady.'

Uncertain whether she should accept his invitation, Jesse looked to Martha Retallick.

After a moment's hesitation, the older woman nodded. 'Yes, you can go, Jesse. It will be a day or two before those hands are fit for work. Why didn't you tell me of the state they were getting into? Come along with me, now. I'll put something on them. I have some salve in my room.'

Later, as Martha Retallick smeared Jesse's lacerated hands with a thick, green, greasy ointment, she gave her some words of advice.

'Walter is my favourite brother and he has a warm and generous nature, but he also has a certain reputation where young girls are concerned. Don't let him take any liberties with you. If he becomes too persistent, tell me. I'll soon put a stop to his nonsense.'

Jesse smiled. 'It's all right, Mrs Retallick. I'll have no trouble with Walter. I know of his reputation, and I don't think he'll put it at risk with me. I'm Ben's girl, and will be until Ben himself tells me he no longer wants me.'

'I wish to heaven we knew where he was, Jesse. If only he had waited to discuss things with one of us . . .'

'He did what he thought was best. He didn't want to get us involved. He'll be back as soon as he learns the truth. I hope that will be soon. I miss him.'

Jesse repeated the same words to Walter the next morning when they had climbed the steep hill out of Mevagissey and were walking along the quiet and narrow track to Gorran Haven.

'Word has gone about that Reuben Holyoak took a severe beating at Ben's hands,' said Walter.

'Yes. Bad enough for Ben to believe he had left him for dead. That's why he went, I'm certain of it.'

Walter looked down at the slim dark girl walking beside him. 'The sooner he learns different the better. You can't be expected to wait for him for ever. Not when there are handsome fishermen like myself waiting to marry a pretty young thing like yourself.'

Jesse grinned at him. 'If marriage was mentioned to you, Walter Dunn, you'd run so fast your boots would catch fire.'

'You shouldn't take notice of village gossip,' Walter smiled back at her. 'All the same, Ben will be foolish to stay away too long.'

At the small fishing-village of Gorran Haven, they had to wait for the St Mawes men to arrive. Walter took the opportunity to discover the extent of the local fishermen's tithe problem.

It was new only in the amount now being demanded. For years the fishermen of Cornwall had been fighting to maintain the pilchard industry against great odds. During the recent Napoleonic wars many of their traditional markets had been closed to them. Coupled with an incredible duty of sixpence a pound on the salt essential for curing the fish, this had reduced many of the fishermen to starvation level. When the war ended, the fishermen tried to overcome the continuing salt duty and regain their old markets. But in recent years the pilchards had not been running in their former numbers. Many thought it was due to the large deep-sea drift-trawlers from the Devon ports, fishing farther offshore. Whatever the reason, times were hard – and the tithe-holders chose this year to increase their tithes.

The custom of paying tithes had begun somewhere in the mists of ancient history, both the lord of the manor and the local priest demanding a share of the catch of fish as their 'tithe'. Grudgingly given at first, it had become an accepted practice over the centuries. More recently, it had been found more practicable for the boat-owners to pay a small sum of money per boat in lieu of tithes. Others paid so much per hogshead of fish caught.

This arrangement had worked well until a needy landowner hit upon the ingenious idea of selling his tithe rights to a speculator. The enterprising purchaser immediately raised the tithes to a level that could be met by only the largest and most efficient fishing-boats. Not to be left behind, many land-owners promptly raised their tithes, too.

This was the problem that had first hit the Gorran Haven fishermen and, more recently, the men of St Mawes. The Mevagissey tithes were owned by Sir Colman Vincent, and Walter knew it was only a matter of time before the baronet followed the others in demanding higher dues.

The Gorran Haven fishermen told Walter they had refused to pay the new rates, but they were a very small community and could not hope to succeed on their own. Only if every fishing-village faced with the same problem followed their example could they hope to break with an ancient custom that had got out of hand. This was why they had invited Walter and the St Mawes fishermen to meet them.

The St Mawes men did not arrive until almost noon. They were in an aggressive and angry mood. Their new tithe-owner had heard of the proposed meeting and, in an attempt to prevent them from attending, had reported them to the local magistrate. He argued that the meeting was treasonable, and would most likely result in a serious breach of public order.

The magistrate, backed by members of the militia, currently stationed at St Mawes Castle, had stopped them on the road outside their village. Fortunately for all concerned, the magistrate was a sensible local man. After questioning the fishermen closely on the purpose of their visit to Gorran Haven, he had allowed them to proceed on their way. The incident served only to anger the St Mawes fishermen and harden their determination to fight the tithe increases.

It was in dealing with such men that Walter Dunn was at his very best. Jesse listened in admiration as he shaped and moulded the men's belligerent mood to suit his own ideas. He finally persuaded them to delay taking any further action until Sir Colman Vincent had shown his hand – as Walter told the men he would, very soon now.

By the time that happened, Walter promised he would have persuaded every fisherman along Cornwall's south coast to withhold his tithes. He insisted that, in the meantime, the fishermen must keep away from the tithe-owners and their agents. He suggested they use their womenfolk to carry out any 'negotiations' that might prove necessary. The fisher-women had a vocabulary every bit as colourful as their men-folk's. What was more, they were quite capable of standing up to any man the tithe-owners cared to send against them, and it was doubtful whether a magistrate would commit the militia to deal with women.

The longer the men from St Mawes talked about Walter's idea, the more enthusiastic they became. There was not a man at the meeting who did not know at least one fisherwoman who was the physical equal of any one of them; but, as a woman, the chances were that her physical prowess would never have to be put to the test.

The St Mawes fishermen left Gorran Haven amused with the thought of setting their women against the tithe-owner's men. They knew that Walter would keep his word to bring every south-coast fisherman into the fight when the time came.

On the way back to Mevagissey, Jesse asked Walter, 'Do you really think Sir Colman will raise the tithe dues?'

'He's already brought in a solicitor to draw up the papers,' declared Walter. 'I have friends at Lamorrack House who keep me in touch with what is going on.'

'Then why did you lie to the men at the meeting? Why keep the news from them?'

'Had I told them the truth there would have been no way of preventing the St Mawes fishermen stirring up more trouble than they can handle on their own. They are in a dangerous mood. There are too few of them to defy the law by themselves – and win. Troops would be brought in from Pendennis Castle to deal the reform movement a blow from which it would never recover. As it is, I can persuade a dozen villages to take action when the time is right. That will increase tenfold the number of men refusing to pay tithes. With the womenfolk dealing with tithe-collectors there will be no men for the troops to arrest and no one to punish as an example. By doing things my way we stand a reasonable chance of succeeding. Success is what this is all about, Jesse. If we win the first battle, the next will be easier. Eventually we'll be able to demand our full rights. The rights of free and equal men . . . The right to have our own man represent us in Parliament.'

Jesse looked at Walter Dunn with something akin to awe. 'Walter Dunn, if I hadn't found Ben first, I might have fallen in love with your clever mind.'

Walter Dunn rubbed his chin ruefully. 'Do you know, you are the first girl who hasn't been charmed by my good looks and splendid body. Ben really *had* better return quickly. You're quite unlike any other girl I've ever known.'

Walter Dunn's affection for Jesse was quite genuine, as Jesse herself quickly realised. By the time she had spent a month in the Dunn house she knew she could not remain there for very much longer. Walter was spending far too much time in her company. He invited her to accompany him to all the villages he visited in connection with the parliamentary reform party and more recently had taken to coming to her room and talking to her for hours.

At first Jesse was grateful to him. She missed Ben dreadfully, especially when she was alone. She had also begun to feel responsible for her mother's death. If she had not allowed her mother to assume the problems of Pengrugla . . . She talked her thoughts out with Walter, and his reassurance helped her a great deal.

But, as time went by, Walter's attentions drew comment from other members of the family, and Jesse knew she had to leave.

Deciding to go was one thing. Implementing the decision without offending the Dunn family – and Walter in particular – was another.

The solution came when Jesse paid a visit to the Happy Union mine. She went there seeking news of Ben and was immediately referred to Captain Loveday Ustick; but this was not the rough belligerent mine captain Ben had known. A huge man he still was, but at the age of fifty Loveday Ustick had been tamed and converted to Wesleyism – by a woman.

Not that Fanny Furse was any ordinary woman. Mevagissey-born, she had been taken at the age of five to hear the aged John Wesley preach. At the end of a characteristically fiery sermon, the great man had picked Fanny out of the crowd and sat her on his knee. Before returning Fanny to her parents, Wesley had urged her to give her future to the Lord.

Neither Fanny nor her parents ever forgot his words. Teaching herself to read, Fanny learned every sermon and scrap of teaching attributed to John Wesley and his brother Charles. Nowhere did she find anything to say that a woman should not emulate the great evangelists. While other young girls walked in pairs around Mevagissey harbour, giggling together and giving boastful young men sly glances from beneath their bonnets, Fanny Furse tramped miles, attending any Wesleyan gathering willing to let her stand up and offer a prayer for their souls.

It was not long before realisation came to Fanny Furse, as it had to Wesley before her, that those most in need of the word of the Lord were the miners of Cornwall. Fanny began a personal crusade in the tough mining communities. The slim five-foot-nothing woman preacher soon became a familiar figure in the shadow of the smoking chimneys of Cornwall's tin mines. She preached her message to hundreds of miners on the cliff-edge mines, pointing to the pounding surf of the Atlantic Ocean as a physical manifestation of the power of *their* Lord. Sometimes she prayed in miners' hovels, bringing comfort to the newly widowed women who wept beside her.

On a rare visit to her home village, Fanny Furse was asked to preach to the miners at the Happy Union mine, up-river from Pentuan. There she met Captain Loveday Ustick. It was a day when the Lord smiled and handed back some of the love He had carefully stored for Fanny Furse during the years she had served Him.

When they married, Loveday Ustick was in his fiftieth year and Fanny Furse was forty – but there was not a happier couple in the whole of Cornwall.

Fanny still preached to the miners, but now she rarely went further than the Crinnis and Polgooth mines, both within walking distance of her new home at Pentuan. She and Loveday set to work to convert a house in the village into a chapel. Here she shared the pulpit on Sundays with itinerant Wesleyan preachers who were always sure of a warm welcome at the house of the Happy Union stream-works' captain and his wife.

Miners too old for underground work were frequent visitors to the Ustick house. They came to the Happy Union seeking to restore their flagging self-respect with employment close enough to mining for self-delusion. Most of these men were beyond any type of work, but in the Ustick house they received a good meal and a powerful prayer. More often than not, a night or two's much needed lodging were thrown in for good measure.

Jesse paid a visit to the Happy Union mine in search of news of Ben in the summer of 1820. Loveday Ustick remembered Ben well, but had not seen him since Ben left to work at the Mevagissey mine, more than a year before. He wished he could have helped, he said. He had liked Ben, but neither Captain Ustick nor any of the men working the stream-works knew his present whereabouts.

At the end of the day's work, Loveday Ustick took Jesse along to his house to meet Fanny. The experienced older woman immediately recognised the unhappiness in Jesse. Before the three of them sat down together for an evening meal, Fanny had learned a great deal about their guest. After a hurried whispered conversation in the kitchen with her husband, she asked Jesse to come and live with them at Pentuan. Loveday Ustick also offered Jesse work, sorting ore at the Happy Union.

Jesse eagerly seized the double opportunity to leave the Dunn house and take work where she was more likely to hear news of Ben. Mining men came to the Ustick house from all over the county. Surely one of them would have word of Ben?

Jesse announced her decision to leave Mevagissey the next evening, when she and the Dunn family were gathered together for their evening meal. The news was received with consternation by Ben's mother.

'Why, Jesse? I thought you were happy here.'

Instinctively, Martha Retallick turned a frown upon Walter, and Jesse hurried to explain.

'I'm going to work at the Happy Union stream-works. I know Ben is working on a mine somewhere, and many miners come to the Happy Union. I'm more likely to hear news of him there than here.'

Much to Jesse's relief, Martha Retallick's suspicions immediately fell away. Her words made sense, and Ben's mother was as eager as Jesse for Ben's return. But Martha Retallick asked Jesse why she could not work at the Happy Union and still live at Mevagissey.

'When Ben and I are married we'll be living among miners,' explained Jesse. 'I would prefer to get used to it now.'

Martha Retallick guiltily approved her decision. She had never really tried to fit in with those about her when Pearson Retallick had taken her to live on the Money Box mine. She admired Jesse's forethought.

Walter took the news very quietly, but later when Jesse walked with him to a reform meeting on Mevagissey quay, he said, 'You're leaving the house because of me, aren't you, Jesse?'

Jesse strenuously denied his accusation, but Walter Dunn knew the truth. 'If you stay, I promise not to bother you. I won't even speak to you, if that's what you wish. But, please . . . don't go.'

'I must, Walter. Finding Ben is the most important thing in my life.'

Walter was reluctant to accept her decision, but he could not persuade her to change her mind. Eventually, he said, 'If you can't find him, or if you change your mind, will you tell me?'

'I promise, Walter.'

'Then I must be satisfied with that – for now. When the right time comes I will have more to say to you. Until then it's better left unsaid.'

'Thank you, Walter. I'll always be grateful to you for the way you've helped me. No one has been kinder.'

Putting a hand gently on his arm, she stood on tiptoe and kissed his cheek.

Rubbing the place where her lips had rested, Walter said, 'Young Ben may think himself a fugitive, but I would willingly change places with him to have what he has.'

Jesse looked to where a noisy crowd milled about the quay. 'If that crowd gets out of hand you may well become a fugitive, Walter. You tread a dangerous path.'

'One day it will prove worth while. Stay and hear what I have to say, Jesse. Much of it concerns Sir Colman Vincent. You'll find it of interest.'

'No doubt, but I have to pack.'

'When are you leaving?'

'Tomorrow.'

'So soon? Surely another week or two will make no difference, Jesse?'

'It could make *all* the difference, Walter, as well you know. Go to your meeting, now. They are calling for you.'

Jesse turned and walked away. Before she went from sight along one of the narrow alleyways leading from the quay, she looked back. As the dejected figure of Walter Dunn approached the crowd who were calling for him, the sagging shoulders straightened, his stride lengthened and he gave them a cheery wave.

Jesse smiled ruefully. Walter had the ability to immerse all his problems in his reform activities and wash them away. Had he been born of a less humble family he would have made a splendid Member of Parliament. As it was, he would probably end his days in the colonies, sent there as an agitator, an exciter of the people. Jesse wondered whether she, or any other woman, could change him. She doubted if it were possible. Walter Dunn had a destiny to fulfil. He would see it through to the end.

On the day Jesse began work at the Happy Union mine, a notice was posted on the quay at Mevagissey. It informed the fishermen that Sir Colman Vincent had raised their tithes from eight shillings to two guineas per boat.

It was the action for which Walter had been waiting. Word went out to all the fishing communities along the south Cornwall coast. The 'tithe revolt' had begun. It quickly spread. One by one, the fishing towns and villages throughout the whole of Cornwall announced their refusal to pay the new tithes imposed upon them. Some made it an outright refusal, others clouded the issue by declaring they were now 'driftnet' fishermen. Traditionally, tithes could only be claimed from those who used a seine-net.

Whatever the alleged reasons behind the refusals, the tithe-holders of Cornwall became thoroughly alarmed. They saw their unearned and totally undeserved incomes slipping away from them.

Only in the port of Falmouth were the refusals accompanied by violence. Then, when the garrison of nearby Pendennis Castle was called out to restore order and arrest the leading troublemakers, it was discovered the so-called 'fishermen' were in fact the crews of the packet boats, using the occasion to air a few grievances of their own.

Elsewhere in Cornwall, many of the tithe-holders hurriedly reverted to the old tithe rates, but Sir Colman Vincent was determined he would not be so easily cowed. He sent Reuben Holyoak to 'talk things over sensibly' with the men of his home village.

When Reuben Holyoak arrived in Mevagissey's village square and called upon the fishermen to gather round and listen to what he had to say, there were few men to be seen. However, there *was* an unusually high number of women. Reuben Holyoak saw nothing sinister in their presence. He spoke to them, urging them to persuade their men to come and hear what he had to say.

'Why don't we do as he says?' shrieked a girl who had worked in the Dunn salting-cellar alongside Jesse. 'Send for Ben Retallick, someone.'

Reuben Holyoak looked angrily at the girl. 'My business is with fishermen. I have nothing to say to Ben Retallick . . . or to you.'

'Oh! Then 'tis a pity you didn't give up talking to women before you drove poor Maude Henna to her death.'

Only when the shouted accusation brought a noisy response from the other women did Reuben Holyoak realise he was surrounded by a very hostile crowd. He tried to push his way through them, but he was already too late. Hands grabbed at his clothing and held him back. The more he struggled, the greater was the determination of the women to hold him. Finally, Reuben Holyoak struck out in a last desperate attempt to break free.

It was the worst thing he could have done. The clutching hands became fists. Pummelled unmercifully Reuben Holyoak was propelled towards the filthy waters of the harbour – and thrown in.

The Mevagissey women cheered loudly as he rose to the surface, coughing and spluttering. 'That's where the money for tithes is earned, and that's where you'll collect it,' shouted one of them. 'You can tell Sir Colman Vincent he'll end up in the same place if he comes down here.'

For an hour Reuben Holyoak alternately trod water and

clung to the stones of the harbour wall, pleading through chattering teeth for the fisherwomen of Mevagissey to allow him out of the cold waters of the harbour. Not until the tide had dropped sufficiently for him to stand up in the muddy harbour did they go on their way, laughing uproariously at the success of their day's work.

Sir Colman Vincent made one final attempt to convince the fishermen of his right to increase tithes. This time he sent a solicitor to talk to the fishermen on his behalf. When the unfortunate lawyer eventually made his escape from Mevagissey, he wore only his long woollen stockings and the tattered remnants of his breeches. His dignity and much of his exposed body had been badly bruised by the coarse fisherwomen and their derisive laughter pursued him along the road to Lamorrack House.

A few days later, after the Sheriff of Cornwall had called upon all the tithe-holders in the county to meet him, notices went up in every village. The fishermen were informed that, with immediate effect, all tithe dues would be charged at the rate applicable twelve months before.

Walter Dunn and his fishermen had won their first battle.

Chapter Twenty-Two

Jesse found working on the mine harder than working in the Dunns' fish-cellar, but there was no salt to aggravate the cuts she sustained on her hands. She also gained a great deal of satisfaction from going home at the end of a day's work thoroughly tired. After performing her share of the household chores, she wanted only to go to bed and sleep until morning, too exhausted for thoughts or dreams.

Occasionally, Fanny Ustick would arrange a prayer meeting for miners and their families at the house. As she spent every spare penny of her money on tea and cakes for her guests, Fanny Ustick's meetings were always well attended.

Jesse helped out at these prayer meetings. It was not for any religious reason, but because it gave her an opportunity to ask newcomers to the mine if they had met with Ben Retallick.

Unfortunately, the Cornish miners were entertained so lavishly with food that they did not wish to disappoint Jesse by saying 'No'. As a result, she received vague reports of young miners answering Ben's description being seen at places as far apart as St Just, Camborne and Kit Hill.

All that first summer Jesse believed someone would soon come to the Happy Union with definite news of Ben's whereabouts, but her hopes were in vain. By the time the fogs and rains of winter spread over the land, Jesse was as miserable as the weather.

Walter Dunn often came to Pentuan to see her. One day, as she walked with him to visit Martha Retallick, he asked her to marry him.

At first, Jesse thought he was joking. But one look at his face was enough to tell her that Walter Dunn was desperately serious.

'I've been patient, Jesse. I respected your feelings towards young Ben. But it's now November. Ben has been gone for eight months without sending word to you. For all you know, he might be dead. How long are you going to keep yourself for him?'

For just a moment Jesse weakened. It would be so easy to say 'Yes' to Walter. He would take care of her and provide her with a home of her own. The Usticks were very kind, but living with them was not the same as having a place where she really belonged.

Then Jesse thought of Ben. She remembered what they had been to each other. Had it not been for her he would have done nothing to run from. He, too, would be enjoying the comfort of his own home. Suddenly her whole being ached for Ben. She knew she would find no real and lasting happiness without him.

'I'll wait for Ben for as long as is necessary, Walter. That means until he returns home.'

Walter shook his head helplessly. 'That's what I thought you would say. Oh, well! I'll ask you the same question next year . . . and the year after. One day you'll weaken. But I warn you, you are missing my best years!'

It was good to be with someone who made her smile. Jesse had grown increasingly fond of both Loveday and Fanny Ustick, but they took themselves and their religion very seriously.

Walter continued his half-teasing banter until they were almost at the Dunn house. Then he said something to prove there was more than romance on his mind.

'I heard an interesting piece of gossip this week. If it's true it will mean the end of Sir Colman Vincent's parliamentary career. It will also provide a powerful argument for reform. It seems Sir Colman purchased the votes in his constituency – a grand total of seven, for fifty pounds apiece!'

'Don't tell me that surprises you, Walter. Every thinking man in Cornwall knows such a practice is commonplace.'

'No, Jesse. It's common practice for a prospective Member of Parliament to "persuade" the voters to elect him and to put up a reasonable amount of expenses towards that end. Handing the mayor of a borough a sum of money to purchase votes is something very different. Even the government we have today dare not ignore this. If I can prove the rumour is true, Sir Colman Vincent will be out and the whole country will scream for parliamentary reform.'

'First you have to provide proof.'

'That shouldn't be too difficult – thanks to Reuben Holyoak. Ah! I thought the mention of his name would interest you. As a reward for his part in the election, Sir Colman granted the mayor of Pengony a parcel of land at a very low rent. Unfortunately for him, the mayor "forgot" to pay any rent at all. He didn't think Sir Colman would chase him for arrears. However, Reuben Holyoak knew nothing of the service rendered by the good gentleman of Pengony. Without reference to

Sir Colman, he repossessed the land and rented it to someone else. He also sold the mayor's livestock and kept the money in lieu of unpaid rent! Can you imagine that? The mayor of Pengony is so furious that he tells the story of Sir Colman Vincent's ingratitude to anyone with the price of a pint of ale and the time to listen.'

'Would he tell the same story in court after Sir Colman has been given the opportunity to speak to him?'

'He wouldn't dare lie, Jesse. I can produce twenty men who have heard what the mayor has said.'

Jesse was not convinced. Anxiously, she said, 'Be very careful, Walter. Sir Colman has much to lose – so much that he'll go to any lengths to silence you.'

'Anything he did would merely confirm his own guilt.'

'Don't be a fool, Walter. Sir Colman won't come after you himself. He gets others to do his work. Remember, with you out of the way there's not another man in Cornwall who would dare try to bring him down.'

Jesse's fears were well founded, but her warning came too late. Walter had already told too many people of the information he had.

Two days after his conversation with Jesse, Walter brought his boat into Mevagissey harbour to find two constables from the nearby town of St Austell awaiting him. They had with them a warrant for his arrest. The charge was preaching sedition.

It was useless for Walter to argue that the whole thing was a ridiculous mistake. The charges were far too serious to be taken lightly. Earlier that same year a group of extremist reformers had plotted to murder the hated Lord Liverpool's entire cabinet. Only a last-minute betrayal by one of their number prevented the desperate plan from being carried out.

Government and judiciary were in a state of jittery vigilance, informers reaping a rich reward for their dubious activities. The merest hint of an organised protest was enough to provoke hasty overreaction.

Walter Dunn was swiftly arraigned before the magistrate at St Austell. Only then did he begin to appreciate the dangerous predicament he was in. Sir Colman Vincent was the examining magistrate. Walter had been arrested on the baronet's warrant.

The proceedings in the magistrate's court were brief. Two hesitant and unsatisfactory witnesses only were called. One was the constable who had arrested him. The other was Reuben Holyoak.

Sir Colman Vincent's estate manager told the court of two speeches he had heard Walter Dunn make at meetings. He failed to add that both had been made more than a year before. On this flimsy 'evidence', Walter was sent to Bodmin Gaol to await an escort to London. There he would face trial on the charges laid against him.

Walter protested loudly, but he was hustled from the court to a waiting covered van which immediately set off for Bodmin at a teeth-rattling gallop. By the time Walter arrived at the prison, his wrists and ankles had been skinned by the heavy irons securing them, and all the protest shaken out of him.

There had been good reason for such indecent haste in removing Walter Dunn from St Austell. So incensed were the fishermen of Mevagissey by his arrest that, after a hastily convened meeting, they were marching on the magistrate's court, determined to secure Walter's release.

Along the way the fishermen were joined by adherents to the reformers' cause from the mines of Polgooth and Crinnis. By the time they arrived at the outskirts of St Austell they were six hundred strong, shouting bold defiance against the magistrate who had ordered the arrest of Walter Dunn.

The marchers never entered the town. Before they reached the first of its houses their way was barred by a troop of blue-uniformed dragoons. Mounted on tall horses, the soldiers waited with swords drawn.

The commander of the troop had selected his position well. The lane at this point crossed a wide common. The soldiers were drawn up in a double line across the full width of the common. There was ample room here for them to ride through the marching column again and again, if need be.

The fishermen and miners were unarmed, and the officer in charge of the dragoons rode to the head of their column, calling on them to disperse quietly and return to their homes.

When the marching men shouted for the release of Walter Dunn, the officer was able to tell them in all honesty that Walter had already been taken to Bodmin Gaol.

This unexpected news threw the would-be rescuers into confusion. A few were for marching on to the county town, but the listening dragoons' officer strongly advised them against such a course of action. He told them that the foot soldiers currently garrisoned in Bodmin had, until recently, been stationed in the Midlands. Many of their number had been injured by rioters there. They would not have the same patience as his own dragoons.

His words had the desired effect. The Mevagissey men had walked six miles from their village on a cold November day. The thought of marching another twelve miles only to be turned back by a company of angry soldiers held out little appeal for them. The brave little army that had set out with such enthusiasm broke up in confusion under the scornful eyes of the dragoons.

* * *

Walter Dunn was not kept in Bodmin Gaol for long, but it turned out to be a harrowing experience for him. The charges against Walter were so serious that his gaolers took no risk of an escape attempt. He was placed in the most secure cell in the prison, sharing it with a prisoner who was to be executed the following day at the end of a hangman's noose. The man was not ready to die and refused to believe that the sentence of the court would be carried out. All night long he wept and pleaded for Walter to give him some glimmer of hope.

An out-of-work miner, Michael Stephens's crime had been to kill a sheep grazing on the moorland. The meat from the stolen animal had been used to keep his starving children alive. Such extenuating circumstances meant little to the Assize Judge, himself a livestock-owner. The law was quite clear. The unlawful killing of a sheep was a capital offence. Michael Stephens was guilty. He must hang. Because he had moved from his own home area in a bid to find work, Michael Stephens had no friends or employer to plead his cause, to urge that the sentence be commuted.

The young miner's abject pleading went on until noon on the day of the execution. Then, struggling and protesting to the end, Michael Stephens was carried to the scaffold by two soldiers and supported whilst the rope was placed about his neck. His terror came to an end when the hangman flung the lever controlling the drop and the sheep-stealing miner was flung into the arms of his Maker.

In the silence that followed the hurried execution, Walter heard a blackbird singing in a nearby tree. Then the voice of the crowd, gathered to witness the death of a felon, swelled to an excited roar. It had been an execution to remember. The reluctance of young Michael Stephens to die would be talked about for a long time.

Through the barred window of his cell, only a short distance from the gatehouse upon which the gallows stood, Walter Dunn winced at the crash of the trapdoor, his manacled hands clenched tightly before him.

Walter Dunn was not a religious man, but when the crowd roared its approval of the spectacle it had just witnessed he fell to his knees and prayed for the soul of the unfortunate young man.

The hours of horror spent in the company of the condemned miner inflicted a deep wound on Walter Dunn's mind. From that time, little that happened had any reality. It was as though he was looking at his own life from a distance, seeing but not feeling the things that happened to him. When he was transferred to a London gaol guarded by a large escort of soldiers, it meant nothing, the journey passing as though it were an unreal dream.

Walter Dunn's family learned of his transfer from Jesse. She walked to Bodmin expecting to see him, the weekend after his arrest.

Her frustration and anger at having undertaken such a long and wasted journey were tempered with concern for Walter. London was a whole world away from Cornwall. Ordinary men and women had no control over the things that happened there. As she made the long return walk to Mevagissey, Jesse tried to think how best she could help the one real friend she had.

It was Sunday evening and the whole Dunn family was gathered in the little house close to the harbour, after attending the evening service in the chapel. Jesse arrived, footsore and tired, and told the family what she had learned. She waited for their anger, but it did not come. Old Mrs Dunn began crying quietly to herself while the grandchildren looked on in consternation. The remainder of the Dunn family received the news in silence. Not one of them muttered a single word of sympathy for Walter.

'Well, what are we going to do to help Walter?'

Mark Dunn shrugged his shoulders. 'What can be done? He was told often enough that a fisherman should tend to his nets and leave changing Parliament to them as understands about such things.'

'What you mean is you'll do nothing.'

Jesse gave Mark Dunn a scornful look, then turned her back on him to speak to his brother.

'How about you, Billy? What do *you* think we should do?'

Billy Dunn looked uncertainly from his scowling brother to Jesse. Before he could reply, his wife answered for him.

'Billy is not going to do anything. He's got me and his children to think about. Mark is right; there's nothing to be done. Besides, what did Walter do for Mark and my Billy when the Revenue men picked them up and carried them off to the Fleet?'

Jesse looked at Billy Dunn's wife in disgust. 'Walter made certain that you and your children – yes, and Mark's family, too – had a roof over your heads and were never short of food. He worked hard so that his brothers had fishing-boats to come home to. *That's* what he did – though why he bothered, I don't know! You are none of you worth an hour of Walter's time.'

Angrily she slammed out of the house.

Tight-lipped, Billy Dunn's wife said, 'It's as well your Ben never married that girl, Martha. We can do without her in this family.'

'Can we?' Martha Retallick picked up her shawl and flung it across her shoulders. 'It's a pity your man hasn't got half the spirit of Jesse Henna. As for marrying Ben . . . if she had, he'd be here now and *he* wouldn't need to be pushed into doing something to help Walter.'

Martha Retallick ran from the house and caught up with a tear-blinded Jesse as she wandered aimlessly at the edge of the harbour.

'I'm sorry if I lost my temper back there,' Jesse said as she clung to Martha Retallick's hand, 'but someone *must* help Walter.'

'You said what needed saying,' declared Martha Retallick. She squeezed Jesse's arm comfortingly and added, 'I wish our Ben was here with us.'

'So do I, Mrs Retallick. So do I.'

Jesse closed her eyes, and for a moment she appeared to be in physical pain. Taking a deep breath, she regained control of herself.

'I'm certain Sir Colman is behind Walter's arrest. Walter knows more than he should of something that could harm Sir Colman. If I am right, no one in Mevagissey can do anything for him. I've thought about it all the way from Bodmin. I know of only one person who might be able to help. Sir Colman's aunt.'

'Help Walter? Against her own nephew?' Martha Retallick was sceptical. 'Why should she want to get Sir Colman into trouble?'

'I don't intend asking her to do anything against Sir Colman; only to see if she can persuade him to have Walter released. Perhaps if he promises to say nothing of what he knows . . .'

Jesse's voice faltered. She saw the weakness of her own argument before Martha Retallick pointed it out to her.

'Walter's a stubborn man. If he believes the information he has will further the aims of his reform movement, he'll use it and damn the consequences. Anyway, the whole thing is out of Sir Colman's hands now Walter is in London.'

'You may be right, Mrs Retallick, but I can't just give up and do nothing. If there is any possible way to help Walter, I'll find it, be sure of that.'

'What if you succeed, Jesse? What will you do then – you and Walter?'

'You know he asked me to marry him?'

'Yes, he thought I should know. Walter is not a guileful man, Jesse.'

'If he were, he wouldn't be in trouble now. Walter has been very kind to me, but I can't marry him. I still love Ben.'

'Ben left here believing he'd killed Reuben Holyoak. There's little reason for him to return to Mevagissey. Ben is my own son, Jesse, but don't waste your life waiting for him.'

They were standing at the harbour steps now, and Jesse remembered how Ben had looked on the day he returned from his very first fishing trip, his face as green as the waters of the English Channel today.

'I'll wait a while yet, Mrs Retallick. I think Ben has a right to expect that from me.'

Eulaliah Vincent had moved into the new house that had been built at Tregassick, the one in which Ben and his mother had lived having been pulled down to make way for the extensive gardens. Although not on the same grand scale as Lamorrack, it was a fine house.

When Jesse arrived, the silver-haired Eulaliah Vincent was in the garden supervising the planting of rose-bushes around a newly seeded lawn. She was delighted to see Jesse.

'Why, child, what a pleasure this is! Have you come to see how I am settling in at the new Tregassick?'

Jesse began to explain the purpose of her visit, but Eulaliah Vincent quickly stopped her.

'This sounds like a story best told behind closed doors.

These are Sir Colman's men working here. Tale-bearers find much favour with my nephew.'

Inside the new house, Eulaliah Vincent ordered a maid to make tea, fussing over Jesse as though she were an invited guest and not a girl whose mother had once been her maid.

Not until tea had been served in front of a roaring fire in the lounge did the old lady settle back to hear what Jesse had to say.

Jesse told her of Walter's long association with the reform movement and of the story he had passed on, concerning Sir Colman's election to the House of Commons.

If Jesse expected Eulaliah Vincent to be shocked she was disappointed.

The landowner's aunt snorted. 'If every man who paid for his votes was thrown out of the House of Commons, Lord Liverpool would not have enough men left to govern – but please go on, child.'

Jesse continued with the story of Walter's arrest and hurried transfer to London.

'You *walked* to Bodmin and back to Mevagissey again just to speak to this Walter Dunn? That is more than thirty miles. What is he to you?'

'He is Ben's uncle. He has helped me a great deal since my mother died.'

'I see. But what of your Ben? You were supposed to be marrying him. Has he changed his mind now you no longer have Pengrugla?'

Jesse told Eulaliah Vincent of Ben's disappearance and the reason why he had left the area so hurriedly. By the time she ended her story the old lady was trembling with rage.

'My nephew has much to answer for – he and that damned upstart estate manager of his!'

Controlling herself with some difficulty, she put a hand on

Jesse's arm and said, 'Try not to hate Sir Colman, Jesse. If you did, it would distress me greatly – though God knows, you have reason enough. One day he will bring about his own downfall by his stupidity. Most of the Members of the House of Commons may have paid for the votes that put them there, but that does not make it legal. If a specific case was brought to his attention, Lord Liverpool would be forced to take action. He is already thoroughly alarmed that this agitation for parliamentary reform is getting out of hand. Oh, you need not look so surprised, child. Do you think your friend Walter Dunn has been carrying on a lone campaign? No, reform fever has the country in as firm a grip as the black plague once had. For this reason I must hold out very little hope of securing Walter Dunn's release. Lord Liverpool is determined to stamp out reform agitation once and for all. He sees it as a greater threat to England than Napoleon ever was. That does not mean you need despair. I will think carefully about what might be done. Sir Colman is in London at present. The first thing I will do is go there and speak to him.'

Jesse protested that such a journey was unnecessary. Surely a letter would suffice? Her concern now was for Eulaliah Vincent. She was a frail old lady, and the journey to London by road would take at least ten days.

Eulaliah Vincent waved Jesse's protests aside.

'Nonsense, child. I have made the journey many times. Besides, it has been far too long since I was last in London. I will make arrangements immediately. I have many friends there, and a personal appeal is worth a hundred letters. Now, where may I find you when I return?'

Jesse left Tregassick wondering yet again why Eulaliah Vincent was prepared to go to such lengths to help her – possibly at the expense of her own nephew. Eulaliah Vincent must have been very fond indeed of her one-time maid.

Jesse did not see Eulaliah Vincent watching her departure from one of the large windows of the house. As Jesse went from sight around a curve of the path, Eulaliah Vincent turned back into the room. Shaking her head, she whispered fiercely, 'The past is coming back to haunt you, Colman Vincent – and this girl will not be as easily bought off as was her mother.'

Chapter Twenty-Three

As the weeks stretched into months, Jesse waited in vain for news of Walter and began to wonder whether Martha Retallick's scepticism about Eulaliah Vincent might not have been well founded.

Then Jesse began to worry that the journey to London had proved too much for the oldest member of the Vincent family. When the snows of winter were decorating the leafless trees and hedgerows, and lying thin and crisp underfoot, Jesse walked from Pentuan to Tregassick. There she enquired after Eulaliah Vincent.

The servants were quickly able to put Jesse's mind at ease. A letter from the mistress of the house had been received only two days before. Eulaliah Vincent was well and enjoying the almost forgotten social pleasures of London. She had written that she did not expect to be returning to Cornwall until a change of weather had brought about an improvement in the condition of the roads. There was no mention in the letter of either Sir Colman Vincent or Walter Dunn.

On the return journey to Pentuan, Jesse did not take the usual path. Instead, she made a slight diversion along an overgrown path that was more sheltered from the cold northerly wind. Along the path she met a young girl hurrying in the opposite direction. It was Judy Lean, the simple-minded daughter of one of the late Sir John Vincent's kitchen maids. Jesse and Judy were of a similar age and had often played together in the woods about Lamorrack House. A straightforward game of hide-and-seek, which might have given a normally restless child half an hour's pleasure, had kept Judy Lean happy and laughing for as long as Jesse had the patience to play with her.

But this was no carefree little girl playing hide-and-seek in the woods today. The simple girl was dressed in a summer frock that was totally inadequate to keep out the cold winds of winter, and the chilblains upon her feet owed much to the broken and ill-fitting shoes she wore. In addition, Judy Lean was dirty – and noticeably pregnant.

Jesse greeted the other girl warmly, but Judy was reluctant to stop and talk. Jesse had to take her by the arm to prevent her from hurrying on her way.

'Judy, it's me . . . Jesse. Surely you remember me? We used to play together, up at the big house.'

For a fleeting moment a shaft of light pierced the tangled darkness of Judy Lean's mind and she smiled. The moment quickly passed, and she became agitated and eager to move on her way.

'Mr Holyoak said I was to hurry back from St Austell and not gossip to anyone. He says local folk are just out to make mischief for me.'

'Reuben Holyoak sent you to St Austell in that condition?' Jesse's anger was fanned by the mention of the estate manager's name. 'What right has he to tell you where you must go and to whom you may speak along the way? Where is your husband . . .?'

'I'm not married.' Judy Lean looked down at the ground beside her broken shoe. 'I work for Mr Holyoak now. I look after his house at Pengrugla. He relies on me . . . he told me so.'

Pity welled up inside Jesse as she stared at the ill-dressed girl standing shivering before her. 'I'm sure he does, Judy. Your mother must be very proud of you now . . .'

The simple girl's expression changed, and Jesse said quickly, 'Your mother . . . she's well, Judy?'

'I don't know.' Judy Lean's bottom lip began to tremble. 'When I went to work for Mr Holyoak she went off with a sailor who worked into Pentuan. They went to Plymouth to get married. She's living there somewhere. Mr Holyoak says she don't care nothing about me now.'

Judy Lean's mother was a widow and had been forced to work very hard to bring up her simple daughter.

'I'm quite sure she *does* care, Judy. She probably thinks about you a great deal – just as I shall now. Look, I am living in Pentuan village, at the house of the captain of the Happy Union mine. I want you to come and visit me there. Will you promise to do that?'

The agitation returned to Judy once more. 'I . . . I can't. Mr Holyoak doesn't let me go visiting. He says I'm better off at home, where he can keep an eye on me.'

'You must meet other people sometimes, Judy. You'll need the help of other women soon' – she looked pointedly towards Judy Lean's distended stomach – 'when the baby comes.'

'Baby? What baby? Mr Holyoak won't have a baby at Pengrugla. He told me so.'

Judy's bewilderment was quite genuine. Jesse realised that this simple girl was not aware that she was pregnant!

When Jesse tried to pursue the matter, Judy Lean became very upset and finally turned and fled along the path, ignoring Jesse's pleas to return.

All the way to Pentuan, Jesse worried about the simple-minded girl, but there was little she could do immediately. She would mention Judy Lean to Eulaliah Vincent – when she returned.

Before then, Jesse had sudden and unexpected news of Ben that drove all thoughts of the unfortunate Judy Lean from her mind.

It came at one of Fanny Ustick's Sunday prayer-meeting teas, attended by a number of men new to the Happy Union mine. One of them, a man in his early forties, was well on the downward path trodden by older miners. Too old to cope with the ladders on the deeper and more prosperous mines, he was now drifting round the county, seeking smaller mines and stream-works. Before long he would be forced to swallow his pride and join the army of odd-job men, willing to undertake any job in order to stay on a mine.

'Ben Retallick?' He frowned in reply to Jesse's routine question, 'Why, yes. I worked with him about four or five months since, on the Luscombe mine, down on Tamarside. I remember him well. A good strong lad. I wouldn't mind working with him again.'

Jesse could hardly believe her luck. 'You actually worked with Ben? Where exactly is the Luscombe mine? Is Ben still there?'

The miner shook his head, and some of the hope died within Jesse.

'No, missie. He left there before I did. He's one of those miners who don't care to stay in one place for long. A month is plenty long enough for the likes of him, I reckon. He'll have worked in another half dozen mines by now.'

Jesse continued to question the miner, gleaning every scrap of information about Ben, until Fanny Ustick called for her assistance in the kitchen.

By the time Jesse came back to the room, the miner had gone. It was the last opportunity she had to talk to him. He, too, was a soldier of the army of drifters. The rumour of an easy surface-job on a deep mine was all he needed to put him on the road to another mine, another district. Jesse never saw him again.

Nevertheless, it was the first positive news of Ben that Jesse had received in almost a year. It now seemed certain that Ben had not left the country, and was probably still in Cornwall.

For the whole of one evening, the patient Fanny Ustick wrote and rewrote a letter to the captain of the Luscombe mine, at Jesse's dictation.

This was a most important letter, and Fanny realised it could not be hurried. Jesse spent so much time trying to make up her mind *exactly* what should be written that Fanny Ustick wrote a brief note of her own to accompany the letter. She begged the mine captain to give them *any* news of Ben.

For weeks, Jesse faced each new morning with the thought that this might be the day when she would have news of Ben. Perhaps Ben himself would arrive, informed by the captain of the Luscombe mine that there was now nothing to keep him away.

Jesse waited in vain. No reply to the letter was ever received.

In the spring of 1821, two young boys were walking along the little-used path where Jesse had met with Judy Lean, when they saw a brightly coloured bundle tucked beneath the leafless hedgerow. Thinking they had discovered some exciting booty, abandoned by the Mevagissey smugglers who used the path, they pounced upon the bundle and unwrapped it with excited anticipation. As the last wrapping was turned back, the boys dropped the bundle quickly, recoiling in horror.

They had found the body of a newly born child, wrapped inside a bloody apron.

News of the grisly find was given to Loveday Ustick by the constable from St Austell when he called at the Happy Union stream-works to water his horse. The constable had been despatched by a St Austell magistrate to view the tiny body and try to establish the cause of its death – and also to seek the dead baby's mother.

Loveday Ustick mentioned the matter quite casually that evening, when he was sitting down to supper with his wife and Jesse. Before he had finished talking, Jesse jumped up from the table, leaving her meal, and announced that she was going out.

'Out? Where are you going at this hour? It will be dark soon.'

'I know, but I must go. I'll tell you all about it when I return.'

Before the Usticks could ask any more questions, Jesse was out of the house. She had no doubt that Judy Lean was the mother of the dead baby. She was equally certain the constable would reach the same conclusion before very long. She wanted to find Judy Lean before he did.

Turning in at the gate of Pengrugla, Jesse had a moment of indecision. She had not seen Reuben Holyoak since she had left this house after her mother's death. She was not happy at the thought of meeting him again now, but it could not be avoided.

The light was failing fast, but it was sufficient for her to see that Sir Colman Vincent's estate manager did not concern himself with the appearance of his own house. Winter gales, heavy with salt from the bay beyond the hill, had scoured much of the paint from doors and window-frames. The house had a sadly neglected air.

There was a light in the kitchen, but when Jesse knocked on the door no sound came from within. She was about to move to the kitchen window to look inside, when a voice spoke from close behind her. Reuben Holyoak had lost none of his gamekeeper's silent ways. Jesse had heard nothing of his approach.

'Well, this is an unexpected pleasure.' Reuben Holyoak looked at her in feigned surprise. He had seen her coming towards the house when she was a quarter of a mile away. 'Welcome back to Pengrugla, Jesse. It's been a great disappointment to me that you should have stayed away for so long. Come into the house.'

Reuben Holyoak went in first and held the door open. Jesse took a single step inside. It was far enough for her to see that the neglect outside had its beginning here. It both saddened and angered her. But she reminded herself that she was not here to take issue with Reuben Holyoak over the condition of the house that had been her home for so long.

'I've come to see Judy Lean. Where is she?'

'Judy?' Jesse had caught Reuben Holyoak off guard, but he recovered quickly. 'I don't know. What's more, I don't care. I sent the slattern packing.'

Jesse was certain he was lying. She said, 'Was that before or after the baby was born?'

'I know nothing of any baby,' Reuben Holyoak blustered. 'What baby? If I learn who has been spreading such rumours, I'll take them before the magistrate.'

'The chances are that you'll have an opportunity to speak to a magistrate sooner than you expect. People around here are not fools. Some of them will have seen Judy. She was with child – and now a dead baby has been found not a stone's throw from here. The constable from St Austell is most likely on his way to this house at this very moment. Now, take me to Judy.'

Jesse sounded far more confident than she felt. She was close enough to Reuben Holyoak to smell the alcohol on his breath, and she knew him well enough to fear him.

'Judy Lean and her baby have nothing to do with me. What that girl does is her own business.'

'Then I've been wasting my time – and yours. I came here to help Judy. I haven't found her and I'm worried. I'll seek out the constable and tell him everything I know.'

Jesse turned to walk from the house.

'Wait!' Reuben Holyoak was not certain how much Jesse really knew, but he did not want her talking to the constable. 'I . . . I'm not sure . . . She may be down at the pigs' house.'

'Why should she be there?' Jesse looked at Reuben Holyoak suspiciously.

'She's been living there for a month or two.' Reuben Holyoak's eyes would not meet hers.

'You mean since you learned she was expecting a child.'

Jesse made no attempt to hide the contempt she felt for Reuben Holyoak. Now she knew for certain he was the father of Judy Lean's dead child. Had he not been, he would have sent her away from Pengrugla the moment he knew she was pregnant.

'Bring a lantern. We'll have need of it if we are to find her.'

Jesse set off down the path in the darkness. Halfway to the pig-sty Reuben Holyoak caught up with her. In his hand he carried a fish-oil lantern that cast a flickering yellow light about them.

'I knew nothing about the baby's death, Jesse. You must believe me.'

Jesse said nothing.

'I swear to you I've done everything in my power to help Judy. I will do so now, but we must keep the constable from learning her whereabouts.'

They arrived at the low windowless building that had once housed the pigs owned by Jesse and her mother. Jesse remembered that Reuben Holyoak had once spent a night here, but the thought raised no smile tonight. The sty was in darkness, but as Jesse pushed the door open on creaking hinges she heard a startled rustle of straw. It was too loud to have been caused by a rat.

'Hold the light up,' Jesse called to Reuben Holyoak.

In the weak yellow light cast by the lamp, she saw that the sty had not been cleaned out since her pigs had been sold.

At first, Jesse could see little in the dark interior of the sty, but as she advanced further inside, with Reuben Holyoak behind her, she made out the shape of someone lying on a heap of last year's straw.

It was Judy Lean.

She lay covered with only the tattered remnants of an old blanket. Her head moved on the straw as she followed the progress of the shadowy figures across the sty towards her. Her face was taut and haggard, but it was her eyes that alarmed Jesse. They were wide and feverish, full of the pain she had borne alone.

Jesse dropped to her knees on the straw and sought to reassure the girl. 'You are going to be all right now, Judy. I've come to help you.'

Judy Lean looked apprehensively towards the lantern held high behind Jesse.

'Don't worry, Judy. That's Mr Holyoak.'

Instead of relaxing, Judy Lean drew an arm from beneath

the blanket and gripped Jesse's arm painfully. 'I didn't do nothing wrong, Jesse. I didn't want to make no trouble for Mr Holyoak. Don't let anyone take me away.'

'Hush, now! No one is going to take you anywhere.'

It was doubtful whether Judy Lean heard her words, so caught up was she in her own tangled fears.

'I'm hurting so, Jesse. It happened along the path . . . I didn't know . . . The baby just came.'

Judy Lean's fingernails dug into Jesse's arm, and Jesse winced with pain.

'I spoke to it, Jesse, but it didn't do nothing. I cuddled it, too, but I don't think it loved me very much. It wouldn't make a sound for me. Then I heard some boys coming along the path. I wrapped the baby in my apron and put it in the hedge. I knew they'd see it . . . I thought it might love them more than it loved me . . .'

Tears were streaming down Judy Lean's face and, before Jesse could prevent her, she struggled to a sitting position. 'I wouldn't have brought the baby to Pengrugla, Mr Holyoak. I remembered what you said to me. If the baby had loved me, I'd have found somewhere else to keep it. I would . . .'

The tattered blanket had slipped from Judy Lean in her agitation, and, as Jesse held the girl close in a bid to calm her, she saw that Judy had lost a great deal of blood.

Over her shoulder, Jesse spoke to Reuben Holyoak. 'Judy needs a doctor. I doubt if he'll want to work in a pig's house. You must help me to take her to Pengrugla.'

'What about the constable? If he finds here there, I'll be in trouble with Sir Colman.'

Jesse snorted angrily. 'Your neck will be safe enough, Reuben Holyoak. So will Judy's if we get a doctor to her quickly. You heard what she just said. The baby must have been dead when it was born. There will be gossip, but that's never bothered you before. Help me lift her up, now – and be careful with her.'

'All right. Hold this lantern.'

Handing the lamp to Jesse, Reuben Holyoak bent down to Judy Lean. With a muffled grunt he lifted her from the straw, avoiding meeting her frightened gaze.

When they reached the house, Reuben Holyoak carried his burden up the narrow stairs to the small bedroom that had once been Jesse's own. It now contained nothing but a hard straw mattress.

Laying Judy Lean on the mattress, he said gruffly, 'I'll find a blanket for her.'

'When you've done that you can go to the village and fetch the doctor. She's still bleeding badly.'

For a moment it looked as though Reuben Holyoak might argue, and Jesse said quickly, 'You'll not want it said you have reason to wish this girl dead, Reuben? Go, now. I have things to do here that you won't want to see.'

Without another word, Reuben Holyoak left the room. A few moments later, much to Jesse's relief, she heard the front door slam shut behind him.

Jesse quickly set to and stripped and bathed Judy Lean ignoring the girl's weak protests. She frowned at the extensive bruising she found on Judy's pale body, but by then Judy Lean was so drowsy she made no reply to Jesse's questions.

Jesse had just completed her task when she heard footsteps on the stairs outside. Thinking it was the doctor, she went out to meet him and have a brief discussion with him before he examined the ill and exhausted Judy Lean.

It was not the doctor but the constable from St Austell.

Looking at Jesse, he said, 'I was told I would find Reuben Holyoak here. Would you be Judy Lean?'

'No, Judy is in there.' Jesse jerked her head at the door behind her.

As the constable made to move past her, Jesse blocked his path, 'Judy Lean is not going to run away, Constable. She's a very sick girl. Reuben Holyoak has gone to Mevagissey to fetch a doctor for her.'

The constable put his head to one side and looked quizzically at Jesse. 'I don't doubt your word, young lady, but I have some questions to put to her.'

'You'll receive no answers from her tonight. Judy is ill and very, very tired. I think I can tell you all you want to know. Yes, the child that was found is hers – but it was dead when it was born.'

'I wouldn't dream of arguing with you, miss. However, the rights of that will be decided at a Coroner's inquest. Have you known Judy Lean for long?'

Jesse nodded. 'We grew up together, but I hadn't seen her for some years until we met again a couple of months ago. It was obvious to anyone that she was expecting a child, yet when I asked her about it she became terribly confused. I'm quite sure she never realised what was happening to her.'

The constable nodded sympathetically. 'That is more or less what others have told me – but someone must have known. The child's father, for instance. Would you have any idea who he is?'

'Thoughts, I might have; but the gossips will already have given you theirs.'

'Perhaps Reuben Holyoak can tell me more.'

'I don't doubt it. Whether he *will* is another matter altogether. But you'll have an opportunity to talk to him soon; I think I hear him.'

When Reuben Holyoak entered the house the doctor from

Mevagissey was with him, complaining bitterly at being called out to roam the countryside in the dark of a moonless night.

Reuben Holyoak came up the stairs behind the doctor. When he saw the constable, he stopped, the blood draining from his face.

The doctor ignored the constable, but to Jesse he said, 'You had better come in the room with me. I may have need of your help.'

The Mevagissey doctor's examination was so crude it came close to brutality. He handled Judy Lean with a roughness that brought screams of pain from her. When he had completed his cursory examination he left her whimpering softly.

As Jesse looked at him in silent disapproval, the doctor wiped his hands on a bloody cloth. 'The bleeding must be stopped if she is to recover. Find some woundwort – there should be plenty growing about here. Make a strong tea from it and give it to her as often as you can force it down.'

'Is that all you can do for her?'

'Go to church and pray if you want a miracle – but I saw a constable outside the door. He will have been sent here by the Reverend Hawkins. Hawkins is a magistrate who pays scant heed to the Bible's dictum of tempering justice with mercy. He has more control over this girl's future than I.'

Jesse said sharply, 'Judy's committed no crime. Her baby was dead when it was born.'

'The Coroner's jury may agree with you, I doubt if their verdict will convince Hawkins. Judy Lean has sinned against the Church by bringing a fatherless child into the world – dead or alive. If he had his way, the Reverend Hawkins would make all such sins capital offences.'

His ablutions completed, the doctor strode from the room and called to Reuben Holyoak as he went down the stairs.

Jesse remained in the bedroom and did her best to comfort

Judy Lean. She did not leave the room until the girl had fallen into a sleep punctuated by long quivering sobs.

When Jesse went downstairs the doctor had left the house. The constable had gone with him.

'Judy will need a woman to look in and help her each day,' she said to Reuben Holyoak.

'Will you come and do whatever needs to be done, Jesse?'

'I have my own work at the Happy Union. You can get a woman from Lamorrack House, but I would like to visit Judy occasionally.'

'You are always welcome, Jesse. You know that.'

Jesse saw the brandy-bottle on the table alongside a half-empty glass. She knew it was time she left.

'I've missed seeing you about, Jesse. It was always my hope that this would remain your home. I've not changed. I still want you here as my wife.'

Jesse looked around her at the neglected and unloved house that held so many memories for her. On her way to the door she paused to throw her words back at Sir Colman Vincent's estate manager.

'This is no longer the house I grew up in, Reuben. You've succeeded in destroying my past; but you'll have no part of my future, I promise you that.'

Chapter Twenty-Four

The Reverend Hawkins sent his constables to Pengrugla to arrest Judy Lean two days after the dead baby had been found. He ordered that she be kept in custody pending the verdict of the coroner's court.

One of the constables was the man who had been to Pengrugla to investigate the death of the baby. He called at the Happy Union mine to give the news to Jesse.

'I wouldn't like you to believe this is any of my doing, miss. To my way of thinking the girl might just as well remain at Pengrugla, but I have to carry out my orders. I'll make sure she is well looked after, don't you worry about that. I've brought along a wagon to carry her to St Austell, and my wife will tend her while she's there. We'll have a doctor look in on her, too, if he's needed.'

Despite the constable's reassuring words, Jesse worried about Judy Lean. She was thinking about the matter on her way home from the stream-works that evening when a passing horseman hailed her. It was Reuben Holyoak, dressed in clothes that would not have disgraced a country gentleman. He told Jesse of Judy Lean's arrest.

Jesse thanked him politely but coolly and continued on her way. Undaunted, Reuben Holyoak swung himself down from the saddle. Leading the horse by the reins, he fell in beside her.

'I've helped Judy as much as I dare, Jesse. Now she has been arrested I can do no more. I have my position to think of. All this is none of my business . . .'

Jesse snorted loudly and walked faster. 'Tell that to those who might believe you, Reuben Holyoak.'

Striding out to keep pace with her, Reuben Holyoak said, 'I was hoping for an opportunity to talk seriously to you, Jesse. As Sir Colman's estate manager I occupy a good position. I have much to offer you. Marry me and you'll be the envy of every girl for miles around. I can give you back Pengrugla. You would have a good life there with me, Jesse.'

Jesse stopped and turned scornfully upon Reuben Holyoak. 'Is that what you told Judy Lean when you bedded her, Reuben? That she would have a good life with you? She's simple enough to have believed you – I am not! Pengrugla means nothing to me without Ben Retallick. You have nothing I want, Reuben Holyoak. Set your fine clothes back in the saddle and find another simpleton to impress.'

'You are angry and upset now, Jesse. We'll talk again another time.'

Reuben Holyoak pulled hard on the rein of his horse as it backed away from him. 'In the meantime I suggest you forget Judy Lean. Allow justice to take its course.'

'Judy Lean needs more than justice right now. She needs friends. I count myself as one of them and I'll do all I can to help her.'

Some of the bal-maidens from the Happy Union stream-works came around a bend in the lane, laughing and joking. Jesse, who was usually content with her own company, waited for them. They had not gone far before Reuben Holyoak rode by, looking neither to left nor right, ignoring the whistles of some of the younger girls.

The inquest on Judy Lean's baby was held in a Mevagissey inn, much to the chagrin of the Reverend Hawkins. He felt the proceedings were robbed of dignity by such surroundings.

No one at the inquest knew why the ecclesiastical magistrate had chosen to attend. Possibly he was expecting to be called upon to give evidence of having arrested Judy Lean.

Jesse was there. So, too, was Reuben Holyoak. He looked ill at ease when called to the witness-box. The estate manager denied knowing that Judy was pregnant. In truth, he solemnly declared, it was not often that he saw the girl. He worked long hours and ate most of his meals at Lamorrack House. Judy Lean had been employed by him to keep Pengrugla clean and cultivate a small vegetable garden there.

According to Reuben Holyoak she was rarely at home when he returned in the evening and he had no idea how she spent her time. He added that Judy's mother had run off with a sailor and he doubted whether Judy's morals were any better . . .

At this point Jesse jumped to her feet and accused Reuben Holyoak of deliberately attempting to blacken the character of Judy Lean.

The coroner was not in the least perturbed by Jesse's interruption. He calmly asked her whether she had something to say to the court. When Jesse said she most certainly had, the coroner asked Reuben Holyoak, 'Have you anything further to say that might help to throw light upon the death of this child, Mr Holyoak?'

Reuben Holyoak shook his head.

'Very well, you may step down and we will hear what this young lady has to tell the court.' The coroner waved Jesse forward.

Jesse's manner was in sharp contrast to Reuben Holyoak's. Firmly and clearly she said she had known Judy Lean since childhood, and she told the coroner of Judy's simple ways. Then she spoke of meeting Judy Lean on the path where the dead baby was found and of her belief that Judy had not realised she was pregnant. Finally, Jesse told of finding Judy Lean in the pig-sty at Pengrugla. Her voice faltered for the first time as she repeated what Judy Lean had said to her about the failure of the baby to move or make a sound.

When Jesse ended, it was apparent to everyone in the improvised court-room that she had made a great impression upon the seven-man jury. But the coroner seized upon another aspect of her story.

'Miss Henna, will you clear up one small point for me? Was Mr Holyoak present when Judy Lean told you about the birth of her baby?'

'He was.'

'I see. Thank you.'

The coroner fixed Reuben Holyoak with a look that made the estate manager squirm. 'No doubt Mr Holyoak has his own reasons for not telling this court such an important piece of evidence.'

Two more witnesses were called by the coroner. One was the constable who had investigated the baby's death; the other was the surgeon who had conducted a post-mortem on the child. Neither man had found any marks of violence on the tiny body.

When the last witness had sat down the jury had a brief discussion then returned a verdict that it had not been proven the baby was alive when born. The coroner recorded their verdict accordingly.

A coroner's jury would rarely bring in a verdict that might lead to criminal proceedings being taken against the mother of a baby found dead under circumstances such as these. If the bastardy laws of England were harsh, the criminal law was pitiless. More than one young girl climbed the steps to a prison gallows, guilty only of earning the disapproval of a jury of her peers, backed up by a stern judge's lack of compassion.

One man in the crowded court-room disagreed with the verdict. The Reverend Hawkins had come to Mevagissey to hear a verdict of 'wilful murder' recorded against Judy Lean. Jumping to his feet, he shouted that Judy Lean had sinned against the Church and that the verdict reached by the jury would offend God himself.

The onlookers responded with a barrage of jeers. When the coroner had succeeded in restoring a degree of order, he addressed the angry magistrate.

'Sir, had it been your wish to address this court I would have been most happy to afford you the opportunity. As it is, the jury has arrived at a verdict with which I am in complete agreement. This hearing is now over.'

The coroner smiled fleetingly at the angry magistrate. 'I am aware that the verdict has placed you in a difficult situation, Reverend Hawkins. You should have waited the finding of my court before making an arrest. I suggest you release the young lady at the earliest opportunity.'

'Damn you, Varcoe. I will do no such thing,' retorted the fiery magistrate in a most unclerical display of bad temper. 'Wickedness must not go unpunished. Indeed, it *will* not! Judy Lean has no employment and no place to live now that Mr Holyoak has dismissed her from his service. I'll not release her to a life of sinful vagrancy, to tempt other men.'

Before the Reverend Hawkins had ended his tirade, Jesse was on her feet again. She shouted, 'Judy Lean is no vagrant, and neither you nor Reuben Holyoak will make her one. She can share my room. There will be work for her, too, when she is well enough.'

When the jury had reached its verdict, the innkeeper had immediately flung open his establishment, anxious not to lose so many prospective customers. Now, with glasses and tankards in their hands, jurors and spectators alike raised a cheer for Jesse, drowning the Reverend Hawkins's angry reply.

Unable to make himself heard above the din, the red-faced magistrate stormed from the inn, calling down the wrath of heaven upon the heads of all those who condoned sinfulness.

Later, the constable released Judy Lean, and she went home with Jesse to the Ustick house. Fanny Ustick had heard all about the unfortunate girl from Jesse and she displayed a great deal more Christian charity than had the Reverend Hawkins. For the first time in many years Judy Lean slept in a house where she was welcome.

It was a full month before Judy Lean was well enough to commence working at the Happy Union mine. She was a hard-working girl, lacking all deceit, and she was well received by the other girls and women with whom she worked.

When Judy Lean had been at the mine a week, she and the other bal-maidens were sorting ore and chattering together when a carriage turned off the road and swayed down the steep pitted track to the workings.

The bal-maidens watched with great interest as Captain Loveday Ustick hurried from his office to meet the carriage and they saw him say something through the open window. Then he turned, shielding his eyes against the light of the sun, and pointed to where the bal-maidens were working.

Jesse knew immediately that the occupant of the carriage must be Eulaliah Vincent. Without waiting to be called, Jesse hurried to where Loveday Ustick was holding the carriage door open.

'Hello, child.' Dressed in clothes that were the height of London fashion, Eulaliah Vincent took Jesse's arm, heedless of the dust that clung to Jesse's coarse dress and apron. 'Walk with me to the far side of the river. I fancy there is less mud underfoot there.'

'You have some news of Walter?' Jesse asked eagerly.

'I have, but I fear it is not the news for which you have been hoping. Walter Dunn has been sentenced to fourteen years' transportation.'

Jesse reeled as though she had been struck, and Eulaliah Vincent's grip tightened on her arm.

'Fourteen years! For what? For speaking the truth?'

'No, child. He was found guilty of sedition. Of advocating violent changes in the order of our society. It is probably the most serious charge that could be levelled against a man in these uncertain times – but there, do not upset yourself so, child. Things might have been much worse for Walter Dunn.'

'But he did nothing . . .' Jesse's voice trailed away in an agony of despair.

'That was not what the evidence implied. Indeed, during the course of the trial it was rumoured that Walter Dunn would suffer the same fate as the Cato Street conspirators.'

Jesse gasped. Even in this remote corner of England news had reached them of Arthur Thistlewood and his misguided fellow-reformers. They were the men who had plotted to murder the whole Cabinet of Lord Liverpool. They had reached an advanced state of preparation when one of their number had betrayed his fellow-conspirators.

Captured and convicted by the due processes of English law, Arthur Thistlewood and four of his lieutenants were hanged by the neck until they were semi-conscious – then removed from the gallows and beheaded by an axeman.

'Fourteen years is a lifetime,' whispered Jesse.

Eulaliah Vincent smiled sadly. 'It is only a lifetime when you reach my age, child. For you it is no more than a passing chapter in the book of life. When Walter Dunn returns to Mevagissey you will still be a beautiful woman – but you must expect very little from him, or I fear you will be terribly upset.'

They had crossed the bridge, and now Eulaliah Vincent turned to Jesse and said gently, 'I went to see Walter Dunn in Newgate prison. I wanted to know if there was anything he needed. Sadly, I fear that imprisonment has proved too much for Walter Dunn to bear. His mind has escaped to the sea and the clean air he loves so much. I am sorry to be the bearer of such sad news, but I felt you should know.'

Jesse was stunned. She had come to believe that Walter was able to cope with anything. Jesse thought of the time she had told him she was leaving the Dunn house. When he walked away from her to the reform meeting, she had admired the way he shrugged off his problems and put them behind him. For such a man to be broken was unthinkable.

Jesse wept openly, and Eulaliah Vincent did her best to comfort her.

When Jesse regained her composure, she walked slowly back to the stream-workings with Eulaliah Vincent. Along the way she thanked her for all she had tried to do. Jesse was convinced Eulaliah Vincent had used her influence to save Walter from the gallows.

When she expressed this opinion to the Dunn family that same evening, only Martha Retallick agreed with her. Billy Dunn said bluntly that, had Jesse not interfered, things might even have gone better for Walter. He told Jesse she had been foolish to expect one Vincent to act against the interests of another.

There was a similar reaction from men who had attended Walter's meetings. When Jesse told them her news and urged them to make some form of protest against his sentence, they did no more than mutter among themselves, carefully avoiding committing themselves to any particular course of action.

Bitterly, Jesse was forced to the conclusion that Sir Colman Vincent's victory was absolute. With Walter Dunn gone from the scene, the reform movement in Cornwall was dead.

Chapter Twenty-Five

To Walter Dunn, his conviction and sentence meant nothing. They were no more real than the surroundings in which he now found himself. He blotted out the words of the Judge, witnesses and court officials as effectively as he did the noises of his rowdy companions in the communal cell of Newgate prison.

It was ironic that Walter Dunn, champion of the rights of others, should be incarcerated in such a place as this. All his life he had bitterly attacked the power of landowners to control the lives of their tenants from birth to the grave. He fervently believed a man had a right to choose his own home, his work, and the wife he took. Now Walter was locked away in a prison, his mode of life dictated by the whim of justice and the mood of his gaolers.

It was the continuous din and the total absence of privacy that Walter found most difficult to bear in Newgate. The noise of crowds was not new to him, but at home he had been able to turn his back upon a reform meeting and walk for an hour or two along a Cornish cliff, with only the wind and the surf as companions.

In his imagination, Walter Dunn spent much of his time there now, looking out to a far horizon across the silver-grey sea he loved so much.

It was a scene he knew well. He had been able to tell the time of day to within minutes, merely by the way the light was reflected from the water beyond Mevagissey.

The sea had provided Walter Dunn with his living. It had also been his barometer, calendar and clock. *That* was Walter Dunn's real world and the place in which his mind sought refuge. Newgate prison was an unreal nightmare.

Walter spent much of his day clinging to the bars of a small window. Three feet away, a dirty grey wall rose higher than he could see, but he knew the sky was up there and he clung to his vantage-point tenaciously, the blows and curses of his fellow-prisoners failing to move him.

During the long months he was in Newgate, Walter Dunn slept little. There was no physical exertion to tire his body, and whenever he closed his eyes he was haunted by the sobs and pleadings of Michael Stephens, as the soldiers dragged him to the gallows from the cell they had shared. Walter would wake to find himself beating the straw-strewn floor with his manacled hands, screaming for them to spare his late companion.

Each week more and more convicted felons were placed in the heavily overcrowded cell. The days passed in constant squabbling and fighting. The area closest to the small barred window, with its relatively fresh air, became the most fought-over site in the cell.

Eventually, Walter Dunn was ousted by some of the more violent newcomers. Pushed to one of the darkest corners, he sat huddled against the wall, his chin sunk upon his chest. He fought only when he was crowded too much, or when food was brought to the cell. There was no comradeship here. Each man had to fight to stay alive.

When it seemed the cell could not possibly accommodate one more prisoner, the transportation agent and his men arrived. They were to convey the convicted men to a prison hulk moored on the River Thames at Woolwich. Here they would await transportation to the penal colonies of Australia.

The enclosed prison-vans were brought into the yard and backed up to the rear of the gaol. The convicts, shuffling clumsily in their irons, were herded into the vans, each man linked to his neighbour, front and rear.

Packed so tightly that they were unable to sit or lie, the convicts complained long and bitterly – yet to Walter it was the most wonderful day he had known for many months. He was jammed against the side of the van, and high above his head was a tiny opening through which he could see the sky.

He stared up at this tiny grey square of freedom for every inch of the bone-shaking journey through the streets of London Town and along narrow lanes beside the River Thames, until the vans drew to a halt by the side of the stinking mudflats of Woolwich Reach.

It was raining hard now. As they were pulled from the vans the convicts slipped and fell about in the black mud, hampered by their heavy chains and cursing their escorts.

The tempers of guards and convicts were not improved by Walter Dunn. He dropped to his knees in the ooze, his mouth wide open to receive the rain that fell upon his upturned face. Holding his shackled hands high in supplication to the dark and stormy sky, Walter wept salt tears that mingled with the rain streaming down his sunken cheeks.

The initial reaction of the guards was to laugh and jeer at Walter, but as the rain continued to beat down on them their merriment turned to anger. When Walter ignored their orders to get to his feet and make his way to the waiting boat with the others, they kicked and pummelled him, then began to beat him with their long wooden staves.

Impervious to their blows, Walter was finally hoisted to his feet and dragged to the waiting boat by his fellow-prisoners.

The prison hulk to which they were taken had once been a proud seventy-four-gun ship-of-the-line, with an honourable record of service. At the Bay of Aboukir she had followed close in the wake of Nelson's *Vanguard*. Later, at the battle of the Nile, she had taken part in the destruction of Napoleon's fleet. Finally, at the battle of Trafalgar, scarred and dismasted, she had been towed clear of the carnage, her guns still spitting anger and defiance at the enemy.

There was little honour in the old warship's present role. With the broken remains of her masts sawn away and stout iron bars securing her gun-ports, she lay in Woolwich Reach, just clear of the foul mud that glistened black at low tide. The quarterdeck, once trodden by the heroes of England, now housed a blood-stained whipping frame where lesser men screamed their pain.

Below decks, the prison-holds were as dark as a Newgate cell – and equally as crowded. It was also indescribably filthy, the guards not daring to go below decks to supervise any cleaning activities.

This would be Walter Dunn's home for the first twelve months of his fourteen-year sentence.

While Walter Dunn was settling into the routine of his new surroundings, Jesse became increasingly depressed because she had received no reply to the letter sent to the captain of the Luscombe mine.

There had been no further news of Ben, and she knew the

difficulties he would experience in trying to let her know where he was and what he was doing. Unable to read or write, Ben would have to entrust a message to anyone he met with who was coming to Mevagissey. Believing himself to be a wanted man, Ben could not afford to trust a complete stranger. Nevertheless, Jesse could not help feeling that Ben would have found *some* means of informing her of his whereabouts – had he wanted to.

Jesse was not aware of Ben's belief that, had Reuben Holyoak lived, she would now be married to the estate manager. Reluctantly, she came to the conclusion that Ben no longer loved her.

There were many who were ready to persuade Jesse that this was so. The bal-maidens with whom she worked told her she was foolish to wait for Ben for so long. Jesse was now a very attractive girl of eighteen years. It was an age when most respectable young women were married and had begun a family.

She would have had no shortage of suitors. A new deep-water dock was under construction at Pentuan. It was planned to use it for the export of china-clay from the rapidly expanding clay industry about St Austell. Young men were flocking to the area from all parts of Cornwall.

For a few Cornishmen it was a prosperous time. Fishing had taken a sudden, albeit brief, upsurge. For years the numbers of the pilchards taken around the Cornish coast had been steadily declining, but this year they returned in huge shoals that ruffled the waters of every bay from Sennen to Rame. The fishermen were kept busy from dawn to dusk.

Mevagissey reeked with the tang of fish, the cobbles of its steep and narrow streets glistening with spilled pilchard oil. If the Dunn brothers ever thought of Walter, it was only to grumble that he was not there to help them with the increased work.

The parliamentary reform movement missed him more. Meetings were still called when an important member from another part of the country visited Cornwall, but they attracted only a fraction of their previous support.

Many reasons could be found for the failing interest. Chief among them was the arrest of Walter Dunn. Shocked and angry at first, men fell silent when the news of his sentence became known, fearful lest the same fate befall them. There were few Cornishmen willing to risk arrest and transportation for a cause they hardly understood. Most believed Sir Colman Vincent had proved his invincibility beyond any doubt. They had no wish to have his wrath turned upon themselves.

At first, Jesse attended the reform meetings in a vain attempt to stir up support for Walter. A few men listened to her, but whenever she tried to address a full meeting she was quickly shouted down. The fishermen of Cornwall were not prepared to listen to a woman who upbraided them for not saving one of their own.

The lack of direction at the few meetings held in the district depressed and saddened Jesse. Eventually she stopped attending them.

Her failure to influence the men at the meetings was not due entirely to the fact that she was a woman. Many a disappointed man had also learned that it needed something more than words to move Cornishmen.

By the end of that year, disillusioned and unhappy, Jesse made up her mind to leave Pentuan and the Happy Union mine. She had gone there because she believed she might hear news of Ben. Now she was ready to admit that he had probably gone for ever. She decided to return to the work she knew and had enjoyed in the past. She would move inland and seek work on a farm. In these difficult days, many farmers preferred to employ women. Taxes were high, profits low, and farmers could not match the wages paid by the mines and clay works about them.

But when Jesse told Fanny Ustick of her decision, the Happy Union captain's wife had a surprise of her own for Jesse.

God had smiled at the Usticks and their settled way of life. At the age of forty-two, Fanny Ustick had become pregnant. She and her huge good-natured husband were absolutely delighted. They accepted it as one of the Lord's miracles and spent much time on their knees, thanking Him for laying His hands upon them.

Now, to Jesse, Fanny Ustick confessed that she was desperately afraid of giving birth to a child. She begged Jesse to remain with her, at least until after the baby was born.

'Loveday and I want this baby so much, Jesse, but I am not a strong young girl to whom child-bearing comes as the most natural thing in the world. I am a staid old woman who should be past this sort of thing – and I am terrified of something going wrong.'

Then Fanny Ustick told Jesse of the reason for her fears.

'My mother died in childbirth when I was ten years old. I can remember lying in my bed crying while my mother screamed and fought for two days and nights to give birth to a child that wouldn't come. I don't believe the Lord will allow me to suffer in the same way, Jesse, but should things be difficult I would like you to be with me.'

Fanny and Loveday Ustick had been very kind to Jesse. After such a plea she could not possibly leave Pentuan until the baby was born.

The child was expected during the first days of June 1822, and Fanny Ustick struggled with an uncomfortable pregnancy through one of the worst winters in living memory. Wild storms raged from end to end of the county, lifting roofs and felling trees that had stood for centuries. For weeks snow blocked the narrow Cornish lanes, cutting off isolated farms and villages, and April arrived ushered in by yet another violent snowstorm. It seemed to the unhappy inhabitants of the county that they had lost the sun for ever.

The snow persisted for most of that month. Dark grey clouds hung low over the countryside from coast to coast and only the most determined of spring flowers showed themselves in the shelter of the hedge-bottoms.

One morning, Jesse and Judy Lean made their way to the stream-works through four inches of snow and all morning sorted ore with fingers stiff from the cold. Loveday Ustick had gone to the St Austell foundry to order some new equipment, and when the midday break came around Jesse decided to return to the Ustick house at Pentuan. She thought Fanny Ustick might need help to clear the snow from about the house. Judy Lean remained behind at the stream-works, her dependence upon Jesse much less now she knew the women with whom she worked.

When Jesse arrived at the house, she received no reply to her first call. She called again. This time she thought she heard a sound in the kitchen. Hurrying there, Jesse found Fanny Ustick seated in an old rocking-chair, clutching her distended stomach, her face the colour of the sky outside.

Shocked by Fanny Ustick's appearance, Jesse crouched down beside her, deeply concerned. 'What's happened, Fanny? What have you done?'

Fanny Ustick was about to reply when a fierce spasm of pain attacked her body. With her face contorted in agony, she fought against the pain for about half a minute. Then she expelled her breath noisily and sank back in the chair.

Slack-mouthed now, Fanny Ustick looked up at Jesse and gasped helplessly. 'I slipped in the snow this morning. I have hurt myself somehow. I think the baby is on its way. Help me, Jesse.'

Jesse had a brief moment of panic, but it passed quickly. She had never before been present at the birth of a child, but she had brought a great many calves and lambs into the world. A baby could not be so very different. Even one that was arriving six weeks before its time.

'We must get you upstairs to your bed. I'll make you comfortable then fetch the mine doctor—'

'You'll do no such thing!' Fanny Ustick spoke through gritted teeth as she struggled to her feet with Jesse's help. 'I'll not have that drunken atheist in my house. I'll go to bed now you are here, but stay with me, Jesse. Please . . . !'

Halfway up the steep and narrow staircase, another spasm caught Fanny Ustick. She was forced to rest on a stair, gasping with pain and clutching her stomach. Jesse realised the baby was well on its way. Coming so much before its time, she wished she were able to call on someone to help her. But there were no other houses within hailing distance, and little likelihood of help until Loveday Ustick or Judy returned to the house. The bal-maidens at the stream-works would miss her, of course, but Judy would tell them she had returned to the house. They would merely assume she had taken the afternoon off work. By the time anyone came to the house it might already be too late . . .

Seated on the dark staircase, Jesse shook off her morbid thoughts. Helping Fanny Ustick to her feet, she half carried her into the bedroom. There she helped Fanny to undress and got her into bed.

The birth of the baby was much closer than Jesse would have wished. Fanny Ustick's muscles were already contracting involuntarily in a powerful bid to expel the child from her body. Fanny Ustick's fear had been that she would suffer a painful labour for days. There was no likelihood of that happening now. Whether the baby would be born alive was another matter.

For the next two hours, Jesse's main problem was preventing Fanny Ustick from throwing herself out of bed as she threshed about wildly, driven on by the ever-increasing labour pains. Jesse had hoped to make hasty preparations for the baby's arrival, but, in constant pain, the older woman would not allow her to leave the bedside.

The child was born as the dark clouds outside lowered over the surrounding hills, hastening the night. The actual birth was over so quickly that Jesse had no time to worry about doing the right things.

At one moment, all that could be seen was the dark damp hair on the crown of the baby's head. The next, it was lying full length in her hands – and very much alive.

With its eyes screwed tight shut, the baby's tiny fists and feet jerkily attacked the stormy world into which it had been so precipitously flung. As Jesse used a finger to clear the baby's mouth, it fought her. Then, sobbing breath into tiny untried lungs, it uttered its first, uncertain cry.

The effect of the sound upon Fanny Ustick was remarkable. The pain of her ordeal immediately forgotten, she struggled to sit up.

Jesse tried to hold her back. 'Lie still, Fanny. There are things to be done yet. The baby is fine.'

'What is it, Jesse? Have I given Loveday a son or a daughter?'

'You have a son, Fanny. A healthy noisy little boy.'

Fanny Ustick sank back on her pillow. Bringing her hands together, she whispered hoarsely, 'Praise be to God! The gift of a son. That is what I will call him, Jesse. Nathaniel . . . the gift of God.'

Jesse felt a great elation. She had successfully brought Fanny

Ustick's baby into the world. Cutting the umbilical cord, she tied it off and bound the baby's stomach. Then, with the after-birth chores completed, Jesse wrapped the tiny wrinkle-faced Nathaniel Ustick in his swaddling-clothes and placed him in the eager arms of his mother.

She was tidying the bedroom when she heard the front door open, and the voices of Loveday Ustick and Judy Lean came to her. Alarmed by the absence of lights downstairs in the house, Loveday Ustick's deep voice boomed through the house as he called to ask where everyone was hiding.

'We're up here, Loveday,' Jesse called. 'Come on up.'

'Is everything all right, Jesse? Judy told me you didn't return to the mine after the midday break.'

The boards creaked noisily as the heavyweight mine captain stumbled clumsily up the stairs in the darkness.

Jesse swung open the bedroom door. Blinking in the light of the lamp, Loveday Ustick saw Fanny lying in the bed. Such was his immediate concern for his pale and exhausted wife that he saw nothing else. Suddenly, hidden by the bed-clothes, the baby stirred and uttered a thin complaining cry of protest.

Loveday Ustick's mouth dropped open in disbelief and he took a quick step to the bedside. Fanny pushed back the blankets and exposed the blotchy red face of their hour-old infant.

Looking down upon his son for the first time, Loveday Ustick's face crumpled. Falling to his knees, he took his wife's hand without once shifting his gaze from the baby. There was such wonder and love in his expression that a great lump rose in Jesse's throat.

Judy Lean had come to the top of the stairs to look silently into the room. Turning her about, Jesse led her down the stairs, leaving the happy couple to enjoy these first shared moments with their newborn son.

Chapter Twenty-Six

Jesse remained at the Ustick house for two weeks after the birth of Fanny's son. The mine captain and his wife urged her to stay longer but, with their family now so blissfully complete, Jesse felt herself more of an interloper in their home than ever.

After a period of uncertainty, Judy Lean decided to accompany Jesse. It was a difficult decision for her to make. She adored Fanny's baby and glowed with happiness whenever she was allowed to help with him. Nevertheless, she felt a fierce loyalty towards Jesse and would not allow her to go from Pentuan alone.

Jesse knew her decision to leave was the right one. Apart from the lack of meaning in her present way of life, Jesse could foresee additional problems coming her way by remaining at the Happy Union stream-workings. Reuben Holyoak had paid two surprise visits to the mine in recent weeks. On both occasions he had carried messages from Sir Colman Vincent to Loveday Ustick. The information contained in them was unimportant; it might have been sent with one of the servants from Lamorrack House.

The messages were merely excuses for Reuben Holyoak to come to the mine, and on both occasions he sought out Jesse. She did not wish to speak to him, and his presence reduced Judy Lean to a quivering wreck, unable either to work or speak. It was apparent to Jesse that Reuben Holyoak had been drinking before both his visits. It was rumoured that just lately Sir Colman Vincent's estate manager was drunk for more hours than he was sober. Jesse had no wish to fall foul of the amorous drunkard.

All the same, Jesse could not dismiss the feeling that by quitting the area she was breaking faith with Ben. She told herself many times that he had been away for two years without sending her a single message. She could not waste her whole life cherishing a dream that Ben Retallick had long abandoned. But still the feeling remained.

Jesse had no fixed plans. She intended striking inland and seeking work on a farm, that was all. Her one big regret was in leaving the sea behind. It was something she would miss. The sea had been no more than a glance away for as long as she could remember.

It was for this reason that on the day before she left Jesse took a long walk along the cliff-top. She went beyond Mevagissey, to a spot where she had spent many hours as a child. On the narrow fern-covered promontory known as Chapel Point she sat down to think.

Jesse stayed there for a long time. When she stood up to return to Pentuan, she saw a large ship under full sail heading westward, about a mile from the shore. As she watched, it suddenly heeled over and turned about in a wide arc, to lie wallowing in the swell of the English Channel, its sails flapping in a most unseamanlike display. There was much unusual activity on the white, holystoned deck, but minutes later the vessel got slowly under way once more and returned to its original course.

Jesse watched until the ship had passed from view beyond the next headland. Then she turned her back upon the sea and slowly made her way homewards.

On board the prison-hulk moored off Woolwich, each day began at five-thirty in the morning. At this hour the convicts were awakened and their dead carried on deck, to be buried in shallow graves in the foul mud of the Thames, as the tide permitted.

At five forty-five, the convicts had their breakfast. Afterwards, it was usual for them to be taken ashore to work on the new docks being built at Woolwich. Unfortunately, no cut stone had been available for many weeks and the convicts remained locked in the holds of the hulk all day.

Life on board the rotting hulk was cruel, degrading, and primitive in the extreme. Many of the convicts were the dregs of human society. With nothing to do to occupy their time, they plotted ridiculously impractical escapes, quarrelled among themselves and bullied those too weak to retaliate. The younger criminals, many of them no more than children, cried themselves to sleep every night and longed for the new land and the promise it held out to them of a better life.

Walter Dunn suffered much at the hands of his fellow-convicts because he was mentally less alert than the others. But after the first few harsh weeks their cruelty became sporadic. There was little pleasure to be gained from tormenting a man to whom all indignities meant nothing.

Walter did all that was necessary to stay alive, but life meant little now. Outwardly he lived. Inside he was already dead. Hate, fear, love, anger – they were all feelings that no longer existed for him. Walter Dunn the man had died when they cut him off from sea and sky. Only Walter Dunn the convict remained.

For a while, hopes were raised on the hulk when rumours began to circulate that a transport was now available to convey the long-term prisoners to Van Diemen's Land, in Australia. It mattered little to the convicts that few of them would ever return. The thought of leaving the stinking overcrowded hulk for the comparative freedom of colonial life filled every man with excitement. Many of them, like Walter Dunn, had already spent a year on board the hulk.

For days, one unsubstantiated rumour followed close on the heels of another. Hopes fluctuated first high and then low in the convict-filled holds. Arguments and fist-fights broke out as men's tempers became frayed with the strain of uncertainty.

The days of eager waiting became weeks, and gradually hope died. Then came the morning when the hatches were not opened at the usual time. Breakfast-time, too, came and went without any movement from above decks. Beating upon the stout wooden planks of their holds, the convicts protested in vain. For an hour it was bedlam below decks. Then, with a crash of complaining timbers, a ship came alongside the hulk, the force of the impact sending convicts sprawling into the dark corners of the prison-holds.

The transport-ship had arrived.

The howls of complaint turned to cheers and hysterical relief. The convicts congratulated each other on surviving the harsh rigours of imprisonment on a convict-hulk. Many had been less fortunate. One in three of the convicts sentenced to terms of transportation were dead before the transports arrived to carry them to the colonies.

A few of the younger men who were leaving families behind them in England wept for the children they would never see again. But they, too, were grateful that their lease on life had been renewed.

They had to wait until after noon before the hatch-covers were removed; then they were herded, two by two, into the harsh light of day.

Under the watchful eyes of heavily armed guards, names were checked and double-checked. Lists were signed and countersigned, and finally passed from the superintendent of the hulk to the mate of the transport *Perseus*. Finally, fetters and chains were carefully inspected and the convicts taken to the Australia-bound ship.

Once on board *Perseus*, half a dozen convicts were segregated from their fellows. Taken to one side, they had the heavy iron chains struck from wrists and ankles. Walter Dunn was one of them.

A boatswain, as gruff and ruffianly in appearance as any convict, explained why they had been singled out for such unexpected treatment.

'The *Perseus* is short of seamen. Good sailors don't want to take a cargo of stinking convicts halfway around the world. They can get better berths, these days. We have to make do with second-best. Even so, we're hard put to make up a full crew. This trip has started worst than most. Half the crew deserted the moment we returned from our last voyage and we've been delayed in London for a week trying to make up a crew. We are still short-handed, so you are going to be put to work. Every one of you has been chosen because he is a seaman, and because your records show you haven't been convicted of violent crimes. Behave yourself on board *Perseus* and you'll enjoy a more comfortable voyage than any one of you has a right to expect. Put a foot wrong and you'll be thrown back into the hold to rot with the others. Do you all understand me?'

The boatswain glared fiercely from man to man. Each newly unfettered convict – with the exception of Walter Dunn – nodded emphatically, eager to please. Walter, rubbing his chafed and emaciated wrists, was gazing up at the sun as though it were the most beautiful object he had ever seen.

The boatswain of *Perseus* took an angry pace forward and jabbed Walter Dunn in the ribs with a calloused finger. 'You! Did you hear what I said?'

Reluctantly, Walter Dunn pulled his gaze away from the bright sun and gave the boatswain a bewildered look.

'He's a bit simple, sir,' explained one of the convicts to the glowering boatswain. 'But he's a good worker and I've never seen him lose his temper. Not even when he's set upon by the others . . .'

For a long fear-filled moment the convict wished he had remained silent as the boatswain switched his scowl to him. 'For your sake, you'd better be right. Keep him working or I'll have you *both* back in the hold.'

The boatswain rubbed his dark stubbled chin and came close to a smile.

'He's not so very different from the rest of the crew on this flat-bottomed scow; they're most of 'em idiots. I must be one myself, or I'd be off earning good wages on a sweet-smelling slaver instead of putting up with the stench of this pig-boat.'

After delivering this parting comment, the boatswain turned his back on the six seamen convicts. They were led away by an armed guard and locked in a cabin until the ship slipped away from the prison-hulk on the late-evening tide.

The next couple of days were happy ones for Walter Dunn. He clambered among the rigging, scrubbed decks and cheerfully carried out every chore he was given, rejoicing in the feel of rain and sunshine on his skin.

On the third day, the ship was sailing close to the coast. Her captain wanted to make a call at the busy Cornish port of Falmouth. Here the ship would take on a final supply of fresh provisions and load mail for the penal colonies of Australia.

The holds, packed with their human cargo, were not yet throwing out the stench that caused strong-stomached sailors to sail well to windward of ships on the transportation run. The captain of *Perseus* set his seamen to scrubbing decks and generally smartening up the ship. Falmouth was his home port and he had no intention of spending the remainder of his career in command of a convict transport. He meant to prove to the ship-owners that he could keep *Perseus* clean and tidy. Any man who could do that with a transport-ship deserved a chance to command one of the fast new packets operating out of the port.

Below decks, Walter Dunn and the other convict seamen were splicing ropes and stitching spare sails. Suddenly, the boatswain's bellowed order sent them clambering to the rigging to furl sail for the run-in to Falmouth harbour.

Walter Dunn obeyed the order eagerly. High in the rigging, with the sea and sky all about him, he felt quite alone in the world. He hurried up the ladder to the deck, smiling as the sunshine touched his face. Breathing in the salt air, he shinned up the rigging of the mainmast and edged his way skilfully out along a yardarm.

Not until then did he take a look about him.

The scene that met his eyes gave him such a tremendous shock that it drove the self-protecting mists from his mind. In an instant it was as though the long months of imprisonment had never happened.

Walter Dunn was looking across a mile of water to where the village of Mevagissey nestled in a fold of the hills, just beyond Chapel Point. It was a scene he had looked upon so many times before. It had been there whenever he raised his head from his nets, or rested on an oar and glanced over his shoulder. It was home.

As he looked spellbound at the unexpected miracle in front of him, the boatswain bellowed to another member of the crew on the bows of the ship – and the spell was broken.

Walter Dunn remembered he was no longer a free fisherman. He was in the rigging of a convict ship heading for a rigorous exile twelve thousand miles away.

The coxswain, at the wheel of *Perseus*, saw Walter Dunn's curving dive into the sea from the rigging. Shouting a warning to the other seamen up aloft, he spun the wheel and put the cumbersome craft into a wide slow turn.

By the time *Perseus* came about and stopped with all sails flapping, there was half a mile of choppy water between the rolling ship and the spot where Walter Dunn had plunged into the sea, and none of the seamen crowding the side of the ship could see him.

As the ship wallowed uncomfortably in the Channel swell, the captain hurried on deck from his cabin. When he was told what had happened, the captain angrily berated the mate who had chosen Walter Dunn to help out with the duties of a seaman. Then, with the Gwineas rocks only a few hundred yards distant, the captain ordered the coxswain to turn the ship to catch the wind and resume course for Falmouth.

'But what about the convict? We can't allow him to escape. Shouldn't we put away a boat and search for him?'

'Escape, you say?' The captain looked at his mate scornfully. 'Look again at that sea, mister. It's a full mile to the shore. The tide is on the ebb and there are strong currents around those rocks inshore. I know of no man who could make such a swim. Enter him in the log as "lost at sea", then forget all about him. A dead convict need be of no concern to anyone.'

* * *

Six days after *Perseus* sailed into Falmouth harbour, two men were walking on lonely Porthluney Beach, not three miles from Mevagissey, when they saw a body floating face downwards in the surf at the edge of the sand. Wading into the water they pulled the body ashore and searched through its clothing in search of something of value. There was nothing.

One of the men was in favour of leaving the body where it lay, but his companion's Christian compassion prevailed. Borrowing two spades from the gatekeeper at the nearby Caerhayes estate, they buried the unidentified body in a shallow grave in the sand of the foreshore.

Neither man recognised the strange garb worn by the dead man as a convict's uniform. Nor did they recognise Walter Dunn, although both men had regularly attended his reform meetings in the past. The year in the convict-hulk had left his face sunken and lined, aging Walter beyond his years.

The anonymous and unmarked grave on the foreshore was one Walter might well have chosen for himself. All about him the waters he had fished for so many years whispered through the sand to him and renewed the seaweed garlands on his grave each day. For his headstone, he had a tall Cornish cliff, carved by God himself.

Walter Dunn had come home to Cornwall, and he was at peace.

Chapter Twenty-Seven

Ben returned to Mevagissey on 8 May 1822. He arrived during the afternoon of one of the busiest days the fishing-village had known for many years. A huge and unseasonable shoal of pilchards had been sighted in the bay that morning and every boat that would float had put out to net them. The fish were brought ashore in tens of thousands and the fisherwomen worked non-stop in the fish-cellars, salting and stacking the fish and making preparations to extract the valuable oil.

As Ben came down the hill towards the village he saw hundreds of gulls, wheeling and shrieking noisily above the teeming harbour.

Martha Retallick was at work in the Dunn fish-cellar with the wives of Billy and Mark, and a number of other women. They and numerous children were all elbow deep in pilchards. Martha Retallick was chattering and laughing as she worked, as excited as anyone at the good fortune that had come to Mevagissey.

Ben stood in the wide doorway of the fish-cellar for some

minutes, and every fisherwoman there saw him before his mother. It was their sudden silence that finally made her look up and seek its cause.

The smile froze on her face when she saw Ben. For long unbelieving moments she looked at him as though she were seeing a ghost. He had been gone for two years, and many times she had doubted if she would ever see him again. Now he was standing here before her.

Of a sudden, she swayed towards the woman standing beside her. Thinking Martha Retallick was about to faint, the other woman reached out a hand to support her.

As suddenly as it had left, the blood rushed back to Martha Retallick's face and she ran across the room to Ben's arms and burst into tears. For many minutes she could only sob uncontrollably in a show of emotion such as Ben had never before seen from her, not even at the time of his father's death. He held her tightly to him while the other women looked on sympathetically.

When Martha Retallick had regained some of her composure, Ben led her away from the fish-cellar to Grandma Dunn's house. Along the way she apologised for the way in which she was behaving.

'It was looking up and seeing you just standing there watching me, Ben. I never had time to prepare myself.'

She began crying softly again, and Ben's arm tightened about her shoulders. Outside the door of Grandma Dunn's house, Martha Retallick paused. Taking out a handkerchief, she blew her nose noisily.

Giving Ben a watery smile, she said, 'I'm weeping like a foolish young girl . . . but you have only yourself to blame. You went from here believing you'd killed Reuben Holyoak, and I thought you must have fled the country. Until that preacher friend of yours came calling, I never expected to see you again. You should have let me know what you were doing . . .'

Ben's surprise at her admonition was genuine. 'I sent as much news as I dared . . . with two men. The first was a miner who left the Tamar valley for Pentuan. The other was a sea-faring man on his way from Plymouth to join a ship at Falmouth. I gave him half a week's pay to call here. I told him if he couldn't find you he should call at Pengrugla. I felt sure Jesse would pass on a message – whatever her situation.'

Ben hesitated, reluctant to ask the question that was burning a hole in his tongue. He searched for words that would not betray his eagerness. 'Is Jesse . . . is she keeping well?'

'She was well enough when I last saw her. But if your message was left at Pengrugla it's not surprising it never reached me. There's no one there with any time for the Retallicks – or for any one else but Reuben Holyoak himself.'

'Jesse didn't marry Reuben Holyoak?'

An overwhelming sense of relief flooded over Ben. He had tried not to build up any hopes after receiving Wrightwick Robert's news. Now he felt ridiculously happy.

'Marry Reuben Holyoak?' Martha Retallick snorted her ridicule. 'Jesse wouldn't marry him if he were the last man left alive in England. No, Reuben Holyoak was as responsible as anyone for the death of her mother . . .'

She saw that Ben knew nothing of Maude Henna's death. 'You'd better come inside, Ben. There is a whole lot of news you should be given – and by the look of you a good meal inside your belly won't come amiss.'

Inside the house, Ben had to submit to the combined fussing of his mother and Grandma Dunn, while his grandfather fired questions at him whenever the two women paused to draw breath.

Not until he was sitting down at the kitchen table with a

heaped plate in front of him could Ben satisfy his own thirst for knowledge.

'What did Jesse say when you gave her Wrightwick's news – that I was alive and well, and in Cornwall?'

This was the question Martha Retallick had known would come – and for which she had no answer. She had seen little of Jesse in recent months. The Dunn family resented Jesse's interference in the matter of Walter's arrest and trial. They would not be convinced that Jesse had done anything but harm in asking Eulaliah Vincent for assistance. Consequently, Jesse had been made less than welcome whenever she called at the house to see Martha Retallick. It was hardly surprising that Jesse soon stopped coming. Martha Retallick *had* intended going to Pentuan to see the girl, but she had not.

'Jesse doesn't know.'

Ben looked at his mother sharply and waited for her to explain. He would have expected her to be eager to pass on the good news to Jesse.

It was Grandma Dunn who made any explanation unnecessary.

'I don't want to hear that girl's name in this house, thank you! The Dunn family has little to thank her for, and our Walter in particular. He might be here now but for her interference. After all he did for her when she was living under this roof, too . . .'

'Where is Jesse now?' Ben interrupted Grandma Dunn's tirade.

'I don't know,' Martha Retallick admitted unhappily. 'When I last met her she was talking of leaving.'

Ben lowered his knife to the plate slowly. 'Leaving? Where would she go? What did she intend doing?'

'She spoke of finding work on a farm. After you left she went to work at the Happy Union stream-works, thinking to hear news of you there. But none ever came. I think she has given up hope of finding you. She waited long enough for you, Ben, I can vouch for that. It wasn't for the want of suitors, either. Our Walter wanted to marry her, for one.'

'Huh! A lot of good it did him,' snorted Grandma Dunn.

Ben ignored her. There were so many things he needed to know. Most would have to wait for now.

'Where has Jesse been living?'

'At Pentuan, with Captain Ustick and his wife. I doubt if she's still there, Ben.'

'I will need to find out before I do, or hear, any more.'

Ben pushed back his chair and stood up from the table.

'But you have only just arrived home. We have so much to talk about . . .'

Ben had a moment of conscience when he saw his mother's distress, but if he stayed here listening to Grandma Dunn's remarks there would be an argument to upset her even more.

'I won't settle until I learn something of Jesse. I'll be back later this evening. We'll talk then.'

When Ben arrived at the Usticks' home he was let into the house by Fanny Ustick. The big mine captain, newly home from the stream-workings, sat in a chair by the kitchen fire, baby Nathaniel cradled in his massive arms. This was a much gentler Loveday Ustick than Ben remembered. Marriage and the birth of his child had mellowed him.

His first words when he saw Ben were: 'You've grown some, boy. You only need a paunch and you'll pass for Loveday Ustick on a dark night.'

It was a blatant exaggeration, but it was the big mine captain's way of acknowledging that Ben had become a man. The good humour of Fanny and Loveday Ustick quickly changed to distress when they learned that Ben had come looking for Jesse. Fanny in particular was most upset.

'Seeing you're here so soon after she left us, I felt sure you were coming with good news. She waited so long for you Ben. She questioned every miner who passed through the Happy Union, in the hope that they might have met with you. Once she met a man who had seen you at the Luscombe mine. I wrote to the captain asking after you, and for weeks Jesse waited for a reply, but we heard nothing.'

'The captain of the Luscombe mine was killed along with five of his men only three months after I left. The boiler burst at the change of shift. The mine was closed down shortly afterwards.'

'We didn't know that.' Fanny Ustick made a helpless gesture with her hands. 'Oh, Ben! If only you had returned three days earlier.'

'There are many things I *should* have done,' said Ben bitterly. 'But I'm not going to spend the rest of my life regretting what *might* have been. I intend finding Jesse as quickly as I can and marrying her. Do you know where she might have gone?'

'No – only that she and Judy were taking the Truro road . . .' Fanny Ustick explained about Judy Lean.

'I'll head for Truro at sunrise,' declared Ben. 'I need to make up for two wasted years – if Jesse will have me.'

Fanny Ustick looked at the determined young man standing before her.

'She'll have you, Ben Retallick. Of that I am quite sure.'

'Bring Jesse back here when you catch up with her, Ben,' said Loveday Ustick. 'Without her I doubt whether my son would be alive to bring me such pleasure today. There is a home for both of you here – and work at the Happy Union should you have need of it.'

Loveday Ustick reached out his hand, trying not to disturb the contented baby sleeping in his arms. 'We wish you luck, Ben. Our prayers go with you.'

Ben left the house warmed by the sincerity of the Usticks and envious of the happiness they had found together.

That night, Ben and his mother sat up until very late, doing their best to fill in the details of the two-year gap in their lives.

Despite his late night, Ben left the house when dawn was no more than a faint glimmer in the east. He had little idea of where he was going, but he headed for Truro because that was the way Jesse had gone.

The sun rose slowly, reluctant to throw off the pale-grey mist that spread inland from the sea, but once it had broken through it held out the promise of a fine warm day.

Ben trudged along high-banked lanes, occasionally stumbling over a hard-baked ridge of earth that only a few weeks before had been buried beneath inches of snow. When he reached the top of a long hill, Ben paused to look about him and ponder on the task he had set himself. Cornwall was a vast patchwork of tiny farms, many of them tucked away in hollows and valleys, unseen from the road. Jesse might have found work on any one of them.

The narrow twisting lane joined the turnpike road to Truro two miles farther on. Ben had intended resting here for a while, but he found, much to his annoyance, that a young man was already there, seated on the rough-hewn granite milestone.

As Ben approached, the young man turned his face towards him and reached down for a fiddle that leaned against the milestone. Tucking the instrument beneath his chin, he drew from it the first bars of a jig, then paused to call to Ben.

'A tune for you, young sir? One to set your feet dancing along the King's highway?'

Ben was feeling hot and irritable, annoyed that this itinerant fiddler had deprived him of the rest he had been anticipating for the last couple of miles. He made no reply.

Before Ben had taken many more paces, the fiddler struck up a solemn dirge and called after him, 'Since the sun and a merry tune have failed to cheer you, I offer a tune to match your thoughts. It will make the miles seem longer, but for a man who wallows in his own misery the road is already overly long. Give me twopence, my fine young friend, and I will sing you words to match my music.'

Scowling, Ben would have gone on his way without speaking had he not noticed the ashes of a fire set back against the hedgerow. Around it were scattered the balladeer's belongings.

Ben stopped and called, 'Are you often at this spot?'

'Often? No, young sir. I have never been here before. However, I arrived here a week ago and have not left since then. Is that the answer you seek?'

'Then you'll have seen everyone who passed this way during that week?' Ben put the question eagerly.

'Alas, no!' the balladeer smiled sadly, 'I have seen nothing since Napoleon's case-shot took my sight at Waterloo. However, my ears have learned to work doubly hard. They tell me now that you are anxiously seeking someone. From the manner of your asking, it can only be a lady. Your wife, perhaps?'

'No . . . but she will be as soon as I find her. We've been parted for a very long time. I returned yesterday only to learn that she had left three days ago.'

'Three days since was fair-day at Grampound. Many young girls passed this way. Some stopped to listen to a tune . . . a few did not. Would she have been travelling alone?'

'No, she has another girl with her.'

'Ah! Then things are not as hopeless as they at first seemed. Many young girls passed by, riding on farm-wagons, or walking in large groups chiding the young men who walked close on their heels. But only two pairs of women came by that day.

The first were early and heavily laden. Farm-women, carrying produce to market. Then, when the sun stood where it is now, two young girls came along. By their step I would put their ages at twenty years, or perhaps a year younger. I remember them well because their walks were so dissimilar. One girl was light on her feet, alert to everything about her. The other was slow of thought and of movement . . . but a kindly girl, for all that. It was she who placed a penny in my hand and thanked me for the tune I played her. Yes, she was a kind girl with a pleasant voice . . . and one who has known much unhappiness, unless I am mistaken.'

The balladeer's description exactly fitted that given Ben of Judy Lean.

'Did they say where they were going? Anything at all that might help me to find them?'

'Nothing at all, young sir – but will you set aside your quest for a few minutes and gather enough twigs for a fire to boil a kettle? I believe I still have a pinch of tea in my bundle.'

'I can do better than that. I have a pie, and some good French brandy to wash it down.'

'God bless you, young sir! You offer me a feast. Accept the hand of Alan Colborne in friendship. You have a name?'

The introductions over, the two men settled down to eat. Alan Colborne ate ravenously. It was evident that balladeering in Cornwall had not kept him well fed.

When they had consumed more than half of the food Martha Retallick had confidently expected to last her son for three days, Alan Colborne leaned back against the grassy roadside bank and savoured the night-traded brandy. It had been a present to Ben from Grandfather Dunn. The balladeer sighed in deep contentment.

'It was a happy chance that brought you my way today, Ben. Tell me, why are you out scouring the countryside for your lady love instead of wedding her in some cool and peaceful village church?'

Warming to the brandy and Alan Colborne's easy companionship, Ben gave the balladeer an outline of the events of the past two years.

By the time he had finished talking he had Alan Colborne's rapt attention, the brandy temporarily forgotten on the ground between them.

'Upon my life, Ben! From such tales as this were the songs of the minstrels of old composed. If I don't make a song of it myself, I do not deserve to call myself a balladeer. But such a quest as yours is not going to be easy.'

Ben's shrug was wasted on the blind man. 'Perhaps not, but by asking at farms and in villages I'll find Jesse one day.'

'You need help, my friend – and you have it! I'll come with you. Between us we will find her. You have my word.'

Ben was not certain he wanted Alan Colborne's company. Guiding a blind man through the narrow lanes of the county would inevitably slow him down. He saw no way in which Alan Colborne could help the search for Jesse.

Alan Colborne spoke as though Ben had voiced his thoughts aloud.

'You doubt my ability to help, Ben? Then listen to me carefully. When did you last see Jesse? Two years ago? Is your memory of her so clear that you could instantly recognise her in the middle of a crowd? No, of course it's not – but mine is! She called out a "Good day!" to me and I heard her speaking in conversation with her friend. I could distinguish her voice from the babble of a hundred others. Then there is her companion – Judy, I believe you said was her name. You would not know her if she stood before you. I certainly would. I know her voice, her walk – even the sweet smell of her hair. I would recognise her if she passed by on the darkest night.'

Alan Colborne paused to take a sip of brandy. 'Such means of recognition may be essential, Ben. Farmers are not doing well at the moment; they will delay taking on workers for as long as possible – until grass-cutting time, perhaps. Your Jesse must attend hiring-fairs, trusting her looks and manners will raise her above the others who seek work. The hiring-fairs are packed with young men and girls, but it is there we must look for her, Ben. Be it Grampound, Truro, Wadebridge – or any one of a dozen other fairs.'

Ben looked at Alan Colborne with a new respect. 'Can you really pick out a single voice from the din of a crowd?'

'That, and much more beside. For instance, I can tell you that approaching us from the direction of St Austell is a gentleman's light carriage.' Alan Colborne paused briefly. 'What's more, it is being pulled by a pair of well-matched horses.'

Ben listened, but could hear nothing. Not until the light open carriage rounded a bend half a minute later did the sounds from it reach Ben's own ears. As Alan Colborne had stated, it was pulled by two high-stepping horses.

'I'll be pleased to have your company, Alan Colborne – if you are quite certain you have nothing else to do.'

The balladeer smiled ruefully. 'I have sat upon this mile-stone growing ever thinner for a full week, and my enquiring fingers have told me we are but nine miles from Truro Town. On the way we pass through Probus, where there is a small fair today. There I will have the opportunity to earn a shilling or two and return your generosity, while you search for Jesse.'

Feeling about him on the ground, Alan Colborne located his scattered belongings and began tying them in a bundle, talking all the while.

'We must waste no time, Ben. If we step out, we can reach Probus in time for the evening's frolics. Tomorrow we will see the fair out and move on to St Columb and Wadebridge and a few other villages, returning to Truro for the big fair in two weeks' time. I have friends in all those places. We *will* find Jesse, Ben. Be assured of that.'

Already, Ben felt better for having met up with the blind balladeer. Finding Jesse would be only a matter of days – perhaps only hours!

By the time the two men reached Probus the serious business of the fair was over. A few men and girls who had been unsuccessful in hiring themselves out still wandered disconsolately about the fair, but Jesse and Judy Lean were not among their number. After asking a few questions, it was clear they had never been there.

Alan Colborne told Ben he must not be disappointed at this first failure. This was one of the smallest fairs in the county, not known to many outside the immediate area.

But, if trading and hiring had ended for the day, the fun was only just beginning. More than a hundred young people were gathered to enjoy such diverse entertainments as juggling, badger-baiting and Cornish wrestling.

Alan Colborne asked Ben to lead him to a quiet spot where he had an open space for a crowd to gather. When Ben found a suitable place, Alan Colborne leaned against a wall, drew the bow across the strings of his fiddle and began to play and sing a tuneful ballad. He had a clear melodic voice, and it was not long before he had wooed many people from the other attractions. When he ended his song, the crowd applauded loudly and called for more.

As coins were flung on the kerchief spread on the ground before Alan Colborne, Ben left him to his work. His audience would not allow him to move from the spot for an hour or two.

Ben wandered about the village for a while. Outside of the fair there was little to interest him. When he saw an ale-house he went inside for a drink.

Before the drink arrived, a frightening din broke out above Ben's head. The ceiling trembled and shook, and clouds of dust drifted down among the customers of the ale-house. Placing a tankard of ale in front of Ben, the landlord smiled at his apprehension. 'Don't you worry, sir. It's only some of they ranters at a meeting upstairs. They don't approve of the goings-on in Probus on fair-day. They're up there telling the Lord of their disapproval.'

The 'ranters' – also known as 'Bryanites' – to whom the landlord had referred, were a Methodist sect which had recently excited some interest by using young women as preachers. Led by a local man, the 'ranters' were notoriously noisy in their particular form of worship.

They were certainly in good voice this night. Their shouts of 'Hallelujah!' and the stamping of their feet made conversation in the ale-house impossible. Before long the dust from the trembling beams and joists formed a choking cloud in the tap-room.

Ben found the noise and the dust intolerable and carried his drink to one of the benches outside the inn door. It was fortunate that most of the other drinkers had already done the same. Ben had just set down his tankard when there was a sudden alarming splintering of timbers. With a mighty crash, the floor of the upstairs room collapsed into the tap-room. The joyous shouts of the 'ranters' quickly changed to screams of terror as they were pitched down through the floor together with tumbling beams, floorboards and fellow-worshippers.

The din attracted a great many revellers from the fair. As each 'ranter' staggered through the doorway, blue serge suit or best Sunday dress torn and covered in dust and plaster, he or she was greeted with ribald howls of derision.

Above the hilarity of the crowd, Ben could hear cries of pain coming from within the collapsed interior of the ale-house.

Calling on a couple of men to follow him, he went back inside. On his way he pushed aside a screaming woman and an equally hysterical man blocking the doorway.

The late-evening light was barely strong enough to penetrate the choking dust inside the building, but it was sufficient for Ben to appreciate the extent of the devastation. Wooden joists had snapped off where they slotted into the damp west wall of the ale-house. Half the floor had fallen into the tap-room; the remainder was hanging down at a crazy angle.

The cries Ben had heard came from a tangle of wood and masonry at the back of the room, and he and his helpers made their way there. A number of men and women were trapped beneath a pile of rubble. As they were dug out each of them was able to stagger to the door. Only one man was seriously hurt; he had suffered a badly broken arm. It hung painfully by his side as Ben helped him out to the street and sat him down on one of the benches.

The crowd of onlookers, disappointed that no one had been killed, or noticeably mangled, soon drifted back to the amusements of the fair. Ben ripped the shirt from the arm of the man who had been the last to be rescued. The break was serious, with white bone protruding through the skin. There was nothing Ben could do to help the man. He needed the attentions of a surgeon. When Ben called for one he was told that a surgeon would have to be brought from Truro.

Ben had seen a great many mine accidents. He was in no doubt that the arm would have to be amputated above the elbow. After expressing his thoughts to the landlord, he suggested that the injured man be kept liberally supplied with strong brandy.

When Ben turned away to go to where he had left Alan Colborne, the injured man called after him. 'Ben! . . . It is Ben Retallick?'

'Yes.' Ben peered at the man's dust-stained face. It was vaguely familiar, but recognition was slow in coming to him. 'You know me?'

'We worked together more than a year since. At the Luscombe mine. My name is Matthew Bolitho.'

This was the man who had worked at the Happy Union mine briefly and had given Jesse the news that Ben had not left the country. Loveday Ustick had told Ben the miner's name.

Ben returned to Matthew Bolitho and clasped his good hand warmly, looking down at him with renewed sympathy. 'I'm sorry to find you in such a sorry state, Matthew. I owe you my gratitude . . . but no mind. What were you doing at a "ranters" meeting? I don't remember you as being a religious man.'

'Today I'm anybody's man, Ben. For a shilling I'll break ore with the maids, and for a free meal I will gladly shout "Allelujah!" with Wesleyan, Protestant, or Papist. I have more breath for praying than for mining, these days. Besides, there was a young girl preaching today. I believe that if a man needs to pray he might as well be looking upon a fair face as on that of a grey-whiskered old man.'

For the first time, Ben noticed the round-shouldered slightness of Matthew Bolitho and saw how the skin was tightly stretched over the bones of his dust-stained face.

'You should have stayed at the Happy Union for a while. Captain Ustick is a good man. He would have kept you on for as long as you were able to hold a shovel.'

Matthew Bolitho's broken left arm was paining him. Unable to disguise his discomfiture, he used his right hand to shift it to a more comfortable position. This done, he leaned back with his eyes closed for so long that Ben thought he had lost consciousness. Then his eyes flickered open, and the pain in them went far deeper than the shattered arm.

It was a look Ben had seen before . . . in his father's eyes.

'I couldn't have stayed at the Happy Union, or anywhere else, Ben. Not for long enough to keep a job. There are too many days when I *can't* hold a shovel. All I can do then is find a hole and crawl inside where no one will find me. One day I'll fail to come out again, I know that. Perhaps I should be thankful I have no one to grieve for me.'

'This is foolish talk, Matthew. If the surgeon hears you, he'll swear the fall has broken your head as well as your arm. You'll feel better when he's tended you.'

Ben hoped he sounded more confident than he felt. In his heart he knew it would not be long before Matthew Bolitho died, unmourned by the world about him. No one cared about a sick and aged miner. Unless he had a family, he rarely remained in one place long enough to qualify for parish relief. He was doomed to spend his useless latter days begging around the mines of Cornwall, an unwanted reminder of the only certain reward to come from underground mining.

Matthew Bolitho was aware of the emptiness of Ben's words.

'When the surgeon has finished with me I'll be good for nothing, Ben. He'll not save this arm.'

The miner gave Ben a weak smile. 'Mind you, it will help me as a beggar. I can claim to be an old soldier who lost an arm in the war with the French.'

Matthew Bolitho gave a short throaty laugh and spat in the dust at his feet. 'Be off with you, Ben. You don't want to be here wasting time on me. You should be down in Falmouth with that girl of yours – the one who asked me about you when I was at the Happy Union. I would have thought you'd have wed her by now. Had her at home looking after your children.'

'You've seen Jesse . . . at Falmouth?'

'If that's her name, I have. Two days ago at Falmouth Fair. She was with another maid. I wished her "Good day", but I could see she hadn't recognised me. Why should she? We met for only a few minutes at Cap'n Ustick's house. I've grown a deal older since then.'

Matthew Bolitho looked very tired. Reaching out his right hand, he gripped Ben's arm. 'You marry her quickly, Ben. Get yourself a family and something worthwhile to live for. Don't end up like me.'

The miner's hand dropped away and he shifted his injured arm yet again.

Ben dropped three bright new guineas into Matthew Bolitho's lap. 'Here, take these. They might be of some help to you. I'll come back and see you when I return from Falmouth.'

Ben hurried away, and Matthew Bolitho called his thanks after him. Although neither man knew it, Ben had just saved the old miner from a pauper's grave.

Chapter Twenty-Eight

Falmouth Fair was much larger than the one at Probus and lasted for a full week. It was the last day of the fair when Ben and Alan Colborne arrived, but the crowds were still big enough to make a search for Jesse difficult. Twice they pushed their way from end to end of the fair. Then Ben made some enquiries of a tall-hatted constable and learned that all the hirings had taken place on the first day of the fair. There had been none since then.

The news came as a great disappointment to Ben. He had believed he would find Jesse here. Now he was more confused than ever. Had Jesse been hired on the first day? Or had she and Judy Lean moved on to some other town? There was, of course, the possibility that Matthew Bolitho had been mistaken. After all, he had met Jesse only once.

Alan Colborne tried to cheer Ben, telling him they had to expect many such disappointments. He repeated his belief that they would find her in the end. Philosophically, he suggested they put their visit to Falmouth to some advantage.

'Find us an inn with a congenial landlord, Ben. One who will offer room and board to a fiddler who knows how to bring in customers. This is a seafarer's town, and there are no more sentimental men than sailors. They are generous, too. Give them a song or two about far-off places and the girls they left behind there and we'll make more money than a week of playing the fairs. I know that is not our reason for being here, Ben, but with full pockets we can search farther and longer than with empty ones.'

Alan Colborne finally settled for a waterfront inn, the Lord Cornwallis. It was named after the old admiral who had once sheltered his fleet in Falmouth harbour during a violent storm, many years before.

Ben had observed before that Alan Colborne had a fine voice. During their evening at the Lord Cornwallis, he learned that the balladeer also had an incredibly wide repertoire. He sang sentimental ballads, stirring songs of brave deeds at sea, and sea-shanties composed to help along such mundane activities as raising an anchor. Alan Colborne knew them all.

Soon, the inn was crowded to over-capacity, the windows rattling to the roar of the singing. Ben was gradually edged into a corner seat. Facing him across a heavy plank table was one of the few unhappy-looking men in the room.

Ben did not join in the singing, because he knew few sea-shanties, but the man across the table thought that Ben disliked singing as much as he did himself. He pulled a face to express his understanding. Afterwards, Ben saw the other man watching him whenever he looked across the table.

'Are you a sailing man?'

The stranger's voice was thick from years of heavy drinking, with an accent that had its origins in East Anglia. Ben shook his head, not eager to make conversation.

'Then what are you doing here in Falmouth Town?'

The stranger banged his tankard down on the table so hard that the dregs shot into the air and speckled his unbearded face.

Ben said nothing. He hoped the angry stranger would get up from the table to refill his tankard. But he was in the company of an experienced drinker. Used to the slow service offered in crowded waterfront taverns, the man facing Ben bought his drinks in pairs. Sliding the empty tankard from him, he reached for its companion.

'I thought this was supposed to be a sailor's town. Sailors . . . ? Ha!'

The snort came when his mouth was only inches from the brimming tankard, and once again the stranger's face was liberally spattered with ale.

'For five days I've been trying to take on hands for a ship as stout as any on the Australian run. So far I haven't found a single one! There's not a seaman here ready to go farther south than Lisbon – and not then unless he has a soft berth on a fast packet. In all my years as a boatswain I've never known anything like it.'

The boatswain sucked in a mouthful of ale and looked speculatively across the table at Ben. 'Are you *sure* you're not a seaman?'

Ben grinned, remembering his brief and inglorious career as a fisherman. 'I'm quite certain.'

The boatswain sighed. 'Then the skipper will have no option but to let some of the convicts up out of the hold to help again. If he doesn't, we'll be anchored in the harbour until most of them have served out their time.'

'Convicts? You've got a shipload of convicts out there in the harbour?'

'Shh! Not so loud, lad. Folk around here would get a mite fidgety if they knew there was a cargo of felons anchored not two hundred yards from their town. They think we'll let them jump over the side during the night and come ashore to murder every one of them in their beds.'

The boatswain wiped ale from his chin. 'I've been on transports for more years than I care to recall, and the only convicts I've seen go over the side are dead ones.'

The boatswain frowned suddenly. 'Until that young fool jumped overboard last Sunday. I still think the skipper should have searched until we found him. For my money he's sitting in front of his own hearth in Mevagissey at this very moment, laughing at us for being as simple as we thought he was. He was no more drowned than I am – and I don't like no convict making a fool of me.'

Ben's interest quickened at the mention of Mevagissey. He was remembering the late-night conversation with his mother the night he arrived there. She had said a great deal about Walter.

'Mevagissey, you say? I have family there. What's the name of this convict?'

'Dunn – though what his first name is I don't know.' The sailor saw the shock on Ben's face. 'You know him?'

Ben nodded. It was a few minutes before he trusted himself to speak. Pushing away his half-finished drink, he rose to his feet. 'Yes, I know Walter Dunn. At least, I did. It seems a great many years ago now.'

As Ben pushed his way through the noisy crowd in the Lord Cornwallis, the boatswain called after him.

'If you see Dunn, you tell him he didn't fool me. I know he's alive.'

Ben knew different. He had left the Dunn house in Mevagissey only thirty-six hours ago. That was four days after Walter had dived over the side of the convict-transport.

Only a dead man would have delayed his homecoming for that long.

* * *

From Falmouth, Ben and Alan Colborne went to the market at nearby Penryn . . . and then they moved on. St Columb, Wadebridge, Bodmin . . . and many small village markets along the way. Finally, they turned their footsteps towards Truro.

It was two weeks since Ben had left his mother at Mevagissey. He now knew how difficult was his self-appointed task. Over the years every market in the country had become a hiring-place for labour. It was carried out on an informal and casual basis. Men and women seeking work would gather in a self-conscious but conspicuous group, close to the ring where the cattle were gathered for sale. The farmers spent much of their time here and had the opportunity to eye prospective employees for as long as they wished. It took only a few words to assure themselves that the man or woman had the experience the farmer needed, and a nod of the head concluded the arrangement.

Only rarely were references offered or asked for. If a hireling proved unsuitable, he or she would be dismissed without notice and a new worker taken on next market-day. There was a considerable army of work-seekers among farm-workers in the county, and Ben saw the same faces at market after market.

On their way back to Truro, Ben stopped at Probus to enquire after Matthew Bolitho. The repairs to the inside of the inn had already been completed, and when Ben spoke to the busy landlord it was a moment or two before the inn-keeper could even bring the injured man to mind.

'Oh! You mean the man who had his arm taken off? Yes, I remember you now, sir. You'd met him before, I believe. Very sad it was. He died while the surgeon was taking off his arm. His breathing was bad, I heard it said. Spent too long working in a mine. Never do know when they are too old to go underground, these miners. Here, have a drink on me, sir – and, if your friend can play that fiddle he has tucked beneath his arm, you are both welcome to as much ale as you can sup.'

Alan Colborne played well that evening, but Ben drank the free ale in a dejected silence. The news of Matthew Bolitho's death, coming as it did after days spent fruitlessly searching for Jesse, depressed him greatly. There had been much about the miner and his illness to remind Ben of his father.

The next morning Ben and Alan Colborne walked into Truro. It was not much of a town, being little larger than Mevagissey, and a whole lot smaller than Bodmin, or the sprawling mining-towns farther west. Yet Truro was a town of which its inhabitants were inordinately proud. Well laid out, and with many fine buildings, its residents boasted that it was the finest in the county. It could do no less than have the greatest fair.

The fair was held in the wide central street, but was so well subscribed that it overflowed into every adjoining lane and alleyway. The crowds were thick in every direction, and Ben felt quite sure the whole of the county must be here.

It was difficult for Alan Colborne to make his way through the densely packed streets. The fair-goers neither knew nor cared that he was blind, so intent were they on their own pleasures.

Eventually Ben found a quiet spot for Alan Colborne, close to the river. Here he sat down with his back to a tree and began to play. When Ben looked back at him before plunging into the mêlée once more, Alan Colborne was already beginning to attract an appreciative crowd of his own.

All that day Ben walked the streets of Truro. He found the place where the young men and girls were offering themselves for hire, but quickly learned that this was not primarily a hiring-fair for farm-workers. Those here were not seeking farm work. They were hoping to be hired as servants in the households of the county gentry, Truro being the centre of Cornwall's society.

By the time dusk fell, Ben had almost seen enough of Truro Fair. Constantly jostled by the huge crowd, carried along with them from one entertainment to the next, he would have liked to leave the overcrowded town behind him. Twice he went to the place where he had left Alan Colborne, but each time he was told by the balladeer that he was not yet ready to leave.

'Give me another hour, Ben,' Alan Colborne pleaded on the last occasion, his face glistening from his musical exertions. Showing Ben the weighty bag of coins tucked beneath his coat, he added, 'I have never known a day like this. Another hour and we'll have enough money to keep us searching for Jesse for a full month. The warm weather and the joys of Truro Fair have turned the heads of your fellow-Cornishmen. They are throwing coins into my hat as though it were a wishing-well.'

Driven from Alan Colborne's riverside concert by the clamour of his audience calling for their favourite ballads, Ben wandered along the still-crowded streets. For twenty minutes he watched two heavily perspiring men wrestling. Stripped to the waist, they grappled and slipped, gouged and swore, while a man with a rasping voice called the crowd's attention to the bout that was to decide who was the 'Champion of Cornwall'. As Ben had seen the same men fighting on at least three occasions that day, it appeared to be a long-disputed title.

Farther along the same road, Ben stopped to listen to a barker inviting the passing crowd to a show in a nearby hall. It was, he shouted, 'The most incredible exhibition to be seen anywhere in the world. Inside, ladies and gentlemen, you will see the *amazing* Monsieur Chabert and his sister, Mademoiselle Chabert, only recently arrived from far-away Russia. Before your eyes they will drink boiling oils and lead, eat flaming torches and perform other, equally impossible feats.'

The barker further declared that the *amazing* Monsieur Chabert could actually remain inside an oven with a joint of meat until it was wholly cooked. Unfortunately for the populace of Truro, it had been impossible to obtain an oven of sufficient size to accommodate him here, in the west of England.

Ben had passed the hall where the show was being held before. On each occasion he had been intrigued by the smoke pouring from the open windows, adding considerable weight to the claims of the promoter. Acting on an impulse, Ben fished in his pocket for the threepence entry-fee and passed into the building.

Many late visitors to the fair shared Ben's curiosity. The hall was well-filled. At the far end of the room curtains separated stage from audience. They were half-drawn, giving the audience a tantalising glimpse of a stage and the many wonders to be seen there.

It was like peeping into Dante's kitchen. Great iron cauldrons sat upon charcoal burners, sending steam swirling about the stage. On a long wooden table were laid out a variety of partly burned torches. Occupying the centre of the stage was a frame made up of thin metal. About six feet square, it had shackles for securing a man's arms and legs. Tied all around the frame were a wide variety of fireworks.

Very soon the hall was filled to capacity and the doors were locked by the barker. This loud-voiced showman appeared to be the only other member of the Chaberts' entourage. He attracted the crowd, took their money, and was now busily preparing the show.

Some minutes later the two stars of the show appeared and the performance began.

Monsieur Chabert was a small bald-headed man with a pointed beard and thin waxed moustache. With many flourishes he sampled the contents of the various cauldrons, grimacing painfully as he held 'boiling oil' and 'hot wax' in his mouth. Then he took a sip from the cauldron of 'molten lead'. After rolling it around on his tongue, he drew from his mouth a piece of solid lead, the size of a musket-ball. Upon completion of this 'amazing' feat, a few of Monsieur Chabert's watchers gasped in astonishment. Others laughed derisively.

The plump Mademoiselle Chabert was a little more impressive, biting off the ends of large flaming torches to extinguish them. Smaller torches were dealt with in an even more contemptuous manner. Mademoiselle Chabert devoured them entirely and earned the applause of the whole audience.

Then it was time for the grand finale of the show.

Striding pompously to the centre of the stage, Monsieur Chabert stepped upon the firework-adorned frame. Adopting a dramatic pose, he allowed himself to be secured to the frame with chains and ropes.

For the first time, Ben noticed that the frame was designed to revolve. With her brother firmly secured, Mademoiselle Chabert gave the wheel a couple of slow, practice revolutions.

Satisfied the apparatus was in working order, Mademoiselle Chabert took a blazing torch from the indispensable barker and ran it around the edge of the frame. The fireworks ignited haphazardly and commenced spitting smoke and flames, whereupon she gripped the frame and spun it with a great deal more vigour than expertise.

The results were spectacular beyond all expectations. A great deal of sulphur had gone into the manufacture of the fireworks and thick pungent yellow smoke belched from them. It was sufficient to overcome the most hostile of audiences. On this occasion, the fireworks did far more. Those on one outside edge of the revolving frame had been secured carelessly and a number of them broke loose.

As the frame revolved the fireworks were flung everywhere, but it was some time before the broadly smiling Mademoiselle Chabert realised the shouts and screams were not the reactions of an unusually appreciative audience. By the time she was able to bring the whirling frame to a halt, flames were climbing high up the colourful curtains and licking at the wooden ceiling of the hall.

With commendable presence of mind, Mademoiselle Chabert raised a cauldron of 'boiling oil' from a charcoal burner and threw its contents over one of the curtains. Most of the lower flames were immediately extinguished, but the flames higher up the curtain were not affected.

While she stood back wondering what to do next, the screams of her brother joined those of the crowd. The oaths he shrieked were no more foreign than those of a Cornish miner. In stopping the wheel, Mademoiselle Chabert had left a broken string of fireworks dangling against the star of the act and his clothing had caught alight.

By now choking smoke filled the whole room, and as pieces of burning curtain and ceiling began to fall among them the audience panicked and surged towards the entrance. They hammered futilely against the locked door, and someone smashed one of the two small windows and screamed for help from outside.

Ben fought his way to the door and, with the help of another man, kicked at it until the lock gave way and the doors crashed open.

Ben stood back, his eyes smarting, as the audience scrambled into the street outside. It did not escape his notice that the still smouldering 'Monsieur Chabert' and his 'sister' were by no means the last to leave the hall.

By the time the last of the audience had fled to safety, the roof of the building was well alight, the flames from it leaping high above the roofs of the town houses.

Ben was the last to leave, but when he stumbled outside into the street his choking was as much from mirth as from the acrid smoke he had breathed into his lungs. It had been a truly memorable show. Ben could not remember when he had ever received better value for his money.

Once clear of the building, he paused to look at the huge crowd that had gathered to view the fire. In the distance the town's fire-bell clanged noisily. Ben knew there would be no shortage of helpers when the engine arrived at the fire and already he was relishing the thought of telling Alan Colborne of the Chaberts' extraordinary performance.

As the crowd closed in about him, Ben heard a shrill voice raised above the hubbub. It called his name.

'Ben! Ben Retallick!' It was a frantic, almost hysterical cry as the owner of the voice fought desperately against the crowd to reach him. Ben turned in stunned disbelief. Then he, too, was fighting the crowd.

Moments later he reached out his arms – and Jesse stumbled into them.

Chapter Twenty-Nine

When the initial shock of the long-anticipated reunion had passed, Ben held Jesse at arm's length from him and they both spoke at once.

'What are you doing—?'

'How did you—?'

They laughed together until a sudden unwonted shyness overcame them. When Ben had left Jesse, two years before, there had still been a girlish ungainliness about her. Now he looked at her and saw a very beautiful young woman. Only the sudden trembling of her lower lip gave Ben a hint of the turmoil inside her. As his arms dropped away from her, she took hold of one of his hands and gripped it fiercely.

'Tell me you are real, Ben. Tell me I won't wake in a few minutes and find I've been dreaming.'

'I'm real, Jesse. I arrived at Mevagissey only three days after you left. I've been searching for you ever since.'

As Ben was talking, he became aware of another girl who had moved up to stand silently behind Jesse. Seeing the direction of his glance, Jesse introduced Judy Lean.

Ben was reminded that he, too, had a friend. Quickly explaining about Alan Colborne, he led Jesse and Judy Lean away from the fiercely burning hall to the ill-lit clearing beside the river. On the way he crushed Jesse's hand in his, afraid that even now she might slip away from him.

Alan Colborne was alone, patiently playing a soft air on his fiddle. In the cover of the trees and bushes beyond the clearing, those courting couples who had not left to look at the fire took full advantage of the darkness and Alan Colborne's romantic music.

As they approached, the music died away. Ben, who had come to know the blind fiddler's mannerisms well, knew he was listening intently. When they were still a few paces from him, Alan Colborne's face lit up in a delighted smile. 'Congratulations, Ben! Your quest is ended. Jesse, Judy, I am delighted to meet you.'

When the introductions and explanations were over, Ben asked Jesse where she and Judy Lean were staying.

Jesse looked nonplussed. 'I haven't had time to think about it. Until this evening Judy and I were working on a farm not more than a mile from here. We took work there while the farmer's wife was a-bed, having a baby. The farmer employed the two of us for the wages of one, but he begrudged us the food we ate. His wife had the baby only a week ago, but this morning he had her out of bed milking the cows before she fed the baby. I feel sorry for her.'

'It's a *lovely* baby,' declared Judy Lean wistfully. 'She deserves a better father.'

These were the first words Ben had heard Judy Lean utter. He did not miss the gentle smile Jesse gave her as she explained, 'Judy is a stout defender of the weak and helpless. She adores all babies.'

'If I don't soon get some food inside me, I will be one

of the world's weak and helpless myself,' complained Alan Colborne. 'Judy, take my arm. We are going to a quiet little inn owned by a friend of mine. There we will celebrate the reunion of Ben and Jesse and raise a glass or two for the ending of two years of loneliness and misunderstanding.'

The White Swan Inn was by no means as quiet as Alan Colborne had predicted, but after greeting Alan Colborne with great delight the landlord led them all to a small private room. Here they would be able to eat in comfort.

When Alan Colborne told the landlord that they had not yet arranged accommodation for the night, he promised there would be two rooms available by the time they finished eating. Two travellers would be turned out of their room to make way for Ben and Alan Colborne. Jesse and Judy Lean could share a room with the landlord's two daughters.

When Ben expressed his gratitude, the landlord brushed them aside.

'I have no need of thanks for doing something for Alan Colborne. But for him I wouldn't be here serving you today. Neither would I be enjoying as fine a life as any man I know. Not seven years ago I was lying sorely wounded on the hillside at Waterloo, with my company cut to ribbons and the French still firing at me. I had given up all hope when Alan came out of the smoke and din of battle to my rescue. He slung me across his shoulders and carried me back to our own lines. When he put me down he took no more than ten paces towards the battle when over came a French shell. It exploded, and Alan staggered back with blood pouring from his face. He hasn't seen a thing since that day. He gave his sight for me, and I owe him my life. In my opinion, Alan Colborne is one of the true heroes of Waterloo.'

'Only old men remember past battles,' joked Alan Colborne. 'Waterloo is now no more than a name. Even the songs that were written about the battle are forgotten – but the songs I sang today were well received.'

He pulled a heavy bag of coins from beneath his coat and handed it to the landlord. 'Will you take these and exchange them for gold coins to tuck inside my belt? And a bottle of your best brandy, if you please. We are going to have a party.'

The four sat down to the finest meal Ben had ever enjoyed, although, seated across the table from Jesse, he found it difficult to keep his mind on food. She was undoubtedly far more beautiful than he remembered. He could hardly believe his good fortune that she had waited so long for him.

Ben and Jesse had little opportunity to discuss personal matters during the meal. Alan Colborne was at his charming and amusing best, and as the brandy brought a ruddy glow to Judy Lean's cheeks she forgot her natural shyness.

Later in the evening they became aware of raised voices in the main bar of the inn. When the hot and harassed landlord looked in upon them, he apologised for the din. It was, he explained, a meeting of the local parliamentary reform committee.

Ben was taken by surprise by Jesse's immediate interest.

'I thought the reform movement was dead in Cornwall,' she commented.

Mopping his brow, the landlord said, 'I wish it were. It went quiet for a while, but since Robert Peel took over the Home Office many of the measures taken against the reformers have been relaxed. They are up to their old tricks again.'

'You mean they are *talking* loudly again,' retorted Jesse scornfully. 'There's not a man among them with the courage to do more.'

'You are more knowledgeable about reform affairs than you were the day we went to the Crinnis mine,' said Ben, his curiosity aroused. 'I seem to remember that you couldn't leave the meeting fast enough.'

'That was before I experienced the need for reform and had Walter Dunn to explain it to me,' replied Jesse. 'No man has done more for reform in Cornwall than Walter. He lived for reform. Perhaps one day he'll be given the justice he deserves.'

Ben was reminded of his conversation with the boatswain of the *Perseus*. Walter had not only lived for reform – he had *died* for it. There would be no justice for Walter Dunn now. But Ben said nothing to Jesse. Grandma Dunn had accused her of being responsible for Walter's transportation. Ben did not want her to feel she was in any way to blame for his death.

When the noise from the reformers showed no sign of abating, Ben suggested to Jesse that they take a walk outside, and she agreed.

Once outside, Jesse took his arm quite naturally. Ben was so absurdly pleased he wished it was daylight, wanting those who passed by to see the beauty of the girl who clung to his arm.

But the darkness had its own compensations. They walked through the town until they reached a tree-lined path by the river. Here, Ben took Jesse in his arms and kissed her. She did not resist him, but there was none of the fiery response that Ben remembered so well and had thought about during many long and lonely nights.

When he reluctantly released her, she whispered, 'Did you mean that, Ben?'

His voice in reply was as husky as her own.

'Then everything will be all right . . . but give me time, Ben. Please!' She kissed him quickly. Then, taking his hand, she set off along the footpath.

It was Ben who broke the long silence that came upon them.

'You and Walter . . . Ma said he wanted to marry you.'

'Yes.'

Jesse seemed to feel that her reply needed no explanation, but Ben could not leave it there.

'And you? What were your feelings for him?'

'I was – and still am – very fond of Walter. He was kind to me when I had no other person with whom I could share my troubles. I told him I couldn't marry him because I was waiting for you. It wasn't easy for me, Ben – especially after the first year. I had no way of knowing whether you would ever come back; whether you *wanted* to come back.'

'I wanted it desperately, Jesse – but whichever way I looked at it, Reuben Holyoak was in the way. At first I was quite certain I'd killed him. I didn't know how he could have lived after the beating I'd given him. I was so mad with him that I *wanted* to kill him. It was frightening! Then – when I realised he must still be alive – I thought you would have been forced to marry him, for the sake of your mother. That was even worse than believing I was a hunted man. The thought of you living with Reuben Holyoak.'

'Poor Ben!' Jesse's own unhappy two years were forgotten in her concern for Ben. Then, softly, she asked, 'Has there been no one else for you, Ben? You must have met a great many girls during your travels.'

Ben hesitated. Guiltily, he wondered if he should tell her about Aileen Brenahan . . .

'No. No one who really meant anything to me.'

His initial hesitation and oblique answer told Jesse much. She did not press him for an explanation now. One day she would know everything that had happened to Ben during the two years he had been away. For now it was enough that he had returned to her.

* * *

They stayed in Truro for a full week. During that time neither Ben nor Jesse mentioned the future. Each was fearful that the other's feelings might have changed. Neither wanted to be the first to risk the happiness they now felt.

It was Alan Colborne who brought the matter into the open. He had done his best to give them as much time together as was possible, making Judy Lean take him out walking for most of every day, whatever the weather.

The four of them were finishing off a quieter-than-usual meal one evening, when the balladeer suddenly downed his knife and turned his sightless eyes in Ben's direction.

'We've been here a whole week now.'

'Yes.'

Ben guessed what was coming and squirmed in his seat.

'Where do we all go from here, Ben? I think the main decision is yours to take.'

Ben took a quick look around the table. Judy Lean was waiting for his reply with undisguised interest, but Jesse had her gaze fixed firmly upon her plate as her knife mounted a half-hearted attack on an unresisting slice of choice ham.

Ben took a deep breath before speaking what was in his heart. 'If Jesse will marry me, I would like to return to mining at Sharptor. I believe the mines there have a great future. As they go deeper they'll find more and more copper. I want to—'

'Ben Retallick!' Jesse's voice was pitched low, but the sound of it stopped Ben short. 'Are you asking me to marry you? Or are you giving us a description of the mines of Sharptor?'

'I'm asking you to marry me, Jesse.'

Alan Colborne stood up quickly. His belt caught the edge of his plate and spilled what remained of his dinner across the table. Reaching out, his fingers touched Judy and he felt for her arm. 'Come, Judy. A man doesn't need an audience when he proposes marriage.'

'Sit down, Judy. You too, Alan,' Jesse said unexpectedly.

As the balladeer sat down obediently, Jesse saw Ben's consternation and she smiled at him. 'I might need witnesses to Ben's proposal should he decide to go away again. Besides, I don't care who hears me say "Yes". Of course I will marry you, Ben, and I will go with you anywhere in the world.'

Judy Lean clapped her hands in delight and Alan Colborne let out a yell that was heard in every corner of the inn.

'Well said, Jesse. As pretty a speech of acceptance as any man will have heard.'

Ben felt so relieved and emotional, he was unable to say anything. He reached across the table, and when Jesse put her hand in his he gripped it so hard he almost crushed her fingers.

The landlord came running into the room, alarmed by Alan Colborne's gleeful shout, and was told the news by his jubilant friend. Before many minutes had passed the room was invaded by well-wishers from the landlord's family and his staff, all of whom knew the story of Ben and Jesse. Soon a very noisy party was in progress in the room.

At its height, Judy Lean guided Alan Colborne to the corner of the room where Ben and Jesse stood together, both slightly bemused by their popularity. Gripping Ben's sleeve, Alan Colborne drew him away from the others. When they were out of hearing, Alan Colborne said very quietly, 'Now you and Jesse are to be married, what will become of Judy?'

Ben looked across the room to where Judy Lean gazed at Jesse, her devotion plain for all to see. 'She'll be all right, Alan. Jesse and I will take her with us to Sharptor. We'll find a house there and she'll live with us, working on the surface at one of the mines.'

Alan Colborne gnawed his lip nervously. 'I'm going to miss her, Ben. She is a simple good-natured girl, and I have enjoyed her company this last week.'

Ben saw the indecision on the face of his friend. 'What are you trying to say, Alan?'

'Damn it Ben! I want Judy to stay with me. To marry me. But I have no right to ask her. I am a man with no eyes.'

'You are as much of a man as any I have ever met – and more than most. You can also earn a good living. But are you certain of this, Alan? You know very little about Judy.'

'I know she is a simple and honest girl. Far too honest to keep a secret for long. She told me about her baby.'

Ben said nothing, ashamed of even thinking that he should tell Alan Colborne about the birth of Judy's baby. Alan Colborne probably knew Judy Lean better than either he or Jesse did.

'I have tried to say something to her about my feelings, Ben, but the words stick in my throat. I have no right to ask any girl to marry me. None. Please forget I've said anything to you. Take Judy with you and Jesse. Look after her as she deserves . . .'

Over Alan Colborne's head, Ben caught Jesse's eye and signalled for her to bring Judy Lean across the room. Alan Colborne heard them coming and tried to make off. In his confusion he went the wrong way. Had Ben not moved quickly, the blind balladeer would have walked into a wall.

'Jesse, Alan has something to ask Judy. It's of great importance to both of them, but for some ridiculous reason he feels he has no right to speak his mind. I think we should lock them in a room together until he comes to his senses.'

Looking at Alan Colborne's consternation, a delighted smile spread across Jesse's face. 'Well, if it's any help to him, I can give him Judy's answer in advance. Since she met Alan she has kept me awake night after night talking about him. Perhaps if he says what's on his mind she'll give me some peace tonight.'

It was enough for Ben. Disregarding Alan Colborne's protests and the startled looks of the landlord and his family, Ben ushered his friend and Judy Lean from the room and took them to the landlord's own sitting-room where he left them together.

It was fifteen minutes before they returned. One look at their faces was enough to tell Ben and Jesse that another wedding was in the offing.

It was a night the customers of the White Swan Inn would remember for a very long time. The night when the landlord supplied free ale, and a blind ex-soldier entertained them with singing such as they had never heard before.

It was also the night Ben Retallick and Jesse Henna came to one another as they had when they were hardly more than children. They confirmed that the only thing they had lost together was time.

Chapter Thirty

When Ben and Jesse set off for Mevagissey, they left Alan Colborne and Judy Lean planning a journey to Plymouth to find Judy's mother and tell her about their wedding plans. The day was oppressively hot, and before Ben and Jesse were half way to the coast they saw heavy black clouds banking up over the English Channel. Hurrying along narrow lanes as the cloud rapidly filled more and more of the sky, they soon realised they had no hope of reaching Mevagissey before the storm broke. It was sweeping inland at a frightening speed.

They were still many miles from the fishing-village when, on a nearby hill-top, they saw the upper branches of a line of giant elms suddenly bow before a ferocious wind. Rain, accompanied by thunder and lightning, moved in behind the wind, and Ben and Jesse sprinted for the shelter of an open-doored barn.

Out of breath, they gained the entrance just as the first heavy raindrops spattered like musket-shots against the barn roof. Inside, a number of heifers had anticipated the storm and sought shelter in a more leisurely fashion. The barn was not large, and Ben did not fancy sharing it with nervous cattle during a thunderstorm. Fortunately, the barn had a hay-loft. Clambering up the ladder first, Ben pulled Jesse up after him and they collapsed on a pile of musty hay as the storm battered the outside of the building.

It was the worst summer storm either of them had ever experienced. As they lay in each other's arms, the wind pummelled the stone walls of the aged barn and tore at the roof. Twice they heard slates scurry down the sloping roof and smash on the ground outside. Water began to leak into the barn in a dozen places, and the beams and joists creaked in protest at the abuse to which they were being subjected.

But it was the thunder and lightning that was most frightening of all. As the heart of the storm came overhead, lightning spat at the trees about the barn with a spiteful sibilance that hung on the air for long seconds, bathing the landscape in an intense white light. Each new flash of lightning was accompanied by a deafening crack of thunder that made the earth tremble and sent the cattle in the barn milling around, snorting in terror. All the time this frightening cacophony was going on, the rain beat against the slate-tiled roof with the noise of a million tiny hammers.

It seemed an age before the wind decreased and the unnatural gloom outside lightened as the storm moved northwards. In fact, the storm had raged for hardly more than an hour.

With the passing of the storm, a stunned hush fell upon the land. Ben and Jesse climbed down the ladder from the loft and went out into a steaming world. At the field-gate they met an anxious farmer hurrying from his home to check his livestock.

'We sheltered in your barn from the storm,' explained Ben. 'We are on our way to Mevagissey.'

The farmer nodded his acceptance of Ben's story. 'It was no weather to be outside. There are three trees down between here and the farmhouse. I reckon the storm took them by surprise. One minute it was miles away, the next it was upon us. If you have friends in Mevagissey, I hope they had more warning than we. There hasn't been a fishing-boat made that could have stayed afloat in such a storm.'

The farmer's gloomy words weighed heavily on Ben's mind until he and Jesse topped the hill above Mevagissey and looked down upon the sheltered little village.

His relief was short-lived. The surrounding hills sheltered the village from all but a south-easterly wind – and the storm had arrived from the south-east.

Coming in behind a high tide, the wind had whipped the sea to a frenzy. All but two of the fishing-boats had returned safely to the tiny harbour, only to be smashed to matchwood by gigantic waves that poured over the harbour wall and flung the boats against the stone quay. Of the two boats that failed to beat the storm, and the seven men aboard them, not a trace was ever found.

Martha Retallick was at the harbour where every ablebodied inhabitant of the village was helping to drag repairable fishing-boats from a mass of shattered wreckage. This was no time for her to express her joy at seeing Ben reunited with Jesse. The storm had been an unprecedented disaster for the fishing community.

Looking about her at the scene of devastation, she raised her hands helplessly. 'What a homecoming! Mevagissey can never recover from this . . .'

'Where are the Dunn boats?'

'Who knows? Mark and Billy brought them in safely, but we haven't found a piece of either boat yet.'

Ben stepped forward to help a group of men heaving at a

rope that disappeared beneath the surface of the debris-littered water. More men and women came to help, and gradually a large fishing-boat was hauled from the depths of the harbour. As they hauled it through the mud to dry land, water poured from a hole the size of a man's head, punched through the boat's planking.

With the others, Ben and Jesse worked until the light began to fade. The falling tide had failed to reveal any more boats in a repairable condition. The destruction of the Mevagissey fishing-fleet was well-nigh complete.

After trudging despondently to Grandma Dunn's house, Ben and Jesse listened to the family gloomily discussing the bleak future that stretched ahead of them now. It would take months, perhaps years, for the fishing-village to recover from the ravages of this June storm.

So wrapped up were the Dunns in their troubles that the presence of Ben and Jesse passed almost unnoticed. Eventually, the two slipped from the house and set off for Pentuan. Jesse hoped to be able to stay with the Usticks until she and Ben went to Sharptor.

The welcome given to them by the Happy Union captain and his wife was as warm as the Dunn's had been indifferent. The night was half gone before Ben left the house to return along the dark road to Mevagissey.

It had been Ben's intention to leave for Sharptor within a day or two, but the problems caused by the storm delayed his departure. There was no work for anyone in Mevagissey. With not a single boat fit to put to sea and hardly a serviceable net along the whole coast, there was no fishing – and no smuggling.

Eventually, after much discussion, Mark Dunn collected every penny the family possessed and went to nearby Fowey, a fishing-town that had missed the worst of the storm. Here he bought a secondhand fishing-boat at a price that only a week before would have seemed ridiculous. Now there was such a demand for boats that customers could be found for anything that would float.

Others in Mevagissey followed the Dunns' example. Any family unable to raise enough money by itself, went into partnership with others and they bought a boat between them.

In church on Sunday, the parson prayed for a fruitful and extended pilchard season. Only this would enable the Mevagissey men to pay off their debts and survive to fish for another season. It might have been better had a prayer been directed to Sir Colman Vincent.

The baronet did not attend their church and he neither knew nor cared about their problems. Only a week after the storm, a lawyer employed by Sir Colman rode on to the quay at Mevagissey, escorted by a large number of militiamen. While the part-time soldiers held back the curious crowd, he posted a notice.

When the fishermen swarmed forward to read it, such a howl went up that it might have been heard in Lamorrack House. They were summarily informed that the tithes had been increased to four guineas for each boat, with an additional two guineas for each seine-net a man possessed. It was more than double the increase successfully resisted by Walter Dunn – and it was payable in advance. Sir Colman Vincent had once again chosen the worst possible moment to increase the tithes of the fishermen.

It was fortunate for the lawyer that he had the forethought to bring the men of the Cornwall Militia with him. They saved him from a severe manhandling – but not from angry abuse. The fishermen and women of Mevagissey called him every name in their wide vocabulary. They rushed to block his escape from the village, and for a time it seemed that anger might overcome common sense. Then the militiamen closed ranks and slowly, but determinedly, eased their way out of Mevagissey.

When they were gone, the villagers split into tight knots of angry gesticulating men and women, all demanding immediate action. Nobody seemed to have any idea what form the action should take, but word soon went round that a meeting was to be called on the quay to discuss the new tithe rates.

For many – and the Dunns were among their number – Sir Colman Vincent's latest action spelled ruin. They had spent every penny they could raise to buy their new boat, and borrowed more to equip it for fishing. They needed another boat urgently. One would earn no more than enough to feed the numerous members of their family and provide them with essential food and clothing – and then only if it was a good season. Until there was another boat they would be unable to pay off their debt. There could also be no thought of paying wages to Martha Retallick. She would be working solely for her keep, and that might not always be forthcoming. Mark and Billy Dunn had a great many mouths to feed.

Grandma Dunn hinted that it might be better for everyone if Martha Retallick went to Sharptor with Ben and Jesse. It was a suggestion that filled Martha with dismay. She hated mining communities.

Ben and Jesse went to the meeting on the quay, but it soon became apparent to both of them that it would provide no solutions to the problems of the village. No one felt inclined to take command of the meeting. After a great deal of argument, an old fisherman was elected to address his fellow-villagers. The choice was a bad one. The old fisherman rambled on about the effects of the storm and the new tithes, concluding with the defeatist observation, 'We shall have to pay the new tithes, be sure of that. Although where the money is to come from, I am sure I don't know.'

'Perhaps Sir Colman will give us time to find the money, if we asked him,' called a voice from the crowd.

Unable to contain her impatience any longer Jesse shouted in a loud voice, 'Have you all forgotten how Walter Dunn dealt with increased tithes, the last time they were raised? Is he the only Mevagissey man with any courage?'

Some of the younger fishermen murmured their agreement with Jesse, but, stung by her words, the old fisherman retorted, 'Would you have the whole village transported along with Walter Dunn? Is that your idea of "winning" an argument with Sir Colman Vincent?'

'Do nothing and you'll find the tithes raised again next year,' called Ben. 'Jesse is right. You have to fight Sir Colman Vincent – and fight to win. Give up now and in a year or two you'll be fishing for him. He'll own your boats, your houses – and you as well.'

'It's easy enough for you to call for action, Ben Retallick,' shouted a voice from the crowd behind Ben. He recognised it as belonging to one of the men who had crewed Walter's boat during Ben's brief fishing career. 'You're not a fisherman. When things get too tough here you can walk out and go off to some mine to earn a living. We must stay and live with whatever decision is reached here today.'

'*If* any decision is reached,' commented Jesse, her voice heavy with sarcasm. 'So far this meeting has been a waste of everyone's time. You might as well have made a collection to pay the tithes to Sir Colman's man when he came here with the militia.'

This time her words stung the fishermen to anger.

'Then why don't you do something to help us?' cried Mark Dunn. 'No doubt Walter taught you some of his tricks, and you have more influence with Sir Colman Vincent than anyone else in Mevagissey.'

Someone in the crowd laughed and others joined in. As Jesse showed her anger, Ben took her arm. 'Come along, Jesse. Leave them to fight their own battles. As they were quick to remind us, there is nothing to keep *us* here.'

White-faced, Jesse shook off his hand and scanned the crowd until she located Mark Dunn. 'All right, I'll go to the big house and speak to Sir Colman. It's what Walter would have done – and I would rather follow his example than the one you have set today.'

Jesse reached for Ben's hand and they walked together from the quay. There was no laughter now. Only the silence of embarrassed men, each too shamefaced to meet the eyes of his neighbour.

Chapter Thirty-One

Time and time again Ben told himself it was foolish to become involved in the problems of the Mevagissey fishermen. Yet there was a nagging voice at the back of his mind that kept reminding him of Walter Dunn. Walter had never allowed expediency to deter him when something really needed to be done – and Ben owed a debt to his late uncle.

Walter Dunn had looked after Ben well when he arrived in Mevagissey as a young boy, fresh from the mines of St Just. He alone of the Dunn family had shown any real concern for Pearson Retallick – and Walter had taken care of Jesse when she desperately needed a friend.

Now Walter Dunn was dead. Sir Colman Vincent was as responsible for his death as surely as if he had ordered his execution. Ben owed it to Walter to do everything in his power to foil the schemes of the baronet and bring about his downfall. He would stay in Mevagissey for a while.

But first Ben needed to find work. The money he had brought with him from Sharptor was almost gone.

This problem was easily solved. Captain Ustick took him on at the Happy Union stream-works. If Ben thought it incongruous that he should accept Sir Colman Vincent's wages whilst plotting his downfall, he never allowed the matter to trouble his conscience.

Ben had reckoned without Reuben Holyoak. Sir Colman Vincent's agent was now involved in every one of the baronet's Cornish interests, and this included his mining ventures.

On Ben's second day at the stream-workings, Reuben Holyoak arrived to collect the account-books while Ben was checking the quality of the tin ore being loaded on the pack-horses. When he saw Ben, Reuben Holyoak's face reddened and Ben thought he was about to burst a blood vessel. Then the agent stormed into Captain Ustick's office, demanding to know why the mine captain had taken on Ben Retallick.

Loveday Ustick lolled behind his desk, the huge bulk of his body overfilling the chair, his hands placed flat on the desk-top, fingers splayed.

'Are you telling me how to run the Happy Union now, Reuben Holyoak?'

'I'm telling you to get rid of Ben Retallick. I don't want to see him anywhere near Sir Colman's property.'

'Stay away from the Happy Union and you won't need to look at him.' Loveday Ustick leaned forward, supporting his great weight on the desk as he glared belligerently at the agent.

For a full minute Reuben Holyoak fought to bring his anger under control. 'I'll go wherever I please on Sir Colman's property,' he said eventually.

'I don't doubt it. But come here telling me how I should operate my stream-workings and you'll leave on the toe of my boot. Now, get out. I have work to do.'

For a moment it looked as though Reuben Holyoak might

stay to argue, but when Loveday Ustick stood up, towering above him, the agent retreated hurriedly to the door.

'You'll hear more of this, Ustick.'

Captain Loveday Ustick slammed the door of his office and went back to his desk, leaving Reuben Holyoak to ride angrily to Lamorrack House – without the account-books.

That Sunday, Ben went to Pengony, the village which had elected Sir Colman Vincent to Parliament. He went alone. It was likely he would need to do some drinking, and women were not allowed in many of the county's ale-houses.

Ben's purpose in going to Pengony was to confirm the story Walter Dunn had told to Jesse shortly before his arrest, about vote-purchasing on the part of Sir Colman Vincent.

There were only two ale-houses in Pengony, and Ben found the man he had hoped to meet in the second. He was certain it was the right man when he heard the landlord sarcastically address the bulbous-nosed customer as 'Your worship'.

Ben carried his drink across the room to the man and sat opposite him.

'I believe you were once the mayor of Pengony?' Ben said when the man looked up at him.

'What's that to you?'

'A friend of yours said that if ever I came here I was to buy you a drink.'

'A friend? What friend? I had plenty of so-called friends when I was mayor, but I can't think of one worthy of the name now.'

'Well . . . perhaps he was not so much a friend of yours as an enemy of Reuben Holyoak.'

The ex-mayor of Pengony scowled. 'Don't mention that name to me. He deprived me of land that is rightfully mine.'

'Rightfully yours?' Ben prodded. 'I heard it belonged to Sir Colman Vincent.'

'Did you, now?' The ex-mayor raised his tankard, spilling some of the contents down his coat. He had already drunk more than was good for him. 'His land it might have been, but Sir Colman gave it to me for my use. He owed it to me, he acknowledged that. It was me who bought the votes that put him in Parliament. Fifty pounds apiece, they cost. Cheap at that, they was. They might have cost him three times as much.'

'From what I have heard since, they probably did.' The landlord had been listening to the conversation; now he came across the room and began swabbing down the already clean table. 'There was more money stuck to your fingers than was ever passed on, I am certain of that.'

Other men in the room were listening to the conversation at Ben's table and one of them chuckled. The landlord did not share in the amusement. 'You'll tell that story once too often, one of these days.'

'Why should you worry?' retorted the drunken ex-mayor. 'It was the easiest fifty pounds you've ever earned. You wait and see how much you are offered next time. You'll see who cheated you then.'

'Next time I might be persuaded to vote for someone else, for less than Sir Colman Vincent has to offer. He does little to help the likes of me.'

Ben listened to the exchanges between the landlord and the ex-mayor of Pengony with a great deal of satisfaction. Downing the last of his drink, he stood up.

'Many men would agree with you, Landlord. The sooner this county gets rid of Sir Colman Vincent, the better it will be for all of us.'

With that, Ben walked out of the ale-house, leaving the

landlord and his customers to speculate on what interest he had in Sir Colman Vincent. Ben's visit to Pengony had been successful. The ex-mayor's resentment at his treatment by the Lamorrack agent still rankled. Reuben might well have laid the foundation of his employer's downfall.

But the day of reckoning seemed a long way off when Sir Colman Vincent and his agent rode up to the Happy Union mine a few days after Ben's visit to Pengony.

Ben was called to the mine captain's office. There he found Sir Colman Vincent in a mood of cold anger. Without any preliminaries, the baronet snapped at him, 'You are dismissed, Retallick. Get off the mine immediately. I suggest you take the opportunity to leave the district. Whether or not you take my advice, I do not wish to see you again.'

This was neither the time nor the place for a showdown with the baronet. Ben turned to go without making any reply.

'Wait a minute, Ben.' Loveday Ustick's voice stopped him. As Ben stood in the doorway, the mine captain addressed Sir Colman Vincent.

'Your father appointed me captain of this stream-works, Sir Colman. I've run it well, both for him and for you. I've made a good profit when similar mines were showing a loss. Leave me to run the mine my way and that is how things will continue. I hire the men I want – and dismiss those I don't. Ben Retallick is a good worker. I want him to stay.'

'If you feel so strongly about the matter, perhaps you had better leave with him, Captain Ustick.'

Sir Colman Vincent gave the ultimatum to Loveday Ustick almost casually, then waited for him to climb down from the ridiculous stand he was making.

Ben knew the mine captain better than did his employer. 'Don't make an issue of this, Loveday. I'll go.'

'Not by yourself, you won't, Ben. This has come about

through Reuben Holyoak's interference. I won't tolerate that. If I am to be captain here, I must run the Happy Union the way I think best. I'll not stay if it's to be otherwise. Do I stay or go, Sir Colman?'

For the first time, Sir Colman Vincent realised he had made an error of judgement, but he could not – and would not – be seen to back down before an employee. Not even the man in charge of the only profit-making venture he owned.

'You heard me, Captain Ustick . . .'

'That's what I thought you would say. Come, Ben.'

The big mine captain clapped a heavy hand on Ben's shoulder and together they walked from the office. Ben was appalled at the consequences Loveday Ustick's action would have for his wife and child. When they were clear of the office he protested strongly to him.

Loveday Ustick's hand tightened on Ben's shoulder. 'Don't take all the blame upon yourself, Ben. Reuben Holyoak has been breathing down my neck for months. He's never forgiven me for taking on Judy Lean after she lost her child. Had you not happened along he'd have found some other way to get rid of me. You mustn't fret. This is Sir Colman's loss, not mine . . . as he'll soon realise. I can walk into any stream-working in Cornwall as a captain. I am the best in the county, and others know it if Sir Colman doesn't.'

Behind them in the mine office, Sir Colman Vincent was seething with anger. He *did* know that Loveday Ustick was the best stream-works captain in Cornwall. He had not wanted to lose him. He could not *afford* to lose him. His financial resources were currently under considerable strain. His income from the Happy Union mine was more important than he would dare to admit to any man.

'Who is the senior man on these workings now?' he snapped at Reuben Holyoak.

'I don't know.'

'Then find out. I want to see him here – immediately!'

Reuben Holyoak hurried from the office and found the tin-streamers gathering together in puzzled groups, looking after their late captain as he walked from the workings with Ben.

'Who usually looks after the mine when Captain Ustick isn't here?' Reuben Holyoak addressed the group of miners nearest him.

'Well, now, that depends . . .' A small bow-legged tin-streamer with a face as knotted as a walnut shell stroked his grey-tinged beard and looked speculatively at the agent. 'How long is Cap'n Ustick likely to be away?'

'For good. Sir Colman Vincent has just dismissed him.'

At Reuben Holyoak's words, a rapidly increasing buzz of anger arose from the listening men. The grizzled tin-streamer stopped stroking his beard.

'Then that leaves me the senior man on the stream-works, but I'll not step into Loveday Ustick's boots. You can go back and tell Sir Colman Vincent he'll need to work the Happy Union himself – with you to help him. I don't know of any man or woman who will stay now Cap'n Ustick has gone. I'll bid you good day and be getting on home now, Mr Holyoak.'

Those men within hearing shouted their agreement with the old tin-streamworker's words. As news of what was happening went around the workings, men and women put down their tools and walked from the mine.

As one man passed Reuben Holyoak, he paused to say, 'I've left the engine running, but you'll need to look at it before an hour has gone by. If it stops, the workings will flood and you won't be taking out any ore for a week or two.'

Thoroughly dismayed, Reuben Holyoak looked on helplessly as the Happy Union tin-streamers moved away along the road in the wake of Loveday Ustick.

'What the devil is going on?' Sir Colman Vincent stormed from the mine office and confronted his agitated agent.

Long before Reuben Holyoak had reached the end of his garbled explanation, Sir Colman Vincent was so enraged that the agent thought he would strike him.

'You fool! This is all your doing. Damn you for involving me in your own petty quarrel with Ustick.' Sir Colman conveniently forgot that he had been as keen as Reuben Holyoak to have Ben dismissed. 'If things are not back to normal by the end of the day, I do not want to see your face at Lamorrack again.'

'But . . . Captain Ustick?'

'Get him back. I don't care if you have to go down on your knees to him. Remember, Holyoak, I can do without you, but I need the Happy Union.'

Reuben Holyoak first practised his persuasive powers on the stream-workers, in a final attempt to get them back to work. They jeered at his words and laughed him down. He was left with no choice but to swallow his pride and seek out Captain Ustick at his home.

The door was opened by Fanny Ustick. Tight-faced, she curtly invited him into the house. Although concerned for the future of young Nathaniel Ustick, she had supported her husband's stand against the interference of Reuben Holyoak and Sir Colman Vincent. She knew how proud Loveday was of his tin-streaming expertise. It was not conceit. It was the pride of a man who had put his God-given talents to their best use.

Reuben Holyoak began hesitantly, suggesting that Sir Colman might be persuaded to take Loveday Ustick back as captain of the Happy Union, if Loveday would make certain concessions.

Loveday Ustick was in no mood to make 'concessions'. He opened the door and ordered Reuben Holyoak from the house. Only then did the agent break down and beg the big man to resume work as captain of the Happy Union mine.

Loveday Ustick's own inclination was to disregard Reuben Holyoak's pleading. He was confident of his ability to find a well-paid post elsewhere. It was Fanny Ustick who eventually stepped in to urge her husband to reconsider his decision.

She liked living at Pentuan and believed she and Loveday were performing a valuable service to God and the Methodist Church there. It was this argument that eventually won her husband over. But Loveday Ustick left Reuben Holyoak in no doubt about the terms on which he would be returning to the stream-workings.

'I'll come back to the Happy Union . . . and so will Ben. Furthermore, I'll have no more interference from you. Keep away from the mine or I will personally heave you in the river.'

Reuben Holyoak agreed to Loveday Ustick's conditions with abject eagerness and hurriedly left the house. He had saved the Happy Union stream-works – and his own position as Sir Colman Vincent's agent. In future Loveday Ustick would be left to run the Happy Union stream-workings in his own way.

Chapter Thirty-Two

True to the promise she had made to the Mevagissey fishermen, Jesse went to Lamorrack House to speak to Sir Colman Vincent. It was the day after the incident at the Happy Union. In spite of her earlier bravado, she was not looking forward to the meeting. It came as a relief to learn that the baronet had left for his Devon estates earlier that very morning. Nevertheless, the issue of the increased tithes would not await his return.

She thought about the matter all that day. When Ben finished work at the Happy Union he found Jesse waiting for him. One look at her was enough to tell him that she had something on her mind. He did not have to wait long to learn what it was.

'I went to Lamorrack House to see Sir Colman this morning. He wasn't there.'

'Perhaps it was just as well. He'd have been in no mood to listen to you. Not after what happened yesterday. When is he expected back?'

'That doesn't matter now. I am going to see Eulaliah Vincent instead. I want you to come with me, this evening.'

'Wearing these clothes?' Dismayed, Ben looked from his dirty working-clothes to Jesse's neat waist-pinching dress.

'No. You'll need to wear your Sunday best. That's why I came to meet you. I want you to tell Eulaliah Vincent everything you have learned about Sir Colman's election to Parliament.'

Ben had not yet made up his mind what to do with the information he had – and today was not a good day to think about anything. He had been working very hard at the stream-works. Because of Loveday Ustick's stand on his behalf, he had felt obliged to work twice as hard as usual. Then Jesse took his hand and smiled up at him, and Ben knew he would do whatever she asked.

When they arrived at Mevagissey together, the Dunn family showed all their earlier cold hostility towards Jesse. Ben bristled with anger. In view of what he and Jesse were doing to help the Mevagissey fishermen, he felt the Dunns might at least behave civilly towards her.

Martha Retallick recognised his anger and hurriedly bundled him from the room, leaving the others sitting around in gloomy silence.

'Go about your business and take no notice of them, Ben,' said his mother when they were outside. 'They haven't got the boat fitted out yet and they are not used to doing nothing all day.'

'Then why don't they get up off their backsides and do something about it . . . as Jesse and I are doing?' Ben retorted angrily. 'It's little wonder that men like Sir Colman Vincent can walk all over the fishermen of Mevagissey. They take everything that is thrown at them and expect someone else to do their dirty work.'

'That's not true, Ben. They are used to fighting. Every one of them has been fighting the sea for a living since he was old enough to sit in a boat, but this tithe business is something they don't understand.

'They lack a leader. Give them one and they'll follow him no matter where he takes them. Walter was such a man; but I want you to remember what happened to him. Don't get any notion of taking his place. The fishermen's troubles are not yours. Marry Jesse and get out of Mevagissey. You're a miner, not a fisherman – you've told me so yourself, many times. I wish to God it were otherwise, but I wasted half a lifetime trying to make your father something he could never be. I'll not waste the other half seeking to change you.'

'If I leave with Jesse, will you come, too?'

'To live on a mine again?' Martha Retallick shook her head emphatically. 'No, Ben. I can think of nothing worse. Mevagissey is my home. I'll stay here.'

'Then the fishermen's battle with Sir Colman Vincent has to be my battle, too. I can't leave until something has been done about the threat he poses to you. Besides, the Dunns and Retallicks have a number of scores to settle with Sir Colman Vincent and Reuben Holyoak. Now I must get washed and changed. Jesse and I are going to see Eulaliah Vincent.'

Martha Retallick looked nervous. 'Say nothing of where you are going to anyone else in this house. They don't trust Sir John's sister. And be careful what you say to her; they may be right.'

It was the first time Ben had seen the new house built on the site of his former home. It was most impressive. The old barn where his father had committed suicide had been pulled down to make way for the sweeping lawns.

Eulaliah Vincent was in the garden of the house. When she

saw her visitors she greeted them warmly, her bright eyes alert and full of a lively inquisitiveness.

'So this is your young man,' she said, when Jesse had introduced him. 'You have been away far too long, Ben Retallick. You are lucky to have found her here waiting for you. Now I suppose you will be rushing her off to be married. Where is the wedding to be?'

'Somewhere near Henwood.' Seeing her blank look, Ben added, 'It's a village on the edge of Bodmin Moor. A friend of mine is the preacher there.'

'Hah! No doubt you will have a meaningless wedding in church before rushing off to a service in some scrubbed and whitewashed chapel, with no flowers or stained-glass windows to look at. It is as well the law does not allow chapel weddings. If it did, some people would never see inside the churches that have been warmed and beautified by centuries of faith.'

'I'm a miner, Miss Vincent. The chapel in Henwood is a miners' chapel. We'll remember our wedding with as much warmth as any that has taken place in church – or cathedral.'

Eulaliah Vincent stared hard at Ben for a moment or two.

'H'm! No doubt you are right. We all have to live our lives in our own way.'

She turned to Jesse. 'What would you like from me as a wedding gift?'

'If you could persuade Sir Colman to withdraw his demand for higher fishing tithes, it would be the best possible wedding present anyone could give us,' Ben said, before Jesse could reply.

'What have fishing tithes to do with either of *you*?' Eulaliah Vincent demanded.

'My mother went to live in Mevagissey, after Sir Colman turned us out of Tregassick,' explained Ben. 'Now she has no work because of the big storm – and Sir Colman's increased tithes. She doesn't want to leave Mevagissey, but unless something happens very soon she'll have to come with Jesse and me when we are married.'

'Is this why you have come to see me?' Eulaliah Vincent had a disconcerting stare, but Ben met it squarely before he inclined his head.

'I see. Then we had better discuss it inside the house. That Holyoak man has a tread like a cat. If we are to discuss my nephew, it needs to be in private.'

Eulaliah Vincent led them to a sitting-room from which they looked out upon a small enclosed garden, richly coloured with rhododendron bushes. After both Ben and Jesse had declined an offer of a drink, Eulaliah Vincent said, 'Now, tell me what this is about. How do you think I can help you? I have very little influence over Sir Colman. He has rarely listened to me in the past; I can think of no reason why he should begin now.'

Ben told Eulaliah Vincent the story of the storm and its disastrous consequences to the fishermen of Mevagissey. Then he told her how Sir Colman's increased tithes had dashed any chance they had of recouping their losses.

After listening very carefully, Eulaliah Vincent commented, 'Sir Colman has chosen a most unfortunate time to raise fishing tithes – but, if I try to tell him so, he will no doubt inform me it is a business matter and nothing to do with me.' She shrugged. 'He would be quite right, of course.'

Then Eulaliah Vincent revealed some of her shrewdness. 'But I feel there is more to this than you have told me. What is it?'

Ben was still not convinced he should tell this aristocratic old woman the details of his conversation with the ex-mayor of Pengony, but at Jesse's insistence he did so.

Eulaliah Vincent listened in silence until he had completed

his story. Then she said quietly, 'These are serious allegations, young man. Be very careful to whom you repeat them. Sir Colman has much to lose.'

'So have the fishermen of Mevagissey. The future of Mevagissey as a fishing-village is at stake – and with it their livelihood.'

'Perhaps. But how many of these fishermen will stand with you and fight for their future? The answer is none! They did not support Walter Dunn, and they will fail you in the same way. Tell me, how do you intend to use this information?'

'To have Sir Colman thrown out of Parliament,' replied Ben defiantly.

Eulaliah Vincent looked at him thoughtfully. 'I believe you will . . . and you may well succeed. If you do, you will bring shame upon a family that has served Cornwall well for a great many years. I will not pretend to like my nephew, but I was very fond of his father – and I am myself a Vincent. Can I persuade you to change your mind?'

Ben shook his head slowly, 'No. Too many people have suffered at Sir Colman's hands. He claims to represent Cornwall in Parliament, but ordinary people mean nothing to him because they have no vote and can't help to elect him. I intend to prove that we *can* have him removed.'

'Are you certain this is *all* you want, Ben Retallick? To remove my nephew from the House of Commons? Or are you seeking lasting fame for yourself as the "ordinary" man who brought a baronet to justice?'

'I want only to stop Sir Colman from making life impossible for the Mevagissey fishermen.'

While he was talking, Eulaliah Vincent did not take her eyes from Ben's face. Now she nodded, apparently satisfied.

'Very well, Ben Retallick. I will trust you. In return you will need to put your faith in me. David Howell is High Sheriff of Cornwall. He is also a close friend. I will give you a letter for him. Tell him everything you know – then say nothing more to anyone. Leave him to take whatever action he feels may be necessary. Your name need never be mentioned. It will be better so – for all of us.'

Ben could not believe that he had succeeded in gaining Eulaliah Vincent's support. It had been too easy.

His puzzlement showed as he said, 'Thank you . . . but why should you help me against your own nephew?'

'I am trying to avert a major scandal,' came the surprising reply. 'My nephew has made a great many enemies, some of them men of influence. One day one of them will learn about Sir Colman's blatant vote-buying and press criminal charges against him. Every man in the country who clamours for parliamentary reform will point to him as an example of all that is wrong with our electoral system. They will raise such a hullabaloo that the Prime Minister will be forced to make an example of Sir Colman. He would go to prison, and the whole Vincent family would share his shame. By doing things my way I hope Sir Colman will fade quickly out of your lives. Is that not what you seek?'

'Yes, but what if he persists in his tithe demands, from sheer spite?'

'David Howell will attend to that. No doubt he will point out to Sir Colman the folly of increasing his unpopularity at such a time.'

Ben tried hard to hide his elation at the thought that Sir Colman Vincent finally stood on the brink of disaster. He began to thank Eulaliah Vincent, but she silenced him brusquely.

'The last thing I want is gratitude for what I am doing. I will need to keep telling myself that this is for the good of the family. Already the name "Judas" springs unwanted to my mind. Go now, both of you, and come back tomorrow for my letter to David Howell.'

When Ben returned to collect the letter, he learned that the High Sheriff had his estate in east Cornwall, not more than six miles from the slopes of Sharptor. It was all the excuse Ben needed to return to the mines on the moor. He told Jesse he would deliver the letter to Mr Howell, then go on to Sharptor to seek work and a cottage for them.

Jesse had other ideas.

'You are not returning to Sharptor without me,' she declared emphatically. 'The last time you left me you were away for two years. I am not going to let that happen again. I'm coming with you.'

Ben did not argue. He could think of nothing he would enjoy more than to have Jesse accompany him on a journey halfway across the breadth of Cornwall.

Martha Retallick did not share his pleasure. With Jesse nearby, she knew he would always return to the district. If Jesse went with him, there was little to bring him back to Mevagissey.

Ben was eventually able to reassure her that he *would* come back. Then he set off to the harbour. He found Mark Dunn sitting on the quay, repairing a storm-damaged seine-net recently recovered from rocks outside the harbour. The shortage of long seine-nets was almost as serious to the fishermen as the loss of their boats.

Mark Dunn acknowledged Ben's presence with a grunt and a barely perceptible nod of his head. 'Have you come to tell me that girl of yours has seen Sir Colman Vincent? Has he agreed to waive all our tithes?' The fisherman snorted derisively. 'He's more likely to raise them again because we've been tardy in paying up.'

'Sir Colman is out of Cornwall, so Jesse hasn't been able to see him. But it means he'll be making no new decisions for a while. That doesn't mean nothing is being done. I am going to east Cornwall to see the High Sheriff. I want you to tell the other fishermen not to pay any increased tithes. They will be reduced again very soon.'

Mark Dunn lowered the seine-net to the ground and stared hard at Ben. 'What nonsense is this? Can you work miracles now?'

'I can't tell you more at the moment.'

'You'll need to do better than that! If you think I am going to tell Mevagissey fishermen to break the law on your say-so, you'd better think again, Ben. You tell them yourself if you want to.'

Mark Dunn's attitude was not unexpected. He was no leader of men as his brother Walter had been. He would follow the example of the others readily enough. He could not be called upon to show them the way.

'All right, I'll speak to them, but it will have to be tonight. I intend leaving in the morning. Will you put out the word that I'll be at the end of the harbour wall shortly before sunset?'

Mark Dunn shrugged. 'I'll tell any man I see. I make no promises about how many will be there.'

Mark Dunn's pessimism proved to be unfounded. The tithe issue was of great importance to the Mevagissey fishermen. They were ready to listen to any one who had something to say.

Ben repeated the message he had given to Mark Dunn, adding that he had something of importance to say to the High Sheriff and was quite sure the demand for higher tithes would not be pursued.

Once again it was Mark Dunn who was sceptical. He asked Ben how he was going to force Sir Colman to change his mind.

'I have told you as much as I can,' replied Ben patiently, 'I can only add that *I* am convinced I'll succeed. Others who are in a position to know feel the same. All I'm asking is that you all hold out a while longer against the tithe increases.'

'It's an easy enough thing for you to ask.' This time the dissenter was Billy Dunn. 'You run no risk of a constable coming to arrest you for debt, seizing everything for which you've worked for years.'

'Would you rather give it all up without a fight?' retorted Ben. 'Is that what Walter would have done?'

'What is there to argue about?' asked another fisherman. 'I doubt whether there are more than two fishermen in the village with the money to pay their tithes. No one is going to pay anything to Sir Colman Vincent. We'll hold out against him for as long as we can. Mind you, when the arrests start, things might be different.'

'Sir Colman Vincent will have dropped his demands long before there are any arrests,' declared Ben confidently. He fervently hoped he would not be proved wrong. 'If justice is done, it will be a very long time before Sir Colman and his agent trouble us again.'

'Amen to that,' said a fisherman who was standing close to Ben. 'But we'll believe it when it comes about.'

Chapter Thirty-Three

David Howell, gentleman and High Sheriff of Cornwall, had his home in a quiet valley through which flowed the River Inny. Walking with Jesse along the long drive leading to the house, Ben was reminded of Lamorrack House. David Howell's house was not as large, but it gave Ben the same feeling in the pit of his stomach. The sensation was heightened when, after handing Eulaliah Vincent's letter to a footman, they were left to wait in a modest inner hallway.

Ben was glad to have Jesse with him, and when he smiled at her she whispered, 'Do you remember when we waited together like this to go in and see Sir John?'

'That was a whole lifetime ago!' There was something about the atmosphere here in the hallway that caused them both to whisper. 'We were only children then.'

Jesse took his hand and squeezed it, releasing it again quickly when a door opened and the footman re-entered the hallway.

'Come with me, please.'

He led them along a narrow corridor and up a half-flight

of stairs to an oak-panelled door set in an angle of the house. Opening the door, the footman motioned for them to go inside.

Once through the doorway, they found themselves in a small and comfortable study. Standing in the centre of the room, David Howell was frowning as he read Eulaliah Vincent's letter for the second time.

Cornwall's High Sheriff was a short, rotund, well-dressed man of middle-age and he was greatly perturbed by what he was reading. Finally, he peered at Ben and Jesse over the top of the pince-nez, balanced halfway down his nose.

'What is all this?' He waved the letter in the air and glared at Ben. 'I gather the accusations are yours? Do you realise their seriousness?'

'I do . . . But they happen to be true.'

'You *believe* them to be true, which is not quite the same thing. Do you mind telling me why you are pursuing these charges against Sir Colman Vincent?'

Ben's hopes had sunk the moment David Howell began to speak. He had the same arrogant manner as Sir Colman Vincent himself. Ben felt he had little chance of a sympathetic hearing from this man. Nevertheless, it was important to try to persuade the High Sheriff to take action against Pengony's Member of Parliament.

'I could give you many reasons. He had my mother put out of her house and took away the farm Sir John Vincent had promised to Jesse and myself – but that is all in the past. The important thing at the moment is to get him to drop the increase in tithes imposed upon the fishermen of Mevagissey. Every boat in the village was smashed by the great storm, and the fishermen are facing ruin. Sir Colman's new tithe rates will take away my mother's livelihood and that of most of Mevagissey's men and women.'

'Are you a member of this Parliamentary Reform Party?'

'No. I belong to no reform movement – yet I must agree with their aims. There is urgent need for reform when men like Sir Colman Vincent can buy their way into Parliament.'

David Howell frowned, but he said nothing for a while. Then suddenly he turned his attention to Jesse.

'Your face is uncommonly familiar. What is your name?'

'Jesse Henna. I have lived all my life at Pengrugla. I don't think we've met before.'

'Probably not. And yet . . . But never mind.'

To Ben he said, 'Why should Eulaliah Vincent be helping you in this matter? I must confess I find all this very difficult to understand.'

'Miss Vincent thinks my information might lead to serious trouble for Sir Colman if it found its way into other hands. She said it might even mean prison for him.'

David Howell nodded non-committally. 'How is it you know Eulaliah Vincent?'

'My mother was her personal maid, and Ben and I are to be married . . .' Jesse's explanation faltered and then stopped as enlightenment came to David Howell.

'*Now* I know why you look so familiar! You are the image of your mother when she was your age. By heaven, but she was a handsome girl.'

Suddenly the High Sheriff's whole attitude towards them changed, his air of suspicion gone.

'Now I understand why Eulaliah is doing all this for you. She looked upon your mother more as a daughter than as a servant. Ah, yes! Eulaliah Vincent has bided her time well . . . All right, Retallick, I will do what I can. It may take a while but, if what you have said is true, I can assure you that Sir Colman Vincent will lose his seat in the House of Commons. No doubt Lord Liverpool will disfranchise Pengony at the same time. Not that it will matter very much to anyone except Sir Colman and his fellow Pengony Member of Parliament. Pengony's need for representation disappeared a great many years ago.'

David Howell showed Ben and Jesse from the house himself and watched from the doorway as they walked hand-in-hand down the long driveway.

When they were almost out of sight, he whispered to himself, 'By God, Colman, be sure your sins are seeking you out now. You sowed the seeds of your own destruction when you bedded Eulaliah's maid all those years ago!'

Ben and Jesse arrived at Henwood weary from a long day's travelling, but it did not prevent Ben from pausing on the road before Henwood village to point out to Jesse the mines, dotted along the slopes of the moor, and clustered together in the valley beyond.

Jesse looked from the vast emptiness of the moor beyond the slopes of Sharptor, to the smoking chimneys and torn turf of the valley bottom.

'Where will we live, Ben?'

'I don't know yet. It will depend on where I find work.'

'I hope it's somewhere up there.' Jesse pointed upwards, to where the rocky mass that was Sharptor towered above the village. 'I don't think I would enjoy living among the smoke and noise of the valley.'

Ben remembered the view across the Tamar valley from his lean-to hut on the moor. He, too, hoped he could find a cottage where he could share the sheer breathtaking beauty of such a view with Jesse.

They walked on in silence until they reached Henwood village, where Ben took Jesse to the Kelynack house. He had already told Jesse of the mining accident that had robbed Mary Kelynack of her husband and every one of her sons. He had mentioned nothing of her daughters.

The door was opened to them by Holly, the youngest of the Kelynack girls. When she saw Ben, she leaped forward and flung her arms about him in a manner that caused Jesse's eyebrows to rise in sharp surprise.

Clutching Ben's hand, Holly Kelynack pulled him in through the doorway, not even noticing Jesse.

'Ma! Ma! Come quickly. It's Ben. Ben's come back.'

Mary Kelynack hurried to the door with Jenny, the second Kelynack daughter, behind her. She did not overlook Jesse, standing silently behind Ben as he hauled back on Holly's arm and halted her eager progress.

'Ben! It's good to see you . . . and you, too.' She reached past Ben and took Jesse by the hand. 'You will be Jesse, of course. We've heard all about you. I wondered if Ben would bring you to see us one day.'

As Mary Kelynack looked quickly at the fingers of Jesse's hand to see if she wore a wedding-ring, Jesse saw the surprise on the faces of the two girls. Mrs Kelynack might have known *all* about her. Her daughters certainly knew far less.

'I was hoping you might be able to put Jesse up for a while,' Ben was saying to Mrs Kelynack. 'I want to find work here, somewhere with a cottage to go along with it. Then Jesse and I will be married.'

'You can *both* stay here. The house seems even emptier since Kate left. I am thinking of looking for a smaller place myself. This house is too large for a widow woman and two girls.'

'Kate's gone? Where?'

Mary Kelynack jerked her head in the direction of Sharptor. 'Up there . . . with Moses Trago.'

Seeing Ben's shocked surprise, she answered his unasked question. 'Oh, she married him properly. Wrightwick Roberts saw to that. I was against the marriage from the start. Kate knew it, but she took no notice of me, nor did she have to. She was a widow and able to choose her own future. For all that, I would be happier if she and Moses had moved into a proper house and not that . . . that *place* on the moor. They say the old men used to bury their dead there, years ago. What sort of home is that for a young girl?'

'If Kate doesn't like it, she might persuade Moses to move down into the village.'

Mary Kelynack let out a loud and meaningful snort. 'Our Kate persuade Moses Trago to do something? They haven't been married much more than a month and she can't keep him at home. He's gone back to his old habits of drinking and fighting in the ale-houses. I feel sorry for our Kate, but I'm not going to interfere. There was a time when I hoped . . . Ah! It is no use talking about it now. Kate knew you wouldn't be coming back – at least, not as a single man. Now sit yourself down, the pair of you. You must be tired out from tramping around the countryside on a day like this. Wait until Wrightwick hears you are back! He's been talking of going to Mevagissey again to find out what happened to you. But he is kept busy around here, although there are still more funerals than weddings or baptisms. It's always the way where there are mines. There were four killed at the Marke Valley mine only last week . . .'

Jesse listened to Mary Kelynack's chatter in silence. Later, when she and Ben were eating with the others, at the table, she answered the questions put to her by the Kelynacks readily enough, but she said little to Ben.

He thought she was probably tired; it had been a long day. However, when she had been taken up to the room that was to be hers during her stay, Ben looked in to see if she was comfortable – and he learned there was another reason for her silence.

After making certain none of the Kelynack family had come upstairs with Ben, Jesse closed the door to her room and rounded on him so suddenly he was taken by surprise.

'What did Mrs Kelynack mean when she said that Kate knew you wouldn't come back as a single man? She good as suggested that Kate might have waited for you had I not been around. What went on between the two of you?'

Ben was astonished. He had never before experienced such jealousy. Coming from Jesse, he found it doubly confusing.

'There was never anything between Kate and myself. When I first visited this house she hadn't long been widowed. She broke down and cried and I comforted her. That was all there ever was. I swear it.'

'Did Kate realise that?'

'Of course she did. Why do you think she married Moses Trago so soon after I'd gone?'

Ben had begun to perspire. Whilst protesting his innocence he had suddenly remembered Aileen Brenahan. What Jesse would do if ever she learned about that episode did not bear thinking about.

'Girls are liable to do some funny things when the man they love is going to marry someone else,' said Jesse darkly. Then her face cleared and she kissed him long and lovingly. 'It's all right, Ben Retallick. I love you – but it will do you no harm to know you are marrying a jealous woman.'

Her words did nothing to help Ben's peace of mind. Gulping down his misgivings, he said, 'I need to find Moses and learn where I might find work and a cottage. I'll take you to meet him and Kate tomorrow evening.'

Ben spent the next day showing Jesse around Henwood and the moors above the village. It was now August, one of the finest months of the year to see the moor, with the fern at its luxuriant best, standing tall and dark green on the lower slopes of Sharptor. Above the fern level, where the heather clung to the granite-grey rock-face, it was a subtle blend of pink and grey.

On the summit of the tor, Jesse leaned back in Ben's arms

and held her breath at the sheer beauty of the view laid out before her. The distant tors and slopes of Dartmoor dominated the horizon. Between the two moors was Kit Hill, surrounded by woodland, with here and there a church-tower standing sentinel over a crumpled patchwork of multi-coloured fields.

'I don't think I have ever seen anywhere quite so lovely as this place, Ben,' Jesse breathed happily.

Ben tightened his arms about her. 'Then you won't mind living here?'

'It will be a wonderful place to bring up a family. A boy could play some marvellous games up here . . .'

'Steady! Saying things like that could put a man off marriage.'

'No, Ben Retallick. Not you. I'll give you a son you'll be proud of – and he will be equally proud of you. But you must promise to bring him up here often. I want him to grow up with the knowledge that there is more to life than a hole in the ground and a mountain of mine-waste.'

'I promise.'

Ben turned Jesse to him and they came together on the moorland tor, surrounded by their future.

When Ben and Jesse arrived at Moses and Kate Trago's moorland home, the sun had moved on beyond the ridge, leaving the ancient cromlech in deep shadow. Jesse was unable to control a shudder as they approached the stone-slab dwelling. She did not know whether it was because they had passed from the sunlight, or whether the sudden chill sprang from a more sinister source. Instinctively, she knew there had been much unhappiness here.

Smoke was pouring from a hole in the stone, indicating that someone was at home, and Ben put his head around the odd-shaped door, built to fit into a gap between the rocks. He called a loud 'Hello', and heard a sound from within. Then the door was pulled wide open and Kate Trago looked out at them.

When she saw Ben, her face showed a mixture of joy and dismay that might have been amusing under different circumstances. Then she saw Jesse, and Kate Trago's hand went instinctively to her hair. It dangled untidily about her face, but neither Jesse nor Ben had eyes for her hair. They were both looking at the ugly bruise that discoloured Kate Trago's left eye and spread over most of her cheek-bone.

'I'm sorry.' Kate Trago took control of herself. 'Won't you come inside? It's not much at the moment . . . but me and Moses will soon get it fixed up. There's been no one to look after the place for so long . . .'

Ben stepped awkwardly through the strange-shaped doorway and helped Jesse in after him. When he turned back to Kate she had tied her long hair hastily into a knot behind her head and was placing a pot of water on the hot ashes of the fire.

'You'll have tea? We've got some. I bought it only yesterday. I'm not so sure about cups. You are my first visitors.'

Kate Trago laughed nervously. It was a sad uncertain sound. When Ben introduced Jesse, Kate gave her a quick smile, trying hard to keep the bruised side of her face away from the other woman.

Eventually, Kate Trago located two cups. With her hand shaking nervously, she poured a weak sugarless brew of tea from the pot and handed the cups to her visitors.

'Where is Moses? I want to talk to him about the mines in the area. I thought he'd be home by now.'

'He . . . he'll be in the ale-house. He's taken to drinking again, this last week or two. He and brother John will be home when they are ready . . . but it probably won't be until late.'

'Ben, you finish your tea and go down to the ale-house for

your talk with Moses. I'll stay up here for a while and chat to Kate.' Jesse's manner was unusually brisk. 'There is no need to come back again. I'll see you at Kate's mother's house.'

Ben had not yet finished his tea, but Jesse took the cup from his hands and shooed him towards the door. Looking over Jesse's shoulder, Ben hardly had time to call 'Goodbye!' to Kate Trago before he was outside. He glimpsed her seated on the far side of the fire, an unhappy forlorn figure. She raised her face to him and then he was gone.

On his way to the village, Ben wondered why Jesse had been so anxious for him to leave the Trago home. He thought about it until the village came into view, then shrugged it away. He accepted that he would never fully understand the workings of Jesse's mind.

Moses was seated in a corner of the ale-house with his brother John when Ben entered. He did not look up until a couple of men from the Wheal Slade greeted Ben and asked him what he was doing back in Henwood. Moses Trago's face lit up in a brief greeting, but it had returned to its customary scowl by the time Ben called for three drinks and sat down opposite the Trago brothers.

'Hello, Moses . . . John. I've just taken Jesse up to your place to see Kate.'

'Oh? Then I expect you've heard all about me blacking her eye?'

'No. Kate said nothing. But as she did her best to hide it from us I knew it must be your doing. Why, Moses? Kate is a good girl.'

Ben spoke quietly, anxious not to anger Moses. He knew that, if he did, Kate would be the one to suffer.

'I didn't mean to hit her. You can believe that, or not.' Moses glared at Ben belligerently.

'I believe you.'

Moses Trago relaxed slightly. 'I'd been drinking,' he admitted. 'She was nagging at me and I meant to push her away. She must have moved.'

Moses gave a gesture of helplessness, then was angry with himself for showing his feelings. He took the drink that was slid in front of him by the landlord and quaffed half of it in one long movement.

'She should have married you, not me. No, don't argue with me. I'm *telling* you. She only took me because she needed a man . . . any man. It was you she really wanted. Between you and that damned dead husband of hers, I don't stand a chance. I work away at her in bed and know she's thinking of you . . . or maybe it's him. I don't know any more – and I don't care.'

'You're wrong, Moses. Kate married you; it's you that she wants. Why don't you get off home and find out for yourself?'

Moses downed the remainder of his ale and bellowed for the landlord to bring more. Snapping his fingers only inches from Ben's nose, he said, 'I don't give *that* whether I am right or wrong! She married me and she'll treat me as a husband and do as I tell her, or I'll know the reason why. She'll have food for me when I get home and I'll take her whenever I want her. For the rest of it, I'll go my own way, just as I have always done. Now forget about Kate. You didn't come all this way just to talk about her – or did you?'

Ben finished his drink slowly and deliberately, then set the empty pot down upon the table.

'No, I didn't come here to talk about your wife, although I doubt if she has anyone else to take her part. Bring her down from the moor, Moses. Move out of that tomb and into a proper house. Give Kate something in which she can take a pride. She'll show you she is a good wife.'

Moses Trago's scowl deepened. 'There's nothing wrong with the place we have now. I am not coming down to the village so

Kate can tell every nosey biddy my business, while her mother keeps an eye on us every minute of the day. No, we'll stay up on the moor, out of the way.'

'Then I have nothing more to say, Moses. Jesse and I will be wed soon. I hope you'll not object to Jesse calling on Kate sometimes?'

Moses shrugged impassively. 'As long as Kate is there when I want her she can see whoever she pleases.'

There was nothing more to be said. Ben could not discuss the prospect of work with Moses Trago while his treatment of Kate stood between them.

Ben looked back from the ale-house doorway and saw Moses shaking his head at something his brother was saying to him. Ben wondered whether John Trago ever took Kate's part during the arguments in the cromlech home. He doubted it very much. Ben had never heard John Trago express any opinion of his own. He was no more than a large, silent, brooding shadow at his brother's side.

When Ben reached the Kelynack house, Jesse had not yet returned. He sat talking to Mary Kelynack while he waited for her. He mentioned seeing Kate, but said nothing about her bruised face.

'Was that husband of hers up there?' Mary Kelynack clattered the dishes for the evening meal.

'No, I met him later in the ale-house.'

Mary Kelynack sniffed. 'He'll no doubt spend all his pay in there – half of Kate's, too, if she isn't careful.'

'I wanted to talk to Moses about finding a mine that could offer me a cottage along with a job.' Ben steered the conversation away from Kate.

'What makes you think Moses would know anything about that? He would probably suggest you make do with a cave, the same as him and my Kate. Anyway, the mines hereabouts will offer you nothing but a low wage. There are more miners seeking work than there are places to be filled. The only way you'll get a cottage is to wait for a man to be killed, then turn out his widow. Even then, you'll find more than one miner ahead of you.'

Mary Kelynack suddenly paused. 'Mind you, now you've mentioned it, I remember Wrightwick saying something about a new mine opening up on Sharptor. He says they are going to work tin when it first opens, but are really after copper. They'll need to build cottages if it is to be any sort of mine at all. It might be worth a try, especially as it doesn't seem to be common knowledge yet.'

'Who is to be the captain? I'll go and see him.' Ben was excited at the news. He had worked for copper in the Tamar valley and stood a good chance of being given work on the new mine.

'I don't think things have gone far enough for the mine to have a captain yet. I do know there will be no adventurers. The mine is to have only one owner – Theophilus Strike. He lives over by Launceston. His family is well known in these parts. Why don't you go to Launceston and speak to him?'

'I will, first thing tomorrow. Thank you for telling me.'

For the next half-hour Ben discussed mining with Mary Kelynack. She declared that the character of the whole area was changing as the mines expanded and took on new men. It had once been possible to walk for five miles in any direction and know every man, woman and child with whom one met. Now, Mary Kelynack said, half the population of Henwood were strangers, all of them bringing strangers' ways to the village with them.

'Before you know it, they'll be complaining about us doing the things we've done here for as along as anyone can remember. Why, only the other day—'

What it was that had happened the other day, Ben never

knew. At that moment Jesse came in, and Mary Kelynack called her two daughters in from the garden and began to dish out the meal.

Only the lively chatter of Jenny and Holly Kelynack prevented the meal from being an unusually serious affair. Ben said little for fear the conversation would return to Kate and Moses. Jesse, too, was strangely silent. It was a relief when the meal was over and Ben and Jesse were able to make an excuse to leave the house and go for a walk together in the late-summer twilight.

They walked along the track that clung precariously to the steep moorland hillside, but it was too dark to see the view. There were only the stars, and the dull red glow from the valley bottom as a furnace door was flung open and coal from the Welsh quarries shovelled inside.

Ben told Jesse what Mary Kelynack had said about the new mine on Sharptor. They tried to imagine what it would be like to live upon the tor on such a night as this with the stars peppering the sky and a bloated moon rising over Bodmin Moor.

As they walked they planned their house and garden, family and future. Then, returning along a different track, they passed close to the home of Kate and Moses Trago and they both fell silent.

Not until they were well beyond all possible hearing did Ben say, 'I wish Moses and Kate had dreams for the future. As things are, I think poor Kate can look forward to nothing but trouble.'

'Far more than we realised,' agreed Jesse quietly. 'Kate is pregnant.'

Chapter Thirty-Four

Theophilus Strike was a large man with a florid complexion and a manner that was blunt to the point of rudeness. When Ben explained his reason for calling upon the mine-owner, Strike frowned. 'Who told you about the Sharptor mine?'

'A widow with whom I lodge. Word gets around quickly when a new mine is to open.'

'Does it, be damned! Then I had better get myself a mine captain quickly, or every out-of-work miner in Cornwall will be banging on my door and begging for work. What do *you* know about copper?'

Ben told Theophilus Strike in some detail, confident he knew more about copper mining than the man standing before him.

Theophilus Strike listened for many minutes before impatiently waving Ben to silence. 'All right! All right! I don't want to learn how to mine copper myself. I just want to be sure the men I employ know what they're doing. No doubt you've mined tin, too?'

'Since I was ten,' Ben declared.

'Very well, I'll employ you. Do you know Tom Shovell, of Henwood?'

Ben's face lit up. 'I know him well. We worked together at the Wheal Slade.'

'You'll be working with him again. He is to be one of my shift captains. Tell him I'm making him responsible for taking on all the men we'll need to open the mine. He can decide for himself how many that should be. I don't want him to bother me until everything is arranged. Right, Retallick, you may go now.'

Ben hesitated, and Theophilus Strike looked at him impatiently. 'What are you waiting for? If it's an advance of pay, you can forget it. I will pay a fair wage for work done, but I'll not give a penny on promises.'

'It's not money, but a cottage. I'm to be married soon . . . as soon as I have a house.'

Theophilus Strike came close to a smile as he looked at Ben's anxious expression. He knew his reply would decide Ben's whole future, yet Ben was doing his utmost not to allow his feelings to show.

Strike liked the look of the serious young man standing before him. He was just the type of miner he hoped to attract to the Wheal Sharptor. Once he was married and settled in a mine-cottage, Ben Retallick would constitute a lifetime's investment.

'You can have your cottage, Retallick. Tell Tom Shovell we will have eight cottages up on the tor, close to the mine. He can build another twelve on the piece of land I own in Henwood village. Let your future bride choose where she wants to live – that should please her. The terms of occupancy will be the usual ones. You build the house yourself from mine materials, and it will remain yours during the lifetimes of three named tenants.'

Ben nodded his agreement. His joy was so overwhelming he

would not trust himself to speak. Theophilus Strike had given him all he wanted. Now there was nothing to prevent him and Jesse from marrying – and they would have their home on Sharptor.

Although it was nine long miles to Henwood from Launceston, it was as much as Ben could do to stop himself running all the way. When he was still more than a mile from the village, a turn in the road brought the grey granite tor into view and Ben could control himself no longer.

He arrived at the Kelynack house too breathless to say anything. Picking up the startled Jesse, he swung her round and round the kitchen until they both collapsed in a laughing giddy tangle on the wooden bench set against the table.

'You've got the job, Ben? Theophilus Strike gave it to you?'

'Yes . . . and much more besides. I can build a house for us. He said you must choose whether it will be up on the tor, or down here in the village.'

Jesse caught Ben's excitement. As she hugged him, she said, 'I can't believe this is really happening, Ben! It's exactly what we were dreaming about when we were up on the tor the other day. How long will a house take to build?'

'That depends how long Tom Shovell takes to find all the miners he needs. There are twenty houses to be built, and the miners will share in their building. Ours will be the first. We can find Wrightwick Roberts and have him arrange a wedding date as soon as you like.'

Tom Shovell was pleased to learn that Ben would be one of his miners at Wheal Sharptor, and he accompanied Ben and Jesse to the site of the mine that same evening.

With Tom Shovell's help, Jesse chose the exact site of the house she and Ben would have. From its windows it would have an uninterrupted view over the wide valley to the east. Behind the cottage, the contours of the moor would not only protect it from the prevailing west wind, but also hide the mine-buildings from view. Ben and Jesse could have found no finer site for a house had they been able to choose anywhere on the eastern moor.

Locating Wrightwick Roberts was more difficult. His Methodist circuit covered a very wide area, his parishioners spread thinly over many miles of moorland. It took in mining communities and farms, Wrightwick's little chapels being dotted here and there around the countryside. After two days of fruitless searching, Ben gave up his quest. He and Jesse would have to wait until the preacher's circuit-riding brought him back to Henwood.

Wrightwick Roberts arrived on the last Sunday of August and joyfully embraced Jesse in his big arms when the happy couple told him they wanted to discuss a wedding.

'I feel I can take some credit for this marriage,' he boomed happily to Jesse. 'It was my news from Mevagissey that sent him scurrying off to find you again – and not before time. He has been wandering Cornwall like a lost soul for far too long. Now, tell me when you would like the wedding to be and I will speak to the vicar at Linkinhorne.'

The Methodist church was in its infancy and the laws of the land did not yet permit Methodist preachers to conduct weddings. Ben and Jesse would have to marry in the parish church, at Linkinhorne. Afterwards, they would return to the tiny Henwood chapel where Wrightwick Roberts would conduct a special service in honour of the occasion.

It was decided that Ben and Jesse would marry when the cottage at Wheal Sharptor was ready to be roofed. Although the first stone had yet to be laid, the time was not as far off as it seemed at the moment.

As soon as Tom Shovell began taking on men, news went around so swiftly that before two days had passed he had a full work-force, drawn from the type of men Theophilus Strike wanted. They, too, were keen on bringing their families to live near the mine and would waste no time in building the cottages. All the stone taken from the ground as they dug the main mine-shaft would be trimmed and utilised in the construction of a cottage that would be built in a month, yet last for two hundred years.

Then, when the Wheal Sharptor shaft had reached a depth of thirty fathoms, and the cottage being built for Ben and Jesse was at bedroom-window height, something happened that threatened to prejudice the secure future they believed was theirs.

A man with a severe limp and an accent that had never before been heard in the area came to Henwood asking for Ben Retallick. He was directed to the Wheal Sharptor.

Ben climbed the ladder at the end of a long shift spent driving the first level at ten fathoms, to find the stranger waiting for him. He introduced himself to Ben as Charles Swindles, from Manchester. A member of the Midlands Parliamentary Reform Party, Swindles' career as a reformer had been assured when he was cut down by a militiaman's sword. It had happened at the great meeting at St Peter's Field, in Manchester, in the year 1819. This was the so-called 'massacre', referred to by the reform militants forever afterwards as 'Peterloo'.

Much to Ben's surprise, Swindles greeted him enthusiastically, pumping his hand and offering his congratulations. 'It's a great honour to meet you, Ben. You've done more for the reform movement by your single-handed action than the rest of us put together. Congratulations!'

Ben was baffled. 'Are you sure you are talking to the right person? What is it I'm supposed to have done?'

'If you're Ben Retallick, then you are the man I've been looking for. Not only have you exposed the sort of vote-buying we know is going on but, with the disfranchisement of Sir Colman Vincent's borough, Manchester and Bradford have gained seats in the House of Commons. We in the Midlands are deeply in your debt.'

'Sir Colman has been thrown out of Parliament? Already?'

'Are you telling me you haven't heard?' Now it was the turn of Charles Swindles to show his astonishment. 'Good Lord, man! This has happened right here in Cornwall, not so many miles from you, yet we in Manchester know about it before you! What sort of an organisation do you have here?'

'I belong to no organisation. I did only what needed to be done. Sir Colman Vincent didn't deserve to be an elected Member of Parliament.'

Even as he replied to the Midlands reformer, Ben wondered how Swindles had learned who had toppled Sir Colman Vincent. David Howell had promised Ben it would remain a secret.

'Sir Colman Vincent can consider himself lucky that our Reform Party didn't learn about him before you. We'd have crucified him. Nailed him to the cross of his own greed and corruption. But what do you intend doing now?'

'Intend doing? I'll finish building my house on Sharptor and be married. Then I hope to work here at the Wheal Sharptor for a great many happy years.'

'You'll spend your life mining, after what you've achieved? That would be a stupid bloody waste – both for you and for the Movement. Stay here by all means, if that's what you really want, but at least take over the leadership of the Parliamentary Reform Movement in Cornwall. Bring it into the National movement. Better still, come back to the Midlands with me and contest one of the parliamentary seats you've given to us. You'll be voted in with an overwhelming majority – the first of a long line of worker-members. It's the chance of a lifetime for you, Ben. You're being given the opportunity to shake this country as though it were an apple-tree. In the shaking, a lot of rotten apples like Sir Colman Vincent will fall. Parliamentary reform is coming, be assured of that. What's more, it will be a far-reaching reform. Men like you and I, and all the poor miners climbing out of that hole in the ground, will have the right to send our own men to speak for us in Parliament. Men of *our* choice. That's what the Parliamentary Reform Party is working for, Ben. You can be a part of it. Tell men what you did – and how you did it. We'll raise such a hullabaloo throughout the land that Lord Liverpool won't dare hold out any longer. He'll have to give us our rights – or we'll take them for ourselves.'

Charles Swindles' words were spoken with a passionate fervour that shone from him like a madness. He made Ben feel uncomfortable. Beliefs meant more to such men than religion – or even life itself. If Ben threw in his lot with Charles Swindles, he would be swept along on an inexorable tide of fanaticism that would eventually overwhelm him. Ben's gaze went from the wide undulating valley laid out before him to the buildings going up about the Sharptor shaft.

'Politics and reform parties are not for me, Mr Swindles. You pursue your dreams wherever they take you. I'll follow tin and copper lodes. They are familiar things to me. I know what they will bring.'

The fire shining from Charles Swindles' eyes burned away as suddenly as it had flared into life. 'I knew you were going to say something like that to me, Ben. As I toiled up here and looked over my shoulder I realised I had little chance of winning you over.'

He swept an arm in an arc that encompassed the whole valley. 'Such beauty as this kills a man's ambition. He needs to be hemmed in by brick walls, surrounded by misery and degradation; the stench of death and disease in his nostrils. That's what makes a man stand up and fight for his rights. He either climbs above everyone else . . . or they climb upon him.'

Charles Swindles gave Ben a rueful smile. 'A radical in Cornwall is crushed to death between John Wesley's teachings and God's own works. However, I'm a man who is used to doing his best with what he has to hand. Will you at least help me to organise a reform meeting, Ben?'

'No, but I'll introduce you to those who will . . .'

Charles Swindles held his meeting the next evening, high on the moor above the mines. If he mourned for the lack of revolutionary enthusiasm, he was, nevertheless, well pleased with the numbers attending his meeting. There must have been four thousand men and women gathered to hear him speak. It was a tremendous crowd for such an isolated spot.

Ben and Jesse went along to hear the Manchester reformer remind his listeners of the aims of his party, and its part in the politics of the new industrial towns of the Midlands. Since the end of the war with France, the working masses had been frequently stirred into violent action against their living and working conditions. The days of wilfully damaging new machinery were past, but when a hostile mob went on the rampage most mill-owners were quick to agree to the demands made upon them. New workers in the industrial areas were immediately drawn into 'societies' or 'unions'.

Then Charles Swindles spoke of the Parliamentary Reform Party's hopes for the future, and told of Ben's part in having Sir Colman Vincent removed from the House of Commons. Swindles went far beyond the true facts of the matter, and Ben edged out of the crowd with Jesse, fearful that the reformer would call him forward and involve him in the meeting against his wishes.

Ben was unable to prevent men from repeating what the

Midland reformer had said, and it was not long before news of Ben's accomplishment reached the ears of Theophilus Strike.

Ben was called to grass from the advancing ten-fathom level of the Wheal Sharptor late one afternoon. He entered the mine office to find Theophilus Strike waiting impatiently for him. The blunt mine-owner wasted no time in coming straight to the point of his visit.

'Word has reached me that you've been involved in deposing the Member of Parliament for Pengony. Is this correct, Retallick?'

'Yes,' Ben replied quietly. His heart sank at the thought of being made to leave Sharptor now, when his cottage was so near to completion. He and Jesse had so much of their future tied up here.

Theophilus Strike waited for Ben to explain. When nothing was forthcoming, he said, 'You are a good miner, Retallick. I have no complaints about your work, but I am starting a new mine here – with my own money. I have taken a big gamble. The last thing I need is to have a troublemaker working for me. If you have any explanation to give, I am ready to listen. If not, you can leave the mine now.'

Theophilus Strike was showing uncharacteristic restraint, and Ben realised he was being given an unexpected opportunity to justify his actions. He also realised he owed Theophilus Strike an explanation.

He began his story with the disaster of the Money Box mine and told of the move to Mevagissey and Pearson Retallick's tragic death at Tregassick. He went on to speak of Sir Colman Vincent's failure to honour Sir John's promise, turning the Retallicks out of their house and attempting to force Jesse to marry Reuben Holyoak. Ben mentioned the two years he had been away from Jesse, during which time Sir Colman had been responsible for having Walter Dunn transported.

He concluded by describing the effects of the storm and Sir Colman's increased tithes on the fishermen of Mevagissey, explaining what it meant to his mother and the Dunn family.

Theophilus Strike listened to Ben's lengthy story without interruption. Feeling a shade more hopeful, Ben added, 'All I wanted was to have Sir Colman Vincent drop his increased tithe charges. Had he not, I would have had to support my mother as well as Jesse and wouldn't have been able to get my marriage off to the start I feel Jesse deserves. I went to see Miss Eulaliah Vincent and she gave me a letter for Mr Howell, the High Sheriff of Cornwall. He did the rest.'

'Eulaliah Vincent? Sir Colman's aunt? She helped you?' Theophilus Strike was incredulous.

Ben repeated Eulaliah Vincent's reason for helping, and Theophilus Strike looked at Ben with a new respect, but he had one more question to ask.

'What about this man from Manchester? The rabblerouser who has been trying to stir up the countryside?'

'He came to me and asked me to join the reform movement. He promised a great future with them and said I might even become a Member of Parliament myself.'

'Oh? And what was your reply to this promise of fame and fortune?'

Ben looked straight at the mine-owner. 'I told him I enjoy my work here. The roof will be on my cottage next week, then Jesse and I will be married. I am a miner, nothing more – and nothing less. I've no wish to involve myself with any reform movement.'

A long silence hung in the room. Abruptly, Theophilus Strike stood up from the corner of the desk upon which he had been seated.

'How is that ten-fathom level coming along, Retallick? When do you think you'll be sending up first-quality ore?'

Only then did Ben realise how tensed he had been. His short fingernails had dug deep grooves in the palms of his hands.

He began to tell Theophilus Strike about the prospects of the ten-fathom level, but the mine-owner did not really want to know. Minutes later Ben was descending the ladder on his way back to work. He had never been so happy to be going down a mine-shaft in all his life.

Chapter Thirty-Five

Ben and Jesse arranged their wedding for Sunday, 10 November 1822. The house was finished and wedding gifts in the form of unwanted pieces of furniture arrived daily, donated by friends who worked on the mine. The furniture helped to take away the bareness of newly whitewashed walls and curtainless windows.

A fortnight before the wedding, Ben went to Mevagissey to inform his mother of the wedding date. On this occasion he did not have to walk. Wrightwick Roberts loaned him his old circuit hack for the journey.

On his arrival in Mevagissey, Ben learned to his great embarrassment that he had become a hero in the eyes of the fishermen. He was greeted with deference by men who had been no more than familiar faces until now. But not until he reached the Dunn house was he told the whole reason for their respect.

Martha Retallick was at home with Grandma Dunn. After they had both hugged him and said how well he was looking, they fussed over him and brought him up to date on the many things that had been happening in Mevagissey.

Sir Colman Vincent's latest tithe demand had been dropped within a fortnight of Ben's visit to the High Sheriff of Cornwall. It was quickly followed by the news that Sir Colman had resigned as Member of Parliament for Pengony. Then Pengony's two seats in the House of Commons had been taken away from the village and given to the industrial Midlands.

All this Ben already knew from his conversation with Charles Swindles. What he had *not* known was that Sir Colman Vincent had sold the whole of his Cornish estates and was withdrawing to his lands in Devon. Ben's victory over the baronet had become a rout! Now he knew why the villagers of Mevagissey had saluted him so respectfully.

No sooner had Martha Retallick finished giving her son the astonishing news than Grandpa Dunn, accompanied by Mark and Billy, arrived home. Ben had to listen to the same news over again. This time it was accompanied by much back-slapping and a familiarity he had never before experienced in the Dunn house.

When there was a quieter moment, Ben asked, 'Does this mean Reuben Holyoak is now without work?'

'No,' replied Martha Retallick regretfully. 'He was. Sir Colman dismissed him before news of the sale came out, but the new owner has taken him back – as a gamekeeper. He's still living up at Pengrugla, by all accounts. He hasn't dared show himself in Mevagissey for many months. Nor will he, if he has any sense left in his head.'

'Is the new owner already in Lamorrack House?' Ben was taken aback by the speed with which things had been happening.

'Yes, and one of the first things he did was to come to Mevagissey to speak to us. He stood on the quay one evening with his young family about him and introduced himself to every fisherman who sailed into the harbour. He said he'd heard of the terrible storm we'd suffered in the summer, and promised he would not be looking for tithes until we were back on our feet again. That's the kind of gentleman we need up at Lamorrack, Ben. We haven't seen the likes of him hereabouts since old Sir John died.'

Mark Dunn had replied to Ben's question and the others all nodded their agreement with his words. It was apparent that the new squire of Lamorrack had made a good first impression upon the fishermen of Mevagissey.

'Don't you be forgetting it was Ben who brought it all about,' said Grandpa Dunn proudly. 'He's a Dunn, and no mistake.'

'It was another Dunn who first obtained the information that finally toppled Sir Colman Vincent,' said Ben. 'If it hadn't been for Walter, none of this might have happened. He has finally been avenged.'

For a moment, Ben wondered if he had made a mistake mentioning Walter. The family might have heard news of his fate. Billy's next words reassured him.

'Walter is on the other side of the world. You are here with us in Mevagissey. Come on down to the Ship Inn, Ben. There's many a fisherman who'd feel honoured to buy you a drink. Things are better now, and no mistake. One more good catch of pilchards and we'll be able to buy our second boat for the next season.'

Ben declined his uncle's invitation, pleading that he needed to make an early start the following day. In spite of their protests he did not weaken. He was going to Tregassick to speak to Eulaliah Vincent, then on to Truro to invite Alan Colborne and Judy Lean to the wedding.

The Dunn family kept Ben talking until late in the night, and he was bleary-eyed when he dismounted from the old circuit horse at the gates of Tregassick House. Eulaliah Vincent was having breakfast and insisted upon Ben joining her at the table.

Ben had expected to find this meeting difficult in view of all that had happened to her nephew and the changes going on about her, but the elderly lady was in high spirits. When Ben told her of the forthcoming wedding, she expressed her satisfaction.

'You will make a handsome couple. Jesse is one of the finest-looking girls in the county, and I can think of no young girl who would not jump at the opportunity of standing at your side before an altar. Now, Ben Retallick, what would you like me to bring for a wedding present?'

'You are coming to the wedding . . . to Henwood?'

'I most certainly am! I would not miss Jesse's wedding if you were marrying her in America. Why? Will I not be welcome?'

'After all you've done for us? We will both be very happy to have you there. But you'll need to stay the night and we have little furniture in the house.'

'You need not worry about me. I will stay with David Howell. I want to thank him for the manner in which he handled your "problem". I will send him a letter today.'

Now the subject had been broached, Ben was able to ask the question that had been troubling him.

'You don't mind that Sir Colman has gone from Lamorrack House and left you here, alone?'

'Mind? My dear young man, I am overjoyed! After all these years I am able to go about my business with no interference. There is no one to tell me what I must or must not do. For the first time in my life I am free to do what I will, without having some member of my family express his disapproval. My only regret is that I am not young enough to enjoy my new-found freedom even more.'

Ben left the house marvelling that Sir Colman Vincent should have such an aunt as Eulaliah Vincent.

Ben reached the White Swan Inn in Truro at noon on a quiet Sunday. It was a very different town from the one he and Alan Colborne had entered on the May fair-day earlier in the year. On that occasion its streets had been crowded with noisy country folk from miles around. Today there was hardly a man, woman or child to be seen, for all that it was a fine autumn day. Even the White Swan Inn had only a few customers, and the landlord sat at a table with a tankard of his own ale before him.

He recognised Ben and greeted him warmly, drawing him an ale from the huge barrel at the back of the room and setting a chair at his own table.

'You've chosen a good day to come visiting, Ben. Today I have time to speak with my friends and nothing to do but sit here and drink the best ale to be had in the town.'

'Where is everyone?' asked Ben. 'I've seen no more than five persons since I rode in. Is something wrong? Has cholera struck the town?'

'No, everyone has gone to Falmouth. My own wife and daughter with them. A ship bound for Holland with a cargo of strange creatures from Africa put into Falmouth to repair storm damage. The animals are being transferred to another ship today, and everyone has gone along to watch. I would have gone myself had I been able to find someone to look after the inn. They do say there are monkeys on board that are almost human. As large as you and I, and nearly as clever. Aye, and creatures as heavy as four farm-wagons, with horns on their noses sharp enough to pierce the side of a ship. There will be talk of nothing else in this part of Cornwall for weeks to come.'

There was a note of deep disappointment in the landlord's voice.

'No doubt Alan and Judy have gone with them?'

The landlord looked startled. 'Alan and Judy? They left for Plymouth three months ago. I thought perhaps you might have news of them. They were going to find Judy's mother and then return to Mevagissey to visit you.'

Ben frowned. 'We're no longer at Mevagissey, but I was there only this morning. I would have been told had anyone been enquiring for me.'

Ben was disappointed. He had hoped that Alan Colborne and Judy Lean would be able to attend the wedding at Sharptor. He had meant it to be a happy surprise for Jesse. After telling the landlord of his wedding plans, to pass on to them, should they return in time, Ben set off on the long return journey to Sharptor.

Chapter Thirty-Six

Alan Colborne and Judy Lean travelled to Plymouth by sea from the quay at Truro. Judy dearly wanted to tell her mother of her forthcoming marriage and receive her approval. Alan Colborne had grave misgivings about the mission, but there had been few pleasures in Judy's young life and he fell in with her wishes.

It was the first time Judy had ever been on a ship. She found the experience exciting, yet at the same time terrifying. There was a favourable wind, and the voyage took ten hours. Along the way Alan Colborne asked Judy to describe the coastline to him. Her excitement when she recognised Mevagissey, tucked between its surrounding hills, delighted Alan Colborne and brought amused smiles from the other passengers.

Eventually, the ship heeled over to pass through a small armada of dusty barges. From them, stone and rubble tumbled into the water at the mouth of Plymouth harbour, forming the foundations of a new breakwater. The short voyage was over.

With Alan Colborne holding her arm as they walked from the docks, Judy Lean looked back wistfully at the ship they had just left. It had been a magic voyage for her, a time to be happy with Alan without anyone expecting anything more from her.

Judy knew she was not as clever as other girls. She had always known it, but it had never before mattered quite so much. Sometimes, she had even found her simple ways to be an advantage. When she did things for which other girls would have been punished, people merely shrugged their shoulders and turned away. It was 'that simple Judy again'.

Now Judy Lean had Alan Colborne. What he thought of her mattered more than anything else in her life. She wanted him to be proud of her, not forced to make excuses for her. Judy loved Alan Colborne with a depth of feeling she had never before experienced.

'Where do we start looking?' Alan Colborne broke in upon Judy's thoughts as they came to a street that was filled with the noises of a busy sea-port.

'I don't know,' Judy confessed. 'Ma came to Plymouth to marry a sailor. He used to come to Pentuan on the boats that loaded china-clay. That's all I know.'

'It's enough for a start.' Alan Colborne made it sound more hopeful than he really felt. Finding an unknown and unnamed sailor in a large port such as this was well-nigh impossible. However, they would try, and they were in no great hurry.

The first thing they had to do was find a place to stay. Alan told Judy to look for a boarding-house, far enough away from the docks to keep them from being disturbed all night by the noisy arrival of seamen and their waterfront women, but not so far that a landlord would ask too many questions.

They eventually found a quiet room in a house above the

jumbled streets of the Barbican. It was a fortunate choice. The landlady had once had a blind son who reached the age of twelve before he was knocked down and killed by a reckless and intoxicated chaise-driver. The driver was the younger son of one of Devon's richest noblemen. The house where she now lived had been a gift to compensate the widow for her tragic loss. Alan Colborne and Judy Lean could have found no more suitable lodgings.

Locating the dock used by the boats engaged in the carriage of china-clay was equally successful. Indeed, it would have been difficult to miss. Spillages in the streets around the dock stained the cobblestones white. Inside the dock, a choking white cloud hung over the ships and drifted on the air to the sensitive nose of the balladeer.

But here the luck of the two seekers ended. For weeks they hung around the docks and adjacent inns, questioning seamen from every boat that tied up at the quay, hoping to find someone who knew of the seaman who had married Nellie Lean from Mevagissey village.

In the evenings, Alan Colborne played his fiddle in a harbourside inn. It was a rough place, and he would not allow Judy to wait for him there. She took him to the door of the inn early every evening, then returned to collect him again at midnight.

It was an arrangement that worked well for a while. Then, one evening, as Judy led Alan Colborne along the uneven Barbican street, there came the noise of running feet behind them. A man shouted, and in the dark doorway of a nearby house a woman began to scream hysterically.

Judy Lean did not know what was happening, but she took hold of Alan Colborne's arm and ran with him towards a dark and narrow alleyway only a couple of dozen paces away. They would have made it to safety had there not been an iron bollard set into the cobbles in the centre of the alleyway opening.

Alan Colborne stumbled over the bollard and fell full length on the ground. In an instant, two uniformed men pounced upon him and dragged him away, ignoring Judy's screams. The press-gangs were out, recruiting seamen for the men-of-war of His Majesty King George IV's navy.

Alan Colborne was hauled to the water's edge and flung into a boat in which a number of other impressed men cowered. Two of them were badly bruised and one was bleeding from a gash on his forehead. At the top of the steps where the boat was moored, the girl Judy and Alan had heard screaming earlier pleaded hysterically for her man to be released. She was noticeably pregnant.

Every time the press-gang returned to the boat with another unfortunate captive, Judy Lean tried to speak to one of the men, but the wails and shrieks of the pregnant girl drowned her own efforts.

When there were a dozen men in the boat, it was evident that the press-gang would soon have as many 'recruits' as they could safely carry. The hysterical pregnant woman realised it, too. When Judy Lean begged her to be silent for a moment, she wailed the louder. Then Judy saw the officer in charge of the press-gang returning with the remainder of his men, two impressed seamen struggling between them.

Judy had to make herself heard now or it would be too late. The pregnant woman still showed no sign of moderating her noise and, in a moment of sheer desperation, Judy lunged at her, pushing her over the edge of the quay into the water. The pregnant woman landed with a mighty splash, her screams cut short as the dirty waters of the harbour closed over her head.

Instantly, there was pandemonium in the press-gang's boat.

Flinging aside the man who tried to hold him, the husband of the pregnant woman leaped over the side, quickly followed by another of the impressed men.

The officer in charge of the press-gang, a limping lieutenant, hobbled to the water's edge and looked down upon the scene of confusion. Rounding on Judy Lean, he said angrily, 'Why did you do that?'

'She wouldn't be quiet. No one could hear me. You must let Alan go – he's blind.'

'Blind? Blind?' The officer looked at Judy Lean suspiciously. 'Are you telling me the truth?'

'Yes. He was blinded in the war, at Waterloo.'

It was some minutes before the officer received any answer to his shouts, such was the noise in the boat. The pregnant woman and her husband had surfaced and were swimming in the wake of the second man to leap from the boat. Heading away from the boat to the far harbour wall, the heavy stomach of the woman was proving no handicap to her swimming.

'Leave them!' the officer ordered. 'We have a good haul this evening. They'll keep for another time. Is there a blind man down there in the boat?'

'There is, sir.' Alan Colborne turned his face up towards the speaker.

'Then why haven't you spoken up before?' As he called out the question, the officer nodded his head almost imperceptibly at his coxswain.

Alan Colborne grinned. 'To whom should I have addressed myself in this floating bedlam, Captain?'

The lieutenant scowled. At that moment, the boat's coxswain, who had been working his way to Alan Colborne's side from the stern of the boat, swung a beefy fist. It stopped only half an inch from the balladeer's nose. Alan Colborne did not flinch.

The lieutenant and his coxswain had operated a press-gang together for many years. This was not the first occasion on which a man had attempted to avoid service to his king and country by pleading blindness.

'Yes, I recognise him now,' called another member of the press-gang. 'He's a blind fiddler who plays in the Mermaid Inn on the Barbican.'

'Then get him up here quickly,' ordered the officer. 'And get the rest of them out to the ship. Hurry, now, or every one of them will have someone swearing that he's an apprentice or an honourably discharged seaman.'

The officer passed Alan Colborne on the quay steps and growled, 'Think yourself lucky, fiddler. Had we not learned you were blind before we reached the ship, you would have been thrown overboard and left to swim ashore – eyes or no.'

With that, the lieutenant put his foot against the bow of the press-gang boat and pushed it angrily away from the steps.

Judy Lean helped Alan Colborne up the last few steps and hurried away with him, fearful that the officer in charge of the press-gang might yet change his mind and decide there was a place in a man-of-war for a blind fiddler.

She was trembling so much that, before they arrived at the inn, Alan Colborne made her stop. In an effort to calm her down, he asked what had happened to cause such a disturbance at the quayside.

By the time Judy had ended her story, Alan Colborne was laughing merrily. Reaching for her face, he cupped it in his hands and kissed her long and hard upon her lips.

'Judy, I will hear no man call you simple again. You were as quick-witted back there as any woman or man I have ever known. I am proud of you. I'll not be content until we are married and no one can take you from me.'

Judy made her way back to their lodgings with so much happiness inside her at Alan's words that she felt she must burst. The happiness shone from her like spring sunshine, and the men and women she passed along the narrow streets found themselves returning her smile and bidding the happy girl 'Good evening'.

A few nights later, when Judy Lean arrived at the Mermaid Inn to take Alan Colborne home, she found him waiting for her beside the open doorway. She kissed him and took an arm to lead him away. Instead of going with her, he held her back.

'Wait, Judy. I don't want to build up your hopes unnecessarily, but I would like you to put your head inside the doorway and look at a woman sitting close to the fire. I heard her called "Nellie" and she speaks with the accent of south Cornwall. She is with a man, but he's not a seaman.'

Filled with excitement, Judy slipped from Alan Colborne's grasp and leaned in through the doorway.

The tobacco smoke hanging in the room stung her eyes and for a few moments she could not see through the blue haze. Then a group of men standing in the middle of the room parted to allow a serving-girl through.

Behind them, seated by the fire, Judy Lean saw her mother.

'It's her, Alan. It *is* my ma!'

Alan Colborne made no answer. He had hoped he might be mistaken. He knew something of the man who was with Nellie Lean. He was one of the ragged band of men who haunted dockside taverns, seizing upon any opportunity to earn a dishonest shilling.

Alan Colborne had also been listening to the conversation of Nellie Lean and her companion. It was apparent to him that the two were living together in something less than harmony.

It was too late for regrets now. Judy Lean had taken his hand and was dragging him behind her across the room, careless of his limitations, so eager was she to reach her mother.

'Ma . . . ! Ma, it's me. Judy.'

Judy Lean came to a halt before her mother, quivering with the emotion of seeing her again after so long. Judy had never considered that her mother might not share her own joy at the reunion. She hardly noticed that her reception was decidedly cool.

In truth, Nellie Lean was both shocked and dismayed to be suddenly confronted with her daughter. Her romance with the sailor she had met at Pentuan had been a brief and violent affair. When it came to an end, Nellie Lean had taken to the tavern life, accepting all it entailed for a woman. After a while, she met up with Aaron Yeo and became deeply infatuated with him. She knew all about his dishonest ways, but he beat her less often than had her former sailor lover. Aaron Yeo was some years younger than Nellie Lean, and the last thing she needed was to have a hitherto unmentioned grown-up daughter arrive and give Aaron Yeo cause to question her age.

Eventually, the absence of a welcome did register with Judy. She looked at her mother in deep distress, and Alan Colborne felt the grip on his hand tighten painfully.

'Aren't you pleased to see me, Ma? I've been looking for you for weeks. I wanted you to meet Alan. Me and him are going to be married. I thought you'd want to know . . .'

'Of course she wants to know . . . don't you, Nellie?'

Aaron Yeo elbowed Nellie Lean in the ribs. Startled, she looked at him and he gave her a sly wink.

'We're both pleased to meet you and your intended . . . ain't we, Nellie?'

Leaning towards Nellie Lean, he whispered, 'Don't you recognise him? It's the fiddler, the blind man who sits in here and plays every evening.'

Nellie Lean was surprised by Aaron Yeo's unexpected acceptance of Judy, but she took her cue from him.

'Why, yes . . . of course we're pleased to see you, Judy. I'm at a loss for words, that's all, my dear.'

'Well said, Nellie. There, can't you see how pleased your ma is, Judy? Why, unless I'm mistaken, them's tears in her eyes. I'm happy, too. My name is Aaron Yeo. I'm a close friend of your ma . . . a *very* close friend.'

Aaron Yeo gave Nellie Lean another wink and a dig in the ribs.

Taking Judy's hand, Aaron Yeo squeezed it and leered at her, secure in the knowledge that Alan Colborne could not see him.

Judy was too happy to notice anything amiss and she did not attempt to withdraw her hand from Aaron Yeo. Nellie Lean did not miss Yeo's attentions and she became more anxious than ever for her unwanted daughter to leave Plymouth.

'You and your ma must have lots to talk about.' Aaron Yeo relinquished Judy's hand after giving it a final squeeze. 'I'll have some more gin brought here. I'll fetch your fiddle from the landlord, too, Alan. This is a happy occasion. One we must celebrate. No, don't you argue with me. This will be an evening you'll not forget in a hurry.'

When his fiddle had been brought to him, Alan Colborne had no alternative but to play. Aaron Yeo's loud voice ensured that everyone in the tavern knew of their 'celebration' – and many of the customers contributed to the gin that appeared on the table before them.

In between tunes, Alan Colborne could hear that the conversation between Judy and her mother was as one-sided as ever, but it seemed not to matter to Judy. She chattered away happily, as though everything in her life was now perfect.

Then Nellie Lean suggested that Alan was being neglected, and Judy came to kneel on the floor beside his chair as he played and sang.

When he ended his ballad, and the applause was at its height, Judy said happily to him, 'You were very clever to find my ma for me, Alan. Do you like her? Is she what you expected?'

'My thoughts are far too occupied with her daughter,' replied Alan Colborne, avoiding a direct answer to her question. 'But if she approves of me perhaps we can set the date for our wedding?'

Judy Lean frowned. She was having difficulty in concentrating on a reply. Aaron Yeo had kept her glass well filled tonight. 'I . . . I think she likes you, Alan. She hasn't said very much. I know it doesn't really matter, but I would like her to say she'll be happy to have you as her son-in-law. I want her to come to our wedding.'

Judy would have continued her indecisive chatter had Alan Colborne not reached down quickly and laid a finger across her lips, 'Shh! I am listening.'

His remarkable hearing had picked up a fragment of Nellie Lean's whispered conversation. Now he strained to hear more, doing his best to ignore the noise all about them.

'I don't want to have Judy stay here in Plymouth. I didn't want her in the first place. I left her working for Reuben Holyoak and thought I'd seen the last of her. All my life she's been in the way of everything I wanted to do. Let her go off with her blind fiddler; she can go as far away as he can take her. I don't want her bothering me *ever* again.'

Nellie Lean's words were slurred, distorted by gin and thick with self-pity. Her voice began to rise above a whisper, but Aaron Yeo was quick to silence her.

'Don't be so hasty, Nellie. Judy's a handsome girl. She could prove a great comfort to you . . . to us both!'

'I knew it! I knew it, Aaron Yeo! You've taken a fancy to my daughter. Now I don't matter to you. I saw the way you were looking at her. Well, let me tell you . . . You'd soon be sick to the craw of her simple ways . . .'

'Shut up, Nellie!' Aaron Yeo's voice rose to a hoarse whisper that Alan Colborne found easier to hear. ''Tis you and me I'm thinking about, not me and your daughter. I'd be lying to you if I didn't say she was handsome. Haven't you seen the way the sailors in here are looking at her? She's simple, you say? Well, so much the better. She'll do exactly what you tell her. Persuade her to be kind to sea-faring men, Nellie. Some of them have been months at sea without seeing a woman and they are in here with pockets filled with money. Judy can take them off to some room and we'll empty their pockets while she keeps them busy. We'll make ourselves a packet, Nellie. Enough for you and me to move away from Plymouth and make a new start together.'

Judy Lean fidgeted and reached a hand up to Alan Colborne's finger, wanting to speak. He pressed his finger tighter to her lips. He had to hear what was said next.

Nellie Lean began snivelling. 'What are you asking me to do, Aaron? She's my own daughter . . .'

'She *owes* it to you, Nellie. You've said yourself how much you've sacrificed for her. She'll do it; she's a simple girl and I can see she's very fond of you. Tell her you're in desperate straits. That unless you get the money to pay off some bad debts you'll be carried off to prison. Say she need only do it once or twice. She'll believe you; you know she will.'

There was such a long silence that Alan Colborne thought

the scheming couple might have moved away. Then, just before one of a large party of seamen cracked a joke that received a noisy reception, he heard Nellie Lean sniff. 'All right. But what about the fiddler? What do we do with him?'

The noise of the seamen destroyed any chance Alan Colborne had of hearing more. He removed his finger from Judy's lips and turned her face up towards his.

'Where are they now, Judy? Your mother and Aaron Yeo? Are they looking at us?'

Judy did not understand the urgency in his voice, but she answered him quickly, 'No. They are talking together. They're not looking.'

'Then take me out of here. *Now!* Hurry, Judy, before anyone can stop us. Move, girl.'

He had never before bullied Judy in this fashion, but it worked. She was hurrying from the tavern with Alan Colborne clutching her hand before she even paused to think.

Once outside, he asked, 'Did you tell your mother where we are lodging?'

'No. Why?'

Judy Lean was a very confused girl.

'It doesn't matter now. Get us back to the lodgings as quickly as you can.'

Out here in the darkness, Alan Colborne's lack of sight was no disadvantage. He hurried Judy away from the tavern, his feet more sure than hers on the cobbled surface.

'But my ma? She'll wonder what's happened to me.'

They turned a corner and Alan pulled Judy to face him. She could just make out his strained face in the light from a nearby bedroom window.

'Judy, do you love me enough to trust me absolutely?'

Judy hesitated, then nodded. Remembering he could not see, she whispered, 'Yes.'

'Then you must believe me when I say we need to get away from here without your mother knowing where we are going. Aaron Yeo has evil plans for you. I heard him persuading your mother to use you to help him to rob seamen. He said there would be no lasting harm in it for you, and your mother believed him. We have to leave Plymouth quickly. You found your mother, and told her we are to be married. Now you must forget her and entrust your future to me. Do you feel able to do that?'

'Yes.'

The sound was forced from Judy Lean's throat.

'Then take us to our lodgings. Hurry, now!'

Alan Colborne had caught the sound of Aaron Yeo's excited voice in the distance. It would not do for him to catch them in this dark and narrow street.

Judy heard the voice, too. Taking Alan's arm she hurried him along narrow alleyways and up steep slippery flights of steps to arrive finally at the house where they were staying.

When they reached the safety of their room, Alan Colborne took Judy in his arms and did his best to soothe away the tears that overwhelmed the desperately unhappy girl.

That day had seen her most cherished dream taken from her and smashed into fragments that could never be put together again.

Chapter Thirty-Seven

Alan Colborne and Judy Lean set off from Plymouth early the next morning. It was grey and cheerless, with a desultory wind blowing through the narrow streets of the port, ruffling the hair of scavenging dogs and sending brittle brown leaves scurrying over the cobblestones.

There was already much movement at the water's edge. The fishing-fleet and a great many merchantmen had ridden in on the early-morning tide. Although it was much too early to expect Aaron Yeo to be abroad, Alan Colborne took no chances. He and Judy made a wide detour round the quays and jetties of the harbour, not approaching the waterfront until they reached the navy yards. Here the River Tamar flowed into the natural harbour of the Sound and they found a ferryman to take them across the river to Cremyll.

When they again set foot on land they were in Cornwall, and Alan Colborne breathed more easily as they set off for Truro. It was his intention that he and Judy should be married there without any more delay.

The weather along the journey was wet and cold, and they made very slow time, staying at a number of inns and taverns where Alan Colborne and his singing and fiddle-playing were welcomed.

Eventually they arrived at St Austell. When Judy mentioned to Alan Colborne that Mevagissey was only a few miles distant, he suggested they pay a surprise visit to Ben and Jesse, believing them to be still in the area.

At first, Judy did not share Alan's enthusiasm for a visit to Mevagissey. Too many unhappy things had happened to her there. Then she thought of the people she knew, servants at Lamorrack House. She could introduce Alan to them; it would compensate her for the heartbreak she had suffered at her mother's hands.

It was already mid-afternoon, but Alan Colborne was so keen to carry his idea into effect that he insisted they set off immediately.

Judy's worry was that darkness would catch up with them before they reached Mevagissey. Her anxiety seemed justified when heavy clouds began to build up overhead, hastening the dusk. Because of this, when they were still a couple of miles from the village, she guided Alan Colborne off the track, on to a path that cut across the shoulder of a steep hill. It passed close to Pengrugla, the place about which she still had occasional nightmares, but it was a quicker route to Mevagissey. She did not wish to lead Alan along a slippery wagon-rutted road in the darkness.

At the top of the hill, they passed through the copse surrounding the house where Judy had lived with Reuben Holyoak, and Judy fell silent, grateful for Alan Colborne's hand in hers.

They were only a matter of yards from the house when Alan pulled Judy to a halt.

'There is someone coming along the path.'

Judy immediately flew into a panic. 'Quick, we must hide.'

'Why? We are hurting no one. It's all right, Judy. I am with you now.'

In spite of Alan Colborne's assurance, Judy stood trembling in the centre of the path, praying that the footsteps did not belong to the man she feared more than anyone else in the world.

Her prayers were offered up too late. Moments later she saw Reuben Holyoak striding along the path towards them, a fowling-piece crooked in his arm. The light was not good beneath the trees and it was evident that Reuben Holyoak had not yet recognised Judy Lean.

'What are you doing here?' he demanded. 'This is private land. You are trespassing.'

From the painful grip of Judy's hand, Alan Colborne realised that she knew and feared this man. Instinctively, he knew that the man now talking to them had been the father of Judy's stillborn child.

'We are on our way to Mevagissey village from St Austell. We came this way in order to reach the village before darkness falls.'

'That alters nothing. You should have set out earlier . . . along the road.'

Reuben Holyoak spoke to Alan Colborne, but he was looking at Judy. There was something familiar about her. He moved closer to see her better.

Alan Colborne smelled the fear that emanated from Judy and he pulled her to him to reassure her. To Reuben Holyoak he said, 'I apologise if we have disturbed you, but we'll not damage any of your property along the way . . .'

'Not so fast. That's Judy, isn't it? Judy Lean?'

Judy nodded with difficulty. Her body was as paralysed with fear as a rabbit confronted by a weasel.

'It's Judy Lean at the moment,' said Alan Colborne, successfully concealing his own unease. 'But it will soon be Judy Colborne. She is marrying me before the month is out.'

'Is that so?' Reuben Holyoak had been watching the way Alan Colborne stood, how he turned his head to hear after he spoke. He realised Alan Colborne was blind – and he immediately dismissed him as being of no account.

'You know you shouldn't use this path, Judy. You'll get into trouble wandering around on other folk's land.'

'We aren't doing no harm, Mr Holyoak. Honest, we aren't.'

Alan Colborne hardly recognised Judy's voice. All the confidence she had gained since leaving Pengrugla had fled from her. She was once again the simple browbeaten girl she had been for all her earlier years.

'We'd better talk about this. You come on into the house with me. You remember Pengrugla, don't you, Judy? The things we did there?'

'Judy is on her way to Mevagissey with me. If you want to discuss anything, you can come down there to do it – although from what I have heard of you, I doubt if you have the courage to show your face to Mevagissey men.'

Reuben Holyoak frowned, then gave a short derisive laugh. 'You have a loose tongue for a man with no sight. Use it as much as you wish, blind man, there is no one to hear you at Pengrugla. Just you sit down on the bank and listen to the birds for a while. When I've finished with Judy I'll let her come back and lead you on your way – like a dog. But don't be too impatient; I want to be sure she's forgotten none of the tricks I taught her.'

Judy was shaking so much Alan Colborne feared she would have a fit. He tightened his grip on her hand and said quietly, 'Move on along the path, Judy, but keep me between yourself and Holyoak.'

Under his prompting, Judy began to move forward slowly, and Alan Colborne went with her. When they were almost level with Reuben Holyoak, Alan Colborne heard him make a move towards Judy. Arms outstretched, he flung himself forward and managed to grip the gamekeeper's coat.

The suddenness of Alan Colborne's move took Reuben Holyoak by surprise. He stumbled and fell to his knees, the fowling-piece slipping from his grasp.

Keeping a tight grip of the gamekeeper, Alan Colborne shouted, 'Run, Judy! Run to Mevagissey and get help from Ben and the fishermen. Tell them Holyoak attacked us—'

A heavy fist caught Alan Colborne in the mouth, splitting his lips and cutting his words short. Releasing one of his hands, Alan Colborne struck out towards Reuben Holyoak's face. The blow struck the gamekeeper in the eye, drawing a sharp grunt of pain from him.

Now Reuben Holyoak became a mad thing. He struck at Alan Colborne again and again, beating him to the ground. Then he knelt over him, punching him in the face, oblivious of the screams of Judy Lean as she saw Alan battered into insensibility.

Judy rushed at the gamekeeper, crying hysterically, and her fingernails raked his face. Cursing, he flung her violently from him. As she fell to the ground, her outflung arm touched the cold steel of the fowling-piece.

Scrambling to her feet, Judy picked up the weapon and pointed the long barrel at Reuben Holyoak. It was one of the new percussion sporting-guns – a weapon she remembered well. Reuben Holyoak had purchased the gun when he was first appointed as Sir Colman Vincent's agent. It had been his most treasured possession. He had cleaned and polished it every night, explaining details of its action to Judy. She had even fired the gun. On the first occasion it had been the result of a generous impulse on Reuben Holyoak's part, but the loud report had terrified her. After that, he had forced her to fire the gun for no other reason than to laugh at her fear.

Terror was in her now, but it had nothing to do with the gun she was holding. Judy Lean's fear was for the life of Alan Colborne, who no longer stirred beneath Reuben Holyoak's blows.

Reuben Holyoak looked up in time to see Judy Lean's finger tighten on the trigger of the gun. He threw up an arm in a vain attempt to ward off the shot and died with a scream in his throat as the charge took him full in the face.

Throwing down the gun, Judy dragged the gamekeeper off Alan Colborne, trying not to look at the ghastly mess that had been Reuben Holyoak's face.

The blind balladeer lay quite still, covered in blood. How much was his own, and how much had come from Reuben Holyoak, Judy did not know.

She tried everything she knew to rouse Alan, but he did not move. He did not even groan, and Judy knew he needed the attentions of a doctor.

Alan Colborne was not a large man, and Judy Lean was a strong girl, accustomed to coping with situations that called for physical strength. After a brief struggle, she lifted him in her arms and set off with him across the fields – away from Reuben Holyoak. She was taking him to a place where he would be certain to receive the best care possible. Lamorrack House.

The arrival of the exhausted bloodstained girl with her unconscious burden caused consternation at the great house. The servant girl who answered the hammering at the kitchen door fled into the house, screaming. Within minutes, the new owner and most of his staff were at the scene.

Judy was immediately recognised, and as she gasped out

her story servants were sent running in all directions. One man hurried to Mevagissey to fetch the doctor. Two more were sent to find Reuben Holyoak – and another rode to St Austell for the magistrate.

The two men who had been to Pengrugla returned first. They were pale and shaken after seeing the result of the violent death meted out to Reuben Holyoak. They avoided looking at Judy Lean. Not until the owner of Lamorrack House drew them outside the room did they give an account of their grisly find. They told him other things, too: of the time Judy had lived at Pengrugla and worked for Reuben Holyoak; of the suspicious circumstances surrounding the birth and death of her child. They also explained that Judy Lean had a limited intelligence.

The two servants exaggerated in the manner of all gossips, leaving the new squire of Lamorrack with the impression that Judy Lean's mental state was akin to madness. He immediately ordered them to lock the door on her and left the two servants to guard the room where she waited by Alan Colborne's side.

The door was unlocked to admit the doctor, and he was still in the room examining the cuts and bruises of the now semi-conscious Alan Colborne when the magistrate arrived.

The Reverend Hawkins was hot from his fast ride and full of the importance of his office. He listened impatiently as the servants who had been to Pengrugla told of finding Reuben Holyoak's body. The magistrate's thoughts were already leapfrogging ahead of their words.

'I remember this girl well,' he told the owner of Lamorrack House. 'I protested that she should have been charged with murder when the inquest upon her child was held. It has taken the death of an innocent man to vindicate my judgement. Mr Holyoak gave evidence against her then. No doubt she has brooded on the matter all this time, and returned with an accomplice to seek revenge.'

The squire of Lamorrack had been thinking along similar lines, but he was surprised at the alacrity with which the St Austell magistrate leaped to such a positive conclusion.

'I must admit there are suspicious circumstances surrounding Holyoak's death. An investigation must be carried out,' he said. 'But had the girl come here bent upon revenge she would hardly have brought her accomplice to my house.'

The Reverend Hawkins shrugged his shoulders, his mind closed to any argument against his theory. 'Who can follow the tortuous workings of a simple mind? I will be obliged if you will keep the girl and her accomplice under guard until my constable arrives, sir. Meanwhile I must return to St Austell and make the arrangements for an early hearing. The Assizes commence before the month's end, and there are no cases of note to be heard. A murder trial should ensure that His Majesty's Judges do not waste their time in Cornwall. I thank you for your help, sir.'

The Reverend Hawkins carried out his promise with almost indecent haste. Judy Lean and Alan Colborne appeared before his bench only two days after their arrest and were swiftly committed to Bodmin Gaol, there to await trial at the forthcoming Assizes.

It would not be a case to excite any great interest or controversy. It was nothing more complicated than the murder of a gamekeeper by a wandering balladeer and his woman. It would not merit even a single paragraph in the national newspapers of the day.

Chapter Thirty-Eight

The wedding of Ben and Jesse was the little mining community's event of the year. Jesse was the envy of every future bride in Henwood. Not only did Martha Retallick attend from Mevagissey, accompanied by her two brothers and their large families, but Fanny and Loveday Ustick came, too, as did Theophilus Strike – and Eulaliah Vincent.

Eulaliah Vincent's carriage was the first light vehicle seen in the village. The roads in the mining area were not suited to the frail wheels and sophisticated springing of a town vehicle.

Waiting in Linkinhorne church for Jesse, Ben felt strange and uncomfortable in a new serge suit and a shirt of stiff cotton. It proved to be particularly difficult when Ben tried to turn his head against the tight collar to get his first glimpse of Jesse in the white wedding dress she had kept a secret from him.

Then she was by his side, with the young Kelynack girls in attendance, looking more beautiful than he had ever seen her.

When the vicar told them to kneel, Ben's boots, new from a Liskeard shoemaker only the day before, were reluctant to bend, creaking with all the noise of a ungreased door. Ben cast an embarrassed sidelong glance at Jesse and was mortified to see that she was smiling. Then she looked up at him and shared her smile, and Ben relaxed.

The vicar of Linkinhorne did not prolong the ceremony. Neither Ben nor Jesse belonged to his church. The ceremony was necessary only to satisfy the letter of the law. Twenty minutes after entering the church, Ben and Jesse left it as Mr and Mrs Retallick and returned to Henwood for a service in Wrightwick Roberts's small chapel.

Eulaliah Vincent had spoken disparagingly to Jesse of a chapel wedding service, but she found little to fault here. The interior had been newly whitewashed, and there was no shortage of flowers to provide a splendid splash of bright colour. Most of the flowers had been gathered from the moorland shrubs, but there were also a few precious late-autumn blooms, picked from the gardens of the miners' wives.

Wrightwick Roberts was not a preacher to give short measure at a church service, whether it celebrated a baptism, a marriage or a funeral. He made quite certain that no one in his chapel was in any doubt about Ben and Jesse Retallick being well and truly married.

Outside the chapel, the young couple faced a barrage of congratulations from friends and wellwishers, many of whom had been unable to make the journey to Linkinhorne or crowd into the tiny chapel.

The greetings over, Ben and Jesse were sent on their way to the new house on Sharptor in Theophilus Strike's small gig.

At the house, a veritable feast was laid out for family and friends, all the food having been provided by neighbours and guests. Theophilus Strike, in particular, had dipped deep into his own pocket to celebrate both the wedding and the completion of the first house on the Wheal Sharptor.

The celebrations went on until late afternoon, when Eulaliah Vincent was the first to say her farewells to the newly wed couple.

'I wish you every happiness for your future together,' she said. 'And I expect you to bring your firstborn to visit me. Not that you need wait until then to come to Mevagissey. With Reuben Holyoak dead there are no bad memories left and no reason why you should not come to see me as often as it pleases you.'

'Reuben Holyoak dead?' Jesse was startled.

'Why, yes, dear. I thought you must have known. He was shot by a young girl whose mother once worked at Lamorrack House. Judy Lean. You must have known her. She was a little – well, simple. She and her lover are to be tried at next week's Assizes in Bodmin. Mrs Retallick will tell you all about it. I must leave before it is too dark. My coachman is not certain of his way, and these lanes will surely shake out whatever sense of direction he has.'

Eulaliah Vincent left the house and climbed into her carriage. As it pulled away, she waved her handkerchief gaily from the window, unaware of the furore she had left behind her.

Jesse was dumbfounded at the news of Reuben Holyoak's death and Ben immediately sought out his mother, taxing her with keeping the news of Judy's arrest from him and Jesse.

'You mustn't blame your mother, Ben.' Loveday Ustick had seen the expression upon Ben's face when he went in search of his mother. Guessing the reason, he had tried unsuccessfully to head him off. 'We all knew about it, but no one wanted to say anything until after the wedding.'

'Judy and Alan wouldn't kill anyone, not even Reuben Holyoak – and, God knows, Judy had just cause for that.'

'The news is true enough,' declared Loveday Ustick. 'One of the maids from Lamorrack House told Fanny about it.

Judy arrived at the big house covered in blood after killing Holyoak.'

'But why?' Jesse asked. 'Why should she kill him? What was she doing anywhere near Lamorrack House?'

Loveday Ustick would have given anything not to have told Ben and Jesse why Judy Lean and Alan Colborne were near Mevagissey, but he was unable to lie. Dropping his glance to the toes of his dusty boots, he said 'She and the young man were on their way to look for you at Mevagissey. That's all I know about the matter. Fanny went to see her in St Austell lock-up before she was sent off to Bodmin Gaol, but she didn't get much sense from the poor girl.'

'Ben, we must go to Bodmin to see them,' Jesse said to Ben.

'You'll need to be quick,' said Mark Dunn, who had been listening to the conversation. 'The Assizes begin this week.'

Ben nodded. It was customary on the mines for a man to be given a week off work when he was married. Ben had intended using the time to improve the cottage. That would now have to wait. 'We'll go to Bodmin tomorrow.'

The news of the arrest of Judy Lean and Alan Colborne brought a swift end to the wedding celebrations and, that night, the bed-talk of the newly married couple was concerned not with their own future, but rather with the present predicament of their friends.

Ben and Jesse's arrival in Bodmin coincided with the ceremonial entry of His Majesty's Judges of Assize. The two judges, resplendent in long red cloaks and wearing shoulder-length, powdered wigs, rode into Bodmin Town in an ornate coach, escorted by a mounted troop of the Cornwall Militia. The judges were met by all the dignitaries of the district, led by the mayor in his robes and with the chain of office about his neck. Behind him, various other officials made up the welcoming committee, each carrying the insignia of his particular office.

This scene of ancient splendour was in sharp contrast to the squalor Ben and Jesse found within the high grey walls of Bodmin's gaol.

The gaol, although not yet fifty years old, was ill-maintained and hopelessly overcrowded. Judy Lean and Alan Colborne were imprisoned in separate parts of the building, and it was only by parting with a hard-earned gold sovereign that Ben was able to persuade a wheezing old turnkey to bring both prisoners together to meet their visitors. It was doubtful whether the single gold coin would have proved sufficient encouragement had the gaoler not been a miner in earlier, healthier years.

The reunion between Alan Colborne and Judy Lean was highly emotional. Judy clung to Alan Colborne and wept as though her heart would break. It was many minutes before she recovered sufficiently to talk. Even then, she clung to Alan Colborne's hand in the manner of a pathetic frightened child.

Alan Colborne told Ben and Jesse the story of their encounter with Reuben Holyoak. There was no doubt in his mind that, had Judy not shot the gamekeeper, Reuben Holyoak would have been in Bodmin Gaol awaiting trial on a murder charge.

Ben was incredulous. 'How can you and Judy possibly be charged with murder? This whole business is absurd!'

'I wish it were, Ben. We are charged with murder, and the magistrate who committed us is determined to prove his case. He was overheard to say that Judy will not escape justice twice.'

'Oh, no!' Jesse let out an involuntary cry of anguish. 'Not the Reverend Hawkins?'

'He said I killed my baby,' Judy Lean suddenly cried. 'I didn't, did I, Jesse? You know it isn't true.'

'Of course it isn't true, Judy. The Reverend Hawkins is a vengeful old man. No one will take any notice of him; you just wait and see.'

Jesse spoke without conviction. The Reverend Hawkins was a magistrate, and a persuasive and passionate speaker. Given the opportunity he might well sway a jury. Judy Lean's present appearance would be on his side. She was wearing the bloody dress in which she had been arrested, and it was doubtful whether she had washed since being thrown into Bodmin Gaol. Far from arousing the sympathy she so desperately needed, Judy looked every inch the murderess the Crown claimed her to be.

Clutching another of Ben's guineas, Jesse hurried from thé gaol and returned within the hour carrying a dress and a cardigan, both of which fitted Judy Lean tolerably well. Then Jesse demanded that the turnkey fetch soap and water. When it was grudgingly brought by the grumbling old gaoler, Jesse embarrassed Judy Lean by making her strip off her old dress, wash all the parts of her body that were visible to the eye, then put on the new dress she had just purchased for her.

The transformation from dirty drab to demure young girl was quite dramatic. Even the ill-humoured old turnkey now looked at Judy with a modicum of respect. While they talked, Jesse also tidied up Judy's hair. When she and Ben left the gaol, Jesse was satisfied that the simple girl could now stand before a jury and not be convicted on her appearance alone.

The trial was due to be held in the Assize Court the next day and, on the way from the gaol, Jesse asked Ben whether he thought Judy and Alan stood any chance of gaining an acquittal.

'I would like to think so,' replied Ben unhappily. 'But the

only fact that cannot be disputed is that Judy killed Reuben Holyoak. *We* know she is telling the truth about what happened. Whether she can convince a judge and jury is another matter. We will just have to wait and see.'

Ben and Jesse spent that night at the White Hart Inn, in the centre of Bodmin Town. Every inn and lodging-house was crowded with court officials and witnesses, brought in from the four corners of the county. Ben and Jesse were obliged to share a room with an asthmatic old man and his wife. The ancient couple had been called to the Assizes to give evidence in a hotly contested tithe dispute between a farmer and the vicar of his parish. They smelled strongly of pigs, and their snoring was reminiscent of the same animal.

Ben and Jesse spent a sleepless night and rose in the morning with an unreasonable hatred for the old couple whose faces beamed amiably at them above the blankets of the bed across the room.

It proved to be a bright and clear late-autumnal day, making the inside of the Assize Court seem even more gloomy than it was. Ben and Jesse arrived there early, to be sure they would not miss the case against Alan and Judy.

It was the first time Ben had been in a court-room, and he found it difficult to adapt to the ritualistic unreality of the proceedings. The judge, barristers and court officers addressed each other with the exaggerated courtesy of the medieval age of chivalry. Ben had the feeling that he was watching stage characters playing out parts they had all carefully rehearsed beforehand.

This feeling was heightened by the atmosphere in the public gallery. Crowded together, shoulder to shoulder, the spectators pronounced their own verdicts on cases still being heard and commented loudly on the physical attributes and mental prowess of all those holding the stage in the well of the court.

So convincing was this air of the theatre that, when the first case was brought to an abrupt conclusion and the judge placed a small square of black cloth upon his head, it was a few moments before Ben understood its implications. It came as a deep shock when he realised that by this simple – almost comic – gesture the Judge of Assize was ordering the execution of the weeping man in the dock.

The charge on which the poor unfortunate had been convicted was stealing a gentleman's purse containing twenty guineas.

The next case on the list received an even briefer hearing than had the first. A woman had broken into the house of her sister-in-law during her absence and stolen two shillings she found on the mantelshelf.

The jury announced their verdict of 'guilty', without retiring – but their foreman added a strong plea for clemency. The convicted woman had been in dire straits. Deserted by her husband, the brother of the robbed woman, she had been left with two young children to feed.

Ignoring the plea of the foreman of the jury, the stern-faced judge awarded the convicted woman the same sentence as the previous prisoner. Donning his 'black cap', he ordered her to be taken away and legally put to death. When the woman was dragged away, screaming for mercy for the sake of her children, the judge drew his lips together in a tight thin line of disapproval.

As the screams died away, Ben thought grimly that Judy Lean could expect little understanding from the man who would try her for her life.

This view was strengthened when the next prisoner, a boy of eleven, was brought up from the cells. Hardly able to see over the edge of the dock, the small boy pleaded guilty in a tremulous voice to the charge of stealing a handful of candles from a mine-store. When the judge was informed that the boy had been convicted of a similar offence two years before, he promptly sentenced him to fourteen years' transportation. On this occasion, the judge explained that the sentence was being passed in the hope of saving the boy from pursuing a useless and criminal way of life.

This sentence brought a brief outbreak of angry murmurs from the spectators in the public gallery, but the sound was swiftly silenced by a stern glance from the judge.

Then it was time for the hearing of the murder charge against Judy Lean and Alan Colborne.

When the two were escorted into the prisoners' dock, chained and manacled, Jesse's hopes sank. The night had undone much of her work. Judy Lean's long hair straggled untidily in front of her face, and she had managed to get the front of her new dress grubby.

Ben was watching the judge and saw the frown of annoyance which crossed his face when both prisoners pleaded not guilty to murdering Reuben Holyoak.

The prosecution's case unfolded rapidly, and the evidence took Ben and Jesse by surprise. It was obvious from Alan Colborne's manner that he, too, had no prior knowledge of the case now being made out against himself and Judy.

It was alleged that Alan Colborne and Judy Lean were on the Lamorrack estate as trespassers on the day of the murder. Their reason for being there, said the prosecuting barrister, was to break into Reuben Holyoak's house and steal whatever they might find. He went on to suggest that Reuben Holyoak had caught them in the act and, after a fight, had been killed in defence of his property.

One of the servants from Lamorrack House gave halting but

honest evidence of finding the body of the gamekeeper on the path, only yards from his house at Pengrugla, clearly killed by a shot from his own gun.

Next, the prosecution called the doctor who had examined Alan Colborne. His report, supported by the bruising still to be seen on Alan Colborne's face, conjured up a picture of a desperate fight.

Then it was the turn of the Reverend Hawkins to give evidence – and his story was the most damning of all. He described Judy Lean as a girl of loose morals, whom he had once arrested for the murder of her bastard child. She had escaped justice on that occasion, he told the court, only because of an irresponsible verdict by a coroner's jury, drawn from men of her home village. Now she had enlisted the aid of an itinerant musician to help her wilfully kill an honourable and respected man . . .

At this point, Jesse could contain her seething indignation no longer. Before Ben could stop her, she had sprung to her feet and called the magistrate a liar.

'Reuben Holyoak was no honourable man,' she shouted angrily. '*He* was the father of Judy Lean's bastard child. He took advantage of a simple-minded girl when she was working for him as a servant . . .'

Jesse had made a similar outburst once before, on Judy Lean's behalf, but this was no coroner's court being held in a village inn. As Ben tried to pull Jesse down to the wooden seat the judge demanded fiercely that she be silent.

'If I have any more of such conduct in my court, I will have you committed to prison until these Assizes are over, and then you will be publicly whipped,' he declared. 'If you have something to say that is relevant to this case, you will wait for the appropriate time. Is that quite clear?'

After staring back at the judge defiantly for some moments,

Jesse nodded her head, once. Sitting down heavily, she turned to Ben and in an angry whisper hissed, 'I'll have something to say, all right. That magistrate is not going to destroy Judy with his lies.'

'You'll say nothing,' said Ben firmly. 'If one of us needs to give evidence for Judy and Alan, I'll do it. You will only get angry and make things worse for them – and for yourself.'

Jesse opened her mouth with a ready retort, but she left it unspoken. Ben was right. She was far too upset to make a useful contribution to Judy's defence.

'All right, Ben. But don't allow the Reverend Hawkins to get away with any one of his lies.'

Ben was relieved that Jesse had given in so easily. Had she insisted on giving evidence, he had no doubt that he and his bride of a few days would have spent the duration of the Assizes separated by a high stone wall.

The Reverend Hawkins continued with his evidence. Whenever he praised Reuben Holyoak, or attacked Judy Lean's character, Jesse writhed with indignation, but she managed to remain silent.

There was little more prosecution evidence and, after an adjournment for lunch, it was the turn of Judy Lean and Alan Colborne to speak on their own behalf.

Judy Lean did not help her cause in any way. She had understood little of the proceedings and was not certain of what she was expected to say. She brought a smile of satisfaction to the face of the prosecuting barrister when she admitted picking up the gun and shooting Reuben Holyoak with it.

Much to Ben's surprise, Alan Colborne showed up little better when his turn came to address the court. The time he had already spent in custody had sapped his confidence. In a hesitant voice, at times barely audible above the noise of the court-room, he told how he and Judy had headed for

Mevagissey and taken a short cut through the Lamorrack estate. When he gave his version of the violent confrontation with Reuben Holyoak, Judy Lean began crying in the dock beside him, making his story even more difficult to follow.

Twice the judge curtly ordered Alan Colborne to speak up. His words brought only momentary improvement. Eventually, the judge sat back in his chair, displaying boredom, his thoughts elsewhere.

When Alan Colborne ended his evidence, he had said nothing to influence the jury in any way.

Peering sternly at the public gallery, the judge sought out Jesse. When he found her, he said, 'Now, young lady. Is there something you wish to say to this court?'

Ben stood up quickly, before Jesse could change her mind.

'I am her husband, my Lord. I would like to speak in her stead.'

'A wise decision,' said the judge. 'Step forward, if you please. I wish to conclude this trial today.'

Ben pushed his way to the front of the court and climbed the steps to the witness-box. He looked at the sea of faces turned towards him. Every man and woman in the court was waiting to hear whether he had any dramatic evidence that would alter the inevitable verdict of the jury.

Looking at the two unfortunates in the dock, Ben wished desperately that he had. Then he began to address the court in a firm and determined manner, telling them something of Judy's background.

He had not been talking for more than two minutes when the judge called him to a halt.

'I am waiting to hear *evidence* from you, Mr Retallick. Character references and excuses may be permitted *after* the jury has reached a verdict.'

Ben was left in some confusion. He wanted to tell the

court the true version of the magistrate's story; to inform the judge and jury that Alan Colborne and Judy Lean were neither murderers nor thieves; to explain that Reuben Holyoak was a bully – and worse. It needed to be said *before* the jury arrived at a verdict. He tried again, telling them about Reuben Holyoak; that he had been the father of Judy Lean's stillborn child.

Once again the judge called him to order, banging the wooden bench in front of him angrily.

'Such allegations directed against a dead man are neither admissible nor viewed with anything but distaste by this court. Is that all you have to offer by way of "evidence", Mr Retallick?'

'I am trying to tell you the kind of man Reuben Holyoak really was. Why, he once attacked my wife . . . !'

'The matter was reported?' The judge looked at Ben from beneath lowered brows.

'No.'

'I expected as much.' The judge leaned back in his chair with a sigh. 'Mr Retallick, you will kindly leave the witness-box. If you wish, you may return to speak for the prisoners after a verdict has been reached.'

Ben hesitated. He thought of his own fights with Reuben Holyoak and of the man's attempts to collect higher tithes and have Ben dismissed from the Happy Union mine. Told here, in this court, it would sound as though Reuben Holyoak had been doing no more than his duty. It would not help Alan Colborne and Judy Lean at all.

Reluctantly, Ben left the witness-box and made his way back to Jesse. He did not look towards the dock when he sat down, totally dejected.

Jesse reached for his hand and squeezed it comfortingly. 'He did not *want* to hear anything said in Judy and Alan's favour,' she hissed angrily. 'He listened readily enough when the Reverend Hawkins spoke *for* Reuben Holyoak.'

The verdict of the jury was never in doubt. In their eyes, Judy Lean was exactly what the magistrate had said she was – an immoral girl. She had given birth to a bastard child and been lucky to escape trial for murder when it died. Since then she had been travelling the country in the company of a wandering musician – and she had admitted shooting Reuben Holyoak.

Alan Colborne and Judy Lean were found guilty of murder.

Once again, Ben was asked if he wished to say anything on behalf of the newly convicted couple.

White-faced at the verdict, Ben returned to the witness-box and made an impassioned plea on behalf of his friends. He spoke of Judy Lean as a simple but truthful girl, who had known little happiness in life until she met Alan Colborne. He spoke of her until he saw the judge showing signs of impatience. Then he told the judge what he knew about Alan Colborne. How he had been blinded by cannon-fire after saving the life of the man who was now landlord of the White Swan Inn, at Truro.

Ben might as well have said nothing. No sooner had he finished talking than the impatient judge reached for the square of black cloth and solemnly sentenced Alan Colborne and Judy Lean to be hanged.

In the cells beneath the court, Ben and Jesse found their friends in a state of shock. Neither of them could believe they were to die at the end of a hangman's rope.

When the tragic pair were taken back to the prison, Ben and Jesse left Bodmin determined to fight for the lives of Alan Colborne and Judy Lean.

First they went to Tregassick to see Eulaliah Vincent and ask yet again for her help. The elderly lady promised to write to her friends in London, but she doubted whether they would be able to set aside the ruling of an Assize Court Judge.

On their return to Sharptor, Ben saw Theophilus Strike and asked for his advice. At first, the mine-owner refused to involve himself in such a matter, but after Ben had told him the full story he promised to do whatever he could.

Next, Ben approached David Howell, only to learn that the High Sheriff of Cornwall had already received a letter from Eulaliah Vincent and had agreed to intercede on behalf of the convicted couple.

Having done all they could, there was nothing for Ben and Jesse to do but wait – and this was the hardest part of all.

The date of the double execution was set for the thirteenth day of December. When the hanging was only a week away and no news of a reprieve had been received, the uncertainty became unbearable.

Then Theophilus Strike rode to the Sharptor mine late one afternoon and sent for Ben.

Ben climbed the ladder to the surface and shivered as the cold air chilled the perspiration that clung to his body beneath the thin working-shirt.

'I have news for you, Ben,' said the grim-faced mine-owner. 'It is not entirely good. Alan Colborne's sentence has been reduced to transportation for life. For that he has to thank the Duke of Wellington, who personally interceded for his life.'

Ben's delight at the news quickly died away as he waited in vain for Theophilus Strike to tell him of a reprieve for Judy Lean.

'You are still waiting for news about Judy . . . ?' Theophilus Strike shook his head. 'The Home Secretary felt unable to make any recommendation on her behalf. She must hang. I am sorry, Ben.'

Chapter Thirty-Nine

On 12 December 1822, Judy Lean was married to Alan Colborne. The ceremony took place in the small prison chapel at Bodmin Gaol. Both prisoners were allowed to wear their own clothing in place of the red and brown patched prison garb.

The prison governor gave the bride away, and Ben and Jesse were witnesses to the ceremony. The prison chaplain was an old man, more used to burying his wretched flock than conducting weddings. He kept forgetting the circumstances of the couple he was marrying and repeatedly alluded to the 'long and fruitful life' they would have together. It caused great embarrassment to everyone except the bride.

Even at this late date, Judy seemed unaware that her life had only a matter of hours to run. She was so happy to be marrying Alan that the hearts of everyone except the confused old chaplain went out to her. After the ceremony, the prison governor gave a small party for the newly-weds in his own house, in the prison grounds, supplying food and drink he had purchased from outside the prison.

Before long, the strain of maintaining an outward show of cheerfulness in the shadow of what the morrow was to bring proved too much for Jesse. She managed to maintain her composure during the harrowing farewell with Judy, but once outside the governor's house, she broke down and wept as though her heart would break.

Ben and Jesse returned to the gaol early the next morning and already the streets of Bodmin were seething with excited sightseers, in town for the hanging. A few were disappointed. They had arrived expecting a double hanging. Their only consolation was that it was the man who had been pardoned and not the woman. The hanging of a woman was always a popular spectacle. Only two other women had been hanged in the preceding fifty years' history of Bodmin Gaol.

The gallows were erected on a platform above the gate of the gaol, and many people were already gathered there to be sure of getting a close view of the hanging. Jesse was incensed to see two house-servants from Lamorrack House among them. They would both have known Judy Lean well.

Prisoners were not usually allowed visitors on execution days, but the understanding governor had given Ben and Jesse special permission to remain with Alan Colborne until after the hangman had earned his fee.

The blind balladeer was seated on his hard wooden bed, his head clutched in his hands, when they entered the cell. He raised his face to them and they saw the haggard look of a man who was suffering mental anguish such as few men had known. More than once during the long terrible night that had just ended, he had prayed that his own reprieve might prove to be a mistake and he be allowed to die on the scaffold beside Judy.

He pleaded with the turnkey who let Ben and Jesse into the

cell to be allowed to visit Judy, but the turnkey had his orders. No one must visit her but the furtive hangman, who would look through the bars of her cell to obtain a rough estimate of her height and weight, and adjust his rope accordingly.

All that morning, Ben and Jesse sat in the cell with Alan Colborne, trying hard to find things to say. Through the barred window, the noise of the crowd gathering outside the prison could be plainly heard. Alan Colborne became increasingly restless. Finally, he stood up and paced the cell with a skill that bespoke many unsleeping hours.

When there were less than fifteen minutes left before the execution-hour of noon, the door of the cell swung open on heavy complaining hinges and the prison governor entered.

Ben and Jesse started to their feet, convinced he had arrived with news of a reprieve to put an end to this nightmare.

There was to be no reprieve. The governor had come to suggest that Ben, Jesse and Alan Colborne spend the remaining minutes of Judy's life in the chapel. There they might pray for Judy's departing soul – and the thick chapel walls would keep out the triumphant roar of the huge crowd when the trapdoor dropped from beneath her feet.

The governor had been in charge of the prison for much of his life, but the hanging of Judy Colborne was the unhappiest task that had ever come his way. It was not only because he had been caught up in the pathos of her tragically short marriage. The governor of Bodmin Gaol believed in the innocence of the convicted girl.

Alan Colborne realised why the prison governor had made his suggestion, but he declined the well-intentioned offer.

'Thank you, no. If there is a God, He will take Judy to him without my prayers. Though why He should allow her to suffer so is beyond my meagre understanding. For myself, I want to know the moment this unjust deed is committed. It is more surely a murder than anything Judy has committed. She is no more guilty than I, Governor. I should be with her on the scaffold, standing by her side. At least allow me to see her once more . . . please!'

Deeply distressed, the governor shook his head. 'It is too late. She is prepared for what is to come. It would be cruel to upset her now. It may be a comfort to you to know she is standing up to her ordeal well. She is a brave girl.'

Alan Colborne banged his fists against the stone wall. 'How can that be a comfort to me? How can anyone find comfort when they know an innocent girl is to die? She killed Holyoak to save my life. If it were not for me . . .'

Ben took Alan Colborne's arm. After a desperate struggle to regain control of himself, the distraught man shook himself free. 'I . . . I am all right now.'

The prison governor pulled a watch self-consciously from his pocket. 'I have to go.' His discomfiture was evident. He had to be present at every execution carried out in his gaol.

'Go!' whispered Alan Colborne fiercely. 'Would that I were going, too. My thoughts are there before you.'

The heavy door slammed shut behind the governor, and his footsteps could be heard hurrying along the stone-flagged corridor towards the condemned cell.

In the cell, nobody spoke for some minutes. Then they heard a murmur of interest rise from ten thousand throats beyond the prison wall.

Alan Colborne turned from the window. 'They have taken Judy to the scaffold . . . Oh, God!'

Jesse was very close to tears but she took his hand. 'Be brave, Alan! Be brave!'

Even from this distance it was possible to feel the excitement of the vast crowd. Their voices buzzed with all the menace of a monstrous swarm of bees.

Suddenly the gaol bell began to toll. It was a deep melancholy sound that reverberated around the stone courtyards and granite buildings. It went on until those in the cell heard a sound that chilled their blood. It was a long-drawn-out muffled scream. The terrified scream of a girl having a dark hood pulled over her head.

The sound was cut off abruptly in the moment that the bell stopped tolling. For long seconds the whole world held its breath at the deed that had been committed in the name of justice.

Then the crowd found its voice with a roar that sent pigeons in panic-stricken flight from trees half a mile beyond the town.

Alan Colborne sank to his knees, his face contorting in agony.

'Judy . . . ! Judy . . . !'

Jesse held his head to her, and Alan Colborne's sightless eyes wept for the wife they had never seen.

Chapter Forty

Alan Colborne was transported in the early spring of 1823, taken direct to a transport-ship waiting out the worst of the winter storms in Falmouth's Carrick Roads.

The prison governor sent word of the impending move to Ben, and he and Jesse went to bid farewell to their friend. It was a distressing experience. Alan Colborne was no longer the cheerful balladeer who had always made light of his blindness. His fiddle, recovered by Ben from the St Austell constables, remained untouched in a corner of his cell.

Alan Colborne behaved almost as though they were strangers, and spent the whole of their visit complaining that a blind man should not be sent to an unknown country where he would be unable to fend for himself. It was as the governor had told them when they arrived for their visit: Alan Colborne had surrendered to his blindness.

There was little Ben and Jesse could do for him. Ben gave him all the money he could spare, but it was accepted with little gratitude. Only when it was time for them to leave the gaol did Alan Colborne show any sign of emotion. For a moment it seemed he would beg them to remain a while longer – but then he turned away and said nothing as the impatient jangling of the gaoler's keys drove them away.

Not until Alan Colborne had gone from Bodmin Gaol did Jesse really recover from the deep shock of Judy's execution. It would have taken longer had not another event occurred to give her something new to think about.

Ben and Jesse were awakened in the darkness of the night by a heavy and persistent banging on the door of their Sharptor cottage. When Ben threw open the window and called to ask who was there, the voice of Moses Trago came up to him from the moonless darkness.

'It's Kate . . . The child is coming, and she's having a hard time. Will Jesse come up and help?'

'Surely! Wait there a moment. I'll be down with a light.'

'Ask Jesse to hurry, Ben. I've left Kate up there with only brother John for company. He is more frightened than she is of what is going on.'

When Ben withdrew his head from the window, Jesse was already dressing. He went down to let Moses Trago into the cottage.

By the time Jesse came downstairs, Moses was pacing the floor impatiently. Ben had not expected him to be in such a state. There had been no noticeable improvement in the relationship between Moses Trago and his wife in recent months.

On the way to the strange home, some of the reason for Moses Trago's concern became apparent. He spoke as though Kate had already given birth to a son. When Jesse suggested the child might be a daughter, Moses fell silent while he thought about it. Then he said, 'No, it will be a son. It has to be. A man needs a son.'

The facilities offered by Moses Trago's moorland home had not improved since Ben and Jesse's first visit. On the contrary, they had deteriorated considerably over the last month. Kate Trago had suffered an uncomfortable pregnancy and been forced to give up work during the eighth month. With no money of her own, and none forthcoming from Moses, household items such as soap had become luxuries that were out of her reach. For the last couple of weeks, Kate had spent much of the day lying on her bed, her aching legs swollen to twice their normal size.

One look at Kate told Jesse that this would not be a simple birth. She was panting uncontrollably, and the eyes she turned up to Jesse were filled with pain. Brushing back perspiration-soaked hair from Kate's face, Jesse knew she must have been in labour for some time, yet there was no sign of the baby arriving yet.

'I need help here,' Jesse said to Moses Trago. 'Is there anyone in Henwood village skilled in delivering a baby?'

Moses looked startled. 'Yes, Mary Crabbe. But she's never been needed for a birth in this house before. My mother—'

'—has gone! And small wonder,' snapped Jesse. 'We kept pigs in a better house than this at Pengrugla, as you know full well. Mary Crabbe is needed here. What's more, Kate needs her mother, too.'

Moses opened his mouth to protest, but Jesse was in no mood for argument.

'If you are too proud to fetch her because you have had words, then Ben can do it for you. I need both Mary Crabbe and Mrs Kelynack to help me, and I need them here – now!'

As both Ben and Moses Trago turned to leave, Jesse called, 'Wait!'

She pointed to where John Trago sat huddled in a corner, a dark blanket wrapped about him. 'You can take him with you.

Then stay away yourself until this is all over, Moses. No man is needed here tonight. Your hour of glory will come when everyone else has done the work. Then you can go to the inn at Henwood and have everyone tell you what a great man you are – for doing something to which you gave little thought at the time, and contributed nothing since.'

Kate Trago groaned from her mattress of heather, and Jesse turned to her, leaving the men to file silently out into the dark night.

'You are welcome to your woman, Ben Retallick,' growled Moses Trago. 'I am damned if I'd let my wife speak like that to any man.'

'She was not speaking to *any* man, Moses,' replied Ben quietly. 'She was speaking to *you* – and she is right. From what I hear, you've put little enough into your marriage since we last spoke together.'

'Hold your tongue,' Moses said angrily. 'Had I wanted such talk I would have fetched the preacher, not you and Jesse. What I do is my own business. You go and do your wife's bidding – but tell Kate's mother I want her out of the house an hour after the baby is born. I'll not put up with *her* tongue wagging at me, too. I'll knock up Mary Crabbe.'

Moses Trago stamped off, with the brooding John Trago following silently behind him.

Mary Kelynack dressed as quickly as she could. After telling her two girls where she was going, she hurried up the hill by Ben's side.

'Did Kate ask for me?' she asked eagerly, when they cleared the village.

'Kate is not well enough to do any asking,' admitted Ben. 'Jesse sent Moses and me out to fetch you and Mary Crabbe.'

'Good for Jesse,' declared Mary Kelynack. 'With Mary Crabbe up there with us we'll manage well enough.'

Ben was working day shift at the Wheal Sharptor. He was ready to leave for work before Jesse returned home to the cottage. Mary Kelynack was with her, and both women looked thoroughly weary.

'Moses has his son,' Jesse managed a weak smile. 'He is a boy of whom Moses can be proud. He arrived fighting the whole world.'

Mary Kelynack snorted. 'He'll need to be able to fight the world with a name like "Morwen"! I have never heard such a name in these parts. But he is his father's son, all right. Not a cry could we raise from him, and he was born with a black scowl on his face that I have seen Moses wear too many times. I feel sorry for the child. What chance does he have in life, being brought up in that cave?'

Mary Kelynack looked about her at Ben and Jesse's home. 'Why can't Moses find my Kate a nice little place like this? Kate has not had an easy time this last year. She deserves more than life has given her. Even her firstborn chose to come into this world backwards.'

'I don't think Moses would settle to a house,' said Ben. 'He prides himself on being different from other men.'

'Pride? Where does that enter the matter? Living in a hovel is no cause for pride!'

'Perhaps he'll change now he has the son he wanted so much.'

'Moses Trago does not *know* what he wants,' said Mary Kelynack bitterly. 'He thought he wanted to leave Sharptor but, after a couple of years away, he ran back here again. He wanted to marry my Kate, but within a month it was plain for everyone to see he'd made a mistake. Now Kate has given him the son he *thinks* he wants. He'll soon learn there is more to being a father than having a son grow up and call you "Pa". A son is the greatest responsibility that God ever gave to a man – and responsibility is the last thing Moses Trago wants. I tremble for my daughter when I think what he'll do when he learns that bitter lesson.'

Mary Kelynack wrung her hands together in despair. She had never before commented on Kate's marriage, but the long fight to bring her first grandchild into the world had breached the wall of her reticence.

'We are Kate's nearest neighbours,' said Jesse gently. 'We'll do what we can for her. She knows she can always call upon us for help.'

'Knowing and calling are two very different things to Kate,' commented Mary Kelynack with much bitterness. 'But it makes me feel better to know you are close to her.'

Mary Kelynack's harsh criticism of Moses Trago was justified before many months had passed. Moses refused to accept that the needs of the baby had to be satisfied before his own. Kate, for her part, made few concessions to her husband's pride. The baby came first with her in all things. This uncompromising attitude earned her a great many beatings.

As soon as Kate Trago recovered from the ordeal of childbirth, she returned to work at the Wheal Sharptor with Jesse. Whilst they and the other bal-maidens worked, breaking down the ore for the stamps, baby Morwen nestled in a wooden box nearby. Wrapped in an old woollen blanket, he lay watching the high and low clouds passing overhead in an unequal race, until he was lulled to sleep by the ringing rhythm of hammer on stone.

On days when the weather was exceptionally bad, Morwen was placed in the shelter of the sorting-sheds. The noise of hammering in such an enclosed space occasionally caused him to blink in sudden alarm. For the remainder of the time, he viewed the underside of the roof above him with as much interest as he gave to the sky outside.

The Wheal Sharptor was proving to be a pleasant and profitable little mine. The miners were fortunate enough to have cut into good tin lodes at shallow levels. This meant that the ladders did not yet need to go down to any great depth. Theophilus Strike was not over-generous to his miners, but neither was he a greedy man. It was not his policy to tear as much ore from the ground as could be brought out in the shortest possible time. By keeping his mine relatively small and shallow, he was making a very useful profit. He would continue to do so when the roofless buildings of many of the larger mines stood in desolation amidst mountains of mine-waste: mute memorials to blood and sweat . . . and avarice.

The miners who worked for Theophilus Strike reflected his attitude in their own work. Almost every one of them was a married man, content to have a steady job for as many years as he dared to look ahead. They were all experienced miners who knew every aspect of mining – and they did it well.

The Wheal Sharptor was a happy mine.

Such a state of affairs was exceptional in the confused and discontented years of the early 1820s. Throughout the country men were clamouring for unprecedented changes in the accepted pattern of life. Paradoxically, many of those who resisted these demands most strongly were the very ones who had brought about the need for change.

Almost unnoticed during the wars of the early nineteenth century, Britain had become the greatest manufacturing country in the world. Men were drawn from the land in their thousands and moved to hurriedly constructed industrial towns. There, in dingy unsanitary conditions, they worked the new machines in huge factories, going home at night to spawn ever-growing families to add to the gross overcrowding and fuel future discontent.

England's glut of cheap labour that utilised husbands, wives and children soon put her years ahead of all her foreign competitors. Huge fortunes were made and remade; but the money was distributed among very few men and, as the country's manufacturing prowess increased, so Britain's agriculture fell behind.

In spite of the momentous switch from agriculture to industry, those who ran the country from Parliament were either landowners, or representatives of landowners. Protecting their landed interests came as naturally to them as drawing breath. Foreign produce coming into the country was taxed to the point where it became hopelessly expensive and beyond the reach of the vast mass of the rapidly increasing population.

Even when the Government was made aware of the problem, it did nothing to alleviate the hunger of the people. Instead, it passed a series of unwise Poor Laws, throwing the burden of feeding the swollen ranks of the poor on to the parish in which they lived. By these means, the Government succeeded in antagonising yet another section of the country's society: all those men who were wealthy enough to pay rates and taxes.

The clamour for reform gathered strength as men of substance called their own meetings. They sent petitions to the Prime Minister calling for an end to the heavy burden of taxation, rates and tithes, under which they reeled. They, too, now demanded the right to elect men to Parliament who had *their* interests at heart.

The mood of these latest recruits to the reform movement was made known to Ben one evening in the late summer of 1823. He was working in the garden of his cottage, stripped to the waist, when a horse and rider turned off the main track to

Henwood and headed up the hill towards the Wheal Sharptor. The horse stepped carefully. The mine-track was torn and scarred by the hoofs of the Wheal Sharptor packhorses which daily slipped and slithered down the hill, laden with ore for the smelting-house. The rider looked up the hill at the group of cottages. Seeing Ben in his garden, he headed in his direction.

When he drew closer, Ben sank the blade of his pointed shovel deep into the earth and leaned upon the long handle, eyeing the horseman. It was rarely that one saw a saddled horse in these parts. Ben was quite sure Sharptor had never seen a more elegant rider. Wearing a coat of soft blue velvet and long black riding-boots, the approaching man reminded Ben of some sleek well-fed mole.

Easing his horse to a halt on the other side of the wall, the rider called, 'I am seeking Ben Retallick. Would you tell me where I might find him?'

'You have,' replied Ben curtly. 'Have we met before? I don't recall you, sir.'

'We have not met before, Mr Retallick, and I doubt if you will have heard my name, but I have heard much of you and am pleased to make your acquaintance.'

Swinging down from his horse, the rider looped the reins over the unpainted gate-post and entered the garden. Extending his hand to Ben, he said, 'I am Richard Hoblyn, of Liskeard.'

Ben shook the outstretched hand, but he had no idea why this well-dressed stranger should have sought him out.

Seeing his puzzlement, Richard Hoblyn explained, 'I have been anxious to meet with you since I first heard of your part in having Sir Colman Vincent's parliamentary seat taken away from him – but may we discuss this matter inside your house?'

Ben frowned. It appeared that the whole of Cornwall was now aware he had been responsible for the downfall of Sir

Colman Vincent. Slipping his shirt over his head he tucked it inside his trousers and led the way inside the cottage. Ahead of him he heard Jesse running upstairs to the bedroom. She had been at the open window watching Ben when Richard Hoblyn came up the hill. She now hurried to change from her working-clothes.

Inviting Richard Hoblyn to take a seat in the best room, Ben said, 'Such stories tend to become exaggerated to suit the mood of the teller, Mr Hoblyn. You mustn't believe all you have heard.'

Carefully adjusting his velvet coat about him on the chair, Richard Hoblyn said quietly, 'Nevertheless, Sir Colman is no longer a Member of the House of Commons. You are wise to be cautious, of course. You have set a dangerous precedent; but it is one I hope to emulate. I am a merchant in Liskeard. I, and many of my friends, are most dissatisfied with the two Members of Parliament who currently represent our borough. Indeed, I stood against them in the last election on the reform issue. As they are both from a titled family I had little chance of success. However, I now have reason to believe that a large sum of money was distributed to buy the votes of men who might otherwise have voted for me.'

'You are probably right, Mr Hoblyn – but what has this to do with me?'

Richard Hoblyn leaned forward in his chair. 'I am here to recruit your aid, Mr Retallick. Certain of my friends in the reform movement are reluctant to take action against our present Members of Parliament. They fear certain . . . retribution? I would like you to attend our next meeting and speak to them. Tell them how you tackled a similar case of electoral bribery – and won!'

Ben shook his head. 'I'm sorry, Mr Hoblyn. I have already refused a similar request, made by a man who travelled all the way here from the Midlands. In Sir Colman's case I became involved because his actions were affecting me and my family. I have no wish to be caught up in the reform issue, or anything else that doesn't concern me.'

Richard Hoblyn looked at Ben in some surprise. Without giving the matter too much thought, he had assumed Ben must be a supporter of the reform movement. Before he could say more, Jesse entered the room. She had put on her best cotton dress and hastily brushed her long black hair down about her shoulders. The transformation from untidy bal-maiden to beautiful woman was astonishing.

Richard Hoblyn sprang to his feet, his expression one of frank admiration as Ben introduced Jesse.

An awkward silence fell upon the room, until Richard Hoblyn began explaining his presence to Jesse, in an attempt to win her support. 'I had hoped to persuade your husband to address a reform meeting in Liskeard, but it seems the idea is not entirely to his liking.'

Jesse glanced quickly at Ben before replying. 'Ben probably knows better than anyone that talking at meetings is a waste of everyone's time. When it comes to making a decision, it takes ten men ten times as long as one.'

Richard Hoblyn conceded that Jesse might have a valid point, but added, 'I already know the course of action *I* must take, but my opponents wield great influence in the county. I need the wholehearted support of my own townsmen. By telling them of his success in the action against Sir Colman Vincent I sincerely believe your husband might win such support for me. The majority of the voters feel as strongly as I about the matter of blatant vote-purchasing, but they are frightened. If we attempt to remove our present Members of Parliament and fail, it could have dire consequences for us all.'

To Ben, Richard Hoblyn said, 'I am prepared to pay you well for your time.'

Ben's pride bridled at the merchant's offer. 'The man from the Midlands promised me a seat in the House of Commons; that, too, failed to tempt me. No, Mr Hoblyn. I sympathise with you, but this is not my quarrel. I want no part of it. I suggest you do as I did last year. Go to see David Howell. He is no longer High Sheriff of Cornwall, but I'm sure he'll be ready to advise you.'

'You know David Howell?' Richard Hoblyn looked at Ben incredulously. His manner towards Ben had so far been condescending. Now he felt he might have underestimated this quiet young man.

'I had a letter of introduction to him. He was most helpful to me. I'm sure he'll know what you should do.'

'He might at that. I believe he is a recent convert to the reform movement. I am obliged to you, Mr Retallick. Perhaps my journey here has not been wasted after all.'

Richard Hoblyn took his leave after casting a final admiring glance at Jesse. At the door, he paused and turned back into the room.

'You will be coming to Liskeard Fair, next week, of course?'

The annual fair was held in Liskeard, to celebrate a saint's day. All the mines in the area ceased operation for the occasion. Ben and Jesse, in common with the other miners and their families from Wheal Sharptor, would be attending.

'Yes, we'll be there.'

'Good! I am keeping open house at my home in Dean Street. I will expect to have the pleasure of welcoming you there.'

Chapter Forty-One

Ben woke before the sun rose, on the day of the fair. Slipping quietly from the bed, he opened the window to check upon the weather. To his great relief, it was dry. A look at the stars, rapidly fading into the grey of morning, told him it was likely to remain so. He and Jesse would be walking to Liskeard, a distance of almost six miles. Rain on a normal fair-day was bad enough. Today it would have proved calamitous. They would be dressing up not only for the annual fair, but also for a visit to the Hoblyn house.

Ben and Jesse took a long time making themselves ready and were still eating breakfast when Wrightwick Roberts came to the door. He had spent the night at Tom Shovell's house and would walk to Liskeard with Ben and Jesse. The big preacher was not given to paying compliments, but so impressed was he with Jesse's appearance that he assured her he would see no more handsome woman at Liskeard Fair.

Jesse dropped him a mock curtsy. 'Thank you, Wrightwick – but don't tell me you are going to Liskeard Fair to look at young women.'

The serious-minded preacher frowned, unaware that Jesse was joking. 'I am not going to the fair to enjoy any sinful pleasures, Jesse. I am going as a dedicated servant of the Lord. My duty is to protect the souls of simple miners. My attentions may not be welcomed by those I seek to save, but that will not turn me aside from my duty. Now, I suggest we hurry, or the fair will be well under way before we arrive.'

When Wrightwick Roberts turned away, Jesse pulled a wry face at Ben behind the preacher's back. Ben grinned in reply. 'We'll be there in plenty of time for you to save souls, Wrightwick. I doubt if any miner will give you a hearing until his money has run out.'

'I'll not wait to be given a hearing, Ben. Rather than see a good man lost to the Devil, I'll give him a drubbing first. He will feel all the better for it tomorrow morning.'

Ben's grin widened. 'Then there will be more than one miner going down from grass tomorrow with sore bones but a happy heart. This should be a fair-day to remember.'

Despite Wrightwick Roberts's anxiety about their tardiness in setting out, it was still early when the trio left Sharptor and headed across the moor to Liskeard.

Soon they met with men from other mines and their families. Some Ben knew, others he did not, but such was the cameraderie among miners that they all walked on together. While the men talked of mines and mining, the women discussed births, marriages and deaths and the children boasted of what they intended doing at the fair.

There was another, less altruistic reason for banding together in a large group. As they drew closer to the town, they met with crowds of farm-workers, also heading for the delights of the fair. With the advantage of numbers on the side of the miners, there was less chance of the farm-workers picking a fight.

Such caution had only been gained by years of hard-won

experience. The farmers and their workers resented the men who tore the heart out of the soil, spoiling good farmland with thousands of tons of useless and unsightly mine-waste. In a similar fashion, the townsmen looked down upon both miners and farm-workers as lacking social graces the townsmen believed came with the refinements of town life.

The sun was still climbing into the sky when Ben, Jesse and Wrightwick Roberts reached Liskeard. Here Wrightwick Roberts took his leave of them. He had matters of religious business to discuss with the local Wesleyan preacher before he could give the fair the full benefit of his disapproval.

Already the streets of the market-town were teeming with miners and farm-workers from outlying communities. Tall-hatted town constables worked valiantly to prevent stalls from blocking the narrow streets, trying in vain to leave room for the noon coach to pass through.

Ben and Jesse moved through the crowd, pausing to express sympathy for an old mangy bear with sore watering eyes. The bear shuffled and swayed at the end of a chain in unrhythmic time to the music of a fife, played by its tinker owner.

They met with more music farther along the road. A small monkey, dressed in red coat and hat, turned somersaults to the tune of a penny whistle played by an ex-sailor.

All around, tempting aromas rose from the food-stalls, and a wide miscellany of goods was offered for sale.

This was the section of the fair that catered for the rag, tag and bobtail of fair-goers. Amongst them, the pickpockets who followed the fair around the countryside carried out their nefarious activities. These pickpockets were an ever-changing band. As petty thieves graduated to their ranks, so others were caught and transported – or occasionally hanged.

In the market-place at the other end of town, the serious business of the fair was conducted. Here were sheep, pigs and cows, brought to the fair for sale or exhibition. Few miners found their way here, and Ben felt out of place among men whose conversation centred around prime beef, milk yields and the size of a prize cow's udder.

Eventually, Ben and Jesse left the fair behind and made their way to the comparative quiet of Dean Street. They were going to take up Richard Hoblyn's invitation, although Ben was not at all certain the merchant would remember extending it to them.

When they arrived at the house, Ben and Jesse saw it was one of the finest in an area of imposing new residences. The house and gardens were crowded with people. Most of the women were over-dressed and ostentatiously bedecked with jewellery. The men wore a variety of styles. Some were dressed as befitted solid prosperous merchants. Others sported the flamboyant fashion favoured by King George IV when he was Prince Regent.

This was the new 'élite' of the country's society: England's middle class; the moneyed ranks of merchants and shop-keepers; men of trade.

In the garden were tables laden with foodstuffs of every description, many of which had never before been seen by the urchins who crowded outside the gate, begging pennies from those who went inside.

Ben and Jesse were stopped inside the gate by a servant who evidently thought they had entered by mistake. Ben was explaining that Richard Hoblyn had invited them, when the host himself came hurrying across the lawns, closely followed by a young man in his late twenties, dressed even more elegantly than Richard Hoblyn.

'Mr and Mrs Retallick! How nice of you to come.'

Turning to the elegant younger man, Richard Hoblyn said, 'May I introduce you to my younger brother, Crispin?'

Crispin Hoblyn took Jesse's hand. Bowing low, he raised it to his lips, 'I am honoured, ma'am. My brother returned from Sharptor singing your praises, but your beauty far surpasses his meagre description.'

Releasing Jesse's hand with exaggerated reluctance, Crispin Hoblyn switched his attentions to Ben and proved he had a surprisingly firm grasp. 'You can be proud of your wife today, sir. She is the fairest flower in this garden.'

Ben was not sure he approved of this foppish young man admiring Jesse so openly, but Crispin Hoblyn had a disarming manner. It was difficult to take lasting offence at him.

Then Ben and Jesse were taken to meet the other guests. Although the Hoblyn brothers had given them a warm welcome, neither Jesse nor Ben felt entirely at ease in such a gathering.

Jesse was fully aware of the lack of quality of her clothes. She had a very attractive slim figure, and her tight-fitting bodice attracted more than one admiring glance from the men, but their wives were fully aware that the dress was home-made, of a cheap cloth.

Ben, too, felt clumsy in his heavy boots and rough serge suit among these men of fashion, but he soon forgot his self-consciousness when he listened to their conversations. By now he had been separated from Jesse and, on the occasions when his host left him for a few minutes, Ben found that the other guests ignored him. They talked together as though he were not within hearing.

It very soon became apparent that the 'reform' sought by these men was not the same as that fought for by the men of the Midlands – or even that of the men of Mevagissey. These men expected to achieve considerable personal gain from an extended franchise. For them it meant no less than the passing of power from the landed gentry to themselves.

They had no thought of giving the vote to *all* men. A vote given to a fisherman, a miner or a farm-worker would be a vote wasted. More, it would be downright dangerous! Tantamount to handing power to the masses. From such foolish ideas were revolutions born.

It was more than an hour before Ben was able to make his escape from Richard Hoblyn, and then not until he had given his promise to attend the reform meeting being held in a field at the edge of the town. Ben realised this was the real reason he had been invited to the house, but he would have preferred to stay away from the meeting.

Ben had not seen Jesse for some time and he was becoming anxious about her. Eventually, he found her, bright-eyed and sparkling, seated on a chair inside the house, surrounded by a number of young men. Of Crispin Hoblyn there was no sign.

Ben plucked Jesse from her admirers with a curt apology to them. Not until they were on their way back to the fair and well clear of the house did he begin to relax.

He grinned at Jesse. 'I would rather spend a day working down a mine than chatting with folk like those at Hoblyn's house. They are not our kind of people, Jesse.'

Jesse gave Ben a sidelong glance. 'You speak for yourself, Ben. Crispin Hoblyn thought otherwise. He even hinted he would like to make me his mistress!'

Ben stopped, his jaw dropping in disbelief. 'He did what!'

Jesse took his arm and hugged him to her. 'There's nothing for you to be angry about, Ben. He put it in such a gentlemanly way that he might have been asking me to stitch a button on his coat.'

'I . . . I'll break his scented neck . . . !'

Jesse looked up at him happily. 'Do you know, this is the first time I've given you cause to be jealous? You needn't worry, Ben. I gave Crispin Hoblyn no encouragement. I'm quite certain he makes a similar approach to every woman he meets . . . In fact, I would have been quite disappointed had he made me an exception!'

Ben looked at Jesse in bewilderment. There were times when he felt he did not know her at all. This was one of them.

Everyone in Liskeard knew of the reform meeting, and most of them attended. The meeting began quietly enough. From a small platform set up at one end of the field, Richard Hoblyn and some of his friends made long dull speeches about the need to slash taxes and review the voting laws of the land.

For perhaps half an hour the meeting followed its predictable path before a number of men elbowed their way through to the front of the listening crowd. With a start of surprise, Ben saw that one of them was Charles Swindles. With him was another man Ben thought he had seen before.

When they and their friends were immediately in front of the platform, they began heckling. At first, the speaker ignored their interruptions. Then he broke the cardinal rule of any speaker. He tried to reply to some of the questions they hurled at him.

Finally, in sheer exasperation, Richard Hoblyn stood up and shouted, 'I don't know who you are, but if you have something to say on the subject of reform one of you may come up here and say his piece. Then perhaps you will allow this meeting to proceed without interruption . . .'

Before Richard Hoblyn had finished talking, the man Ben had seen before was being helped on to the platform amidst noisy applause from his supporters. He was a stout red-faced man with long grey hair turning to white.

'Gentlemen – and ladies – of Cornwall. You may have heard of me. My name is William Cobbett . . .'

An excited murmur went through the crowd, and suddenly

Ben remembered where he had seen the man. He had been addressing the huge gathering at the Crinnis mine, years before, when Ben and Jesse had attended their first reform meeting with Walter Dunn.

Cobbett was a well-known reformer and political dissident, and Ben saw Richard Hoblyn's discomfiture. The merchant could not have anticipated that his meeting would attract the attentions of such a man. He would certainly not welcome his presence. Both men claimed to speak for the ideals of 'reform', but they had little in common.

Speaking with a powerful voice, rich with a rustic, country accent, William Cobbett had none of the rambling ineptitude of Richard Hoblyn's reformers. His voice was heard by every man and woman in the five-thousand-strong crowd, his words blunt, spoken without regard for his listeners' sensitivities.

William Cobbett's views went far beyond the reform of Parliament. He called for the abolition of the House of Lords and all the privileges that sprang from the possession of land and wealth. Pointing to the heavens, he roared, 'All men are equal in the sight of God! Is that not a Christian precept? Yes, it is . . . and Wesley did his fellow-men a disservice by urging them to accept their lot in this world in exchange for a vague promise to improve their status in the next. There is nothing in the Bible that says a man must stay poor and work twice as hard as he should – just to make another Christian rich!'

Cornwall was a staunch stronghold of Wesleyan Methodism. Cobbett's criticism of the founder of the Methodist Church provoked an angry outburst from many of his listeners. Immediately, the men who had pushed their way to the front with Cobbett closed in on the platform and turned to face the crowd. They were neither miners nor Cornishmen. Ben guessed correctly that William Cobbett travelled with an escort of men of his own convictions – and they all looked tough.

The crowd's displeasure did not bother Cobbett. Still in full flow, he castigated all forms of authority and urged the miners of Cornwall to join together in a 'Union of Miners'. He told them their labour was a powerful weapon in the fight against all that was wrong with the country's parliamentary system. The miners in the North of England had already set the precedent. Now Cornwall was being given the opportunity to join the national fight.

William Cobbett knew how to rouse the miners of the North, and he could whip the industrial workers of the Midlands into a frenzy – but he knew nothing of the Cornish miner, neither his method of working nor his stubborn independent nature.

The vast majority of the miners here were 'tributers'. Tributing was a traditional method of mining that made each man virtually self-employed. They bid against each other for a particular working-area in a mine, after which the miner's own skill and hard work determined how much he earned.

Some mine captains paid lower rates than others, and a few mines skimped on the matters for which they were responsible. Inadequate shaft work and poor maintenance were the cause of too many deaths, but the miners usually managed to set things to rights without any outside help.

Suddenly, a hand gripped Ben's arm and a voice shouted, 'Here is someone who can tell you how to topple authority. One of your own kind. Ben Retallick – a miner.'

Charles Swindles had recognised Ben in the crowd and, unnoticed by him, had made his way from the platform to Ben's side. Now he pushed him towards the platform while the crowd gave him an uncertain reception and Jesse stood tight-lipped and disapproving behind him.

Ben began to struggle against Charles Swindles' grip, but then he looked about him at the miners in the crowd. He had seen many of them emerging from a mine shaft, filthy and exhausted at the end of a shift. Others he had watched giving away their hard-won money to the landlord of an inn or beer-house.

On the platform in front of them now were men who were prepared to use the miners and take just as much from them, but in a more subtle and dishonest way. Neither Hoblyn nor Cobbett cared about those to whom they were appealing. The miners and farm-workers would be used, and then discarded, as expediency and ambition dictated.

'All right, I'll speak.'

Ben shook off the hand of Charles Swindles and made his way to the platform. He ignored the proffered hand of William Cobbett and sprang on to the wooden platform.

His arrival brought a few genuine cheers from miners in the crowd who knew Ben, or had seen him in their district.

Standing on the platform, looking out over the sea of faces extending over the full length and breadth of the field, Ben experienced a moment of panic. Then he remembered some of the snippets of conversation he had overheard at Richard Hoblyn's house, and he began to speak to the crowd.

'As Charles Swindles has just told you, I am a miner, as are most of you here.' Ben drew in a deep breath and said firmly, 'They are the only true words I've heard spoken today.'

A startled hush fell upon the huge crowd and Ben was quick to follow up his initial impact.

'This meeting has been called to discuss parliamentary reform. There cannot be anyone here who doubts that reform is needed. It's not right for a few landowners to control the lives of thousands of men and women from the day they are born to the moment they die; to tell them where they must live, what work they will do – even who they are allowed to marry. In a moment of anger, one of these landowners can dismiss a man and turn his family out to starve to death. He can bring pressure to bear on the adventurers and close any mine in the country. Not one of us is safe from men with such power.'

The applause that greeted these words was led by the men on the platform. Alarmed by Ben's opening words, they were now convinced Ben had used them only to gain the attention of the restless crowd.

Ben swiftly disillusioned them.

'Yes, we all want reform. But what exactly is this "reform"? What will it give *us*, the miners and farm-workers of Cornwall? Richard Hoblyn and his friends see it as a chance to put *themselves* into Parliament; to have bills passed to ease *their* taxes and make life better for the merchants and shopkeepers of the country . . .'

'Well said, Ben!' cried Charles Swindles gleefully. He had hardly got the words out before Ben switched his attack to include the Midlands' Chartist and his travelling companion.

'William Cobbett is no better. He wants to lead us to a revolution, with himself standing behind us as an English Napoleon. He says we must all stand up and fight . . . but for what? For William Cobbett? He has no knowledge of the way we Cornish miners work and is interested only in the trouble we can stir up to help *his* cause.'

From the corner of his eye, Ben saw William Cobbett signalling to some of his men. A couple of them moved hurriedly towards the platform.

'Yes, we need reform – but not just for the sake of change.'

One of William Cobbett's men reached on to the platform and grasped Ben's ankle. Shaking him off, Ben shouted his final words to the crowd, who were now cheering him wildly.

'My advice to you is to refuse to be pushed into doing something you'll all regret. Do nothing until a man comes along who knows our ways. Our problems . . .'

Two of William Cobbett's men gained the platform and

rushed Ben in an attempt to throw him off. Ben's fist dropped the first of them to his knees. The second man swung a punch which caught Ben on the side of his head and made him stagger. He recovered quickly and, taking his attacker by the collar, dumped him unceremoniously in the lap of William Cobbett.

Ben leaped from the platform to the ground and was immediately surrounded by Cobbett's men. For a few minutes he fought valiantly to defend himself before Wrightwick Robert's voice roared, 'I'm with you, Ben,' and the preacher fought his way to Ben's side. At the same time, a figure leaped from the platform, knocking two of Ben's assailants to the ground.

It was Crispin Hoblyn. Scrambling to his feet, the elegant young man adopted the exaggerated stance of a prizefighter. Exaggerated or not, he swung a beautiful right hook to down another of Cobbett's men. Now many of the miners in the crowd surged forward and the odds swung overwhelmingly in Ben's favour. The men from the Midlands were chased from the field.

Ben grinned as Wrightwick Roberts dabbed his bloody nose, looking indignantly at the blood staining his handkerchief.

'You were right, Ben,' the preacher said nasally. 'No God-fearing Cornishman could possibly follow a man who insults John Wesley and is ready to spill the blood of a servant of the Lord.'

Jesse fought her way through the excited crowd to Ben's side and looked anxiously at the graze along his cheekbone. Over her head, Ben met Crispin Hoblyn's eyes.

'I'm obliged to you,' Ben said stiffly, remembering his advances to Jesse.

'The pleasure is all mine,' Crispin Hoblyn produced his

infectious grin once more. 'Though I doubt if my brother will agree with me. He certainly did *not* agree with you.'

Crispin Hoblyn rubbed his knuckles proudly. 'Tom Cribb, the prizefighter, taught me his art. This is the first opportunity I have had to put his teaching to the test.' He looked down at one of William Cobbett's followers who knelt on the ground with bowed head, groaning loudly. 'I owe Tom a night out when next we meet.'

Crispin Hoblyn looked beyond the crowd to where a large body of bright-coated horsemen rode down the track to the field. 'I think we had all better leave now. It would seem the magistrate has called out the militia. It would be a sad end to a wonderful day to spend it sharing a cell with some of Cobbett's rabble.'

Ben and Jesse arrived within sight of Sharptor when the sun was sinking low behind the high moor, sending long fingers of shadow far out across the valley.

There had been little opportunity to talk on their way home from Liskeard. Many miners walked the same rough roads, full of excitement at the eventful meeting they had attended. They attached themselves to Jesse and Ben, talking all the while of what had occurred at the Liskeard Fair reform meeting.

Some miners who had left the meeting after Ben and Jesse overtook them along the way, passing on the disturbing news that a few of the young hot-headed miners had stoned the militia. They said there had been a number of arrests. Minutes later, another miner caught up with them. He had later news. The disturbance had been caused by a small group of drunken farm-workers. Only two arrests had been made, both by the constables, and both for drunkenness.

Shortly before Sharptor was reached, the track divided. The upper route went to the Wheal Sharptor, the lower to the Marke

Valley mines. Here the last of Ben and Jesse's companions left them. They were alone for the first time since leaving Liskeard.

Rounding a shoulder of the hill, they paused to gaze eastwards, to where the patchwork of tiny fields and spinneys blended with the mauve haze of distance. Ben looked at Jesse, but she was seeking something in the valley.

'There's Linkinhorne church steeple . . . in among those trees.'

'I'm sorry, Jesse.'

'Sorry?' she turned to face him. 'Sorry for what?'

'For breaking up the reform meeting. I'm not a reformer at heart – and I don't like people using me. Hoblyn, Cobbett and Charles Swindles are not reformers, either. Each of them uses the reform cause to achieve his own ends. Walter must have been the only honest man in the whole of the reform movement. It really meant something to him. It would break his heart if he could see what has happened to the cause for which he gave so much.'

'It broke his heart soon after his arrest,' said Jesse huskily. 'Not one of the many men Walter helped had the courage to raise his voice in protest on Walter's behalf. Had you spoken in favour of reform today you would have been setting out on the same road that Walter took – a road to unhappiness and broken promises. No, Ben, you told the men at that meeting how you felt, and I'm proud of you for doing it. Besides, I don't want a husband who thinks more of an ideal than of me. I love you, Ben. I want you to love me . . . with all your heart.'

Ben kissed Jesse and as they walked slowly along the path with their arms about each other. Ben looked up the hill to their little grey cottage, tucked in a fold of the moor.

'This is what I want from life, Jesse. I have a job I enjoy, a home in one of the most beautiful spots in the land . . . and a wife who is fancied by the gentlemen of the county.'

Ben grinned happily at Jesse. 'One day we'll have a family of our own. Then I'll have all that any man could need.'

Jesse stopped suddenly. When Ben looked down at her he saw she was smiling at him in delight.

'You couldn't have said anything to make me happier, Ben. I've been waiting for the right moment to tell you my news. Now you've given it to me. Ben Retallick, you are going to be a father. Soon both our lives will be complete. May God give us many years to enjoy them – together.'

Chase the Wind

History lives on in these ruined walls
Sagging with age and troubled thought.
Stone-wept tears around mossed feet.
Yesterday's hero. Apart. Forlorn.

Once proud and tall above the moor,
Its chimney smoke would chase the wind
High over mounds of broken ore
That gave to man his daily bread.

But who was last to close the door?
Did he look back with sad regret
Or, turning, laugh and hurl the key
And climb towards the setting sun?

But no man lives who knew it then
And gaping doors no secrets hold.
While scouring time and moorland gorse
Eradicate our yesterdays.

Chapter One

Ninety fathoms below grass, in the darkness at the bottom of the main vertical shaft of Wheal Sharptor copper mine, Joshua Retallick stepped from the ladder on to the ore-strewn floor. He took a couple of shaky steps, his legs trembling from the climb down.

Above him, so far up that the clean, star-studded sky could not be seen, was a small rough-square hole. Through this was hoisted the copper ore that would make one man rich and send fifty more to a premature grave.

Josh moved to one side as boots scraped on the wooden rungs above him. The night shift was coming on duty. As each man stepped to the floor he would flex his arms, easing the muscles in his shoulders. Muscles knotted by the fear of falling that made a man grip each rung just a little too tightly.

The miners passed through the openings into the tunnels that sloped gently away from the main shaft. They stooped, automatically but unnecessarily, used to smaller tunnels than these. Once inside they paused to light the yellow candles that each man relied upon to give him light by which to work and warning of foul air.

Josh followed one of the miners along the tunnel where he knew his father was working. At first, the tunnel was narrow, with water oozing from walls shored up in a haphazard here-and-there manner. Then, suddenly and dramatically, it opened out into a huge vault, eighty feet wide and thirty high. Here there had been a seam of near-pure copper. Now it was a rock-walled emptiness – the ore long since fed into the belly of a Swansea smelting-house and disgorged as blocks of gleaming metal, each tinged with the colour of the furnace, to be shipped in tall-rigged vessels to a world eager for high-grade Cornish copper.

In the vast chamber clouds of dust hung on the heavy air. The shadows of the new arrivals flickered and were distorted, moulded by the smoking flames from two candles standing in niches in the rough-hewn wall.

A dirty sweating figure, stripped to the waist, appeared from a small tunnel, pushing a laden wheelbarrow ahead of him. Seeing the new arrivals he rested the wheelbarrow, added another streak of dirt to his face with the back of his hand and called back down the tunnel from which he had emerged.

'Time to wrap it up, Ben. Night shift are here.'

The call was taken up by unseen men in other tunnels, 'Knock it off! Night men are here!'

Men cramped in unnatural postures gratefully eased their way back from exploratory borings and headed towards the main shaft to begin the long climb to air and home, to comparative comfort and company, where there was not a million tons of rock and earth packed above them.

The miner who had first signalled the arrival of the relief shift grinned at Josh. ''Tis a bit late to be coming down to help us. Has Preacher Thackeray given up trying to learn you? Does he think you should be working below ground wi' us?'

'No.' Josh grinned. 'There's a meeting of the Benefit Union at the chapel tonight. Lessons ended early.'

'I wouldn't mention anything about it to your dad. He's not too happy wi' talk about Thackeray's "Union".'

Budge Pearn towelled his body with his rough-spun shirt before pulling the crumpled garment over his head and tucking the end inside his trousers. At eighteen he was four years older than Josh. His mother had died in childbirth. When his father was killed in a mining accident Budge was seven years old and had been taken into the Retallick household.

'When are you coming up to see Jenny and the baby?' He pronounced it as 'bebby'. 'She's right handsome now. Plenty of hair, too.'

'I know. Jenny brought Gwen down home today. That reminds me. You'd better not be late home. Mum gave Jenny some boiling bacon for your supper.'

'I'll be up on the moor before your dad sets foot on the ladder.' Budge pocketed the stubs of half a dozen candles. 'Give my love to your mum.' Then with a cheery wave he was gone.

Further along the tunnel, Ben Retallick welcomed the arrival of the night shift with grateful relief. At thirty-five years of age he was reckoned an 'old man' by mining standards. It was an era when a miner who had seen his fortieth birthday below ground was something of a rarity.

Climbing over a heap of newly dug ore he crawled backwards along a tunnel scarcely three feet high and only as wide as his shoulders. It would be widened eventually – the copper seam was quite broad here – but he had been burrowing his way forward in an attempt to determine its direction and value.

Ben Retallick had been working in Cornish mines since he was ten years of age and was one of the most experienced miners on Wheal Sharptor. He had worked two-men shallow streamings on the high moor and the great labyrinths that extended beneath the sea in the far west of the county. He might well have been a captain for one of those tin mines had not Theophilus Strike asked him to come and work as a tribute worker on the newly discovered copper seams of the Wheal Sharptor. This meant that Ben Retallick would become a free-lance miner, contracting on a piece-work basis for the right to remove the ore for the mine-owner at so much per ton. This was why it was so important to know the direction and value of a seam of ore.

It was said that Ben Retallick could follow a rich seam even when it leap-frogged a twelve-foot barrier of granite. He would not be deluded by a tempting stretch of momentarily rich ore which petered out within a few yards.

Outside, in the wide tunnel, Ben Retallick stood upright slowly. The cramped muscles had knotted his limbs into a crouched position, and it was a painful adjustment. The damp from the walls of a mine worked its way into a man's joints and caused them to swell.

He looked up to see the sympathy on Josh's face and grimaced. 'A boy shouldn't see his father when he's fighting the cramps, Josh. What are you doing down here?'

Josh shrugged and tried to sound nonchalant. 'My lesson finished early. I thought I'd come down to meet you.'

Ben Retallick saw the half-filled wheelbarrow and the long-handled shovel cast hastily aside and frowned. Budge Pearn had been in a hurry to finish work. It was time he learned that a man always emptied his own wheelbarrow below ground. Then Ben smiled at his own thoughts. Budge had plenty of time to learn. With a pretty wife and baby daughter waiting for him at home there was more reason for a young man to be on the surface than trundling barrow-loads of another man's ore down here for three pounds a month.

'Come on, son. Let's go up top and taste some fresh air.'

At the foot of the ladder there was a great deal of good-natured banter and jostling between the men working another seam. Ben put a hand on Josh's shoulder and stood back from it. At the end of a shift he had neither the energy of the youngsters nor patience with them.

Another man also lacked patience. Heavy-browed, dark-eyed and scowling, Moses Trago elbowed his irritable way through to the ladder. Broad-shouldered and brutal, he cared for no man's opinion, using his fists in arguments where other men would use words. Behind him, walking in his brother's shadow, the quieter John Trago loomed just as large.

The arrival of the two men put an end to the outburst of good humour and Ben and Josh shuffled forward with the other miners.

This was the part of mining that Ben found more difficult with each passing day. From ninety fathoms down there were five hundred and forty ladder-rungs to be climbed before a man's head rose from the hole in the ground. Ben knew the number. There had been a time when he would count them. But no more. These days he gritted his teeth, kept his face turned downwards and climbed numbly. Occasionally the man above him might be climbing too slowly, or would slip because of his own weakness and step upon Ben's fingers. Then he would feel an unreasonable fury – almost a black rage – against the unseen miner. The feeling would sustain him, drive him on until he stumbled out on to earth that was open to the sky.

Once on the ladders all talking ceased. A man would regret each mouthful of wasted air when he arrived, lungs roaring for oxygen, at the top of the shaft.

Josh was aware of this and he climbed steadily and carefully ahead of his father.

Never a pleasant experience, tonight the climb suddenly became a frightening nightmare. Josh and Ben were on the fourth ladder, almost fifty feet from the bottom of the shaft when there was a blood-freezing scream from high above them and the confused shouts of men.

Josh had no idea what was happening, but it was an experience that Ben had known many times before. His ''Ware below!' rang out and he used the same breath to clamber up to share a rung with Josh. 'Swing behind the ladder,' he hissed. When Josh obeyed him hurriedly, Ben Retallick closed his arms about his son and held him tight against the ladder with arms and knees. His back pressed against the uneven rock of the shaft.

Most times a falling man would mercifully smash his head against the side of the shaft and know no more. This one was not so fortunate. The scream had died to a low inhuman sound in his throat as he flailed past Josh and his father, but he remained conscious until the moment he crashed on to the floor of the shaft. Josh would remember the sound of it for as long as he lived. His hands about the ladder gripped so tightly that his nails drew blood from his palms.

For two full seconds there was silence. It was broken by the clattering of boots as the men on the lower ladders scrambled back down.

'Ben! Ben Retallick!' The cry went up as Josh followed his father down.

'I'm here. Who was it who fell?'

'Budge Pearn.'

'Oh my God! His poor maid.'

Josh heard the agonised whisper from his father as his own legs threatened to buckle beneath him. The miner dropped to the floor of the shaft where flickering candle-light added to the gruesome scene, then turned back to shield Josh from it. He was only partly successful.

'Wait for me at the fifty-fathom level, Josh,' he said.

Josh could only nod his agreement. He was not sure whether the lump in his throat would make him cry or be sick.

Ben put a hand on his son's shoulder. 'Go on up. There's nothing you can do here.'

Josh turned and climbed blindly, the lump still lodged in his windpipe. Budge Pearn had been as a big brother to him.

Behind him, Ben looked down at the smashed body. Miraculously, there was not a mark on Budge's face. Reaching down he closed the lids on fear-filled eyes. 'Poor maid!' he repeated. Though only a few weeks past her seventeenth birthday, Jenny Pearn was now a widow with a baby to support. Like Budge she was an orphan, her father having died in an identical accident. Ben looked down at the body and thought of the young wasted life. He felt suddenly old and tired. The boy had so much to live for.

Tom Shovell, the shift captain, swung off the ladder and bent down over the body. Then he looked sympathetically at Ben. 'You get on home. We'll do what's necessary here. Budge will go up in the ore-sling.'

Ben nodded numbly.

'We'll take him on to the chapel from there. I'd be obliged if you would take it on yourself to tell Jenny. You – or Jesse.' Jesse was Ben's wife. 'I needn't tell you how sorry I am, Ben. He was a well-liked lad.'

'There's little comfort in that for poor Jenny.'

Ben Retallick began the climb to the surface once more. At the fifty-fathom level Josh joined him and they completed the climb in silence.

There was a chill east wind blowing on the moor. Normally Ben would have shivered and hurried along the path to his cottage when the breath had returned to him. Tonight there was no speed in his legs. The small group of miners clustered around the top of the shaft murmured their sympathy, but that was all. They saved their questions for those who came to the surface behind him.

It was early March and quite dark as they took the path that wound over the shoulder of the tor towards the small cluster of slate and granite cottages huddled against the wind in a shallow depression on the east-facing slope. As they walked they could hear the heavy hollow thudding of the great pumping engine at the Wheal Phoenix in the valley beyond the cottages. Once, there was a red glow which flared up behind church-like windows as one of the furnace doors was swung open.

'How . . . how do you think it happened?' Josh asked, speaking for the first time since they had both stood by the shattered body in the shaft.

'I expect Budge was in a hurry. Probably trod on a loose rung. It's an easy thing to do. I've seen it happen too often.'

'But why to Budge?'

He had to make it sound fierce or his voice would have betrayed him.

'I don't know the answer to that.' Ben put an understanding arm across his son's shoulders. 'Why do so many men die in the mines? You're the one getting the schooling. Think of some way to save miners' lives and you'll be blessed by every mother and wife in Cornwall.'

He stopped talking as they heard the sound of someone running and stumbling along the path towards them. The footsteps were too light to belong to a man.

'Who's there?' Ben called.

'Ben! Is that you?'

'Jesse! What are you doing out here?'

'Oh, Ben! Thank God you're safe! Thank God!' She clung to him, shaking violently. 'They told me there'd been an accident. That you'd fallen.' She buried her face in his rough shirt, grasping the material tight with her fingers.

'Who told you that?' Ben put his hand beneath her chin and lifted her head.

'Moses Trago. I left everything and ran. Your dinner! It will be ruined.'

'Moses Trago is quicker to carry bad news than to offer help.' Ben Retallick was angry. Moses Trago must have heard his name being called and assumed that it was he who had fallen.

'Then there was an accident. What happened? Was anyone hurt?'

'It was Budge, Mum.'

Ben felt Jesse stiffen in his arms as Josh spoke. 'He fell from the ladder.'

'He's dead, then.' It was a statement of fact rather than a question.

'Yes,' said Ben gently. 'Jenny hasn't been told yet. I was going to see her myself but it might be better if you did it.'

Jesse was silent for so long that Ben thought she might not feel capable of breaking the news to Budge's wife. Then she burst out, 'Why? Why did it have to happen to Budge? The two of them had found so much happiness together. Oh! Poor Budge! Poor Jenny!'

'It was an accident, Jesse. They happen.'

'It's that damned mine. Worn ladders, frayed ropes . . . !'

'Enough now, Jesse. It gives us our living.'

'Try to tell that to Budge – God rest his soul.' She sobbed once. A long uneven breath. But she slipped from Ben's arms when he tried to comfort her.

'I'll go to Jenny now. Before she hears the news from someone else.' She paused alongside Josh. 'If you ever become a miner, Joshua Retallick, I'll never forgive you.'

She moved away along the path, and her voice came to them from the darkness.

'Ben?'

'Yes?'

'I'm not forgetting to thank God it wasn't you.'

As she hurried away Ben said, 'One day you'll be looking for a wife, Josh. If you find one who is half the woman your mother is you'll be a lucky man.'

His own parents would have disputed that when he first told them he was going to marry her. They were staunch Methodists and had brought Ben up in the same faith. Jesse shared the same religion – up to a certain point. But she possessed an impetuosity, a disconcerting habit of saying exactly what she thought when the thought came to her. It was not kindly accepted by her elders. It did not happen so often now; the years had mellowed her. But once in a while she would say, or do, something to remind Ben of the girl she had been when he married her. Wilful and stubborn his parents may have thought her, but Ben loved her for it and had never sought to change her.

In the kitchen of the small granite cottage Josh swung the cooking-pot off the fire while Ben eased his boots off. Small, but spotless, the kitchen served as dining- and living-room. There was one other downstairs room where all the 'best' possessions were housed. It was kept for special occasions and the formal visits of people outside their immediate circle of friends.

Josh ladled stew into two bowls, and they sat at the table eating in silence. Josh was thinking of having more when the door banged open and Jesse Retallick bundled inside a thin pale girl who looked hardly old enough to be the mother of the kicking, wailing infant she clutched to her. Jesse kept an arm about Jenny and took her straight through into the 'best' room.

A minute later she was back in the doorway. 'Josh. Upstairs and move your things into our room. Make yourself up a bed on the floor. Jenny will be moving into yours. Ben, bring some fire into the other room.'

She went back to look after Jenny, and two chairs scraped back as Ben and Josh moved to carry out Jesse's orders.

As Ben was filling a bucket with live coals from the kitchen stove, Jesse came back into the room and deposited a pile of baby-clothes on a chair.

'Hurry and get in there with her, Ben,' she said. 'She hasn't started crying yet. When it comes it will be all the worse for the waiting.'

When Ben took the coals in, Jenny was seated on the faded horse-hair sofa that had been a wedding-present from his father. Dry-eyed and taut, she was not even aware of his presence and continued to stare vacantly in front of her.

He poured the coals into the fire-place and piled wood on top of it before standing up and looking down at the pathetic young window. He wanted to say something to her, give her some words of comfort; but she was as cold as rock, totally withdrawn from the world of the living.

'Is that fire going?' Jesse swept into the room and, picking up the baby, placed her on the floor in the corner of the room. 'Leave us now, Ben.' She moved to the sofa where Jenny was sitting unseeing. With a last pained look at the girl, Ben returned to the kitchen.

Josh made his bed – an untidy heap in a corner of his parents' bedroom – and climbed into it, pulling the blanket up to his chin. He was lying there, his face turned away from the door, when his father came into the darkened room. Ben saw the glitter of tears on his cheek.

He said nothing but walked to the window and looked down into the valley where Henwood village lay. There was light shining from the large windows of the chapel, and he guessed the body of Budge Pearn had arrived there.

Then he heard the sound from the room downstairs. It startled him before he realised fully what it was. Starting as a low moan it quickly swelled and expanded until it burst out as a sob. Then Jenny began crying noisily. Painful as it was to listen to, Ben yet felt a sense of relief. Now Jenny was a young girl who had lost her man. A widow with a small child. Someone with whom to feel sympathy and for Jesse to comfort. Before, she had been unapproachable, locked away in a place where no other human could join her or share her pain.

Ben went downstairs, put on his boots and coat, and let himself out of the house to walk to the village.

Despite the darkness and the chill east wind a great many villagers were gathered about the entrance to the chapel. The insularity of the small moorland communities had been changed by the influx of miners from other parts of Cornwall – and even from beyond the Tamar. But a fatal accident, like any other deviation from the norm of everyday life, was an event to be shared by all.

There were enquiries from all sides about Jenny as Ben strode to the chapel door. Some stemmed from mere curiosity, but most from genuine concern for her. The women in the crowd knew that tomorrow, or the next day, it might be their turn. The mines were notorious widow-makers. Accidents were all too frequent. Even when a man thought he had won, and gave up the life of a miner, he discovered that the mine had passed on a fatal legacy to him. He had spent years toiling in air sometimes so foul it would scarcely support life, breathing in dust for the whole of a shift. Then the sudden change of temperature at the end of a shift when his labouring lungs exchanged the heat of the mine for the chill of a winter night. They all took their toll of him. Few ex-miners survived to spin yarns of their exploits to their grandchildren.

The inside of the small chapel was clean and starkly bereft of ostentation. Ben was surprised to see the preacher inside, distributing hymn- and prayer-books thinly along the benches.

The Reverend Wrightwick Roberts was not a resident preacher. He rode the North Hill Methodist circuit. Methodism was still a young religion, dependent entirely upon the Sunday collections for its income. Only the larger mining communities like St Cleer, where Josh went for his lessons, could afford to support a resident preacher.

The North Hill circuit minister was himself an ex-miner and his shoulders were almost as broad as Moses Trago's, but when he spoke his voice was strangely soft coming from such a big man.

'It's a night for grieving, Ben. The Lord's ways are beyond

the understanding of mortals.' He nodded towards a closed door at the far end of the chapel. 'Budge is through there. Mary Crabbe is with him.'

Mary Crabbe had been taking charge of births and deaths in the district since before Ben was born. He nodded his acknowledgement. 'It's been a sad day, Wrightwick.'

The preacher doled out the last of the prayer-books. 'Every mine accident brings sadness to someone. How is Jenny taking it?'

Ben sat down on the end of a bench. 'Hard. But Jesse is looking after her.' He suddenly felt old, and the preacher saw it in the sag of his shoulders. 'Josh is taking it badly too. They were like brothers.'

'And you, Ben?' The preacher asked the question softly. Ben and Jesse had looked upon Budge Pearn as another son.

'Yes, and me.' It was as much as he would ever say on the subject and more than any other man would hear from him.

'You'll see to things, Wrightwick? Take the service for him? I'll be paying.'

'And what about the men on the mine? Don't they collect for such happenings?'

'Sharptor isn't the Caradon – or even Wheal Phoenix. We are still small. I want whatever is collected to go to Jenny. It won't be much. A few guineas aren't going to go far with a baby to feed and clothe.'

'Then what about Theophilus Strike? Won't he give anything?'

Ben managed a faint smile. 'That sounded like young Preacher Thackeray talking. Theophilus Strike pays wages, Wrightwick. Jenny will collect whatever was due to Budge – and a guinea or two besides.'

Wrightwick Roberts frowned at the mention of William Thackeray. The fiery young St Cleer preacher was fast establishing a reputation as a miners' champion, and the younger men flocked to hear his sermons on Sundays, packing the large St Cleer chapel to capacity.

'Why do you let Josh stay at Thackeray's school, Ben? He's not a good influence.'

Ben shrugged. 'His lessons are cheap – and good. Josh has learned to read the Bible and can work out sums that leave me with my jaw hanging. Is that bad, Wrightwick?'

'No. But that isn't what I am talking about. Thackeray teaches things that you won't find in any schoolbook. He feeds his ideas to young miners who know no better. Telling them to band into a "union" and demand more money is dangerous talk, Ben. It shouldn't come from a man who serves God.'

'All I've heard is rumours. None of them from Josh,' said Ben, standing up. 'But I do know the boy is learning things I would dearly love to have been taught. I am grateful to Preacher Thackeray for that. Josh will have a chance in life, Wrightwick. He won't have to go down a mine because he knows nothing else. And he won't end up on a table in your chapel with Mary Crabbe straightening his broken limbs.'

He stopped and drew a deep breath. 'I'll be away now before I say more than I should.'

'We've been friends too long for me to take offence,' said the preacher. 'And I'll walk up with you. I'd like to see Jenny.'

He held open the door and followed Ben outside. There were only a few of the older women still waiting and they bobbed their heads at the preacher.

The two men walked side by side along the street and on to the twin-rutted track that climbed towards the mine, passing close to the Retallick cottage.

Ben's tiredness was telling on him now, and the preacher slowed his pace to stay with him.

'How many years have you been mining now, Ben?'

'Most of my life, it seems. I've been underground since I was ten.'

'It's the underground part that takes it out of a man,' said Wrightwick Roberts. 'Don't you think it's time you thought about a surface job?'

Ben snorted. 'For what? A woman's pay?'

Wrightwick Roberts knew better than to pursue the matter. For Ben to give up working below ground would be an admission of defeat, an acknowledgement that he was too old to beat the ladders. But it was always the ladders that scored the final victory.

'How about an engine? Is the Sharptor going to get one?'

'I don't know. Only Strike can answer that. If it means spending money the answer is "No". Besides, we won't need one for a year or two.'

'What's money got to do with it? With the mine and its shop Theophilus Strike is making more money than he knows how to spend.'

'Likely you're right,' replied Ben. 'I wouldn't know.' They had arrived at the cottage. Ben opened the door, and both men went inside.

'How is she?' asked Wrightwick Roberts as Ben sat down gratefully.

Jesse had been bustling about the kitchen when they arrived and she said, 'As well as any woman who has just lost her man. And when she begins to get over it she'll begin to worry about the future for herself and the baby. She's no home because the cottage belongs to the mine and she's no family to turn to.'

'She has us,' said Ben. 'She can move in here. I hope you didn't wait to hear it from me to tell her.'

'No, I didn't. But it's nice to hear you say it.'

Wrightwick Roberts left the kitchen, and as Ben leaned back in his chair, relaxing a little, an unintelligible murmur started up in the other downstairs room.

'It will be strange having a baby about the house again.'

'Budge would be happy to know we are looking after the pair of them,' said Jesse. There was a break in her voice. Ben reached across to where she was standing by the table and took her hand.

The inquest on Budge Pearn was a brief perfunctory affair. It was held in the chapel, and the coroner was feeling the cold. It was his second inquest into the death of a miner that day and there were two more that afternoon.

He was experienced in dealing with mine fatalities, the previous year having supplied him with seventy-four – twenty-two of them the result of a single disaster.

Such fatalities were no longer of interest to even the most morbid, and the newspapers gave them only a passing paragraph. This being so, the coroner wasted no time in accepting the facts as they were presented to him. He recorded a verdict that one Budge Pearn, miner, had met with an accidental death whilst leaving his place of employment, namely the Wheal Sharptor. Then, there being no local gentry in the mining village of Henwood, the coroner immediately set off in his trap to lunch at Linkinhorne vicarage.

Budge Pearn was buried that same afternoon, on a day as grey as the occasion. The persistent easterly wind helped tears flow the more easily for the women and made casual mourners restless to return to their firesides.

But Wrightwick Roberts was not a preacher to cut corners at a man's funeral. Budge Pearn went on his way to the hereafter with as good a reference as any man could receive. In the same sermon the preacher damned a mine that allowed a man to fall to his death and then failed to send a representative to his funeral.

In all fairness, Theophilus Strike *had* delegated someone. His senior mine captain had been told to go, but Herman Schmidt could think of better ways to spend an afternoon than standing on a windswept hillside, listening to a sermon in a language he barely understood in praise of one of the workers he regarded as little better than animals.

Instead, Schmidt was shut inside his house in the nearby town of Liskeard. He was already in a state of alcoholic stupor. He was in the habit of spending much less time at the Wheal Sharptor than Theophilus Strike was aware of, but Schmidt's knowledge of mining had been learned with a Germanic thoroughness.

There was little that any man in Cornwall could tell him about copper-mining.

Once a week Herman Schmidt carried out a full inspection of the mine, and it was a day the miners had come to dread. If he found the slightest thing that was not to his liking, there would be miners seeking work elsewhere on the following day. There was very little that escaped his attention and, if his hangover was worse than usual, he was quite capable of inventing a reason for dismissing a man.

From his weekly visit the mine captain was able to compile his reports and direct the operations that kept Wheal Sharptor a profit-making mine.

Captain Herman Schmidt was a brilliant mine captain. He was also a foreigner, an atheist and a drunkard. The miners of Wheal Sharptor hated him.

Chapter Two

'Very well done, Josh. Your reading is greatly improved. Keep it up.'

Josh looked down in embarrassed pleasure at the book from which he had just finished reading. The Reverend William Thackeray was not given to handing out unearned praise to his pupils. They were all, like Josh, the sons of miners – each of them eager to learn, grateful for the opportunity of receiving the education denied to their fathers.

Starting these classes had been one of the first tasks William Thackeray had set himself upon taking up his appointment at St Cleer. A slight, stooped, consumptive-looking figure, he had accepted many years before that he was no physical match for his fellow-men. So he had chosen words as weapons to fight his way through life. Then he had discovered the Lord and recognised in him an unending source of ammunition. Sent to Cornwall, he saw the abject poverty so many miners lived in, the appalling rigours of work below ground. It was inevitable that he should become a social reformer. With his power of oratory he quickly earned the enmity of the mine-owners and 'adventurers' – those who held shares in the mines. He cared little for any of them. His sermons drew men to the chapel. Once inside, William Thackeray made sure that some of the Lord's teachings got through to them. He had also followed the fortunes of the 'Chartists' with considerable interest. Preacher Thackeray advocated the formation of a 'union' of miners in Cornwall to pursue the same quarry – the betterment of the working miner.

He spoke to Josh again. 'Yes, young man, you have it in you to become as educated as anyone in these parts.'

He suddenly stopped and jabbed a long sensitive finger at the air an inch from Josh's nose. 'But that is only the beginning. The important thing is *what* are you going to do with that education?'

The question and the finger took Josh by surprise. 'I don't know, sir – but I'm not going to be a miner.'

The menacing finger was lowered. 'I am pleased to hear *that*.' The preacher glowered around the room. 'How about the rest of you?'

He began pacing the width of the room in front of the class with short jerky steps. 'You are all the sons of enlightened men. Miners who started their life without the benefit of any education whatsoever, but who are determined their sons will be better equipped to go out and earn their livings. You will not have to go underground to support a family simply because you are unable to do anything else. Never forget that you owe it to your fathers to make something of your lives. You owe it to *me*. To *yourselves*. And you owe it to *God*! Never forget to thank him for giving you a preacher who is also a teacher. But the best way for you to show your gratitude is to take full advantage of your education.'

He stopped in front of Josh once more. 'Now, I will ask you once again. What will you do when your education is completed?'

'Well . . . I think I would like to be an engineer.'

William Thackeray's eyebrows rose an inch. 'An admirable ambition. Does any other boy know what he would like to be?'

The hands rose hesitantly and sporadically.

'H'm! We seem beset by uncertainty.'

He thumped the table in front of Josh with his fist, making him jump again. 'But to become anything worth while in this world you must *work* and *work* and *work*!' The words were emphasised with his fist, and at each thump Josh blinked involuntarily.

William Thackeray's eyes were aglow with the fires of enthusiasm. 'If a half – no, only a quarter – of those who raised their hands became teachers and educated the sons of working men, I would fall on my knees and thank the Lord for bringing success to my mission.'

He looked around the room at the tousle-headed ragged boys, and the fire dulled. 'But, for all my teaching, I have no doubt most of you will waste your knowledge – using it to count barrow-loads of ore, or perhaps to work out the percentage of copper to the ton.'

He shrugged. 'At least you won't be cheated by a dishonest mine captain. All right, boys, school is over for today. I will see you at the same time tomorrow – Wait!'

The sudden noise died away again as the twenty-two boys in the class closed their eyes and stood with bowed heads.

'Lord, may the wisdom and learning I have attempted to instil into these boys be used always to the glory of Thy name and the benefit of those who, though created in Thy image, have dug deep into the good earth Thou gavest to us and moved closer to the Devil and his evil ways. For the sake of Jesus Christ, our Lord. Amen.'

There was a mumbled 'Amen' in answer to his prayer, the briefest of pauses, and then a flood of boys surged out through the door. Leaving William Thackeray alone in the room with his thoughts.

The track wandered aimlessly in the general direction of Sharptor, skirting the Caradon mines and dipping down to where the great shaft of the Wheal Phoenix yawned deep in the shadowed valley. Josh ignored the track and went straight across country. Avoiding the few walled fields, cleared of gorse and fern by forgotten generations of farmers, he toiled up on to the high lonely moor.

This was the place that Josh loved above all others. It was a vast landscape of sweeping emptiness, uncompromising in its seasonal moods. The stunted bushes, bowing to the east, were evidence of the prevailing winds of winter. Now the gorse was a tangle of yellow blossom. Here and there a lacework of streams left the turf soft and sponge-like underfoot. The whole tangled moor was criss-crossed with the tracks of centuries of badgers and foxes. Above it all, blunt-winged buzzards circled remorselessly in search of their live prey.

That was how Josh saw the moor today. With the scattered houses, mines and creaking ore-wagons out of sight he could think, create his own future. He wondered what life was like away from the mining community, beyond the valley of the Tamar, further even than the dark highlands of Dartmoor dominating the horizon twenty miles to the east.

He had told Preacher Thackeray he wanted to be an engineer. In truth, he knew little about mechanical things. He had looked at the engines in the Caradon and Phoenix mines and had been very impressed by their size and noise, and the power of the hissing steam, but he knew nothing of their workings. He decided he would find out.

Josh was on the high moor proper now. He skirted the roofless ivy-clad engine-house and gaping shaft of a mine abandoned a few decades before owing to insurmountable drainage problems.

He paused to watch the aerobatics of a buzzard which had strayed into the territory of a pair of crows. The large black birds were working as a fighting team. While one harassed from close range, the second bird climbed high above them, dropping into the battle area with wings closed in a vain attempt to decide the issue. The buzzard, sure in the knowledge of its superiority, continued unhurriedly on its course. Only occasionally did it take a positive stand. It would roll on to its back to meet the threat from above with outstretched talons, capable of bringing the battle to an end with one ripping blow. Then it was the turn of the crows to take hurried evasive action. Courageous they were, but they knew the limited extent of their harassment.

Josh liked to see the buzzards. They enjoyed complete freedom of the great moor. A freedom he would dearly love to possess. But, except for the long summer evenings and occasions like this, there was little time for exploring. In the morning he worked at the mine, dressing the ore at the surface with the women and other children. In the afternoon he attended the school at St Cleer. Most evenings he would help with the household chores before settling down to more schoolwork, often working by the light of a tallow candle until bedtime.

The evening schooling had become more difficult since Jenny and the baby had come to live with them. He found the noise from the kitchen distracting wherever he was in the house. Usually he worked in the bedroom he now shared with his parents, but baby Gwen was put down to sleep in the next room. She had begun to cut her first teeth and cried a lot.

Josh could see the small group of cottages well down on the slope from the moor. Another ten minutes and he would be home. But first he had to pass the Tragos' home – and Morwen Trago was sitting astride a long rounded boulder outside the entrance.

The Tragos were a strange brooding family and their house very much in keeping with their image. It was comprised of a number of gigantic slabs of rock. Those for the front and side walls were laid upon their edge with three more balancing on them to form the roof. The rear of the roof, together with the back wall, was buried in the hillside. The doorway was a crevice between the rocks with an odd-shaped wooden frame surrounding a door seven feet high and designed to fit the space. Here lived Moses Trago and his wife and children, together with his unmarried brother John.

The 'house' had not been built by the Tragos. Some of the older inhabitants of Henwood could remember when Moses Trago's father had moved into it. Superstition had it that it had once been a burial-place for the 'old men' whose shallow diggings scarred the moor.

Morwen Trago was the eldest son of Moses. He was almost two years older than Josh. Sliding from the rock, he took up a position straddle-legged across the path in front of him.

Josh approached him warily, stopping when he was still ten feet away.

'What do you want, Morwen?'

'What do I want?' The bigger boy feigned surprise. 'I live here, Josh Retallick. There's nothing that says I can't stand outside my own home if I want to.'

'Then you'll let me past?' Josh's face felt taut.

'Of course I will – once I've seen what you have in that bag.'

Josh's grip on his canvas schoolbag tightened. 'It's only school-books. They belong to Preacher Thackeray.'

'Do they, now? A preacher's books! Preachers ought to look after their own books. Not use them to stop other folks from working. Religious nonsense, that's what books are.'

Morwen was echoing his father's words. They had been accompanied by a stinging cuff on his ear when Morwen had asked him whether he could take reading lessons with Preacher Thackeray. That had been when Morwen was working on the surface with Josh and some of the other boys. Since then Moses had found work underground for his son. Morwen was on the morning shift at the Wheal Phoenix where Moses and John now worked.

'Books are only nonsense if you can't read them,' Josh retorted. 'And they are staying in my bag.'

'We'll see about that . . .'

Morwen began to advance towards Josh along the path. He stopped when Josh stooped and picked up a broken piece of granite weighing about two pounds.

Morwen Trago looked at Josh standing with the piece of stone in his hand and weighed up his chances of tackling him. Just when it seemed he might ignore the odds, a barefoot girl with tangled long black hair and wearing a tattered dress ran between them.

'Stop it, you two! Josh, put down that stone.'

'No. Not until I'm past Morwen.'

She turned to the other boy. 'Let him go, Morwen. You're older than he is. Ma wouldn't like it if I told her you were bullying.'

Miriam Trago was the same age as Josh, but her shrill young voice carried the air of authority that came with being her father's favourite.

'He won't stop me,' said Josh defiantly. 'If he tries, I'll hit him with this.' He raised the hand holding the stone.

Morwen Trago looked from his sister to Josh. With a scornful shrug of his shoulders, he said, 'Keep your books. Only cissies and preachers read books.' He turned away and strolled towards the rock house.

Josh dropped the stone to the ground and mumbled, 'Thank you, Miriam – though he wouldn't have stopped me.'

'I don't care about that. I didn't want to see Morwen's head split open. That's all.'

With a look almost as scornful as her brother's she too turned away and walked towards her home.

'That's not true, Miriam Trago.' Josh called after her. 'You stopped us from fighting because you thought I might get hurt. You can't help being a Trago. You just don't want people to think you're nice, that's all.'

Miriam swung round to face him and glared for perhaps five seconds. Then she bent down, took hold of the bottom of her ragged dress and raised her hands above her head.

She was wearing nothing beneath it.

Josh's face went scarlet. He turned and fled down the path with Miriam's derisive laughter chasing him most of the way. Miriam Trago was as wild and untamed as the moor itself.

Chapter Three

The wet cold days soon gave way to warmer ones as the spring advanced into summer. The seasons of the year made little difference to the miners. Below the ground it was hot and wet the whole year round. But it did mean that when they climbed to the top of the ladders at the end of a shift they sucked in warm air. Consequently fewer of them contracted pneumonia.

For Josh, the longer days meant he was able to spend more time on the moor. Far more than he had in previous years. He rarely came home from the chapel school by the same path and, as the evenings stretched out, so did his walks. He avoided the Trago home as much as possible, but would often see Miriam in the distance. If she were close enough to recognise him, she would wave. He ignored her greetings. Miriam had wandered the moors from her earliest days and knew the whole wild area better than any man, woman or child. She worked a full day shift with her mother on the grading-floor at the Wheal Phoenix, but her evenings were spent out on the moor. There she felt free – free from her home environment, and free from the disapproving looks of the women in the village, who frowned at her bare feet and her lack of meekness and modesty.

Although Josh and Miriam would occasionally see each

other on the moor, the next encounter between the Trago and Retallick families occurred at a more senior level. It was a brief and violent meeting.

The Sunday evening was warm and pleasant. Ben, Jesse and Josh, a few paces ahead of Tom Shovell, Jenny and baby Gwen, took a slow walk homewards from Henwood chapel. Along the way they occasionally paused to chat to other miners and their families who were also making the most of an opportunity to feel the sun on their faces.

At the edge of the village the Reverend Wrightwick Roberts caught up with them. His perspiration was as much the result of a fiery sermon as it was due to the weather.

Ben Retallick said as much.

'It could be, Ben. It could be!' The preacher mopped his face energetically. 'But it's the Lord's work. I can't put less into it than you put into digging out copper ore for Theophilus Strike.'

Ben smiled. 'From the look of the collection we are digging copper for the Lord too, Wrightwick. There was no silver there.'

'It's a poor community, Ben.' The preacher carefully folded his damp and lifeless handkerchief before tucking it away into a jacket pocket. 'There is precious little money left over when a family has been fed these days.'

'I'll agree with that.' Jesse was walking with Josh. 'Unless something is done soon a month's pay won't buy a bag of flour.'

The two men nodded their agreement. 'It's a bad law that prevents corn from entering the country then sends half our own corn elsewhere,' said Ben bitterly. 'Unless Parliament does something we'll see the troubles of twenty years ago with us again.'

'We don't need any troops in Cornwall,' said the preacher.

Josh, his imagination fired at the thought of seeing mounted and uniformed troops riding into the village, moved closer to hear their talk.

'Parliament's never been slow to send in troops against the Cornish, Ben. You must know that.'

'But we've got a young queen on the throne now. She won't want to start her reign by spilling the blood of her own people.'

'She's only a girl,' replied the preacher. 'She will do what her advisers tell her. But we'll need the Lord's help if ever troops are sent in. We've got a hundred thousand miners, and hotheads aplenty to rouse them. There are even some of the Lord's servants who use His house for such unholy work.'

He looked accusingly at Ben. 'By sending Josh to learn from Thackeray you give him support, Ben. Don't you worry that Josh might get mixed up in the politics of his teacher?'

Ben shrugged. 'Let Thackeray preach what he wishes to men. He teaches schooling to children. It's thanks to him that Josh is able to read the Bible to us on a Sunday evening.'

Wrightwick Roberts chose to make no reply.

They reached a steep part of the track and, taking baby Gwen from Jenny, Tom Shovell tucked the infant into the crook of one arm. He made light work of the gradient, despite the extra pounds that Gwen had put on in recent weeks. In sharp contrast, Jenny had wasted away since Budge's tragic death. She was thin to the point of frailness, and her skin had developed a translucent paleness that attracted attention wherever she went. She had been a pretty girl before. Grief had changed her into a woman possessed of an unusual haunting beauty.

When they arrived at the cottage, Ben, Jesse and Jenny went inside with the baby. Josh stayed outside with the preacher, who was talking to Tom Shovell.

They had not been there for many minutes when a bellow from the direction of the higher moor brought their conversation to an abrupt halt. They turned to see Kate Trago, the wife of Moses Trago, running wildly towards them. Her long hair streamed behind her and the left half of her dress was ripped to the waist, exposing a distended and emaciated breast flapping pendulously as she ran.

Fifty yards behind her Moses Trago lurched around a turn in the path, running unsteadily with a wide-legged gait.

Kate Trago stumbled and fell in front of the startled group.

As Wrightwick Roberts went to help her she heaved herself up from the ground. They saw that one eye was swollen with an ugly graze beneath it.

Taking the preacher's arm, she pulled him towards the house. She signalled the others to come with quick movements of her free hand.

'Hurry! Get into the house,' she pleaded. 'Moses is mad drunk. Get inside or he'll kill me – and you!'

The preacher freed his arm. 'Take her into the cottage and you go with them, Josh.'

'Let me try to reason with him,' said Tom Shovell. 'I know him, Wrightwick. He'll listen to me.'

'He won't listen to anyone in his state. Get everyone inside. Quickly!'

The door banged at his back as the preacher turned to face the drunken miner.

Moses slipped on the same patch of mud as his wife, but steadied himself palm downwards on the path.

'Get out of my way. I want my wife.' Moses Trago's eyes were as unsteady as his voice.

'Go home and sleep it off, Moses.' The preacher's voice was pitched low and coaxing.

'I said I want my wife!'

'Leave her be. She's inside talking to Jesse Retallick.'

'I don't care who she's talking to. She's a lazy idle slut. No, she's worse than that. She's a thief. A thief!'

Moses lurched forward. He stopped so close that Wrightwick Roberts winced at the gin fumes the drunken miner belched into his face as he spoke.

'You know what she did? Do you want to know what that bloody woman did?'

Wrightwick Roberts avoided the thick dirty finger waving only inches from his nose.

'I'll tell you what she did.' He screwed his mouth up and blinked stupidly. 'I'll tell you what she did. She took money from my pocket. That's what she did. Took it when she thought I was asleep. What do you think of that, Preacher Wrightwick-bloody-Roberts?'

'I expect she had need of it.' The preacher's voice was calm and even, though Moses had thrust his face to within inches of his own. The sickly smell of the cheap alcohol made the teetotal Methodist preacher feel like retching.

'You expect she had need of it?' The miner's unshaven upper lip curled back in a sneer. 'I'll tell you what she has need of. I don't have to go to chapel to learn how to run my life. I'll do it my way. So will she!'

He lunged towards the door, but Wrightwick Roberts was too quick for him. He stooped under the other man's arm and, as Moses fumbled for the latch, put his shoulder beneath his armpit and heaved. Moses Trago took eight or nine uncontrolled backward paces on his heels before crashing to the ground.

Rolling over quickly he looked up at the preacher, sheer rage sobering him momentarily. 'I'll kill you for that!'

He came up from the ground with unexpected speed. Quick as he was, someone else was faster. The door behind the preacher was jerked open, and he was thrust aside as Ben Retallick took the headlong rush of Moses Trago with outstretched arms, closing them around the drunken miner as the two men came together. Finding his arms pinned to his sides, Moses Trago opened his mouth to roar. Ben Retallick's muscles strained and he cut off the sound.

Moses Trago was no stranger to fighting and he was not to be overwhelmed so easily. In an effort to break the other man's grip he staggered around until he tripped on a stone. Both men fell heavily to the ground.

Ben Retallick fell awkwardly, and his grip slackened for an instant. It was enough. Flinging his wide shoulders back, Moses Trago broke the encircling grip and scrambled to his feet.

Ben was still on his knees when Moses Trago's boot took him on the shoulder and knocked him rolling down again. The kick had been aimed at his head, but drink and exertion had taken their toll on the burly miner's faculties. It was fortunate for Ben. Had the viciously swung boot connected with its target he would not have risen again. Moses Trago moved quickly around him as he tried to rise, kicking him in the ribs, in the kidneys, aiming for his head. It was one of Moses Trago's wilder kicks that proved his undoing. It missed completely. Ben was quick enough to grasp the foot and with a twist and a heave he sent Moses Trago crashing to the ground once more.

Ben Retallick was on his feet in an instant. As his opponent began to rise he crashed a rock-hard fist against his temple. The miner fell face first on to the earth. It must have been a purely reflex stupidity which brought him half on to his feet again. This time Ben's punch swung up into Moses Trago's face. The force of it straightened him up before he dropped backwards to lie prostrate with arms flung wide.

'Now there's as fine a punch as ever I have seen,' said Wrightwick Roberts in admiration. 'It would have felled a bullock.'

'It needed to,' replied Ben, rubbing his knuckles. 'Moses Trago is a powerful man. But a man always fights harder on his own ground.'

He kneeled down beside the unconscious man. 'Bring some water, Wrightwick. It worries me to see him lying here like this.' He put an ear against Moses Trago's chest and looked relieved. 'His heart is going like a stamp-hammer. There's little enough wrong with him.'

Jesse came out of the house with a bucket of water and unceremoniously flung the contents over Moses Trago's face.

'There's no need for you to stand around here as though Ben had done something wonderful, Wrightwick Roberts,' she said. 'So you can take that unholy grin from your face. I don't approve of a man fighting in front of his family. On a Sunday too.'

Wrightwick Roberts' jaw dropped. 'He did it to protect his family,' he protested. 'If Moses had got into the house he would have smashed it up; he was fighting drunk. You should be thankful that the Lord was on Ben's side!'

'Ben has never needed anyone on his side when it came to fighting,' Jesse said, her jaw thrust out. 'You should remember that, Wrightwick. You knew him before we were married.'

This was all new to Josh. He looked at his father with new admiration.

'Anyway, a man protecting his family is one thing. There's no need for him to look as though he enjoyed it.'

Her words were harder than the look she gave her husband before she went back inside the house.

It took three more bucketfuls of water to make Moses Trago stir. It was like watching a young child wakening from a deep sleep. He twitched, shuddered, rolled his head from side to side and then slowly sat up. The last movement was almost too much for his abused body. It sent a protest via every nerve to the brain. Moses Trago clutched his head between his hands and let out a loud groan.

'You may think you are suffering now, Moses. One day you'll have to answer to the Lord for your misdeeds. This drubbing will be as a gentle tap on the hand compared with what will happen to you on that day.'

Moses Trago's reply was an expressive oath accompanied by another groan.

'If I hear any more of that sort of language from you, I'll forget I am a preacher and do the Lord's work for him . . .'

Moses Trago got unsteadily to his feet. He stood swaying and glaring at Wrightwick Roberts, Ben Retallick and Tom Shovell.

'I won't be forgetting this day in a hurry,' he said. 'You'll live to regret it, Ben Retallick. So will you, Preacher.' He raised his voice to be sure it carried into the house. 'You can tell that woman of mine if she dares show her face inside my home I'll break every bone in her body.'

He turned and staggered away along the path towards the high moor. Only Josh saw a small tangle-haired figure in a torn dress slip from the bushes on the far side of the house and vanish into the ferns on the hillside.

'You'd best be careful of him, Ben,' said the shift captain. 'Moses is a dangerous man. He cares little for the standards other men set for themselves.'

'Tom is right. You keep clear of him or he'll do you a mischief.'

Kate Trago had come from the house peering painfully through her one good eye. The swelling about the other had caused it to close completely.

'I'll not upset Moses. Neither will I go out of my way to avoid him,' declared Ben. 'He'll be all right when he sobers up. We were boys together, Kate. I know Moses Trago as well as any man.'

'No!' Kate Trago shook her head. 'Moses is not the man you once knew, Ben Retallick. He's changed. In the last few years he's changed. Oh, I know he's always been a rough man with his fighting and drinking; but there's more to it now. He's turned sour inside. He believes he's owed something. He'll never get it because he doesn't even know what it is! It's money and yet more than money. He envies you more than anyone else, Ben. You've got all the things that Moses hasn't. Respect. A house. You're part of something that we don't belong to. I know it must sound stupid but he really hates you for being something that he's scorned to be all his life.'

She stopped talking abruptly and there was an uncomfortable silence.

'I've said far too much. Take heed of it and I'll have thanked you for helping me. I must go now.'

'You can't go yet!' Ben Retallick protested. 'Moses is still raving drunk. He'll kill you if you go near him.'

'He won't.' She shook her head. 'He'll go home, stumble on to his bed just as he is and sleep until morn. Then he'll get up and go to the mine. That's all there is in his life. Drink, sleep and work. But he won't hurt me anymore.' There was a gleam of a tear in her eye. 'Besides, I'm his wife. I've got to go back to him.'

She started off up the path, pausing to call back, 'Thank you again for your help. Thank you.'

She went on her way without looking back. In spite of her cheap and well-patched clothes there was something about her walk that was too proud for one in her station of life. Only Jesse Retallick might guess at her innermost thoughts and she could have wept for her.

* * *

Three days after the fight Miriam Trago waylaid Josh on his way home from the St Cleer chapel school. She must have been watching for him from the top of the tor to have known which way he would come. She stepped out from the tall fern into his path when he was on the high flat moor, hidden from the cottages on the other side of the tor.

'Hello.' It was a casual greeting. As though the meeting were completely accidental.

'Hello.' Josh's reply was more cautious. His small feud with Morwen Trago had exploded into something far more serious and violent now their fathers were involved, and he knew Miriam had seen the fight.

But Miriam had not sought him out to extend the feud.

'Have you been to the chapel school?' It was an unnecessary question. They both knew it.

'Yes.'

'What do you learn there?'

'Oh, lots of things. Reading. Writing. Sums.'

'Do you like it?'

He nodded his head. 'Yes, I do.'

'I wish I could learn to read and write. I'd like to know how to write my name.'

'Why don't you ask your dad to let you go?'

She shook her head. 'I did ask him. He says there's no need of such fancy ways for girls. They should get out and make money before they get married. Not waste time on such things. That's what he said.'

The mention of Moses Trago brought about a long uncomfortable silence.

'He's not all bad, you know.'

'Who?' Josh was anxious to avert a clash with this naturally wild girl who was behaving in an uncharacteristically polite and quiet manner.

'My dad. He's not all bad.'

As she spoke she looked down at her dirty toes. Her bare feet had long been a subject of disapproval among the villagers of Henwood. They boasted that, no matter how poor they might be, there was not a child in the village who did not have boots for its feet. Had they voiced their disapproval to Miriam she would have been genuinely astounded. She enjoyed feeling the springy turf of the moor beneath her feet.

'He drinks – but so do lots of miners. And he doesn't hit me very often. When he does he's always sorry afterwards.'

Josh said nothing.

'He works hard. Even your dad says he's a good worker.'

'So he might be. But he gets very quarrelsome when he's been drinking.'

Her head came up and her dark eyes clashed with his. He thought he ought to have maintained his silence. Then the challenge subsided.

'That's his way. He doesn't mean anything by it.' She touched the corner of one of the books that protruded from his canvas shoulder-bag. 'What's this?'

'It's a writing book.'

'Writing? Show me. I want to see what your writing looks like.'

Josh hesitated. Despite Miriam's excitement and apparent interest he was wary of her. She could be trying to trick him into something.

'Please!'

'All right.' He extracted the book from the flat canvas bag with exaggerated carefulness. Flicking through the pages, he opened it to disclose a handwriting that was small and not too neat.

The untidiness meant nothing to Miriam; she was very impressed. 'There's such a lot of it. Did you write it all?'

He nodded, absurdly pleased at her praise. 'There's lots more. Almost a whole book full.'

She extended a long brown finger and gently touched the written words with the tip of it.

'What does it say?'

He turned the book up the other way and began to read: '"He said unto him, the third time, Simon, son of Joseph, lovest thou me? He saith unto him, Yea Lord . . ."' Josh read two pages before closing the book.

'That was from the Bible,' he said, embarrassed by the adulation on her face.

'It was beautiful!' Her expression was full of wonder. For the first time he noticed that she had very dark eyes, fringed by the longest eyelashes he had ever seen.

'I wish I could read and write.' There was no doubting her sincerity now.

'It wouldn't take you long if you took lessons.'

'Could you write my name – Miriam?'

Josh nodded. 'Yes.'

'Then write it for me. Please, Josh! Write it for me.'

'All right.'

He rummaged in his bag and came out with a scrap of paper. 'I need something to rest this on.'

'I know just the thing; it's a flat rock.' She took his hand and, full of excitement, pulled him after her as she left the path and plunged into the ferns and bushes.

'It's a secret place. Nobody but me knows of it.' Miriam took him uphill, through patches of undergrowth where tall ferns touched Josh's face and brushed coarse fingers through his hair while tangled brambles threatened to trip him.

When they reached an apparently impenetrable barrier of gorse, she released his hand and dropping to her knees signalled for him to do the same.

'Follow me.'

She disappeared into a low gorse-tunnel. As he followed her a carpet of blunt gorse-needles attacked his knees and the palms of his hands.

The dark tunnel twisted and turned for twenty feet before he was out into sparkling sunlight once more. Thick gorse was all around, but here in its centre was a large flat rock. Two others leaning against one another formed a small triangular cave. When he stood up he could see the whole of the Phoenix valley through the thin top branches of one of the gorse-bushes, but it would have been impossible for anyone to see the two children from below.

'Here, rest the book on this rock.'

She sat cross-legged on the granite, her skirt tucked between her legs, the thin thighs and calloused knees as brown as a gipsy's.

Josh unslung his bag and taking out a book placed it on the rock. Then he smoothed out a piece of paper and laid it upon the book. Taking out a thick-leaded pencil, he knelt down beside the rock. Carefully and elaborately he wrote the letters, calling them aloud as he went.

'M-I-R-I-A-M. Miriam. There you are!'

She had been watching him, hardly daring to breathe. Now she took the paper from him as though it was a magic formula for all the riches of the world.

'This really is my name? It says "Miriam"?'

'Yes.' Her reaction was most satisfactory.

'Can I keep it?'

'Of course you can. It's of no use to me.'

'This is the first time I've ever seen my name written down. I'll keep it for ever and always.'

He thought it was a small enough thing to give her so much pleasure.

'I'll teach you to write it for yourself if you like.'

Her reaction alarmed him. For a second it looked as though she might throw her arms about him. Instead, she dropped down on to the rock beside him and gripped his arm.

'Oh please!'

He first had to show her how to hold the pencil; then how to form the letters, with his hand clenched over hers. Her hair was very close to his face and it smelled like the fern.

It took a long time and the final result was far from satisfactory. Although Josh insisted that it was fine, Miriam knew better.

'No,' she said, clutching the piece of paper with Josh's effort on it. 'This is much better. But I'll do it properly one day, if you'll learn me.'

'I don't know,' said Josh uncertainly, not wishing to sacrifice all the long lone summer evenings on the moor he had planned.

'You can use this place for your own,' she persisted. 'And, if you'll try to learn me, I'll show you a badger's set.'

Josh wavered. Sensing the weak spot in his determination, Miriam prised it wide open. 'The badgers have babies.'

Josh's resolution crumbled and blew to the wind.

'All right. I'll teach you reading and writing. But I want to see the badgers first.'

'Come on, then.' Miriam was elated. For months she had watched Josh returning from St Cleer. Her whole being ached with wanting to learn the things he was learning. Her father would not allow her to attend the chapel school, so she had decided her only chance to achieve an education lay with Josh. She had been prepared to offer him anything in return for lessons. He had settled for a sight of the badgers. After the big build-up to this moment in her own mind it had come as an anti-climax. But she was still very happy.

Josh followed her through the gorse-tunnel once more and they headed across the moor, away from the Phoenix valley. Miriam took him on a direct course, deviating only once in order to avoid a patch of bog. He would not even have seen it but for her warning.

'If you got in there, you'd never get out,' she said. 'I saw a sheep caught there last winter. It was too far in for me to help it. In five minutes it sank out of sight. It was horrible!'

Josh shuddered. He took careful note of the position of the bog for his future ramblings. A little further on they dropped into a deep gully, about forty feet wide with a weed-covered stagnant pool at the far end of it. This, Miriam said, had once been a gold mine. Worked by the 'old men'.

'We must go quietly now.' She laid a hand on his arm and Josh edged forward, holding his breath, expecting to be confronted by a badger at any moment. He was apprehensive of the outcome as he had never seen a badger. His scant knowledge of them came from the tales of other boys who most probably had never seen the animal for themselves. In their tales the badger was as strong as a ram, as bold as a fox, and armed with claws the length of a boy's fingers.

'Here, sit down by me and don't say a word,' Miriam whispered as she pulled him down beside her on to a rough grassy bank with the level of the moor overhanging twelve feet above them.

Josh did as he was told and furtively looked about him. He could see nothing.

'Where are they?' It came out as a hoarse whisper.

'Shh! Their set is over there.' She pointed to a spot twelve feet away, where a sprawling thorn-bush grew from a substantial mound of earth. 'See the paths?'

Now she had drawn his attention to them, Josh was able to see three – no, four – well-worn tracks leading into the bush from four different directions. They were so well defined they could have been made by the feet of men.

'But where are the badgers?' His whisper was as low as hers had been.

'They'll be out soon. Usually they don't come out until after dark but lately they have been bringing their babies up for a while at this time of day.'

They sat in silence for a long time, but it was difficult to become too impatient. The evening was warm and peaceful, the drone of a bumble bee and the far high song of a skylark the only sounds that could be heard from the gully. Josh even found it pleasant being seated arm to arm with Miriam. There was a nice smell to her. It was not only her hair. The whole of her carried the scent of fern and heather. It was as though, while still retaining her human status, she had become a part of the moor on which she spent so much of her time.

He gave her a sidelong glance. Perfectly relaxed, she sat with her eyes half-closed, the long dark lashes almost meeting. Her thick black hair fell around her shoulders, as wild and unruly as a blackberry thicket.

Her eyes opened suddenly and she clutched at him. 'There! Did you hear that?'

'No. What am I listening for?'

'That thumping noise below us. In the ground. It's the badgers; they always do that. There, now!'

He heard it this time. It was like the warning thump of a rabbit far below them, deep in the earth.

'That means they'll be coming out now.'

Josh stared at the bush intently, not daring to blink until the whole bush swam before his glazed eyes. Then Miriam's grip on his arm tightened painfully and his eyes focused again. From the hole in the bush a long head, clearly marked with wide black and white stripes, came into view. The badger raised its nose and sniffed first to the west, then to the north and finally to the south. Satisfied so far, the animal advanced a foot from the bush, bringing its long-haired grey-brown body into view. The badger peered around cautiously but not timidly. It was larger than Josh had imagined. As large as a medium-sized dog. Suddenly, as quickly as it had appeared, the badger turned and was gone.

'It saw us!' exclaimed Josh, bitterly disappointed.

'Shh!' Miriam's fingernails dug into his arm again. 'It didn't see you. I don't think badgers can see anything very well. It always does this to make sure it's quite safe for the babies. They'll all come out now.'

She had hardly finished speaking when the badgers did exactly as she had said. There was no hesitation this time. The male badger lumbered straight out from the bush closely followed by two cubs. The female, rather more cautious, brought up the rear.

Josh held his breath until he thought he would burst. The badgers moved along their chosen path for about twenty feet before the male paused for a prolonged scratch. The two cubs took this opportunity to explore a nearby forest of ferns. It was Josh's efforts to follow their progress that brought the badger-watching to an abrupt end. He felt the stone turn beneath his hand as he leaned sideways. He grabbed at it but was not quick enough to save it. The stone bounced down the small embankment. With a startled squeak the female badger sent the cubs in headlong flight back to the set. She was close behind them. The male quartered the ground after them, emitting grunts and squeaks. He paused when level with Josh and raised a reproachful nose in his direction. Then he too was gone.

'I'm sorry,' said Josh sheepishly.

Miriam jumped down to the floor of the gully. 'It doesn't

matter. I've seen them lots of times before.' She looked at him suspiciously. 'But I showed them to you like I promised. You'll still learn me to read and write?'

Josh nodded. 'Yes. You meet me on my way home from the chapel and I'll give you a lesson. Not every day, though.'

'How many days, then – four?'

Josh shook his head. 'No. Two perhaps.'

They finally settled for three days a week and Josh shrugged the strap of his bag more firmly on to his shoulder. 'Are you coming?'

Miriam shook her head. 'Not yet. There's a full moon tonight and I want to watch it from up there.' She pointed to where the great rock mass that was Sharp Tor rose stark and grey above the moor. 'Why don't you stop and see it with me?'

'No, I must get back for supper. Mum will be wondering where I am.'

'Mummy's boy!' Her voice mocked him as he scrambled from the gully and set off home across the moor.

'Josh! Josh Retallick!'

He turned to see her standing wide-legged on an uneven rock above the gully.

'If you come up Sharp Tor with me I'll let you kiss me.'

'I don't want to.' He turned his back on her and walked away.

'You will one day, Josh Retallick. You will one day!'

Josh need not have been in a hurry to get home. Nobody had noticed how late he was. Besides, the family knew he was in the habit of deviating from the direct route. But this evening they hardly acknowledged his arrival. The house was full of people. Among them were most of the miners from Ben Retallick's shift, including Tom Shovell. Also there, and looking uncomfortably out of place inside a house, was Nehemeziah Lancellis, the mine hostler who had no home of his own and shared the stables of the horses he tended. Small of stature, he had ridden horses for gentry in his younger days. Until a fall left him with an ill-mended broken leg.

Wrightwick Roberts was also in the room. It was his booming voice that met Josh's ears when he went in.

'I am not happy about this trip into Bodmin. To go to see a public hanging is shameful enough. With it taking place on a fair-day there will be all manner of sinful things to entice our young men.'

'But it's a holiday,' argued one of the men. 'And it's a double hanging of miners. Men from the Kit Mill mine. Some of us know them, have worked with them.'

'There's nothing to be proud of in knowing convicted murderers,' retorted Wrightwick Roberts. 'There are more than enough Christians you *don't* know!'

'It's too late to stop it now,' said Ben Retallick quietly. 'Theophilus Strike has agreed to loan us the horses and ore-carts for the day. Even though Captain Schmidt was against it.'

Nehemeziah Lancellis nodded vigorously.

'Best accept it, Wrightwick,' went on Ben. 'See it as a chance to say a prayer for the souls of the two men who are to be hanged.'

'I can do that in any one of my chapels,' snorted the preacher. 'If every man here came to chapel instead of Bodmin, we'd pray the both of them straight into heaven.'

'They'll make it, even without our prayers,' said Jesse Retallick from the kitchen doorway. 'From what I hear, others were more to blame than them for the killing. A militiaman, wasn't it?'

There was a growl of assent from many of the miners.

'There can be little excuse for killing a man, Jesse,' said Wrightwick Roberts. 'A man's life is sacred.'

'And so is a man's family!' Jesse Retallick retorted, her face flushed with emotion and hands planted firmly on her hips. 'Did the adventurers worry about that? Didn't they lock the men out? Stopped them from working, then wouldn't give them the money they were due? It's not surprising the miners got angry. But even then the adventurers wouldn't stand up to them like men. They called in the militia to do their dirty work for them.'

'These are things you don't understand, Jesse,' said Wrightwick Roberts, and Ben Retallick looked up at the ceiling, waiting for the explosion he knew the preacher's words would provoke. 'The men wanted a charter. They spoke of uniting all the miners in the district. It's dangerous talk, Jesse. Such things are bound to lead to trouble.'

'I may not understand about charters and uniting the miners, Wrightwick Roberts. I do know how a man would feel if he saw his family starving, knowing the adventurers' store was full of food and them owing him money. I wouldn't give a snuffed candle-flame for the chances of any man who tried to stop him. There isn't a miner here who wouldn't do the same. That includes my Ben.'

The murmur of agreement grew louder, and Jesse raised her voice to say, 'You be there to lead the prayers for their souls, Wrightwick Roberts, or I'll shame you by doing it for you.'

Red-faced, with eyes flashing angrily, Jesse Retallick turned her back on the crowded room. Josh slipped into the kitchen before she slammed the door shut.

'I could have told you it wasn't wise to tell Jesse she "didn't understand". Not when she feels so strong about something,' chuckled Ben Retallick. The preacher ran a handkerchief around the inside of his collar, and conversation in the room got under way again.

'Better an honest direct woman than one who hides her thoughts and practises slyness,' said the preacher. 'It says so in the good book.'

He put his handkerchief away and held up a big hand for silence. 'All right, men. Now we've decided to go to Bodmin . . .' – he paused until the spontaneous laughter died away – '. . . we'll get down to details. Nehemeziah, how many wagons will we have? You've done the trip by wagon before, haven't you? How long will it take?'

Nehemeziah was not used to being at the centre of a discussion, far less being called upon to speak, but he did his best.

'Ah! Well, now. There's Bessie and Flower can take the oldest ore wagon. Tinker and Satan – begging your pardon, Preacher.

That's the name of the horse. He's called that 'cos of an evil temper. I didn't name him, o'course. Called that when I bought him from Liskeard market, he was.'

Satisfied that he had made his point, Nehemeziah Lancellis continued with the list of horses and the wagons they would pull. It was an impressive tally. The Wheal Sharptor had more than forty prime horses and half that number of wagons, ranging from the great ore wagons usually pulled by a team of six to the small governess-cart in which Herman Schmidt was riding to the execution.

The talking dragged on until late in the evening. Josh had his supper in the kitchen with Jenny and his mother, who was still smouldering after her outburst.

'Do you really think a union is a good thing, Mum?' asked Josh between mouthfuls.

'If it will force the adventurers to treat a miner as a man – then, yes, it's a good thing.'

'That's what Preacher Thackeray says. He told us that man is made in God's image and so we are all equal.'

'Equal? One man kills himself in a hole in the ground to make money while another man sits in a big house thinking up ways to spend it. That's being equal?'

There was a sudden outburst of noise from the next room and Jesse Retallick said, 'Listen to them! You'd think we were going off for a month instead of a day. It's always the same with men. All they've got to do is hitch up the horses and take us to Bodmin, then bring us back in the evening. They'll spend hours talking and arguing about it when they already know what has to be done.'

'Have you been to Bodmin before?' asked Jenny.

'Oh yes!' replied Jesse Retallick. 'This will be the fourth time.'

'What is it like?'

'Well . . . it's hard to describe. Lots of houses. Streets full of carts and carriages. Drunkenness. More people than we'd see hereabouts in a lifetime. Then there's the prison. A huge, ugly, grey place – enough to give you the shivers to look at it. I always think of the poor wretches kept inside for years.

It must be awful for them. But why don't you come and see for yourself?'

Jenny shook her head. 'I don't want to go to see two poor men die. No, me and Gwen will stay here and enjoy the sunshine. It will be nice and quiet with everyone else away. There'll hardly be one person left in Henwood village.'

'No, all those who can walk will be in Bodmin. Even Mary Crabbe – tho' I would have thought she'd seen enough dead men.'

'How about the Tragos?' Jenny asked.

'Miriam and Morwen are going,' replied Josh without thinking. 'But Moses Trago has some business to attend to.' He was repeating what Miriam had told him during one of her lessons on the moor.

'His business will be with the innkeeper,' retorted his mother. 'But how is it you know so much about the doings of the Trago family?'

'I expect it's that Miriam,' teased Jenny as she saw the colour creep up into his face. 'A pretty little maid for all that she's a bit wild.'

'You keep away from that family,' warned Jesse Retallick. 'They'll bring nothing but trouble. Every one of them.'

Another upsurge of sound from the next room indicated that the meeting was breaking up. Taking advantage of the distraction, Josh murmured his 'Good night' and made his way upstairs to bed.

Chapter Four

The day of the execution dawned bright and clear. The sun rose on the wagons loaded with miners and their families, being pulled by the toiling horses up the steep track from the Sharptor mine. There was an air of subdued excitement among the passengers. It was rare indeed for them to get together in this way for a social outing. The chapel-goers were used to praying together, the drinkers often found themselves in each other's company in one or other of the inns in nearby villages, but no one could remember them all going out on such a jaunt as this.

Even today there was a dividing-line between them. The chapel folk had possession of the front half of the convoy, and the standard deteriorated towards the rear, the last two wagons being filled with the younger miners, among whom bottles of gin were already being passed. Such behaviour did not pass unnoticed. The bonneted women in the leading wagons tuttutted disapprovingly, and old Nehemeziah Lancellis cursed the fact that he was in charge of the very first wagon. He would make certain he brought up the rear on the way home.

Most of the older children were riding in two wagons. Josh found himself sitting close to Miriam and her brother Morwen. But this was a different Miriam to the one he met on the moor.

True, she wore no shoes on her feet, but her hair had been brushed back tidily and the dress she had on was made from new calico. But it was her manner that Josh found so strange. He had said, 'Hello,' to her when he climbed aboard the wagon and she had scarcely answered. Morwen scowled deeply and succeeded in looking very like his father.

Miriam stayed quiet when the other children were talking and singing. They swayed together in gleeful exaggeration whenever the driver got a trot from his heavy horses on the rutted and pot-holed track.

Halfway to the Assize town the wagons passed a tin mine which was still operating, although it was a county holiday. There was much catcalling and ribaldry from the rear wagons, especially when they saw the women and girls at the shaft-head sorting the tin ore.

'You'll never find out what you're seeking there, m'dear,' shouted one wag. 'Come over here and I'll let you share what copper-mining's given to me.'

'I'll show 'ee what tin'll do for thee,' shouted the girl and, as the young miners whooped with laughter, she picked up a piece of rock the size of her fist and threw it hard and high. Her aim was good. As it plummeted down into the crowded wagon there was a great commotion. Some of the young men were pushed over the side by the efforts of those within to escape the missile.

The women laughed and cackled. The laughter changed to shrieks of simulated terror when a Sharptor lad shouted, 'Come on. We'll show these tinner-girls what a real man is.' The young men leaped from the wagons and began chasing the fleeing girls and women.

It was unfortunate that half the underground shift of tinminers were still in the boiler-house, changing their clothes before going below. As the Sharptor lads passed the engine-house the tinners spilled out amongst them. In the free-for-all that followed most of the young men from the other wagons jumped down to assist the hard-pressed Sharptor miners.

Morwen Trago was among them. When Josh tried to follow he was deliberately tripped – he suspected it was by Miriam

– then sat upon, his arms and legs pinned to the floor of the wagon.

'Let me up! Get off! I'm suffocating!'

'Shut up!'

One of the village girls, a buxom seventeen-year-old, raised the edge of her skirt to look at his face. 'Better dust in your nose than a lump of tin in your teeth.'

Jesse Retallick called from the next wagon, and to Josh's eternal shame the well-proportioned girl shouted. 'It's all right, Mrs Retallick! I'm sitting on him. He'll learn more down there than some of they fools over there.'

Josh fumed impotently at the shrieks of laughter that went up from the women.

After a few seconds the edge of the skirt was lifted again. This time it was Miriam's face peering anxiously into his own. 'Are you all right really, Josh?'

'No!' he hissed between clenched teeth. 'She's caving – my – ribs – in.'

'Oh! So you're saying I'm overweight, then?' said the fat girl. She bounced up and down on him, making the breath rasp noisily from his throat. So concerned was Miriam that she pulled the big girl backwards by the shoulders. She fell with her feet waving in the air and her skirts tumbled about her wide hips.

The others pinning Josh down were dealt with equally effectively. As Josh struggled up, sucking the breath back into his lungs, Miriam helped him to the front of the wagon. She sat him down with his back against the high board beneath the grinning driver.

The fight was over at the pit-head by now and the copper-miners were jumping back into their wagons. Morwen took his place in the rear wagons with them.

With her brother gone Miriam was her usual self. Once she had made sure that Josh was all right she kept up a steady stream of chatter. The chagrined Josh said little in reply.

Soon the wagons began passing many people afoot, all of them heading for Bodmin town. There were couples and families, old and young, miners and ploughmen, shepherds and pig-farmers, cowmen and hostlers. Others, tinkers and musicians and the traders and pickpockets, were already there.

When someone called that Bodmin could be seen up ahead, Josh was as excited as Miriam. He knelt up beside her, looking between the straddled legs of the driver on his high seat.

Over the broad sweating flanks of the horses they saw the slate roofs and jumbled streets of Bodmin town.

The wagon swayed and jolted down off the dirt track and on to teeth-rattling cobbled streets. The shod hoofs of the blowing horses struck sparks from the stones as the wagoner held them back down the steep approach to the county town.

Now there were sights aplenty to be seen as the slanting rays of the morning sun woke a million window-panes. The streets were at times so narrow that the upstairs of the houses leaned towards each other as though sharing a secret. Here and there the streets opened out into squares where stalls and sideshows, tinkers' carts, and livestock of all descriptions tangled together. To one side of the town stood the gaunt grim walls of Bodmin Jail. But above all there were people. Thousands and thousands of people! They were everywhere. Like disturbed ants. And still they poured into the town.

All this Josh and Miriam saw all too briefly before a town constable, perspiring in tall dark hat and heavy blue uniform, waved the mine wagons off the road. They trundled down a lane that led them away from the town again until they turned into a churned-up field three-parts full of wagons.

The unfamiliar and overwhelming nearness of the town had overawed the mining people. They milled around in their groups talking unnecessarily and laughing loudly and nervously, all waiting for someone to take the initiative.

Once again it was the young men who showed the way. Whooping and shouting, they moved off in a rowdy bunch, eager to sample the delights of the town – delights which the Reverend Wrightwick Roberts feared would prove sinful. He watched them go with a sad heart.

'Now, Josh, what are you going to do? Will you come

with us?' Jesse Retallick broke away from a small party that included Ben, Wrightwick Roberts and Tom Shovell.

'No.' Josh was aware of the disapproving look his mother was giving to the barefooted Miriam, who was pretending to be too interested in the town to notice. 'I'll have a walk about the town and see what's going on.'

'Well, you mind you behave yourself and don't go getting into any mischief.'

Jesse looked at the girl again and sniffed. 'Miriam, have you got any money to spend?'

'Money? No. But I don't need any,' she hurriedly added as a purse appeared in Jesse Retallick's hand.

'Nonsense! Everyone needs money on a fair-day. Here's threepence for you. Josh, have you still got that shilling?'

He held it out towards here, grinning happily.

'Good. Don't lose it. Off you go now, you two. Enjoy yourselves and be back here at six o'clock.'

Miriam transferred her astonished gaze from Mrs Retallick to the copper coins in her hand. 'She gave me money! Your mother gave me some money!'

'Don't sound so surprised. Mum is like that. She may sound a bit gruff at times but she never means anything by it.'

'And I thought she never liked me!'

Miriam's gratitude was beginning to be embarrassing.

'Oh, come on. Let's look around Bodmin. Everyone else has gone.'

Certainly, all the Sharptor and Henwood residents had gone, but more and more wagons were trundling into the field, and the roads from the surrounding countryside were jammed with people.

Josh and Miriam found themselves moving into Bodmin with the human flow. They passed stalls and shops that displayed everything imaginable for sale. From shoes to saddles and sweets to horses. Miriam spent a farthing at the first stall on some sweets which turned out to be even stickier than they had looked. They wandered along in bulged-cheeked silence until they found themselves before a great iron-studded gate, set into the high grey wall of the prison. Here the gallows had been erected on a raised platform and two oiled and pre-stretched ropes hung from the stout cross-beam, their noosed ends swinging gently and ominously in the faintest of breezes.

It was here, where the morning shadow of the gallows fell across the earth, that the crowd was thickest. Not everyone had been drawn to the spot by morbid curiosity. Wrightwick Roberts was not the only preacher with the idea of being on hand to pray for the condemned men's souls. Four or five Methodist ministers from the mining communities and many of their parishioners were also there. They formed a party of about two hundred strong, occupying the area immediately adjacent to the gallows platform. Their presence did not please the officer in charge of the military guard. He paced about on the platform, shouting to keep a clear passage between the prison gate and the gallows.

He eventually called to a sergeant. During the course of an earnest conversation they looked often towards the group of Methodists who were on their knees praying.

Nodding in acknowledgement, the sergeant turned away and walked to where his soldiers lounged against the prison gate. There was still a long time before the execution, but at the sergeant's shouted command the soldiers ceased their lounging. Unslinging their muskets, they moved to take up positions surrounding the platform. Significantly, there were twice as many soldiers on the side nearest the praying Methodists as on any other.

As nothing else seemed to be happening, Josh and Miriam took another walk about Bodmin and returned shortly before noon. The crowd had swelled to fill the whole vast space in front of the prison and overflowed halfway up the slope of the opposite hill.

At five minutes to twelve the huge studded prison gates swung open. Led by a single drummer, two columns of soldiers resplendent in bright red coats and white cross-belts marched slowly from the dusty courtyard within, the sun gleaming on the steel bayonets fixed to the ends of their long muskets.

Shuffling between the lines of soldiers were the two wretched miners, heavily manacled and chained to each other, clothes ragged, eyes fixed on the ground at their feet.

Their appearance was the signal for a murmur of excitement from the crowd. It quickly gave way to a growl of anger from the miners when it could be seen what condition the unfortunate prisoners were in.

The condemned men paused at the steps leading to the platform, aware for the first time of the vast size of the crowd. A soldier prodded them none too gently and one of the two tripped, dragging his companion to the ground at the very edge of the platform.

The crowd's growl became a roar, and the soldiers fingered their guns uneasily. The sergeant helped the prisoners to their feet with more sympathy than they had received at the hands of the soldiers, and the angry noise from the crowd died away. The hangman now stepped forward. Keeping his hooded head turned from the crowd, he moved to the men he was soon to execute.

'Brothers!' The voice of Wrightwick Roberts boomed out so loudly that there could have been few of the vast crowd who did not hear him. 'Brothers! Join me in a prayer for these two sinners who are nearing the judgement of the Lord. Let us appeal for His mercy. Pray that their sins be forgiven, their punishment end here on earth. Down on your knees and pray with me.'

There was a rippling movement through the crowd as all of the women and most of the men dropped to their knees or, as they were wearing Sunday clothes, squatted so as not to be conspicuous above the others.

The two condemned men also fell to their knees, grateful for the extra few minutes of life Wrightwick Roberts had won for them.

Josh was kneeling with the others but he had to reach up and pull a bewildered Miriam down beside him.

'Kneel down!' he hissed at her.

The voice of Wrightwick Roberts boomed out his thanks to the Lord on behalf of the two men. 'Lord, we thank thee for this opportunity to ask Your forgiveness for these miserable sinners . . .'

'What's happening?' Miriam asked in a hoarse whisper. 'Aren't they going to hang them after all?'

'Of course they are going to hang them. Just keep quiet!'

'Why is Preacher Thackeray thanking God, then?'

'Shut up!'

A woman kneeling in front of them turned her head to give them a withering glance, and they fell silent. Preacher Roberts' prayer was a long one, and when he had finished he ordered the crowd to stand and sing a hymn with him.

As the words of the hymn rose from ten thousand throats the officer of the soldiers found it difficult to contain his impatience. The whole thing was a nightmare for him. The sooner it was over the happier he would be. He looked for the hangman and saw him standing beside the condemned men. His hands were clasped in front of him and his chin thrust forward inside his hood. He was behaving as though he was in chapel.

When the third verse began, the officer spoke to the sergeant and the two prisoners were thrust forward until their faces were touching the rope of the nooses. The hangman was aroused from his religious fervour and persuaded to place the nooses about the necks of the two men. His action caused the voices of the crowd to falter. As he tightened the nooses and carefully positioned the knot beneath the left ear of each man the singing died away altogether. While the hangman was doing this the sergeant unlocked the chains that bound the men together and their arms were pinioned securely by the soldiers.

The officer stepped forward. His voice, nerve-tight, had but a fraction of the strength of Wrightwick Roberts'.

'Silence!' He called. 'Silence in the name of the Queen!'

The noise from the crowd subsided quickly.

'It is my duty to see that the sentence of death passed upon Thomas Arthur Sleedon and William Joseph Darling is carried out in accordance with the laws of this realm. They have been found guilty by a jury of fellow-men of the murder of Henry

Talbot, a militiaman, whilst he was carrying out his duties. Her Majesty's Judge of Assize has ordered that they be hanged by the neck until dead. Before the sentence is carried out they may speak their last words. May God rest their souls.'

'And may he rot yours and the souls of all those who oppress the miners of this county.'

An astonished Josh recognised the voice of his teacher, William Thackeray. The preacher was not a big man. He could not be seen in the midst of the group of agitated miners who stamped and shouted less than twenty yards from the gallows.

There was a murmur of agreement from the crowd, but William Thackeray had more to say.

'The militia is supposed to uphold the Law – not carry out the orders of the adventurers who keep miners poor in order to line their own pockets.'

The response this time was a roar of approval that alarmed the officer.

'What would we do if our families were starving? If food was deliberately kept from them? Wouldn't we take it?'

'Yes! Take it! Take it!' replied a thousand voices.

'The wrong men are on the scaffold,' shouted William Thackeray. 'It should be the adventurers! The mine-owners!'

'Take them down! Release them!' The cries came from all parts of the crowd as it seemed to sway forwards towards the gallows platform.

The officer rapped out an order and the soldiers brought muskets to their shoulders. At the same time the hangman reached forward. His shaking hand gripped a large wooden lever set close to one of the uprights of the gibbet.

Above the shouting and general hullabaloo a woman's voice could be heard screaming, 'Thomas! Oh God! Thomas!'

One of the condemned men, a look of anguish on his face, took a step forward – and trod into eternity. The trap-door dropped down on oiled hinges and the condemned men fell until the rope jerked them to a fatal halt. They hung with heads and shoulders visible to the crowd, their heads sideways as though listening, while the taut ropes quivered above them.

So sudden was the moment of execution it was seconds before the crowd fully appreciated that it was over.

When they did there was a sudden hush as though the world had stopped breathing. Then the woman who had screamed for Thomas Sleedon let out a long animal howl and Josh became aware that Miriam was clutching his arm, her fingernails biting into his wrist painfully.

A great gust of sound broke from the crowd and fists were waved angrily in the air.

'It was horrible! Horrible!' Miriam began sobbing. 'Why did they do it? Why did the officer kill them?'

Josh tried to tell her that it was not the officer's order but the court's, but too much was happening about them. The crowd was angry. Their feelings, like Miriam's, were turned upon the officer. As the soldiers cut down the two dead men a stone flew through the air, landing with a thud on the platform. It was followed by another – and another. Soon the air around the gallows was thick with missiles.

As the soldiers carrying the two bodies retreated towards the prison gate, the hangman cowered down alongside them. The remainder formed a tight line facing the crowd and retreated step by step. As they neared the gate those on the extreme ends of the line came under attack from the bolder young miners. This provoked their officer into showing them the authority of the Army. With blood trickling from a cut on his face, he snapped out an order. The line of soldiers stopped retreating and half of them dropped to one knee, their muskets pointing at their tormentors. As the crowd faltered, those exposed to the soldier's aim pushing back against the others behind them, the officer raised his sword. It fell, a flash of silver in the sun, and the muskets spoke.

At the last moment the soldiers raised their weapons and the musket-balls sped harmlessly above the heads of the crowd. But the volley had a salutary effect. The mob was thrown into near-panic, the frightened screams of the women nearest the soldiers leading those further away to believe they had been shot. Long before the truth became known, thousands were fleeing the field, while the soldiers and their grisly burdens were secure inside the prison. Indeed, there were many folk who never did know that the shots had not been aimed into the crowd. Tales of the murdering soldiers who shot at unarmed Cornish folk swept the county from end to end, doing nothing to enhance the fast-flagging popularity of the military.

Holding Miriam's hand, Josh ran with the crowd, not stopping until they reached the safety of the narrow thoroughfares.

His feeling of relief was almost immediately replaced by a sense of foolishness. No soldiers were pursuing them and there had been no second volley. But Miriam's tear-stained face was real enough. She was in a state of near-shock.

'Oh, come on,' said Josh, more harshly than he intended because of the discovery that he was still holding her hand. 'It's all over now.'

Miriam drew the back of her hand across her eyes and succeeded in producing horizontal smudges to add to the perpendicular ones.

She could not remove the sight of the hanged men from her mind. One minute they had been alive, men with thoughts and feelings; the next . . .

She had been watching the face of the one who had taken the pace forward at the moment the hangman pulled the lever. She had seen his utter surprise. Horrified, she had still been looking when the rope snapped taut and death displaced surprise. She would have nightmares about it for the remainder of her life.

'It's all right now. I'll buy you some more sweets – and we'll go in to watch the dancing bear.' The animal was just one of many entertainments on offer in the crowded fair.

They saw the bear, an unhappy, degraded and flea-bothered animal, and they bought more fruit and sweets. By late afternoon Miriam had succeeded in pushing thoughts of the hanging to the back of her mind.

As it was a special holiday the town's inns were open all day. There were many who took full advantage of the fact. Drunken men, and not a few women, became commonplace as the day wore on. In the ale-houses the loud and ribald singing drove smoke and the sweet heavy smell of beer and gin out through open windows and doors.

Those who had already drunk too much, unused to the town's brew, lay sprawled outside in the gutters amidst the litter of the day. The lucky ones were those who fell drunk in the main street. They were quickly removed by friends or the constables specially sworn in for this day. Those who were not so fortunate staggered far enough away to fall in some more inconspicuous alley. Here they were quickly relieved of everything of value by the gangs of young villains who followed them from the inns, fighting off similar-minded rivals.

There were many other fights for lesser reasons. The miners would be talking about them for weeks to come.

Josh and Miriam saw Morwen Trago in one such brawl and Josh had to drag Miriam away while she shrieked at her brother to stop. He was only just in time. A band of the special constables came on the run, laying about them with their long staves, driving off the able-bodied and arresting those who lay unconscious on the ground. Morwen was one of the runners.

But it was trouble of a different and unlooked-for kind that caught up with Miriam and Josh. It came in the person of Herman Schmidt, Sharptor mine captain.

Yet another fight had erupted in the town's main street. Josh took Miriam down a narrow alleyway in an attempt to bypass the trouble-area and return to the main street closer to the country dancing being held at the far end of Bodmin town.

The alleyway led into another – and yet one more until they were lost. Josh was about to suggest they turn around and retrace their steps when they saw a thick-set man standing straddle-legged close to the wall of a house. He had his back towards them and a stream of urine ran past him to the gutter.

Josh's instinct was to hurry past as fast as they could, but the man heard them coming. Turning, he blocked their way in the narrow alleyway. It was Herman Schmidt and the German had not bothered to button his trousers.

'Well, well! And what have we here, eh?' The accent was

thick and guttural and in no way helped by the amount of alcohol he had drunk. He peered down at them drunkenly and took a staggering step forward.

'What you want?' He was talking to Miriam. 'You looking for a man? All right, Cornish whore. How much you charge, eh? How much?'

Josh edged backwards and tried to pull Miriam with him, but the German reached out and took her arm in a grip that made her draw in her breath with pain. 'You hear me, Cornish whore? I am more of a man than your peasant farmer or poor miner. How much do you want?'

'One guinea.'

Josh looked at Miriam in amazement, unable to believe he had heard her correctly.

'A guinea! What you take me for? One guinea! It is maybe made of gold, Ja?' He snorted derisively, then stooped down to look more closely at her. The gin fumes on his breath were enough to make Josh wince and he was half a pace behind Miriam.

'Um! You are young, still. You have a room?'

She nodded.

'Then I give you half a guinea.'

'A guinea.'

'Half a guinea!' the German roared. 'No woman is worth a whole guinea. Not even a German virgin.' He cursed in coarse German and spat upon the ground.

'Miriam, what are you saying? Come away.'

Without turning around she waved her free hand behind her back, signalling for Josh to go. The mine captain, fumbling in a waistcoat pocket for a half-guinea, paused and spoke to him.

'What arc you doing here, boy? Go away.' He peered at Josh, trying to focus his bloodshot eyes. 'Don't I know you?' He shook his head heavily. 'I should know you, perhaps. But go away. Run off.'

But Josh stood his ground. The mine captain pulled a golden coin from his pocket. He had no more success focusing his eyes upon it than he had trying to identify Josh. He held the coin up before Miriam's face. 'Here. Is this a half-guinea?'

She snatched it from him. 'Yes.'

'Come on, then. We are wasting time. Where do you live?'

Josh caught Miriam's hand, thoroughly alarmed. 'Don't go with him, Miriam. He'll hurt you. Don't go—'

Herman Schmidt said angrily, 'When I give an order it is meant to be obeyed.' The back of his heavy hand swung and caught Josh on the side of his head, knocking him off balance. He thought he heard Miriam scream, but the sound was lost in the blaze of lights that flashed in front of his eyes as his head struck a wall. Then everything went black.

When he opened his eyes he believed that he had been only temporarily dazed, but Miriam and Schmidt were gone. He felt sick. Whether it was from the blow to his head or the thought of what the German and the small girl were doing together he did not want to know.

He scoured the alleyways in the immediate vicinity, but there was no sign of them. Soon he found himself out on the main street again. The shadows were beginning to grow long when Josh gave up looking. There were still far too many people in Bodmin to make anything like a thorough search possible.

Despondently he made his way back to the field where the wagons were parked. This too was a scene of some activity now. The Sharptor contingent was not the only one to have travelled a considerable distance to witness the execution. Wagons were trundling off, late-comers running to get themselves hoisted aboard.

A couple of the Sharptor wagons had already left. In others there were drunken miners, placed there by their friends to sleep off their excesses. The wagon on which Josh and Miriam had come to Bodmin was empty. Josh clambered on to it and squatted near the front, the tall driver's-box blotting out his view of the noisy loathsome town. Gloomily he looked out across the fields towards the moor that lay between Bodmin and home.

Gradually more and more of the Henwood and Sharptor villagers arrived, but it was nearer eight o'clock than six o'clock when they were ready to move off. He had seen his mother and father arrive, Jesse flushed with the excitement of the day and carrying lots of packages of once-in-a-lifetime frivolous purchases. She looked for Josh, saw he was safely on a wagon and waved cheerily. He raised his hand in acknowledgement, glad that she did not come across to talk to him.

Suddenly from the corner of his eye he saw a flash of brown skin and the familiar long black hair of Miriam as she scrambled up beside him. He stiffened involuntarily, not sure whether he was relieved or angry. But Miriam was bubbling over with happiness, as though nothing untoward had taken place.

'Oh, Josh! You don't know how glad I am to see you. When you fell I thought Schmidt had killed you. As soon as I could I came back to look for you, but you'd gone. Where have you been? I've been looking everywhere for you.'

There was no stopping her. The words just poured out. 'Look! I've been shopping. I bought a comb for my ma. Some tobacco for Dad. A new cap for Morwen – he's always wanted one. There's some ribbon for me . . .' She paused. 'And I've bought this for you.'

She held something out towards him. When he made no move to take it from her she took his hand and dropped the object into it.

He tried not to, but he had to look down at it. It was a pocket-knife. A bone-handled knife with two spring blades that folded into it. He was tempted, very tempted; but stiffly he returned it, dropping the knife into her lap.

'I don't wan't it.'

Miriam's mouth dropped open in surprise. 'But it's a present . . .' Her eyes suddenly opened wide. 'You don't think . . . ?' You don't believe I went with that – that *animal*?'

A couple of women looked around at the vehemence of her words. After giving them a withering look Miriam lowered her voice. 'I wasn't going to let him get away with the things he said to me. I took his money – and it was a whole guinea, not a half-guinea. When I found a house with the door open I took him inside and told him to go upstairs and wait for me in the bedroom. It was quite a big house. I expect he's still there.'

She smiled, epecting Josh to smile in return. That would make everything all right again. But Josh's thoughts were in a turmoil. He wanted to believe her. He did believe her. But Miriam had led Captain Schmidt on.

'Taking his money was stealing. You should have come away with me when I wanted you to.'

'It was *not* stealing. Not after what he said to me. Besides, he hit you. He deserved to pay for that. Anyway, he had hold of my arm, remember? I couldn't have got away. If I'd struggled he would have hit me too and then something bad *would* have happened.'

The wagon had filled up fast and now the wagon-driver returned and made them all crowd closer together to allow even more passengers to get on. When he thought there were enough he climbed on to the seat and cracked his long whip over the backs of the horses. With many 'Hups!' and 'Heave hos', the horses strained into the harness. As the wagon creaked its way out on to the road to begin the climb away from the town the lights were beginning to glow in the windows of the houses. On they went, up the track to the high moors where a light hazy mist was beginning to blunt the craggy tors.

Everyone was in a very happy mood – everyone except Miriam and Josh. The singing rolled back and forth along the line of wagons.

In the crowded swaying wagon, Josh sat with his arms wrapped around his drawn-up knees. Miriam could do little else but lean and bump against him, miserably staring in front of her. Once or twice Josh stole a glance at her face, half-hidden by her straggling black hair. Although it was not possible to be sure, he thought he saw tears trembling on the brink of her eyelashes.

He was thoroughly miserable. It was made all the worse by the belief, hidden beneath a lot of other feelings, that Miriam was right. Captain Schmidt *had* been holding her arm. He would certainly have been violent had she tried to run away.

A dull ache at the back of Josh's head was proof enough of that. The captain also deserved to be separated from his money – that too Josh accepted. The thing that bothered him most was that Miriam should have been immediately aware of what the German was talking about, when Josh himself had not been really sure. He was still vague on some of the issues raised by the incident.

He thought of the mine captain, tricked into entering somebody's house; tried to imagine what had happened when he discovered his mistake. Perhaps he had been found in the house.

He looked again at Miriam but it was too dark to see her face now.

'Miriam, I'm sorry.'

There was no reply.

'I don't think you did anything wrong – and the knife is a lovely present.'

She grasped his hand, sniffed noisily and heavily, then rubbed her eyes against the shoulder of his coat. Without a word the pocket-knife was replaced in his hand.

'I wonder what old Schmidt is doing now?'

It was a very shaky laugh, but she managed it. He squeezed her hand awkwardly. 'I wasn't much help, was I?'

'That wasn't your fault,' she said indignantly. 'He hit you.'

There was silence between them for a few minutes and a new song was started in the next wagon. The wagoner cracked his whip for the horses to close up on the sound. Ahead of the first wagon a miner had jumped down and was leading the way with a lantern swinging in his hand.

'Do you really like the knife?'

'Yes. It's the best present I've ever been given.' He meant it.

'It was the first present I've ever bought for anyone.'

'I bet it cost a lot of money.'

'Yes, it did, but I've still got half a guinea left.'

She contorted her body and retrieved the coin from somewhere beneath her clothes.

'Here! You can have it. I don't need it.'

The warm coin was pressed into his hand, but he pushed it back and closed her hand about it.

'No, you keep it. One day you'll want to buy yourself something special.'

She contorted again, and the coin was gone once more.

She hugged his arm between both her hands. As the singing gradually died away only the soft clumping of the horses' hoofs and the squeak and creak of the wagons broke the silence of the night. Her head drooped to rest on his shoulder.

'Josh?' Her voice sounded sleepy.

'What?' he whispered.

'I wouldn't do bad things with anyone, Josh.'

'No?'

'No – only with you, and they wouldn't be bad then.'

There were strange stirrings in his young body and he felt very grown-up and protective towards the young but disturbingly mature girl who slumbered quietly on his shoulder as the wagons rolled homewards.

Chapter Five

William Thackeray rode back to St Cleer in an excited mood. He knew his words had stirred the huge crowd. Had the soldiers' officer not acted so quickly, he might have incited them to storm the gallows and release the two condemned miners.

The thought that he might have been partly responsible for the act which had sent them to the gallows never crossed his mind, although he knew they had attended the meeting he had called at Kit Hill when their troubles first started. But Preacher Thackeray was to be found wherever the miners had trouble. He would address them in the open air, hemmed in by the gorse and fern, or within the stone walls of a barracks-like sorting-shed. He cared little for his surroundings as long as there were men who would listen – and there were always men ready to listen to William Thackeray. Every Sunday he attracted huge congregations. It was as much for this reason as any other that his church did not withdraw him from Cornwall, for the words that he preached were not all drawn from the Bible. Not for Preacher Thackeray the comfortable meaningless jargon that country parsons had served to their flocks for generations past. He was concerned for the souls of his people, but he saw no reason why they should suffer unnecessary hardships in this life in order to enter the same heaven to which their far more comfortable employers were bound.

And so Preacher Thackeray urged the miners to join together to improve their lot in life. This was why he preached 'union'. This was why he was feared and hated by mine-adventurers and those whose fortunes were swelled by the poverty of the miner. 'Union' was a word he used in every sermon he preached. Union with the Lord. Union against the practice of paying miners with mine tokens redeemable only in the mine's own store. Union with every other Cornish miner. They needed it to negotiate terms of employment that would raise the status of the miner from near-serfdom to valued employee, with due recognition for his skills.

Thackeray advocated that the men should fight for their rights in any and every possible way. If it were necessary to use violence, then Jesus Christ himself had set a precedent. If a few tables had to be overturned – then so be it.

It was for this type of preaching that men came to hear him. He was as popular with miners as he was unpopular with mine-owners and Cornish gentry – for his preaching was not directed against the adventurers alone. He slated the Government for its short-sighted agricultural policies – policies which sent food prices soaring. He pointed a stern finger at farmers who took advantage of bad laws to withhold corn from the markets, raising corn prices to a level that miners' families found impossible to afford.

There had been little enough of Preacher Thackeray physically when he first crossed the Tamar into Cornwall. His continuous crusade among the mining communities of east Cornwall trimmed his weight still further. As Jesse Retallick once remarked, he had no more flesh on him than a weasel. It was a good description. Small and wiry, he possessed boundless energy. He also had the weasel's uncanny ability to hold the attention of an audience when he so wished.

He was almost halfway to St Cleer when he met up with one more group of men travelling in the same direction as himself. He would have passed through them with no more than an echoed 'Good night' had not one of them called to him.

'Is that Preacher Thackeray?'

'Unless I'm mistaken that's John Kittow. What do you want with me?'

The small group of miners closed about him, and John Kittow lowered his voice, for sounds carry far at night on the high moor.

'We'd like a word with you, Preacher. Somewhere quiet.'

'I'll meet you any time you like, John. Won't it do here?'

'No.' William Thackeray could detect the shaking of heads around him. 'No, Preacher. Better if 'tis said where there's light to see who's listening and walls to stop them as shouldn't be.'

'Then you'd better make it the chapel. Tomorrow night?'

'Right after the late shift comes up, if that suits you.'

'That's all right with me, John.' His horse threw back its head and danced sideways. Thackeray yanked it to a halt again. 'But won't you tell me something of what it's about?'

The movements of the horse had taken him a little distance from the men and there was a noticeable hesitation before the voice came from the darkness.

'Corn, Preacher. That's it in one word. Corn!'

Herman Schmidt did not put in an appearance at the Sharptor mine next day. There was nothing out of the ordinary in this and no one – with the exception of Josh – would have thought anything of it had not Theophilus Strike called in at the mine in the late afternoon. Then the word went around like chaff in an east wind. The German mine captain had been arrested by the Bodmin constable and kept in the town's lock-up overnight. It seemed he would have been there still, had he not got word to the Sharptor mine-owner of his plight.

Theophilus Strike had gone straight to Bodmin and eventually managed to smooth over what would otherwise have been a very serious situation for the German. He had been arrested on a charge of entering a dwelling-house with intent to commit a felony. There was also an additional charge of assaulting the constable called to arrest him.

With a great deal of diplomacy, backed up by a few gold

coins, Strike had persuaded the tenants of the house where Schmidt had inexplicably found himself to withdraw their complaint. The constable too was a reasonable man, appreciative of the purchasing power of a brace of guineas. He had the additional satisfaction of knowing that, whereas the wild swings of the mine captain had not found their target, his own beefy fists had left their mark on Schmidt's features.

Herman Schmidt pleaded 'guilty' before the magistrate to a charge of being drunk and disorderly and was fined five shillings, the magistrate adding a stern warning for him to steer clear of the Bodmin hostelries in the future.

During the time his battered face was healing the mine captain kept away from the mine as much as possible. For what remained of that summer he was a quieter, more reasonable man. Nevertheless, it was some weeks before Josh was able to see the mine captain's approach without a sinking feeling in his stomach. He need not have worried. Herman Schmidt could remember nothing of the events that had led to his arrest

The lights were burning until well into the night in the St Cleer Methodist church for the meeting between Preacher William Thackeray and the miners of Caradon led by John Kittow. It should have been one of the nights when Josh stayed late for his studies but he was ushered out by the preacher and, after looking at the faces of the men who began to arrive while he collected his books together, he wasted no time in going.

Only selected miners were allowed into the hall that evening. Others who called to see the preacher found the door guarded by two burly Caradon men. They were curtly told to conduct their business on another, more convenient occasion. Nobody questioned it. Far better to accept whatever the preacher was doing and forget about it.

Even so, there were many who wondered about the secret meeting, but they would not be kept in suspense for long.

The shortage of corn had been growing steadily worse throughout England. It had not been helped by the government laws which prevented corn from being imported, in a misguided attempt to protect the interests of the farmers. It certainly helped the farmer, but at the expense of the poor worker. He was unable to afford the astronomical prices the corn was fetching on the open market.

When Josh mentioned the unusual happenings at the St Cleer chapel to his father, the miner knew immediately what it was about. Rumour had been rife lately that miners' action was imminent. Ben Retallick was sitting in the doorway of the cottage enjoying the late-evening air and he frowned at the thought of more trouble. Thackeray's meddling with affairs outside the chapel did not please him. He could see nothing but trouble coming from it.

'You'd best forget you saw anything tonight,' he said. 'And be quite sure that I'm the last one you tell of it.'

The miners of Caradon had determined to do more than talk about their problems and had already formulated a rough plan of action. They were having this meeting with Preacher Thackeray in order to give his quick and clever mind a chance to work out the details and smooth out some difficulties. John Kittow wanted to be sure that as little as possible could go wrong, for it was a bold plan the miners were embarking upon. . . .

Callington market was smaller than many others in the county, being overshadowed by the nearness of the greater market-towns of Liskeard, Launceston and Saltash. But trade was usually brisk for all that, and lately it had become a collection centre for farm produce. From here it would be hauled to Cotehele quay and shipped down-river to the seaport of Plymouth.

This particular market-day began much like any other and, although the observant onlooker might have noticed an unusually high proportion of miners about the market-place, it excited little interest. The farming community deliberately avoided noticing them at all.

There had always been miners on the moor. For longer than there had ever been farmers, in fact. But those early miners – the 'old men' of legend – had done no more than scratch the ground and search the streams for their ore. They lived a solitary furtive life and had little contact with men outside their own kind.

These 'new' miners were a different breed altogether. They dug deep into the very bowels of the earth, raising mountains of rubble around their shafts. The thump and clanking of their steam-engines reverberated over the countryside, frightening cattle and worrying the sheep. Even at night they worked, the glow from their furnaces flickering along the ridges like the watch-fires of hell. Neither were they partial to the solitary life. Instead, they roamed the lanes in noisy boisterous groups. It was a brave countrywoman who would venture past one of the many inns frequented by them.

No, the miner and the farmer were different breeds of men and there was a wide gulf between them.

All morning the farm-wagons trundled into Callington loaded with produce and livestock and among the produce was – corn!

The corn-market was at the very centre of the town, outside a stone-built granary. Here a man's occupation was forgotten as miner, countryman and town-dweller crowded around the auctioneer as he called loudly for bids.

As the bidding began the calls came quickly and eagerly from those who most needed the grain. 'Sixty shillings! Sixty-five! Seventy!' There was very little grain allowed to be sold on the home market. At seventy-five shillings for a quarter the bids were still coming in from all sides. At eighty shillings men began to shake their heads. By the time it had made ninety all but the most determined had dropped out, including the combines of ordinary people who had pooled their cash in an effort to get at least some corn to take home. When the corn reached a calling-price of one hundred and five shillings only the merchants remained – and none of them was from Cornwall.

The bidding slowed down noticeably now, rising in pence. 'One hundred and five shillings and four pence I am bid. It is best-quality corn and will fetch much more in the city – or even in Plymouth. Do I hear one hundred and six? Who will bid one hundred and six?'

'Eighty shillings, and I'll take the lot.' The voice, deep and very Cornish, came from towards the back of the crowd.

The auctioneer smiled derisively. 'I'm sorry, sir, you're a little late. The bidding has reached one hundred and five shillings and four pence – or did I hear one hundred and six?'

'You heard eighty shillings, and that's all you'll be getting. I'll take the lot.'

John Kittow pushed his way through the bidders to the front and a broad wedge of miners split the crowd behind him.

'You can't do this! I've been bid more than one hundred and five shillings. I am honour bound to sell at the best price.'

'There's nothing honourable in keeping food from the mouths of those who need it. Nor in robbing those who can pay more. Eighty shillings is a fair price for a quarter and that's what it will be sold for.'

The auctioneer began to protest once more, and John Kittow pushed him from his auctioneer's perch into the midst of the miners. The man disappeared momentarily and re-appeared to be raised high above the heads of the miners. Too terrified to struggle, he was passed over the heads of the cheering men to the rear of the crowd.

'Now!' John Kittow put up his hands for silence. 'We're selling corn to whoever wants it. At eighty shillings a quarter. There will be no bidding. It's a case of "first come, first served". Is it agreed that eighty shillings is a fair price?'

There was a majority shout of assent, but one man called out, 'The farmers have made enough profit from corn. Sell it at sixty shillings. Forty, even!'

'There will be none of that talk!' John Kittow put a stop to the murmur before it spread. 'There's been work put into the growing of it. A man is entitled to his living. Eighty shillings has been agreed and that's what it will be sold for. Nobody will be turned away if he has the money to pay for it. Come on, now! What are you waiting for?'

The crowd surged forward to buy a bushel or two. It was an opportunity that was hardly likely to be repeated. Word went quickly through the whole market of what was happening, and crowds thronged to the corn-sale. It was not only the townsfolk and the miners who came. Stalls were left unattended as traders deserted them for the chance of buying corn. It had been missing from their diet for so long that there were young children in some families who had never known the taste of it.

A few of the farmers whose produce was up for sale protested at the unorthodox method of sale, but when sections of the crowd turned on them they withdrew, angry and sullen.

One or two of the more aggrieved among them decided to ride from the town to summon the military from Launceston and Liskeard. They got no further than the town's limits. Formidable pickets of miners armed with pick-axe handles guarded every exit from Callington. The corn-sale would continue in their way for as long as was deemed necessary.

The sale of immediate stocks did not last the hour, but then the shout went up that there was plenty more corn stored in the granary. In ten minutes the doors had been battered down and spilling bags of corn were being passed out to enable the sale to continue.

The whole affair was conducted in a most efficient manner, proving that the hours spent in discussion in the St Cleer chapel had not been wasted. The miners worked in threes – one man measuring the corn, the second taking the money from the customer and placing it into the canvas bag held by the third. Other miners, sweat running down their grinning faces, humped corn from the granary and shouldered it to the sellers.

John Kittow was acting as general supervisor, calling up more corn for this trio; directing eager buyers to another where they would be served more quickly. At one stage he saw an old woman, wrinkled face anxious beneath her widow's shawl, moving from one group to the next, watching the proceedings from the edge of the would-be buyers, but not pushing her way through to the front.

'Is it corn you're wanting, mother?' asked Kittow, taking her gently by the elbow. 'You come over here with me and we'll see that you get it without waiting.'

'Ah, will I now?' The woman's voice was as old as her face.

'And what d'you think I'll be paying you with? Wanting's one thing, m'dear – buying's another.'

John Kittow noticed for the first time the frayed patches of her shawl and the all-but-threadbare black cardigan beneath it.

'You'll be a widow, then, mother?'

'These twenty years,' she replied. 'And he went the same way that you'll go. With his lungs full of dust from the mine.'

'We'll all go when the time comes,' said John Kittow, guiding her forward once more. 'But there'll be no miner's widow leaving here today without corn to fill her belly for a day or two.'

He spoke to a miner who looked up from a half-empty sack. 'Some corn for a miner's widow. As much as she can carry away.'

He drew some coins from his pocket and threw them into the money-bag being held by another miner. 'If any more widows, or others in need, come for corn give it to them. Pay for it from your own pockets. You'll get it back from the mine fund. But make sure the money goes into the bag. I'll have no one saying there has been any dishonesty here today.'

John Kittow proved himself a man of his word. When the last bushel of corn had been sold the money was brought to him and he passed it on to the farmers who had brought in the corn. They grumbled that they would have received more from the merchants but were so relieved to be receiving any money at all that they made little fuss.

The balance of the money was counted with the granary agent and he reluctantly gave the miners a receipt for it, agreeing that it tallied with the amount of corn sold at the miners' price.

Their business concluded, the miners of Caradon withdrew their pickets from around the town and, as peacefully as they arrived, they quitted Callington.

The military was called out and a troop of soldiers rode into Callington the next day, but there was very little that they could, or would, do. The business had been conducted in a scrupulously honest manner. Though the price was not what the farmers expected, they still made a good profit from it.

There was another reason for the tardiness of the soldiers in taking action. They were due for a tour of duty abroad, where there would be a chance of 'real' action, with possibly battle honours for the regiment and a title for its colonel. He had no wish to blow up a relatively minor rural incident into a people's uprising. There was no glory to be gained in quelling a civil disturbance.

Chapter Six

The remainder of that summer went quickly and there were many who were glad to see it pass. For others – and Josh was one – it was a year to gather in and cherish, and he hoped it might never come to an end. But the long happy evenings spent on the moor with Miriam grew shorter and became memories. They had searched the bracken for nests, watched the badgers live out their ordered lives bringing up a healthy family, envied the gliding, circling buzzard and twice disturbed a fox drinking from brackish water in a moorland hollow. The fox displayed no fear and its slow retreat from them could have been interpreted as insolence. But on the second occasion, when they tried to follow it through the undergrowth, the animal vanished without a leaf or blade of grass trembling to show which way it had gone.

Miriam said the fox was probably a witch in one of her many disguises. Although Josh laughed at her foolishness, he was true Cornish and the countless generations of superstition that had gone into his breeding made him glance uneasily over his shoulder more than once as he hurried home in the dusk.

Then, almost before they realised it, summer had gone. The winter wind rattled the leafless branches of the hunch-backed bushes and laid the dry bracken flat to the ground, and the horses working the mine-whims blew steam from wide nostrils as they trudged around in circles on their long road to nowhere.

'It's hard to believe that Christmas is only two weeks away.'

Jesse Retallick beat up the mixture for the pudding she was preparing.

'It's Gwen's first Christmas,' said Jenny. 'I hope we will have some snow for her to see.'

'She's a fine baby. It's such a pity her father isn't alive to see her face when she opens her presents on Christmas morning.'

The deep sense of loss was still there, but it was now possible to talk about Budge to Jenny without having her dissolve into tears.

'I believe Budge *will* see her face,' said Jenny quietly with absolute conviction. Tom Shovell was a religious man and he had been a constant visitor to the house since the summer. His simple faith had restored a great deal of her self-confidence and brought her peace of mind, much to Jesse Retallick's relief. There had been a time when she feared the girl would never return to normal.

Jesse turned to Josh, who was sitting reading a schoolbook in a corner close to the fire. 'With Christmas over life will be very different for you, young man.'

Her manner was jocular but there was sadness deep inside. The year 1839 would see great changes in the Retallick household. Josh was going away on an apprenticeship. Thanks to his education, Theophilus Strike had offered him the chance to become a mine-engineer.

Josh would be away for close on three years at Harvey's foundry and engineering works at Hayle. There he would learn how to build and look after engines of the type Theophilus Strike planned to install in the Sharptor mine. An engine would not be necessary for three years because there was plenty of copper in the shallow drier levels. The mine-owner saw little sense in spending money to erect an engine to drain deeper shafts when the men could be digging out the existing ore and bringing money in.

As the Hayle foundry was to build the engine Josh would be involved with it from the beginning. When he returned he would possess a greater knowledge of engines than anyone in the district. His presence on the mine would avoid the necessity of calling out an engineer from Hayle when something went wrong. Theophilus Strike had costed the whole operation very carefully. Eventually, Josh's apprenticeship would save him a great deal of money.

He had not, of course, told Josh about this when he called him in for an interview. Instead, he had checked Josh's reading, his writing and his knowledge of arithmetic. Then, satisfied, he offered him the chance of three years at Hayle in return for an undertaking by Josh to work at the Sharptor mine for the following ten years. To his astonishment and Ben Retallick's dismay Josh had refused this offer. It was a desperate gamble. Josh now wanted to be an engineer more than anything else in the world. But ten years was a long time to be tied to one employer. He was now fourteen years old. It meant that he would be almost thirty before he was free of his commitment. Although he might not want to move elsewhere, the very thought of the restriction would be constantly at the back of his mind. It would always rankle. Five years' tied employment with the guarantee of a reasonable salary constituted his terms of acceptance.

Strike's astonishment had quickly turned to anger but it did not last. He knew there was not another boy available at Sharptor with Josh's standard of education, and without an engineer he believed it would be foolish to buy an engine. Without an engineer being readily available a major breakdown could spell disaster for a deep mine.

He agreed to Josh's terms. But Josh was left in no doubt about his part of the agreement. He was expected to return from Hayle with the best engine in Cornwall, and his commencing salary would depend entirely upon the report that Strike received of Josh's proficiency at the end of his training.

When Josh and Ben Retallick left the mine-owner's office the miner had taken off his hat and regarded his son with incredulous respect.

'I never thought I'd live to see the day when a son of mine would be offered the chance of a lifetime by a mine-owner and turn it down like that! And then to go on and call your own tune! Josh, if cheek is what matters you'll go far in this world.'

'It wasn't cheek,' Josh said, hiding his own elation. 'It was simple arithmetic. I know what I will be worth to Theophilus Strike. He knows it too. I could have asked for more without being greedy.'

It was true. He and Preacher Thackeray had spent a whole evening discussing the matter, and the preacher had finally proved his case by using simple mathematics. Thus Josh had been able to attend the interview armed with the same facts as the mine-owner. Josh intended to work hard during the three years he would be at Hayle, and Theophilus Strike would receive value for his investment. But Josh had plans for his own advance into manhood. Only single men could exist on low wages.

'I don't know, I'm sure,' Ben Retallick had said. 'It looks as though this schooling of yours is beginning to pay off already!'

Josh looked affectionately at his mother as she busied herself with the pudding mixture. 'Don't let's talk about my going away until Christmas is over.'

'And why not? It's something to be pleased about. You are getting a better chance in life than your father. Be thankful he doesn't want his son to follow him down the mine. There's many who can't wait to get their children below ground. Some of the mites are hardly big enough to hold a shovel. Moses Trago never wasted any time with his Morwen.'

There was silence for a few minutes, but the mention of Moses Trago had reminded Jesse Retallick of something that had been on her mind for some days.

'I haven't seen that Trago girl lately. Do you still meet her?'

'Miriam? Yes, now and again.'

This was rather more than a white lie. He saw her every time he came out from the chapel school at St Cleer. During the dark winter nights she was always waiting nearby in the shadows. They would walk together to their hideout on the moors where, by candlelight, he would teach her as much of his evening's lesson as he could remember.

Jesse Retallick knew that the two spent a lot of time in each other's company. She had seen them herself. Had she not, she would have known by the Henwood villages' thinly veiled innuendoes about it being 'unhealthy' for a boy and girl to spend so much time alone together, away from the influence of adults.

In a quiet indirect way she had found out from Josh about the schooling he was giving to Miriam and she approved of it. Miriam Trago had more about her than most other girls of her age. If she could escape from the influence of the remainder of the Trago family, then she wished the girl luck.

'What is she doing for Christmas?'

Josh looked surprised at the question. 'I don't know. Probably nothing at all. Miriam told me once they don't keep Christmas. Moses Trago says it's just another day.'

'Then it's time she learned different. Tell her that she's welcome here for Christmas Day. That's if you'd like to have her here?'

Astonishment and pleasure wrestled for supremacy on his face, and a stab of pain went through Jesse Retallick as she realised that he would not be a boy for very much longer. She doubted whether he would remain with his parents for very long after he returned from Hayle.

'Can I tell her now?' He slammed his book shut.

It was her turn to show surprise. 'At this time of night? You're not going up to that Trago place?'

He shook his head. 'No, she won't be there, but I know where to find her.'

Jesse Retallick bit back a refusal and began beating the pudding with unnecessary vigour. 'All right. But be back before your father comes home from the chapel meeting.'

He was gone by the time she had finished talking, and as the door banged noisily behind him Jenny smiled. 'Now, there's a young romance for you!'

'Nonsense! He's still a child. Both of them are.'

'Maybe, Jesse. But I was married when I was only two years older than they are now. There's nothing wrong with it. Despite her family Miriam is a good sensible girl, and she thinks the world of Josh.'

Jesse Retallick said nothing, but her Christmas pudding was stirred more thoroughly than it had ever been in any previous year.

It was dark on the hillside and a heavy chill hung in the air, but Josh was too happy to notice. He left the path a hundred yards from the cottage and followed a badger track up on to the high moor. There he struck off into the undergrowth and the going was harder. Twice he thought he had reached the hideout before he saw the faint outline of a boulder in front of him and knew he was there.

He crawled quietly and carefully along the tunnel through the gorse until he saw a soft glimmer of light ahead. It went out before he reached the end of the tunnel and he knew that Miriam was there and she had heard him.

'Miriam! It's me,' he called in a hoarse whisper.

Josh rose from the narrow gorse-tunnel and advanced into the space between the rocks. The candle was tucked into a small recess so that it was well sheltered from the wind and as little light as possible escaped from the hideaway. Beside the fat home-made candle were jammed a couple of books, old and in an advanced state of deterioration. Behind them was a pile of paper filled with Miriam's crowded untidy writing.

'What are you doing here at this time of the night? Is something wrong?' Her eyes were even darker than usual in the candlelight.

'No, there's nothing wrong. He held it back for as long as he could. 'I just wondered what you'll be doing on Christmas Day?'

She looked at him in amazement. 'You came all the way up here in the dark to ask me that? I've already told you. Christmas is the same as any other day for us. Except that my dad doesn't work. I expect he will be drinking all day.'

'Well . . .' He could not control the grin that threatened to split his face in two. 'How would you like to spend the day with us? Come to the cottage in the morning and stay all day? Have Christmas dinner with us and everything?'

Her expression made the journey in the dark worth while.

'Honest? Who said I could come? Your mother?'

He nodded.

Josh had become used to her impetuosity by now and, after submitting to the first onslaught of violent hugging, he broke free.

'You'll come?'

'Of course! As it's just an ordinary day for us I'll be able to come and go as I like. Nobody will ask where I'm going.'

'Then that's all settled. I'll go back and tell Mum you'll be coming.'

'Can't you stay for a while and help me? There are lots of long words in this book. I don't understand them.'

'No. Dad will be home from the chapel meeting soon. I don't want to upset him before Christmas.' He shivered. 'It's freezing cold up here. I don't know how you can learn anything in this weather.'

'Where else can I go? I don't mind the cold but I don't like the rain very much.'

She carefully placed her books in a tin box she had managed to acquire and tucked it well back into a crevice between the rocks. Then she snuffed out the candle and crawled through the tunnel behind Josh. Once out on to the moor she took his hand in a perfectly natural gesture. They often held hands when they walked on the moor in the dark. It was practical as well as companionable. If one stumbled or slipped, the other was able to prevent a fall. But once off the moor, or in daylight, Josh would not have been seen dead holding hands with anyone.

'Didn't your mother mind you coming out to see me this time of night?'

'Of course not. Why?'

She shrugged. ''Cos people talk. Do you remember one evening in summer we met Nehemeziah on the path below here?'

'Yes. One of his horses had got loose and wandered up here. What about it?'

'A few nights later I heard him telling old Mary Crabbe about seeing us together on the moor.'

'That doesn't matter. We weren't doing anything wrong.'

'*We* know that. I doubt anyone else would believe it. I know Mary Crabbe didn't. I heard what she said to Nehemeziah and she didn't care whether I heard her or not.'

'What did she say?'

Miriam did not answer immediately and Josh pulled her to a halt.

'What did she say?' he repeated.

A gust of wind from the west caught Miriam's long black hair and blew it forward, the ends of it flicking across his face.

She released her hand and pulled the hair back, knotting it behind her neck.

'She said I'd end up in trouble one day. She said if it wasn't you who laid me in the fern it would be someone else.'

'The nasty-minded old bitch!' Josh bristled with indignation.

Miriam took his hand again and squeezed it. They moved off along the path once more.

'Anyway, Mum doesn't believe that. She wouldn't have asked you home for Christmas if she did.'

'I've always wanted to have a *real* Christmas. What's it like?'

He told her. Of the holly-wreaths decorating the pictures and the mantelshelf. The small presents and the large meals. Prayers at lunch-time. The singing around the fire in the evening. And he tried to put into words the atmosphere of Christmas, of being part of a family and belonging. She listened in thoughtful silence until they arrived at the track that led downwards to the cottage and up to the Trago home.

'Are you sure I won't be in the way. If it's a family thing, I mean?'

'Of course you won't. You've been invited. Jenny and the baby will be there. Wrightwick Roberts will be coming in the evening. Tom Shovell too, I expect. Besides, I want you to come.'

'That's all right, then.' She was happy again.

'I've got to go now. I'll see you tomorrow at St Cleer – same time?'

'Yes.' She leaned forward and kissed him on the lips. For all the clumsy inexperience of it, he went hot inside.

'Good night, then.'

'Good night.'

Josh walked home without feeling the cold, as tall as any man.

Christmas came, as it usually does, with a great rush. After weeks of anticipation and fretfulness and much planning on the part of Jesse Retallick, all was very nearly ready. On the day before Christmas Eve a cart-load of miners' wives, Jesse Retallick among them, went into Liskeard market. They returned laden with meat, vegetables and mysterious parcels that were promptly tucked at the back of cupboards, accompanied by dire threats directed against anyone curious enough to want to seek them out.

Then, on Christmas Eve, just before dusk, the Sharptor mine ceased working. The men came to the surface to be greeted by Theophilus Strike, who handed to each man a large fat goose, freshly killed, and a half-guinea. Beside him was Herman Schmidt, his cheeks aglow with pre-Christmas drinking and offering his hand to each miner together with a guttural 'Merry Christmas!' But even at this time of goodwill he was not able to hide his contempt for the men under his control. It had been his intention to work the men until midnight, but there was not a miner in Cornwall who would remain underground after dark on Christmas Eve. This was the night when strange things happened in a mine; when mysterious lights cast their glow in the deepest and most remote tunnels and Christmas hymns might be heard, sung by choirs who had no place in the world of humans. The miners put the strange happenings down to the 'knockers', the little men who lived unseen beneath the ground and whose mining activities had frightened generations of mining men who had given these underground 'piskies' their descriptive name. But whoever, or whatever, was responsible for these Christmas Eve happenings not a single miner could be found who would stay below grass when dusk began to fall over the moor. Some of the older miners even went so far as to take extra food on shift with them and leave it behind when they quitted the mine for the Christmas period.

But, once on the surface, the miners put the mine behind them and trudged off down the hill, the married men to their homes and the excitement of Christmas, the remainder to the equally cheerful but less inhibited pleasures of the inns.

Ben Retallick had his meal and then went off to help Wrightwick Roberts prepare the chapel, leaving Josh and Jenny to decorate the house while Jesse prepared the food for the one day in the year when the menu was not controlled by economy. The large jar on the kitchen mantelshelf was the source of this annual bonus. Every week Jesse Retallick put a few pence into it, the amount dependent upon current commitments. This had been a particularly good year, Josh and Jenny adding their share. The young widow was now working at the Sharptor mine, sorting the ore with Josh. They had become very close of late, like brother and sister. It pleased Jesse Retallick. Josh was an only child and, although she and Ben had tried not to spoil him, he had received far more attention than was usual in that age and place. It was partly due to Sharptor's isolation. Up there on the slope there was nobody of his own age, apart from the Tragos. Jesse tried to make up for it by interesting herself in what he was doing. This isolation had made Josh used to doing things on his own and helped him to develop the love he had for the high lonely moor where he was so much at home.

This too was why Jesse had not discouraged Josh's friendship with Miriam, despite her grave misgivings about the wisdom of Josh becoming involved with any member of that unconventional family. They were wild and unpredictable like the tough shaggy cattle that roamed the moor with no control and scant regard for the boundaries that were set up for them. But she had invited the Trago girl to spend Christmas with them in order that she might start the new year with a better knowledge of her. Then she would decide whether the friendship should continue.

All this was going through Jesse's mind as she mixed pastry and rattled steaming pots on the kitchen range.

'There, now!' said Jenny, stepping back to admire the ivy that she had draped around the window-frame. 'Do you think that will please your sweetheart, Josh?'

He went red. 'She's just a friend, that's all.'

'Of course she is.' Her eyes twinkled and Jenny looked happier than Josh had seen her for many months. 'That's all Budge and I claimed we were. Right up to the day we married we were just "friends"!'

She laughed at his discomfiture. 'Don't worry, Josh. I won't make your cheeks go red tomorrow. Not in front of Miriam. Mind, I've found some kissing-berry for over the door. You'd best use it when Miriam comes into the house. It's the custom. We'll not have you breaking it.'

'It's a stupid custom!'

'No!' said Jenny firmly. 'Girls put great store by such things. You want Miriam to have as good a Christmas as any other maid, don't you? Never mind, you've got a few years to learn about what Miriam likes. Come on, let's go and try one of your ma's mince pies. If we stay here your face will set fire to my decorations.'

Christmas Day dawned damp and grey, with low cloud looking in at the windows of the cottage. Josh rose before first light to begin building up the fire in readiness for the day. Usually this was the time when the presents would be opened, but today they were waiting until Miriam arrived.

His mother was next downstairs. Then his father and finally Jenny, carrying the baby. Everyone was made to walk around the room with her so as not to miss the baby's reaction to the decorations. Gwen was fascinated most by the huge candle which Jesse had lit when she got up. It would burn until the last of the family went to bed that night.

'I hope Miriam won't be too late,' said Jesse Retallick as she began to fry breakfast on the kitchen range. 'I can't wait to see the baby's face when she opens her presents.'

Josh walked to the window and caught a glimpse of colour out in the grey mist. 'Here's Miriam,' he cried and went to the door. He opened it and stepped outside expecting to see her coming down the path. But he could see nothing. Puzzled, he walked out to the gate and once again caught the glimpse of colour that he knew was her best dress.

'Miriam!' As he scrambled up the slope from the path she came out from behind the gorse-thicket where she had been hiding.

'What are you doing up here? We have been waiting for you. We can't open any presents until you're there. Come on! The baby's busting to get started.'

Miriam shrugged her shoulders. 'You didn't tell me what time to come. I haven't seen you for a couple of days. I thought your mum might have forgotten she invited me. Or your dad might have said I couldn't come.'

'What would he say that for? Hurry up! Everyone's waiting.'

'Just a minute.' Miriam bent down behind the bush and picked up a small pile of badly wrapped parcels.

'What are they?'

Miriam hugged the packages close to her and her chin went up. 'They're presents. Everyone gives presents at Christmas.' She did not add that it was a custom unknown in the Trago household. She had gone to a great deal of trouble to ask questions of everyone with whom she could claim the slightest acquaintance in order to find out what went on in more orthodox houses at Christmas-time.

'What have you got for me?'

'Wait and see.'

Now that she was quite sure that she was going to spend Christmas in a house with people who celebrated it in a way she had only heard about, Miriam allowed some of her excitement to shake itself loose.

Only her mother knew that she would be spending the day

with the Retallicks, and the secret was safe with her. Miriam was up and dressed long before dawn to go to her hillside hideout where she had concealed the presents. Since then she had been waiting in the bushes near the cottage, willing Josh to come out and look for her, shivering with cold and anticipation.

Jesse stood in the cottage doorway watching Miriam coming along the path with Josh, and she understood far more of the girl's feelings than Miriam realised or would have been happy to have her know.

As they approached his mother Josh could see the uncertainty begin in Miriam's face and he touched her elbow gently. 'It's all right,' he whispered. 'They are all waiting for you.'

It was doubtful whether his reassurance did anything to make her feel more at ease. But Jesse Retallick's first words jolted her to an immediate halt.

'Stop there and don't come inside!'

Josh was as startled as Miriam.

'It's bad luck to have anyone enter the house with bare feet at Christmas,' said Jesse. She had been straight-faced until now, but seeing Miriam's dismay she smiled. 'So we'll just have to do something about that. Here, child, open this.' Reaching behind her she picked up a parcel from a chair just inside the doorway and handed it to Miriam. 'A very happy Christmas to you, Miriam.'

'Well, don't just stand there gawking like a loon,' she said to Josh. 'Take her parcels from her while she looks at her present.'

Speechless, Josh did as he was told while Miriam undid the ribbons on her present and carefully opened out the wrappings.

Inside was a pair of shiny black shoes, made in soft leather.

Miriam's eyes said everything. 'Thank you! Thank you, Mrs Retallick.'

Jesse sniffed. 'Well, put them on, then – and be sure they fit. It's time we went in to breakfast.'

Hurriedly Miriam placed the shoes on the ground, slipped

her feet into them. They were a good fit, and Jesse nodded her head in satisfaction. 'I didn't think they would be far out,' she said. 'And they are made of soft leather so as not to hurt your feet.'

'They're beautiful,' said Miriam happily, trying not to walk awkwardly in them.

'Come on in and have some breakfast, child, before we let all the warm air out of the house.'

As Miriam crossed the step, Jesse squeezed an arm about her shoulders. 'It's nice to have you with us for the day, Miriam.'

'Don't let her pass under that kissing-berry until Josh has done his duty,' Jenny called from the kitchen.

'I'd almost forgotten that!' exclaimed Jesse. 'Come on now, young man. Miriam is your guest. You'll do the proper thing or there will be no Christmas presents for you.'

With flaming cheeks, aware of the grinning faces of his father and Jenny, Josh gave Miriam a quick peck on her cheek.

'That wasn't much of a kiss,' said his mother, 'but I suppose it will have to do for now.'

From the kitchen doorway Jenny let out a loud groan. 'The young men of today aren't what they used to be, and that's a fact. If Budge had kissed me like that I'd have wanted to know what I'd done wrong.'

Miriam smiled happily at Josh as she was ushered into the kitchen for breakfast. The initial awkwardness had been broken through and Miriam had been made to feel completely at home.

Her appetite was astonishing. She cleared her plate of a meal that would have set a miner up for the day, and then she accepted the offer of a second helping.

Immediately after breakfast they all adjourned to the best room and it was time for the presents to be opened. The baby provided the centre of attraction, but to her young mind an empty box was equally as interesting as the coat it had contained.

Miriam had some anxious moments when each of the

presents she had bought was opened, fearing that it might not be acceptable. There was a leather purse with a picture of Launceston Castle embossed on it for Mrs Retallick, and Jesse was clearly delighted with it. The gifts for Josh's father, Jenny and the baby were equally well received. For Josh there was a neckerchief in bright colours.

'You shouldn't have spent so much money on such things,' said Jesse Retallick. 'I'm sure you work hard enough for it.'

Miriam kept her face averted from Josh, and he knew what had happened to the remainder of Herman Schmidt's guinea.

Presents were exchanged all round and Miriam received more small gifts from the rest of the family. Then Josh brought out his present for her, and Miriam knew by the way the others lapsed into silence that it was something special. When she held it in her hands she thought it felt like a book – a thick book.

It was. When the wrappings were taken off she held a beautiful leather-bound Bible in her hands. 'Thank you, Josh,' sounded totally inadequate but it was all she was able to say.

'Josh said you were learning to read. We thought it would be a sensible and useful present,' said Jesse.

'You won't find better reading than is in there,' said Ben seriously. 'Everything you will ever need to know about life is in that book.'

Miriam opened the cover. Inside was written, 'To Miriam Trago from Josh Retallick,' and it pleased her almost as much as the Bible itself.

'Talking about the good book . . . It's time to be thinking of chapel,' said Ben Retallick, rising to his feet. There was general movement in the room and Miriam felt uncertain about what was expected of her, but Jesse came to her rescue.

'We'll let them go off to the chapel,' she said. 'You can help me with the Christmas dinner.' To the others she said, 'And don't you let that Wrightwick Roberts ramble on until everyone in the chapel has a spoiled meal waiting for him at home. There will be nothing here for him to eat tonight if he does.'

Wrightwick Roberts considered it his duty to visit those of his parishioners who were either sick or too old to come to chapel, but his evening meal was something he shared with the Retallick family.

Those who were going to chapel were soon ready and as they went down the hill Josh turned to wave to his mother and Miriam who were standing in the doorway.

He knew that his mother had arranged things this way. By the time he and the others returned from chapel she would have thoroughly assessed Miriam's character. The thought of it kept him fidgeting all through a service which seemed to go on for ever. Actually it was hardly any longer than the regular Sunday service. Preacher Robert's sermons were notorious for lasting overlong but he had a lot ahead of him today.

Then, with the service over, it was as though everyone in the village wanted to say 'Merry Christmas' to Ben Retallick and Tom Shovell.

Jenny grinned at Josh's impatience. 'For a shy and backward lad you're a mite eager to be back with your girlfriend.'

He scowled and said nothing.

'Don't worry, Josh. Miriam and your mum will get on well. Jesse's bound to take to her. You'd go a long way to find a girl like Miriam around here.'

Ben Retallick and Tom Shovell said their last 'Happy Christmas!' and they made their way up the track into the low damp cloud that still hung around the tor.

'You're just in time,' said Jesse Retallick as they stamped on the mat and filed into the house. She was smiling, and the whole atmosphere in the house was evidence that whatever Jesse had been looking for in their guest she had found. Now there was one Trago who would find a welcome in the Retallick household.

The meal that Jesse served up was gigantic, with the stuffed goose as the centre-piece. Even Miriam had to admit defeat. Afterwards they sat around talking and playing word- and guessing-games – except for Ben Retallick, who sat in his chair by the fire snoring gently for most of the afternoon.

Wrightwick Roberts arrived in the early evening, stamping

his feet on the doormat like some great wagon-horse. His eyebrows were raised at the sight of Miriam Trago, but he made a point of singling her out for special attention later when they had eaten yet again and were gathered around the roaring fire to sing hymns. Miriam had never been to chapel but she knew snatches of the hymns and was quick to pick up a tune. The words she read from Preacher Robert's hymn-book.

'You sing like a lark, girl,' said Wrightwick Roberts. 'A voice like that should be singing the praises of the Lord every Sunday. You come to chapel and there's not a girl in the village but wouldn't envy you and wish she could sing half as sweetly.'

Miriam was glad he did not persist in his talk about her going to chapel; she would have found that difficult to keep from her father for very long.

All too soon Jesse and Jenny began yawning, the preacher and Tom Shovell put on their coats and went out into the night and it was time for Miriam to go home. Christmas Day did not have many minutes to run but it was probably the happiest day she had ever spent and she had been half-hoping that a miracle would come along to make it last for ever.

Before she left, Jesse Retallick hurried into the kitchen and came back with a basket laden with food which she had handed to Josh. 'Here, you carry this up the hill for Miriam. There's heaps of food left. It's a shame to see it go to waste.'

At the door Miriam's reluctance to leave was so apparent that Jesse's heart went out to her and she hugged her in a way that left nobody in doubt as to her feelings about her.

'I'm sorry you have to go, my dear. It's been lovely having you. Mind you come here often to see us. I shall be very hurt if you don't.'

Miriam kissed her impulsively and with everyone's 'Good night' ringing in her ears she set off with Josh into the darkness.

Once out of the light of the cottage she took Josh's arm and hugged it to her. 'Oh, Josh! It's been such a wonderful day! The best in my whole life!'

'Mum liked you a lot,' he said, his teeth showing white in the darkness.

'You really think so? She was wonderful to me.' Still holding his arm, she gave a happy skip. 'She promised to teach me to cook properly. On a stove.'

'Haven't you got a stove at home?'

'No.' She stopped skipping, and some of the happiness escaped from her. 'There are lots of things we haven't got at home.'

They walked on in silence for a while. Then she stopped. 'I'll take the basket now.'

'It's all right. I'll carry it all the way for you. It's heavy.'

'No. My dad or Morwen might not be asleep. I'll go the rest of the way on my own now.'

'What's the matter, Miriam? Have I said something to make you unhappy?'

'No, it's nothing anyone's said to me. It's been such a happy day. Too happy. Nothing will ever be quite the same again. Now I'll have to go back to doing all the same things as always.'

'You can come down to the cottage now, though. Whenever you like. Mum said she would be hurt if you didn't come. She meant it.'

'I know. I'm grateful to her for that. Good night for now, Josh.'

She leaned forward and kissed him hard on the lips. Then she was gone into the darkness.

He stood there for a full minute, until there was no sound but the wind blowing down from the rocky tor, then he turned and went home.

Miriam pushed the make-shift door aside stealthily and eased her way into the damp interior of her home. The sour smell of exhaled alcohol fumes greeted her. Noisy snores came from the corner where Moses lay. They were echoed from Morwen's bunk in another corner. Now he was working full time he was doing his best to drink like a man.

'That you, Miriam?' her mother whispered from the gloom.

'Yes.'

'Did you have a nice day?'

'Yes.'

'That's good, but don't tell your father where you've been. He brought a bottle home and was shouting for you to come and have a Christmas drink with him. He got into quite a temper because you weren't here.'

Miriam said nothing.

'You hear me?'

'Yes.'

'Well, just remember it or we'll all suffer. Good night now.'

'Good night, Ma.'

Miriam pushed the basket behind her rough mattress and undressed slowly. Then, sliding between her blankets, she lay on her back, eyes wide open for a few minutes before turning suddenly to bury her head in the straw pillow.

Chapter Seven

Christmas with the Retallicks was supposed to have been a secret, but Miriam was not clever enough to keep it away from the remainder of the Trago family for long and she suffered cruelly when Moses Trago found out.

It was Kate Trago who brought the news to the Retallicks. She knocked on the door of the cottage on New Year's Eve at the height of a rainstorm. Even then she would not have come beyond the doorstep had not Jesse dragged her inside.

'I'm not standing out there to catch my death of cold for anyone,' she said. 'If you've something to say, then for goodness' sake say it inside. Now, sit down by the fire and get warm. I'll give you a cup of broth. It will take the chill from your insides.'

She ladled out a mugful of steaming brown soup from the pot on the fire, brushing aside Kate Trago's protests. 'Get it down and stop arguing. You look as though you have need of it. Right, what's this about Miriam?'

'I – I was hoping she would be here.'

'Well, she isn't. What's happened?'

Josh was studying in the best room. Hearing voices he came through to the kitchen and was taken aback to see who it was.

Kate Trago gulped down a mouthful of soup. It was very hot and set her coughing.

When the fit passed, she said, 'It was Moses. He found out she had spent Christmas in this house and there was a terrible scene.'

'Oh! And who told him she was here?'

'He found the shoes you gave her. I tried to stop her saying anything about them, but she was too worked up to listen. All she kept doing was shouting at him to give them back to her. Then it came out. She said she'd spent Christmas Day here. It was the best day of her life, she told him. Said that your Ben had got a proper house for his family. And . . . but, oh! she said so many things. The more he laid into her the more she shouted defiance at him.'

Jesse listened as though it was herself taking the blows. Josh's face had gone the colour of chalk.

'Did he beat her bad?'

'I don't know!' Kate Trago was close to tears. 'I was screaming at him to stop, but when I tried to pull him away he knocked me down.' She paused and looked from one to the other. 'If it hadn't been for our Morwen I think Moses would have killed her.'

'Morwen stopped his father?' Jesse knew the boy was big for his age. Even so, he was no match for Moses.

'Yes.' Kate Trago's hand began to tremble so violently that she had to hold the cup in her lap with both hands to prevent the contents from spilling. 'He took a pick-handle to him. While they fought, Miriam was able to get out. I haven't seen her since.'

The whole thing was beyond Jesse's understanding. 'When did this happen?'

Kate Trago looked shamefaced, 'Night before last.'

'*What!* And you haven't looked for her before this? The poor girl could be dying somewhere.'

'I know – but I was so sure that she would be here.' Her voice broke and the trembling got so out of hand that Jesse had to rescue the cup of soup.

'Josh, have you seen Miriam?'

'No.' It was quite true. She had not met him for two nights; but, although not usual, it had sometimes happened before.

She would find some animal to watch by moonlight, or even have to work late at the Phoenix mine. 'But I think I know where to find her.'

He was already putting on his boots.

'Don't forget your coat. It's bitter out there.'

Kate Trago stood up.

'You're not going before you've seen whether Josh finds Miriam?'

'I must. I've left the younger ones alone up there. Take care of her – and tell her it's all right to come home. Moses won't touch her again. He's sorry for what he did. He wouldn't say it to anyone, but I know it. He's a hard man, Mrs Retallick, but there's some good in him still and he loves that girl.'

'We won't argue about that now.' Jesse's lips drew into a tight line, relaxing only to call to Josh, 'Go careful. We don't want anything happening to you.'

Josh banged out of the house and into the night. It was bitterly cold and the wind bit at his ears. He crashed through the undergrowth, and now that he had time to think he dreaded what he might find at the hideout. He blamed himself for not going there before tonight. He should have known that Miriam would not have missed seeing him for two nights with his departure for the engineering works only a couple of weeks away.

He found the faint path that passed close to the hideout and followed it, relying on luck rather than sight, although a pale moon occasionally slid out of the heavy grey clouds.

At the entrance to the narrow gorse-tunnel he paused and listened. He thought he could hear a sound from within, but when he called softly there was no reply. Halfway along the tunnel he was sure of the sound and when he came into the hideout he recognised it for what it was. A cold chill went through him. It was shallow, rasping breathing. He had heard it once before, when Grandfather Retallick was fighting his last losing battle with death.

Josh fumbled on the rock with cold useless fingers for the candle. When he found it he had even greater difficulty in lighting it. But it finally lit and cast its flickering light across the shadows. To Josh's imaginative mind the candle-flame had more strength in it than Miriam's body. She was slumped in a corner, sheltered from the wind, with her back against the rock and her chin resting on her chest. It was this that was the cause of her bubbling breathing as much as anything else, but Josh did not know this.

He believed that she was dying, and the state of her face was sufficient justification for his belief. Her left eye was puffed up like an apple and he could not see whether it was open or closed. A bloody graze extended from the bridge of her nose back across her forehead, and the dark shadows on her face had nothing to do with the dancing candle-flame.

He dropped to one knee beside her and, putting one hand gently beneath her chin, he lifted her head.

Weakly she tried to jerk it away from him and the movement caused her to groan painfully.

'Miriam. It's me. Josh.'

He could see now that both her eyes were swollen and tight closed. She must have been lying here, completely blind, for two days and nights.

'Miriam! Can you hear? It's me. Josh.'

'I hurt! I hurt!' She whimpered.

'It's all right now. I'll get you out of here.'

'I hurt!' She subsided into silence again. Her chin fell forward on to her chest as Josh removed his hand.

Telling her that he would get her out was one thing. Carrying out his promise was something else.

When he tried to lift her to her feet he touched one of her ribs, low down on her chest, and it grated beneath his fingers. Miriam cried out in pain.

The next few minutes were a nightmare. In dragging her to the mouth of the hideout he knocked over the candle. Then by dragging, pushing and heaving in the darkness he finally succeeded in getting her out on to the moor. Doing his best to ignore her half-conscious protests and nerve-racking dry sobs he got her on to her feet. With her arm hooked about his shoulders he staggered downwards across the slope of the moor, heading in the general direction of the cottage. More than once he fell, taking Miriam with him. Each time he climbed back to his feet. Brushing the stinging gorse-needles from the palms of his hands, he would heave Miriam up again and struggle on. Sweat began to run down his backbone, making a liar of the weather.

Then, during a swaying pause for breath, he heard someone. More than one person. They were crashing through the undergrowth towards him. Thinking that it might be Moses Trago or one of his family, Josh lowered Miriam quietly to the ground. Trying to control his laboured breathing, he sank down beside her. Whoever it was began to move away. Up the slope to his left.

'It must have been Josh; it was too noisy for a pony.'

Josh recognised the voice of Tom Shovell and then his father's soft-voiced reply.

'Dad! Over here.'

Within seconds two heavy dark shapes loomed out of the darkness in front of him.

'What are you playing at? Have you found the girl?'

'Yes, but I thought you might be Moses. Be careful; she is hurt badly.'

'All right, Ben. Gently now. I have her.'

The big shift captain cradled Miriam in his arms as though she were a baby.

Ben Retallick's hand found his son's shoulder, 'Are you all right?'

'Yes. But you – you wait until you see her. Her face. . . .'

The grip tightened. 'Don't worry. She'll be looked after now. Well done, Josh.'

Josh gulped back the tears that threatened to well up in his eyes. Now that Miriam had been given into the care of more capable hands, his knees felt weak and shaky and the perspiration that had soaked into the back of his shirt lay across his shoulder-blades like ice.

When they entered the cottage they were greeted with gasps of horror from Jesse and Jenny. As Tom Shovell laid his burden down on the sofa the bruises on Miriam's face showed scarlet and purple in the light.

Ben Retallick sucked in his cheeks with anger, and the heavy breathing of the shift captain had nothing to do with the effort of carrying Miriam.

'I think she has a broken rib,' said Josh. 'Low down on the right side.'

'She'd best have a doctor see her,' declared Jesse. 'Tom, will you go out for one? Get the man from the Caradon. He's more likely to be sober than the Phoenix doctor. Ben, put pots of water to boiling. Jenny and I will get this mite to bed.'

She began unbuttoning the tattered cardigan that Miriam wore.

'And you can stop gawping!' This to Josh. 'You've done your bit. Now we've got our work to do. I'll be making up a bed in our room. You'll have to sleep downstairs until she's well. Unless I'm mistaken this one will be laid up for a couple of weeks.'

Jesse underestimated by a week. For the first four days the mine doctor from the Caradon group of mines was a daily visitor. He strapped up Miriam's ribs – two of them were broken – and worked on Miriam's face. He feared that her nose was also broken, but when the swelling around her eyes began to go down he was pleased to acknowledge that he had been wrong.

On the fifth day Miriam could see from one eye and progressed steadily thereafter. News of her beating swept through Henwood village like an east wind. There was a steady flow of visitors to the cottage door bringing gifts. They consisted mainly of cast-off clothing, the donors angling for an invitation inside to have a look at Miriam's battered face. Thanks to the firmness of Jesse Retallick few of them were successful. Yet all of them returned to the village with wild descriptions of the injuries she was supposed to have sustained.

Kate Trago was a frequent visitor. She always came after dark and would sit next to her daughter's bed saying scarcely a word and wringing her hands nervously the whole time.

But when Miriam was able to sit out of bed for an hour or so each day she received a visitor who caused great consternation in the Retallick house. He too came after dark, but the very fact that he knocked gently at the door and waited quietly for it to be opened was sufficiently unusual in itself.

Josh opened the door – and as promptly slammed it shut again. Turning to his father in alarm, he said, 'It's Moses.'

Ben Retallick leaped from his chair and Jesse reached for the heavy iron poker kept alongside the stove. Moses knocked again. It was not an impatient knocking, but neither was it timid.

Ben motioned for Josh to move further into the room before going to open the door himself.

Moses stood before him, his hat held in his two hands. 'I've come to take Miriam home.'

It was a bald matter-of-fact statement.

'Then you've had a wasted journey.' Ben Retallick controlled his anger admirably.

Jesse was less reticent as she moved up alongside her husband. 'You take one step into this house, Moses Trago, and you'll feel this poker across your head. That girl has suffered enough at your hands. You'll not get the chance to do it again.'

'I haven't come here to quarrel, Mrs Retallick. What has happened is done. It can't be forgotten, but it won't happen again.'

It was an effort for Moses to appear humble before anybody, but he managed it.

'It won't happen again because she stops here,' said Ben Retallick firmly. 'When she's well enough we'll discuss her future. Not before.'

'Ben, I came here tonight determined to keep my temper. What I did was wrong and I'm sorry. I could blame the drink but I'm not using that as an excuse. All the same, Miriam is my daughter and I want her home.'

The poker wagged at him like an accusing finger. 'You broke two of her ribs, did your best to disfigure her for life, then let her wander off on to the moor – to die, for all you knew. And you stand here and talk of wanting her? Moses Trago, you are a hypocrite. A big, bullying, lying hypocrite.'

Moses Trago fought hard to maintain control of himself and

the strain showed. Then a voice from the stairs made them all look in that direction.

'Mrs Retallick, please let him come in to speak to me.'

Miriam's face was still discoloured and she clung to the hand-rail unsteadily.

'What are you doing up? You shouldn't be out of bed.' The poker was lowered and Jesse went to her.

'Please! Please let him come in.'

A look passed between Jesse and Ben, then Ben stood back from the door. 'You can go upstairs to see her. But, father or not, she'll not leave this house until she's well.'

Moses Trago stepped inside, his shoulders filling the doorway. There was movement behind him and he said, 'Morwen and brother John are outside.'

'They can stay there,' said Jesse brusquely. 'You're coming in only because it will upset the girl more to have a scene, but you'll not stay long. She's still a sick girl and I'm not pretending that you are welcome in this house.'

Moses mumbled something that might or might not have been his thanks, then he went up the stairs, following Miriam in to the room where she slept.

Downstairs the only sound for a long time was the crackling of wood on the fire and the murmur of voices from the bedroom.

Suddenly Josh said fiercely, 'He's not taking her with him.'

'Don't go climbing hedges until they are built,' said Ben.

'But he said he's come for her.'

'And we said she isn't ready to go,' said Jesse firmly. 'Miriam isn't fit to go, and nobody is going to force her.'

They heard the bedroom door opening, and Moses Trago came clumping heavily down the stairs.

He stopped in the centre of the room and looked from one to the other, finally settling his gaze on Jenny.

'She says she'll be coming home when she's well,' he said. 'Until then I'd be obliged if you'd have her here. I'll pay for her keep.'

'You'll keep your money and your insults to yourself,' retorted Jesse. 'She'll stay because we want her.'

'I owe you for the doctor too,' Moses persisted doggedly. He slapped two coins on the table. 'Here are two guineas. That should pay for everything.'

Jesse was on her feet and had thrust one of the coins back at him before he could say more. 'We'll take one guinea for the doctor. You caused her injuries. There's no reason why anyone else should pay for that. Whatever else we have done has been because we are fond of the girl. We want none of your money for that.'

'I pay my debts.' Moses Trago flushed angrily. 'I'll be under no obligation to anyone.'

'You have a debt to the Lord,' said Ben Retallick. 'It was only His will that kept her alive until she was found.'

'Then give this other guinea to the boy. I hear he found her.'

Josh felt his heart pounding inside him as he stood up. 'I did that for Miriam. Not for your money. Buy her some new shoes with it to make up for those you burned.'

He felt his mother's eyes on him. Kate Trago had not told her that during the fight in the Trago home Moses had thrown Miriam's shoes on to the fire in his rage. Miriam had told Josh and been more upset about it than she was for her injuries.

'You've got spirit but no money-sense,' said Moses looking at him from beneath shaggy brows. 'I've already promised Miriam some new shoes. I've also told her she can have schooling from that preacher at St Cleer. I don't like the Trago family being under obligation to anyone for anything. I've said what I came for. When Miriam is well enough to come home her mother and Morwen will come for her. Good night, Mrs Retallick. Ben. Boy.'

His look passed on to Jenny. He nodded, then turned and was gone.

'The cheek of the man!' Jesse all but exploded. 'Of all the nerve . . . !'

'Hush, now,' said Ben. 'Moses Trago cannot change what he is. Keeping his temper tonight cost him much. Give him credit for that.'

In the middle of their conversation Josh went upstairs to

find out from Miriam what had been said by her to gain such concessions from her father.

Jenny Pearn said nothing. Something in Moses Trago's eyes when he looked at her had frightened her. Tonight he had been reasonable enough. He was certainly more sober than she had ever seen him before – but there was an evilness about him that went much deeper than drunkenness. It was an animal brutality – and yet still something more. With a shiver, Jenny arrived at the conclusion that Moses Trago was close to madness and she feared what this might bring to all of them.

Chapter Eight

Miriam left the cottage and returned to the Trago home one week before Josh was due to begin his apprenticeship at Hayle. Both departures hit Jesse Retallick hard. She had become very fond of the girl. Her quick wit and an ever-ready willingness to listen and learn something new endeared her to the whole household. Even baby Gwen was always pleased to go to her.

It was like losing one of the family to watch her walking away up the hill with Morwen Trago beside her. Her brother felt awkward and was impatient at having to stop and wait each time she turned round to wave.

Then, with Miriam out of the house, it was time to pack and repack, stitch and iron, and generally prepare Josh for a stay in a town which, although hardly fifty miles distant, was as remote as the Highlands of Scotland to Jesse.

Josh himself put off thinking about it until the very last minute. He had finished his schooling with the Reverend William Thackeray, and as a parting gift the preacher had given him an old wood-and-leather chest to carry his belongings. He had also given him some words of advice.

They stood in the chill evening wind outside the little house behind the chapel where the bachelor preacher lived.

'You will be carrying my best wishes with you, Josh. But,

what is far more important, you will be looked to as an example of what education can do for every miner's son. You'll become a symbol of escape for every boy who longs for more from life than a daily shift in a mine. Don't let us down, Josh.'

They walked along the path to the gate and Preacher Thackeray opened it, pausing to look intently at Josh.

'While you're away you'll be learning new things and meeting new people. Never let them make you forget where you come from or the men who remain here – working and dying in wretched conditions. Always keep them in mind. If during the course of your apprenticeship you hear of something that might make life easier for them, then follow it up. Work hard at whatever you do. If you hear anyone at Hayle talking about a union of miners, listen to him. I would like to know the strength of feeling about it in the far west. Talk to the other apprentices, Josh. Find out about unions in other parts of the country. It's gained a strong foothold in some parts and I'm convinced that's where the future of the miner lies. With a strong union he could live a better and fuller life – that and brains like yours to seek ways to make his job safer. He would be able to take his place in the community, Josh, a proud man with a special skill, not some sort of animal to burrow in the ground all day and go home drunk to sire brats all night.'

He held out his hand. 'Goodbye and good luck, Josh. May God be with you.'

Josh made his way homewards filled with a resolve to work hard and justify the preacher's faith in him. He would also serve the miner in every way possible. It was a resolution that was to remain with him for a great many years.

His next farewell was with Miriam. Josh had not been looking forward to it. He had thought about it for a long time, imagining it as a parting that would be full of emotion. He could not have been more wrong. Miriam had caught a nasty cold in the few days that she had been home. It was this that was choking her, not emotion. The tip of her nose glowed like a blacksmith's iron, and she shivered and sniffled constantly as they stood together on the path between their two homes.

'I'll write and tell you all about Hayle and my journey as soon as I arrive,' declared Josh. He was travelling by sea from Looe harbour.

'And I'll write back straightaway,' Miriam said nasally.

'Well . . . I'll say goodbye, then.'

'Goodbye, Josh.' Her eyes were watering in the bitter wind. She shivered and felt thoroughly miserable as Josh held her briefly to kiss her goodbye. She turned her head from him and he kissed her cheek

'I don't want you to catch my cold to go away with.'

'No. Take care of yourself, Miriam.'

'And you, Josh. I shall miss you terribly.'

He realised that he was going to miss her more than anything else at Sharptor. He would have liked to tell her so but did not know how to begin. When he looked at her shivering he knew it would be cruel to keep her out in the cold until he found the right words. He turned and walked away. Looking back once he saw her standing on the path, a teeth-chattering little figure who waved bravely through tears and cold until he was out of sight.

That left only his family the following morning. Jesse fussed about him, tucking in his scarf and pulling up his collar as he sat on the driving-seat of the ore-wagon beside Nehemeziah Lancellis.

'You be good, mind. No fighting with the others – and write often.'

'Yes, Mum.'

The aged hostler flicked the reins and the wagon creaked away. Josh waved until the huddled group of his mother and father, Jenny and the baby, Tom Shovell and Miriam disappeared from view around a curve in the track. Miriam had been unable to let him go without seeing him once more, in spite of her cold.

As Josh had never before been away from home for more than one night he set off on the journey to Hayle with very mixed feelings. He and Nehemeziah were on the first wagon of the day to leave the mine for Moorswater. This was the inland terminal of the canal linking the mining area with the seaport of Looe.

As they bumped along he looked at the driver, huddled into his heavy coat beside him, but the strange old hostler had eyes only for the great steaming horses. Josh took advantage of the silence to collect his thoughts.

The silence lasted for almost two hours and then Nehemeziah cleared his throat noisily, spat over the side of the wagon and said, 'There be the canal, down the hill apiece. 'Tis a fair busy place.'

At the water's edge Josh could see pack-horses and wagons lining up to be weighed before discharging their loads into the long, blunt-nosed barges.

As they pulled into line behind another wagon Nehemeziah called to a little man seated on the leading barge with his arms folded across the stout tiller. 'There's someone to ride with 'ee today, Tom.'

'Oh? And who says so?' scowled the man past his pipe.

''Tis Ben Retallick's boy,' said the hostler. 'Going down to Hayle foundry on the *Helen and Stephen* from Looe.'

'Well, why didn't you say so in the first place?' The man on the barge stood up awkwardly. 'Any member of Ben Retallick's family is welcome to anything that Tom Taylor can do for 'em. Come aboard, son. We'll be away in a few minutes.'

Fascinated, Josh looked at the man's right leg. It was a wooden peg from the knee down.

'Ah! You can look at it, young man. If it wasn't for your father I wouldn't be alive to wear a peg-leg. Heave your things aboard and sit down on this side. Watch the dust don't blow all over you when the last load is dropped aboard.'

Josh swung his trunk on to the barge and raised a hand in farewell to the Sharptor hostler. So began the second stage of his journey to Hayle. Ten minutes later the barge was under way. It was towed by a sorry-looking barge-horse which plodded along, head down, on the canal path.

'And how are things at Wheal Sharptor?' asked Tom Taylor as the barge slipped silently through the water.

'The mine is doing quite well,' replied Josh. 'They have hit good ore in the new south-east adit and won't need to go any deeper for a long time. When they do they will need an engine. That's why I'm off to Hayle. I'm going to become an engineer. But how do you know the mine? I've never seen you there.' The visit of a man with a wooden leg would certainly not have passed unnoticed.

'It was before you were old enough to know about it,' said the bargee. 'And I know it all right. That's where I lost this leg.' He banged his knuckles on the wooden limb. 'Carrying out the orders of that drunken German and using his gunpowder. It was when the mine first opened. We were cutting the twenty-fathom level. The roof came down on me. If your father hadn't been there to dig me out, I'd be buried there now for all that Captain Schmidt cared about it. If Theophilus Strike had any sense, he'd have made your father captain of Wheal Sharptor years ago. Ben should have left Strike and gone to the Phoenix years ago, when they wanted him as their captain.'

This was news to Josh. Nothing had ever been said in his hearing about his father having the opportunity to take charge of the great Phoenix mine.

'He stayed at Sharptor more to please your mother than anything else,' the bargee went on. 'But he'd never admit it. Jesse's always loved it up there. So she should; it's beautiful. I can remember how it would be on a fine day. You could look from your door and see every part of Cornwall that matters. Half of Devon as well. As I remember, you were no more than a year or two old then.'

He pulled on the tiller to take the barge out slightly from the bank. 'We had one of the cottages alongside yours. Tom Shovell has it now. We liked it there too, the missus and me. Of course, we had to go after the accident. A one-legged man is no good to Strike and his German captain. Not a penny did I get from him, although it was more than a year before I got this job. But I've always said it was leaving that cottage that killed my missus. She loved it there. Just like your mother.'

Josh murmured his sympathy, but the bargee was not

listening. 'Yes, beautiful it were up there in the summer-time. With the swifts nesting in the eaves of the cottage and the flowers all out in the garden. . . .'

He fell silent for a time and then said, 'Perhaps Ben knew what he was doing when he chose to stay at the Wheal Sharptor, after all.'

The barge eased gently into a lock, and for some minutes the ex-miner was busy casting a rope up to the lock-keeper and easing the boat through the narrow lock.

The whole process of locking fascinated Josh. He held tight to the barge when the gates at the lower end of the lock were opened, expecting the boat to be swept out like a leaf in a moorland stream. All that happened was that the barge settled down to the new level. The horse took the strain of the barge-rope and they moved slowly along the peaceful waterway towards their destination once more.

All the way to Looe the one-legged ex-miner regaled Josh with tales of the 'old days' at the Sharptor mine. Most of his yarns had to do with the sudden deaths that had occurred. As though trying to prove – as much to himself as to Josh – how lucky he was to be a live bargee, when he might so easily have been a dead miner.

Every so often his memory would dredge up a name and he would digress to talk about him. Most he dismissed scornfully as being fit only to grade the ore and not skilled enough to dig for it. A few – Ben Retallick and Moses Trago were two – he regarded as experts in the field of mining.

'How about Mary Crabbe – is she still alive?'

Josh assured him that she was.

'She's a witch, if ever I've seen one,' said Tom Taylor seriously. 'She's there for the birth of every child and the death of every man. Yes, she's a witch, lad. I've known her to arrive at a house ready to lay a body out at the minute he takes his last breath. She knows when it's time but it's no human voice that tells her.'

He caught Josh's expression. 'You don't believe me? Well, never mind, but just remember what I've told you. One day you will see for yourself. Calls the raven her brother, does Mary Crabbe.'

It was after noon when they tied up alongside the ore jetty at Looe. It was a busy and noisy part of the docks – and a very dirty one. There was ore dust on everything above ground and thick as mud underfoot. With the rattle of tackle and the creaking of the cranes it was not surprising that the fishermen of Looe had fought hard to have the canal elsewhere. It did little to improve their livelihood.

'You'll find the *Helen and Stephen* over the other side,' said the bargee. 'One of the fishermen will row you across. Don't give him more than a penny, though he'll ask for more. And, lad. . . .' He looked embarrassed. 'Be careful of Captain Henry of the *Helen and Stephen*. He's an evil man. I wish you were travelling to Hayle on any other boat.'

Josh had no idea what the bargee was trying to tell him but he thanked him and assured him that he would take care; then, struggling with his trunk, he set off along the busy jetty.

Before he had gone twenty yards a boy of about his own age, wearing an oversize ragged fisherman's jumper, appeared alongside. 'I'll carry your trunk for you for six pence.'

'You won't,' puffed Josh. 'I could hire a horse for that money.' He put the trunk down and took a breather.

'You're no sailor,' said the boy, looking at Josh's serge suit and heavy miner's boots. 'But you're not from around here.'

'From up on the moor. I'm taking passage on the *Helen and Stephen* to Hayle.'

'Then you'll be needing my boat,' said the boy, 'and as you're from these parts it will cost you no more than three pence.'

'It's not your lucky day,' grinned Josh. 'I've heard there is someone hereabouts who charges only a penny. I'll wait until I find him.'

The boy groaned. 'All right, a penny it is. Now, I'd better give you a hand with this trunk or it will take us half the day to get there and I'll lose all my good fares. I heard that folk from up on the moor sewed their pockets up before they came down to the towns.'

The boat was a small aged affair with three inches of water slopping inside it, but the boy handled the boat well and it was not long before they were bumping against some stone steps in the lee of the *Helen and Stephen*'s weathered stern.

She was much larger than Josh had imagined she would be, and when he stepped from the high quay on to the dirty rope- and tackle-tangled deck he was awed by the height of the masts. For all that, this was an ore-carrying boat. A pack-horse of the coastal waters. There was nothing glamorous about her role or her appearance.

He had an ugly moment when, heeding the urgent shouts of one of the sailors, he ducked quickly as a cargo-jib swung inboard, missing his head by inches.

The dust rose in clouds from the ore that rumbled and thudded down the chutes into the hold and there was a choking pall hanging over the ship. The men on the deck were fully occupied with loading, and Josh felt at a loss, wondering to whom he should report his presence.

He was rescued by a small balding man who appeared from out of nowhere and took Josh's arm, propelling him towards the stern of the boat while he dragged the trunk behind him with his other hand.

'Come on in here, boyo,' he said in a sing-song voice, guiding Josh through a door. 'You'll find a ladder along there a little way. Go down it and yours is the cabin on the right.'

'How do you know—?' Josh began, but the other man broke in, 'How do I know you are Master Retallick? That's easy, my lad. First, you come on board with your trunk and stand in a place where you are likely to have your head knocked off by the loading-jib. That means you are no sailor. So you must be a passenger – right?'

Josh nodded as the man pointed to a ladder, 'Go down there. Now, secondly, a passenger is something of a novelty on board this scow. So you must be Retallick. Simple when you fit all the facts together, you see.'

He pushed a door open and heaved the trunk into a space that was scarcely six feet square. 'Here you are, now. Not up to the accommodation I've known on East India Company ships. But it's a bed, boyo. It's a bed!'

He gave Josh a lop-sided grin. 'I'm Taffy Williams. Steward, cook and Captain's whipping-boy. Like this leaking old ship I've known better days, but we both keep going. You make yourself at home. I'll let the Captain know that you're aboard.' His face took on a serious expression. 'That's if he hasn't been drinking. . . .'

He gave Josh a thoughtful look. 'I think it might be better if you stay in your cabin as much as possible while you're aboard. I'll bring your meals down to you. There's too much work going on up top at the moment, anyway. The Mate won't want you wandering around.'

Everything was bewilderingly strange to Josh and, although he did not relish the thought of being confined to the cell-like cabin for the whole of the journey, he did not argue. Instead, he asked when the ship would be putting to sea.

'Everyone is working in order to catch tonight's tide,' replied the steward. 'But a lot depends on whether the wind holds its direction. If it moves any further to westward we'll be obliged to stay here for a while longer. Now, you just unpack the things you're going to need for today and tomorrow. With a good wind we might make Hayle tomorrow night, but I've known us to battle it out for a week or more – then end up closer to Ireland than to Cornwall.'

When the little Welshman had left Josh sat down on the edge of the narrow bunk and looked about him. There was little to see. A bed, a stool and table, all securely fastened to the floor, and a cupboard. It was as spartan as a hermit's cell. There was not even a port-hole to look through.

When the Welsh steward returned to the cabin Josh was lying on the bunk, reading.

'A young man of learning, I see!' The steward chattered as he transferred steaming dishes from the tray to the table. 'How I envy you. You young men today have opportunities that were never around when I was a boy.' The last plate on the table, he said, 'Sit yourself down here and get some of this food inside you. Good solid food it is. I cooked it myself. Especially for you.'

He fussed around as Josh seated himself and began to fork the food to his mouth. The steward was right. It was good.

'No, when I was a boy, schooling was beyond the reach of the likes of me. And of course there was a war to be fought then. That made things very different indeed.'

'Were you in the war?' Josh looked at the steward with new interest.

'Was I in the war? Why, bless you, boy, I was not ten feet from Admiral Nelson himself when he fell dying. Oh yes, and many's the cup of gruel I've taken up to him at night when he paced the quarter-deck while we chased the Frenchie Admiral halfway round the world. "Taffy," he said to me many a time, "Taffy, if it wasn't for you making sure I had me victuals I'd forget for sure and one day I would collapse and die. Then England would be lost." Ah. Those were glorious days, young Master Retallick. England will never see the like of Admiral Nelson again. There wasn't a dry eye in the Fleet when the news of his death got around.'

Josh was suitably impressed.

'There's plenty I could tell you about the war. But it would take longer than you'll have aboard this lump of driftwood.'

Then, although the door of the cabin was closed and there was no chance that anyone could see them, Taffy Williams looked over his shoulder furtively before pulling a bottle from his pocket and pouring some of its contents into a mug on the table in front of Josh. 'Here, have a drink of this. It's as good a rum as you'll get anywhere. Captain Henry keeps it hidden in his cabin.'

The fumes rising from the mug that Taffy Williams held up to his face caused Josh to jerk his head back hurriedly. 'No, thank you. I haven't drunk rum before.'

'You haven't drunk—? No man ever refuses good rum when he's on board a ship! You get it down you. It stops you from getting the scurvy. Necessary at sea, is rum.'

Josh had never heard of scurvy, but it had an ominous ring to it so he obeyed the steward and lifted the mug to his mouth. Doing his best to ignore the pungent fumes, he took a mouthful and swallowed. The liquid hit the back of his throat and there was a brief period of shock as the rum cut off the supply of air to his lungs. Then the blood rushed to his face and Josh choked and gagged and coughed all at the same time.

It was an incredible performance. As Taffy Williams pummelled his back the steward sounded satisfied. 'There, I told you it was some good stuff, didn't I, now?'

Eventually the fit subsided and Josh was able to wipe the tears from his eyes.

'I think you are trying to poison me,' he croaked.

'Now, there's a thing to say. The lop-sided grin was there again. 'I bring you a drop of the Captain's best rum – at great risk to myself – and you say that. Never mind, boyo. You get the rest of it down and it will keep the bad weather outside of you.'

Josh tried another sip. This time it did not choke him. It burned a fiery trail down his gullet, and he gulped air like a fish.

'That's better,' said the steward. 'We'll make a sailor of you yet. Mind you. . . .' He looked quizzically at the heavy miner's boots Josh was wearing. 'We'd better keep you below. If ever you went over the side wearing those on your feet you would sink like the ship's anchor.' He winked cheerfully at Josh and was gone, the cabin door closing softly behind him.

Josh decided he liked the little Welsh steward and his cheerful breezy manner.

Whether it was the rum or the excitement of the day Josh never knew, but he lay down on his bunk intending to read his book and it was not many minutes before his eyelids drew together and he fell into a deep sleep.

He awoke to an unaccustomed sense of movement, and sitting up he became aware of the creaking of timbers all about him. He swung his feet to the floor and stood up, only to crash against the opposite wall. Then, seconds later, he was tumbled backwards on to his bunk again.

They were at sea, and it was not a comfortable feeling!

Josh rose to his feet once more, only to be flung back immediately.

At the third attempt he clung first to the edge of the bunk and then grasped a stanchion before making it to the door. Twice he opened it, and twice it swung back on to his fingers. Then he lurched out into the passageway and, advancing hand over hand along the rail running the length of the narrow unlit corridor, he arrived at the ladder. Here he could feel the cold air coming down to meet him. At that moment a small figure clattered down the ladder and collided with him.

'Is that you, young Master Retallick?'

'Yes.'

The single word came out distorted, first drawn out as the deck dropped beneath him, and then clipped off as the ship rose as suddenly, compressing his stomach.

'I think I'm going to be sick.'

'I'm not surprised; the wind's a bit fresh. Come up here with me. No, you go first.'

The steward supported him up the ladder, holding him when the ship's antics threatened to throw him back into the corridor.

On deck there was a sharp cold wind, and spray stung Josh's face and tasted salty on his lips.

'Let me tie this around your waist.'

The steward passed a rope about Josh, fastening the other end to something at the top of the ladder. He was not a moment too soon. The ship heeled heavily to one side, Josh's feet shot from under him and he skidded down to the side of the ship to be brought up with a sudden jerk within inches of the sea that surged past below the guard-rail.

'What did I tell you about those boots?' Chuckling, Taffy Williams began pulling him in like a fish on a line, but before he had brought in his 'catch' Josh pulled away from him and, lunging as far the rope would allow, fell to his knees and threw up in the direction of the sea.

Three times he was sick. Then, trembling, he scrambled back to the top of the ladder and sat down groggily.

'You'll be all right now.' The steward's hand gripped his shoulder comfortingly.

'Is it going to be like this all the way to Hayle?' The words came out in rhythm with the ship's movements.

'Bless you, no!' Taffy Williams exclaimed. 'We are beating into a beam sea at the moment. Once we get past St George's Island and clear the Ranneys we'll be turning down-channel with the sea behind us. You won't know we're moving then.'

Secretly Josh doubted whether he would survive long enough to prove the truth of the steward's statement. But after he had suffered another rasping bout of sea-sickness the ship heeled over and lay at an acute angle for some minutes, then straightened up and was heading down-channel. Although it was by no means a smooth passage, the ship had lost most of the see-saw cork-screw movement and life was much more comfortable. Now Josh could hear the voices of unseen sailors raised above the wail of the wind in the rigging.

'Now, you come down below again and get into a warm bed. I promise you that by morning the wind will have dropped and you'll wish that you could spend all your life at sea.'

Josh felt too weak to argue and allowed himself to be led below. Getting into the bunk he did his best to ignore the motion of the ship, although it was emphasised by the flickering oil-lamp which hung from a beam above him and obeyed the law of gravity, while the ship danced around it.

But Taffy Williams had been telling the truth. When he bustled into the cabin the next morning carrying a bowl of steaming porridge, with two boiled eggs rattling together in a dish, the ship was gliding along steadily. There was only a gentle rocking movement to show that they were still at sea. The events of the previous evening could all have been part of an unpleasant dream.

Not only that, but Josh also discovered he had an appetite and the porridge smelled good.

'Where are we?' he asked as he swung his legs to the ground. 'Are we close to Hayle?'

'Why? Are you in a hurry to get there?' queried the steward.

'Because, if you are, you've chosen the wrong means of transport. A horse would have been quicker. No, boyo, you can't hurry the wind. It blew even stronger for a while after you had turned in and we had to go with it. We were almost at the Scillies before it died down and we were able to turn. We're heading for Hayle now but it will be after midday before we sight Cornwall, I shouldn't wonder. The wind must have blown itself right out. There's scarce enough now to float a feather on. But when you've finished your breakfast I'll take you up to see for yourself.'

He was as good as his word, and when Josh had eaten and washed in the hot water the steward left outside the door Taffy Williams came down for him.

'When I take you on deck we'll go for'ard. Beyond the cargo-holds. Then even if the Captain goes on to the quarter-deck he won't see you.'

'Why shouldn't the Captain see me? He knows I'm aboard, and Mr Strike paid my fare. There's no reason why he can't meet me.'

Taffy Williams avoided meeting Josh's eyes. 'Captain Henry is a strange man,' he replied. 'I've served in this ship a few years and I know. Just take my word for it and keep clear of him. Things will be better that way.'

Josh shrugged. His curiosity had been aroused by the way everyone spoke of the mysterious Captain Henry. But he would not be on the ship for very long and, if he did not meet him, it would not bother him. He followed Taffy Williams up on to the deck without saying any more.

Halfway along the main deck Josh was straining his neck to look up at the men working on the yard-arms when there was a loud bellow from behind them.

'Steward! What the hell are you doing? Come here!'

Josh looked behind and saw a stocky black-bearded man standing straddle-legged on a small raised deck beside the helmsman.

'I'm just attending to the passenger, sir. I'll see him for'ard and be with you right away.'

'You'll come when you are damn well called, mister –

and bring the passenger with you. He's entitled to meet the man who is responsible for his well-being and safety while he's aboard. It's common courtesy for a captain to greet his passengers. Come along. What's the matter with you?' he bellowed as the steward hesitated.

Reluctantly, Taffy Williams led Josh back along the deck towards the helmsman's position.

As they drew near Josh thought that Captain Henry was not at all the kind of man he had imagined the captain of a ship would be. His 'uniform' was a large blue sweater, frayed at the cuffs and with a hole in one elbow. It sagged low over a pair of dirty blue serge trousers. Most incongruous of all, the Captain wore soft carpet-slippers on his feet.

'I should think so!' Captain Henry rumbled as they approached him.

His hand was hot and clammy in Josh's and the dark-brown eyes that looked at him were red-rimmed. Above a dark beard, his cheeks were a skein of tiny blue and red veins.

'Now, there's a fine-looking lad,' said Captain Henry quietly. 'He should have been brought to me as soon as he came aboard, Williams.'

Josh wondered whether it was his imagination or if the Captain's words really did carry more menace than the shouting of a few minutes before.

'Well now, boy,' said Captain Henry. 'And how did you sleep last night? Was the weather too rough for you?'

'It was a bit,' admitted Josh. 'Is it often like that?'

'I wish it was,' said the Captain. 'That was little more than a good breeze. You don't get any bad storms around home waters. Down in the Antarctic, now, that's something different again. When I was down there whaling I saw waves as tall as one of your mine-chimneys. That's real weather for you.'

He broke off to glare at Taffy Williams. 'Come now, steward. Don't hang around here. You've got work to do.' Then, as the little Welshman turned to go, 'The boy will have his lunch with me in my cabin.'

Taffy Williams looked unhappy as he went away, but the

Captain turned back to Josh. 'Now, boy, is this your first time in a ship?'

Josh said that it was.

'Then we'd better show you what goes on.' He pointed to the horizon where a few low islands could be seen low down on the skyline.

'Over there you can see the Scillies. A dangerous place to sail close to. The further away they stay the happier any sailor will be.'

Captain Henry went on to tell Josh of the ships that had foundered on the Scilly Isles. When he had exhausted that subject, he talked of whaling in the Antarctic. He showed Josh how the compass worked and even allowed him to steer the vessel. It was not long before Josh was wondering why both Taffy Williams and the one-legged bargee had been so concerned about his meeting the captain of the *Helen and Stephen*. He was interesting and entertaining company.

It seemed no time at all before the ship's bell was clanging to announce midday.

'That's the signal for lunch,' said Captain Henry, clapping Josh on the shoulder. 'Come down to my cabin. We'll have a meal in surroundings more fitting to a fare-paying passenger than that hen-coop of a cabin you slept in last night.'

He led the way along the main deck and steered Josh into a short corridor. The corridor ended at a red mahogany door with a gleaming brass handle.

The Captain turned the handle and swung the door open, waving Josh inside. 'There you are, boy. You won't find a cabin to compare with this even on those new-fangled steamers that the big companies are playing with. It's a captain's cabin, as good as any on an Atlantic packet. When the sea is your home you have to make your own comfort. D'you like it?'

'Like' was a totally inadequate word. The cabin was more luxurious than anything Josh had ever seen. The walls were panelled in polished rosewood with gleaming brass lanterns spaced at intervals along three of them. The fourth 'wall' was completely taken up by a long narrow window. It must have been tucked tight beneath the stern of the *Helen and Stephen*.

There was a fine carpet on the floor, while the furniture, at first sight appearing sparse, was cleverly designed to blend into the cabin.

'You don't mind if I change before we eat?'

Without waiting for a reply the Captain walked to one of a series of cupboards cunningly built into one of the rosewood walls. He opened it to reveal a rail of clothes quite out of keeping with his present rough appearance and station in life. There were shirts and waistcoats of silk, breeches of fine linen and coats that a gentleman would have been proud to possess.

'Don't look so surprised, boy. You don't think I've always been skipper of a gash-boat like this, do you? No, I've been master of some of the finest ships ever to have voyaged to India. In those days no man was ashamed to say he'd been a guest at Captain Henry's table.'

'Then why are you on the *Helen and Stephen* now instead of in one of those ships?'

'Well you may ask,' said Captain Henry, pushing a silken shirt inside corduroy breeches. 'But it's a long tale and better left in the past.'

Josh had seen many men change their clothing at the mine. When they came up from a wet shaft most men would strip naked and towel off before putting on their home-going clothes. In the rough mine surroundings a naked man was a perfectly natural thing. Josh had scarcely thought about it before. But here in this sumptuous unfamiliar cabin it embarrassed him. He looked away from the Captain, examining the remainder of the cabin.

There was much to see. A barometer standing fully five feet tall and set in soft golden brass; a globe of the world with mountain ranges raised in relief and coloured as though there was snow on the highest peaks. Harpoons stapled to the wall. . . .

'Well? Is it, or is it not, the finest cabin you've ever seen?'

'It's a very fine cabin,' Josh agreed.

'You're damned right it is!' Captain Henry strode across the cabin and briefly draped an arm about Josh's shoulders. Josh stiffened instinctively.

'You're all right, boy.' The arm tightened momentarily, then was taken away, much to Josh's relief.

The Captain now moved to another cupboard. Pulling out a key that hung on a long silver chain about his neck, he inserted it into the cupboard door.

The Captain reached inside and with much clinking of glass lifted a bottle and glass tumblers on to the table.

'Now, this is something else I enjoy. A good drink – and I mean "good". None of your cheap wines for me. I learned about good liquor when I was a real skipper. I had passengers aboard the whole time then. Men and women of family and breeding – not a hold full of grubby ore. Hah! Those were the good days.'

He poured golden liquid into two glasses. 'You try this, boy. The best sherry from Spain. You won't find its equal anywhere.'

'I don't really drink. . . .'

'Nonsense! I take it as a personal insult when a guest in my cabin refuses to drink with me. Come in!' he called in answer to a knock upon the cabin door.

The door swung open. Taffy Williams, dressed in a once-white coat came in carrying two bowls of soup on a tray.

'About time too,' grumbled Captain Henry. 'All right, boy, sit up to the table. That's it; the chair over there. I'll sit here where I can see you. What wine do you want – white or red?'

Taffy Williams was standing behind the Captain's chair and signalling to Josh he mouthed the word 'white'. Josh accepted his cue, although he did not want any wine at all.

'White wine?' The Captain sniffed his disapproval. 'I never drink anything but red. But it's your choice to make.'

He swung around upon the little Welshman. 'Are you still here? Get off and bring us some wine. Move yourself! By God! One day I'll get a real steward to take your place.'

He lifted his sherry and with a single quick movement tossed the contents of the glass down his throat. He immediately reached for the bottle to refill it. Waving the bottle in his hand he called, 'Drink up, boy. Tell me whether it's to your liking.'

Josh took a sip and was relieved to find that it lacked the fire of the drink Taffy had given to him the previous evening. This was quite pleasant. He said as much.

'Good!' The Captain filled his own glass for the third time. 'You'll enjoy the wine too.' He picked up a spoon from beside his plate, and Josh followed his example. The number of knives, forks and spoons on the table bothered him. He did not want to make a glaring error in front of his host. He need not have worried. For all his fine wardrobe and affected gracious living, Captain Henry ate his food with a gusto that would have disgusted a fastidious eater. The noise of the soup disappearing into his mouth curtailed all intelligible conversation.

Taffy Williams returned to the cabin carrying two heavy flagons. One he put down before Captain Henry and the other in front of Josh. Then, without uttering a word, he turned to go.

'Come back here. I didn't tell you to leave!' Captain Henry's shout made Josh drop a spoonful of his soup on to the tablecloth.

'Pour the drinks. What sort of a steward do you think you are? I've had ignorant savages who could do the job better.'

'I don't suppose they had to do the cooking as well,' retorted the steward in his sing-song Welsh voice.

In the silence that followed Josh thought that fire would belch forth from Captain Henry's nose.

'Damn you, Williams!' His voice vibrated with anger. 'I'll have you off this ship when we reach harbour. There won't be a skipper in the country who will take you on. No, not even on a stinking Irish pig-boat!'

Taffy Williams appeared to be completely unconcerned at the Captain's outburst. He calmly filled Josh's glass from the flagon before leaving the cabin. Ignoring Captain Henry's malevolent look.

'Insolent lout. I'll have him flogged if he's not careful.'

Josh observed that the skin between the Captain's beard and his eyes had turned an ugly purple.

'Well, is the wine to your liking, boy?'

Josh lifted his glass hurriedly and took a cautious swig. His astonishment showed before he could conceal it, and the Captain thrust his jaw forward aggressively. 'What's the matter? Is it vinegary? Damned steward. I'll murder him.'

'No.' Josh took a large mouthful. 'It's fine. It really is. I like it.' He emptied the glass and refilled it from the flagon.

Captain Henry beamed. 'That's the stuff, boy. You drink it down.' He poured red wine into his own glass until it overflowed on to the cloth. 'Wine was never meant to be any other colour but red. However, each to his own taste, I say. Drink up, boy. There's plenty more where this came from.'

Josh breathed a sigh of relief and took another drink from his glass. He could match the Captain drink for drink with this 'wine'. Taffy Williams had filled the flagon with pure water.

As the meal progressed Captain Henry became louder in his speech and more careless with the pouring of his wine. During the brief silences that interspersed his outbursts he fixed his bleary eyes on his guest. It made Josh more and more uncomfortable. By now he was eager to get the meal over. Breathing a sigh of relief he laid down his last spoon. Captain Henry did the same.

'Enjoy your meal, boy?'

'Yes, thank you. It was very nice. I'll be going now. . . .'

'Sit down! Sit down! That was as good a meal as you'll get at sea. Better than the swill we feed to the crew, eh?' He laughed uproariously, hiccuped, then belched.

'Sit down, I say. You've got to let food digest properly. What you need is a brandy. *Williams!*' He bellowed like an angry bull and the steward appeared so quickly that he must have been standing just outside the door.

'Clear this filth away. And get out the brandy. The good brandy, none of your new rubbish. They haven't made a good drop of brandy in France since they packed Napoleon off to St Helena.'

Josh began to edge towards the door but Captain Henry's

eye caught him and pinned him to the spot like a harpoon. 'Come over here and sit down. When this Welsh layabout has cleared away and put out the brandy we'll have a drink and talk together.'

He propelled Josh into a seat by the stern window, stumbling on the way and leaning heavily on him for support. Josh looked at the steward, appealing silently for his assistance. But before Taffy Williams could show any sign of acknowledgement Captain Henry turned on him.

'Are you still here? Get out, you lazy good-for-nothing.' He lunged at the frail little steward, who promptly fled through the doorway. Captain Henry slammed the door shut after him and drove home the bolt. 'That will keep him out,' he said. 'I'll get the brandy myself.' He staggered to the liquor cupboard, leaning against the imagined roll of the ship.

Listening to the Captain muttering to himself as he sent bottles crashing against each other in the cupboard, Josh was thoroughly alarmed. Captain Henry was roaring drunk. Josh had begun to realise why he had been warned about him. He was no normal man.

Lurching back to the table, Captain Henry placed a brandy bottle and two pot-bellied glasses in front of Josh.

'Here we are! The best brandy you can buy. This will put fire in your belly.'

'I won't have any more, thank you,' said Josh, determined to keep his voice steady.

'Of course you'll have some!' the Captain's voice thundered out, his beard jutting forward once more. 'Do you want to be taken for an unsociable lout?'

For a full minute he glowered, and Josh did his best to meet his eyes. Then the Captain's manner underwent a complete change.

'You mustn't take any notice of me, boy. I wouldn't hurt you. Just have a small drop so that I am not drinking alone. You'll enjoy it, I promise you.' He slopped the brandy into the two goblets and reached across the table to place one beside Josh.

As his arm went out it rested on the table alongside Josh's

own. The contrast was striking. One arm dark and hairy, Josh's smooth and light brown.

'Look at that, now,' said the Captain, pushing his arm against Josh's to make the contrast even more noticeable. 'You wouldn't think both these arms belonged to men, would you, now?'

He lifted his hand and ran his fingers slowly along Josh's bare arm from wrist to elbow. 'Smooth, like a girl's. Soft, too, I'll wager.' He took Josh's arm between finger and thumb and gently squeezed it.

Josh looked up at Captain Henry's face and his stomach turned over at the expression he saw there. Pulling his arm away, he stood up hurriedly.

'I'm going out for some fresh air. I think I'm going to be sick.'

Quick as he was, Captain Henry was faster, and with his back to the door he barred Josh's way.

'You can't go now, boy.' His tone was wheedling. 'Here, sit down and drink your brandy.' Beads of sweat stood out from his temples, but Josh stood his ground and the Captain's eyes began to glitter angrily. 'Where do you think you can go if you leave this cabin? You are on my ship. I could have you brought back here in irons if I wanted to. I am the captain and my crew do as I tell them.' Then his voice became low and persuasive once more. 'But there won't be any need for that, will there? You're an intelligent lad; I can see it in your face. You be nice to me and I won't hurt you. More than that, you'll find I can be generous to those I like and I'm beginning to like you, boy. Come along. Be sensible.'

Josh's heart was thumping in his chest as he assessed his position. There was no way out of the cabin while the Captain stood against the door. Physical force was out of the question. He turned back to the table. 'What is it you want?'

'That's better. I knew you for a bright boy as soon as I saw you!'

Josh avoided looking up into the leering face.

'As to what I want. Why, nothing more than for us to be friends. Men on board ships need to have friends. It's a strange life at sea, boy. A man needs someone to share things with. To help him with his problems. You know what I am talking about.'

Josh sat down, and the Captain came across the room to stand beside his chair. Josh could smell the animal smell of the seaman's body. A hand came down and touched his forehead. 'You're hot, boy. So am I. Undo your shirt; you'll feel cooler.'

The hand moved down further. Past his face and down to his chest. Josh looked up at Captain Henry. His fingers closed around the brandy glass and suddenly he hurled the contents straight at the bloodshot eyes. The glass shattered in his hand as Captain Henry staggered backwards with both hands to his face. Josh dived for the door.

Had the bolt not been so stiff he would have had it drawn and been out of the cabin before the Captain recovered. But while he frantically levered it up and down Captain Henry leaped at him. Pinning his hands to his side, he swung Josh away from the door.

'I'll teach you to pull a trick like that on me. You'll suffer for that, boy. I'll break you. Have you screaming for mercy. Damned if I won't.'

He dragged Josh towards the bed in the corner of the cabin. Just before they reached it Josh kicked backward with the steel-tipped heel of his miner's boot. He felt it strike home and scraped it hard down the Captain's shin. Captain Henry's grip broke, but Josh's flight was blocked by the table. Before he could get around it the enraged sea captain once more barred his way.

Looking for something with which to defend himself, Josh seized the half-full flagon of red wine. As Captain Henry lunged towards him, Josh swung it. Face and flagon met with a sickening smash, and as the flagon disintegrated the captain crashed to the floor.

Josh wrenched open the door and looking back saw Captain Henry lying with his head turned to one side. Blood poured from a jagged wound on his forehead.

In the corridor outside the cabin he collided with Taffy Williams and the First Mate.

'I've killed him! I've killed him!'

'Shut up!' The Mate went into the cabin and Taffy Williams rounded on Josh. 'Go back to your cabin. Leave us to deal with this. Don't stop on the way and say nothing to anyone. Not a word. You hear?'

Josh stumbled out into the winter sunshine and took the few steps to the guard-rail. There he fell on to his knees and was more sick than he had been during the storm of the previous night. Oblivious of the ribald laughter of the crew he finally cuffed the back of his hand across his mouth. Getting to his feet he made his way to his cabin.

Once inside he closed the door and sat down heavily on his bunk. The thought of what had just taken place in the Captain's cabin caused him to bury his head in his hands. It had to be a nightmare. It could not really have happened. Then he remembered the blood on the Captain's face as he lay motionless on the floor. It had been only too real.

He recalled the public hanging at Bodmin, visualising a re-enactment of the same scene with himself standing on the scaffold, the noose about his neck. The shame of it would kill his mother. She—

There were footsteps outside the cabin and he started to his feet. It was Taffy Williams.

'Sit down. Sit down,' he said, and correctly interpreted Josh's expression. 'Oh, he's not dead! More's the pity.'

Josh could not believe him. 'But the blood on his face? His head . . . ?'

'Yes, he's got a nasty cut on his forehead,' said the steward. 'He'll always carry a scar to remember you by.' He chuckled. 'That's a different memory to the one he thought he would have, I'll wager.'

The relief was so overwhelming Josh had to sit down again. 'What will happen to me now? What will he do?'

'He'll do nothing – except perhaps consider himself lucky to get away with only a cut head. The Mate made that clear to him. He promised Captain Henry that if anything came of this he would end his days looking at the sea through the bars of a prison hulk.'

He grinned. 'It was the Mate's happiest day aboard this ship. He leaves us at the end of this trip to take over his own command. He has been waiting for something like this to happen. It gave him the chance to tell the Captain what he thinks of him without fear of reprisal.'

'This is what you and the bargeman were trying to warn me about. I should have paid more attention.'

'I don't know about any bargeman. I certainly was. Captain Henry's reputation is well known among sailing men.'

'Why do you stay with him?'

Taffy Williams looked embarrassed, 'Well . . . I suppose I'm getting on a bit now, you see. It wouldn't be easy for me to find a new berth.'

He turned to go but paused in the doorway. 'We'll be putting into Hayle at first light tomorrow morning. Stay in your cabin until then. I'll bring your supper and anything else you might need. You came out of this scrape well – but don't let that go to your head. It could just as easily have gone the other way. Sheer luck decided it. Remember that.'

Chapter Nine

As Taffy Williams had predicted, dawn found the *Helen and Stephen* riding the tide into Hayle harbour. Josh was anxious to go ashore, and his packed trunk stood in the passageway outside his cabin. He himself stood at the top of the ladder to the deck, sheltered from the gaze of anyone at the wheel. He shivered in the cold mist which drifted low across the wide glistening mud-flats of the Hayle river estuary.

It was a dull unprepossessing scene, flat and dreary. On the far bank were the ugly stone buildings of the works that was to be his home for the next three years. Smoke from the foundry and smelting-chimneys belched forth thick and dirty, darkening the mist. Although it was early, there was much activity on the foundry jetty. Another boat was going in ahead of them. Two others tied alongside hurried to batten down to catch the tide. The *Helen and Stephen* herself would be staying only long enough to off-load a small quantity of iron ore for the Harvey foundry. The bulk of her cargo was copper ore bound for the Swansea smelters.

With the help of a longboat, the ship edged in towards the jetty. At the last minute the unpredictable tide caused the ship to swing in hard. She met the jetty with a crash that had Josh clinging to the guard-rail for support.

He hurried down the ladder for his trunk, but Taffy Williams beat him to it.

'Leave it to me, boyo. I'll carry this for you.' When Josh protested that it was too heavy, the little steward heaved it up and got his shoulder underneath it with an ease that belied his years. It was indicative of many years' practice carrying passengers' baggage in earlier days.

With the tide not yet full and the *Helen and Stephen* low in the water, there was no need of a gangway to connect the boat with the shore. A section of the guard-rail had been removed and Josh stepped direct from the deck of the ship on to the stone jetty. He shot a quick glance back to the stern-deck of the ship, but Captain Henry was nowhere to be seen – only the First Mate, who raised an arm in a cheerful farewell.

At the far edge of the jetty the steward lowered the trunk to the ground. 'This is where I leave you, Master Retallick.' He held out his hand and Josh shook it warmly.

'I don't think you will forget your first sea trip in a hurry.' The Welshman grimaced. 'But don't judge all skippers by Captain Henry. Most of them are fine men.'

Josh felt that he had known the little steward a lifetime instead of a scant two days. 'Thank you for all your help. It's a good thing you were around. Without you I don't know what would have happened. Thank you again.'

Taffy Williams smiled. 'I should be thanking you. The story of how Captain Henry got his scar will grow with every telling. I shall be able to enjoy free drinks for the rest of my sea-time on the strength of having been there when it happened. Take care of yourself, young man. Learn all they have to teach you here. It isn't only the mines that need steam-engines for pulling carts along the rails. Steam-engines are going to change things. You are getting in at the beginning of something very important. I wish I was your age so I could do something like it myself.'

He was not used to making such long speeches, and with a half-wave of his hand he turned and was gone.

'You Joshua Retallick?' Although Josh did not recognise the accent it was pure Cockney. The voice belonged to a boy of about his own age.

'Yes.'

'You'd better come with me, then. Tom Fiddler's the name. I've been sent to meet you.'

He made no move to help as Josh picked up his trunk. Carrying it before him, Josh walked stiff-legged after the other boy.

When they reached the corner of the main foundry building Josh put the trunk down to take a rest. The other boy stopped with him.

'Didn't see Captain Henry on deck when the *Helen and Stephen* came in. Is he still in command?'

'I expect he was in his cabin.'

'Did you meet him?'

Josh met the curious blue eyes with a hard stare. 'Yes. Why?'

Tom Fiddler shrugged his shoulders. 'Just wondered. I've heard talk about him. A bloke I know of reckoned as how he'd got a few funny ideas.'

'He's still got them. We didn't get on very well.'

The other boy grinned at Josh, his manner becoming suddenly friendly. 'Pleased to hear it. 'Ere, let me help you with that trunk.'

Taking one of the handles he let the trunk swing at arm's length between them and chatted away as they walked on.

'You'll like it here all right. Harvey's makes the best engines in the world. Mind you, it's best to keep out of the way of the Copperhouse lot. They'll fight you to try to prove theirs are better.'

He pointed to the far end of the long narrow creek to the east. Black acrid smoke belched from a series of tall grimy chimneys. 'That's their works. Most of the river bank belongs to them. They had the only quay too and did their best to put us out of business. But Old Man Harvey showed them. He built his own docks here, then thumbed his nose at them. Never forgiven him for that, Copperhouse haven't.'

They skirted the edge of a huge granite-block building, treading a muddy path between piles of rough ore, rusting girders and new-cast boiler parts, pockmarked and heat-stained. As they passed an opening as wide and tall as a miner's cottage, a furnace door was opened. The heat and roar from within gave Josh an almost physical blow and sent him staggering. 'You'll soon get used to that,' said his companion. 'But at first you'll be gasping for breath whenever they open a furnace door near you.'

Before they passed into the building that served as a dormitory Tom Fiddler pointed out the house of the works manager. It lay between the dormitory and the gate. Tom said this made it well-nigh impossible for any of the apprentices to get past the house without some member of the household observing them.

The dormitory itself was comfortable enough. It even had a wood floor – a rare luxury for a single-storey building – plus a partitioned-off dining-area just inside the entrance. Along the whole length of the building, spaced out against the two long walls, were a dozen beds. A fair-sized locker stood alongside each.

Tom pointed out the empty bed and locker allocated to Josh. This would be his for the next three years. But Josh was not given any time to settle into his new surroundings. Tom Fiddler waited while he changed into working clothes, then took him to meet the works manager.

William Carlyon was a tall, hook-nosed, no-nonsense man who frowned at Josh as though he disliked all boys – and new apprentices in particular. Dismissing Tom with a peremptory wave of his hand, he kept Josh waiting for some minutes while he completed a letter and sealed it down. This done, he leaned well back in his chair. Placing his fingertips together in front of his chest he looked coldly at Josh.

'I understand you are a boy with a fondness for violence?'

Josh was momentarily startled and then his spirits sank. News of his encounter with the master of the *Helen and Stephen* had not been slow in circulating.

'Well, Retallick, is it true or is not? Are you a young man who practises violence?'

'No, sir.'

It came out as an unhappy mumble.

'Speak up! You are saying that nothing happened on the *Helen and Stephen*? You never struck Captain Henry a blow that severely gashed his head?'

Josh searched desperately for the right words. 'I hit him with a wine flagon – but it was. . . . I didn't want to have to do it.'

William Carlyon nodded, his eyes not leaving Josh's face. 'Perhaps you would care to enlarge upon that statement?'

Josh hesitated and then shook his head. He did not want to relive the nightmare afternoon on the ship, even if it meant being sent home to Sharptor in disgrace.

'I see! You are quite certain you will not talk about it?'

'Yes, sir.'

'Very well.' The manager stood up and walked to the window that opened out over the untidy foundry yard and stood with his back to Josh.

'If you take my advice, you will maintain that attitude, Retallick. Knocking Captain Henry unconscious may make you something of a hero in the eyes of a great many people hereabouts, but I have no room for a troublemaker among my apprentices. However, Captain Henry has gained a certain unfortunate notoriety and the fact that he has laid no charges against you weighs heavily in your favour.'

He turned to face Josh. 'Do we understand each other?'

Josh could scarcely hide his relief. 'Yes, sir. Thank you.'

'Then we will consider the matter forgotten. Unless you yourself commit some act to remind me.'

He frowned again, but his face no longer looked quite so formidable to Josh. 'Now we begin the task of turning you into an engineer. All in three short years!' He sniffed derisively. 'That is scarcely enough time to teach you to work an engine, let alone build or repair one.'

He walked to the door, beckoning Josh to follow him. 'But we'll make a start and teach you your trade from the very beginning.'

An hour later, sweating and coal-grimy, Josh was helping a toothless old ex-miner to shovel Welsh coal into the greedy furnaces and bring them up to a heat that would boil iron.

For a week Josh carried out this task and developed muscles that had lain dormant until now. He learned that there was more to maintaining the correct temperature in a furnace than just heaving coal through the fire-door. The raking and banking, clearing and de-clinkering were of equal importance.

His return to the dormitory at the end of each working day was the signal for a great deal of good-natured banter from the other apprentices. They had each been initiated into the engineering trade in the same hard manner. The bantering was not as rough as it might have been. William Carlyon was not the only person in the Hayle engineering works who had heard of the fight on the *Helen and Stephen*. The news had earned Josh a cautious respect from the others. But, this apart, they were a friendly enough group of boys. They all worked a long day in different sections of the foundry. In the evenings they spent a couple of hours writing notes or studying plans of engines – past and proposed. Because of this there was little opportunity for Josh to get to know them quickly. The exception was Tom Fiddler, who took upon himself the task of teaching Josh the Harvey routine.

Every one of the boys was totally dedicated to becoming a steam-engineer. Listening to them discussing problems and theories in the evenings, Josh envied them their knowledge and seniority. It would be some time before he could get down to actual engineering. At the end of his week as a stoker he would be helping to load the ore into the furnaces.

Then he would learn how to handle the steaming molten metal that poured like a brew from hell into the waiting moulds. Following that he would become involved with the moulding itself. Boilers, pipes, beams and tramway lines, all were made at Harvey's Hayle foundry, in addition to the parts that were made in the works' own smithy – another link in the chain of Josh's learning.

The apprentices worked a six-day week, the seventh day being theirs to do with as they wished, provided they did not miss the two-hour service held in Hayle Methodist chapel in the morning.

Washed and wearing the best clothes they possessed, they assembled outside the works manager's house to escort the Carlyon family to chapel. William and Molly Carlyon had wanted a son to continue the Carlyon line. Instead, they had produced two daughters. Sarah and Mary. Sarah was Josh's own age, but Mary was only six, spoiled by family and apprentices alike.

Josh took an immediate liking to her and she to him. All the way to the chapel she chattered away. He found himself having more to say than he had for the whole of the time he had been at Hayle. Before they fell silent to pass in through the chapel door she had elicited details of his home, parents and a great deal more besides. This information seemed to interest her sister too.

Inside the chapel Josh had his first taste of the deep division between the two foundries established in the small town. In Henwood he had been used to sitting in the pews to the left of the aisle and he instinctively went in that direction. He was hurriedly pushed to the other side by Tom Fiddler.

'We sit over here,' he hissed into Josh's ear. 'That side's for Copperhouse.'

Josh sat behind the Carlyon girls. He could not help noticing the whiteness of the backs of their necks and the fair hair drawn back in identical tidy plaits. Paradoxically, it made him think of Miriam – of her brown skin and long, untidy black hair. He wondered what she was doing at that very moment. As the weather was fine she would most probably be somewhere on the moor, scuffing her feet through the dead brown fern; or perhaps she was in the hideout, reading, or writing to him.

The service was long and boring. More than once Mary Carlyon turned to smile at him, to be sharply elbowed into conformity by her sister.

When the service finally came to an end the apprentices were allowed to walk around the town until lunch-time. It was during this period, according to Tom Fiddler, that they enjoyed slanging matches with the Copperhouse apprentices, occasionally goading them into a fight. Despite Tom's enthusiasm Josh did not join them. He remembered William Carlyon's warning and had no wish to become involved in any fight.

He had thought to make his own way back to the engineering works, but the Carlyon family were only a short distance ahead and Mary saw him. She called out to him and they waited until he caught up.

Mrs Carlyon queried the fact that he was not staying in town with the other apprentices. Josh made the excuse that he wanted to write home. This was partly true. He knew his mother would be worrying about him. Miriam too. He would address the letter to his parents, and Miriam could read it to them. But it was difficult to think of letter-writing when he was surrounded by the Carlyon family. From them he learned that it was part of the apprentices' Sunday afternoon routine to have tea with the family.

When he left them and went into the dormitory the unaccustomed silence in the empty building was unbearable. He began his letter in a mood of homesickness that remained with him throughout the whole three pages. During that time he wanted nothing more than to be on the moor, wandering across the green wind-swept expanse.

The mood did not leave him until the others returned, noisy and happy. They had achieved a rowdy confrontation with the Copperhouse boys. No blows had been struck on either side, but in the verbal battle the Harvey apprentices were in no doubt that they had won the exchange of insults.

'They don't know nothing about engines,' scoffed Tom Fiddler. 'You could suck more water out of a mine with a straw than one of their engines could raise. And we told them so.'

There was renewed laughter when Josh asked what the reply had been.

'Their faces went as red as a runner's waistcoat,' said Tom. 'But they didn't have no answer. Harvey's engines are the best in the world.'

This was a belief that Josh was to find throughout the

works. From the old man who cleaned the clinker from the furnaces to the company's top designer, each and every man was genuinely convinced that Harvey's products had no equal.

Josh enclosed a brief note to Miriam with his letter, asking about some of the things that mattered only to them – or that mattered not at all. These few lines took longer to put together than the whole of the letter to his parents. He sealed them down and put them safely in his locker. Tomorrow they would go out with one of the ore boats to Looe, then up-canal with a bargeman to end the journey in the pocket of a Sharptor wagoner.

Josh had not been away from home a week; yet already, when the other boys were around him, Sharptor seemed like another world in another time. Tea in the Carlyon house, however, was one part of his new life he would gladly have forgone. He began to feel ill at ease when he sat down at the huge table with its white cloth, silver cutlery and ordered appearance. It might have had something to do with his recent experience of similar refinements. It would have been less of an ordeal had he been seated in the midst of the other boys. As he was the newest apprentice Mrs Carlyon wanted to find out something of his background. So he was seated between herself and Sarah.

This only added to his feeling of awkwardness and made him more clumsy than usual. During the past week coal dust had become engrained in his fingers and beneath the nails, and he tried to keep his hands beneath the table as much as possible. Because of this he quickly crammed his mouth overfull whenever he had to use his hands. This was always the moment when either Sarah or her mother asked him a question. He would have to gobble like a turkey and swallow greedily to give them an answer.

Mrs Carlyon quickly established that his father was a miner in one of the smaller mines and Josh would be tied to the same mine for a number of years after his apprenticeship. After that she lost a certain amount of interest. Not so Sarah.

To the Cornish of the far west, Bodmin Moor was something

vague and mysterious, shrouded in mist and legend. Sarah was curious to know more about it.

When he began to talk about the moor, Josh temporarily forgot his shyness. By the time he had finished telling Sarah about the badgers and their habits he found that the whole company had been listening to him.

'You know your badgers and Bodmin Moor well, Josh,' said William Carlyon. 'You also have the ability to talk about them. Take the same interest in engineering and Mr Strike won't be sorry he sent you to Hayle.'

He stood up. 'Now it is time to send you all back to your dormitory to prepare for tomorrow. Work hard during the coming week. We look forward to having the pleasure of your company next Sunday.'

During the next weeks Josh's life settled into a pattern that varied only in the work he was doing. Gradually he began to enjoy his Sundays with the Carlyons more than he had that first one. If Mrs Carlyon was not happy because Sarah spent most of the time talking only to Josh, neither she nor William ever mentioned it.

That was a mild winter. When it gave way without a struggle to spring, Easter had arrived.

This was a weekend that Josh had been looking forward to for two very good reasons. One was that after the weekend his apprenticeship would start in earnest and he would begin to learn about the working of steam-engines. The second was that the boys were being given a four-day holiday, and he was going home. Not by sea, but overland in a coach. Travelling with no less a personage than Francis Trevithick, son of the great Cornish engineer and inventor Richard Trevithick. Like his father, Francis Trevithick's influence extended beyond the field of mine-engineering. Richard had married into the Harvey family, and his son had learned his skills with them. He was currently working on steam locomotion.

It had caused more than a passing stir among the apprentices when they saw him at chapel one Sunday morning. Later they met him at the Carlyon house. It was there he made his offer to take Josh as far as Launceston in his own coach. He was travelling to Bristol where a Harvey steam-engine was to power a new transatlantic paddle-steamer being built in the Bristol docks. He was to act as an adviser on its installation.

Shivering by the gate of the works in the early Good Friday dawn, Josh began to worry whether Francis Trevithick might have forgotten his promise. Then, at hardly a minute past six o'clock, the carriage swung around the corner, pulled by a pair of fine horses.

Josh started to clamber up on to the driving-seat with the liveried coachman but the carriage door swung open and the gruff voice of Trevithick called to him, 'In here, lad. You'll freeze to death up there in those clothes. Besides, I want to find out whether they are teaching apprentices anything these days.'

Josh climbed inside and sat on the shiny black leather seat opposite the master-engineer.

'You'd better make yourself comfortable and enjoy the ride while you can,' grumbled Trevithick as the horses gathered speed and the coach swayed in rhythm with their gait. 'There's little enough good road this side of Wadebridge. Now, tell me what you've learned about engineering at Harvey's.'

Josh started to say that he had not been at the works for many months and had learned hardly anything at all, but Trevithick waved his excuses aside with an impatient gesture. 'Nonsense! You will have learned quite a lot, I am sure. How do you bank a furnace to get the maximum heat from it? And what do you do to keep it at the highest possible temperature using the minimum of coal? Then what about moulding – you've done some of that? Good, then what must you be most careful of when you pour into the mould? Presume there is a flaw in the metal, how would you know it was there if you couldn't see it on the surface?'

Josh gave Trevithick the answers he was looking for – briefly at first, but the engineer demanded more detail, probing the limits of Josh's knowledge.

'And what are you going to do when you leave Hayle?'

Josh told him about Theophilus Strike and the Sharptor mine.

'This mine of yours – it's still being pumped by a horse-whim?' Trevithick spat the question out. 'What depth has the mine reached? How many men are working it?'

Josh told him.

'Then Strike ought to be horse-whipped! What sort of a mine captain does he have to allow the mine to operate in such a primitive fashion?

'A German, you say!' He snorted. 'They've killed as many Cornishmen by their ignorance as the whole of the French Army with their bullets. What type of engine will you install there? Do you know?'

Theophilus Strike had ordered a beam-engine of proven performance. A type that had been used in local mines for more than thirty years.

Trevithick snorted derisively yet again. 'In three or four years' time all those engines will be as out-dated as the rag-and-chain pump. Any we have on the shelf will be sold off abroad. You listen to me, lad. If you can persuade this Theophilus Strike to buy one of the new-pattern engines – say a forty- or fifty-inch model, with a central-flue cylindrical boiler, he'll never regret it. What's more, he will save enough coal in the first year to pay the difference in price. Here, I'll show you what I mean.'

He pulled a small case out from beneath the seat and, producing paper and pencil, proceeded to illustrate his point, proving it with the aid of masses of figures. Most of the technical details were beyond Josh's understanding, but he realised that this was a unique opportunity and took possession of each sheet of drawings as Trevithick discarded it. He knew that one day it might prove invaluable.

When the engineer had exhausted the subject of the engine, he said, 'What provision is there for a man-hoist?'

Josh confessed that he had heard no mention of it – adding that he was determined to do something about it when he possessed more knowledge.

'Good for you. With a German in charge you will find it hard work. To him the Cornishman is of less importance than the horse on the whim. If he dies it is a nuisance – but no more than a nuisance. How long does it take a man to reach the surface from a deep shaft? Twenty minutes? Half an hour? An hour even? By the time a man has climbed for that long he is thoroughly exhausted. If his hand slips he doesn't have the strength left to save himself. If he survives the climb to crawl out of this hole like some sweating dirty creature the cold air is going to tear at his lungs as though it were a steel rasp. My God, boy! Our miners – yours and mine – they deserve better than that. Look here. I'll show you the way an ordinary pumping-engine can be used to bring men to the surface without interfering with its primary purpose. My father designed it. It's the simplest principle imaginable. If the mine-owner needs any convincing, as most of them do, I will give you some figures to prove how much energy a miner expends on climbing *down* a ladder. That should make him interested. Save that energy and he gets more ore for his money. It will also prolong a miner's working life by ten years. I am perfectly serious about this, young Retallic. Get a man-engine working in your mine whatever else you forgo. This is as worthy a crusade as any that has ever been embarked upon. Persuade all mine-owners to provide a lift for their miners and you are halfway towards forcing them to accept that they are employing men. Here, look at this. You don't have to be a fully trained engineer to understand it.'

Trevithick explained his father's idea in the simplest possible terms. He had been correct; it was an amazingly simple idea.

'Why every mine does not have one is quite beyond my understanding,' he said. 'I believe that it is worth any cost involved to save one single life. Yet here is something that costs very little and nobody wants to know it.'

Josh thought of Budge Pearn. Had there been a man-hoist in Sharptor mine, Jenny would not be a widow today.

'Preacher Thackeray is always saying the very same thing,' said Josh, now completely at his ease with the engineer.

'Preacher Thackeray?' frowned Trevithick. 'I've heard talk of him. He's the man who wants all miners to unite. That's dangerous talk, young Retallick. Help to make the miners' lot an easier one by all means. That is Christian charity. But don't try to put ideas into a man's head that he is the equal of his employer. It's talk like that in the North that has caused so much trouble. "Unionism", I believe they call it. "Dangerous nonsense" is more like it. Put power into irresponsible hands and there is but one outcome. The sort of bloodbath that swept France not very many years past. I defy your preacher to stop that with words once it's begun.'

Francis Trevithick was merely saying what every middle-class man in England honestly believed to be true. Treat the workers as equals and they would turn and cut their employers' throats. It would be many years before the shadow of the French Revolution ceased to darken social progress.

'But politics holds no interest for me. Nor you, if you have sense. Do you understand the principle of the lift now?'

Josh did. The thought that he would probably be able to build one when he got back to Sharptor at the end of his apprenticeship filled him with enthusiasm. As well as preventing the deaths of miners like Budge Pearn it would stop scenes like those he had seen around the top of the shaft in winter. Miners coming off shift – his father amongst them – would sit or lie helplessly on the ground, coughing and gasping with pain as their labouring lungs drew in cold air. He asked a few questions. Trevithick answered him and drew quick live diagrams, cursing as the coach bumped and jolted, making the drawing of accurate lines impossible.

'There you are,' he said finally, handing his last drawing to Josh. 'Somewhere I have a detailed set of plans that my father once drew up. I will send them to you at Hayle. It is far too bumpy now for drawing. Tell me what little you know of the principles of a steam-engine.'

Helped along by Trevithick's sympathetic questioning, Josh discovered that he knew far more than he had realised. Most of it had been gleaned from the arguments and discussions that went on every evening in the dormitory between the more advanced apprentices.

And so the hours and the miles sped by until they arrived at the toll-gate at Bold Venture. Here Josh left the coach.

Trevithick climbed down with him, shading his eyes against the sun in a vain effort to pick out Josh's destination. All he could see was an apparently rugged moorland. When Josh explained that he would be striking straight across the moor to his home, Trevithick patted him encouragingly on the shoulder and got back into the coach.

Smiling through the open window he said, 'For my part, I would be as incapable on that moor as you might be designing a double-action steam-boiler. But you have time to learn. I doubt I have.'

He signalled to the driver, and with a crack of the coachman's long whip the coach heaved away. Josh waved goodbye to the engineer who, a few weeks later, had full sets of plans for no fewer than four different types of man-lift delivered to Josh at Hayle, each of them with details of its advantages and drawbacks listed in Trevithick's own handwriting.

When the coach was well on its way, Josh turned off the road on to a barely discernible track leading across the moor. It was not really necessary to follow any path, being too early in the year for the grass to have grown to any height. The fern that would soon be shoulder-high was no more than a series of large green staples pegging the ground. Only the gorse was thick and yellow-flowered, but this grew more sparsely when he reached the higher moor.

It was a bright clear day, and Josh could see the balancing stones by Sharptor from three miles away. He was not the only one able to see for such a distance. Before he had gone another half-mile a figure was running to meet him. A few minutes later a laughing, panting Miriam threw herself upon him.

'Josh! I knew it was you! I had been seeing cattle, sheep and ponies and all sorts of things that I thought were you. Then suddenly I saw you and there was no doubt. Let me look at you. You have grown taller and broader! You have, don't laugh.'

Josh hugged her, still laughing. He had not realised just how much he had missed her. There were changes in her too.

'What's been going on while I've been away? Your hair! You've had it cut.' It had been brushed so much it shone.

'And that's a new dress. You didn't have that when I left – and shoes! I must have been away much longer than I realised. You're not the same Miriam.'

'Josh Retallick!' Her expression was that of the other Miriam. 'Don't you think I might have done all this because I was meeting you? Because I wanted to look nice for you?'

'Have you? Dressed and made yourself look nice for me, I mean?'

She looked at him for a moment, then laughed. 'No. William said I must tidy myself if I wanted him to teach me.'

It came as a shock to realise she was talking of Preacher Thackeray. Josh had been taught by Thackeray for years without referring to him by his Christian name. Miriam was prattling on. '. . . Jenny washed my hair and cut it for me. This dress was one of hers. Do you like it?'

She pirouetted around in front of him, finally extending one foot in front of her. 'And my dad bought these shoes for me.'

She saw his face and stopped. 'What's the matter, Josh? Don't you like me as I am now? Do you want me to take off my shoes?' As she bent to untie them he stopped her. 'No, Miriam.'

'What is it, then?' she pleaded.

Josh wondered himself. 'I – I don't know. I think it might be because you have grown up so much while I have been away.'

'I thought you wanted me to grow up. Wanted us both to grow quickly.' She spoke quietly, but the unhappiness had fled and her dark eyes were shining.

'Yes.' Josh felt awkward, tongue-tied. 'It's come as a bit of a surprise. That's all.'

She took his hand and spoke, looking down at the ground. 'It's a special sort of surprise, Josh – and only for you.'

She squeezed his fingers. 'Come on, now. Your mother has a wonderful dinner cooking for you and I'm invited. Don't let it spoil.'

It was better then, walking home across the moor, linked hands swinging between them. Miriam told him of the badgers, and of the old blind pony that had started following her across the moor when she went for her daily schooling.

By the time they reached the cottage there was the same easy companionship between them that had always been there, and after a few minutes inside the house it was as though he had never been away, except that there was more to talk about around the table. His mother fussed about him excessively, unwilling to believe that he could possibly be fit and well after more than three months away from her care.

Ben Retallick said very little after his initial handshake, but he looked well satisfied with life and occasionally had a smile at the way Jesse was fussing around their son.

The remainder of the day passed very quickly. At dusk Josh accompanied Miriam to within sight of her home. On his way back along the path, whistling softly to himself, he saw someone standing ahead of him. He stopped whistling and took his hands from his pockets. He relaxed his clenched fists when his father's voice called, 'That you, Josh?'

'Yes, I wondered who it was standing there. I thought it might be Morwen.'

'I came out for some air,' said Ben Retallick. 'There's little enough of that down below in Wheal Sharptor. The sooner you come back with that engine the better. We are going down another twenty fathoms next month. I'll wager that we won't be far from water at that level.'

Josh slowed his pace to match that of his father.

'Haven't they dug another adit to take the water off?'

'No, and the horse-pump can't cope with much more than we've got now.'

'Whose idea is it to go down further? Schmidt's?'

'Yes. Don't you agree with it?'

'No. Do you?'

His father shook his head, and Josh went on, 'When I left Sharptor everyone was talking about the rich ore they had found on the present level. They said they wouldn't need to go deeper for years. So why go down now? Why not wait for the engine?'

'I don't know, Josh. Only Schmidt knows the answer to that.'

They had arrived at the gate of the cottage now and Ben Retallick stopped. 'I hear tell you ran into a spot of bother on the way to Hayle.'

Josh went cold. 'Yes.'

'Did that ship's captain hurt you?'

'No, I hit him first.'

'Good. That's all I wanted to know.'

Josh gulped. 'You heard what I did? I hit him with a flagon of wine. At the time I thought I had killed him.'

'Lucky it was you and not me who hit him. Likely as not I'd have made a job of it.'

Josh felt vaguely relieved. The thought of his parents finding out about the incident with Captain Henry had worried him.

'Does Mum know?'

'No! If she ever found out she'd be waiting for that sea captain with the kitchen cleaver the next time he came into Looe town. I think this is one secret we had better keep to ourselves. I wanted you to know that I believe you did what had to be done. We'll let the matter lie there and not bring it up again. If I thought too much about it, I might be the one waiting at Looe for him.'

The weekend went all too quickly. Most of the time was spent around the house with his family, or on the moor discovering the signs of spring with Miriam.

She walked as far as St Cleer with him on his return. From St Cleer he was travelling on the recently established coach service as far as Truro. The trip had been a surprise present from his father. The money he had saved was only sufficient for Josh to travel on the outside of the coach, but without it Josh would have had to set off at dawn and walk. Either that or trust to the generosity of farmers with their slow-moving carts. As it was, he would have a seventeen-mile walk from Truro to the works; but in Cornwall, in the early part of the nineteenth century, the ordinary Cornish man or woman was well used to walking.

At St Cleer they called in to see Preacher Thackeray and he

greeted Josh enthusiastically. He frowned when he was told what Josh's apprenticeship had consisted of so far, and said it was 'a waste of valuable teaching time'. But he waxed enthusiastic when Josh spoke of his conversation with Trevithick.

'He is absolutely right, of course,' said the preacher. 'I am glad to hear of a man of his standing in society so concerned with humanity. But why doesn't he express his views to the mine-owners – the adventurers? If he persuaded his relatives, the Harveys, not to sell an engine without a man-hoist being installed at the same time, every mine in Cornwall would have one in no time.

'It will come eventually,' he went on. 'When the men start pulling together for their mutual benefit. They proved what could be done when corn was short. If only they would join together in one strong union they could right all the wrongs in the mines.'

This was Preacher Thackeray's self-appointed mission in life, the crusade that he believed he had been ordained for. But there was no need to preach his beliefs to Josh. He had been converted long before. At this very moment he was wishing that the preacher might have had other business to attend to. It would soon be time for the coach to leave, and there were a few things he wanted to say to Miriam.

But Preacher Thackeray had no other pressing business.

'You learn all you can about those man-hoists while you are at Hayle, Josh, and about anything else that will ease the lot of men like your father too. It's a great opportunity that will never be repeated.'

'I wish I could do the same,' said Miriam. She had nodded her agreement while the preacher was talking. 'You are teaching me schooling. To what use can I put it?'

'That depends on the husband you choose,' said Thackeray. 'Marry a miner or a farm-worker and your education will be wasted. Education won't bring a baby into the world and it will not cook a meal. Find a man whose mind matches your own quick brain. Between you there should be no limit to what can be achieved. You must find a man who recognises that a woman is capable of thinking for herself – a rarity in these parts, I am afraid.'

'Miriam, can we . . . ?' Josh made a vain effort to get Miriam away, but it was already too late. From outside the inn the coachman's horn called on travellers to board the coach.

Josh shook the preacher's hand then walked the few yards to the coach with neither the time nor, of a sudden, the words to say what he had been wanting to say. Now it was too late and he was miserable.

'Don't you want to go, Josh?'

They stopped at the coach and he looked at her. She had been studying his face. There was understanding in her eyes.

'It's not that I don't want to go. It's . . .' He shrugged helplessly as the coachman sounded a final warning.

'Is it because of me?'

He nodded. 'Yes.'

'Then you've no need to worry, Josh. I will be counting the days until you are back. But quickly now; the coach is leaving.'

He snatched a quick kiss and jumped upon the coach as the coachman cracked his whip. The horses strained against the leather of the harnesses.

'I'll write, Josh. I'll write.'

Miriam ran to the corner after the coach, and he waved until the trot of the horses became a canter and St Cleer and Miriam receded over the brow of the hill. Josh dug his hands into his pockets and mulled over the words that should have been said.

Chapter Ten

There was little time for brooding in the days and weeks that lay ahead of Josh. William Carlyon was determined that the engineers trained at the Harvey works should match the engines for which they would be responsible. When he handed the plans for the man-hoists to Josh he asked him why Trevithick should be sending them to him. As a result of his reply William Carlyon not only saw that Josh received the fullest possible training as an engineer but also that he was fully conversant with all the latest developments in man-hoist design.

In his own way Carlyon was as enthusiastic as Trevithick had been, but for a different reason. The works manager saw that by getting miners to and from the working areas more quickly they would be extracting more ore and the mines would be going deeper. This is turn meant more pumping would be required. And pumping meant engines. It was not only Harvey's that depended upon rich and efficient mines. The whole economy of Cornwall was propped up by the mining industry, but as explorers and colonisers advanced across the face of the earth they were discovering huge deposits of copper and tin in areas where cheap labour was readily available. Thus the need for greater efficiency was becoming a very important factor in Cornish mining.

Josh did not mind the extra work resulting from his expressed interest in the man-hoist idea. If engineers are born and not made, then Josh was a born engineer. He had an instinct for mechanical things which was apparent to everyone responsible for his training.

His letters to Miriam and his family were full of his newly discovered skills and interests. Even on Sundays in the company of the Carlyon family he could speak of little else, and it did not always please Sarah. One Sunday in midsummer they were returning from chapel. He was in the middle of extolling the virtues of Harvey's latest thirty-two-inch engine which was proving to be far more efficient than previous engines twice its size. Sarah suddenly stopped and stamped her foot angrily. 'I am sick of engines! Sick of the sound of them. Sick of hearing about them and sick of living in the middle of a foundry. I'm surrounded by the smell of engines, bits of engines and men who work with engines. I *hate* engines!'

With that she lifted her chin and flounced off, leaving a stunned Josh staring after her.

Mrs Carlyon had caught the end of her outburst. 'My daughter has always been one for speaking her mind, Josh. It may not be a fault but it can be very disconcerting at times. Take no notice; she will be better tempered this afternoon.'

Since she had learned that Trevithick was taking a personal interest in Josh, and William Carlyon had marked him out as an outstanding future engineer, Mrs Carlyon's attitude towards him had warmed considerably. 'I understand her feelings, though,' she said with a glance at William Carlyon, who was trying not to smile. 'There are times when I feel like screaming too. All the men I meet here believe that the whole world revolves around the Harvey works. There are other things in a woman's life. Of course, you can't be expected to understand about that yet.'

It was with some trepidation that Josh went to tea that day with the Carlyons, but Sarah behaved as though nothing had happened. All the same, Josh was very careful not to talk about engines. Soon the conversation turned to horse-riding, Sarah's latest interest. The Carlyon girls had owned ponies for years, but for her recent birthday Sarah had been given a full-blooded hunter. It was a beautiful spirited horse. Sarah thought there was no better horse in the county, but her mother was terrified of it. She felt sure that Sarah would not be able to control it.

'Have you ever ridden?' Sarah asked Josh over tea.

'No. Except bareback on the mules and cart-horses at the mine,' he replied. 'And then only when Nehemeziah wasn't around.'

Then he had to explain about the little mine hostler who shared the horses' stables and lived for little else but his charges.

'Wouldn't you like to learn to ride properly?'

'Yes.' It was an unthinking reply. 'But I could never find the time.'

'Of course you could.' Sarah had him firmly on the hook. 'Daddy, Josh says he would love to learn to ride but doesn't have time. He could ride Pedlar on Sundays, couldn't he?' Pedlar was the pony which had been succeeded by Hector, as her new hunter was named.

'If Josh thinks he can fit it in with his engineering studies I have no objections.' He looked from his daughter to Josh and back again. 'Besides, I think it might do him a great deal of good to have an interest outside his work. Providing, as I've already said, that it doesn't interfere with his studies.'

The grins of Josh's fellow-apprentices were tinged with envy. Quite apart from the break with routine, Sarah was a very attractive girl.

'Tonight, then. Can we start tonight?'

'If you wish. But I won't have the stable lads turning to because you want to go riding, Sarah.'

'There is no need for them to do anything. Josh and I will saddle up and rub down the horses when we come back.'

'Then what are you waiting for?'

'I have nothing to wear for riding,' protested Josh. 'I can't go as I am. Not in my best trousers. And I certainly can't wear these boots on a horse.'

'Daddy, you never wear your riding clothes now. Can Josh borrow them?'

'There is no need for him to borrow them,' said William Carlyon. 'He can *have* them. I doubt if I shall want to go riding again.'

He grinned at Josh. 'It's no use, Josh. Sarah has decided that you are to have a riding lesson. I would never hear the last of it if I were responsible for spoiling her plans. Come along with me.'

Josh followed him upstairs to return after a time wearing riding breeches that were a shade too large. Tucked inside tall shiny riding boots it did not show too much. The jacket was slightly overfilled across the shoulders, but the whole outfit looked quite smart.

The apprentices thought so too and whistled their approval, defying Mrs Carlyon's attempts to silence them.

'You look a right toff in that get-up,' said Tom. 'We'd better draw straws to see who gets his hands dirty on that old ninety-two-inch engine tomorrow. I can see it isn't going to be you – sir.'

Josh took a menacing step towards the grinning Cockney, and Mrs Carlyon hurriedly stepped between them. 'Now, you boys, just stop it.' She took Josh's arm. 'Take no notice of them, Josh. You look splendid.'

So too did Sarah when she came into the room where the boys were gathered. At that moment there was not one of them who would not have been eager to change places with Josh. The high-heeled boots she wore beneath her long dark-brown riding skirt made her look taller. She was a naturally slim girl and the effect was emphasised by the braiding of her long blonde hair at the back of her neck.

Josh felt awkward walking from the house in his newly acquired riding boots. He was keenly aware that the Carlyon family and the other apprentices were watching from the house. There was another chorus of whistles when Sarah took his arm to cross the slippery foundry yard, but once out of sight of the house Josh relaxed.

At the stables he saddled the two horses under Sarah's instruction. He had some trouble with Hector until Sarah took the thoroughbred's head between her hands and talked to him as Josh threw the saddle on to his back. After she had checked the girth-straps, Josh led the big horse outside and helped Sarah to mount. He then led out the pony and swung into its saddle. Wheeling it around he followed her out of the works.

They took the road which led away from the town, going towards Lelant Down, and were soon cantering across open grassy country.

Drawing in beside him, Sarah said, 'Why did you tell me you couldn't ride? You are doing splendidly.'

'It's just like riding the mine horses,' replied Josh. 'In fact it's easier; there is something to hold on to and somewhere for your feet.'

'Come on, then!' cried Sarah. 'I'll race you to the top of that hill.' She dug her heels into the hunter's ribs, and in three bounds it was as many lengths ahead of the pony.

Josh followed suit, and Pedlar responded readily. It was now that Josh learned the difference between riding a slow-jogging pony and trying to sit one that is galloping. He managed to stay with it but it felt as though his arms and legs were going in four different directions while his body bounced between them. At one moment, his face was buried in the coarse hairs of the horse's mane. The next, his head was jerked back on his neck and all he could see was sky.

Fortunately the pony found it almost as uncomfortable to have such an uncontrolled weight upon its back. It slowed, dancing in a half-circle, shaking its head, not sure what to do. Josh was able to bring it quickly back under control and he took it up the hill at a more leisurely pace.

Sarah had dismounted and was waiting for him, flushed from the gallop. Her hair had fallen loose and was hanging about her shoulders.

'I won! Why didn't you give Pedlar his head? He enjoys a good run.'

'He didn't enjoy it today,' declared Josh, swinging gratefully to the ground. 'I wasn't doing any of the things he is used to his riders doing.'

Sarah laughed. 'You'll learn. I'll show you on the way back

what you should have done. But look over there. Isn't that worth coming up here to see?'

She pointed to the north where the farmland sloped away to the edge of St Ives Bay and the sea beyond. A few red-sailed fishing-boats leaned away from the wind in the middle distance. Closer to the horizon two packets crowded on full sail without apparently moving and were overtaken by a wisp of lace-cloud.

'It's beautiful up here, isn't it?' said Sarah as Hector chomped grass behind her, reins loose over his head.

'Yes, it is,' agreed Josh. 'But you have to see the moor to really know what beauty is.'

'I've seen it,' said Sarah. 'We went to Barnstaple once and crossed over it. It's a bleak dreary place.'

'It isn't! I expect you took a road over a flat part of the moor. Get away from the road and you'll find the rivers and the tors and the valleys. The whole of it's alive with more animal and plant life than you will ever have seen in one place before.'

'You really love the moor, don't you?'

Josh nodded, thinking of it as it would be at this time of the year.

'And have you discovered all these birds and animals and plants by yourself?' Sarah was looking at him as she asked her question and she caught his expression. 'Who do you explore the moor with?'

He cleared his throat before answering. 'Sometimes by myself. Sometimes with Miriam.'

Sarah crouched down and stroked Hector's nose as he pulled the grass. 'Who is Miriam? What is she like?'

He tried to describe the wild moorland girl but was aware that his word-picture was a mere skeleton of the real girl. He did not know whether the fault lay in his telling, or because it was impossible to describe Miriam without having the moor near at hand. He never thought of the one without the other. It was the first time he had realised the fact. He thought it strange that the realisation should come now, when he was high on a hill, looking out across the sea in the company of another girl – a girl who was so different from Miriam.

'I think we ought to go home now.'

Sarah flicked the reins back over Hector's head and had swung up to the saddle before Josh could make a move to help her.

She was not silent on the return journey. She told Josh how he should hold himself and move with the movement of the pony, yet there was a certain reserve that had not been present before.

Back in the stable he rubbed down both horses and on the way back to the house he thanked her for the lesson.

'Will we be able to go again next Sunday?'

'Would you like to?' She looked at him, knowing that she was able to read his thoughts by his expression. Josh had never mastered the art of lying.

'Yes. Very much.'

Some of the sparkle returned to her. 'All right. We'll make it a regular Sunday treat. We can go out early, before breakfast, when everyone else is still in bed. That's the time I enjoy riding best. It feels sometimes as though there is nobody else in the whole world – especially up there on the hill. Come along into the house and have something to eat and drink before you go back to the others.'

And so riding became part of Josh's routine. He enjoyed both the ride and Sarah's company. The other apprentices grudgingly came to accept his good fortune and special relationship with the Carlyon family. If they did not resent it, then it was because Josh never let up on his engineering studies. More than that, it was apparent to everyone that William Carlyon demanded a higher standard of work from Josh than from the others.

During these first months at Harvey's boys completed their apprenticeships and went out to take their places in the world. Others joined the works and the cycle was completed. But it still came as a shock to Josh when Tom Fiddler's training came to an end in the late autumn, although he would only have stayed until Christmas anyway. Tom's father was an enterprising butler in the household of the Lord Mayor of London. It so happened that during the course of his duties the Mayor was called upon to entertain a very wealthy Chilean mine-owner, and the Cockney boy's father found an opportunity to talk to him. He spoke with such effect that not only did he secure a highly paid post for Tom in Chile, but the mine-owner also travelled all the way to Hayle to meet him. Before leaving he placed a large order for mine equipment. Tom would be required to accompany it to South America.

Until the equipment was ready Tom was going to London to spend the remainder of the time with his parents. Then he and the machinery would take passage in one of the huge steam-powered ships Trevithick and his contemporaries had helped to design.

Officially there was no such thing as a farewell party for an apprentice. But, on the day before the newly qualified engineer was due to leave, William Carlyon would let it be known that he had other business to attend to and would not be carrying out his customary 'lights out' inspection of the dormitory.

As soon as darkness had fallen the departing engineer and his closest friends would slip quietly from the dormitory. Scaling the high foundry wall via the roof of the stables, they would make their way to one of the many inns of the town.

John Wesley was still remembered by many Cornishmen around Hayle, and his Methodism was a powerful force in the county, but Hayle was a seaport as well as a mining centre. In spite of the many pressures brought to bear by the Methodists there were many hostelries that catered for the tastes of the non-religious miner, or the sailor intent on spending all his pay in one uproarious night lest his next trip prove to be his last.

The Boot Inn was just such a place and it was to this infamous haunt that Tom, Josh and three other apprentices made their way from the works. It was the first such visit for Josh, not because he held any deep religious convictions but because of his habit of studying hard – this and memories of his only previous drinking session, aboard the *Helen and Stephen*.

On the other hand, Tom boasted that he had not missed one farewell party during his three years' apprenticeship at

Harvey's works. This was borne out by the reaction of the pot-girl who came to swab off their table as they squeezed into an empty corner of the noisy smoke-filled bar.

'What, you here again?' she said to him. 'They must have apprentices piled two deep inside those walls, the number of farewells you'm having.'

'Ah! But this is a special one,' said Tom, giving the girl a lewd wink. 'It'll break your heart to hear it. It's for me, Rosie. I'm off to South America to make my fortune.'

'You'll never do that down any mine,' sniffed the girl, hitching up a shoulder of the dress that threatened to slip down and expose what little of her bosom could not already be seen. 'And as for breaking my heart! It will be a sight quieter around here, I dare say. I won't be going to bed with bruises on my backside where you've pinched me. If that's missing you, then good riddance to you, I say.'

Despite this off-hand speech the first ale that Tom had was a present from the pot-girl. ''Cos I'm so glad to be seeing the back of you,' she explained.

The boys, Tom especially, talked a great deal and made a lot of noise, but they were not drinking heavily. For one thing, their pockets would not run to it. In the main they came from homes like Josh's own. It was a sacrifice for their families to keep them at the engineering works.

Josh found himself fascinated by the other customers of the inn. Sailors for the most part. They were a loud and boisterous crowd, and the jokes they told were bawdy in the extreme.

Suddenly a hand was clapped on his shoulder, 'Well, I never did! If it isn't Master Retallick. And what might you be doing inside a place like this?'

Josh swung around to see Taffy Williams smiling behind him. The little steward looked much frailer than Josh remembered, and when he stood up he towered over the little Welshman.

'Taffy! It's grand to see you again. I've often wondered how you were. How long are you here? Are you still on the *Helen and Stephen*? But don't stand there, come and join us.'

'Well, there's enough questions for one breath. No, I won't

come and join you, thank you. I can see that you and your friends are having a little celebration.' He nodded to Tom and the others in a vague cheery way. 'Besides, I am with a friend over there at the end of the bar. He and I were shipmates on the American run when we were both no more than lads.'

'Well, at least let me come across and buy you both a drink,' said Josh, fingering the coins in his pocket, hoping he would have enough for the extra ales.

'I'll be back with you in a minute,' he said to Tom.

Taffy's friend was a small man with a permanent blink and a head devoid of hair except for a thin bushy fringe around the edges.

'Willy, I would like you to meet a young friend of mine, Josh Retallick.'

A limp hand was placed briefly into Josh's.

'H'm! He's a big lad,' murmured Willy in a soft disinterested voice, his sing-song accent indicating that he too came from across the waters of the Bristol Channel.

'He's the one I have told you about so often. The one who scarred Captain Henry.'

'Is he now?' The lack of interest disappeared immediately. 'In that case I am *very* pleased to meet you, young sir. You did something that should have been done many years before. I don't know how Taffy managed to stay with him for as long as he did.'

'You've left the *Helen and Stephen*?' Josh queried.

'No,' Taffy shook his head, 'but Captain Henry has. I think the Mate must have said something to the agent after he'd taken over his new ship. When we docked in Falmouth three weeks later Captain Henry was sent for by the owners. He never came back! When a new captain came aboard two days later we packed his gear, sent it ashore – and that was that!'

'Where did he go?'

Josh paid for the two tankards of ale and Taffy lifted his to Josh. 'Your very best health. Where's he gone, you ask? Now, that's a question, that is. He's certainly not sailing these waters. I've heard rumours that he's master of a small ship trading between the west coast of Africa and the Caribbean.'

There was a murmur from Willy. 'We know what cargo he'll be carrying on that run. Slaves. Battened down in a stinking hold. Treated worse than pigs from Ireland, they are. Yes, Captain Henry's found his place in life. One day he'll burn in hell for it.'

'I thought slave-trading had ended,' said Josh.

'It has in this country,' said Taffy. 'But they still have slaves in the Americas. There's a ready market for them anywhere over there. While there's money to be made and men like Captain Henry to sail the ships, the trade will go on.'

'Poor wretches,' sighed Willy. 'I once saw a slave ship come into New Orleans. The slaves, poor souls, were brought out of the hold chained together, all trying to protect their eyes from the light that they hadn't seen for months. And the smell! It was unbelievable. The crew kept a gap between the ship and the jetty when they berthed. As the slaves came ashore they were pushed into the water and held under with a long pole. I was surprised some of them didn't drown. But it did get rid of some of the smell. After that they were all taken off to be auctioned.'

Willy shuddered in an exaggerated manner, oblivious of the amused looks some of the seamen were giving him.

Josh made his excuses, shook hands once again with the two little Welshman and returned to the table to rejoin his friends.

'Where'd you dig those two up from?' asked Tom with great interest. 'They're bleedin' pansies. Faded ones at that! I shouldn't have thought they were your type?'

'I met Taffy on the *Helen and Stephen*,' said Josh, glaring at Tom. 'If it hadn't been for him I'd have been in real trouble. He proved to be a good friend at a time when I most needed one.'

'Fair enough! I'm sorry,' said Tom hastily. 'No offence meant, Josh.'

Josh relaxed and grinned. 'None taken, Tom.'

'Whew! I'm glad about that,' said Tom. 'For a minute I thought you might take me by the throat and shake me. Here, it's my turn to buy another round. It's no use you trying to make that ale last any longer. Rosie! Let's be having some service here. Can't have you getting fat and lazy.'

'I wish you was as particular about not wanting me to get fat for other reasons,' said Rosie, gathering up the tankards noisily. 'I could do with one of they chastity-belts, working in here. And a foundry-cast backside would be a help. If I had a guinea for every pinch I gets, I'd be able to buy an inn of me own.'

'It's a shame, Rosie,' said Tom, when the laughter had died away. 'But if you can't afford your own inn you can at least have a drink with me. Take for them all from that.'

He slapped a half-guinea down on the table.

'Thank you, Tom. I'll take the money and have the drink later, when things are bit quieter. But you mind what you're doing with your money. I'll wager this half-guinea was given you for your fare home. Spend it and you'll be walking to London. You miss that boat to South America and there'll be no fortune for you.'

'Don't worry about me, Rosie, my love. Tom Fiddler will never be short of money in his pocket.'

Rosie gave him a shrewd look. 'No, I don't suppose you'll ever want for anything, Tom. I can see it in your face. You'm born lucky – and that's sight better than being born rich. But what am I doing standing here talking to you? I'll find myself out of a job if I don't serve some of the other customers pretty quick.'

'Now there's an ambition for a man,' said Tom, watching her make her way across the bar-room away from them. The inn was very full now. As she elbowed her way through the noisy half-drunken crowd more than one hand patted her well-rounded buttocks.

'Hey! It looks as though that friend of yours is in some sort of an argument, Josh,' said lanky Nick Doid, the only other Cornishman among the Harvey boys 'There's quite a crowd about him over in the far corner.'

Josh tried to get a better view of what was happening, but it was Tom who exclaimed, 'It's the Copperhouse apprentices.' In an instant the five of them were on their feet.

The Copperhouse boys had probably been drinking elsewhere before coming to the Boot Inn. In the noise and general activity none of the Harvey apprentices had seen them arrive.

One of them, a large ginger-haired youth of about seventeen, was mincing around the little Welsh steward, one hand held behind his head and the other on his hip. His companions whooped and shouted encouragement. The ginger-haired youth tried to persuade Taffy to dance with him. When he refused, another of the Copperhouse crowd pushed him from behind and sent him staggering forward. The big youth caught him and dragged him around in a rough imitation of a dance. Meanwhile Willy shrank back further into the corner, his eyelids fluttering frantically.

Josh waited to see no more. There had been a look of physical pain on Taffy's face as the ginger-haired youth grabbed hold of him. Ploughing through the crowded bar, Josh's anger reached flash-point as he arrived in the midst of the Copperhouse party. Taking the ginger-haired apprentice by the collar he tugged him violently backwards, forcing him to release the steward. Then Josh swung him round and using him as a protesting battering-ram cleared a path to the door, and flung him headlong into the street.

Tom's cheers were echoed by some of the seamen who had watched what was happening. They were short-lived. The remainder of the Copperhouse apprentices were on Josh before he could return to the table. He was borne to the ground, fists and boots flailing, by the sheer weight of their numbers.

Within seconds the Harvey apprentices rushed headlong into the fray. As the grappling, fighting youths rolled around on the floor the other occupants of the inn became involved, accidentally or otherwise. In two minutes the inn had erupted into a heaving, seething mass of battling customers.

On his knees, Josh came face to face with Tom. 'Are you all right?' he shouted.

'Fine!' Tom bellowed in return. 'Look.' He opened his hand to reveal a fistful of coins. There was copper, silver – and even a gold piece glinting among them.

'They're all over the place!' He grinned. 'Look for yourself.'

A sailor reeling back from a blow fell over the outstretched arm and the coins were scattered to the four corners of the room.

'You bloody fool!' Tom shouted and struck out at the sailor as he regained his feet. The blow caught him behind the knee and he fell down again, cursing and flailing about him.

Josh got to his feet and was swapping punches with one of the Copperhouse apprentices when the cry went up that the town constables were on their way. There was an immediate stampede for the door. The constables were notorious for cracking heads and lodging disturbers of the peace in the lock-up for a night prior to an introduction to the magistrate. With the prospect of thirty days on the treadmill in Bodmin Jail looming over him plus certain dismissal from Harvey's Josh was one of the first through the door.

He ran through the darkened streets, over the foundry wall and down the sloping roof of the stable, not stopping until he was safely inside the dormitory. The others came in one by one until, in the dim light from a taper, Josh saw that they were all present. With the exception of Tom!

'Oh, you needn't worry about him,' said Nick Doid. 'I saw him going out through the back door of the inn with Rosie. There'll be little sleep for the rats in the hay-loft of the Boot Inn stables tonight.'

It was a sorry parade of apprentices who bade farewell to a smirking Tom Fiddler the following morning.

'I've never known such a night for accidents,' commented William Carlyon, turning Josh's head towards him in order to see his swollen and discoloured eye the better. 'It's a wonder there are any doors left standing in the place judging by the number of you who have collided with them. Didn't you have an accident, Tom?'

'I hope not!'

Tom's grin lasted until he was out of sight on the carrier's cart. Turning away, Josh knew he was going to miss the cheery Cockney.

Chapter Eleven

Josh found little time to mope about the departure of his friend. It seemed that the more he learned, the more he found to learn. It was an accumulative process.

When his first year ended Josh spent a short Christmas interlude with his family and Miriam at Sharptor. He enjoyed being with them, but with so much to talk about the time passed all too quickly. Even so, his mind was constantly slipping away to tackle an engineering problem, real or theoretical. He told Miriam about it when she commented on his preoccupied air. She accepted it proudly. She believed that Josh would one day be a brilliant mine-engineer.

It was the summer of 1840 when a disaster occurred at Sharptor which might well have altered Josh's planned career. It brought home to him, as nothing else could have done, the dangers which exist in even the best-run mine.

Josh was in Harvey's foundry yard, helping to repair a huge ninety-inch boiler, when a horseman came clattering through the works gates. The rider was in as much of a lather as the horse he was riding. As he slipped to the ground it was with a sense of foreboding that Josh recognised him as Nehemeziah Lancellis.

The gnarled little hostler saw Josh hurrying towards him and started to gasp out his story.

'Josh! Josh, boy. I've brought bad news for 'ee. Best get home. Be quick 'bout it.'

'What is it? What's happened?'

A crowd was beginning to gather about them now.

'Stand back and give him some room,' ordered William Carlyon, arriving on the scene. 'And bring something for him to sit on,' he added as Nehemeziah staggered and Josh put a supporting arm about him.

'Don't bide for me, Josh. 'Tis Ben. . . . He was working on a new adit . . . off the main shaft. New man on the black powder. Set off a bad explosion. . . . Roof's down with Ben and three more 'neath it. Schmidt won't have rescue work. He's back on the drink. . . . No sense in 'im. Best get there . . . sort it out, Josh. Hurry, or they'll be none of 'em out alive.'

'I'll go now, Mr Carlyon. I'll take Nehemeziah's horse.'

'No!' Nehemeziah waved a hand to emphasise the word as Josh lowered him on to a stool that had been produced. 'He'm clapped, Josh! Wouldn't last half a mile. 'Tis one of Strike's too. I took'n from stables. Borrowed him, like. I'll be taken in for horse-stealing if'n he dies.'

'Josh.' It was Sarah. She had run from the house in time to hear most of what had been said. 'Take Hector. He's the fastest horse you'll find.'

'Can I?' Josh turned to William Carlyon.

'Of course! It's Sarah's horse to do with as she wishes. I can think of no more important work he'll ever be called on to do. Take Theophilus Strike's horse to the stables when you go. Tell the stable boy to walk him around for a while. He's had a hard ride.'

'I'll take 'en and do it meself, if it's all the same to 'ee,' said Nehemeziah, rising stiffly to his feet. 'Then I won't worry none 'bout the way 'tis done. Don't wait for me, Josh. Get off now.'

Josh hurried away to throw off his working clothes and put on the riding trousers and boots given to him by the Carlyons. He would never manage Hector wearing his heavy mining boots.

Quick as he was changing, Sarah was leading the big

horse fully saddled from the stable by the time he arrived there.

He was now a competent rider with no fear of the stallion. As he mounted, Sarah whispered to the horse, 'Run fast and take care of him, Hector.'

As Josh wheeled the stallion about, William Carlyon handed a number of small coins up to him.

'For the turnpikes,' he explained.

Then, to a chorus of good wishes, Josh clattered out of Harvey's. He waited only until he was clear of Hayle town before shaking out the reins and allowing the big horse to stretch out into a mile-consuming gallop.

While Josh was on the road between Hayle and Sharptor things were happening at the mine.

Herman Schmidt, red-faced and angry, stood at the entrance to the collapsed adit facing a sullen crowd of copper-miners.

'Go back to work, all of you.' His words were made harsher by the gutteral German accent. 'It is doing no good to stand around here. The roof has collapsed. The men inside are dead. There is nothing else to be done. We'll start another adit somewhere else.'

The angry murmurings of the crowd grew louder and Schmidt glared at them. 'You are doubting my word? The word of a German mine captain? You are as nothing compared with me. You know nothing but the pick and shovel. I, Herman Schmidt, am in charge here. I say the men are dead. So? I am sorry. Now we go back to work.'

Thomas Shovell stepped from the crowd. 'With all due respects to you, Captain Schmidt, that isn't our way. Ben Retallick and the others might well be dead, but we'll see that they have a decent burial. We owe them that.'

'Them you owe nothing! Me you owe everything!' Schmidt shouted. 'And I say you work – you hear? Work! Work! Work! If anyone tries to go into this adit, he is no longer employed at the Sharptor mine. I will make damn sure he works in no other mine anywhere in Cornwall. The men in there are as buried as they will ever be.'

Tom Shovell's face had paled but he had no intention of retreating. 'No, Captain Schmidt. We will dig out the adit until we find those men. Dead or alive.'

There was a sudden commotion in the crowd and men were pushed out of the way as Wrightwick Roberts came to the front.

'What is this, a meeting? Hold your meetings later. What we need now are men with picks and strong arms. Come on. Give me something to dig with and follow me into that adit.'

'Nobody goes in there. I have said so,' Schmidt repeated. 'They must go back to work.'

The angry preacher looked from the mine captain to the miners and the reason for the inactivity became clear.

'They'll go back to work when they've brought out Ben Retallick and the others,' said Wrightwick Roberts. 'Come on, Tom. In we go.'

With a nod the shift captain fell in behind the preacher. Schmidt moved to block their path and was sent reeling from the entrance by a push from Wrightwick Roberts. Before he had recovered his balance the entrance to the adit was crowded with miners. Soon candles were being lit and passed forward for the preacher and the shift captain as they advanced further into the adit.

'Schmidt is going to stir up big trouble in the Wheal Sharptor over this,' said Tom Shovell.

'He's lucky I was able to get enough women together to keep Jesse Retallick at home,' retorted the preacher. 'Had she come up here, she'd have torn Schmidt to pieces.'

A hundred feet into the hillside they came to a tumbled barrier of rock that completely blocked the tunnel. It spilled down from the broken roof, carpeting the floor with boulders at a distance of twenty yards from the fall itself.

'This doesn't look good,' said Wrightwick Roberts, indicating the rock-fall ahead of them. 'What do you know about this adit, Tom? Is it loose rock right through?'

Tom Shovell looked crestfallen. 'I don't know as much as I should, Wrightwick,' he confessed. 'The men have been digging the adit as the opportunity arose while I've been kept busy with a drainage problem at the bottom of the main shaft. When they came across a seam of copper I sent Ben along to check on whether it was worth working. He must have wanted to get at a bit more of it than he could see. The man on the powder was a new man from the Kit Hill workings. He told me he was used to black-powder blasting.'

He nodded, indicating the fallen rock, sending a shower of wax to the floor from the candle attached to his helmet. 'But this isn't the work of an experienced man.' He looked thoughtful. 'I can remember them saying a few days ago that they had a tricky patch of loose rock to get through. How far it went I just don't know.'

'Then we'd better get at it and find out,' said the preacher. Lighting other candles from the one held in his hand, he placed them on rough ledges hacked into the adit walls. 'There'll not be room for more than one man to work a way through here, Tom. I'll have first turn and you pass back the rocks I get out.'

'We'll need a bit of shoring-up here and there,' said the shift captain, turning a professional eye to the job in hand. 'Pass the word back along the tunnel,' he called over his shoulder. 'Fetch in some timber for shoring-up, and saws for cutting it down to size.'

Wrightwick Roberts strained at a large block of granite that, like an iceberg, had most of its bulk hidden from view. When it was reluctantly prised free a trickle of smaller rocks showered into the place it had occupied. These were soon cleared, and the preacher climbed into the hole. He worked loose another boulder that, like the first, would require two miners to carry it back along the adit to the entrance.

Gradually, slowly, Wrightwick Roberts disappeared from view into the hole he was making. The shift captain moved candles forward with him.

As the preacher advanced, his progress slowed considerably. With his great strength he was able to work loose large chunks of rock, but then he had to manhandle them back to the beginning of the fall himself. There was room for only one man inside the tunnel he was clearing and no other Sharptor miner possessed his strength. However, the answer to this problem presented itself in the form of the three male members of the Trago family – Moses, his brother John and young Morwen, who was already beginning to outstrip his father in size and uncertain temper.

Wrightwick Roberts had advanced only some eight yards when Moses called in to him.

'Come out here and give these weaklings a hand, Preacher. I'll take a spell in there.'

Wrightwick Roberts, his fingers torn and bleeding from clawing for a grip on the rough granite, submitted gratefully. Backing out into the comparative spaciousness of the two-man-width adit he straightened up painfully. But there was little time for relaxation. Moses scrambled inside the narrow tunnel dug by the preacher's hands and continued the work as though his own life depended upon it.

With such giants of men spearheading the rescue the rate of advance increased rapidly. By the time Josh slithered the frothing, sweat-darkened Hector to a halt at the mouth of the adit, the amount of rock being brought out from inside was more than during a normal working day.

One of the boys from the Sharptor mine took the horse from him eagerly and led it away towards the mine stables. Sarah's horse had galloped its great heart out on the road from Hayle. Now with hanging head and stiff-legged gait it allowed itself to be led away as meekly as though it were an old mine hack.

Josh hurried along the adit-tunnel, impatient with the many delays he encountered as the miners brought the results of the rescuers' efforts to the surface. When he reached the place where the fall began he came face to face with Morwen Trago who, sweating and covered in dirt, had just heaved himself out of the rescue-tunnel. The two were much of a build now.

'Have you found anything . . . ?' Josh began the question, but Morwen shook his head.

'There's no sign of the end of the fall yet. That's if there is any end. It's beginning to look as though the whole length of roof has come down.'

He looked at Josh's riding habit and a trace of a sneer raised the edge of his mouth. 'You'd better wait out on grass. This is no place for gentry down here.'

Josh's reply was to strip off his jacket and shirt. Bare to the waist, he crawled into the hole, working his way forward to where Tom Shovell, Wrightwick Roberts and John Trago were backing up Moses.

The shift captain was scarcely recognisable beneath a layer of dust. 'There's nothing hopeful to be said, I'm afraid, Josh. Things are looking bad. Unless we get to the end of this fall very soon there'll be no hope at all of finding anyone alive.'

'So they said outside. I'd rather dig than think about it. I'm going up to take over from Moses for a while.'

'There'll be nobody giving up,' said Wrightwick Roberts. 'But there's no sense in raising false hopes.'

'Is Schmidt still outside?' asked Tom Shovell.

'No. They said he was off to Launceston to find Theophilus Strike.'

'What are you doing back there? Having a bloody tea-party? Take this rock from me before I lose it.' It was Moses Trago.

'Josh Retallick has just arrived,' called Tom Shovell, as the preacher wrestled with a two-hundred-pound rock. 'He's coming up to take over for a while.'

'Tell him to stay back there and save his breath for heaving stones. There's more than enough of them here. Whoever cut out this adit should be gibbeted. The shoring-up would have been better had they used hazel-twigs.'

'The team who did it are somewhere up ahead, with Ben,' said Tom Shovell, as he took the rock from Josh.

The voices of the men were hoarse as a result of the dust-laden air in the cramped tunnel.

The man at the front would often be forced to stop, coughing and choking in the cloud of dust he had raised. This in itself was unusual. Most of the mine-tunnels on this slope were excessively wet. It was quite likely that this peculiarity had contributed to the extent of the adit-collapse, the rock being more inclined to crumble.

The tunnel had progressed another twenty yards, and John

Trago was in the lead when he stopped digging and called on the men to listen. The call went back along the adit until all was quiet except for the rattle of a wheelbarrow somewhere far behind.

Then the waiting and listening men heard the sound of metal upon rock, as though a pick-axe were being used – ahead of them!

'It might be the knockers,' John Trago whispered fearfully, referring to the unseen little men of miners' folklore.

'Knockers be damned,' growled Moses Trago. 'I bet it's Ben Retallick. Here! Let me come up there.' Pushing past his brother and Josh he began attacking the fallen rock with renewed vigour. As the rocks were handed back along the tunnel at an increased rate the sound of metal against stone became clearer. Soon it was close enough for Moses Trago to stop digging and try a booming, 'Hello!'

There was a muffled shout of reply, and Moses renewed his efforts. Ten minutes later, after a struggle with a large slab of rock, there was a cascade of shale and stones away from them. When the dust cleared the excited rescuers saw the drawn face of a man who has come too close to death peering at them from the underground tomb.

'Thank God! Thank God!' The face began to contort and it looked as though the man would burst into tears.

'Thank him later, if you must.' Moses Trago slithered into the open tunnel beside the man. 'Where are the others?'

The rescued miner pointed behind him into the adit, and Moses Trago groped his way past. Josh slid down the pile of loose rubble behind Moses and followed, a flickering candle held in his hand.

Thirty feet on they came upon a second roof-fall. Protruding from beneath this pile of rock a man lay face downwards, the lower part of his body hidden by rocks. It was Ben Retallick.

He looked dead, but as Josh dropped to his knees beside him he stirred and pushed his head and shoulders up from the ground with a groan of pain.

'Aaagh! Who's that?'

The light from Josh's candle bothered him and he tried to ward it off with his hand.

'It's all right, Dad. Don't try to move. We'll soon have you out of there.'

'Josh! What are you doing here? Aaagh!'

The cry of pain came with a shifting of stones amidst the roof-fall.

'Bear with it a while longer, Ben. We'll have you out of there in a few minutes. Where does it hurt most?'

Wrightwick Roberts crouched alongside Josh.

'It's the weight on my legs.' Ben Retallick gritted his teeth. 'I think my right leg is broken. But you get on with what you have to do. The pain isn't that bad. John Maddiver took the full force of the fall, with his brother. I think one of them is lying across my feet.'

There was another slide of stones as the Tragos eased a huge slab of rock from the pile. Ben Retallick winced again, and Josh took his hand.

'Pity they can't teach you down at Harvey's how to stop such happenings,' said his father.

'It doesn't need an engineer to see that the timber work in here isn't as it should be,' said Josh.

'The boy is right,' said Wrightwick Roberts, who was standing by to wedge a fair-sized rock beneath the stone slab when the Tragos had it high enough. 'I'm surprised you didn't go straight up top and report it unsafe when you first saw it.'

Ben Retallick coughed out a harsh laugh. 'Have you tried to have a conversation with Herman Schmidt lately? That man gets rid of a miner if he so much as looks at him. There's no point in telling him about something he doesn't want to know.'

There was the sound of voices from the rescue-tunnel and Tom Shovell came into the light, followed by a tall thin man whom Josh recognised as the Wheal Phoenix mine doctor.

'It's a great relief to see you alive, Ben,' said the shift captain. 'You nearly had more company in here. Jesse's outside. She wouldn't stay home after someone went and told her Josh had arrived and was in here too.'

'We'll have him out in a few seconds,' called Moses Trago. 'Preacher, give us some of your strength on this rock. You'd best call on your Lord to help us too. Josh, pull out your father as soon as he's free. Make sure of it the first time. There's no telling what might happen once we let go of this again.'

The first attempt was abortive. Nothing moved. At the second attempt Moses and John Trago stood shoulder to shoulder with Morwen and Wrightwick Roberts. They strained together, muscles cracking until slowly the thick slab of granite began to rise, inch by agonising inch. At last, assisted by Tom Shovell and the doctor, Josh was able to pull his father clear.

As the slab of rock was lowered again Josh saw the fingers of a man protruding from beneath it, at the place where his father's legs had been.

The doctor had to do little ripping to get at Ben Retallick's leg. The trousers were already torn from ankle to thigh. As the doctor examined the swollen and discoloured leg, Josh began to thank Moses Trago. 'I don't need your thanks,' said the big miner churlishly. 'And you are not beholden to me. I owed the Retallicks a debt for what you once did for my Miriam. That debt is now paid. The Trago family owe nothing to anybody.'

After hearing the doctor's opinion that the fracture was a simple one with no visible complications, Josh left his father with Tom Shovell and Wrightwick Roberts helping to splint the leg. He made his way to the surface. Arriving there he was blinded by the sunlight and almost bowled over by his mother as she flung herself at him.

'Josh, what's going on in there? Have they found him yet – and how did you get here?'

His eyes were more accustomed to the light now, and Josh saw that it was Miriam who was gripping his arm while Jenny stood on his other side. Disentangling himself from his mother, Josh said, 'The man they brought out. Didn't he tell you?'

'Tell me what? The man was a blubbering wreck. Not able to speak a single intelligent word.'

'Dad's all right.' His mother sagged in his arms with relief.

'He's got a broken leg. But he's cheerful and the doctor is with him now.'

'A broken leg? How bad . . . ?'

'Now, Mum! I've said he's all right. I've been speaking to him. The doctor says it's a simple break that will soon mend.'

'How about the other two who were with your father?' asked one of the miners in the crowd.

'There's little chance of them still being alive,' replied Josh, remembering the fingers beneath the pile of rock. 'They were closer to the blast. It looks as though the roof came down on top of them. But Moses and the others are still digging.'

A woman in the crowd began to cry loudly.

'The price of being a miner's wife,' said Miriam bitterly as she watched the woman being led away. 'Her husband gone, a family to support, and within the month she'll have to be out of her mine cottage. If she's lucky, the poor-house will take her. If not, she'll sell herself to drunken miners to get food for her children. That's the system her husband gave his life for.'

Josh looked at her in quick surprise. She was learning more than mathematics and English at the St Cleer Chapel school. It could have been the Reverend William Thackeray himself talking.

'Hush, Miriam! Such talk will do nobody any good,' said Jenny Pearn. But Josh had heard the growls of agreement from the miners at her words. They were not all Sharptor men. It was apparent that the seeds of discontent were scattered further afield than any one mine.

Twenty minutes later Ben Retallick was carried from the adit and the Trago men came out with him. Moses singled out Mary Crabbe, standing on the edge of the crowd.

'There's work for you, Mary.'

'Both of them?' Her face was devoid of all emotion.

'Both of them. Dead because the Wheal Sharptor employs second-rate men to do its blasting.'

He said this deliberately loudly as Theophilus Strike came through the crowd. The mine-owner heard, but chose to ignore the remark. At least, for the moment. He made his way to where Ben Retallick lay.

'I'm pleased to see you safe, Ben. Herman Schmidt told me you were dead.'

'And so he would have been had it been left to that German,' put in Moses Trago.

'You've learned nothing about holding your tongue since you left my mine,' said Strike, looking directly at the big miner for the first time. 'What are you doing here now? The Wheal Sharptor has enough men to carry out its own rescue operations.'

'It should have,' retorted Moses Trago. 'But freeing trapped miners isn't part of a day's work anymore in the Wheal Sharptor.'

There were angry shouts of agreement from the crowd. Theophilus Strike flushed and pursed his lips. He turned to Tom Shovell. 'Captain Schmidt came to me with some garbled story of a roof-fall. Four men killed and you refusing to obey his orders, he said. What is it all about?'

'There's one of his "dead" men,' said the shift captain, pointing to Ben Retallick. 'Another of them has walked home. The other two are dead. Captain Schmidt wanted us to abandon any rescue attempt. He said it wasn't worth while. We Cornish don't do things that way, Mr Strike.'

'Thank God for that!' ejaculated Jesse Retallick, the crowd agreeing with her.

'There seems to be a few matters here that need clearing up,' said the mine-owner. He turned back to the Tragos. 'There will be a guinea for each of you at the mine office tomorrow. It comes with the thanks of the Wheal Sharptor.'

'You can give my guinea to the families of the dead men,' said Morwen Trago, and turning his back on the mine-owner he walked away.

There was a pleased look on Moses Trago's face as he watched his son go on his way.

'The boy's spoken for all of us,' he said. 'I've no doubt Norah Maddiver will have need of the money. She'll get precious little from those who should be giving.' He spat on the ground just in front of Theophilus Strike's riding boots. Then he and his brother swaggered away through a crowd that parted respectfully for them.

'And what are you doing here? Why aren't you at Hayle?' Strike snapped at Josh.

'I was brought word of what had happened and came straightway.'

Strike took in the filthy trousers, scuffed boots and remainder of his riding habit. 'Then you had better get back there again and not waste good learning-time.'

'My horse will be ready to ride in the morning. I'll go then.'

Strike raised his eyebrows. '*Your* horse, eh? I'm paying for you to become an engineer, Retallick. Not to learn how to be a gentleman and own horses.'

'It's not my own horse and I've learned to ride on Sundays, when there are no lessons,' said Josh defiantly. He was angrier than he should have been, but he did not like being spoken down to in front of Miriam. But the conversation had moved away from any discussion on how word had reached Josh. He would not have given much for Nehemeziah Lancellis' prospects of continued employment had the mine-owner learned the facts in his present mood.

'You are a young man, Retallick, and young men are not renowned for good manners. I will allow your insolence to pass on this occasion. But I suggest you learn how to address your employer before you return to work here or you may well find life very very difficult. Now go home and take your mother with you. I want to speak to your father before he is taken home. You too, Captain Shovell.'

Next he turned his attention to the crowd. 'The rest of you can go about your business. Anyone who is here without due cause in ten minutes' time will be prosecuted for trespass.'

'Pig!' hissed Miriam as she went off with Josh, Jenny and Jesse Retallick.

'Shh!' said Jesse. 'Theophilus Strike could have been far harsher than he was.'

'He could also have expressed some sympathy for those

who had been killed,' said Jenny bitterly. 'I don't think he even cares.'

Jesse Retallick knew the thoughts that must be going through Jenny's mind and she put a motherly arm about her 'I'm sure he cares, Jenny. It's just that Theophilus Strike doesn't know how to express kind thoughts. He feels more comfortable showing people the hard side of his character. Some men are like that.'

Miriam sniffed loudly and then grinned at Josh when Jesse went on to say, 'And you two are a fine pair of rebels to take to meet the mine-owner!' But Jesse's heart was light inside her. She had gone to the mine expecting the worst. But Ben was alive, his injury far less serious than she had dared hope. Then her son was home for a night. She missed him far more than she would admit to anyone and would be overjoyed when his course had ended, though it was apparent to all who saw Josh and Miriam together that he would not remain at home with his mother for long.

Ben came home carried between Tom Shovell and Wrightwick Roberts and escorted as far as the gate by a crowd of off-duty miners. 'Every one of them grinning like a sheep,' commented Jesse Retallick. It was with very good reason.

'Come along, Jesse,' said Ben, his face all smiles despite his injury. 'Don't be slow opening the door when your husband is carried home by the new mine captain.'

'You, Tom?' His face betrayed the answer and Jesse hugged him impulsively. 'Oh, I'm so glad for you! And for the mine. But what has happened to Herman Schmidt?'

'Theophilus Strike says he won't be back. It seems he reeked of alcohol when he barged in on a meeting Theophilus Strike was having with some business friends. He said a few things that one doesn't say to a mine-owner. Josh, take note!'

'That's wonderful news,' said Josh. 'Sharptor will be a happier mine now.'

'But that's not all the news, lad,' said Wrightwick Roberts. 'Ask your father who is to take Tom's place as shift captain – when his leg has mended.'

'Ben! You've not been made shift captain after all these years?' cried Jesse.

Ben Retallick nodded, then had to ward off his wife as she hugged him too. 'Steady now, Jesse. Remember my leg.'

'It's a pity it took two deaths to make Theophilus Strike see sense,' said Miriam.

Wrightwick Roberts' face lost its smile.

'True. But God works in His own way, as I hope you will come to accept one day.'

Miriam stared at him defiantly until the preacher's glance dropped, then she threw up her chin and went into the kitchen where she began noisily to stoke up the fire, which had been allowed to burn low in the excitement of the day.

'My God!' said Ben Retallick with admiration in his voice. 'Every time I look at that girl I see Jesse as she was when she was young. There's spirit there.'

'Too much for my liking,' said the new mine captain. 'I think women should be gentler altogether.' His gaze followed Jenny Pearn as she too went into the kitchen.

There were times later that evening when Josh too wished that Miriam were a more conventional girl with a less enquiring mind. The talk around the table over the meal moved to Josh's ride home. He had to tell them about Hector, who was now safe in Sharptor stables, and how his riding lessons had begun with the acquisition of riding clothes. Miriam asked him a number of questions, but it was not until he was walking her home that she pursued the subject of Sarah Carlyon.

'Why did she pick you out for riding lessons?' she asked.

Josh shrugged into the darkness. 'I don't know. I think it might have been because I was telling them about Nehemeziah and his horses. It just sort of happened. Besides, I don't think any of the others know much about horses.'

'Is Sarah very beautiful?' asked Miriam suddenly, after a long silence.

'No.' Josh was aware he was lying. 'Well . . . she's quite pretty, I suppose.'

'More beautiful than me, Josh?'

'No.' He was able to say it with complete honesty.

'Have you ever kissed her?'

'Of course not! She means nothing to me, Miriam. She is the works manager's daughter, that's all. I expect she only taught me to ride because there was no one else to go riding with her.'

'That's all right, then.' Miriam turned to him suddenly and threw her arms about him. As Josh drew her into his arms she responded fiercely. Lips and bodies met in a passionate kiss that made Josh feel as though his whole body was on fire.

The same heat was in Miriam, and his hands made their first voyage of discovery on her body. Gently at first and then more demanding. She responded with low moans and teeth that plucked at his skin. Then, as quickly as it had begun, she was pushing him away. 'No, Josh. No! Not now. Please – Josh!'

She slipped out of his grasp and held him at arm's length as he tried to pull her to him again.

'No, Josh. Don't let it be like that with me.'

He felt both ashamed and frustrated and let his arms fall to his sides. 'I'm sorry.'

Immediately she was back again. 'No, don't feel sorry. I want you to need me like that. But please try to wait a while longer. It won't be too long, will it, Josh?'

'No, only until the year I come home and start earning.'

She kissed him again, until his hands began roving once more.

'I must go now, Josh.'

'All right.'

'Josh?'

'Yes?'

'I love you. I love you so much that I could burst with it.'

'I love you too, Miriam.' It sounded strange now that he had finally put his thoughts into words.

'Honest?'

'Honest.'

She came back to him, fiercer than before. 'Then you can. If you really want to.'

'No.' It came easier now that it was his decision. 'We'll wait until we are properly married.'

'I'm glad. Good night, Josh.'

'Good night, Miriam.'

Another embrace and she slipped away into the darkness. On the way home to the cottage Josh heard Moses and Morwen going up the path to the moorland cave-house, coming from the direction of the village. They were both singing drunkenly. He wished his apprenticeship was already over so that he could marry Miriam and take her away to be with him.

Chapter Twelve

Josh was on his way at dawn. So too was Nehemeziah Lancellis. Hector was stiff from his long ride the previous day and, though he soon loosened up, Josh kept him in check. He met up with the Sharptor hostler not far from the Indian Queen Inn.

The little hostler was overjoyed to hear of Ben Retallick's escape from the adit. When Josh told him of the departure of Herman Schmidt and the resulting promotions, he thought the old man's face would split in two.

'Things'll be better now, Josh. Ar, Sharp Tor will be an 'andsome bal now.'

'No doubt about it, Nehemeziah,' grinned Josh. 'Now, you'd better be getting that horse back or you won't be around to enjoy the changes. Don't let Theophilus Strike know you borrowed his horse to come and fetch me. He wasn't too pleased to see me!'

Nehemeziah Lancellis waved his greasy old hat in acknowledgement, and with a smile Josh wheeled Hector westwards. There was some cloud building up way out over the sea. It heralded rain, so Josh let Hector have his head. The big horse chose a fast mile-eating gallop that brought the tall smoking chimneys of Harvey's foundry into view before the midday steam-whistle sounded.

Josh eased the horse down to an easy canter to enter Hayle. Turning in at the foundry gates he rode past the works manager's house and straight on to the stables. Here he dismounted, his legs far stiffer than those of the horse.

As he pulled the saddle from Hector's sweating back he heard his name called. Turning he saw Sarah running across the stable yard towards him, holding her skirt high to clear the mud.

'Josh, what happened?' She stepped close to him, looking up into his face, trying to read his expression. 'Is your father all right?'

He nodded happily. 'And, thanks to Hector, I was home in time to help dig him free from the roof-fall.'

'Oh, Josh, I'm so pleased!'

Impulsively she stood on tiptoe with hands resting briefly on his shoulders, and kissed him quickly on the mouth. He remembered Miriam's question of scarcely more than twelve hours before. But there was little time to dwell on that. William and Molly Carlyon arrived together with most of the apprentices. All began asking their own questions.

It was William Carlyon who rescued him. 'Come to the house, Josh. You can tell us about it over a meal. I expect you could do with some solid food inside you after your ride.'

While they were eating, he told the family about the rescue and subsequent events.

'Your father must be very highly thought of,' said Mrs Carlyon speculatively. 'He might even become the mine captain himself, one day.'

'He could do the job well enough,' said Josh proudly. 'But Tom Shovell is a good man too.'

'From what I have heard, Theophilus Strike is fortunate to have a man with your father's experience working in such a small mine,' said William Carlyon. 'His promotion doesn't come before time. There are many mine adventurers who would have made him their mine captain had he a mind to move away from Sharptor.'

Josh was considerably impressed. He had not been aware that William Carlyon knew anything about Ben Retallick.

While they were eating, Sarah called attention to Josh's hands and it caused him some embarrassment. He had done his share of removing rock from the fall and his fingers were bruised and cut from tearing out the rough granite. Despite his protests Mrs Carlyon and Sarah insisted on bathing them for him and rubbing in an antiseptic ointment.

He was relieved when the 'resume work' hooter sounded. He was able to leave the house with William Carlyon and make for the apprentices' dormitory, to change into his working clothes.

'Our Sarah was very worried about you last night, Josh,' said William Carlyon as he closed the gate after them and set off across the yard. 'She is very fond of you in her own quiet way.'

'She's a fine girl,' said Josh. 'I'm very grateful to her for allowing me to go home on Hector.'

William Carlyon gave Josh a searching look. 'I started work down a tin mine when I was ten, Josh. Don't get to imagining that the Carlyons are any better – or any worse – than the Retallicks. One day you will be an outstanding engineer, unless I am mistaken. Plan your future now, while you can see it more clearly than you will once you return to Sharptor. You'll not always be engineer to Theophilus Strike. This is the time to lay the foundations for the future, while you are here. Good Cornish engineers will never be short of work, anywhere in the world. There are copper mines opening up in South America. Tin mines too. There is no reason why you should limit yourself to copper. They will have need of mine-engineers everywhere. Some of the ship's captains I speak to these days are full of the new discoveries being made abroad. More than one of them has brought me samples of ore to check on. Most of it is good quality, Josh. If you decide that your future still lies here in Cornwall, you will need to be good to keep us on top. If we ever allow our efficiency to slide, then we will lose out to these overseas producers. Mines depend on engines, but the best engines in the world are only as good as the engineers who make and maintain them – as you have heard me say many times before.'

Josh nodded. He preferred talking engines to discussing the works manager's daughter.

'But standing here chatting is not going to qualify you as an engineer. Away you go and change. I am very pleased that things at Sharptor turned out so well after all.'

The weeks and months went by at Hayle. Lost in sheer hard work summer slipped into autumn and autumn surrendered in its turn to winter. By November, Josh was considered to be sufficiently well trained to go with a team of Harvey's engineers to a local tin mine. In this way he gained practical knowledge of installing mine machinery.

It was the best possible experience for him. He found immense satisfaction in helping to solve problems that ranged from transporting a huge seventy-inch boiler across rough uneven country to the testing and acceptance of the building that was to house the engine. The main wall of the house had to be strong enough to support the weight of the thirty-ton rocking-beam that topped the column of wooden 'plungers'. It alternately drove them into the depths of the main shaft and pulled them up again, pumping out the water from the lower levels.

The work had only just been completed when the snows came. There was not a man or woman alive in Cornwall who could remember when there had been a winter like it. The snow hid the toll-roads and spread a thick blanket on the fields and tors. And still it came down.

Hayle harbour was unnaturally still and silent, jammed with ships unable to move out because of the blinding snow that whirled in from the east. Not a single ship was able to enter or leave for two weeks. Most of those unfortunate enough to be caught at sea when the blizzard started foundered on the inhospitable coast. Others vanished without trace somewhere out in the unseen storm-tossed sea.

For Josh it meant that he was unable to make the journey home to spend Christmas at Sharptor. It was a great disappointment. He and the other apprentices had enjoyed a lucrative business clearing pathways through the deep snow between the ships and the town. The money had been spent on unexpected presents for those at home.

Neither was there any way of informing them at Sharptor that he would not be coming. Ben and Jesse knew in their hearts that travel through the snow was quite impossible and they had voiced this opinion many times throughout Christmas Eve. Only Miriam continued to nurse the hope that some miracle would occur to allow Josh to come home.

'Perhaps it is only up here on the moor that the snow is so bad,' she said. 'It might be better further west.'

She was wearing a new dress of coloured gingham pinched in at the waist the better to show off her slim developing figure to advantage. The dress had been specially bought for Josh's homecoming.

'No, it's the same all over the country,' said Ben Retallick, reclining in the rocking-chair close to the roaring fire. 'Not even a seagull could get home in weather like this. Nehemeziah tried to take two mules down to Liskeard for some mine stores. He hadn't got as far as the lower path before one of the mules slipped and went into a snowdrift. It swallowed up the animal completely. Even when Nehemeziah and the other mule had dragged it clear and turned round it was as much as they could do to follow their tracks back to the mine. I don't suppose there is anyone in the county stirring beyond his doorstep this Christmas.'

'Poor Josh,' said Miriam miserably. 'He was so looking forward to coming home. His last letter was full of it.'

'I wonder what sort of Christmas he will have at Hayle?' put in Jenny as she lifted a large steaming kettle from the fire.

'Oh, he'll do well enough,' said Ben Retallick. 'William Carlyon and his family will see to that. I think they've taken quite a fancy to our Josh. Theophilus Strike was talking to me about it the other day. He met Carlyon at some mining meeting in Camborne. Strike also said that Josh was regarded as one of the most promising young engineers they've ever had at Hayle. He sounded well pleased about it.'

'And so he should be,' said Miriam, grasping at an outlet for her unhappiness. 'He will be paying near-starvation wages for a skilled man who could go anywhere and earn good money.'

'That's as may be,' frowned Ben Retallick, 'but don't lose sight of the fact that without Theophilus Strike's money to pay for his training Josh would be slogging his life away down a mine, just like your brother.'

Jenny came across the room and put a comforting arm about Miriam. 'Never mind. Josh will be just as upset at not being able to be with you. I'm quite sure he will be home as soon as he can.'

'It's all right for you,' said Miriam. 'Tom Shovell will be here for his Christmas meal.' But the edge had gone from her voice and she managed a smile. Jenny was a very gentle loving girl. Nobody was happier than Miriam at the romance that had sprung up between the middle-aged mine captain and the young widow. While neither of them had yet broached the subject of marriage, gossip in the village had it that this would be the last Christmas that Jenny and baby Gwen would spend in someone else's house.

All the same, Miriam did not enjoy her Christmas. Not only was there the disappointment of not having Josh, there was also the misery of jealousy eating at her insides. Josh was spending Christmas with a girl Miriam instinctively knew was in love with him. Josh might not be aware of it but he could not fail to compare what Sarah had to offer with Miriam's lack of family background and possessions.

It was a continuation of this feeling that spoiled the New Year weekend for both of them. The weather broke mid-week and within forty-eight hours the snow had gone from all but the highest and most sheltered hedges of the tors. A blustery south wind helped to dry out the saturated land.

Once again Josh arrived home on Hector. Sarah had offered the horse almost casually, commenting that it would give the big horse some much needed exercise after being confined to the stable during the snows. Josh wore the new complete riding outfit that had been a Christmas present from the Carlyon family. It was actually a present from Sarah alone, but Mrs Carlyon had wisely persuaded Sarah to offer it as coming from the whole family, thus avoiding any embarrassment. As she carefully explained to Sarah, Josh was at the very beginning of his career and had little money of his own. His Cornish pride might cause him to reject an expensive present from a girl for whom he could not buy a gift of equal value.

This ploy might have fooled Josh, but Miriam immediately guessed the true source of the gift. It overshadowed her modest gift to him, and nothing seemed right from then on. It was a miserable weekend, without sufficient time for them to overcome this initial misunderstanding.

It was two very unhappy young people who said goodbye to each other on the Sunday evening, Josh to make the long lonely ride to Hayle and Miriam to spend an hour crying in the hideout on the moor before going home to face yet another violent quarrel between her long-suffering mother and drunken father.

For the next two months the letters between Hayle and Sharptor were full of self-recrimination for a wasted weekend that could never be recalled.

The year 1841 sped along as though it was in a hurry to get somewhere, and the Sharptor engine became an exciting reality for Josh. By late summer it was being assembled. It was rare for a mine-engineer to be involved in the manufacture of his own engine. In this Josh was lucky. His involvement began with a personal selection of the firestores for crushing and smelting. Then followed the careful mixing and pouring of the liquid metal into the cast which Josh had given a minute inspection. In this way was born the boiler, flawless and of the finest metal. Not for Josh the constant gnawing fear of a boiler-burst; or of working with a boiler in which there was a known flaw, unable to close down and renew it because of the loss of work for the mine. Not that every mine captain would even contemplate such a course of action.

It was often far easier to dismiss an engineer and employ another, less skilled and less aware. One who relied on a bottle or two of gin a day to help him ignore the probability of an explosion.

There were many such 'engineers' working in the mines of Cornwall. Explosions were all too frequent.

But the boiler was only part of the engine; there was also the massive beam and numerous pipes, gears and wheels associated with a shaft-head working. It was now that Josh found William Carlyon to be a tremendous help. The works manager had a background of practical mining experience. By applying this experience to the task of engine-building he was able to eliminate years of trial and error. Josh realised that the works manager was taking special pains over this engine as a particular favour to him. Harvey's was riding the crest of a great business wave, and William Carlyon had more than enough administrative work to occupy his days.

Finally, all that could be done at Hayle was completed and the equipment loaded on to a ship to be carried around the coast to Looe. There Josh would meet it and accompany the engine on the difficult overland journey to Sharptor.

Suddenly all the years of studying at Hayle were over. He was an engineer going out into the world of working men, his off-duty time his own and no necessity to spend his evenings studying. It was a strange feeling. Even leaving Hayle would be something of a wrench. For almost three years it had been everything to him – home, work and occasional recreation. But he had long since outgrown the newer apprentices. They were no longer such a tight-knit little group as they had seemed on his arrival at Hayle. Consequently, his farewell party was a quiet affair compared with that of Tom Fiddler, and he had hardly a trace of a hangover when he went to the Carlyon house to say goodbye.

This was a difficult parting. William and Molly Carlyon had treated him as though he was a son. He had become genuinely fond of the family – especially, he had to admit, of Sarah. It was not the same feeling as the one he had for Miriam. That was a tempestuous emotion, a smouldering feeling that threatened to ignite one day with an all-consuming roar of flame. His feelings for Sarah were gentler, feelings of deep affection.

When Mrs Carlyon had hugged him and given him a motherly kiss, she said, 'Surely you are not going without saying goodbye to the horses? Sarah, take Josh down to the stables. You have both had many happy hours riding together. I am quite sure the horses won't get nearly as much exercise now.'

Josh walked with Sarah in silence to the stables. He opened the door and they went inside, into the warm and familiar smell. The stables were empty except for the Carlyons' riding ponies and Hector. All the other horses were working between the foundry and the jetty.

'Goodbye, Hector, old chap,' said Josh, patting the horse's neck as the big animal nuzzled his ear. 'I'm going to miss you.'

'Will you miss me too, Josh? Just a little?' It was a very unhappy little plea.

'I'll miss you a lot, Sarah. You've been very very kind to me while I've been here.'

She turned away from him so he could not see her face. It was only when her shoulders started to heave that he knew she was crying.

'Sarah! Don't.' He touched her shoulders and she turned into him, letting the sobs come noisily.

'Please don't cry.' Her tears were wet and warm on his chest, through his shirt, and he held her close as she clung to him. Then he was kissing her, and she was responding with a hunger that made his body react as it had once before. In another place. With Miriam.

He tried to pull away, but she clung to him in fierce desperation. 'Don't go, Josh. Don't leave me.'

'I must, Sarah. My apprenticeship is over now. I have work to do. You know that.'

'I only know that I can't face life here without you,' Sarah cried.

'You mustn't talk like that,' he said gently. 'Your family have been very good to me, Sarah. If I thought I was repaying them by making you unhappy I would be very upset.'

Sarah pulled away from him and looked down at the ground. 'I'm making a fool of myself, aren't I, Josh?'

'No, of course you're not.'

She nodded her head violently. 'Yes. Yes, I am. I'm sorry.'

She fumbled in her sleeve for a handkerchief, and he handed her his own. After dabbing her eyes she blew her nose violently. 'I'm all right now,' she said thickly.

'That's good. Come on. . . .' He put out a hand to take her arm, but she stepped back.

'No, don't touch me, Josh. I shall only do something foolish again, if you do.'

'We'd better go now,' he said. 'The men will be waiting for me.'

'You go. I want to stay here for a while.'

'Sarah, I can't leave you like this.'

'It's better, Josh. Really it is.'

He hesitated. This was harder than he had ever imagined it would be. 'All right. Goodbye, Sarah.'

'Goodbye . . . Josh!'

He stopped and turned at the door.

'Will you write to me? Tell me how you are getting on?' Sarah asked.

'Of course I will. Not only that; I might even be coming back here for a while. Your father thinks we ought to have a steam-whim at Sharptor for raising the ore. If I can persuade Theophilus Strike, I'll come here myself and arrange it.'

'I would like that. Goodbye, Josh. Think of me sometimes.'

He went outside and the sunshine burned his eyes.

The men were in the wagon. As soon as he climbed on board the driver whipped up the horses and they trundled off. Harvey's was supplying a team of four men to install the engine and they were travelling with all the tools they would need for the job.

They arrived at Sharptor the following day. After a brief reunion with his family – Miriam was at work at the Wheal Phoenix – Josh hurried away to Looe. He meant to ensure that sufficient care was taken with the engine on its way up the canal to Moorswater. He left the Harvey team to inspect the newly constructed engine-house and prepare for his arrival with the machinery.

The boiler looked huge sitting on the jetty alongside the

ship that had carried it. But it was the massive beam that was the most difficult item to handle. It's thirty-ton bulk was formidable. Special equipment would have to be used throughout the whole of its journey. Josh had expressed doubts about carrying it up the canal, but the canal company had a barge which had been built for this very purpose. The Wheal Caradon had used it two years before when they had expanded their workings.

Josh thought that, if the Wheal Caradon had needed a special barge for their beam, they would probably have a wagon too. When the beam had been secured aboard the barge, Josh rode off to enquire.

'The Wheal Sharptor, eh?'

The pinch-faced Captain Frisby had responsibility for the largest copper-mining complex in east Cornwall.

'How far are you expanding? I'm not lending mine equipment to another mine that might very well put us out of business.'

Josh looked around at the highly industrialised Caradon complex, its numerous tall black-smoked chimneys and general air of bustle and industry. It was more like a small town than a mine. He could count at least a half-dozen engines of different types and sizes. The Caradon mines employed more than a thousand men. Wheal Sharptor was not in the same class, and Josh said as much.

'We'll never be able to compete with the Caradon,' he added. 'We don't have to pay shareholders, and Theophilus Strike has too many other interests to want to make us very much bigger.'

'That may be the way it is now,' said the Caradon captain, 'but who knows what may happen next year? Or the year after?' For the first time Josh recognised the fact that he might be refused the loan of the special wagon.

'From what I heard during the time I was at Hayle there just isn't enough copper being produced to meet the demand for it,' he said, choosing his words carefully and keeping a tight grip on the anger boiling up within him. Many mines were rivals, but it was unheard of for one mine to refuse to help another when it would cost nothing and was within its power to do so. But this man was not Cornish and that made a difference.

'I don't think Sharptor will ever be a big mine,' Josh repeated. 'We are too crowded. With the Phoenix to the south and east of us and Darley to the north we have only two alternatives: work to the west or sink deeper shafts. The west side has been checked out pretty thoroughly and there is not much there. So we must go down. With the money that will cost him Theophilus Strike is not going to make a fortune from it.'

This statement repeated almost word for word a conversation he had overheard between his father and Tom Shovell during Josh's last weekend at home.

'Apart from anything else,' Josh went on, 'even the biggest mines sometimes need help. One day you might need another engineer. You'll always be able to call on me.'

'If ever I need another engineer I won't send for a boy to do the job,' retorted the Caradon captain. All the same, he looked at Josh with a new interest. 'Where did you pick up engineering? Loafing about in some boiler-house and watching the fireman?'

'No, I learned it properly at Harvey's of Hayle,' replied Josh. 'The engine on its way up the canal from Looe is one that I helped to build. That's why I am here asking for your help and not the Sharptor captain.'

'Is that offer of yours a firm promise?' asked the captain. 'If ever we have need of you, we can call on you?'

'If you ever need help, I'm quite sure Tom Shovell will be happy for me to come, whether we owe you a favour or not.'

'H'm! Well, it's my experience that you get nothing given to you in this life,' said the Caradon captain. 'So if ever we are stuck for an engineer I will hold you to your promise. You can take the wagon. But you'll have to provide your own horses. I'm not wearing out my mine's horses for the Wheal Sharptor.'

Josh was quite happy with the arrangement. The Sharptor

mine had no shortage of good horses. When he inspected the wagon he knew he would need all of them. It was a very heavy low-slung construction of iron and huge wood beams. The iron wheels had rims on them as wide as a man, to prevent the wagon from sinking into the ground. Even so, Josh knew that careful thought would have to be given to mapping out a safe route for the wagon when it was fully laden.

Captain Tom Shovell could not hide his amazement when Josh told him that he was borrowing the Wheal Caradon's wagon and of the deal that had been made.

'He'll call on your services one day, you can depend on that,' he said. 'But it's a rare thing to have got something from Captain Frisby. He's the meanest man you'll find in Cornwall. You'd better go and tell Nehemeziah to give you the horses before Frisby changes his mind.'

The hostler was happy for the opportunity to do something out of the ordinary and show off all his horses. He was always bragging that they were the best in east Cornwall. Now he would prove it. In fact, Sharptor had been the first mine in the area to use horses and wagons to carry ore. The mines had always made do with a varied collection of ponies and mules to carry it. Balancing a pair of open-mouthed bags, one each side, they had picked their way from mine to port for many years. Trudging out deep narrow trails across moor and heath that would remain for more than a hundred years.

Leaving only enough horses to work the winding-whims that brought the ore to the surface, Nehemeziah and his stable-boys were able to muster seventeen pairs of horses. They were an impressive sight. Theophilus Strike had started his stable with three mares and a stallion from the shires. By careful selection and breeding Nehemeziah had expanded his working stock to its present proportions. There was not a mine hostler in Cornwall who did not know of Nehemeziah and his great shire-horses.

As the double line of horses jangled their brass-embellished harness along the track into the Caradon mine all surface work came to a halt, the women, boys and old men stopping to watch them. Nehemeziah, riding on the back of the leading pair, was fully aware of the impression he was creating. He shouted his orders to the horses with the authority of a cavalry officer. The beasts did not let him down. They halted, wheeled and backed as though each one carried a rider.

With four pairs of horses pulling and the remainder bringing up the rear the heavy wagon was hauled away from the mine with such ease that it might have been a pony-cart.

Captain Frisby watched the performance with great interest. While Josh was checking and greasing the thick axles he got into earnest conversation with the Sharptor hostler.

As they left the Caradon mine behind them Josh rode up alongside the old man. Nehemeziah was wearing a grin that showed off his shortage of teeth.

'You've got plenty to smile about,' said Josh. 'They've never seen horses like these at the Caradon before.'

'Reckon that's so,' agreed the old man. 'And they won't see the likes again – even though Cap'n Frisby said as how he'd match 'em if I went to work for the Caradon. Give me a sight more money too, so he would.'

'Well?'

Nehemeziah chuckled but said nothing.

'What was your reply? Are you going to accept his offer?'

'An' leave these beauties? 'Sides, I told 'en what 'twould cost. Came damn near to choking of 'en.'

'Captain Shovell said he doesn't like to spend money. It might put him off calling on me to do any odd jobs that he thinks of. I'll tell him you're thinking of taking up his offer, say you mentioned the hundred pair of shires he'll be buying for you. He'll have nightmares about it and won't want to see or hear anyone from Sharptor for fear they have a message from you.'

'Cap'n Frisby'd get his money back from more than they,' said Nehemeziah. 'His pack-'orses don't carry more'n a spoonful apiece. Two o' these pullin' a wagon do the work of twenty o' they.'

'Don't tell Frisby that.' Josh kneed his horse forward. 'The day might come when I'll need something to frighten him off with. I'm going on ahead now to see that barge in.

Use the brakes down the hill to Moorswater; that's a heavy wagon.'

'Engine's your'n. 'Orses is mine,' the old man growled.

Josh grinned and waved cheerfully.

The beam was as difficult to transfer from barge to wagon as Josh had feared. He used hoists and the only available crane, but the ropes parted. The beam crashed down, smashing a line of stone paving-slabs as though they were biscuits. Then some heavy chains were produced and the work was quickly completed. With the beam on the special wagon and the boiler on one of the three long carts they began the slow return to Sharptor.

Darkness travelled faster than the wagon, as it was forced to take a long route in order to keep firm ground beneath the wheels. Nehemeziah announced his intention of spending the night where he was, with the horses. Two of the stable-lads stayed with him.

Josh rode home with one of the wagon-drivers up behind him and it was midnight before they were back at Sharptor.

The family was waiting up for him but, despite the late hour, he was surprised that Miriam was not with them. He commented on it while he was eating.

His mother was unusually evasive. 'I don't suppose she knows you're home,' she said.

'I can't believe that. There isn't one person in Sharptor or Henwood who doesn't know the engine's here. Half the county turned out to see Nehemeziah's horses. Besides, Miriam used to spend more time here than she did at her own home. What's happened?'

'Miriam doesn't spend much time at Sharptor these days,' explained his mother. 'She puts in a full day's work down at the Wheal Phoenix, then she goes to St Cleer to do her schooling, as you once did. We've seen very little of her these last two months.'

'No, it isn't Miriam's fault, Josh,' said Ben Retallick. 'She's staying away in order to save us from any unpleasantness, that's all.'

'I don't understand. What unpleasantness? I thought you

enjoyed having her here. She's almost family, and once we're married. . . .'

'Well, bless my soul!' exclaimed Jesse Retallick. 'I thought the boy was never going to say he'd marry her. It's not before time.'

'Miriam knows,' said Josh. 'But that doesn't explain what is happening.'

'It's all my fault, Josh.' Jenny Pearn rose from her seat in the corner.

Now Jenny . . .,' Jesse Retallick began, but the young widow waved her into silence.

'Yes, it is, in a way. You've been away a long time, Josh. You don't know what Moses Trago is like now.'

'He's an animal!' exclaimed Jesse Retallick.

'That's as good a description of him as any,' agreed Jenny. 'You remember how he used to be when he had been drinking?'

Josh nodded.

'Now he's far worse. It's as though the drink has drowned the normal part of his mind.'

Jenny sat down on the stool in front of the fire. 'He came to the house when your mother was in the kitchen and must have thought I was here alone. He started mauling me. Your mother had to threaten him with the meat cleaver before he would let me alone and go.' She shuddered. 'He's evil.'

'But that's not all of it,' put in Jesse. 'He began coming to the door to ask for Miriam and made more than one scene when she wasn't here. It meant nothing to him whether she was here or not. It was an excuse to leer at Jenny. It ended with another fight between him and your father. It was lucky for Moses that your father didn't know until afterwards how much of a nuisance he'd been or he would have done more than throw him out.'

'He's not a sane man anymore,' said Ben Retallick quietly. 'He's sick in his mind.'

'He has the devil in him,' said Jesse Retallick.

'And now Miriam is staying away so that he'll have no

excuse for coming here.' It was a statement rather than a question.

'Yes. I'm sorry, Josh.'

'It's none of your doing,' Josh said to Jenny. 'But I feel sorry for Miriam.'

'Then the sooner you marry her the better,' said Jesse Retallick. 'But it's way past the time to go to bed. You're home now and there will be plenty of time to talk to Miriam. Now, if you want to set off early for that engine of yours, you'd better be getting some sleep.'

Josh let himself out of the cottage into the hill mist that promised a fine day. At the gate a silent figure darted forward, and the next moment he was holding Miriam.

'I'd almost given you up for lost,' he said, holding her at arm's length in order to look at her. 'Where have you been?'

'Me?' she asked indignantly. 'I waited out here last night for so long that I almost fell asleep on my feet. I finally decided that you must be spending the night at Looe and went home. But I got up early this morning to come down here, just in case you'd come home.'

'You should have gone indoors. Mum misses you, Miriam.'

'No, I didn't want to do that. I expect she's told you what happened. I'm not going to bring trouble on them again, Josh.'

'Miriam, that's foolish. They are very fond of you and—'

Miriam silenced him with a kiss on his lips. 'We won't argue about it – especially now. Where are you going? Can I walk with you?'

'I'm going to the Sharptor stables. Then out to meet Nehemeziah. We'll have the parts for the engine back here by noon. Then I can begin to put it together. It's a fine engine, Miriam.'

'I'm quite sure it is if you've helped to build it.' She laughed happily and clung to his arm and chattered as they swung along the path in the grey morning.

They skirted the indistinct shell of the new engine-house and halted a short distance from the almost empty stables.

'Will you see me tonight, Josh?'

'I'll do my best, but it will be difficult for a couple of days. The men from Harvey's want to see the engine working by Saturday so they can return home. That means working from dawn to dusk and beyond. If it's at all possible, I'll make the time. If not, then I'll meet you on Sunday. We'll spend the day on the moor.' He smiled at her. 'I'm home now, Miriam. We have a lifetime ahead of us.'

'I know, I'm so happy I could bust. I won't wait around tonight. I'll let you get on with putting your engine together. I'll go straight on to my lessons after work. You must go to talk with William; he is always asking about you. He says you've proved to be one of his most successful pupils.'

It still sounded strange to hear her call the Reverend William Thackeray 'William'. 'Give him my regards,' he said. 'Tell him I might seek his advice on how best to convince Theophilus Strike that he needs a second engine – one that I can use to hoist men to grass at the end of a shift.'

'He'll be very happy to help. There is more than mere talk of a union of miners now, Josh. The Wheal Phoenix men are for it, and Caradon miners are talking about stopping work if the mine shop prices rise any more.'

'That's probably just what's needed.' The mist was thinning out as the sun rose over Dartmoor, well to the east, beginning to colour the sky. 'I must go now. I have a way to go.'

''Bye, Josh.'

He kissed her quickly, then strode away to the stables. He could almost imagine they were married already and that Miriam would be waiting for him at the end of a working day. But the bells that fate was planning to ring were not for a wedding.

Chapter Thirteen

As Josh had anticipated, the work of building the engine kept him working at a frenzied pace for the remainder of that week. His meetings with Miriam were brief. But the thrill of watching the engine take on working shape beneath his hands was an experience to drive away all other thoughts for much of each day.

Awkwardly, he tried to express his thoughts to the engineer in charge of the Harvey team as the engine neared completion. The engineer nodded knowingly. 'You'll never know another feeling like it, Josh. It's the nearest thing to being God that a man will ever achieve. All these parts we brought up from the foundry were just pieces of manufactured metal. Now we've put them together and given them life. You've seen the whole thing grow from nothing. For ever more this engine will have something of you in it. All engines have life and character. No one who works with them would deny that. But this engine will be something special for you. It's your creation. You'll come to know its every mood and its strength and weaknesses. I'm telling you, Josh, a man can fall in love with an engine and need not be ashamed of it.'

The engine was scheduled for completion on Saturday afternoon, although it would be another week before the long plungers would extend to the bottom of the shaft and link up with the water-pump. But on Saturday the boiler would be filled, the fire started and the shiny piston-rod would set the great beam rocking on its pivot.

During the final few hours a leak in the main steam-pipe caused some concern. A flurry of activity put it right, and by four o'clock that afternoon Theophilus Strike and some of his gentlemen friends were inside the boiler-room watching the pressure-gauge register for the first time. Outside the door, and peering in at the windows, were the families of every miner who worked on the mine, together with those miners who were off duty.

Ben Retallick and Jesse were well to the front, standing with Wrightwick Roberts. Jenny should have been with them but she had stayed at home. Young Gwen was recovering from a bad bout of measles and was not yet fit enough to leave the house.

The steam-pressure reached working level. The black smoke spewed forth from the tall stone chimney and chased the wind up the slope. The water began rattling in the pipes as the Hayle engineer tapped each one of them, checking the joints for leaks. Then, as the needle hovered halfway across the dial of the gauge, he decided it was time. 'All right, Josh. Open them now.'

Jenny Pearn filled the kettle and set it on the fire in the kitchen. She pushed it well down so that no movement of the coals would cause it to overbalance.

Behind her she thought she heard the latch on the outside door click shut.

'Is that you, Jesse? That was over quickly. How was Josh's engine? Will it . . . ? Oh my God!'

Standing swaying inside the room, his chest heaving, was Moses Trago. His face was black with underground dirt and streaked with the sweat of a long shift.

Jenny put her left hand to her throat. The other felt behind her for the door-frame. She drew support from it for a moment, then her hand felt along the wall. Slowly, very slowly, she moved along with it. She had no coherent thoughts in her mind. She only knew she had to get away from Moses, get upstairs to Gwen.

Moses followed her with his eyes, red-rimmed eyes that were as dark as fifty fathoms.

As far as the corner of the room Jenny was moving away from him, but edging along the far wall brought her closer. Moses took two lurching steps into the room, and Jenny flattened herself against the wall; arms stretched out as though she were being crucified.

Moses made a drunken unintelligible movement with his hand. 'Come here!' The words were scarcely more recognisable than the gesture.

Jenny did not move.

Moses lumbered another couple of heavy paces towards her. Now he was close enough for her to know the strong animal smell that reached out from his body and the stale gin on his breath. But it was his eyes that made her shudder with horror. There was no light in them, only a blackness as deep as the grave.

'Please, Moses, no,' Jenny begged. 'My babe. Don't . . . !' He grabbed at her as she tried desperately to slip past and he caught her dress at the shoulder.

She struggled to break free, but his grip held and the fabric parted, baring half her upper body to the waist.

Moses held her like a dog on a ragged lead, and pulling her roughly towards him, reached out with his other hand and it closed bruisingly around her flesh.

Jenny screamed, and Moses released her torn dress to strike her across the face with the back of his hand.

She screamed again, and this time his fist cut it short. The sight of blood on her lips turned Moses into a mad thing. Again and again he struck her until she slumped to the floor. Moses went down with her, his knees straddling hers while his hands ripped the remnants of her dress from her body.

Josh twisted the steam-valve, and with oiled precision the piston rose slowly from its casing, pushing the end of the thirty-ton beam with it. At the end of its stroke it returned equally slowly, with a faint sigh of escaping steam.

There were shouts and cheers from outside, and Theophilus Strike looked surprised as the engine repeated its action.

'It's incredibly silent,' he said. 'I thought it would make a din you could hear for miles.'

'You'll hear enough from it when it's driving the pumping-rods into the shaft,' answered the Hayle engineer. 'But she'll never be a noisy engine. You can thank your own engineer for that. He supervised the building of it well, Mr Strike.'

Theophilus Strike gave Josh a hard look. 'I'm pleased to hear it. Do you feel confident that you can keep it running as well?'

'If I can't, you've wasted a lot of money and I've wasted a lot of time, Mr Strike.' He held the mine-owner's gaze for a long moment before adding, 'There will be no trouble with this engine.'

Theophilus Strike nodded, expressionless, and turned back to the Hayle engineer. 'I thank you. You and your men are free to go whenever you wish. I am well pleased.' There was a dull jingle of coins from the bag he dropped into the engineer's hand.

'Now,' he turned to his friends, 'shall we go and leave things in the hands of those whose job it is to keep the mine running?'

He filed out with the others without another look at the Wheal Sharptor's engine.

When the mine-owner had gone the miners and their families crowded into the building to have a closer inspection of the working engine. Josh allowed them in but made sure they stayed away from the moving parts.

Jesse Retallick looked from the engine to her son with undisguised pride. 'It's a wonderful thing,' she said loudly. 'And to think that Josh built it. It's a proud day, Ben.'

Ben Retallick smiled understandingly and rested a hand on Jesse's shoulder. 'It is. When the engine starts pumping it's going to make life much more comfortable for the men working down below. We're getting down too deep for the horse-pumps to keep up with us. You'll be everyone's favourite then, Josh.'

'We'll have that part completed and working by the end of next week,' said Josh. 'Two of Harvey's men who specialise in pumps are coming on Monday when they've finished a repair job at Kit Hill.'

More and more miners and their families crowded into the boiler-room and engine-room. Before long the heat had become oppressive. Jesse Retallick announced her intention of going home. She had seen the engine, heard the admiring remarks about Josh's skill; now it was time to go.

'I'll come with you,' said Ben. 'I see enough of this place all week. Will you be coming soon, Josh?'

'Not for a while. As soon as everyone has left I'll douse the fire and empty the boiler. We won't be firing it again until the rods are in place.'

When his mother and father had left Josh was kept busy answering the questions put to him by the miners. Some of the questions were put from politeness but others went beyond mere curiosity. The miners realised the considerable effect the engine would have upon their lives and the future of the mine. Those miners who had worked in other mines where there had been an engine were surprisingly knowledgeable about them. Josh enjoyed pointing out all the refinements of the Sharptor engine which he knew the earlier engines had not possessed.

Tom Shovell had remained in the engine-house chatting with the miners and their families and was close to the engine when one of the Henwood boys came panting up to the door.

'Captain Shovell! Captain Shovell!' The urgency in the boy's voice killed the laughter at a joke someone had just told.

'Yes, what is it?' Captain Shovell pushed his way to the door.

'Ben Retallick says will you get down to his place. Quick as you can.'

'Why, what's happened?'

'I don't know, but he looked terrible fierce. I could hear someone crying inside the house.'

Tom Shovell set off at a run as Josh grabbed a shovel and began pulling out the coals from beneath the boiler. 'I'll be down as soon as I've cleared this,' he called.

The water from the boiler was tantalisingly slow in draining through the pipes, but as soon as he felt it was safe to leave Josh ran along the path to the cottage.

There were half a dozen or so men inside, amongst them Wrightwick Roberts and Tom Shovell. The remainder were some of the mature miners who frequently shared an evening with the Retallick family.

But this was no social gathering. When Josh entered the room they stopped talking. In the silence he heard a sound like the moaning of the wind on an autumn night. It came from the bedroom.

'Who's upstairs? What's happened?' Nobody answered him, and Josh started for the stairs. His father's arm barred his way.

'No, Josh.'

'But why? Will someone tell me what's going on? Is it Mum?'

'No, it's not your mother,' said Ben Retallick. 'It's Jenny.' His eyes were on Tom Shovell as he spoke. 'Moses Trago was here while we were all up at the Wheal Sharptor.'

The mine captain's hands closed into fists that trembled with the ferocity of his grip and he fought for control of his face.

'Evil!' he muttered. 'Evil follows Moses Trago like an evening shadow.'

'We've got to find him,' said another man. 'The Lord only knows what he might do if we don't get him quickly.'

'Is Jenny hurt bad?' Josh's throat felt dry and pinched.

'That's something only your mother and Jenny will know,' answered his father. 'It looks bad. We found her lying unconscious on the floor with most of her clothes ripped from her. She'd taken as bad a beating as I've seen for a long time.'

Tom Shovell's fists twitched again.

'We're wasting time,' said a gruff voice. 'Let's get out and find him.'

'Yes.' It was a reluctant Ben Retallick who moved away from the stairs. 'It's something that must be done.'

'There can be no other way,' said Wrightwick Roberts softly.

'I'll come with you,' Josh cried. There was a disaster looming here; he could feel it.

'No. You'll stay home.'

'Your father's right.' It was the miner with the gruff voice again. 'The fewer who know of this day's work the better. For everyone.'

'You'll need all the help you can get to bring Moses back,' insisted Josh.

'There will be no bringing him back . . .,' began one of the men, but Ben Retallick silenced him with a look.

'I want you to stay here, Josh. Moses Trago is no longer normal. He might come back. If we're not back before dark, you're to lock the doors and not open up unless you're quite sure it's one of us. You'd best get the axe from the shed. Don't hesitate to use it if you have to. Do you understand?'

'But. . . .' Josh felt as though he were teetering on the edge of a yawning crevasse with the earth crumbling beneath his feet, not sure whether to jump or go back.

'There are no "buts". This is a thing I ought to have done something about long ago and you're needed here.'

He swung away and left the house, the other men following. Tom Shovell walked like a man in a bad dream, hoping that he might wake up with the next step.

'Ben!' It was Jesse Retallick calling from the bedroom.

'He's gone out with the others.'

'To find Moses? Oh my God! Hasn't there been tragedy enough for one day? Josh, go and find them and stop them.'

'Dad said I was to stop here.' Josh looked at his mother. 'And he's right.'

'Right? There will be no right done this day. What do you think is going to happen when they find Moses? Do you believe he is going to say, "I'm sorry. I'll come back and let the judge put me in prison for the rest of my days"? Do you think your father and those other men will even try to speak to him? And I hope you looked at Wrightwick Roberts' face. If a godly man is capable of such an expression as I saw there, who's going to stand up for what's right?'

She stood in front of him, looking up into his face, pleading. 'Josh, don't think I am worried for Moses Trago's safety. He's forfeited all claim to human sympathy by his actions today. But if your father and the others do what they have in mind they'll spill his evil on to all of us. It should be locked away, Josh. Please go and stop them. I beg you!'

His mother's passionate outburst conjured up a series of confused and disjointed pictures in his mind. But his father's words had left no room for argument. 'I want you to stay here,' he had said. If he left the house now, and Moses did return, Josh could only blame himself. He could not go and he said so once more.

Jesse Retallick started to say something but she stopped abruptly, her hands falling helplessly to her sides. She knew her two men well enough to realise when they could be persuaded and when they could not. Then all other thoughts were forgotten as a drawn-out moan came from the bedroom accompanied by a loud thud. Jesse Retallick ran up the stairs followed by Josh.

Jenny Pearn lay on the floor by the open door. Josh bent down beside his mother and drew back in revulsion. Her face was puffed and bruised to such an extent as to be unrecognisable. Josh was appalled. He had forgotten what Moses Trago's handiwork could look like.

'Here. Help me lift her back into bed.' Jesse Retallick had an arm about Jenny's shoulders.

'Leave her. I'll do it.' Bending down, Josh lifted the beaten girl and carried her to the bed. As he laid her down she struggled to sit up.

'No! No, Moses! Please don't. You're hurting me!' Her voice rose to a scream, and Jesse held her down to prevent her from falling from the bed again, talking soothingly to her all the while. 'Hush! It's all right, Jenny. It's all right, my love. It's me, Jesse. You're all right. Hush now!'

Jenny stopped struggling, and the cries became sobs as she clung to the other woman. 'I couldn't stop him. He was too strong, Jesse. He did it to me. I couldn't stop him. Oh, Jesse what am I going to do? What will happen to me now?'

'Shh! Everything will be all right.' As she was talking, Jesse dismissed Josh with a movement of her head. 'We'll have you better in no time. All of this will be behind you like a bad dream.'

Even downstairs Josh could hear Jenny's crying and he went outside for the axe. Out here the thick walls and the distance muffled the sounds.

He looked up the hillside, expecting to see some of the men, but there was nothing. Nothing except for the slow-moving train of pack mules moving southwards along the slope, coming down from a new mining venture high on the moor itself.

Beyond the rocky heights of Sharptor there was a build-up of dark-grey cloud and the distant shimmer of a lightning-flash. Josh collected the axe and returned to the cottage.

By dusk there was no sign of Ben Retallick or the other men and the storm had moved closer. There was little conversation in the Retallick cottage. As the thunder rumbled outside, Jesse busied herself in the kitchen. Josh paced from window to door to hearth and back again. Growing more restless with every minute that passed.

It had been dark an hour before there was the scraping of boots on stone outside and the soft voices of men talking in whispers. Josh hurriedly unlocked the door, and Jesse came from the kitchen, drying her hands upon her apron.

The men entered the cottage grim-faced and silent, except for the miner with the hoarse voice. 'There'll be no need to lock the door against Moses Trago again,' he said triumphantly.

'He's dead?' Jesse Retallick's question was an accusation.

'Yes, he's dead,' replied Tom Shovell. 'His body is lying at the bottom of the old diggings up on Cheesewring Hill.'

'So you found him,' said Jesse Retallick, flatly. 'You found him and you were judge and jury – and God himself.'

'It wasn't like that.' Ben Retallick looked an old man. 'He fell. It was an accident.'

'An accident? Ben Retallick, I've known you for a lifetime and I don't believe you. Do you expect a jury of strangers will think differently?'

'It was an accident, Jesse.' Wrightwick Roberts' big fingers tangled and untangled themselves jerkily. 'We had him cornered at the top of the old shaft and called on him to give himself up to us. He was throwing rocks to keep us back. As he stooped to pick up one from the edge of the shaft he slipped and fell down it.'

'Are you telling me you actually saw this with your own eyes, Wrightwick Roberts? Or did one of you who was closer to Moses say that's what happened and you all agreed it must be so?'

There was an uncomfortable silence during which Jesse Retallick looked at each of the men in turn, hoping that one of them would meet her gaze.

'Tom, you'd better go upstairs to that poor girl. If she's awake she'll have need of your kindness. Say nothing of what's happened to Moses. I only hope there were no witnesses to this night's work.'

Again the men looked uncomfortable, and Jesse gasped, 'For God's sake! Someone did see you! Who was it?'

'There was no other to see what happened.' This from Wrightwick Roberts. 'Although the Trago girl was following us shortly before. But it really was an accident, Jesse.'

Josh never waited to hear the last part of the sentence. He could imagine Miriam following the men who were hunting her father, hoping to find him first and warn him. Then to witness his death – however it occurred. He had no doubt that she had seen it. He reached for his coat and bolted through the door before anyone was able to say anything to him.

The storm was almost overhead now. Between the rumbling thunder the lightning picked out the bushes and rocks of the moor, enlarging them and giving them long trembling shadows.

As he stumbled through the undergrowth, Josh reproached himself bitterly. If he had not been so completely wrapped up in the Sharptor engine he might have heard something from Miriam of her father's state of mind. There might even have been a way of averting today's series of tragedies.

He heard a movement in the undergrowth ahead of him and stopped, suddenly fearful of what else might be abroad on this wild night. It was one of the shaggy moorland cattle, stunted like a tree on the high moor and equally as wild.

The cottage had been sheltered by the bulk of the tor from the north-easterly wind. Up here it was much more exposed. The uneven gusts of wind ripped through the green undergrowth like a prophet spreading the gospel of the storm to come.

Finally Josh reached his destination. On hands and knees he crawled through the gorse-tunnel into the rock hideout. It was silent inside and he thought he had guessed wrong. Perhaps Miriam no longer used her old hideaway. Then a sustained web of lightning broke up the sky and he saw her. She was crouching in the corner where he had once found her with a face as badly battered as the one he had seen today.

'Miriam! I thought you would be here.' He dropped down beside her. 'I'm sorry. I really am.'

He had hoped – expected – that she would fall into his arms and cling to him, that he would comfort her and wipe away her tears; but she was showing no emotion. Her body was stiff and rigid. Only her lips moved.

'They killed him. They cornered him like a dog in a sheep-pen. Then they killed him.'

'Try not to think about it, Miriam.' His hands went out to her shoulders. 'They didn't mean to do it. He slipped.'

'No!' She spat the word out. 'They killed him. I saw it.'

'They wanted to take him back. He had to be caught after what he did to Jenny today. Nobody wanted it to end that way.'

'Yes, they did. That was exactly how they wanted it to end.'

His arms were about her now. He tried to draw her to him, but she did not unbend.

'Miriam, don't hold the pain in like this. Cry, scream, shout, do anything, but don't just shut yourself off from me.'

She remained stiff for another minute, and in the light from another flickering lightning-flash he saw her face turn to him, her eyes dark hidden shadows. Then suddenly, without any warning at all, she brought her mouth up to his. Her arms went about him, fierce and demanding.

It took him by surprise, but he responded immediately and eagerly. He had known that she would listen to him. Her mouth moved wildly beneath his before her teeth sank into his lower lip. He tasted blood. She slipped sideways to lie on the grass of the hideout, and he went down with her. Side by side their bodies strained to each other. Her hands slipped inside his jacket and began plucking his shirt loose from his trousers. Then her hands were clutching, clawing at the skin of his back.

His hand pushed clumsily inside her dress and closed about the firmness of one of her breasts. She moaned. The sound grew louder as, button by undone button, his hand worked down her dress. Her body writhed. Throbbed warm beneath him.

Then he was fumbling at his trousers, inexpertly and hurriedly. When he rolled on to her she strained to receive him. Thunder and lightning was all about them, their bodies the hub of the storm, everything radiating outwards from them. The storm grew fiercer and more violent, reaching its climax in a vibrating roll of thunder that left the earth trembling. Josh shuddered with it, gasping for breath.

When it died away he lay still for a long time, moving only when he felt the rain pounding against his near-naked body.

He stood up slowly, reluctant to leave her. Self-consciously he pulled his clothes together.

Miriam lay where he had left her, not moving, her white skin glistening with rain in the light of the now passing lightning.

Josh was uneasy. Something was not right.

'Here. Take my jacket. You're getting soaked.' It was a stupid meaningless thing to say. But he took off his jacket and laid it over her. She ignored it and rose to her knees. The jacket slid to the ground. Then slowly she got to her feet.

'Miriam, are you all right?'

He reached out a hand to her, but she flinched back as though he had tried to strike her.

'Don't touch me!'

'What's the matter? Did I hurt you? I'm sorry, but you wanted it to happen as much as I did, didn't you?'

She moved back from him. 'Did I, Josh? Are you quite sure? When I tell Morwen and Uncle John what happened up here will they believe you – or me? You can't deny it happened. There's blood to prove it because I've never been with another man, Josh. What do you think they will do when I tell them you forced me? Held me down and took me. Will they get the Wheal Phoenix men out to hunt you? Carrying sticks and shouting like huntsmen when they see you? Perhaps they'll drive you backwards and surround you at the top of some mine shaft. They'll give you a choice, Josh. Face their stones and flailing sticks – or back to the hole in the ground. The hole with crumbling edges. Tell them they've made a mistake, Josh. Tell them we both wanted to do it. Do you think they'll believe you? Do you think they'll even listen?'

'Miriam, you don't know what you're saying. We're going to be married—'

'No!'

The thunder rumbled away in the background. Miriam's hair lay long and wet down her face and over her shoulders as she shrugged herself back into her limp dress. 'How can I marry you? Your father killed mine.'

Josh attempted to deny it, but her voice was a scream that cut him short.

'He did! He did! He murdered him. I can't marry you now.' Her voice broke. 'It's over between us, Josh. Finished. I told you once that you would be the first man to have me, and I've kept my promise.' She tried to swallow the sob that rose into her throat, but it escaped.

Josh took hold of her, but she broke free, slipping beneath his arms. Before he could stop her she had gone, into the gorse-tunnel.

'Miriam, come back!' A flash of lightning ripped the sky, blinding him, and the thunder laughed as he stumbled into the pin-sharp gorse.

Beyond the tunnel, away from the hideaway, he called again. The wind threw the words back in his teeth.

He wandered the moors searching and calling until the storm tired of playing with him and, drawing its cloak of rain about itself, moved on. Later still the moon showed itself, pale and weak, but it was almost dawn before Josh went home to the cottage, thankful for the grey darkness. He sat in his father's rocking-chair in the kitchen and watched the dawn come in through the window. When he heard stirring upstairs he let himself out and made his way to the Sharptor mine and the Harvey engine.

Chapter Fourteen

Moses Trago was buried at St Cleer with only his family and a couple of inquisitive miners present. The Reverend William Thackeray took the service and he spoke of the 'tragic accident' that had taken Moses from them. Morwen scowled angrily and was about to dispute the preacher's statement when his mother put a restraining hand on his arm. She did not relax it until the uncomfortable eulogy came to an end and the first spadeful of earth rained down upon the rough-planed coffin lid.

Miriam, looking ill and strained, continued to stand gazing unseeingly into the narrow trench until William Thackeray put a comforting arm about her shoulders and led her from the graveside.

'We'll all go back to my cottage for some refreshment,' he said to Kate Trago. 'There's something I wish to say. It may not be altogether proper at this sad time, but there is little sense in delaying it.'

Miriam's shoulders heaved beneath William Thackery's arm as she noisily fought back a sob, and Kate Trago moved forward to comfort her with soft words. John Trago followed in her wake, but the scowling Morwen turned and walked away with neither a word nor a backward glance.

Josh knew about the funeral and that Miriam would be

there; but, though he desperately wanted to speak to her, he knew better than to attempt it.

He was still bewildered and unable to think straight about Miriam and himself. For a couple of days after the night of the storm his unhappiness had been mingled with fear. But there had been no knock at the door, no crowd of angry miners eager to avenge the seduction of a young girl. Now only the uncertainty remained.

He tried to intercept Miriam on her way home from her work at the Wheal Phoenix, but she never came. When he enquired he found she had not been to work since the death of her father.

He made various attempts to see her again after the funeral but never caught so much as a glimpse of her. Then he changed his tactics and waited near the Tragos' rock home. Here he came into violent contact with another member of the Trago family.

Josh was watching the path from the cover of an ivy-clad rock when he heard the faintest of sounds from the undergrowth to one side of him. He turned to see Morwen Trago coming at him.

Declining to give ground, Josh waited as Morwen crashed through the last few yards of fern to face him.

'What are you spying on us for, Josh Retallick? Haven't you and your lot done enough? What are you after now?'

'I came up here to see Miriam,' said Josh.

'Did you, now?' Morwen Trago mocked. 'Then you'll have a very long wait because Miriam isn't here. I don't suppose you'll ever see her here again.'

'What do you mean? Where is she? I must see her.'

'Must? Who do you think you are? Just because you've been away to learn about engines and come home wearing fancy clothes and riding a horse with a saddle, you needn't think that everyone is going to jump to do your bidding. The Trago family has suffered enough at the hands of the Retallicks and their friends. Go away and leave Miriam alone. She's showing some sense at last. She doesn't want to see you again.'

He turned to go, but Josh caught his sleeve. 'You're lying, Morwen. She'd never say that. Where is she?'

The expression on Morwen's face was as venomous as his father's had ever been and he knocked Josh's hand from his sleeve. 'No Retallick calls me a liar. I've told you to leave Miriam alone. This should help you remember it.'

Josh was expecting a blow from Morwen's fist, but it was his booted foot that lashed out first. Josh managed to twist his body enough to prevent the steel-rimmed heel from sinking into his groin, but it raked painfully across the front of his thigh.

Josh grabbed at the boot and twisted, bringing Morwen to the ground. As he tried to rise Josh hit him in the face before closing in and grappling with him. Wrestling and gouging, they rolled crashing down the slope to land with a breath-shaking thud on the hard-packed earth of the path.

Morwen was a stone heavier than Josh, but there was little to choose between them when it came to actual strength. Few blows were struck on either side. Instead, it was a mauling, wrestling fight. Neither of the participants had been more than bruised when the hands of a man stronger than either of them reached down and prised them apart with a stranglehold on their collars.

'Hasn't there been enough fighting between our two families? Is it going to be carried on by the sons now?'

It was John Trago, the brother of Moses.

Morwen began to struggle as John lifted them both to their feet, but John shook his nephew until his teeth rattled.

'Stop it, I say!'

Morwen ceased his struggles, and John Trago released them both.

'Now, what's this all about?' The big man's voice was surprisingly soft. Perhaps it was because Josh had never really listened to him before today. John Trago had always walked in the shadow of his elder brother. Moses had made the decisions and said all that was necessary. John had usually stood silently by, with no evident thoughts or opinions of his own.

'I caught him snooping around, spying on us,' said a surly Morwen.

'I was trying to see Miriam.'

'You won't find her here anymore,' said John Trago.

'I told him that,' put in Morwen.

'Then where is she? I must see her.'

'She's at St Cleer, staying at Preacher Thackeray's house.'

'Thank you. That's all I wanted to know.'

'Josh!'

He had turned to go when the call stopped him.

'You must leave her be, now.'

'Why? We have something that needs talking about.'

'She's getting married this coming week.'

Shock and disbelief hit Josh with a near-physical blow, and he reeled under the impact.

'Married? It isn't possible! Who . . . ?'

'The preacher. She's marrying Preacher Thackeray.'

Josh's mouth hung open like an idiot's. William Thackeray had been his friend and tutor. He had taught Josh not only how to read and write, but even how to think.

It had been his guide-lines that Josh had followed through recent years. Furthermore, the preacher had known of Josh's love for Miriam. He could not be marrying her. It would be a complete and utter betrayal. He hardly heard the rest of John Trago's words.

'Don't try to see her there, Josh. It would only distress her. This is a good marriage for Miriam, a chance to get away from the past and lead a normal happy life. If you think anything at all of her, don't take that chance away.'

Josh stumbled away along the path, followed by Morwen's derision. His mind was in a turmoil. He did not choose his direction and walked unknowingly, aimlessly. When he did become aware of things around him he looked up to see the rock hideout just ahead. He crawled gratefully into its shelter.

He needed to think, to find some way out of this incredible nightmare. Engineering problems he had been taught to deal with. Human ones were something new.

He sat looking at the spot where he had lain with Miriam on that stormy night less than a week before. He had believed that the act of making love would bind them closer together. Even her outburst afterwards could be explained away. She was so terribly grieved and upset by the events of the day; but he had always believed she would come back to him, that he would be allowed to make up for all the bad things that had happened in the past. But to marry William Thackeray – it was unthinkable.

He raised his head and saw something metallic gleaming in a crevice between the rocks. It was a tin box. Lifting it down, he prised off the lid and saw it was full of papers. He pulled them out and looked at them and found that he held in his hands a full record of the relationship between himself and Miriam. Not only were there all the letters he had sent to her while he was at Hayle but also the pages of arithmetic he had taught her, the names of towns and countries he had written for her. Finally, on a scrap of paper he found a faded word that had once brought such pleasure to Miriam. It was her name. 'Miriam.' She had been happy that day, delighted at seeing her name in writing for the first time. 'I'll keep it for ever,' she had said. It seemed that the 'for ever' had come to an end.

For the next few days Josh drove himself hard at the mine, helping to get the pump working. He drove others too, and after two days during which he rounded on anyone at the slightest provocation he was called to the mine captain's office.

Tom Shovell came immediately to the point. 'I've called you in here because you are upsetting the men who are working with you. They haven't complained to me, but I've got eyes and ears to find out things for myself. All right, so you've got problems. I know about them and so does every other man on the mine. I suspect that's the only reason someone has not tried to knock your angry young head off. I've known you a very long time, Josh. My friendship with your father is something I value highly. But I'm not having your personal problems interfering with the efficient running of the Wheal

Sharptor. Nobody here is in any way to blame for them. I suggest you do something about sorting it out at source. If it means taking a day off, then do it. It will save me more hours in the long run.'

Walking away from the office, Josh had to admit that the mine captain was right. When he returned to the shaft he apologised to the men working with him. Because he was liked, his apologies were waved aside. But the men were relieved to see him behaving normally again.

Josh did not go straight home that evening. When work was over he set off in the opposite direction – to St Cleer. Tom Shovell had mentioned the source of the trouble, and Josh was on his way to see the Reverend William Thackeray.

At the gate to the preacher's small stone cottage, situated behind the chapel, Josh hesitated. Coming across the moor he had rehearsed what he would say to the preacher. He would tell him that for Miriam to marry anyone but himself would be a dreadful mistake. They, Miriam and Josh, loved each other and always had. They had promised themselves to each other. He had thought of saying that they had already given themselves to each other but decided to keep that as a last desperate bid to prevent the marriage.

Then, as he squared his shoulders for the coming confrontation, a sudden thought made a coward of him. What if Miriam opened the door? He had no speech rehearsed for that eventuality. The wrong words could ruin the future for both of them.

While he hesitated, the problem was solved for him. William Thackeray came out of the cottage. Closing the door behind him, he walked down the path towards his former pupil.

'Josh! How wonderful to see you. How are you?'

Josh ignored the preacher's outstretched hand. William Thackeray dropped it to his side without changing his expression. 'I knew you were home and was hoping you would find time to come and see me. I have also heard how busy you are working.'

'Is there some place where we can talk?'

The preacher indicated the books beneath his arm. 'I am on

my way into the chapel to do some teaching. It's something I do every evening at this time. Surely you hadn't forgotten?'

'No. That is – I hadn't thought about it.' In fact he had forgotten, but it was not this which disconcerted him. It was the aura of complete confidence which always surrounded William Thackeray. For Josh this was a violently emotional problem. He could not understand how the preacher was able to maintain such a calm composure.

'I want to speak to you about Miriam,' he blurted out, feeling awkward and adolescent, a pupil with the master.

'Yes, I know.' Preacher Thackeray stopped and looked at Josh. 'But talking will not change anything. Miriam and I are to be married.'

Josh drew in a great gulp of air. It was out in the open now. William Thackeray had set the fact out in front of him as though it were a mathematical problem to which he already knew the answer but wanted to see what sort of a hash Josh would make of it.

'She was going to marry me,' he said, totally inadequately.

'Yes, I know. That is why I am glad you have come to see me, Josh. We have been friends for a very long time. I would have been unhappy in the knowledge that someone we both care so much for had come between us. I know Miriam feels the same way.'

'She said so?'

'Not in so many words, but the feeling is there nevertheless.'

'Where is she now?'

'I'm sorry, Josh. That is something I am not willing to tell you.'

'I want to see her. I want her to tell me herself that everything is over between us. I'll believe it then.'

'No. It would serve no useful purpose, and she has suffered quite enough recently. Don't you agree?'

'I only want to hear her say the words. I'll accept it then.'

'You will have to accept it from me, Josh. Miriam is going to be my wife.'

Josh towered over the preacher, but William Thackeray was

well experienced in facing angry men. They held no terror for him.

'I don't believe this has just happened,' Josh said angrily. 'You've been working towards this all the time I've been away. Miriam was desperate to learn things and to get an education. You've taken advantage of it.'

'You just told me yourself that she was going to marry you. Circumstances have changed only in the last couple of weeks, Josh. I can hardly be blamed for the reasons behind that change.'

The preacher's quiet reasonable tone only served to make Josh angrier. 'She can't marry you! She can't! Ask her about—' Josh was going to tell him about the events of the night of the storm, but the words stuck in his throat.

'She has told me all I want to hear and we will be married on Sunday. I think—'

'I don't give a damn what you think!' Josh blurted angrily.

'We really won't achieve anything pursuing this conversation.' William Thackeray turned in towards the chapel. 'I would like you to come into the chapel with me, Josh.'

Josh stopped and the preacher looked back at him sorrowfully.

'I'm sorry, Josh. I'll pray for your peace of mind.'

Josh turned away, angry and ashamed at the tears that stung his eyes. William Thackeray had won. Josh was not proud of himself for having even contemplated mentioning that night in the hideout with Miriam, but he would not allow this man who had once been his friend to witness his humiliation.

But someone else witnessed his defeat. Miriam saw it in his step and the abject droop to his shoulders as he walked away from the chapel. Her eyes burned for him.

From her room upstairs in the preacher's home she had watched him approach the house, until suddenly her knees had become so weak she had to cling to the brass upright of the bed for support.

At the same time she heard William rushing to gather books from the study and leave the house, heading off Josh before he reached the door.

While the two men were talking at the gate she felt physically sick, not wanting to look at them standing together, yet unable to turn away.

Then, as they moved off, she almost screamed at them to come back, to remain where she could see them.

Now, as Josh walked away hunched in his unhappiness, it was his misery she shared, not William Thackeray's victory.

When he passed from her view she laid her forehead against the cold metal of the bed. Closing her eyes she wept as she never had before. Now there could be no turning back. Her tears were for Josh's today and both their tomorrows.

There were two weddings that month. In the chapel at St Cleer, William Thackeray was married to Miriam Trago; while, in the little whitewashed chapel at Henwood, Jenny Pearn became Mrs Shovell.

Josh went to neither wedding. He made the weak excuse to Jenny that there were last-minute adjustments to be made to the pumps in the Wheal Sharptor. He could not have sat through the service without torturing himself with thoughts of the other wedding taking place only a few miles away.

Although his absence was for emotional reasons, there *was* something he was working on in the mine – and it was being done without the knowledge of Theophilus Strike.

The pump was worked by a series of huge wooden rods, alternately pushed down and drawn up by the movement of a rocking-beam. They extended from the grass to the bottom of the shaft and rose and fell extremely slowly, at a rate of scarcely more than five strokes a minute.

Inspired by the plans given to him by Francis Trevithick, Josh was using this slow speed to provide a simple means of raising men to the surface.

The idea was starkly simple: The length of the engine's stroke was some twelve feet, and Josh had bolted blocks of wood to the rods at a distance of twelve feet apart. At the same intervals up the shaft he had built tiny platforms into the wooden framework. It would be a simple matter for a man to step on to a block and ride up for twelve feet. Then he would step off and wait for the next stroke of the pump to ride up the next twelve feet in the same manner.

The experiment had Tom Shovell's blessing, even though he lacked Josh's conviction that the mine-owner would appreciate the advantages to be gained from the experiment.

As it happened, he did not have to wait long to discover the mine-owner's reaction. Theophilus Strike arrived to see the inauguration of the pumping operation, this time without his retinue of friends.

The engine-men who would be operating the engine on a shift basis were all experienced. Josh had satisfied himself that they knew what they were doing before he allowed them to operate his engine.

The fire had been stoked up from early morning and the hissing of steam from the escape-valve was a new sound in the Sharptor air. When Strike, Tom Shovell and the shift captains were assembled, Josh signalled for the engine-man to set the pumping-engine in motion. With a gentle hiss of steam and protesting creaks from the wooden rods, each one a foot in diameter, the horse-operated water-pump became a piece of history and steam took over. Without ceremony and with no fuss it had all the ingredients of an anti-climax.

'So now we have become a modern mine,' said Theophilus Strike to Tom Shovell. 'How is it looking down below?'

'Why not go down and see for yourself, Mr Strike?'

Theophilus Strike looked at Josh, who had made the suggestion, not quite certain whether it smacked of insolence.

'I've built a new idea into the pumping system,' Josh went on. 'It means that the men will be able to come up from the levels without using the ladders.'

'What the devil do you mean?' Strike blazed. 'Your job was to put in the engine and pumping system and see that they keep working. Not install some fool idea of your own.'

'It's not exactly my own idea,' said Josh, realising that Theophilus Strike was capable of dismissing him on the spot. 'It was Richard Trevithick's idea. His son gave me the drawings.'

'Francis Trevithick?' There was an immediate change of

attitude. The Cornish engineering family was highly respected in the county. 'When did he come to Sharptor?'

'He didn't. I met him at Hayle and we discussed means of lifting men to surface. He told me that when I installed the engine into Sharptor I was to be sure to build a man-lift into it. He even sent me a completely detailed set of plans his father had drawn up.'

The mine-owner's look searched Josh's face. 'And how much did this idea cost?'

'It cost virtually nothing,' Tom Shovell broke into the conversation. 'We made use of materials that were already to hand.'

'So you knew about it too? Your job is to keep me informed about Wheal Sharptor, Shovell, not to do things behind my back. Now, you!' He pointed a finger at Josh. 'How is this new idea supposed to work?'

Josh explained, and Theophilus Strike listened intently. 'And how many mines are using this method to bring their men to the surface?'

'Wheal Sharptor will be the first in Cornwall,' Josh said proudly.

'All right, take me down to the fifty-fathom level and I'll see for myself how it works. Give me a hard hat, someone.'

Hurriedly Tom Shovell sent one man to find a hard hat and another to take candles to place by each platform in the shaft down to the fifty-fathom level.

Josh explained the workings once again at the edge of the shaft where the objects of his labours could be seen. He pointed out the huge iron staples driven into the rods at shoulder level to provide a hand-grip.

The primitive man-lift was totally lacking in safety measures, but it was less dangerous than a narrow wet ladder to a tired man.

There was a certain reluctance to be the first man to use the man-lift and so Josh led the way, stepping on to the block as it came up to its maximum height. It was easier than even he had thought it would be. The platform were sufficiently large and the low speed of the engine eliminated much of the danger.

Theophilus Strike followed him, and his appearance in the fifty-fathom working tunnel startled the miners. It was the first time the mine-owner had visited a working area that was not directly accessible via a horizontal adit.

When his tour of inspection was over Theophilus Strike returned above ground. The minute he stepped on to grass once again it was obvious to everyone he had enjoyed the novel experience.

'I approve of your work, Josh. You have done well. Thanks, I have no doubt, to Trevithick's plans. It pleases me that the Wheal Sharptor is able to show the way to other mines. I only hope your lift is not going to make my miners soft.'

'At the end of a shift a man is already tired,' said Josh quietly but intensely. 'Anyone who has ever seen a man lying gasping for breath after climbing the ladders would never think it soft to find another way to get them up. Why, when they had an expert look at the new treadmill in Bodmin Jail he said that no prisoner should have to tread more than twelve hundred rungs in one day's work, yet a miner working at three hundred fathoms climbs eighteen hundred – *after* he's finished his day's work. Doing away with that can do nothing but great good.'

'Joshua Retallick, I like your initiative, and I'm satisfied with your skill as an engineer, but you will keep your radical thinking to yourself. I will agree to allow the men to use this "man lift" as you call it, but I do not need to be lectured on the lot of the miner. On the Wheal Sharptor a man is paid a fair wage for a fair day's work. No one is forcing him to stay. I've heard all about these people who mutter about a "union of miners" and try to tell mine-owners what their men can and can not do. I'll have none of that talk here. Anyone who thinks differently would be well advised to leave now. Do I make myself quite clear?'

'I think Josh was only trying to explain that we'll be able to use our more experienced men at the deeper levels now we have the man-lift,' put in Tom Shovell. 'We haven't been able to use them before because the climb back up was too much.'

'I'm fully aware of what he was saying,' replied the mine-owner. 'I hope he is equally certain of my meaning. There is quite enough discontent in this area. I'll have none of it at the Wheal Sharptor. Now we'll go to the office. I have some business to discuss with you.'

'You'll have to watch that tongue of yours,' said Ben Retallick when the mine-owner and his captain had gone beyond hearing. 'Wag it if you must, but not when Theophilus Strike is about.'

'What did I say?' protested Josh. 'I only spoke the truth. I've seen you on the ground by the shaft gasping for air like a drowning man. And a hundred others beside.'

'Strike doesn't want to know about that,' Ben Retallick said. 'While you've been away your friend the preacher at St Cleer has been out and about complaining of the miners' conditions. Wherever he goes there is trouble. Strike knows you were schooled by him and it bothers him. Learn to choose your words when he's near. He may be a bit touchy but he's a good man to work for.'

'He needn't worry about my association with Preacher Thackeray,' said Josh bitterly. 'He's no friend of mine.'

Josh may have considered his friendship with William Thackeray to be at an end, but every evening a prayer for him went up from the preacher's house.

Kneeling by the bed she shared with her husband, Miriam first prayed to be given the strength to make William Thackeray a good wife although she did not love him, accepting that she needed to work hard at it because of her hunger for Josh. It was a Trago curse passed on from her father. As he had craved after Jenny, so she wanted Josh. But Josh must never know of her feelings, and because of this she also prayed for forgiveness for the hurt she had inflicted on him.

This private evening ritual was a penance she accepted. It continued even when kneeling was a feat of will-power made daily more difficult by the new life swelling inside her – the child of the moor with no birthright in this house.

Chapter Fifteen

As close as the weddings of Miriam and Jenny had been, the births of their respective babies in the middle of 1842 were closer. Both children chose to enter the world in the dark of the same night – hoping, some said, that the absence of light might hide their secrets.

Miriam's son was born after twelve hours of painful labour. She writhed on the bed in the cottage behind the chapel, arching her back as she gripped the head-posts, fighting to bite back the screams that each labour-pain drew from her and the name that was on her tongue.

Not until the pain had almost sapped the last of her strength and caused the women attending her to send out an urgent call for a doctor did the baby finally make his way into the world, adding his cries to the gasps of his mother.

Jenny had an easier time, if such events are measured only in terms of physical pain. It began not long before midnight. By the time Mary Crabbe arrived to perform the duties of midwife, the birth was well under way.

The old crone took complete charge of the proceedings. Hustling the women neighbours from the room, she opened the door only in order to receive the boiling water that was passed through in bucket and kettle. By two o'clock in the morning it was all over. But there were no baby sounds heard in Tom Shovell's house, no admiring women to cluster about the bed. The baby, also a boy, was still-born. Its death brought about by an umbilical cord wrapped about its neck.

There was sympathy for Jenny, but little sorrow at the loss of the innocent child. Those who saw it said it had the scowl of Moses Trago on its screwed-up face. Others described the expression as more evil than a scowl. But a strangled child is never a pretty sight.

All the women agreed about one thing. The baby's death had been no more natural than Moses Trago's. It was no secret that Mary Crabbe had hated Moses. But the women kept their thoughts about the death of the child to low whispers, passed on only behind closed doors. Mary Crabbe could cure a coughing cow with the breath from her own mouth. She could touch a wart with her fingertips and it would shrivel and fall off. There were few who had not drunk one of her potions when they were sick. But after Nehemeziah's old dog had got among her chickens, killing half of them, it had begun to waste away for no apparent reason. Within a month it was dead. So there was not a woman who would willingly risk her displeasure.

Less discreet was the talk about Miriam's child. That it was conceived out of wedlock was unanimously agreed. The only point at issue was whether or not the Reverend William Thackeray was the child's father. Most of the gossips had it that he was, but there were others who gave knowing looks in Josh's direction. For his part he gave no sign that he knew of their opinions. Or cared, if he did.

The engine at the mine was running well, carrying out both its primary and secondary tasks. Although many of the older miners had scoffed at the idea at first, more and more of them were now using Josh's man-lift to ride to grass. The womenfolk of those who worked in the lowest levels no longer had to delay a meal until their men regained enough energy to eat. They blessed Josh for his innovation.

As word of Josh's man-lift spread around the area it became commonplace to see off-duty miners from the Wheal Phoenix and Caradon mines crowding around the top of the main

Sharptor shaft, watching the lights from the candles on the hats of the ascending miners come slowly to the surface. They would gasp in disbelief when, in answer to their questioning, a comparatively fresh man would state he had come up from the two-hundred-fathom level.

It was not long before Captain Frisby from the Wheal Caradon sent a messenger asking Josh if he would call to see him.

Josh went after work that same day. The Caradon captain came immediately to the point.

'Tell me about this man-lift idea of yours,' he said. 'How much would it cost to put one into the Caradon for me?'

Josh grinned. 'It would cost next to nothing. But since when has the Wheal Caradon been so concerned about its men?'

'You don't want to believe everything you hear, young man,' snapped the captain. 'I can't help it if the Wheal Caradon has more than its share of trouble-makers. We are a big mine, not a little family concern like the Sharptor. We can't be so fussy about who we take on.'

'You get what you pay for,' retorted Josh. It was well known that, for all its great size and high production, the men working for the Wheal Caradon were amongst the worst-paid miners in the country. And it showed in the amount of ore brought out per man.

'You sound like a union man,' said Captain Frisby angrily. 'I get enough of that every day. But I didn't bring you here to quarrel. I'm asking you to do this job for me. Convert the main pump into a man-lift – if it doesn't cost too much. Perhaps that might stop some of the grumbling. I do my best for them and that's what I want to do now.'

Josh looked at the mine captain suspiciously. His words did not fit in with the stories that Josh had heard about him.

'Let's go and have a look at the pump-rods,' said Josh. 'A lot depends on their type and the way they've been fitted.'

On the way Josh questioned the mine captain about the main shaft. Unlike the Wheal Sharptor, the Caradon shaft was not entirely perpendicular. In places the pump-rods worked along an incline, resting on rollers. The men would have to use ladders for these parts of the climb. For the remainder of the way it would present no problems. The pumping-engine could be adapted in the same way as at the Wheal Sharptor.

He said as much to Frisby and the mine captain was well pleased. 'Good! Good! When can you make a start on it?'

'I can't,' said Josh. 'But send a couple of your carpenters and fitters across to the Sharptor tomorrow and I'll show them what to do. Then they can come back here and do it themselves.'

Frisby frowned. 'I suppose that will have to do. Will you inspect it when it's done? I don't want any mistakes caused by shoddy workmanship or by men not knowing exactly what they are about.'

'Yes, I'll do that,' agreed Josh. 'But what's wrong with your own engineer? He'll be able to tell whether it's a good job or not.'

'Caradon hasn't got a proper engineer at the moment,' said Frisby. 'You could have the job if you wanted it. I'll pay you half as much again as you are getting now. There would be no shortage of work. We have plenty of equipment here and more engines than you'll ever see at Sharptor.'

'I don't doubt there would be the work. How many *new* engines do you have?'

This was a blow in a sensitive spot and Josh knew it. The two most recent engines acquired by the Caradon mine had been bought from a tin mine near Truro. There they had already performed many years' service.

'You want me to buy all new equipment as well as pay you a good wage? Young man, if I bought new engines I wouldn't *need* an engineer!'

Josh smiled. 'Sorry, Captain Frisby. I appreciate your offer but Sharptor suits me for now. I wouldn't fancy working on an unhappy mine. Pay half as much again to all your men and you wouldn't have to look for engineers. They'd be banging on your door.'

'Yes, and so would the shareholders. Thank you for nothing. Perhaps it is just as well you won't come to work for me. I have no shortage of men to preach about fair pay for the miner and about their union. Bah! It's just another way of getting more for doing less.'

He was still grumbling about the union when Josh left him.

But Captain Frisby was not the only one to become increasingly aware of union talk. It was something that had been discussed in a half-hearted way wherever miners gathered for years, yet there had been no positive moves to unite the miners until Preacher Thackeray came to St Cleer. It was his dedication to unionism as much as to religion which had made the talk reality. He was an eloquent speaker, yet down to earth enough to get through to the uneducated miner. Neither was poverty any stranger to him. It had been a persistent foe throughout his childhood days in the East End of London. But, always bright, he had been singled out for special education by the City Road Mission, later being sent to work and preach in the black coal valleys and iron hills of Wales. There he had seen the violence that erupted when men sought to better themselves. He came to recognise the power that ordinary men wielded when they united in common purpose. Unity. Union. It was the same thing.

William Thackeray had become a keen convert to their cause, travelling many miles to address meetings. Then he had been abruptly transferred to Cornwall. He had been told that the Cornish system of mining, with each man seemingly his own master, made the Cornish miner less likely to be interested in the ideals he preached. William Thackeray was proving them wrong. At least in east Cornwall. When he spoke of unionism men listened. When they returned for the next meeting they brought friends with them. They came to him with their problems, asked his advice.

During the years he had been taught by him, Josh had assimilated many of Preacher Thackeray's beliefs. He was never reluctant to argue the cause of a miners' union with anyone who had a point of view to put forward.

He had even recently attended one of William Thackeray's open-air meetings. In a crowd of almost a thousand his anonymity was assured, but there were many times during the preacher's speech when he felt he had been singled out as the target for a particular phrase or remark. It was this, he realised, that was the secret of Thackeray's power of oratory. Every man there left the meeting believing that the preacher had been speaking personally to him.

The reason that Josh had not attended any more meetings was because Miriam now occasionally delivered a speech with her husband. Josh did not feel able to face her, although it had been more than a year since her marriage.

The time had brought changes for the whole of the Trago family. Soon after Miriam's wedding John Trago had come down the hill to the Retallick cottage. He stood in the doorway, changing his considerable weight from foot to foot, big and awkward. Although every broad inch of him was a Trago, he lacked the ambient menace that had always travelled with his older brother.

'Well, come on in, man,' said Jesse Retallick. 'Though I can't think of a Trago who's crossed this doorstep without bringing trouble into the house.'

'I hope all that is past, Jesse,' said the big miner. 'That's what I've come to speak to you and Ben about.'

'Then take a seat,' said Ben. 'You're so big you're blocking out the light.'

'I'm sorry.' John Trago obligingly moved across the room to place his back against a blank wall. 'But I won't sit down. I'm not stopping.'

He cleared his throat noisily. 'I wanted to tell you that I hold no grudge against you, Ben, or against any of your family. No more does Kate. We neither of us believe that the death of Moses was deliberate.'

It was Ben Retallick's turn to look ill at ease.

'Not that anyone could have blamed you had it been otherwise. He did a terrible thing to Jenny in your house. There's nothing can be said on his part for that. The drink had got him so bad he wasn't living his own life, Ben. How any of us put up with him I don't know – especially Kate. He would hit her around cruelly if we weren't there to stop him.'

John Trago cleared his throat nervously once more. 'I'm

going to marry Kate and look after her and the children. I'll try to give them a bit more of life than they've been used to up to now.'

'That's a fine thing, John,' said Jesse. 'And I'm sure that you'll make a job of it.'

'Thank you, Jesse. I'll do my best.' His face was red and he was perspiring. Talking came harder to him than physical labour.

'You have my good wishes too,' said Ben. 'But you haven't come here today because you want us to be the first to congratulate you. What else is on your mind?'

'There is something else, Ben. You see, I think the children should be brought up to feel they are just like everyone else. Not some strange beings who live in a cave on the moor. There's a house to rent in Henwood that I've been promised. That's a start. But I want it to be a real beginning, Ben. I want Kate and the children to make friends and live without people pointing a finger at them, whispering that they're the family of Moses Trago, the man who raped Jenny and ended his days in a mine-shaft, hunted by the men of Wheal Sharptor.'

Ben nodded seriously. 'That makes good sense. How can I help?'

'You're a respected man in the village. If you put it about that you have no argument with us, everyone else will do the same.'

'We'll do that willingly,' Jesse Retallick said firmly. 'And tell Kate I'll help her to move in. It will be Tillie Coryton's old cottage you are talking about?'

John Trago nodded. 'Yes. It'll need a bit of work doing to it, but I'll see to that.'

'You'll need some bits of furniture to put in there too,' said Jesse. 'We've got a few things to spare now that Jenny has gone. You can have them. I'll get Ben and Josh to take them down for you.'

'I'm grateful to you,' said John Trago. 'Kate will be too. She thought . . . well, that you probably wouldn't want anything more to do with us, what with Moses, then Miriam marrying that preacher from St Cleer.'

'We won't talk about that,' said Jesse Retallick firmly, her lips narrowing into a tight line, 'or I might forget all my good intentions. She did something that has hit our Josh hard. It hurts me to see how he looks sometimes.'

'It came as just as much of a shock to us,' said John Trago. 'It didn't make any sense. Miriam had always been keen for Josh and she isn't the sort of girl to change her mind overnight. Kate went over to stay with her the night before the wedding. She woke up in the night and heard Miriam crying fit to bust, but the girl had locked her door and wouldn't let her mother in.'

'What does Morwen think about this new arrangement of yours?' Ben Retallick made an effort to change the subject.

John Trago shook his head. 'I don't think he's too happy about it. He has some idea in his head that it's breaking faith with his father. I am afraid there is a lot of Moses in that boy, Ben. But it doesn't much matter now; Morwen's gone. He left yesterday for Bodmin to take the Queen's shilling. He thinks a soldier's life has more to offer him than being down a mine. I can't say that he's wrong. We parted on good terms. I doubt if we'd have done that had he stayed any longer. He has his father's weakness for drink. But I'll say no more about him. He's left. I wish him well in the service of the Queen.'

He edged his way to the door. 'I'm very obliged to you both for listening, and for your kind offer, Jesse. I know it will make Kate very happy.'

'She'll be happy enough already in knowing she'll have a good man to look after her,' said Jesse. 'Tell her to come down and see me tomorrow. I expect we'll find a few more things to come in handy in that new cottage of yours.'

Chapter Sixteen

By the year 1843 the copper mines were going through a boom such as they had never known. Demand for copper ore far exceeded supply, keeping prices up. Expansion was the order of the day. But the boom was not indicative of the country – or even Cornwall – as a whole.

Corn was once again short. Why, nobody knew. The market was there but there was little corn to be harvested and many farm-workers were on the parish, out of work with families to support. In Cornwall the situation was aggravated by a slump in the market for tin. The tin-miners wandered the county in search of work and food. Many of them found temporary lodgings with relatives and friends who earned a living digging copper. Some of them were given work on the copper mines – not the regular underground work to which they were accustomed, but part-time work on the surface, grading and sorting the ore. Women's work. Children's work. But for those tin-miners prepared to swallow their pride it meant they could afford a meal and a drink. The Wheal Sharptor had a dozen of them digging a new shaft, more to give them employment than because the need was there.

A few mines – and the Caradon was one – saw the plight of the tinners as something from which to gain advantage. In an effort to increase their profits they took them on at low wages and then cut back the pay of their own men. It aroused great anger among the established miners, but they dared do little but talk. For every copper-miner who left there were fifty out-of-work tinners clamouring to take his place, however low the wage. It took a man like Captain Frisby to wring the full advantage from the situation.

The tinners were in the habit of crowding around outside a mine, waiting for someone to be dismissed or for an accident to occur. Twice fights broke out between the Caradon miners and the waiting tinners. It did nothing for an injured man's peace of mind to see men scrambling for his job as he was carried homewards. It made the miners jittery. They felt the tinners were putting an evil influence on them, wishing them ill.

When Captain Frisby first began to take on the tin-miners at a lower wage some of the Caradon men asked Josh to intercede with the mine captain on their behalf. He refused. He realised that it would merely have given Frisby an excuse for widespread sackings. There was nothing for the miners to do but to grit their teeth and sweat it out. It set out a strong case for a union of miners. Had one been in existence such a situation would never have arisen.

When Josh would not help, the men went to Preacher Thackeray. He gave them the same advice. Thackeray had already held fruitless meetings with the tin-miners. They had been well attended. The tinners had little else to do with their time.

They listened to what he had to say, agreed there was a need for all miners to show a solid front if they were to better themselves; then, if an hour later they were offered a job of work at half-pay, they jumped at it without a twinge of conscience. Principles do not sit well in the stomach of a hungry man.

Another result of the slump in tin-mining was that the demand for mine-engines dropped and the Cornish engine works had to search out new customers.

Josh was in the engine-house of the Sharptor mine, reassembling a steam-valve he had stripped down, when a voice from the doorway said, 'I'm pleased to see you haven't forgotten everything you learned at Harvey's, Josh.'

Swinging around, Josh saw William Carlyon standing in the doorway. Then Sarah pushed past her father. Rushing across the engine-room she flung her arms about Josh's neck and kissed him. The engine-man and two of the Sharptor miners looked on with great interest. Rumours would not be slow in going around Henwood tonight.

Josh was unable to ward Sarah off because his hands were black with grease. He had to stand with arms extended to his sides to avoid spoiling her clothes. There was nothing to do but enjoy her embrace.

'A little grease never hurt anyone,' said William Carlyon and he grasped Josh's hand when Sarah finally released him.

'What are you doing here?' Josh spoke to the Harvey manager, but his eyes were on Sarah. She had grown taller since he last saw her. With her long blonde ringlets tied behind her neck she was a strikingly beautiful girl. Her clothes too were of a quality seldom seen in this area.

'We came here especially to see you,' teased Sarah happily. 'You hadn't written to me for so long I became worried about you. So here we are!'

Josh looked at her father for confirmation and William Carlyon smiled. 'It's all right, Josh. That isn't true. I have to go to Bristol on business. We want to make the boilers for a new ship they are planning. I thought it a good opportunity to give the family a holiday. Mary and Mrs Carlyon are with your mother at the cottage.'

As they talked Josh rubbed the grease from his hands with a piece of rag.

'I rode all the way here on Hector,' said Sarah. 'And Mary rode part of the way on the pony you used to ride when you were at Hayle. The rest of the time she rode in the coach with Mother.'

'You rode Hector wearing that dress?'

'No. I changed when we reached your cottage. It's a new dress. Brought specially from London for me by one of the ship's captains. Do you like it?' She struck a pose, holding the full skirt out to her sides.

'It's a beautiful dress,' he said truthfully. 'Far too good to wear in an engine-house.'

'That's what I told her,' said William Carlyon, 'but she would take no notice of me.'

He nodded towards the engine, its exposed metalwork bright beneath a sheen of grease. 'I can see you are keeping it in good order. If every one of our engines was looked after as well there would be little go wrong with them.'

Josh was pleased at his words. They too would be repeated many times by the listening Sharptor men. William Carlyon's name was well known in the mining fraternity, his opinion respected. If he praised Josh there could be no doubt that the Wheal Sharptor had an engineer to be reckoned with.

'I would like to meet your father and Captain Shovell,' said the Harvey manager. 'One of the men outside told me they were together at the explosives store. Where will I find that?'

Josh started to lead the way but William Carlyon stopped him with a gesture. 'No, just point me in the right direction. I'll find it. You see that Sarah gets back to the cottage. It's all right. We spent last evening dining with Theophilus Strike. I told him we should be robbing him of his engineer for as long as we were here. He made no objection.'

Josh sent one of the miners to guide William Carlyon to the explosives store. It stood some distance away from the mine buildings. Then, after giving instructions to his engine-man, he washed his hands and set off down the track with Sarah.

'Are you pleased to see me, Josh?' Sarah looked up at him provocatively.

'If you are fishing for compliments, then the answer is "Yes". I am pleased to see you. You are even more beautiful than I remembered.'

The Josh she had known at Hayle would not have had the nerve to pay her such a compliment and for a moment Sarah was taken aback, not at all sure that she enjoyed such blatant flattery. Then she looked again at Josh and saw the new confidence in him. He was a young man with the knowledge of his own ability as an engineer, and a man to whom others looked for leadership, respecting his learning. Josh would be a leader in whatever he set out to do. Some men develop in that way without being able to help themselves.

Because of this Sarah accepted the compliment and was stirred by the strength in him.

'You have changed, Josh.'

'Is that good? Or bad?' His smile was a challenge.

'I'm not sure. For you it is probably good. For me . . . ?' She shrugged and there was a moment of silence between them. Then she smiled, removing all tension between them. 'Come on, Josh. If I don't get you home soon Mary will come looking for you. She has talked of nothing but coming to see you for days.'

For the remainder of the way they spoke of people they had both known at Hayle, of the foundry staff, apprentices long gone, and newer ones of whom Sarah despaired. 'They are all so young and terribly serious about their work.'

When they arrived at the cottage Mary ran out and flung herself at him. She seemed hardly to have grown at all.

Mrs Carlyon made the right noises about Josh having 'filled out', and she had a speculative look in her eyes when she watched Sarah and Josh together. Jesse too showed more than a passing interest in the lovely young girl from Hayle. It was a relief when Sarah asked Josh if he would like to go for a ride to show her something of the moor. Josh protested that he would have forgotten how to ride, but he allowed himself to be persuaded and soon he was riding Mary's pony along the path to the high moor, while Sarah followed on Hector.

Once above the ridge, they rode knee to knee through the bracken. 'This is heaven!' Sarah took a deep breath and closed her eyes. 'There is no smell quite like that of fern and heather.'

She gave Josh a warm smile. 'This is just like old times. You don't know how much I have missed riding with you. Have you done much riding since you left Hayle, Josh?'

He looked at her sharply. Did she really understand so little about life in a mining community? Or was she joking?

He saw that she was quite serious.

'No. I haven't ridden since the day I brought the boiler and beam up from Looe. I'm a working man now, Sarah. I have little time to ride and no horse to use if I wanted to.'

'You could ask Mr Strike,' Sarah said seriously. 'I am quite sure he would loan you one of his horses. He is a very nice man.'

'He's a mine-owner. What is more, he owns the mine where I work. He pays me a wage for doing a job of work. I don't think he would take kindly to a request from me to borrow one of his horses for my pleasure.'

'I am sure he would,' replied Sarah. 'But it is far too lovely a day to have an argument. I'll race you to that circle of stones over there.'

The circle of stones was a mile away, and Sarah and Hector arrived a hundred yards ahead of Josh.

'Phew! I'd forgotten a lot of things about riding. One of them was that unless you are in practice it leaves you as blown as the horse.' He dismounted, throwing the reins over the horse's head before helping Sarah to the ground.

She rested her hands on his shoulders and jumped down lightly. But when she landed on the springy turf she did not remove her hands immediately.

Josh looked down at her and she came to him, arms meeting about his neck. For a few minutes, as they kissed, her ardour matched his own. Then he slid one hand up to enclose her breast through her dress. She breathed heavily against it for perhaps ten seconds. Then a tremor went through her body and gently but firmly she took his hand away and placed it behind her back.

'Don't do that, Josh.'

He put the arm back around her and she kissed him wildly. Finally, breasts heaving, she rested her head on his chest, still holding him tightly.

'Oh, Josh! I have missed you terribly.'

'I think you really mean it.'

'You know very well I do. I told you so in every one of my letters. Didn't you read them?'

He had received a letter from her every week and had written perhaps five or six in reply.

'Yes, of course. I wish I could write letters as well as you.'

She pushed away from him and smiled. 'Oh well! A girl can't have everything. At least you had not forgotten me.'

She took his hand and began to lead him towards the stones.

'What are they?'

'Just some stones that the "old men" put up. Legend has it they were people who played football on a Sunday and were turned to stone for their sins.'

'Poor people,' said Sarah. She stooped and picked up a raven's feather from the ground, twiddling it, black and glossy, between her fingers.

'Are you really pleased to see me, Josh?'

'Very pleased.'

He was.

'What about that girl you used to write to when you were at Hayle? The one you told me about. Miriam? Do you still see her?'

'No.'

It was too positive. Too sharp an answer. Sarah looked up quickly.

'She married a preacher. Preacher Thackeray. They live in a village not far from here.'

'Preacher Thackeray!' She was happy again. 'Mr Strike was telling Daddy about him last night. He preaches for a union of all the miners, doesn't he?'

'He says that miners and their families should have fair wages and reasonable working conditions,' said Josh.

'Well, it was something like that,' said Sarah. 'Mr Strike said that Preacher Thackeray is a pain in the neck and ought to be moved to one of the cities. Well away from Cornwall.'

'I told you, Theophilus Strike is an employer. He's bound to oppose Thackeray.'

'Don't tell me you agree with this preacher?' Sarah was only half bantering.

Josh stopped and pulled her gently round to face him.

'Sarah, I don't think you understand. Of course I agree with him. I'm bound to agree with him. He's trying to help men like me. I'm a miner. My father is a miner. All my friends are miners!'

'No. You are not like those creatures we saw coming out of a shaft on our way here. They were filthy dirty, horribly coarse men. You are an engineer, Josh, and your father is a captain.'

Josh was about to argue further. Instead he looked at Sarah and shrugged his shoulders. 'It doesn't matter. We agreed not to argue.'

'Silly! There is nothing to argue about. I think it is a splendid thing for you to care about the miners. I am sure they need someone like you to take an interest in them. It is a pity, though, that they do not have a bit more pride in themselves. Try to keep themselves clean and tidy.'

Sarah had absolutely no conception of conditions below ground in dark, wet, dirty tunnels. Life for her was quite straightforward. When she got dirt on her hands she washed. When she was hungry she ate. Josh doubted whether she was aware that miners' children frequently died from malnutrition, but he had no wish to spoil her day by explaining the facts of mining life to her. She was far too happy. She was also very lovely.

'One day I'll take you down a mine,' he promised. 'Then you'll see for yourself how difficult it is for a man to keep clean when he's working.'

'I will keep you to that, Josh Retallick. But right now I want you to show me Dozmary Pool. That is where King Arthur's sword is supposed to have been thrown when he was dying. Did you know that?'

'No.'

'I read about it recently. That reminds me. I have had a beautiful book of poems given to me. I will send it to you with my next letter.'

'Thank you.' Josh would be pleased to have something fresh to read. Because of his rift with Preacher Thackeray he had not been able to obtain any new books. He missed them. At Hayle he had been able to help himself to whatever books he fancied from William Carlyon's house.

He helped Sarah into her saddle and they rode together to Dozmary Pool and looked down at it from the top of a low hill. To Josh there was nothing mysterious about it. It was simply a small lake with low muddy edges.

'It isn't much to look at,' he said aloud.

'No, but it has an incredible atmosphere.' Sarah shivered. 'It is such a dark brooding place. Don't you feel it, Josh?'

He felt nothing but wisely kept quiet.

'I have heard that it is so deep that no one will ever be able to find the bottom of it. Any animal that strays into it is lost for ever.'

'You could say the same about a lot of the marshes on the moor. If an animal starts sinking into them it's not safe for a man to go in after it. One of the moor farmers was lost that way when I was a boy. He sank so fast that he was gone before his friends could get a rope to him.'

'Ugh! How horrible. I think your moor is a cruel place, Josh.'

'It's a hard place,' he admitted. 'But I wouldn't live anywhere else.'

'Then what do you intend doing, Josh? Surely you aren't going to stay as the engineer on the Sharptor mine? You would be wasting your training and your ability if you did that. The Sharptor isn't even a big mine.'

'I don't know.' They had turned their horses now and were riding slowly back across the moor. 'I enjoy working here.'

'We had a letter from Tom Fiddler a couple of months ago.'

Josh grinned, remembering Tom's hectic farewell party. He had heard nothing of the Cockney since then.

'He is doing very well in South America. He has made a lot of money and bought a half-share in a gold mine. He hopes to be coming home for a holiday in two years' time. He says he will probably be a rich man by then.'

'I'm sure he will be,' said Josh. 'Tom has both the nerve and the luck to become rich. I'd like to see him again if he ever came to this part of the country.'

'Wouldn't you like to work in a place like South America, Josh?'

'I don't think so.'

'I would love to travel and see the world. That's where men are so much luckier. Unless a girl has a husband to take her with him on his travels she can never go anywhere.'

What Josh's reply might have been was never known. At that moment a fox broke from the cover of a gorse-thicket not twenty yards ahead of them. With a yell Josh kicked his heels into the ribs of his startled pony and gave chase. Sarah was slower off the mark, but Hector quickly overtook Josh's mount. The fox dodged first one way and then the other, leaping through spaces between granite boulders that they had to circle around. It was a hot hectic chase that ended in the gully where Josh had once watched badgers. The fox scrambled up the bank into an area of jumbled broken rock where the horses could not follow and was quickly lost to sight.

Sarah thoroughly enjoyed the gallop and they arrived back at the cottage hot and pink. Sarah gave the two families a dramatic version of the pursuit of the fox, and Mary pouted with envy.

'If I had been there I'd have caught it.'

'I'm quite sure you would,' agreed Josh.

'I can ride as well as Sarah,' said Mary, determined to impress him. 'You come and watch me when I go out riding at home.'

'I wish I could,' replied Josh.

'You'll get that chance sooner than you expect,' said William Carlyon. 'That's the reason I wanted to see Captain Shovell today. I had a long discussion with Theophilus Strike last night. I managed to pick up some business from him. He said that, if Tom Shovell thought it a good idea, the Wheal Sharptor should have a whim-engine. Tom thought it an excellent suggestion. He is to hasten the digging of the new shaft, and when it's finished it will be used exclusively for hoisting ore to the surface. It will speed things up enormously.'

Josh felt he should have been consulted on the matter of the engine. But any resentment he might have felt was dispelled by William Carlyon's next words.

'It was entirely my idea, Josh. I persuaded Theophilus that it would make sense to have another engine. He said that if Captain Shovell thought we needed another engine, then he would leave the choosing of it to you. He wants you to come to Hayle to supervise the making of it – just as you did for your present engine. He is very pleased with the way that one has done its work. He feels its success is due entirely to the personal interest you had in its manufacture.'

While William Carlyon was talking, Jesse Retallick had been watching Sarah. She saw her face light up when her father said that Josh would be going to Hayle. Jesse was both pleased and saddened. Josh might not be aware of it yet, but she knew she was going to lose her son to this girl one day. She successfully shrugged off the vague feeling of uneasiness it gave her.

Chapter Seventeen

Josh travelled to Hayle early the following month, riding a horse from Theophilus Strike's stable. As William Carlyon had told him, he had a completely free choice in engines. More, there was a promise of a rise in salary upon his return – for 'increased responsibility'.

What Josh did not know was that when the tin mines had crashed many of their engineers had taken posts abroad. Most of them in various South American countries where mining was on the increase. Now there was a slight upsurge in the demand for tin, and some tin mines had begun working on a small scale once again. Unfortunately, the lay-off had not improved the condition of the engines. Engineers were at a premium. Furthermore, Josh's ideas on man-engines to bring the miners to the surface had captured the imagination of both miners and mine-owners. His reputation had spread far beyond his experience. Theophilus Strike had no intention of losing his engineer because he was not paid enough.

Although Harvey's foundry had not changed, Josh was no longer an apprentice and life was very different for him. Now he was a guest in the works manager's home with ample spare time on his hands. He discussed engines and the latest modifications with William Carlyon and Harvey's designers, and although he lacked years his ideas were taken seriously by the Harvey men.

It was not merely that Josh represented a customer. William Carlyon had once said that the Sharptor engineer was a particularly gifted apprentice. It was true. Engineering came as naturally to him as did singing to some other men. Training had been necessary, but the gift was there to begin with. Harvey's top men realised that Josh was cast in the Richard Trevithick mould, lacking only that great man's burning ambition to make his mark on the world.

But the time Josh spent at Hayle was not devoted entirely to work. One evening he accompanied Sarah and Mary to a concert, given in the large chapel by a touring orchestra.

Sarah pouted and threw a tantrum when her mother insisted that Mary accompany them. 'Why does she have to come? She is too young to appreciate the music. We manage very well without her when we go riding. We don't need a chaperon.'

'Not when you're riding, although many parents would insist upon that. But riding is a family matter; this is not. All the people we know will be there. If you were to be seen accompanied only by Josh there would be gossip. You would be regarded as . . . well, as not a nice girl. I'm quite sure you don't want that. Neither does Josh.'

So Mary went with them. But Josh had other problems to cope with at the concert. He was wearing his Sunday clothes, bought since he had begun to earn. He was, he felt, a well-dressed man of the world, proudly escorting an attractive girl to a concert. But when they entered the chapel he was brought sharply down to earth. William Carlyon had obtained the tickets for them and they were in the most expensive seats.

It was a mistake.

The men around them here were not just well dressed. They were elegant! Amongst them Josh felt a shoddily dressed lout, his Sunday suit of good stout dark-blue serge shown up for what it was – an ill-fitting outfit of cheap cloth and poor workmanship. He could see it for himself. He did not need the thinly disguised contempt on the faces of numerous well-dressed young men to tell him. They called their greetings to the Carlyon girls, ignoring him.

It was a relief when the music began and he had something else to think about. It helped too when Sarah's hand found his own. After squeezing it reassuringly she kept tight hold of it as the music swelled and filled the building.

It was a Beethoven programme, and as the strains of his great Eroica Symphony rose and fell Josh found himself in a new land, his cheap suit forgotten. He had discovered music.

'Isn't it beautiful?' Sarah whispered, and he could only nod in agreement, not daring to speak. When the music ended Josh applauded in numbed amazement. He returned to earth only when they left the chapel and went outside – to the world of belching chimneys, clattering hoofs and the smell of the mud of a falling tide.

The return was made harder because with it came the knowledge that he would probably never attend another concert. Such an event had nothing in common with his life at Sharptor. No, it had been a once-in-a-lifetime experience, and he felt richer for it.

'What is the matter, Josh? Didn't you enjoy the concert? You are looking very unhappy.'

'I enjoyed it very much. If I was looking sad it must have been because I was thinking that I might never attend another.'

'Why not? We have a concert at Hayle a couple of times every year.'

'But I'm not working at Hayle,' he reminded her.

'You could be,' Sarah declared pointedly. 'Daddy would be very happy for you to join the engineering staff at Harvey's. He has said so more than once.'

'Yes, Josh, come and work here,' said Mary excitedly. 'Then we would be able to see lots more of you. If you don't we will have to come all the way to Sharptor to see you and Sarah if you get—'

'Mary!'

The young girl bit back her words and looked fearfully at Josh, as though expecting him to flee from their company.

To Mary's relief and Sarah's embarrassment he laughed. The thought of marriage to Sarah had been with him as a vague shapeless thought ever since her visit to Sharptor. He did not love her – certainly not in the tempestuous way he had loved Miriam. But he was fond of her. Very fond. And he was desperately lonely, deep inside. He had his work, his engine and his inventive ideas, but they were all at the Wheal Sharptor. Outside of the mine he led a solitary life. The cottage seemed empty without Jenny and baby Gwen. And he met too many memories walking alone on the moor.

Marriage was one way out of the cocoon of loneliness Fate had weaved about him, and Sarah was a very lovely girl. . . .

'That's all right, Mary. I think you might have done me a very big favour.'

Looking back on it later, Josh knew that if it had not been for Mary's words he would never have made his decision. He would have been unable to summon up the courage had he not been aware that Sarah had herself discussed it – if only with her young sister.

'I want you to go home by yourself, Mary. I'm taking Sarah for a walk by the river.'

'Mummy said I was to come with you or people would talk.'

'That was at the concert, stupid! Go on home.'

'It's all right, Mary. I'll explain it to your mother when we get home.'

Mary watched as Josh and Sarah turned off into a lane that led to the river, then she ran home as fast as she could go.

'Why did you insist that Mary went home?' Sarah released his arm and took his hand.

'I only asked her. You insisted.'

Sarah's face reflected the pink of the sky above the distant sea. 'You know very well what I mean,' she said.

'And I think you know why I wanted her to leave us,' replied Josh.

Sarah said nothing.

'But there are a few things that must be made clear before I can say what's on my mind, Sarah.'

She looked up at him, but he avoided her eyes as they walked slowly on, hand in hand.

'We come from very different backgrounds, you and I,' he began.

'Wrong, Josh! You know yourself that Daddy is always talking of his mining background. He is very proud of it.'

'Yes, but you've never had to live on a miner's pay. You've been brought up to expect things like a large house, nice furniture and a horse. A miner could never give you all that.'

'Daddy never had all that when he married. The first home he took Mummy to was a one-up-and-one-down house in a terrace. But you keep talking of miners, Josh. You are an engineer.'

'True.' He remembered the rise in pay that Theophilus Strike had promised him on his return to Sharptor. It would place him almost on a par with his own father. 'But I live and work in a mining community. I'm one of them and there is no getting away from that. There would be no horse, no concerts like tonight.'

'Concerts are nice but they are not essential. I disagree about a horse. It would cost little to feed Hector if there were some grazing available. There is no shortage of that about Sharptor.'

'There are other things too. I spend hours at the mine, and you would have no one to talk to – at least, no one of your own intelligence. You would probably become bored and unhappy. I wouldn't like to see that happen.'

They stopped at the water's edge. The sun had gone and the curved slice of pale moon had the sky to itself.

'Josh!' Sarah turned to face him, the moon at her back hiding her face in shadow. Only her voice, low and husky, gave away her deep emotions. 'Josh, you are taking a great many things for granted, whatever it is you are trying to say. Either you don't know me as well as I thought – as I hoped – or you are trying to argue yourself out of something. Either way I don't think you should say any more. When you have made up your mind you will know what to do, and how to find the answers to your questions. Right now I think we had better be getting home. I am sorry if Mary made you feel that you had to say something. You don't, and I promise I will try not to embarrass you in any way. Now, shall we go?'

Her voice broke a little on the last word, but she held her head high.

'No.' He believed she must be able to hear his heart pounding. 'I have already made up my mind. But it's a big step to ask you to take. I don't want you going into something that might not measure up to your expectations. What I am trying to say is . . . Sarah, will you marry me?'

'You mean it, Josh? You really mean it?'

'Yes, Sarah. I mean it.'

'Oh yes, Josh! Yes! Yes! Yes!'

She clung to him and he could feel tears running warm and wet down her cheeks.

'I thought you had decided that you didn't want to marry me, Josh. I was trying to be brave and sensible about it but I was so unhappy inside.' She clung to him as though he might run away from her. 'Josh, I love you so very very much.'

'I'll try to make you happy, Sarah. I'll try very hard.'

She kissed him hungrily. 'And I will make you a good wife. I can cook and sew and housekeep – and I will get rid of Hector.'

'No, you won't. We'll find some way to keep him. Some day we might even get another horse. I won't have anyone saying that you lowered yourself to marry me. A man has to try to better himself, not stay down at the level of the lowest.'

Sarah laughed through the tears of happiness. 'Oh, Josh, you are funny! Just now you were saying that I couldn't have a horse. That you were a miner and wouldn't have much money. Now you are reversing your argument.'

'It wasn't so much arguing as thinking aloud.'

Now the decision had been taken, the all-important question asked, Josh felt a nervous elation. He had been accepted. By

Sarah, if not by her father. But nothing was formally settled. William Carlyon might refuse to allow Sarah to marry him. She was only nineteen and there was little that could be done if the Harvey manager had other plans for the future of his elder daughter.

He voiced his thoughts to Sarah as they made their way homewards, his arm about her waist, her head resting back against his shoulder.

'Daddy won't refuse.'

'You sound very sure.'

'I am.'

She looked up at him and he saw the white gleam of her teeth. 'He has known of my feelings for you since you first came to Harvey's as a new apprentice. I have loved you for a very long time, Josh. But when you left Hayle I thought you had gone back to your girl at Sharptor. I was very unhappy. For a long time I thought I had lost you, although I realised I had no claim on you. I am glad that Miriam married someone else. That left the way clear for me, and I knew I would get you sooner or later.'

The mention of Miriam jolted Josh, and the fact that it could alarmed him. Then he thought of something else. Should he tell Sarah of that last night on the moor? Of the baby? He decided against it. Nothing good could come of it. The secret was his. And Miriam's.

'You have gone very quiet, Josh.' They had arrived at the edge of the town now, and as he took his arm from her waist she clasped her two hands about it. 'Are you worried about speaking to Daddy?'

'Yes.' It was the truth. He tried to think of what he would say, but his mind refused to function along the right lines.

At the door of the house Sarah turned to him, smoothing down the lapels of his jacket. 'He won't dare refuse. He knows if he does his whole family will never speak to him again.' She kissed him. 'That one is for luck.'

The Carlyon family were sitting in the large lounge. They all looked up when Josh walked in with Sarah and there was an air of expectancy in the room. Certainly Mrs Carlyon gave both he and Sarah a questioning look. Sarah seated herself on the sofa beside her mother and looked down at her hands clasped tightly in her lap.

Mrs Carlyon's expression changed to a deep frown.

'Sit down, Josh. There's plenty of room. Take the chair over there.' William Carlyon pointed through the smoke from his pipe to the armchair that faced his own.

'I'd rather stand, if you don't mind. There's something I would like to say – I mean, to ask.'

Relief flooded into Mrs Carlyon's face.

'That's all right, Josh. Sit down and feel free to ask.'

Josh looked around the room and licked his lips. They had become inexplicably dry.

Instantly, Mrs Carlyon was on her feet. She ushered Sarah and the vigorously protesting Mary from the room.

Josh continued to stand and cleared his throat twice before William Carlyon said, 'For goodness' sake come and sit down, Josh. If I have to keep looking at you over my shoulder I'll end up cricking my neck. All right. You want to marry Sarah. Now I've said it for you. It need choke you no more. Sit down and we'll talk about it.'

William Carlyon looked at Josh in sympathetic amusement as he moved across the room to perch on the edge of the armchair.

'That's better. Now, what do we have to discuss? I know you. I know your family. I am aware of your capabilities and I have a shrewd idea of your future. What more should a prospective father-in-law want to know? You've already asked Sarah, of course?'

Josh nodded. 'Yes.'

'There's no need to ask what she said. I'm surprised she hasn't proposed to you long before this.'

There was a silence lasting a few minutes before William Carlyon said, 'Do you have any idea where you might live?'

Josh had not.

'Good. That's what I was hoping you might say. Now, don't think I'm interfering, but Sarah is used to a little more material comfort than you are able to provide for her at the moment

– though it's far more than I would have been able to offer when I was your age.'

'I'm aware of that. I said so to Sarah.'

'Then you'll understand my thoughts on the subject. What I have to say is this. When I was at Sharptor I noticed a derelict house a couple of hundred yards up the hill from where the new shaft is to be sunk. It seemed to be quite a big place, with a couple of cleared fields behind it. Do you know where I mean?'

'Yes, that's the idle farm – at least, that's what it's called in the village. It's never been lived in during my lifetime.'

'Who owns it?'

'I couldn't be sure, but I think it belongs to Theophilus Strike. I seem to remember there being some talk about his buying it when I was a boy.'

'That couldn't be better. Josh, you and Sarah have my blessing for your marriage. And if that derelict farm and the two fields belong to Theophilus Strike I'll buy it for you and Sarah as a wedding present. We'll also give you a houseful of furniture to go with it. All I expect of you is that you will get your miners together and put the house in order.'

When Josh protested the works manager was being too generous, William Carlyon cut him short, 'I'm a reasonably wealthy man, Josh, and the house and land will be cheap. But it does mean that Sarah will be able to keep that horse of hers. There will also be room for one of your own if you feel later that you want one. The house itself is larger than a miner's cottage and will give you a status that all engineers should enjoy. As for the rebuilding of it – well, you can incorporate your own ideas in that. It will give me a great deal of pleasure to make you a gift of your first home.'

William Carlyon beamed. 'Now, that's settled. I'll write to Theophilus Strike in the morning and your wedding can take place when the house is completed. That means that the date is entirely in your own hands.'

'I can hardly believe it!' exclaimed a dazed Josh. 'Sarah will be as excited as I am.'

'Then let's tell her! Call everyone back into the room while

I bring out the brandy. I'm not a great drinking man, but I feel this occasion calls for a celebration.'

Sarah had told Josh that her father would raise no objection to their marrying, but after leaving them together it seemed a very long time before Josh came out to call her and the family back into the lounge. One look at his face told her all that she wanted to know.

'Molly! For some quite inexplicable reason this young man wants to marry our daughter. I thought it better to say yes, to humour him.'

Sarah was so happy she did not know whether to rush to Josh or her father first. She eventually hugged Josh quickly and then ran across the room to fling herself at her father. He managed to ward her off long enough to place the glasses he held on to a table, then he clasped her to him and told her how pleased he was for her.

Meanwhile Josh was receiving the excited congratulations of Mary and the less exuberant embrace of Mrs Carlyon. Afterwards the glasses were handed around and William Carlyon proposed a toast.

'To Sarah and Josh. May they share happiness, prosperity and a long life together.'

His words were echoed, the toasts were drunk and everyone began chattering at once. Josh tried to tell Sarah about the house on the slope above the mine, but it seemed that all her family wanted to talk to her at the same time.

He returned home to Sharptor earlier than he had planned to break the news to his family.

Jesse was delighted. 'She'll make you a good wife, Josh. She's a fine girl. A daughter I'll be pleased to welcome.'

It was a proud day too for Ben Retallick. Josh would be making a good marriage – far better than Ben could ever have predicted. Not only that; his son was to become a land-owner, with room for a couple of cows and any other livestock he might want. It would give Josh a degree of independence unique in a mining community.

Theophilus Strike was happy to sell the old farm to William

Carlyon at a fair price. His own contribution to the wedding present was a generous one. He undertook to supply all the building materials necessary for its renovation. He had recently bought the granite quarry on the tor, so there would be no shortage of stone. Wood too was plentiful in the mine store.

Later that weekend Josh inspected the farmhouse in company with his father.

'It's going to be a major job,' said Ben Retallick when the tour of inspection was over. 'It needs new floors, roof, doors and windows. You've got little more than a shell of a house to work on; but the walls are as stout as you'll find anywhere.'

The house was larger than Josh had expected. It had four rooms downstairs and five up. In addition, there were a number of outbuildings in better condition than the house itself.

'You'll live like a king up here, lad,' said Ben Retallick. 'When it's finished and your mother comes visiting she'll be putting on her chapel clothes.'

'As long as she doesn't expect a formal greeting when she gets here,' smiled Josh. 'But I can't see it ever being ready to live in. There is so much to do and I'll be away for a few weeks yet supervising the building of the new engine. There just won't be the time.'

He looked ruefully at the stark grey stone walls and heaps of disintegrating timbers.

'Nonsense! The first thing needed is a roof to keep the weather out. There are thousands of slates piled up at the back of the Wheal Sharptor building-store. Theophilus Strike has said we can take whatever is needed to put the place to rights. We'll have that done by the time you come home with the new engine. We might even have the floors down too.'

Ben Retallick was better than his word. When Josh brought the new engine around the edge of the hill, above the Wheal Phoenix, he saw the once idle farmhouse standing proud and tall with new roof and doors, and windows that reflected the sun. The men from the mine had completed everything but the plastering inside.

By working really hard at it Josh could have the house finished and be married to Sarah in little more than a month.

But before he was able to make a start on the house, he had to install the whim-engine. This would take longer than usual because he wanted to experiment with a new tipping arrangement. He had designed it himself to speed up work at the head of the shaft. There was another reason. Another man-lift. This one would be incorporated in the ore-hoist and, if successful, would mean the men coming to the surface in one continuous hoist. He was convinced it would work, as were the engineers at Hayle with whom he had discussed it. But there were still a few safety innovations to be perfected before he brought it to Theophilus Strike's attention.

The whim-engine and new shaft were inaugurated with more ceremony than the previous engine had enjoyed. Sarah and her family came to Sharptor for it. As Josh's future wife, Sarah was generally acclaimed by the miners to be a 'fine-looking maid'.

She was thrilled with the progress on the farmhouse. 'It's just too wonderful, Josh. I can't believe it has been built up so quickly. Why, we could move in tomorrow!'

'Not quite!' But he was pleased at her enthusiasm. 'There's still a lot of work to be done inside, and I have to do that myself.'

She pouted in a very characteristic manner. 'I think you are deliberately putting off marrying me for as long as you can.'

He took her hand and led her away from the others, up the stairs to the bedroom cluttered with plasterers' tools and material. Here he took her into his arms and kissed her until she was breathing like a winded doe and pushed him away.

'Josh Retallick! This is not our bedroom yet. Stop! Someone is coming upstairs.'

She hurriedly patted her hair into place as a miner took some timber into another upstairs room.

'I thought you needed convincing that I wasn't trying to put off the wedding.'

'All right, I'm convinced. I am also very happy. This is the first room in the house where we have kissed. I want it to be our own bedroom.'

Josh nodded. 'So be it. I'll decorate it accordingly.'

'We will have the bed here,' said Sarah, pointing to the back of the room. 'Then we can wake up in the morning and see to Kit Hill and the Devon hills.'

'I envy you both,' said Mrs Carlyon, who had entered the room quietly while Sarah was talking. 'You have a house in a beautiful setting and are beginning a new future together.' There was a wistful note in her voice as she added, 'There is so much to be got out of life.'

She went to the window as her husband came upstairs. 'Look out there, William. Will you ever be content to gaze out at grimy foundry walls after seeing this view?'

William Carlyon smiled happily. 'I fell in love with this place the first time I saw it. I thought then how wonderful it would be to live here. I toyed with the idea of buying it, but there are many years to go before I retire. It would be a crime to leave such a house derelict and unloved for so long. Now we've found the perfect answer. I shall be happy knowing that Sarah and Josh are living here.'

'Oh, Daddy! It's a marvellous present. It really is.' Sarah hugged her father. 'And I am so happy.'

He squeezed her close for a few seconds. 'That's how it should be. Now, let's have a look at the bedroom your mother and I will have when we visit you. I want a room with a view that includes Sharptor. I haven't seen a rocky peak like that anywhere else.'

That evening the wedding arrangements were finalised. The ceremony would take place at Hayle at Easter-time. In the meantime Josh would complete the inside of the house. Sarah would be sending furniture to the house as it was purchased. They had discussed what they wanted and Sarah was to organise the buying of it. Between now and the wedding day Josh would make the journey to Hayle on at least two occasions. Sarah would visit Sharptor once more, when the house was quite ready.

There was plenty to keep Josh busy. He now had two

engines and was responsible for training two young lads in the rudiments of engineering. As if this were not enough, an unforeseen incident occurred at the Caradon and Josh became involved in it.

Captain Frisby had continued his policy of taking on destitute tin-miners desperate for work. Their numbers now equalled those of the thoroughly disgruntled copper-miners, who were bearing the brunt of any tasks requiring skill and knowledge in copper-mining. It was at this stage that Frisby played his joker. He declared that the wages of the copper-miners would be cut to correspond with that paid to the ex-tinners. The smouldering anger of the copper-miners exploded into action. They downed tools and a noisy crowd assembled in front of Frisby's office, demanding that the decision be reversed.

His answer was to declare that all those miners not willing to accept the new rates of pay were dismissed. He would take on tinners in their place, he said. One miner was as good as another to Frisby. If half his work-force was content to work for less pay, then the others must follow suit – or go.

Word went around quickly that there would be vacancies at the mine, but the out-of-work tinners who hurried there found the way to Captain Frisby's office blocked by a determined group of Caradon miners. They wisely decided that a hungry belly was preferable to a cracked skull.

But worse was to follow. The Reverend William Thackeray heard of the troubles and hurried to the mine. He arrived in time to catch Frisby's night shift of ex-tinners reluctant to pass the angry copper-miners.

Thackeray seized the opportunity to call a meeting of the men. They gathered within sight of Frisby yet far enough away to prevent their words from carrying to the pale-faced but determined mine captain.

William Thackeray sympathised with the copper-miners and applauded their actions. Standing on a rock so he could be seen by everyone, he also praised their courage.

'It's fallen to you, the miners of Caradon, to make a stand against greed and injustice. What you do here today will be a yard-stick for every mine captain and miner in Cornwall. If justice prevails you'll have struck a blow that will be felt throughout the county. Fail, and twenty years of fighting for better conditions will have been wasted. You've proved your determination. Now, remember that it's your very livelihood you're fighting for – the future not only of yourselves but of your families.'

'Tell that to the tinners!' called a voice from the crowd and there was loud agreement.

'While there are "tinners" and "copper-men" you'll never achieve anything,' replied Preacher Thackeray. 'When you accept that you're all miners you will have won a major battle. There are differences between you now that should never be. No man from Cornwall must keep another from working merely because he gained his experience in a different type of mine. Any more than a stranger has the right to come here and take away another man's livelihood by selling himself cheap.'

Banging palm with fist to emphasise his words, he shouted, 'Until you can greet each other simply as "Miner" you are playing the adventurer's game. Boosting his profits and ensuring that you remain poor men.'

The roar of approval was interrupted by a shout from one of the tinners.

'That's easy to say when you've got a full belly, Preacher. When you've been without food for a week and hear your kids crying night after night because hunger pains won't let them sleep, you'll work for food alone. We've seen hard times from too close.'

Now it was the copper-miners' turn to remain silent and listen to the tinners backing up their spokesman.

'But in the long term your way only helps the few. Can't you see that? If only you would all join together the mine-owners wouldn't dare to lower wages for anyone. If they tried you could down tools and hold out for a fair wage. One that might even go up as profits rose. You could start a miners' fund. The men who were in work would pay into it while those who were out of work could draw enough to buy food for their families.'

Agreement and derision were equally divided between the miners this time.

'This is all very well, Preacher Thackeray, but all this talk of union is tomorrow talk. We've had our pay cut today. What do we do?'

The words came from John Kittow, the man who had masterminded the sale of corn in Callington market some years before. He had been at the Wheal Caradon since the day they had first begun mining copper. As well as being an excellent miner and a much respected man he was pointed out to newcomers as a man who had survived three roof-falls. Perhaps it was this – being alive after three times beating the odds – that made him contemptuous of pretension. He spoke his mind and went his own way. Whether other men followed meant little to him.

The muttering in the crowd swelled loud again.

'You do what you please,' shouted one of the ex-tinners. 'We're going on shift.'

The noise that went up from the men who had downed tools was an ugly one. The main body of them surged around in a movement that took them across the line of anyone with a mind to go to the shaft.

'There'll be no work done tonight,' called a Caradon man.

'Not unless a tinner wants his head busted by a copper-man's shovel,' called another.

'No violence!' called Preacher Thackeray. 'No fighting, or Frisby will call the militia in.'

'Their heads will dent as easy as a tinner's,' called the copper-man who had just spoken. The others hooted their approval. The angry Caradon copper-men outnumbered the night shift of tinners by four to one. It would have taken a brave man to be the first to push his way through to the head of the shaft.

'Please, no fighting!' pleaded Preacher Thackeray. 'You need to show a united front to beat Captain Frisby.'

He turned his attention to the incoming shift. 'This is your chance to show Frisby he can't set miner against miner. Call off your shift tonight.'

'They can't do anything else,' called one of the copper-men. 'They won't get past us.'

There was uncertainty amongst the tinners, and Thackeray seized eagerly upon it. 'Turn around and go home,' he said. 'You can't be blamed for not working tonight.'

'That's all very well,' growled one of the night shift. 'But Captain Frisby won't pay us for what we don't do. We've got to live.'

'I'm pleading with you not to try to work below ground tonight,' Thackeray repeated. 'Turn around and I'll speak to Captain Frisby. I'll tell him I've suggested there be no work done tonight.'

There was an earnest conversation among the night shift, a few lifted shoulders and general nodding of heads.

'All right,' said their spokesman grudgingly. 'But we'll be back for work tomorrow.'

'Bless you!' said Thackeray. 'You've avoided violence and struck a blow against those who want to see the miner stay poor.'

'We'll never get rich if we can't work,' retorted the miner, but he and the remainder of the night shift of miners turned away and slowly made their way from the mine.

From his office Captain Frisby watched them leave and anger boiled up inside him. Most of it directed at Preacher Thackeray. He had been unable to hear what was being said but he put his own interpretation on what he was able to see. He was in no doubt that the preacher had turned back the men who wanted to work. Thackeray's sympathies were well known to lie with the others – the trouble-makers.

With Captain Frisby in this frame of mind there was no chance of Preacher Thackeray negotiating with him on the men's behalf. When the object of his anger came to the office in an attempt to speak to him Frisby turned the key in the lock and refused to open the door, ignoring all the preacher's pleas.

'You can say what you've got to say from there, Preacher Thackeray. You'll not come in here with your seditious talk.

I've heard all about you and tonight I've seen it for myself. Preventing honest men from working, and stirring up trouble. That's what your talk is all about.'

'I stopped the night shift from working to prevent trouble,' said William Thackeray. 'The men were so incensed they would have fought a bitter and bloody battle.'

'If they were it was because of what you had been telling them. Go away. Go to your chapel and do some praying for your soul. Leave the running of a mine to someone who knows something about it.'

'It was your way of running the Caradon that caused them to stop work in the first place. But I've not come here to quarrel with you, Captain Frisby. I'm here to discuss the men's grievances. It would be far easier if you opened this door and let me in.'

'I've nothing to say to you, or to those men out there. As far as I'm concerned they no longer work at the Wheal Caradon. Tomorrow I'll take on new men to fill their places. There's no shortage of good miners.'

'Captain Frisby, let me in and we'll talk this matter over sensibly—'

'There's nothing more to be said. I've done talking. Go away!'

For a few minutes more William Thackeray tried to persuade the mine captain to change his mind, but Captain Frisby refused to acknowledge his presence, and eventually the preacher went back to the miners.

'He's angry tonight,' he said. 'Give him time to cool off and he'll talk. If you can be here to stop the morning shift from starting work he'll know you mean business. I'll come back to see him later in the day. If he realises that the mine is going to lose production he'll agree to whatever demands you care to make.'

'Preacher Thackeray!' John Kittow spat on the ground. 'I don't like all this talk of "demands" and scoring victories. All we want to do is to go back to work for the pay we were getting before today. None of your long words is going to do that for us.'

'Aren't you forgetting the tinners, John?' demanded Thackeray. 'Were they getting a fair wage?'

'I care as much about the tinners as they care about me,' stated Kittow, meeting the preacher's eyes. 'They would have come in and taken our jobs for half the pay and not cared what happened to us. If that's the way they feel I don't give a damn about them. If you have their interests at heart I suggest you go and see them. Warn them not to try to come into work until our pay is back to what it was. If they don't listen they'll be walking straight into big trouble.'

'And that's your answer to Frisby? To cause trouble? To give him an excuse to bring the magistrates out here and call in the militia?'

'No, Preacher Thackeray, I'm on my way now to ask someone to come to talk to Captain Frisby for us.'

'I don't think Captain Frisby is in the mood to talk to anyone,' said William Thackeray. 'He went so far as to say he no longer considers any of you to be employed at the Wheal Caradon.'

'Then we've nothing to lose,' said John Kittow matter-of-factly. 'But if Joshua Retallick will agree to talk for us I think Captain Frisby might listen. He's a great deal of respect for him.'

Thackeray's surprise at the mention of Josh's name was apparent, but after a while he began nodding thoughtfully. 'Yes. Yes, I'll concede that Captain Frisby might listen to Josh. But it's a lot to ask a young man to take upon his shoulders.'

'You may be right. But his shoulders are broad and he's nobody's fool. I can't think of anyone else who can help us.'

He turned to the other miners. 'You stay here. I'll go and find Josh and try to get him over here tonight. The longer this drags on, the harder it will be for any of us to give way to the other. Just make sure Captain Frisby stays in his office until I get back.'

'There seems to be little I can do here at the moment,' said William Thackeray. 'If you need me I'll be at my home. I wish you luck in your efforts. But I had hoped you might see the wider issues involved. You in particular, John.'

''Tis hard to see past the next pay-day these days,' said one of the men. 'Especially when there's little 'uns at home depending on you. But you've done your best for us and we're grateful for it. If you've a mind to offer up a prayer for us when you get back to the chapel we'd take it kindly.'

The gratitude of the miners was genuine enough. But as William Thackeray rode home he felt he had suffered a personal defeat. It was a bitter and unusual taste in his mouth. The formation of a powerful union was a personal crusade, something too great to be entrusted to any other man. Yet at a crucial moment the power in him had failed. Nothing he could say or do would make any difference. He had allowed the initiative to slip from his hands and pass to someone else.

The truth was that the foundations of Thackeray's dream had been built on unsafe ground. Men, unlike bricks, are not of a uniform size, to be laid one upon the other in order to build a solid structure. They have to be shaped by time and cemented together by circumstance. The time was not yet and circumstances were against Thackeray's ideas of unity. Miners are slow to accept new ideas, Cornish miners more than most. Preacher Thackeray still had much to learn about them.

Miriam tried to tell him something of this when he reached home. But William Thackeray was tired and short of patience.

'They'll have to learn to accept new ideas if they want to improve conditions. I doubt whether Josh will have any more success with them.'

William Thackeray's back was turned to his wife and he missed her expression.

'Josh was there? You saw him?'

He turned quickly but she had bent low over the bread she was slicing.

'No, he wasn't there, but the miners are going to call him in to speak for them. I wish him well.'

'We both wish him well, William,' Miriam said quietly.

* * *

Josh was in the kitchen of the Retallick cottage talking to his father when John Kittow arrived. To the best of his knowledge Josh had never spoken to the man and he was puzzled when Kittow said he would like to speak to him.

'It's to ask a favour of you,' the miner added.

'A favour? Something to do with engineering? I'll be happy to help if I can.'

'No, it's not to do with engineering.' The miner looked at Jesse Retallick, unhappy that she was listening.

'Is it something that you'd like to say to me in private? We can go outside . . .'

'No. No, it doesn't matter. Word will be about soon enough. There's trouble at the Wheal Caradon. Bad trouble. I think – and the other miners agree with me – you are the only man likely to be able to help us.'

Josh was no wiser, but, gaining confidence, John Kittow went on to tell him about the events that had followed Captain Frisby's announcement of the wages-cut.

'Why, the mean old skinflint!' Jesse Retallick was unable to contain her anger. 'It's hard enough for a man's family to manage on a full week's pay these days, without having it cut down.'

Ben Retallick waved his wife into silence. 'The man's a fool,' he said. 'There's more to running a mine than getting copper above ground. But Theophilus Strike won't be happy about you getting mixed up in the Caradon's troubles, Josh.'

'It isn't in Strike's time,' retorted Josh. To John Kittow he said, 'How do you think I can help? Preacher Thackeray is a more persuasive talker than I am. If he failed . . . !' He shrugged his shoulders.

'The preacher might be more used to talking,' agreed John Kittow, 'but Captain Frisby knows you. He'll listen to anything you have to say. You know our problems. You've been brought up in mining and you've done a great deal of learning. There's none of us is good enough to state our case to Captain Frisby. There might be something we don't know about, something he won't tell us. The other men agree that whatever you decide is best we'll go along with. We're in need of help and there's no one else we can turn to. We've got to work because we've families to keep, but that doesn't mean we have to be trodden into the ground. If we don't work, then the Caradon doesn't work. Even if it means cracking a few heads along the way.'

There was a long silence when he stopped talking. It lasted until Josh said, 'All right, I'll come up to the mine with you.'

'Good boy!' said Jesse Retallick, and John Kittow looked greatly relieved.

'Don't get too involved,' warned Ben Retallick as his son prepared to leave the cottage with the Caradon miner. 'You'll make more enemies than friends by taking up other men's disputes. Having said that, I wish you luck.'

'Take no notice of your father,' whispered Jesse as she stepped outside the door with Josh. 'He'll be the proudest man on this side of the moor if you can get those men back to work again.'

On the way to the Wheal Caradon, Josh kept John Kittow talking. By the time they arrived he had built up a sound background of the way the mine had been changing in recent months. It was not a happy picture and reminded Josh of the Sharptor mine during the last period of Herman Schmidt's reign.

It was quite dark now, but few miners had gone home. They sat around bonfires near to the main shaft. The earlier excitement had worn off, and the shadowy faces in the firelight were those of worried but determined men. Behind them the beam of the big pumping engine rocked slowly on its axle. Irrelevantly, Josh's engineer's mind noted that behind the steady thump of the engine there was another, less usual, noise. The packing on the huge piston was disintegrating.

'I'll go over to see Frisby on my own,' he said to John Kittow. Waiting until the self-appointed spokesman had joined the others around the top of the shaft, he headed towards the mine captain's office.

There was a light inside but it had been turned down too low for anyone to be visible.

Josh knocked heavily on the door. When he received no immediate reply he knocked again.

'Who is it?' Captain Frisby's voice was thick and surprised. The voice of a man who had either been dozing or very deep in thought.

'It's Josh Retallick. Can I come and speak to you?'

'What for? If you come from that preacher you're wasting your time. I've nothing to say.'

'Preacher Thackeray is quite capable of talking for himself,' Josh said sharply. 'I'm not running his errands. Your miners asked me to speak to you. Out of regard for both yourself and them I agreed.'

'Those men out there are not my miners,' shouted Captain Frisby. 'They ceased to be employed here when they stopped work.'

'And the Caradon mine will cease to exist if you don't do something to save it,' retorted Josh. 'But I'm not standing out here trying to hold a conversation with you through a closed door. Will you let me in, Captain Frisby? Or shall I go home and attend to my own business and forget about your troubles?'

There was no reply, and Josh was about to turn away when a key grated in the lock and the door swung open. Two steps inside and the door was slammed shut and locked behind him. Josh waited in the gloom until Captain Frisby had turned the wick of the lamp up. Then he took a seat to face the weary Caradon mine captain across the breadth of the large desk.

Captain Frisby's first words were defiant.

'I'm prepared to talk to you, but I've no intention of going back on my decision. I'll not be dictated to by the rabble outside.'

'Captain, that "rabble" has built the Wheal Caradon up into one of the largest copper mines in Cornwall. They can just as easily destroy it again. With a little help from you.'

'What do you mean, "destroy it"? I'll get the militia in. They won't get away with smashing equipment on this mine.'

'Nobody will have to touch a thing,' said Josh. His quiet confidence made the mine captain listen. 'The piston-packing is going on the pumping engine. I give it twenty-four hours before it breaks down completely. You haven't an engineer at the mine at the moment, have you?'

'The engine-man can carry out simple repairs like that,' said Frisby quickly. 'I don't need an engineer.'

'You've just cut the engine-man's wages with the others,' replied Josh. 'They're keeping the engines running at the moment, but I can't see them doing any repairs unless matters are settled very quickly.'

As Frisby thought about it, Josh added, 'I believe your deepest level is rich but wet, Captain. How long would it take to become flooded?'

Captain Frisby looked at him and licked his lips. It had been a very wet season. A mere forty-eight hours without pumping would be sufficient to stop the new level from being worked for a very long time. Longer than that and the workings might be under water for months. Josh knew it too.

'All right. Tell the engine-men their pay stays the same. But that only applies to the engine-men.'

'I'm sorry,' said Josh. 'But they have no alternative now. They must go along with the miners. Your action today has done more to bind the copper-men together than all the speeches Preacher Thackeray has ever made.'

'Then I hope it keeps their families fed. They won't have a job to do it for them.'

'I'm sure you're right.' Josh changed his tactics. 'And I don't suppose you'll find it easy to get another job after this.'

The mine captain's head snapped up.

'Me find another job? The shareholders won't dismiss me for doing what I'm paid for.'

'How do you see your job, Captain Frisby?'

'The same as every mine captain. To run my mine, bring up the maximum ore and make a good profit for the shareholders.'

He said it as though it was a maxim he repeated to himself every day of his life.

'That's exactly why today's events will mean your looking for work somewhere else.'

'Don't try to frighten me, Josh Retallick. I know what I'm

doing. It's those good-for-nothing miners out there who'll be looking for somewhere else to work. There are more miners than there is work. They must take what they can get and be grateful to be working at all. I'll give a job to the cheapest man and he'll work harder because he's frightened to lose it. The result is more ore, lower costs and higher profits.'

Josh looked at the mine captain with distaste. If he hadn't heard it for himself he would have scoffed at anyone else repeating such a statement. To Captain Frisby miners were not men with thoughts, ambitions and problems. They were units on a balance-sheet. Even so, the mine captain's mathematics were wrong. Josh lost no time in telling him so.

'How much have your profits risen since last year?' he asked.

'They haven't,' admitted Captain Frisby. 'But they've not fallen, and a lot of man-hours have gone into opening up the new deep level. With this cut in the men's wages there might even be a slight increase by the end of the year.'

'Not if the engine breaks down and the deep level is flooded.'

'That's something that no mine captain can anticipate. Look, Josh, you know the engine-men. Get them to put that piston right and I'll give them an extra two days' pay as well as keeping them on at the old rate.'

Josh ignored this plea. 'The Wheal Sharptor has gone deeper to open a new level. Yet the profit for this year is running fifty per cent above last.'

'The Sharptor's a small mine. You can't compare it with the Caradon.'

'Then take the Wheal Phoenix. Their profit is up a hundred per cent.'

'Sheer luck!' argued Frisby. 'They drove into a rich lode.'

'No, Captain. There's never been such a boom in copper. Every mine in the county is riding high. When your shareholders see their dividends at the end of this year they're going to start asking questions. I don't think you have any of the answers.'

Josh had put his finger on the root of the trouble at the

Wheal Caradon, Frisby's real reason for cutting the miners' pay. It was a last desperate attempt by him to bring the mine profits up.

'It's the men,' Captain Frisby mumbled desperately. 'They're lazy. I should have cut their pay months ago. If I paid them what they're worth their families would all go hungry.'

'No, you're wrong.' Josh stood up and paced restlessly back and forth across the office. 'You have good men here, Captain. They're as good as miners anywhere in Cornwall, a great deal better than most.'

He stopped to look down at the mine captain. 'Why don't you bring back the tribute system? That way you couldn't lose, and the men would be happy.'

'Tributing' was a traditionally Cornish method of mining. The miners, working in small teams, would bid for a particular section of the mine. They would be paid a percentage of what the ore they brought to the surface fetched. If it were a particularly good section and they were exceptionally hard workers the team would make good money. If they had chosen badly they had a lean time of it. Either way the mine was never the loser. It was a system with an element of chance that satisfied the fierce independence of the Cornishman. Working as a tributer he felt he was his own master.

'The shareholders are against tributing,' said Frisby. 'They said that everyone was fighting for the best levels and the mine wasn't expanding as it should.'

Josh could hardly point out that a good mine captain would have been exploring and tunnelling, seeking new and profitable lodes, using his experience to read the signs and follow the copper.

'Then you need to keep good miners,' he said. 'And you must face the fact that your methods have failed. Pay low wages and you get a second-rate man. The good miner will go where he's paid for his experience. You still have a few of them left. Pay them well and let them set the standard. When other men become experienced enough, then raise their money too. Give them a few shillings extra when the tonnage is up and they'll have something to work hard for.'

Josh expected Frisby to argue, but he stayed silent. Encouraged, Josh went on.

'There are still a few months to go before the dividend is called. Give your miners some encouragement. There's a good chance that your profit will be up enough to satisfy all but the greediest shareholder.'

He paused.

'Stay stubborn, put down the pay of your best men and there can be only one possible result. The Wheal Caradon will be the only established copper mine to lose money this year. You'll be dismissed and you'll leave with a reputation to keep you out of mining for the remainder of your life.'

Josh could see the uncertainty on Captain Frisby's face. He had almost won. It was time to take his greatest gamble.

'Well, I've said all I have to say. I'll be going now. I have my own job to get up for in the morning. Good night, Captain Frisby.'

'Wait!'

The cry was one of sheer desperation.

'Don't go just yet.' Captain Frisby was on his feet. He moved across the office to stand between Josh and the door. 'Josh, you must see how it is with me. If I agree to do the things you've mentioned, the men will think they've beaten me. I wouldn't be able to hold my head up on the Wheal Caradon. I'd see the scorn in their eyes every time I gave one of them an order.'

Josh shook his head. 'That won't happen if you take the men into your confidence. Tell them you made the decision to cut their wages because the Wheal Caradon is the only mine not to have a rise in profits. Tell them if they are prepared to raise production you will keep their wages at the present level – and might even throw in a small bonus. Try to get them working with you instead of against you.' He had a sudden thought. 'Who are your shift captains?'

Captain Frisby avoided Josh's gaze again. 'I haven't any just at the moment. They've all left. I don't have men with enough experience to replace them.'

Josh shook his head incredulously. 'Captain, I'm surprised

you've managed to keep the Caradon running at all. Do you know John Kittow?'

'Yes. He's one of the men out there, isn't he?'

'He's the man who came to ask me to help,' said Josh. 'He realises that there are two sides to every dispute. He even suggested there might be some reason why you cut the miners' money. What better opening could you want to explain your point of view? Tell John Kittow you've reconsidered the situation. He's a good sound miner. I've heard others say so. Make him your senior shift captain. Explain things to him. He'll do the rest. Well, Captain, what's it to be?'

It took the captain a full minute to make up his mind. He nodded. 'All right. If Kittow will guarantee to raise the tonnage I'll agree to try things your way. But I want it known that I've not given in to any threats. I've reconsidered my position, that's all.'

'The men will be too grateful to think about anyone giving in, or winning. You've made a wise decision, Captain Frisby. I'm sure you won't regret it.'

'I hope not,' growled Captain Frisby. 'Tell Kittow to come and see me now. We might as well get things sorted out tonight. Then I can go home to bed.'

The men seated about the fires rose to their feet as Josh came into the light of the flickering yellow flames. There was little optimism on their faces. He sought out John Kittow. 'Can I have a word with you, John?'

'Have we still got a job here, Mr Retallick?' The question was asked by an anxious fifteen-year-old, the sole wage-earner for his mother, two younger sisters and a mine-crippled father.

'You'll be back at work tomorrow,' said Josh, and as he and John Kittow left the firelight there was a buzz of excitement behind them.

'Is that true? Has Captain Frisby agreed to take us back on full pay?'

'He's done more than that. . . .' Josh told the miner of his conversation with Captain Frisby. 'So take things easy with him. Don't let him feel he's given in to anyone. He has his pride, for all he has some peculiar ways.'

'Josh, we owe you a very big debt for tonight's work. I'll make sure the Caradon men never forget it.' The miner shook Josh's hand gratefully.

'Never mind about that. Get in there to see Frisby before he changes his mind.'

As John Kittow headed for the mine office Josh walked away from the Caradon feeling elated at having been able to solve the miners' problem.

Jesse Retallick was overjoyed. 'There! And you succeeded where Preacher Thackeray failed, in spite of all his learning.' She looked at Josh with pride. 'They won't be talking of anything else in Henwood or St Cleer for days.'

'You did well for the men, Josh,' said his father more soberly. 'It was time someone put Captain Frisby right. But I doubt if that's the end of it for you. Now you'll be called into every dispute that breaks out around here. Getting yourself known as the men's spokesman isn't going to help further your career as an engineer. It won't put you into favour with everyone.'

There was a prophetic ring to his words, but on this night Josh was too pleased at having achieved something worth while to give it any thought.

Chapter Eighteen

As the wedding date neared, the house on the hill occupied most of Josh's spare time. The plastering was almost finished, but there were still fire-grates to be built, doors to be hung and a hundred other improvements to be carried out. All of these Josh was doing himself, now that the major building work had been completed.

Sometimes he would go up to the house when there was not enough light left by which to work and just sit at the window. Watching the darkness advance over the land, he tried to identify the pin-points of light that loosely speckled the countryside. On the distant horizon a rash of lights marked the great city of Plymouth. Josh had never been there, but he had built up a mental picture from the tales he had heard and the lights that could be seen.

He wondered what it would be like living in this house and looking out on all this with Sarah. More, sharing his whole life with her. There were times when he had grave doubts about their future together, but he had heard this was a natural premarital state.

One day, early in March, he was called from his bed at four o'clock in the morning because a rod had broken in the whim-engine. It took him until midday to complete the repair. Then he carried on with routine work until four o'clock in the afternoon, when he stopped work for the day. Instead of going back to the cottage, he cut across the moor to the farmhouse. A cartload of furniture had arrived from Hayle the day before. After carrying it upstairs he began to paint one of the bedroom doors.

He had almost finished when he heard the kitchen door open downstairs. It did not surprise him. His mother was a frequent visitor and always used that door. He waited for her to come upstairs or call out to him. Instead, he heard a sound he could not place. It was a low gurgling noise. He waited and it was repeated, but this time from a different room.

He was about to investigate when he heard the stairs creek. Moving quietly back into the shadows, he waited as the complaining stairs reported the progress of the mysterious visitor.

Then a head appeared above the hand-rail, and seconds later Miriam was standing at the top of the stairs, her young son in her arms.

She was the last person he had expected to see. The surprise was so complete he dropped the paint-brush to the floor.

The sound brought Miriam to an abrupt halt. Even in the poor light at the head of the stairs he could see changes in her face as the blood first drained away and then came rushing back to her cheeks.

'Josh?'

'Wh-what are you doing here?'

'I'm sorry. I came to Henwood to visit my mother. I thought – I'd heard about your house. I wanted to see it. I shouldn't have come. But I didn't think you'd be here at this time of day.'

The words came tumbling out, tripping over each other. In her arms the baby gurgled away completely unconcerned.

Miriam turned quickly as though to run down the stairs.

'No, don't go! I mean. . . . You can look around if you want to.'

He did not know why he said it, why he never remained silent and allowed her to go, but his heart was pounding so hard inside him he would not have heard the voice of reason had it shouted at him.

'I would rather not, Josh. Not with you here.'

'I'll go if it makes you feel any easier.'

'Don't be silly!' Her laugh was softer, less uninhibited than he remembered. 'It's your house, not mine.'

'Yes.'

She looked at him as he moved forward to stand by the open bedroom doorway, the light shining in upon his face.

'You're looking well.'

'Am I?'

He felt awkward, tongue-tied, not able to think of anything to say, yet not wanting her to leave.

She slowly walked down the stairs and he followed. Stopping in the kitchen, she ran her finger over the dust on top of the range that had been cast in the Harvery foundry.

'This is a fine stove, Josh. Sarah will be able to cook some grand meals on it for you.'

'It was specially made at Hayle. But who told you her name?'

'You did, a long time ago. I always wondered whether you might marry her one day.'

'That's funny.' His expression belied the statement. 'She always thought I would marry you. . . .'

Her finger stopped tracing in the dust.

'. . . and so did I.'

She turned to face him, and he thought she was angry. Then he saw the expression on her face was anguish. 'I couldn't have married you, not after everything. Couldn't you see that?'

'No. I would have accepted that you couldn't marry me right away. But to marry Preacher Thackeray within a few weeks of. . . .'

His voice trailed off as she turned away from him.

'Josh, don't talk about it now. Please! We shouldn't be saying such things at all. Not in this house. This is where you and Sarah will live. Oh! I shouldn't have come. I'm sorry, Josh.'

The baby tugged at the white woollen bonnet he was wearing, pulling it off and dropping it to the floor.

Josh stepped across the room and retrieved it. Tiny fingers reached for it and he handed it over. The baby was chubby and contented, his eyes as blue as Josh's own.

'What do you call him?' The baby had his finger in his grasp now.

'Daniel.'

'Hello, Daniel.' He jigged his finger up and down and the child chuckled.

Miriam pulled the baby away from him.

'Don't, Josh. Don't!'

He beat her to the door and put his back against it. 'Why not, Miriam? Why mustn't I play with him?'

Tears stood out from her eyes as she shook her head. 'Don't make me say it, Josh. Please don't make me say it.'

The tears broke free from her eyes and she crumbled. 'Oh God! Why did I come here? I must be mad!' She sank down on to the wide window-seat.

Josh moved away from the door and stood over her, his face working. He had wanted to hurt her, wanted to get some reaction from her, some recognition of what had once been between them. But seeing her cry like this threatened to tear him apart.

'I'm sorry, Miriam. I shouldn't have pushed you into that.'

She was shaking now and it alarmed the baby.

'Here. Let me take him.' Dropping to one knee, he took Daniel from her, holding him as though he was made of delicate china. He laid him on the floor on a pile of cloth that had been used to protect the newly delivered furniture.

Miriam fumbled in her sleeve for a handkerchief. When she found it she crumpled it in her hand, crying and talking and occasionally drawing in great shivering gulps of air.

'William has been very good to me – to us, Josh. He's a kind man who still talks well of you. He was so proud of what you did at the Wheal Caradon. He thought their cause had been lost. But you saved it, he says. He has wanted to invite you to our meetings, but I dreaded seeing you again. I didn't know what I might do if we ever came face to face. I was frightened. I didn't know what you would say or do.'

She bit at her lip in an effort at self-control, and Josh desperately wanted to help, wanted to stop her baring her heart.

'Don't say any more, Miriam.' He put a hand on her shoulder.

She raised her eyes to meet his and he tried to read what was in them, but all the emotions he thought he could see there were his own. Yet her eyes drew him on like magnets. It was madness! He knew it – and disregarded it. He swayed towards her and suddenly he was holding her. His mouth crushed hers and her arms were about him, pulling him to her.

It stopped as suddenly at it had begun and they drew apart, both shocked with the force of the impact.

'I'm sorry,' he said lamely.

'It was as much my fault as yours.' A strange calmness fell between them as the emotion drained away.

'Now I don't need to ask myself what I might do if I were to meet you,' she said. 'I have my answer.'

She picked up the baby and gave Josh a warm gentle look.

'Don't go yet,' he said. 'Stay for a while longer.'

She shook her head. 'No, Josh. I'm married now. You too have your future to think of.'

'What future? I can't marry Sarah. Not now I know how I feel. . . .'

'Shh!' She silenced him. 'You felt sorry for me, that's all. Of course you'll marry Sarah and both be very happy in this lovely house. But I'm glad you've seen Daniel. It has worried me – trying to decide whether you should see him or not.'

She smiled at him. 'I'm glad I came here after all, Josh. There's been a lot of pain and bad thoughts inside me. They've gone now.'

'You just can't walk out of my life, Miriam – not again.'

She was in complete control of herself now. 'You know I must, for everyone's sake. Be happy, Josh. I'll pray for that. Be happy.' She opened the door and was gone. He called after her, but she never turned. He knew if he ran after her there would be a scene that could only end in complete humiliation for him. Miriam had made up her mind.

He watched her until she was out of sight, lost in the shadows of the tall bracken of the moor.

Miriam knew he was watching and she willed herself not to turn around for one last glimpse of him. Nobody else would ever know what it had cost her to push Josh away when every part of her being was screaming out for him. She had wanted him physically and emotionally. But she had been the cause of great unhappiness to him once. She was determined not to repeat it. Miriam had paid for her treatment of him, paid in the agony of childbirth, bringing his baby into the world to take another man's name. She paid every day when she looked into Daniel's eyes and saw Josh in them. And she paid by being married to a man she had never really loved and never would.

Josh did not go near the house for a week after the meeting with Miriam. Then more furniture arrived from Hayle and he was forced to help place it. The house was almost ready when, with the wedding less than a month away, Sarah came to inspect it.

She was delighted with what she saw – and promptly ordered a major change-around of the furniture. Sarah had very decided views on where everything was to be positioned.

'I've planned it out very carefully,' she said when Josh was taking a breather after moving almost every single piece of upstairs furniture into different rooms. 'As each piece was sent on its way I made a note of where it would go.' She paused. 'I am not very sure about that wash-stand, though. I feel it might look better against the wall over there.'

Josh groaned and she squeezed his arm sympathetically. 'Poor darling. You are having to do so much. But it will be worth it when it is all finished. It is very exciting, isn't it?'

'Yes.' It came out a lie.

'Well, try to sound a tiny bit enthusiastic about it!'

'I think you have enough enthusiasm for both of us.'

'I suppose that is true. But marriage is such a great event in a girl's life. She gets her own home, a place where she makes the decisions about what goes where, what she will cook for every meal – even how she does the housework! I suppose it is different for a man. When he gets married he gives up the right to do whatever he pleases.'

She looked up at him. 'I will work hard for you, Josh. I will try to make you a good wife.'

'I'm sure you will.' Her sincerity touched him. Then he looked past her, through the window and across the moor. 'I only hope I prove to be as good a husband. . . .'

The wedding was proclaimed the event of the year in Hayle. The chapel, decorated with hundreds of flowers for the event, was packed with guests. Included in their ranks were Theophilus Strike, Tom Shovell and Jenny from Sharptor, and Wrightwick Roberts was there to help the Hayle preacher with the service.

As a mark of respect to William Carlyon, most of the Harvey family were present, looking well dressed and well bred. But Ben Retallick would not allow Jesse to be over-awed by them. 'We're God-fearing folks who owe nothing to anyone and we have a son any of them would be proud to own today.'

The ceremony was simple and moving. When it was over Josh and Sarah returned to the Carlyon house in a gaily decorated pony-trap.

In the house the presents were on view, among them a silver dish from Francis Trevithick. During the reception Josh discovered that the mine-owners and engineers in this part of Cornwall had heard of his man-lift innovations. He was asked many questions about it by men who were complete strangers to him.

'It is wonderful to have a famous husband,' teased Sarah, rescuing him from a small group of ex-Harvey apprentices who were asking technical details about Josh's latest lift. 'But I am quite sure that it will keep until after our wedding day.'

'I don't mind,' said Josh. 'If even one of those engineers goes back to his own mine and puts in a man-lift, it will save many men who otherwise would not be at the wedding of their sons.'

'Josh, I am sure that my whole life will soon be tied up with mine-engines, boilers and all the other things that are important to a very clever engineer. But this is my wedding day and I want to enjoy every minute of it.'

Josh gave in without further argument. He was soon shaking hands and making smalltalk with young men who all looked alike and young women who gave him and Sarah shy knowing glances.

Eventually the guests began to drift away. Soon only family were left standing between mounds of dirty crockery and dejected foodstuffs. Then they adjourned into another room and everyone talked until well after their usual bedtimes. Finally, in an agony of embarrassment, the newly-weds were ushered upstairs to the room they were to occupy for that night.

Spending the first night of their married life beneath the Carlyon roof was a mistake. Sarah's initial shyness was so acute it only just fell short of terror. Although she snuggled up to Josh in the luxurious bed which was usually occupied by her parents, she would not allow Josh to consummate their marriage that night.

'I just couldn't!' she whispered. 'Not here in their bed. In this house. It – it just wouldn't seem right somehow. You do understand, don't you, Josh?'

He managed to convey the fact that he was offended in a single grunt.

'I am sorry. But tomorrow night we will be in our own house. Just you and me. It will be different then.'

They travelled to Sharptor by coach the following day. Alone. Jesse Retallick protested that it was unnecessary extravagance to use two coaches when they were all going to the same place; but William Carlyon stayed firm, and Sarah and Josh went ahead of the others in a light fast carriage.

The newly-weds arrived at their future home to discover it had been cleaned that very morning. A fire was burning in the lounge and there were fresh spring flowers everywhere, all provided by the wives of the Sharptor miners. This was a traditional homecoming, the wives' way of welcoming Sarah to their midst.

There was something else too and it pleased Josh out of all proportion to its value. It was a grandmother clock, standing conspicuously on the table in the lounge – a present from the miners at the Wheal Caradon.

Much later that night Josh lay in bed, thinking about the future. Beside him Sarah was curled up, asleep, the tears on her cheeks now dry. They had made love for the first time together. Sarah had given her all to him but it was not a wildly passionate union. Even the tears she had shed were more of relief because the act had not caused her as much pain as she was expecting. In a whisper Sarah had told her new husband that it had been wonderful, all she had hoped it would be. But Josh realised then that love-making for Sarah would be more a wifely duty than an abandoned pouring out of her love for him.

But lack of enthusiasm in bed was the only criticism he could possibly have levelled against Sarah. She was a promising cook, a good housekeeper, and she genuinely loved Josh.

'You've got a good wife there, Josh,' said Ben Retallick one evening as he and Josh walked down the hill in the dark after Ben had called in on his way home from the mine. 'Mind you take good care of her.'

Josh confirmed that he would.

'Have you seen anything of Miriam since you've been wed?'

Josh answered quite truthfully that he had not.

'Good! From all accounts she's leading her husband a merry dance. You were wise to break with her when you did.'

Josh did not correct him. Instead he asked, 'In what way is she leading Preacher Thackeray a dance?'

'By making him look a fool in front of his own parishioners, taking meetings of miners, trying to tell grown men about the benefits of this "union". Some folk seem to think it would cure all the ills of the miner, change him from what he is into something he can never be. Telling him he is as good as the men who give him his living.'

'You surprise me, Dad. I always thought you were on the side of the miner.'

'So I am,' retorted Ben. 'Which is more than I can say for anyone who fills his head with a lot of dangerous nonsense. Not that many of them take in what she's saying. All they go to her meetings for is to see her getting excited about something that's none of her business.'

Josh laughed. 'Have you heard Preacher Thackeray complaining about it?'

'No. I wouldn't expect to. But I can imagine what he says to her in private.'

'I think he's well pleased with her. Preacher Thackeray believes not only in the equality of all men – but women as well.'

'Then he's more of a fool than I would have taken him for. It's not a woman's place to be talking to a crowd of men. It's not decent.'

'Preacher Thackeray is a man who will use all the means at his disposal to put his beliefs across to the miners. And what he preaches is perfectly right.'

'I'd rather not hear that talk from you, Josh. Especially now. You've moved up in the world. You have a good skill at your fingertips and a wife from a good family. Be thankful for it. Don't go getting mixed up in any of Preacher Thackeray's doings.'

'But that's just it, Dad. Don't you see? What you've said proves how right Preacher Thackeray is. He taught me to read and write and do sums. He also taught me to think for myself. That's a right that every miner's son should have. But if it hadn't been for him I would never have been able to go to Hayle and learn how to be an engineer. His arguments are sound. Do you think Theophilus Strike is a better man than you? I don't. Neither should you.'

'Theophilus Strike is the mine-owner. As such we owe him our respect. I for one am indebted to him, for making me shift captain.'

'Dad! That argument won't hold water. I respect Theophilus Strike as I respect any other man. But he gave you the shift captain's job because you're the best man for it. Any Sharptor miner would tell you that. By appointing you shift captain he was doing what's best for the mine, and for himself. I'm grateful to him for giving me the opportunity to become a mine-engineer, but I'll repay his investment by keeping his engines trouble-free. Theophilus Strike is in a position to do what he has for you and me because of money he never had to work for. We're proving that we can do things without having that sort of money to help us. How does that make him better than us?'

'I don't like to hear you talk like this, Josh. When you settled the trouble at the Caradon mine I was pleased. It saved a great many jobs. But I've heard since that Preacher Thackeray uses it to prove to miners what they can get if they stand up to those who give the orders. It's dangerous talk, Josh, and I'd be pleased to hear you speak against it.'

'I'm sorry, Dad. I can't speak against something I believe in. Preacher Thackeray is telling the truth. If the Sharptor miners hadn't defied Captain Schmidt you wouldn't be here today talking to me.'

'Things have a habit of sorting themselves out, given time,' said Ben stubbornly, determined not to be convinced. 'All I ask is that you don't concern yourself with Preacher Thackeray's doings. You've got a wife and position to think of.'

'I'll remember that,' said Josh. 'But I'll still speak up for things I believe in.'

There was a resigned sigh from Ben Retallick. 'That's just what I said your reply would be.'

'"Said" . . . ? To who?'

'To Theophilus Strike, Josh. I was hoping to get you to see sense without bringing his name into it. Since my arguments don't move you I'd better tell you his words. He inspected the mine this morning. He tried out your new man-lift and thought it could prove useful, though he seemed to prefer the first one. He had a good deal to say about your engineering and said he was well satisfied with your work.'

Ben Retallick paused and crossed himself quickly as a star dropped diagonally across the sky to be swallowed up in the vastness of time and space.

'He also said he was disturbed – no, "concerned" was the word he used – concerned at some of the talk he'd heard about men coming to you with their problems. He said he'd even heard it rumoured you were for a miners' union. He was mightily relieved when I told him that, while I couldn't know who might have sought your advice, I could say there was no truth in the talk of you preaching for a union.'

'Dad, I haven't preached for a union – yet! If I was asked to I'd think seriously about it. As for giving men advice – yes, I have. Whenever I've been asked for it. I don't have to ask Theophilus Strike for his permission. He pays me a wage for a day's work. Whatever else I do is none of his business!'

'All right, Josh. Don't get angry with me. I've only told you what has been said. All I ask is you give it some thought. There's no sense in stirring up Strike. He's a good man; but he likes to think he's getting his own way – whether he is, or not. Now, I've kept you away from Sarah for long enough. I'll bid you good night. Don't forget you're both eating with us this Sunday.'

He walked away down the hill to the Retallick cottage, leaving Josh struggling to shrug off his anger. He considered the mine-owner's comments to be undue interference in his private life. He could not believe it was coincidence that it came at a time when the union of the miners was becoming more than a preacher's dream.

The movement was a long way from having the unanimous approval of every miner, but it was gaining ground. Each mine now had a small nucleus of men who met regularly and exchanged ideas with men from other mines. They elected members to attend meetings presided over by Preacher Thackeray and report back to their own committees. These were not the open 'conversation' meetings that Preacher Thackeray held to gain recruits, but a gathering of dedicated 'unionists' – men who gave their time and application to bringing about a revolution in the miner's way of life.

Josh was interested in the movement but he had taken no active part in the affairs of the miners since the trouble at the Wheal Caradon. It was for this reason as much as anything that he considered Theophilus Strike's words to be particularly unfair. He smarted under them all the way back to the house.

Chapter Nineteen

'What are you thinking about?'

It was a sultry late-summer night and the bedroom was filled with soft silver moonlight. Sarah turned on to her side to face Josh and slipped her arm over his chest.

'I thought you were asleep,' Josh replied quietly. 'Did I wake you?'

'No. I have been lying here trying to read your thoughts. Is something worrying you, Josh?'

'No.' He pulled her towards him. 'I can't sleep, that's all.'

'Are you quite sure, Josh? You aren't tired of me already?'

He snorted with amusement. 'That's a fine thing to say after only four months of marriage! Ask me again after four years.'

'I'm glad.' She snuggled closer to him. 'I am very happy. But something is bothering you. Is it anything to do with that man who called to see you this evening?'

'John Kittow? Not entirely. The miners over at Kit Hill are having some sort of trouble. He wants me to go to a meeting they're holding at Kelly Bray tomorrow night.'

She rose on one elbow to look down at him. 'You are not going?'

'I told John Kittow I would.'

'But why? It has nothing to do with you. Whatever trouble

they have there concerns neither you nor the Wheal Sharptor. Why get involved in it?'

'I'm not getting involved. I've simply been asked to go to a meeting. I'm going because I'm interested.'

'Theophilus Strike won't like it.'

'Sarah, I don't *care* what Theophilus Strike likes. This is none of his business.'

'And the Kit Hill miners are none of *your* business, but that is not going to prevent you from going to their meeting.'

Josh said nothing. It was their first argument. He felt the unhappiness knotting itself inside her. They lay side by side in silence for a long time before Josh felt a tremor run through Sarah's body. It was followed a few seconds later by a strangled sob that racked her body for the second time.

'Sarah, please don't cry.'

'Oh, Josh! I'm so miserable!'

He turned and put his arms about her and she clung to him, tears coursing down her face and soaking his shoulder.

He held her for a long time, soothing her and brushing the hair back from her face until she stopped crying.

'I'm sorry, Josh. That was silly of me.

'No!' She stopped him as he was about to protest that it was his fault. 'You must do what you feel you should do. I have no right to object.'

'You're my wife, Sarah. You have every right to express your opinion. All I wish is that you were interested enough to want to know what it's all about, instead of condemning my involvement out of hand.'

'I don't want to know, Josh. I probably wouldn't understand it anyway. But you know what you are doing. I accept that. Now, don't be angry with me anymore.'

She drew him to her and that night their love making found the fervour that had been missing before.

Josh rode Hector to Kelly Bray with John Kittow behind him. The meeting was held in a clearing behind a miners' inn and was well attended.

The men's grievance was with the mine store. Every mine

ran its own store and it invariably gained a stranglehold on the miners and their families. When a man started work on a mine he rarely had the money to see him through the first month. The only place he could obtain credit was the mine store. His tools came from there, together with the essential items of furniture to set up home. The cost was higher than elsewhere, but few men had any choice. It suited the mine-owners – who also ran the store. A man had to work hard to keep up with his indebtedness. He was fearful of losing his job. It also meant that, as soon as he was paid, the money was returned to the mine-owners via the store.

Occasionally it happened that the owners became greedy, especially if they thought some of the miners' money was escaping them. Then they simply increased the store prices.

This was the problem at Kit Hill. The men had complained of high prices to no avail. So deeply in debt were they that few of them could afford to break the vicious circle by buying elsewhere. Two men who had walked the miles to a Gunnislake mine store on pay-day had been dismissed and told they were lucky not to have been taken before the magistrate for attempting to obtain 'false' credit.

Incredible though the allegation was, had it gone before the local magistrate there would have been a conviction. Magistrates were well-to-do local men, most of them with shares in at least one mine.

It was against this background that the meeting had been called.

It got off to a slow start. When Josh and John Kittow arrived there must have been a hundred and fifty men in the wide piece of open ground. Men stood in small groups, some arguing among themselves, others looking embarrassed at being there at all.

John Kittow and Josh picked their way through the crowd, the Caradon shift captain occasionally greeting an acquaintance. When they reached a heap of mine waste that would serve as a platform Josh looked about them and said, 'John, this is a complete waste of time. Unless someone starts talking to the men they'll all begin to leave. I'll probably go with them. Who called the meeting?'

'A miner named Harry Reeve,' said John Kittow. 'I can't see him here.'

'Well, if he can't bother to turn up for his own meeting I see no sense in staying.'

'Give him a few minutes,' pleaded John Kittow. 'Something must have happened to keep him away. He's a reliable man, or so I'm told. I must admit I don't know him well.'

They began moving slowly back towards the place where Josh had left his horse when there was a sudden upheaval in the crowd in front of them and voices raised in anger. A red-faced man, perspiration tracking down his face, pushed past them, heading for the heap of mine waste. When he reached it he turned to the crowd, holding his hands aloft, calling for silence.

'Quiet, please! Listen! Listen to me! Shut up a minute!'

The noise died down and the hot newcomer, who seemed to have the greatest difficulty in standing still, raised his voice and shouted unnecessarily loudly.

'Harry Reeve won't be coming here to speak to us tonight . . .'

An angry buzz from the crowd drowned his words and he waved his arms wildly again until the miners fell into a near-silence.

'It's not his fault. He's been arrested.'

There was complete stunned silence.

'Not only Harry Reeve, but also Richard Crossentine, Daniel Trehane, Sam Maddiver and Wesley Barnicott along with him.'

The crowd erupted into anger as the miners took up the cry of 'Why? Why?'

'I'll tell you why,' shouted the sweating man. 'It's because the adventurers heard there was to be a meeting about the store. They thought they'd put a stop to it by having Harry Reeve and the others arrested. They are to be taken before the magistrate and charged with "incitement to riot"!'

There was another roar from the assembly and a second man

scrambled up on to the rubble. He had difficulty in maintaining his balance. Josh thought he was probably drunk.

'We'll show them what a riot is,' he shouted. 'We'll go and get Harry out.'

The crowd was for leaving on a rescue mission there and then. But the first man tried to bring some order to the meeting. 'No! We mustn't do anything just yet. Someone went from Callington to fetch Preacher Thackeray as soon as we found out they had Harry and the others in the lock-up there. He'll be here soon. He'll know what to do.'

'We already know what to do,' said the second man, intent on rousing the crowd. 'We don't need a bloody preacher to tell us. If he wants to talk he'll find us at Callington lock-up, getting Harry Reeve and the others out!'

Once again he had the crowd's approval and there were shouts of 'Come on. What are we waiting for? One and all! One and all!'

This was the age-old cry of the Cornishman and had preceded more than one bloody riot.

Josh pushed his way roughly through the miners and climbed up to join the other two on the waste-mound. He was big enough to gain the attention of the miners without using any tricks, and they fell silent as he called to them.

'Wait! If you go to Callington and break into the lock-up there's not a court in the county will find Harry Reeve and the others not guilty. You'd condemn them by your actions.'

There were catcalls and some shouts of 'Who are you?'

'This is none of your business. Leave it to those of us who are friends of Harry Reeve.' This from the man who had advocated rescuing the arrested men.

'Don't do anything you'll regret,' Josh reasoned. 'You met here to talk of union, of action to right a wrong. Don't let this panic you into doing something that will give the adventurers an excuse for taking action against unionism.'

'And what's arresting Harry Reeve if it isn't taking action against us?' The man on the mound beside Josh pushed his face towards him. His breath confirmed Josh's earlier opinion that he had been drinking. At the same time Josh heard his own name being spoken among the crowd of miners.

'Get off here and let me talk to them.'

The drunken miner pushed Josh, but in a quick move Josh took hold of the man's arm. Swinging him around to face the crowd he pushed him off instead. His action brought a cheer from the miners at the back of the clearing. When he tried to make himself heard above the hubbub someone called, 'It's Joshua Retallick. Let him speak.' Others took up the call, and when he spoke he had their full attention.

'The worst thing you could possibly do is use violence. That will solve nothing. There are other ways of achieving your ends. But you must decide here and now what it is you want. Then make sure every last man in the Kit Hill mine is with you. If you don't show complete unity you might as well walk away from here right now and forget about helping either Harry Reeve or yourselves.'

'That's the soundest advice I've heard at any meeting. You are absolutely right, Josh.'

It was the Reverend William Thackeray. During the argument he had arrived unnoticed, his neat little gig making no sound as it approached across the soft grass.

But it was not the preacher who caused Josh to become suddenly tongue-tied. It was Miriam, seated beside him.

Miriam was just as surprised to see Josh at the meeting but she managed a faint smile that gave no hint of her inner turmoil. With her long loose hair blown by the wind and her face flushed with excitement she still had all the wild beauty of the young girl Josh had explored the moor with. There was not a man at the meeting who was not stirred by her presence.

But this type of gathering was William Thackeray's natural environment. Giving the reins to a nearby miner, he handed his wife from the gig and pushed his way to the front of the crowd with Miriam following.

As the man who had brought the news of Harry Reeve's arrest reached down to help them on to the rock platform, Josh began to climb down, not wishing to be confronted by Miriam in such a confined area. It was William Thackeray who stopped him. Gripping Josh's arm, he spoke to him in an urgent whisper. 'Stay here, Josh. We have need of you.'

To the crowd he cried, 'You've heard what Josh Retallick said. I endorse his every word. Is there any man here who has other ideas?'

There were a number of dissenters but not as many as had enthusiastically supported a march on Callington lock-up.

'Then let's hear them. You! The bearded man at the front here. What do you suggest we do?'

The bearded miner was unhappy at being singled out for attention. He looked about him for some visible sign of support, but men avoided his eyes.

'I say we march on Callington and release Harry Reeve.' It was said hesitantly and without conviction but there was a degree of agreement in the crowd.

William Thackeray turned to Miriam in a routine that would have had a familiar pattern to any miner who had attended some of their previous meetings. 'He suggests this band of good men . . .' He waved his hand in a gesture that took in every miner. 'This crowd of – how many? One hundred? Two, perhaps?'

Miriam nodded seriously.

'All right, let's say that two hundred miners were to march on Callington. What do you think would happen?'

Miriam looked slowly over the crowd and nodded her head again. 'They are fine men. I doubt if you could pick better anywhere. Each one capable of holding his own in a fist fight with any man.'

Her clear voice rang out so that not one man missed her words. Josh was impressed by the self-assured manner in which she held their attention. Then he remembered an evening when as a young girl she had prevented a fight between Morwen and himself by projecting just such an authority.

Preacher Thackeray was talking again. 'Two hundred brave Cornishmen, prepared to storm the Callington lock-up and release their friends.'

Some of the miners were looking puzzled. The preacher

and his wife seemed to be contradicting William Thackeray's earlier statement, agreeing that a march on Callington would succeed after all.

'Yes. We'll do it too!' someone shouted.

Miriam stepped in front of her husband and reaching down inside the front of her dress pulled out a small linen bag attached to a long drawstring looped about her neck. The curious crowd fell silent.

'You are brave men,' agreed Miriam. 'Any man who earns his living below ground has courage. None could deny it.'

She held up the small linen bag for all to see, and her next words rang out with all the power she could put into them. 'Yet this small bag would hold enough musket-balls to kill every one of you!'

The men were looking puzzled again, but Miriam did not leave them in suspense for long.

'You wonder what this has to do with you? Then I'll tell you. At this very moment a full company of soldiers, regular disciplined troops – more than a hundred of them – are riding post-haste from Bodmin barracks to Callington. *Every single one of those soldiers carries this many musket-balls!*'

In the stunned silence that followed the miners stared at Miriam in disbelief.

'Yes, a full company of soldiers will be in Callington before nightfall.'

Pushing the bag back inside her dress, Miriam struck a pose with hands on hips. 'Do you take the Callington magistrate for a fool? He knew what the rest of you would do when he arrested the leading Kit Hill unionists. There was a horseman on his way to Bodmin for soldiers before the ink was dry on the warrant for Harry Reeve's arrest!'

Josh was as surprised as the miners. His object in preventing them from marching on Callington was so as not to prejudice the case of the men held in custody. He had never envisaged the military becoming involved.

'Then what can we do?' called one of the miners. 'We can't just stand back and do nothing.'

This was a cue William Thackeray had been waiting for.

'That must be for you to decide,' he declared. 'I can only advise you on ways to achieve the aims of all Kit Hill miners. But, first, how many of them are *not* at this meeting?'

'Not more than fifty,' replied the miner beside him.

'I suggest you make certain those fifty join with you to stop all work in the Kit Hill mine.'

This provoked noisy mutterings among the miners. 'How are we supposed to live while we're out of work?' asked one, and others echoed his question.

Miriam glared angrily at the crowd. 'Men are in prison for no other reason than that they tried to help you. They face trial – for you. I know you have families to think of. So does Harry Reeve. Who will feed his five children?'

'My wife is right,' said William Thackeray. 'Conditions won't improve without some sacrifices being made by everyone. Stopping work at the mine will hurt your pockets, yes. But it will hit the pockets of the adventurers too. They won't allow such a state of affairs to go on for long.'

'What do you say, Retallick?' one of the miners called.

Josh had been standing at the rear of the group on the mound, happy to allow the others to do the talking. Now, as they stood aside for him, he stepped forward, avoiding meeting Miriam's gaze. Instead he looked down at the anxious faces in the crowd, aware that his answer would decide the miners' actions and choosing his words carefully.

'I say do as Preacher Thackeray suggests. Get the others with you. Tell the captain you'll allow the engine-men to go in for one week only. By the end of that time the prices in the mine store must have been lowered and Harry Reeve and the others released. If they haven't, tell him the engine-men will shut off the pumps and allow the mine to flood.'

Josh's words received noisy approval.

'But you must have a leader,' declared William Thackeray. 'Someone you can trust to carry your decisions – to the adventurers, if necessary – without being cowed by them. Do you have such a man?'

A number of men called the name 'John Trehane'.

'Is John Trehane here?' asked William Thackeray.

'That's me, Preacher,' said the miner on the mound with them.

'Then the meeting is all yours, John Trehane. I wish you good luck. If you need help or advice you know where to find me.'

'Thank you, Preacher – and Mistress Thackeray. You too, Mr Retallick. You're well thought of by the men and we appreciate your coming to show support for us.'

Miriam was being helped to the ground by William Thackeray and John Trehane when John Kittow pushed his way through to them.

'I'd like to have a word with the men before you go,' he said, and Josh helped him up on to the stones before joining Miriam and William Thackeray on the ground.

John Kittow came straight to the point. 'I've brought an answer to one of your problems,' his deep voice boomed out over the assembly. 'You wanted to know how your families would manage to live if you weren't working. I'll tell you. We've been through troubles ourselves at the Wheal Caradon, as Josh Retallick could tell you. Because we know what it means to have support at a time like this we held a meeting at the Caradon last night. It was agreed by our men that they would each give a shilling a week to help during the time you're not working.'

The cheering and shouting showed what the men of the Kit Hill mine thought of the gesture. But John Kittow had not finished.

'Not only that – listen now! Not only that. The Wheal Phoenix men have told me to tell you they'll each give sixpence a week too.'

'We've done it! Miriam. Josh. We've done it!' William Thackeray was pumping Miriam's and Josh's hands and literally dancing up and down. 'A union of miners has become a reality in this part of Cornwall. There'll be no stopping us now. This is what I've been working towards for all these years.'

His elation was almost matched by that of the miners. With the threat of starvation removed they knew they could win the fight against the high mine-store prices.

Josh was still not comfortable in Miriam's presence but it was difficult not to get caught up in the infectious enthusiasm of the crowd.

'All we need now is the acquittal of those men in custody at Callington. Then it will be a victory,' he said.

'Of course, Josh. But come. We must talk about these exciting happenings over a glass of wine. No, Josh! The evening will turn sour if you don't come home with us.'

Miriam felt as apprehensive as Josh but she managed a 'Please, Josh,' and was not certain whether she wanted him to accept or refuse.

'Of course he'll come. He's been absent from our circle of friends for far too long. This evening's happenings have been brought about as much by what he did for the miners of Wheal Caradon as by my own efforts. Come, Miriam. We'll ride in the gig and Josh can accompany us on that fine horse of his.'

As John Kittow declared his intention of remaining with the Kit Hill men and finding his own way home later, Josh was unable to make an acceptable excuse for not going to St Cleer.

The preacher drove his horse along at a fast trot and it was not long before they reached St Cleer and drew up outside the preacher's house.

'Now, you two go into the house while I put the gig away. Leave your horse tied up at the gate, Josh. I'll give him some water. When I come in I'll open a very special bottle of port wine. I've been saving it for just such an occasion as this. Go on inside now.'

Dusk was not far off, and inside the house it was dark and quiet. Josh followed Miriam into the comfortable lounge and, when she had lit a lamp, seated himself in the corner furthest from it.

After a heavy silence, Miriam said, 'It's nice to see you here in this house, Josh.'

'Is it?'

'Yes, it makes me very happy. I'm quite sure William feels the same. He's missed your friendship. We both have.'

'Don't you think friendship might be difficult in the circumstances?'

'No, Josh. There are many things William doesn't know – and needn't know. But even if he did I feel sure he'd forgive both of us. As a preacher he's well aware of the weaknesses of men and women. It would distress him, but I'm sure he would find forgiveness. Especially if the interests of the union were involved. That comes before anything with William.'

Josh looked for some sign of bitterness in her face, but there was none.

'What about Daniel?'

Miriam drew in a deep breath. 'Daniel is part of William's family. He loves him very much. I don't believe anyone would be cruel enough to destroy that feeling.'

There were words in Josh's throat but they caught there. Instead he said, 'Where is Daniel now?'

'With my mother for a few days. . . .' Miriam looked at him and bit her lip. 'Josh, let's not make tonight unhappy. I really am pleased to have you here. I feel as though I am singing in here.' She put a hand to her breast. 'William is happy too – and you can't tell me that you aren't very proud of your part in what has been achieved today.'

She moved closer to him. 'Do you realise what it means? Now the miners are strong enough to stand against the mine-owners. By joining together they can improve their living standards, get a fair wage, and will not have to accept the many unfair conditions that go with their work.'

William Thackeray had entered the room quietly. He saw the look on Miriam's face as her hand rested on Josh's chair for a brief second but he said nothing. Going straight to a cupboard he took out three glasses and filled them from the bottle he carried in his hand.

Handing the glasses around he raised his in a salute.

'To the Union. To the Miners' Fund and to a better understanding between all Christian men, whatever their lot in life. May they all be as God made them – equal!'

'I'd like to propose another toast,' said Josh gravely. 'To the freedom of the men who were arrested today for trying to exercise that equality.'

* * *

That very night the Kit Hill mine store was burned to the ground. It was difficult to say when the fire started because the mine was not being worked and the engine-man spent most of the night dozing. It was left to the Callington town watchman to raise the alarm when he saw the flames lighting the sky-line atop the hill, as though it was the Midsummer Night bonfire.

The fire brought the military to the mine. They stayed for a week. There were angry words exchanged between soldier and miner but, although they came close to blows on more than one occasion, the peace was kept.

There were few miners who regretted the destruction of the store and they made no secret of their feelings. But the incident sealed the fate of the five union leaders held in custody. There had been hopes that they would be brought before the magistrate on a trifling charge and be summarily dealt with once the miners' terms had been met. But the fire made the matter far more serious. They were sent in custody to Bodmin Jail to await trial at the next Assize, charged with conspiring to destroy property. It was generally recognised that they had little chance of an acquittal now.

'Whoever set fire to that store convicted them as surely as though he were the Assize judge himself,' said William Thackeray when he rode over to the Sharptor mine to tell Josh the news. Josh already knew; the store-burning had relegated all other news of the day in the area.

'Is there nothing that can be done for them?' asked Josh.

William Thackeray shook his head. 'Nothing. The miners are collecting to engage counsel for them, but it will be a token defence only. The judge will be determined to make an example of Harry Reeve and the others. The mine-owners must be rubbing their hands at such an opportunity.'

They were seated in the lounge of Josh's Sharptor house. Sarah came into the room bearing a tray with tea and cakes upon it. She was pleased at the opportunity to be a hostess. A minister was of sufficient status to warrant more formality than the friends and acquaintances from the mine who occasionally called in to see them.

'We are discussing the plight of the men from Kit Hill mine held for trial at Bodmin, Mrs Retallick,' said William Thackeray, seeking to draw her into their conversation.

'I am quite sure they will get their just deserts,' said Sarah icily. 'I wish that Josh would keep well out of it. No good can come from such goings-on.'

She was pouring tea and so was unaware of the slightly raised eyebrow as the Reverend William Thackeray looked from Sarah to her embarrassed husband.

'Sarah is the complete boss's daughter,' said Josh.

'I am not a snob, Josh,' Sarah said. 'The Cornish miner is the best in the world. I have heard my father and his friends say so many times. But he should keep to working in a mine and leave the running of it to those who are experienced in such things.'

Preacher Thackeray recognised there was a basic difference of opinion between the couple and he launched into the sort of traditional smalltalk that Sarah was used to hearing from the Hayle preachers.

William Thackeray only briefly mentioned Sarah's attitude. That was when Josh walked beside the minister's pony as far as the Sharptor mine. 'Your wife is a charming girl, Josh. She shows her breeding. I don't think you'll have an easy time convincing her of the justice of unionism.'

'Sarah will think differently about it when she understands it better. The only talk she has heard until now has been against it.'

'I ought to send Miriam on a visit to convert her,' said the preacher as he dug his heels into the pony's ribs.

Watching as pony and rider merged with the dark shadows along the path, Josh thought it might be as well if Sarah and Miriam did not meet. He knew instinctively they would strike sparks from each other.

Sarah was not the only one to be unhappy at Josh's involvement with the unionists. But Theophilus Strike had none of Sarah's charm to offset his displeasure. Josh had never seen the mine-owner in an angrier mood.

He went for Josh as soon as he arrived at the Wheal Sharptor, a few days after the Kit Hill fire.

When Josh entered the office he was standing behind the mine captain's large desk.

'Joshua!' Strike's voice was normally loud and now his words fairly thundered out. 'What's this nonsense I've heard about you being involved with the criminals who burned down the Kit Hill mine shop?'

'I know nothing about the burning-down of the Kit Hill store,' Josh replied, meeting the mine-owner's eyes and keeping his voice normal.

'Don't lie to me, Joshua. I have it from a very reliable source that you were at the meeting that preceded the burning of the shop.'

'Then your reliable source will have told you I warned the miners against taking any unlawful action.'

'So you don't deny attending this meeting of Kit Hill riff-raff?'

'I don't deny it, Mr Strike. I'm of the opinion the Kit Hill miners have a just grievance.'

Theophilus Strike looked at him in amazement. 'Do you realise what you are saying? You have the nerve to stand there and tell me quite blatantly that you support men who burn a building to the ground? Five rogues are due to stand trial for just such support. Are you quite mad, Joshua?'

'I'm not mad, Mr Strike, any more than those five miners are guilty of involvement in the burning of the mine store. They were arrested before the meeting. The only thing of which they are guilty is of speaking their minds about the prices in the Kit Hill mine store.'

Theophilus Strike leaned forward across the desk, supporting his weight on clenched fists.

'I've a good mind to dismiss you here and now. Anyone who condones violence among miners and refuses to deplore the destruction of mine property is a dangerous man to have around.'

Josh paled at the threat but he refused to be cowed by the mine-owner.

'I've never condoned violence or supported the destruction of any property. I'm in sympathy with the Kit Hill miners because they have a just grievance. I don't expect you to understand; the Wheal Sharptor has never been run along Kit Hill lines. The miners here earn a good wage and the shop prices are fair. That's why this mine is free from trouble. A fair wage for a fair day's work is all that any miner wants.'

The mine-owner continued to glare but waited for Josh to continue.

'Perhaps if I quote some prices charged at the Kit Hill store you'll begin to understand.' He began with the prices of foodstuffs – they were roughly twice the normal. Then he mentioned candles, and the tools a miner needed below ground – some were almost four times the fair price. Theophilus Strike was a merchant, aware of the wholesale prices of the items Josh mentioned.

'That's preposterous!' he declared when Josh had finished. 'I don't believe it.'

'It's easy enough to prove,' replied Josh. 'Ask any of the men who had to pay those prices. Then add the interest that the store-keeper levied on those whose payments fell behind.'

Josh had succeeded in shaking Strike, but he was an owner, not a miner.

'Even if the Kit Hill miners were being robbed, what business is it of yours? You're an engineer, not a miner. Why did you go to this meeting?'

'I was asked to go with a friend from the Wheal Caradon,' replied Josh. 'I went because I'm interested in miners. I try to make their work easier by introducing such things as the man-lift. I'll do anything within my power to help them lead safer and more comfortable lives.'

Taking a deep breath he put into words what he had hardly been able to channel into conscious thought before.

'I'm an engineer now, Mr Strike. I have you to thank for that. But long before I learned to be an engineer I was a miner's son. I would take food to him on the days when sheer exhaustion caused him to oversleep and rush off to work without anything to eat. I've crawled along tunnels scarcely high enough for me to wriggle through. If there had recently been an explosion there was more dust than air. In side-tunnels all the way along I could hear the echoes of men coughing up what was left of their lungs.

'I can remember my father crushing me against the wall of the shaft so I wouldn't be knocked off the ladder, as a man – no, a boy – one who'd been like a brother to me – fell to his death because his hands were too numb to keep a grasp on the rungs. Then I went home and spent the night listening to the heart-break of a widow only a couple of years older than myself.

'Then there were the evenings when I went to the top of the shaft to wait for my father to come up from shift. The good days were the ones when he was working on one of the upper levels. He might be able to manage a "Hello, son," after ten or fifteen minutes. The bad days were the ones when he was down at the deeper levels, when he wouldn't even see me. He'd crawl from the shaft and collapse on to his belly, sucking in air with such a noise I feared his lungs might burst. It would take him half an hour to regain the strength and breath to get to his feet and walk home with me. Sometimes I couldn't bear to stand and watch him and I'd run off on to the moor. When I got home he'd ask me why I hadn't met him. I'd lie and say I'd forgotten.

'No son should see his father in that condition, Mr Strike – defeated, crawling like a wounded animal from a hole in the ground. Those evenings when I ran away from watching him on the ground I'd walk on the moor, begging God to give me the opportunity to help him and the other men like him. Some of the older men were in an even worse condition. They would try desperately to get to their feet at the same time as the younger men, frightened that the mine captain might see them and decide they were too old to work at the bottom levels where the money could be earned.

'I worked at Hayle, Mr Strike. I was determined to master engineering. It was a way of making sure my sons would never have to see me lying on the ground at the top of a mine shaft. That's why, when Trevithick gave me the plans for a man-lift,

I built it without asking anyone – in case you tried to stop me. But it doesn't end there. Other things in a miner's life are just as wrong. If he's lucky he might live to be forty-five years old. For every one of those years he's had to put up with unbelievable hardships at work and little enough comfort at home.

'I've seen that there's more to life than that. I've ridden in a coach, galloped a horse – one with a saddle on it. I've been to a concert and heard music I never knew existed. I've seen what life is like outside a mine. I'm realistic enough to know that every miner can't become a gentleman overnight. But there must be more for him than bed, drink and work.

'Maybe that's why I went to that meeting. Perhaps I wanted to tell them something of what I've just told you.'

'It's as well you didn't, Joshua. They would probably have laughed at you. You are too young and too sensitive to take that.'

Strike was looking at Josh in a strange way. 'You're a humanitarian, Joshua. I fear you'll find it an unrewarding field of endeavour.'

His anger had completely gone.

'I respect your motives, but I question the effect they will have upon the men and upon you – especially upon you. I'll be perfectly honest with you, Joshua. I rode here with the express intention of dismissing you. I had no thought of giving you a hearing. Now I have and I can respect your sincerity. But I must doubt your cause and I feel sure I'll be called upon to defend my tolerance in the future. However, just so long as I have no trouble in the Wheal Sharptor I will accept your right to pursue your beliefs.'

Josh began to thank the mine-owner, but Theophilus Strike cut him short with an impatient gesture. 'Don't thank me, Joshua. I'm doing you no favour. In all probability I would be helping you more if I were to give you an ultimatum: forget your ideas or lose your post here. But I believe you have to work out your own destiny – and God help you!'

With that Theophilus Strike strode out of the office, leaving Josh feeling as though he had spent a long day working in the heat of the boiler-room.

Chapter Twenty

The Kit Hill miners kept the mine idle for a full week before an extraordinary meeting of the mine-adventurers was called. There it was reported that the engine-men were ready to join the miners.

The shareholders hurriedly arrived at a solution whereby the whole of the blame for the men's grievances was placed upon the mine captain. It was grossly unfair. The mine captain had done nothing more than follow the instructions of the adventurers. But this was an accepted hazard of a mine captain's job. With their scapegoat out of the way a settlement was agreed and the miners resumed work immediately. A new store went up on the site of the old one, with the promise that the prices of the goods sold would not exceed those of other mine stores.

But there was to be no happy ending for Harry Reeve and those arrested with him. When the miners demanded their release they were told the matter was out of the adventurers' hands. The miners' leaders had been arrested by the soldiers and sent for trial by the magistrate. Now the Law must pursue its ponderous relentless course. As the mine captain had been dismissed as a sop to the miners, so would their own leaders be arraigned as a reminder that there was always a price to be paid for each 'victory'.

The Law exacted a cruel price from the miners.

Preacher Thackeray attended the trial and late on the second day Josh saw him coming down from the high moor, riding direct from Bodmin.

When the preacher pulled his pony to a halt it was well lathered.

'The court found them guilty, Josh.'

It came as no surprise. The whole countryside had been expecting it.

'And the sentence?'

'Fourteen years' transportation!'

Josh winced. It was a vicious sentence. Except in very very rare cases such a punishment meant banishment for life. A man was shipped abroad, usually to Australia, to work as a convict for the duration of his sentence. Upon its expiration he was 'free' to work for his fare home – if he could find someone to pay him more than a subsistence wage and was able to keep his money safe for the years it would take him to save the fare.

'What are we going to do about it?'

'That's what I hoped you would say, Josh. Fetch your horse and we'll go to see the men at Kit Hill. I would like to see a march on Bodmin Jail. We'll show the judges that the miners will not accept this without a struggle.'

Josh saddled Hector and rode out to join William Thackeray, closing his ears to Sarah's protests. Her dislike of unionism had hardened since a weekend visit home two weeks before and she made no secret of her disapproval. Neither would she speak to Preacher Thackeray now.

But, if William Thackeray expected the Kit Hill miners to down tools and make an immediate protest at the sentence inflicted on their colleagues, he was bitterly disappointed.

The miners were sorry to hear the news. Shocked even. It was a 'shame'. But when action was suggested they looked down at the ground, up at the sky, and shuffled their feet uncomfortably.

''Tis difficult, you see,' said one of the miners, summing up the situation. 'We'd love to do something to help 'em.

But we've got to think about our families now, haven't we? I mean, we didn't have a proper week's pay when we was striking. We've got to make that up. Besides, the adventurers might not take it kindly if we stopped work again.'

'But Harry Reeve and the others have families too,' said Josh. 'And their children are receiving no money. All this because they wanted to help you!'

''Tis sad, I agree,' said the spokesman. 'But it won't help them if we lose our jobs as well. Will it, now?'

Josh bit back the retort that the imprisoned men had lost far more than their jobs on behalf of the Kit Hill miners. There was no moving them.

The most that William Thackeray could get from the miners was a half-promise to attend a prayer-meeting outside the Jail gates the next Sunday afternoon. It had to be designated a prayer-meeting. All other public meetings were banned on a Sunday.

Not surprisingly, the other mines in the area were not prepared to give Preacher Thackeray more support than the Kit Hill miners. He had to be content with the projected prayer-meeting. The Caradon miners promising him a hundred-per-cent turn-out.

As the horses' heads were turned towards St Cleer, Josh expressed his disgust at the attitude of the Kit Hill miners.

The preacher shook his head sorrowfully. 'I learned long ago not to be surprised or disappointed at anything. When there should be gratitude there is complete indifference. Good deeds are repaid with bad, and there sometimes seems very little sense in preaching the fellowship of man. But it must be done or the world will slide back into darkness. It's a new experience for you. One not easy to accept. But don't blame the Kit Hill miners too much. They came close to losing their livelihoods. It brought them face to face with the realities of its consequences. They don't care to risk it again for fear their luck might not hold good.'

'What about the men who have been sentenced to transportation for their sakes? Don't they count for anything?'

'Of course they do. But they knew what might happen to

them because of their beliefs. They accepted it. There will be others who'll suffer for the same cause. But one day we'll win. We must win in order to stop miners risking their lives thousands of feet below ground without getting reasonable pay and conditions. That's what this is all about, Josh. Each tiny victory, no matter how small, is another step closer to that goal.'

Josh did not go on to St Cleer with William Thackeray. Instead he turned off and took a short cut to Sharptor.

Sarah was busying herself in the kitchen, and the exaggerated clatter of tins told Josh that she was not in the best of moods. Nevertheless, he told her the results of his trip to Kit Hill with William Thackeray.

'Well! What else did you expect?' she snapped. 'You don't think anyone will thank you for meddling in their affairs, do you? They burned down the store and they know that someone must be punished for it. You are a fool to get yourself involved with them. Mother thinks so too.'

Josh paused in the act of putting a mug of water to his lips.

'What has your mother got to do with it?'

'We spoke about it when I was home.'

'Oh?'

Sarah flushed. 'Isn't it natural for a girl to talk over her problems with her mother?'

'I hadn't realised I was a problem.'

Sarah looked hurt. 'You know very well what I mean, Josh. It worries me to see you mixed up with something like this. It's dangerous.'

'It worried Theophilus Strike too. But at least he heard me out and tried to understand why I feel so strongly about the union. That's more than you'll do. You've decided to close your mind to anything connected with unionism and that's the truth of it.'

'I have more important things to occupy my mind,' said Sarah.

'What sort of things? Whether to do the washing on a Tuesday instead of a Monday? Wondering whether the blue dress looks nicer than the pink one to wear into Launceston market?'

It was spiteful and he knew it, but it was out before he could bite it back.

Sarah placed the pan she was holding carefully in the cupboard and dried her hands upon her apron before answering him.

'No. The sort of thing that is occupying my mind at the moment is whether I will bear you a son or a daughter.'

Josh's expression of utter astonishment was very satisfying.

'You – you're pregnant?'

'Yes.'

'But why didn't you tell me? Why didn't you say something about it before?'

'You have been so involved with this silly union business that I was scarcely able to gain your attention for long enough to tell you anything. Anyway, I wasn't absolutely sure. That's why I went home to see Mother.'

'You could have spoken to my mother about it. She would have told you anything you wanted to know.'

'I couldn't have asked her about something like this, Josh. It was difficult enough to discuss with my own mother. Dr Scott examined me and told me for sure, though.'

'Why did you see the doctor? Is something wrong?'

His concern brought an answering smile from Sarah and she was no longer angry with him. 'Of course not. It is usual for a woman who is having a baby to see a doctor. And I have known Dr Scott all of my life.'

'Jenny didn't see a doctor when she was expecting.'

'Well, I am not Jenny,' said Sarah sharply. 'And I want a doctor to be with me when I have my baby.' She looked suddenly unhappy. 'You haven't even said you are pleased about it!'

'Of course I'm pleased.'

He took her into his arms and kissed her very gently. 'And I think you're very clever. What's more, if I like it I'll allow you to have lots more . . .'

* * *

Jesse and Ben Retallick were delighted with the news when Sarah and Josh visited the cottage the following evening and told them.

'I've expected it for some weeks,' exclaimed Jesse as she beamed at her daughter-in-law.

'How?' Sarah glanced quickly down at her stomach. 'There is nothing to see yet.'

'I've seen it in your face. That's where it shows first.'

'You'll find life is a bit different with a baby around,' said Ben Retallick, grinning from the comfort of his armchair. 'You can forget what a good night's sleep is like for a start.'

'Nonsense!' Josh said. 'You're forgetting I was here when Jenny had little Gwen with her. She was no trouble at all.'

'Not to you, she wasn't,' said Jesse. 'You slept through most of her crying. You can't do that when it's your own.'

She put a tea-pot on the table and looked pointedly at Josh. 'And perhaps having a child around will keep you home in the evenings.'

'What's that supposed to mean?' asked Josh.

'You know well enough. Gallivanting off with that preacher from St Cleer. I breathed a sigh of relief when you came back from Hayle and saw nothing of him for a while. But from what I hear you've taken up with him again, riding around to meetings of miners and stirring up trouble. It's a pity he doesn't spend more time preaching and less time urging miners to do things they wouldn't think of left to themselves.'

'Then you'll be pleased to hear he is holding a special prayer-meeting tomorrow,' said Josh. 'Outside Bodmin Jail. To pray for the five men who have been sentenced to transportation. He hopes to gather as many people as possible so their singing might give encouragement to the men inside.'

'That sounds as though it has all the promise of a mob,' said Ben Retallick seriously.

'No, Preacher Thackeray will keep it in hand. There'll be no violence.'

'You are not going?' This from Sarah.

'Yes. I've promised Preacher Thackeray I'll be there. But I'm so certain nothing bad is intended that you can come along with me and see for yourself.'

'I'll have no part of any of Preacher Thackeray's meetings,' declared Sarah, and Jesse agreed with her.

On the way home that evening Sarah asked, 'Will Preacher Thackeray's wife be going to the meeting tomorrow?'

'I doubt it. Why do you ask?'

'No special reason,' said Sarah, much too casually. 'But I heard she often speaks at meetings. I wondered . . .'

'This is a prayer-meeting, a service,' answered Josh. 'I expect Miriam will have other things to do. But why don't you come along and see for yourself?'

Sarah did not go, and Josh was wrong. Miriam was very much in evidence.

She had persuaded Mrs Reeve, wife of the imprisoned union leader, to come with her, together with three score miners' wives.

There was a huge attendance at the 'prayer-meeting'. By the time Preacher Thackeray was ready to begin the service there must have been close to a thousand miners standing in the shadow of the high grey prison wall. They had come from Kit Hill, Caradon, St Austell and as far west as Redruth. On the edge of the crowd, their cloaks and dresses rustling in the wind, the women formed a small group.

A number of interested townspeople hung about the fringe of the gathering, curious to hear what Preacher Thackeray would have to say. They did not stay long. News of the proposed service had reached official ears, and no sooner had the preacher called, 'Let us pray,' than the huge iron-studded gates of the prison swung open and an infantry officer marched out at the head of forty soldiers. The townsfolk immediately scattered to watch the proceedings from a safer distance.

The soldiers left the prison in a double file, marching along the road into Bodmin town until they had cleared the edge of the crowd. Then, at an order from the officer, they wheeled left, keeping a distance of twenty yards between themselves and the miners. The officer barked out another order and one file of twenty men began marking time while the other column carried on. When they formed one single line with the others they too began marking time until the whole line was called to a smart halt.

At the command 'Left turn!' the soldiers faced inwards towards the miners. Only the spongy grass prevented the precision of their movement being fully appreciated as their feet stamped down in unison.

Ignoring the military presence Preacher Thackeray called upon his vast congregation to pray with him.

They had hardly begun murmuring the Lord's Prayer when the harsh parade-ground voice of the officer rang out.

'Attention there! By assembling here today you are breaking the law which forbids such gatherings on a Sunday. As an officer of Her Majesty's Army I order you to disperse peaceably in the name of the Queen. If you refuse I will carry out my duty and break up this illegal meeting.'

Preacher Thackeray continued in his prayer until the 'Amen' was said.

'Do you hear me? I order you to disperse immediately.'

There was a long silence before the officer called his men to come to attention and 'order arms', a command which brought their musket-butts down on the ground.

Quietly and deliberately Miriam led the women to form a line between the soldiers and the miners. The move caused the soldiers to glance uneasily at their officer.

'At the command "Take up firing positions" . . .,' the officer called, but Preacher Thackeray interrupted him in a voice as authoritative as his own.

'By what law do you seek to break up a service of divine worship?'

'The by-laws of this borough. I am empowered to order you in the Queen's name to abandon this meeting and go home in an orderly and quiet manner.'

'Do the by-laws of this borough override the laws of England? Since when has the misuse of Her Majesty's name been sufficient to flout the will of Parliament? This is not a "meeting" as you will persist in calling it. I am a minister of the Methodist Church and am conducting a perfectly legal religious service. Furthermore, if you persist in your interruptions I will call the Constable and have you arrested for the contemptuous disturbance of persons assembled for religious worship. Since you appear to be sadly lacking in knowledge of the Law I will tell you. It is an offence punishable at the Court of Quarter Sessions and you will be held in custody until the day of the trial.'

There was nervous laughter from a section of the miners. It ceased immediately when Preacher Thackeray frowned in their direction.

The officer was perplexed, but he had started something and his training told him that once a course of action had been decided upon it should be carried through to a conclusion, however wrong it might ultimately prove to be. He barked out an order and forty muskets came to the firing position, albeit reluctantly and with less precision than the soldiers had shown until now.

The women in front of the miners closed ranks determinedly, and their move caused more unease among the soldiers.

'We can't shoot at women . . .'

'Silence!' It was the same voice, but the face behind it was the pallor of the granite walls.

'If you fire and kill anyone in this congregation you will hang for it. Each one of you who pulls a trigger will be guilty of as foul a murder as any to have been tried in the courts of this country.'

The breeze was not strong, and the forty muskets waved more violently than the ribbons of the women who faced them.

'Sarge, we can't shoot them, can we? He can't order us to do that.'

'Shut up!' The soldier with three gold stripes on his arm spoke in a hoarse whisper that carried to the miners. 'He's the one who's giving the orders. If anyone's neck is going to be stretched it'll be his, not yours.'

The uncertain silence that followed was broken by the even voice of Preacher Thackeray.

'We will sing our praises to the Lord.'

He began to sing, taking the first line on his own until the clear voice of Miriam joined him. Other women and miners followed, and the words of the hymn hung heavy in the air.

Halfway through the second verse the singing swelled to a powerful and triumphant crescendo. The soldiers were leaving! Looking neither to right nor left the officer led his men back on to the road. Pausing only to form twos, the bright-coated infantrymen marched back into the jail and the heavy doors banged shut behind them.

The service went on for another hour and a half but it was now something of an anti-climax. The miners had witnessed an incident that would be told and retold in every mine in Cornwall. Inside the forbidding jail, in that mysterious way imprisoned men have of gleaning and passing on every single crumb of information from that faraway world outside the high walls, the prisoners knew of the miners' triumph over the military long before the service had ended.

It was news that would have gladdened the hearts of Henry Reeve and his fellow-unionists had they been there to hear it. But, unknown to those outside Bodmin Jail, they had been moved the previous day and were now being held in the foul-smelling, rotting prison-hulk lying off Devonport. They had set foot on Cornish soil for the last time.

The miners had scored a small point. The game had gone to the other side.

Chapter Twenty-One

By December in that year of 1844 the exiled miners were three months distant from England. Cornwall had experienced more than twice its normal winter rainfall, and it still wanted a week to Christmas. The clouds hung around the crags of Sharptor like a veil. For months there had not been two consecutive dry days. Water poured from the high moor in a thousand angry rivulets, forming deep dangerous ponds in the 'old men's' ancient diggings. In the depths of the working mines the water oozed from wall and roof as though the rock were a sodden sponge.

Josh should have been leaving with Sarah to spend Christmas with her parents at Hayle, but the abnormally wet state of the deeper shafts was causing some concern in the Wheal Sharptor. The great engine was pumping at twice its normal speed yet barely managing to hold its own against the water. A pump-rod cracked with the extra strain placed upon it, threatening to tip the scales against the men who worked the mine. Had it broken without warning it would have wiped out the mine's profits for a whole year. As it was, Josh and his helpers had the pump-rod changed inside two hours.

In these conditions, Josh felt he could not leave the mine without an engineer. In spite of Sarah's sulking and bad humour he decided to stay on at the mine for a while longer.

'You don't *have* to stay!' she said for the fifth time that morning.

'I *do* have to stay,' he repeated patiently. 'If the pump stopped for very long the mine would flood beyond recovery. You've left Hector for me. I'll ride him to Hayle on Christmas Eve to join you.'

'I shouldn't have to travel alone in my condition,' Sarah said petulantly. 'Anything could happen.'

'You'll be in a coach with other people. The baby isn't due for nearly five months. If the travelling worries you so much, then don't go. Stay here and we'll have Christmas in our own home.'

'No. It has been ages since I saw my family and I have had enough of Sharptor this winter. If I don't get out of this cloud for a few days I will go insane.'

Some women glow with a new vitality and happiness when they become pregnant. Sarah was not one of these. She felt heavy and awkward, and tired very easily. It had not helped her humour when old Mary Crabbe came up to the house to pay her customary pre-natal visit. It was part of local tradition. No village woman was ever entirely convinced she was going to have a baby until Mary Crabbe had been to the house.

But Sarah was impressed by neither the old crone's reputation nor her appearance.

'I will not have that woman delivering my baby!' she declared when Mary Crabbe had left the house. 'Did you see her hands? They were absolutely filthy; her nails looked as though she had been sorting ore!'

'Those were the hands that delivered me,' replied Josh, 'and just about every other baby in the district.'

'That may be so, but she won't be delivering my baby!'

Whether or not Sarah's undisguised displeasure was the reason, Mary Crabbe paid only the one visit to the house. Some days later she was talking to Jesse Retallick and, when the coming baby was mentioned, Mary Crabbe turned away without a word, leaving Josh's mother standing alone in the village street looking after her.

A light carriage sent by Theophilus Strike took Sarah to St

Cleer. There she transferred to the bulky post-carriage that would carry her the remainder of the way. Josh loaded her cases and fussed about her, settling her into her seat with a blanket wrapped about her legs.

'Now, you take care,' he said, 'and keep well wrapped. I'll be with you on Christmas Eve and will bring your presents with me.'

'I wish you were coming with me now,' declared Sarah. All at once she looked very young and vulnerable.

'So do I,' said Josh honestly, 'but it won't be long. In the meantime you'll be surrounded by your family. They'll make you feel like the Queen.'

'Not until you join me, Josh.' She kissed him and clung to him for so long he became embarrassed for the coachman standing waiting patiently. But Sarah had seen the door of the preacher's house swing open and, though she could not see who was standing back from the doorway, she did not release her hold until the door was closed again.

Josh waited until the coach swayed from view at the bottom of the hill before turning and heading back to Sharptor.

Sarah will feel better for a few days' rest, he thought as he arrived back at the house and changed into his working clothes to go to the mine. She'll be her old bright and happy self when I see her again on Christmas Eve.

But for the second time in his life the weather spoiled his Christmas plans and decreed that it would be longer than a few days before they met once more. The day after Sarah left the wind changed direction and the temperature dropped rapidly. The snow began to fall at dusk and gradually put a covering on the sodden ground. It snowed until the rivulets were no more than thin cracks of water a foot below the crust of the snow. Then the wind increased, and snow and wind vied in their efforts to outdo each other.

The equal battle raged for five days before a brief truce was called on Christmas Eve. From the bedroom window of the house Josh looked down the slope of the moor and along the valley beyond. It was a pure white featureless world, with neither track nor hedge showing through the snow. The wind had banked the snow against the walls of the few cottages within view. Had he not known exactly where they were situated he would not have been able to pick them out from any other mound of snow.

Josh had tried to leave the house and make his way to the mine earlier. For half an hour he had dug from the front doorway to clear what he at first thought was a drift, only to discover that the snow was lying to a depth of four feet on that east-facing slope. He had never known a snowfall like it.

At ten o'clock Nehemeziah arrived at the house, plodding behind two big shire-horses harnessed in line to stamp out a path from the mine to the house.

'Never known such weather,' said the wizened old hostler as they made their way together to the mine. 'And there's more'n a bucketful up there.' He raised his eyes to the heavy dark sky.

Ben Retallick was warming his hands at the boiler fire when Josh arrived.

'There will be no Christmas at Hayle for you this year, Josh.'

'No,' Josh agreed. 'And Sarah won't be too pleased about that. She tried hard to get me to go with her last weekend.'

'You couldn't have done that – not with the weather we've been having and the water in the mine.'

'That's what I told Sarah. She wasn't convinced then – and she certainly won't be today!'

'Never mind, Josh.' Ben Retallick could not suppress a sympathetic smile at Josh's forlorn expression. 'If women weren't so contrary they wouldn't be women. I was going to add that you'd learn that one day, but you won't. Your mother can still surprise me by taking off after something I've said in all innocence. You'll be spending Christmas with us, of course?'

Josh nodded.

'Good! That will please your mother. Jenny and Tom will be there with young Gwen. And Wrightwick.'

'I won't be down until midday,' said Josh. 'If I'm not going to Hayle I'll come down here and spend the morning firing the furnace. The engine-man can have the morning with his family.'

Tapping one of the boiler-gauges he said, 'How is the water in the lower levels? I'd like to slow the pump down a bit if possible. It was never built for high-speed work.'

'We should get a few easier days before the thaw,' said Ben Retallick. 'But I'm going down there now. I'll let you know whether the water is tailing off when I come back up.'

'You'll be better off down below than outside, Cap'n Retallick,' said an old surface-worker, pounding snow from his clothing as he came into the engine-house. 'It's started snowing again.'

When he got home that evening Josh cleared a path to the stables across the old farmyard and forked plenty of hay down from the loft for Hector. It was as well he did. By morning another eighteen inches of snow had fallen and Josh floundered to the mine along the path cleared by Nehemeziah the previous day.

The engine-man had been drinking, and the fire was much lower than it should have been. Josh made no complaint. He knew that the man would have spent the whole night singing to prevent himself from hearing the sound of the 'knockers', who were reputed to take over the mine workings on this special night. If the engine-man needed something to help him keep up his courage there was no one who would criticise him for it. It was a brave man who would defy generations of superstitious fear and remain alone in the vicinity of a mine for the whole of Christmas Eve night.

The morning passed quickly for Josh, and when the relief engine-man arrived at lunch-time he walked to the Retallick cottage in a light flurry of snow.

It was a Christmas like so many others that Josh had shared with his family, but his thoughts kept turning towards Hayle and the Christmas he should have been having with his wife. He could not help feeling guilty about not being with her.

'You're not going to frighten the snow away by looking out there,' said Jenny as he glanced out of the window for the dozenth time.

'No, I suppose not,' he grinned wryly. 'I only hope there's snow like this at Hayle.'

'Don't worry yourself about that,' said Ben. 'This goes a bit further than Hayle. I doubt whether there is a passable road in the country. It's worse than the time when you were an apprentice and couldn't get home for Christmas. The way the wind has set there'll be little change for a week or two.'

'Sarah will be all right, Josh,' said his mother. 'She'll be snug and warm in that nice house, with her family to look after her and spoil her a little.'

'Yes. We must all count our blessings,' said Wrightwick Roberts pompously. 'There are a great many folk in far more uncomfortable circumstances than ourselves and those we love.'

'The Kit Hill miners on their way to Botany Bay, for instance,' said Josh.

Wrightwick Roberts did not agree with unionism and he disapproved most strongly of the actions of his fellow-preacher at St Cleer.

'They received what they deserved,' he said. 'They knew the law.'

'And they broke no law.' Josh thought an argument with the preacher might take his mind off Sarah. 'It was an improper trial. Harry Reeve and the others committed no crime because they were in the Callington lock-up when the Kit Hill store was burned down. They never incited anyone else to do it because they were arrested before they had a chance to speak to their men.'

'The Law must be upheld,' said Wrightwick Roberts dogmatically. 'The courts of this land are there to administer justice. They do it well enough.'

'Just as they did with the young boy at the last Launceston Assizes,' retorted Josh. 'You remember it, Wrightwick? Thirteen years old, wasn't he? Caught stealing two gallons of potatoes to help keep his family from starving. It was the Lord Chief Justice himself who judged that case. Supposedly the fairest man in the land. What sentence did he pass on that boy? Tell us, Wrightwick?'

The preacher squirmed in his seat.

'Yes, I see you remember. It's something no man in Cornwall should ever forget. Penal servitude for life – at the age of thirteen! Some might argue that such a sentence is justice, but it was tempered with precious little mercy.'

'Now then, you two. What sort of a conversation is this for Christmas Day? Ben, put another couple of logs on that fire and Jenny will give us a verse of a Christmas hymn. One we can join in with.'

Wrightwick Roberts smiled sheepishly and the family Christmas resumed, the harmony broken only when little Gwen got a piece of Jesse's special cake lodged in her throat. She had to be up-ended while Tom Shovell thumped on her back.

It was the new year before a gentle thaw set in. Not until the sixth day of January was Josh able to send a letter off to Sarah with the coach from St Cleer. Afterwards he called in to visit William Thackeray, but he had gone to Liskeard to meet a preacher from London passing through *en route* for the port of Falmouth.

Miriam invited Josh into the house and he sat in the kitchen while she made him tea and gave him the latest news of the local unions. There was increasing support for it from the miners. But as support grew, so did the opposition of the mine-adventurers.

'They fear the power the miners will hold,' reported Miriam. 'And so they should.'

Watching her move about the kitchen Josh was once more stirred by the cross-current of feelings she provoked in him. There was something almost boyish in the free way she moved, her strides long and certain. But the masculinity ended there. Her figure was completely feminine: slim and firm.

'We've got to get every miner into the union,' she went on fiercely, unaware of his appraisal. 'When the last man joins life will begin anew for everyone. The miner will enjoy a standard of life he's not yet aware of.'

'Not all mine-owners breathe fire, and drink miners' blood for breakfast, Miriam.'

She smiled as she handed him his tea. 'Working for Theophilus Strike is inhibiting your enthusiasm. He's the one flaw in our argument against the adventurers. But mining is a family business for him. He takes an interest in the way things are run, not merely in how much profit goes into his pocket.'

She stood in the centre of the kitchen and her smile became the cheeky grin of a younger Miriam. 'But he hasn't always been a good judge of men. Do you remember Herman Schmidt and that day in Bodmin?'

'I remember. He had a very heavy hand.'

'Poor Josh!' Her look was warm. 'All to defend the honour you thought I was anxious to sell.'

'No, I realised what you were doing. I was only worried that his eagerness might prove stronger than your cunning.'

'Shame! I wasn't worth it, was I? It would have been better had you walked away, not caring whether Schmidt did what he wanted with me. It would have saved us both a lot of hurt if you hadn't cared so much.'

'Didn't you care just as much, Miriam? Or did I imagine your tears when we were returning on the wagon?'

'Yes, I cared. I cared so much that when I needed to I was incapable of thinking straight. Caring is a painful emotion, Josh. It makes you so much more sensitive and puts life under a magnifying-glass, making it larger than it really is.'

It was perhaps fortunate that there was a diversion at this juncture. It came in the form of a loud cry from another room. Miriam said, 'That's Daniel.'

Josh had not seen the boy since the day Miriam had visited the house at Sharptor, almost a year before. Usually when Josh called Daniel was 'in bed' or 'with his grandmother'.

Before Miriam returned to the room he could hear her talking in low endearing tones. When she opened the door she bore in her arms a sturdy little boy, no longer a baby but a child with stabbing fingers and big blue eyes.

'Hello, Daniel. My, but you've grown into a tough little chap!'

Daniel tucked his chin in and pretended not to look at Josh.

'I believe you're shy!'

Daniel turned and grabbed his mother for safety and she hugged him to her.

'Are you hoping Sarah will have a son, Josh?'

He looked startled and she laughed. 'Oh, Josh! Don't tell me you're surprised that I know Sarah is carrying a baby? My mother lives in Henwood. Nothing happens there that isn't immediately common knowledge.'

He gave her a sheepish grin. 'I wasn't thinking. No, Miriam, I am hoping that Sarah will have a girl.'

Miriam was about to say that she thought a man always wanted sons to perpetuate his own image but she stopped herself quickly. It might direct the conversation to dangerous ground. It was not long before the sight of Miriam hugging Daniel to her, and having the boy looking at him from his Cornish blue eyes, began to cause an emotional upheaval inside Josh that he had no wish to analyse. He stood up to go.

'Won't you stay until William comes home, Josh? He should return within the hour. He'll be very sorry to have missed you. Stay and have a meal with us.'

Josh shook his head. 'Thank you, but I've got some work to do at the Wheal Sharptor. I shouldn't have come away but I wanted to send a letter.'

'Well, if you must. But come again soon, Josh.'

At the gate Miriam said something to the child in her arms and Daniel waved to him. Josh returned the wave before swinging into the saddle of Hector and heading the horse towards the Wheal Sharptor. He had to fight the animal all the way. During the bad weather Hector had been kept inside without exercise and now he wanted to run. But the ground was in too treacherous a state for an uncontrolled gallop. So it was a thoroughly bad-tempered beast that Josh shut into the stable when he arrived home.

The house felt big and empty without Sarah. The emptiness

made Josh restless, unable to settle anywhere. He had hoped she would come home as soon as the roads were passable, but the snow thawed and a strong drying wind blew in from the east and still she did not return.

He was beginning to get anxious when a letter arrived with a wagoner. It had been sent from Hayle with one of the ore-boat captains. The sailor had scribbled a note on the outside of it apologising for the time it had taken to arrive – due, the captain had written, to conditions of the sea over which he had no control and which was as like to have driven the boat to the Americas as bring it to Looe.

Sarah's letter was a lengthy tale of woe. Her Christmas had been spoiled because Josh was not there with her. Her unhappiness had been infectious and spread to the whole family. She went on to chide Josh for not having come with her as she had begged him to before the snows came. Also, she said, she had been expecting a letter from him long before it actually arrived, as the snows at Hayle were cleared away before the turn of the year. Finally, she stated that worrying about Josh had brought her so low her mother had refused to allow her to travel until she was fully recovered in health and spirits.

The tone of the letter so alarmed Josh that he set off on Hector to ride to Hayle that weekend. Galloping across the moor and then along the open wind-swept road, he had only the turnpikes to think about. He reproached himself for not having considered Sarah more, for not leaving the Wheal Sharptor to cope without him for a few days. The mine employed enough sensible men to keep things running in the temporary absence of their engineer. Even that cracked pumping-rod might have been repaired after a fashion to await his return. There were too many other things that had occupied his mind when his main concern should rightly have been for his wife. He promised himself that he would make up to Sarah for his thoughtlessness.

After his resolutions and good intentions it came as an anticlimax to arrive at the Carlyon home and find nobody there. The shift foreman told him the family had gone out to visit friends. Who the friends were and at what time they might return the foreman was unable to say.

It was dusk and the light beginning to light up the windows of Hayle before the Carlyons' small coach rumbled in through the works gate.

Sarah did not look ill. She alighted laughing gaily with her sister. When he opened the front door of the house there was a confused silence before Sarah flung herself at him.

'Josh! What are you doing here?'

'I came because I received your letter telling me how ill you were.'

Sarah looked embarrassed, but her mother came to her rescue. 'And so she has been ill. So much so we were all most worried about her. Poor Sarah was so upset that you weren't here at Christmas she worked herself up into a terrible state. Today is the first day she has been anything like her old self. I thought a visit to St Ives to see her cousins would be good for her. And so it was. Getting out of the house and into the sea air has worked wonders. Poor child! But I expect she will be better now you are here.'

Sarah squeezed his arm affectionately. 'It's lovely to see you, Josh.'

'I'm very relieved to see you looking well,' he replied. 'I've been imagining all sorts of things as I rode down here.'

William Carlyon had been driving the carriage, and after handing it over to an hostler he came into the house and shook Josh's hand warmly. 'It's good to see you again, my boy. I've been surrounded by these women since before Christmas. I wondered how long it would be before you came to my rescue. Now, since no one else seems to be able to leave your side I'll get you a drink myself. What will you have?'

'I'll get them! I'll get them!' Mary ran to the cabinet which held the drinks and William Carlyon sighed, 'There you are, Josh. I spend a fortune educating the child and the only thing she really enjoys doing is serving drinks!'

Josh said he would have a brandy, and Mary selected the correct glass, poured the drink and handed it to him.

'I hear the weather has been quite severe on the moor,' said the works manager. 'Far worse than we experienced here – and we were unable to move far from the house.'

Josh told him of the snow and its results – of the small mines which had been forced to stop work completely, their stocks of coal exhausted; of the sheep, frozen to death and not discovered until the thaw uncovered the gullies where they had taken shelter.

'Yes, it's the worst weather in memory,' agreed the works manager. 'If we hadn't stockpiled iron ore the foundry would have been out of business. For ten days not a ship moved in or out of Hayle. It was a ghost port.'

'How is the house?' asked Sarah. 'Is there any damage from the storms?' Josh reassured her that the house and its outbuildings had stood up to the weather.

'Will you be able to stay with us for long?' asked William Carlyon.

Josh shook his head. 'Until Sunday only.'

There was an immediate outcry from the two girls, and Sarah said, 'Why, Josh? Why can't you stay for longer? Surely the mine can spare you for a few days?'

Josh put down his brandy and turned to face her. 'I thought you would want to come back with me. If you are feeling well enough.'

Mrs Carlyon threw up her hands in horror. 'It would be madness. The poor girl has been so ill. She shouldn't make a long journey while she is carrying a child.'

Since his arrival Josh had been nursing a suspicion that Sarah's mother was trying to arrange things so Sarah should have the baby at Hayle.

'The journey would be worse for her next week. Even more so the week after. I think the sooner she comes home the better.'

'Why not let her have her baby here, Josh?'

He had been right. Now it was out in the open.

'It would be much, much better from Sarah's point of view.' Mrs Carlyon waxed enthusiastic. 'Just think. Someone would be here to care for her *all* the time. Dr Scott would be on hand. He's known Sarah since she was a child, and he's very good at delivering babies. Not only that; she would be more comfortable here. I mean no offence, of course. Your house is lovely and you're lucky to have it. But there are things here it takes years to gather together.'

'You have a very nice home, Mrs Carlyon. But it's not *our* home. That's at Sharptor. When it's near the time for the baby to come I'm sure my mother won't spend much time away from the house. And we have doctors there too.'

'I hope you're not referring to mine doctors,' Mrs Carlyon snorted. 'I wouldn't trust one of them to deliver a litter of pigs.'

'Josh is right.'

William Carlyon stood up and went to the drinks cupboard. On the way he paused by Sarah and gently ruffled her hair. 'Your mother finds it difficult to realise you're not still a little girl. You are a married woman now and your place is with your husband. Especially for the birth of your first child.'

He refilled his glass and looked towards his wife. 'Can you imagine what I would have said to your mother had she suggested you go home to her when you were expecting Sarah?'

It looked as though Mrs Carlyon was thinking up a further argument, so Josh said quickly, 'You are quite welcome to come and stay with us when it's nearly time.'

'No, Josh.' William Carlyon shook his head. 'It's your life. Yours and Sarah's. And it's your child. Nobody has the right to interfere with your arrangements for that. Sarah will come home with you on Sunday. The works hostler will take her in my carriage.'

He held up a hand to silence his wife as she was about to speak. 'I know Sarah hasn't been too well, but there's nothing wrong with her now.'

'Well! I'm only trying to do my best for Sarah. If that's going to be considered interference there's nothing more to be said, I'm sure! Come along, Mary. Upstairs and change your dress before you get it filthy playing about.'

She swept out of the room followed by Mary, who gave Josh a shy smile of support before she too went out.

'I think that could be termed a "royal exit",' commented William Carlyon. 'Now, if you'll excuse me, I need to check with the foreman that everything is well in the foundry.'

Sarah and Josh were silent for a few minutes after he left the room.

'Don't you want to come home, Sarah?' Josh said at last.

'Oh, Josh, of course I do!' Her eyes filled with tears and she gripped her hands in her lap. He reached for them and pulled her around to face him.

'Then what is it? Have you changed your mind about me? Don't you love me?'

'O-o-oh!' she wailed and leaned towards him, and he held her close.

'Then what is it? Something's very wrong. Won't you try to tell me?'

She pulled away from him and looked down at her hands from eyes that threatened to overflow.

'I'm scared, Josh.'

'Scared! Of what?'

She shrugged helplessly. 'Of everything. Of spending so much time on my own in the house. Of the moor. Of having the baby. Most of all having the baby.'

'But why haven't you told me this before? I thought you were happy. Don't you want the baby?'

'Yes! Yes, of course I do. I want it more than anything. It's just. . . . Oh, I don't know, Josh. I don't seem to have got to know anyone at Sharptor. Or in Henwood village. I feel as though I am a complete stranger there.'

'But, Sarah, you've only lived there for a short while. The folk are no better and no worse than they are anywhere else. They wouldn't force themselves upon you because they're afraid they might not be welcome, but if ever you were in trouble they would help without having to be asked. They are concerned about you. There isn't one of them who hasn't asked after you since news got around about the baby. Why, they've even asked after you as far off as St Cleer village.'

Sarah looked at him quickly. 'You mean Miriam?'

'Yes.'

She continued to look at him as he explained, 'I saw her when I put your letter on the coach. She already knew about the baby.'

'Do you wish you had married her instead of me?' Her bluntness took him by surprise.

'Is that what you believe?'

'I don't know what to believe. I only know that I get knotted up inside when you are off somewhere with that preacher because I think you might be talking to her. I imagine you will compare us and wish you had married her instead of me.'

He was relieved when she dropped her gaze.

'Sarah, I married you because I wanted to. Nobody forced me to do it. I was – and am – very proud to have you for my wife. I've known Miriam all my life. I couldn't forget her if I wanted to. But you are my wife and Miriam is married to my friend. Need I say any more?'

'No. I'm sorry, Josh. It isn't anything you have done. It's me. Don't take any notice. Women get like this when they are pregnant. Come upstairs with me while I change into something more comfortable. This dress was made for a slim young girl. Not a pregnant wife. It is cutting me in two. When I have changed we will see if we can put Mother in a good mood again.'

She rose from her chair and, taking Josh's hand, pulled him to his feet. She was far more relaxed now. 'Poor Josh, I've given you a bad time, haven't I? Never mind, we'll go back to Sharptor and I will be a good and dutiful wife to you.' She managed a pale but happy smile. 'And I do love you. Husband.'

They went home to Sharptor as planned on the Sunday and the next months were very happy ones for both of them. It snowed sporadically until the end of February but the snow rarely hung around for longer than two days at a time, and it was pleasant to sit indoors in front of a crackling log-fire with snow floating down outside. During these months the house on Sharptor became a home.

There was no shortage of work at the Sharptor mine. The

main pump needed an overhaul, and Josh worked hard with his trainees to complete it in record time. Meanwhile the water was kept under control by an emergency system that Josh rigged up.

Then there was his latest man-lift innovation in the secondary shaft. It was a cage-lift with improved gearing and a sophisticated indicating system enabling the winchman to know just where the cage was during the whole winching period. The gearing also meant that at shift-change time when there was no ore being carried the men could be taken down to the working levels and the off-going shift brought to grass in record time. In an emergency it could prove invaluable.

Josh showed the plans to Theophilus Strike, describing how it would work, one afternoon when the mine-owner was visiting Sharptor. Strike waxed enthusiastic about its potential.

'It's a great piece of engineering design,' he said. 'I can see it having uses in mines far beyond the Cornish border. You must patent it.'

Josh protested that it was merely an idea and would have to be proved first. But Theophilus Strike was not to be put off.

'It will work. Anyone with the slightest knowledge of mines can see that. And because it will work well it will be copied. If you won't patent it, then I'll do it for you. You sit down and copy out that plan you've shown to me. I'll do the rest.'

He was as good as his word. Later, when the system was installed in the Sharptor mine and had proved itself, he frequently brought fellow mine-owners to watch it at work. Within three months of its first trial run a mine-engineering company in the North of England negotiated with Josh to install similar systems in mines in their area. Josh was to receive a fair percentage of the profits they made on it.

The atrocious weather of the winter and the subsequent difficulties in travelling and communications meant that unionism remained in a near-dormant state, Josh not once venturing as far as St Cleer.

This pleased Sarah, mainly because it kept him away from

Miriam. In her present condition Sarah had become obsessive about William Thackeray's wife, although she managed to keep it from Josh. But she also thought Josh foolish to dabble in such dangerous nonsense when he could be working on new designs and inventions. Her father had told her Josh would rapidly become the world's foremost expert on mine safety equipment if he devoted more time and energy to it. Sarah wanted to push him into doing what she thought was right. She was too inexperienced as a woman to understand that Josh was one of those men who might be easily led in certain directions but who would never be pushed into anything.

Then, early in March, on a day when the moorland scrub was bowing before the fierce winds, the brief period of contentment came to an end in the house on Sharptor. Josh arrived home from the mine as it was growing dark to find Sarah lying back in the rocking-chair in the kitchen. Her face was pale and frightened, beads of perspiration standing out on her forehead and upper lip.

'Thank God you are here, Josh!' She rolled her head from side to side, wide-eyed, thoroughly alarming Josh. 'The baby. I think it's coming!'

A spasm of pain gripped her as she finished speaking. 'Oh! Josh, help me. Help me! Please!' Her shoulders hunched and a cry of agony broke from her lips as the muscles of her stomach contracted with fierce strength.

Josh gripped her forearms and shared her agony until the pain passed away.

'Don't move, Sarah. Stay here and I'll go and find the doctor.'

'No!' she screamed at him as he moved towards the door. 'Don't leave me, Josh! Don't leave me!'

'I must get help, Sarah. You need someone with you who knows what's happening.'

'No, stay with me, Josh . . .' Her voice rose and ended in a cry of animal anguish as the pain came back yet again.

Josh was in a terrible quandary. Sarah needed help. The baby was not due for another seven weeks, but there seemed little doubt that it was coming now. Something was seriously wrong, yet if he left her alone even for a short while she might become hysterical and do something to cause herself injury.

Then he heard a sound from the track that went past the house on to the moor. He opened the door and in the gloom made out the shape of a cart going up the hill towards Ward-brook, the farm situated a mile away on the moor.

'Hey! Stop!' He ran from the house, waving his arms, and the cart creaked to a halt. It was being driven by a lad of about sixteen, one of the Wardbrook farmer's sons.

'I need your help,' said Josh. 'My wife is in the house and our baby is coming two months too soon. Do you know where Captain Retallick lives?'

The boy shook his head. 'No, we don't have anything to do with mine folk. Pa says they're a blight on good farming land.'

He was slow of speech and far from bright, but he was Josh's only hope.

'Never mind.' He dug into his pocket and came out with a silver coin. 'Look! Here's a shilling for you. Run down to the mine and tell them that Sarah Retallick up at Idle Farm is starting her baby and needs help quickly. Have you got that?'

'I've got it.' He snatched the coin from Josh's fingers. 'But what about my horse and wagon?'

'Leave it. It won't go anywhere except home.'

Behind him in the house he could hear Sarah screaming again. 'Hurry, now. It's very urgent. I'm depending on you.'

The boy heard Sarah too. Jumping down from the cart he set off at an awkward lope along the path to the mine while Josh rushed back into the house to find Sarah struggling to her feet.

'I thought you had gone. Oh God, Josh, I'm scared! Help me.'

He held her tight until the latest spasm passed. Then he guided her gently upstairs to their bedroom. He turned back the bedclothes, talking all the time, telling her that help was coming, that soon everything would be all right.

'I think help will be too late, Josh. The waters have already burst. The baby is coming now.'

He undressed her and helped her into the special nightdress she had set aside for this occasion. The pains came twice more before she was safely in bed. By this time he was perspiring as much as Sarah.

He lit the lamps in the room and brought in two more.

'I'm just going down to put as much water on the stove as I can. That's what they did when young Gwen was born.'

'Don't be long, Josh. Don't leave me alone up here.'

He hurried downstairs, threw logs on to the fire and put all the pots and kettles he could find on the stove. Every few seconds he looked through the window, expecting to see help arriving.

Then an agonised scream from Sarah sent him rushing upstairs again.

'It's coming! It's coming! I can feel it! Help me! Help me!'

It was the last thing in the world that Josh felt capable of doing, but there was no alternative. Sarah was looking at him from eyes as large and frightened as a cornered doe.

'It's all right, Sarah. Lie back and try not to throw yourself about too much.'

'No! The baby. It's coming. I know it is.'

Her back arched with pain and she threw the bedclothes off her body.

Josh drew them right down and saw that Sarah was not exaggerating. Her frenzied thrashing had caused her nightdress to work up about her waist, and there, just emerging from her body, was the damp dark head of a baby. There was no time for nervousness now. He went to take hold of the baby's head but Sarah's body relaxed for an instant and the head returned inside her. Twice more contractions of pain threatened to force the baby from her, and twice it returned. Then, the third time, there was no denying it. The pain had her rolling and screaming in agony, but there was no return for the baby now. Josh had its head between his hands. He was never sure whether it was his doing or whether Nature supplied the twist that turned its shoulders. But suddenly the baby was there. He was holding it. A tiny damp bloody object, attached to the body in which it had grown by a thin, ridiculously long umbilical cord.

Sarah lay back on the bed, sucking in great noisy gulps of air and Josh was left wondering what to do with the motionless baby when belated help arrived. He heard the door open downstairs and his mother called, 'Josh! Sarah! Are you up there?'

'Come quickly. The baby's here.'

Jesse Retallick ran up the stairs and into the bedroom and saw Josh crouched holding the baby clear of Sarah's legs, frightened to straighten up.

'Has it cried yet?'

Josh looked startled.

'The baby. Have you made it cry?'

'No.' Josh shook his head, not comprehending.

Throwing off her cloak, Jesse Retallick took the baby from his hands and, hanging it head downwards by its ankles, slapped it on the backside. Once. Twice. Three times.

With a frown she put a finger inside its mouth checking that its tongue was down and the throat clear. Then she smacked it again. The fourth slap brought forth a low strangled cry. At the fifth its body jerked feebly and it gave another weak cry.

Jesse Retallick looked worried and Josh said, 'What's the matter. It's all right, isn't it? It's alive. It made a noise.'

The cry had been like the feeble mewing of a weak kitten. Jesse Retallick was unhappy.

'I wish Mary Crabbe was here,' she said. 'But she went to Callington for her brother's funeral and hasn't returned yet.'

'Shall I fetch a doctor?'

'Your father's gone for the mine doctor at the Phoenix. He's the nearest.'

'Josh. What is it? Is it a boy? Have I given you a son?'

Poor Sarah, exhausted by the pain and effort, opened her eyes as though coming out of a drugged sleep.

'It's a boy,' said Jesse Retallick.

'I'm glad,' Sarah murmured wearily. 'Can I hold him now?'

'Not yet, my love.' Jesse turned to Josh. 'Get me some of that hot water I saw on the stove. And some towels. I've got to cut the cord, and the afterbirth will have to be brought away. Hurry, now.'

Josh was only too pleased to have someone else to give the orders. Childbirth was a time for women. Men should have no part in it. Besides, there was something wrong. Whatever it was, his mother was far more capable of dealing with it than himself.

He ran up and down the stairs, carrying hot water and towels up and empty pots down to be refilled and set back on the stove.

After one such trip he arrived in the bedroom to discover that the baby now had a separate existence. Jesse was winding a strip of linen about the tiny waist, hiding the bloody knot that sealed off the severed umbilical cord.

She placed the baby in the small cot that was still not fully completed. As she tucked tiny blankets about it she said to Josh, 'I want hot-water bottles filled and brought up. You hear me?'

Josh nodded.

'Good. They are for the baby. While you fetch them I'll get on and help Sarah.'

Ben Retallick came into the kitchen as Josh was filling the earthenware bottles from the large kettle.

'It's a boy,' said Josh. 'I delivered it.' Then he noticed the angry frown on his father's face. 'Where's the doctor?'

'He was too drunk to get any sense out of. I wouldn't have let him touch a moorland sheep in that state. Are Sarah and the baby all right?'

'I don't think Mum is very happy with either of them. You'd better go and see her.'

Screwing the stopper into the second bottle he went up the stairs ahead of his father.

In the bedroom Jesse Retallick was kneading Sarah's stomach as though it was a pile of dough and without pausing in her efforts she looked questioningly at Ben.

'The doctor wasn't available,' he said, going across to the cot. 'Is this our grandson? Is he all right, Jesse?'

Jesse looked down at Sarah, making sure her eyes were firmly closed before shaking her head vigorously.

She left Sarah for a minute and, taking the hot-water bottles from Josh, wrapped them up well and pushed them down the side of the cot beside the still infant.

'There's no sense in trying to hide it.' She spoke in a whisper that would not carry across the room. 'The baby has come much too soon. It's a weakling. But I'm more worried about Sarah. She must have been in labour for a long time. She's desperately tired. The afterbirth has got to come away, but I'm getting no help from the poor girl. We must get a doctor from somewhere.'

'There's a new doctor at St Cleer,' said Josh. 'I'll saddle Hector and go and fetch him.'

'Hurry, Josh. I don't want to alarm you but I think Sarah's condition is serious. Oh! If only Mary Crabbe was here.'

Josh was already out of the room and on his way to the stable. Hector was not used to being disturbed after dark and having a saddle slung roughly on to his back. He showed his disapproval in no uncertain manner.

'Steady, boy! Steady! That's better. We've work to do tonight. You'll need the speed of the west wind. Come on, now.' Leading the horse from the stable he sprang into the saddle.

Fortunately there was a good moon. Fifty yards down the track Josh swung Hector on to the narrow path he had used when he went to St Cleer for his schooling. Hector took it at a fast canter, not rearing at shadows, though he once protested when a startled badger made a noisy departure from the path ahead of them.

The door of Dr McKinley's house was opened by his wife and Josh hurriedly explained the emergency.

'The doctor's visiting Preacher Thackeray,' she said. 'Tell him I'll have his bag ready and his horse saddled by the time he gets back here.'

Miriam opened the door to Josh but her warm welcoming greeting fell away before his enquiry for the doctor.

'He's playing chess in the lounge with William. What is it, Josh? Your father? Is it a mine accident?'

'No. It's Sarah and the baby. . . .'

Both men looked up in surprise as Josh flung open the lounge door.

'Why, Josh. . . .' William Thackeray rose to his feet. 'You look as wild as the moor. What is it?'

'I came for the doctor, William. Would you ride out to Sharptor with me, Dr McKinley? Our baby has arrived nearly two months before time. My mother says it's a weakling and there's something wrong with my wife. The afterbirth won't come. My father went for the Phoenix mine doctor but he was as drunk as a tinner when he found him.'

'You can tell me about it on the way.'

Dr McKinley was new to St Cleer. He was a young man and a keen doctor. 'I'll play you again another night, William.'

'I'll fetch your coat.' Miriam rushed away and returned with the doctor's coat and hat.

'Josh.' She took his arm. 'I hope things go well for Sarah and the baby. I really do.'

'Thank you.' He was impatient to be on his way with the doctor.

'We will pray for them both,' said Preacher William Thackeray.

But God must have had business elsewhere that night. In spite of all that Dr McKinley tried the baby died before the sun rose.

Neither did he have any more success with Sarah's afterbirth. He used methods that had Sarah screaming in pain and made Jesse Retallick's tired face turn even paler. Josh and his father were keeping a vigil in the kitchen, and the shift captain did his best to talk loudly whenever the sounds from above became too alarming.

When the dawn was dusting a thin pale crust on the distant sky-line it was a very weary doctor who made his way downstairs.

'I'm sorry,' he said. 'I've done all that I can. All that remains is surgery. That will require greater skills than I possess.'

'But where can we find a surgeon?' Josh pleaded. 'She's too ill to stand up to a long journey.'

Dr McKinley shook his head. 'I don't know. The only thing I am sure of is that if she doesn't see a surgeon soon she'll die.'

'Then we must take her by coach to Plymouth,' said Josh as Jesse came into the room tying up the strings at the throat of her cloak.

'You leave that girl where she is until I come back,' she ordered in a voice that allowed for no argument.

'Where are you going?'

'To fetch Mary Crabbe,' Jesse announced firmly. 'No disrespect to you, Doctor. I saw for myself that you did your best. But Mary Crabbe has brought more children into this world than any doctor. If she can't do anything, then it will have to be the surgeon.'

'Believe me, I welcome anything that might save that girl upstairs from the surgeon's knife,' said Dr McKinley in a tired voice. 'But delay will be dangerous.'

'I won't be many minutes. Josh, go up and sit with Sarah. Keep her forehead cool. She's in a fever.'

Sarah's appearance shocked Josh. When he had last seen her she was tired after the hard childbirth. But now she was gaunt and haggard, her cheekbones unhealthily prominent and perspiration standing out on her forehead. He spoke to her, but she seemed not to hear. As he bathed her forehead he tried not to let his gaze wander to the sheet-draped cot in which lay the body of their child.

Sarah had not stirred when he heard Mary Crabbe's wheezing breathing and his mother's voice coming from the stairs.

The old lady came into the room with uncombed hair, wearing an ill assortment of clothing; indicative of the haste with which Jesse Retallick had roused her from her bed.

She stood in the doorway gazing about her and waiting for her breathing to become less laboured.

'Get out!' she snapped at Josh. 'And take that with you.'

She pointed to the draped cot. 'It's ill-luck to have death in the room with a sick mother. Hurry up! And boil up lots of water. We'll need all you can heat. And a bowl – two bowls. Jesse, help me prop up this maid. Go on, boy. What are you waiting for? Move yourself.'

Josh carried the cot into another bedroom and placed it down gently. There was something pathetic about the lack of weight in his burden and it brought a lump to his throat. Here beneath the creased sheet was the body of the child that had always been a little unreal to him.

But for Sarah it was to have been a great fulfilment. For seven months she had carried the developing life in her body and a dream in her mind.

Sarah had always held a fear that Josh was unsettled with life and with her; that he had married her but had not really settled down into a married state. The baby was meant to change that. She believed that giving Josh a child would put her ahead of Miriam and tip the scales in her favour. With his child here in the house she was sure Josh would stay at home, having less to do with William Thackeray, his unionism – and his wife.

Josh did not know all these things, but he was aware that having the baby was very important to her. Now it was dead.

Only Dr McKinley remained when Josh went down to the kitchen. When he asked, the doctor told him that Ben Retallick had gone to send a rider to Hayle. The Carlyons needed to be told of the night's happenings.

'Yes, it's right they should know,' muttered Josh, though he knew before the end of the day Mrs Carlyon would be at Sharptor with recriminations and hostile glances. He had taken Sarah from her care and the birth had not gone well.

Ben Retallick returned to the house with Jenny Shovell. She made tea for the men before going upstairs to join the other women.

The men were talking quietly among themselves, and Dr McKinley had said for the third time, 'We must get that girl to a surgeon,' when there were noisy footsteps on the stairs and Jenny hurried in for another pot of water.

'It's all right!' she announced. 'Mary Crabbe's done it. Sarah will be all right now.'

The relief in the room was enormous, but in the case of the doctor it was swamped by incredulous disbelief.

'You mean the afterbirth has come away?'

Jenny nodded. 'Yes.'

'But how? How did this woman do it? I tried everything I'd learned at medical school . . . !'

'I think it was herbs, mostly,' said Jenny.

'I must see this for myself, or I shall refuse to believe it.' Dr McKinley left the kitchen talking to himself and shaking his head.

'Can I see her now, Jenny?' Josh asked.

'Not just yet, Josh. Sarah will be all right, but wait until Mary Crabbe has finished all she needs to do.'

It was a matter of moments only before the doctor returned, more amused than indignant at being ordered from the bedroom by Mary Crabbe. 'She has certainly succeeded where I failed,' he admitted. 'And after all my years of medical training . . . ! I find it very hard to understand.'

'I shouldn't try, Doctor,' said Ben Retallick. 'I've known Mary all my life. There are some things I've heard of her doing that I'd be frightened of knowing too much about.'

'If she was a younger woman I would ask her to help me with my maternity cases,' Dr McKinley declared. 'A woman like that is worth her weight in gold.'

'Mary Crabbe never worked for any man,' said Ben Retallick. 'And she's upset as many women as she's helped.'

'All the same . . .,' Dr McKinely mused. 'But there is nothing more I can do here.' He looked at Josh. 'I'm sorry about the baby. There was nothing you could have done better. The poor little chap came into the world too soon, that's all.'

'Or too late!'

Nobody had heard Mary Crabbe come down the stairs. She stood in the doorway, hair awry, standing as solid as a toad. 'There are few eldest sons in these parts who weren't begotten in the fern of the moor.' She cackled. 'There's more love to be found there.'

The three men looked at each other but Mary Crabbe had not finished. 'And there will be precious little love to be found in this house. Shame, yes. And more. But you'll find out. Oh yes! You'll find out soon enough!'

Pulling her dirty shawl about her shoulders she shuffled out of the house. In the silence that followed they could hear her talking to herself as she walked out to the track on her way back to the village.

'I think her mind has finally gone,' said Ben Retallick after he had cleared his throat noisily. Josh was standing pale with fatigue and shaken by the old woman's words. 'Take no notice of her, Josh. She is so old she doesn't know what she is saying half the time. Forget her words and remember only her deeds. You owe her Sarah's life.'

'Yes.'

Josh nodded his head, tiredly trying to shake out the chill thoughts Mary Crabbe had placed there. Turning abruptly from the others, he said, 'I'm going up to Sarah.'

Sarah was lying quite still. Her eyes were closed and she looked very weak. Josh felt her forehead. It was quite cool now.

'Josh?' Her lips hardly moved.

'Yes. I'm here, Sarah.'

'I'm sorry, Josh.'

'Shh! You've done nothing to be sorry about. You're a very brave girl and I'm proud of you.'

A tear crept from the corner of her eye and tracked rapidly down her face. 'No. It wasn't meant to be, Josh. It should have been Miriam here bearing your child. I've always known that. She belongs to the moor as you do. I have no place here. I don't belong. I don't! I don't!'

'Now, what kind of talk is this?'

Jesse Retallick had been gathering towels and soiled bedding. Heaping it on the floor, she crossed to the bed and gently brushed back a wisp of fair hair from Sarah's face. 'You shouldn't be thinking such strange thoughts.'

Sarah's head rolled from side to side on the pillow and, moving away, Jesse took Josh's arm and led him to the door.

'Leave her now, Josh. She's had a bad time and needs sleep. Having you here is disturbing her. Go off somewhere and rest yourself. It's been a bad night for you too. I'll stay and look after Sarah.'

When he went back to the kitchen it was empty. Dr McKinley had gone and in the distance Josh saw the broad back of his father walking wearily down the path to the Wheal Sharptor.

Josh went out of the kitchen, across the yard and up the hill to the high moor. It was a clear spring morning, the birds busy and singing. On the rocks of Sharptor two ravens croaked. A pair of buzzards drifted across the sky, disdainful of the crows who noisily and jealously defended the square of sky they regarded as their own.

But Josh saw none of the things he usually looked for on the moor.

Mary Crabbe's words had disturbed him greatly, but Sarah's had upset him more. He could not put them out of his mind.

He walked alone on the moor for three hours. Then, after looking in at the house where Sarah now lay in a deep sleep, he went to the mine.

At home he felt helpless and his mind was too active to allow him to sleep. What anguish must Sarah have been going through for her to say what she had? And what was the meaning of Mary Crabbe's predictions, so vague and disquieting? His tired brain did not want to think about them.

In the mine were things he knew, tangible things. His skill as an engineer was something of which he was sure. Here, surrounded by familiar objects, he put the pieces of his mind back into place and became less troubled.

In St Cleer, Miriam saw the weary doctor's return and hurried out to hear the news. She returned to the chapel cottage choked with grief for Josh. It was a generous and sincere emotion. She had prayed so often for his happiness.

But she also longed for the impossible – to be able to comfort Josh for the dead child another woman had borne him.

Chapter Twenty-Two

It was dark when the coach carrying Mrs Carlyon rolled into the yard of the old farmhouse. Seconds later Sarah's mother swept through the house and up the stairs to the bedroom where Sarah still lay in an exhausted sleep.

Jesse Retallick met her at the bedroom door and held a finger to her lips. With only the briefest of nods Josh's mother-in-law went directly to the bedside. It was with difficulty she restrained herself from tucking in the corner of blanket that hung to the floor.

Tight-lipped, Molly Carlyon shook her head in a gesture of displeasure and walked from the room ahead of Jesse Retallick.

Jesse closed the door and in the passageway outside said, 'I'm pleased you're here. I only wish it was in happier circumstances.'

'Where is the baby?'

Jesse Retallick hesitated and the other woman said impatiently, 'I know the child is dead. But I would like to look at my first grandchild.'

'*Our* first grandchild,' Jesse Retallick corrected her quietly. The fact that Sarah's mother had not even greeted her civilly had not gone unnoticed. 'He's along here. Such a tiny scrap of a boy.'

Standing by the other woman as she turned back the sheet covering the baby, Jesse Retallick felt intense sadness at the sight of the cold wrinkled little face. It was such a terrible waste of a new life. The baby had left behind so many undiscovered things.

Mrs Carlyon replaced the sheet and the two women went downstairs. Josh had been in the outhouse having an all-over wash when the coach drew up. Now, dressed in clean clothes, he was making some tea.

'A fine mess you've made of looking after my daughter. . . .' Mrs Carlyon launched straight into the attack.

The kettle banged and popped noisily as Josh replaced it carefully on the stove.

'"We have doctors at Sharptor too", you said when I wanted Sarah to stay at Hayle. What of your doctors now?'

'There was nothing the best doctors in the world could have done . . .,' Jesse began, but Josh waved her into silence.

'Mrs Carlyon, the baby was so early that nobody was ready. It all happened so quickly I had to deliver the baby myself. I did my best. If that wasn't enough, then I must be responsible for the death of my own son. But I don't think I could have done more.'

'He did well,' said Jesse. 'I held the baby when he made his first cry. I knew then he was too tiny to live.'

'And what about Sarah? She is lying up there a very sick girl.'

'Sarah is an exhausted woman,' said Josh. 'She had a very difficult time. But she'll be all right if you don't upset her.'

'Upset my own daughter!' Molly Carlyon bristled with rage. 'I came here with a reckless coachman, bounced about until I'm covered in bruises, and I arrive here to be told I mustn't upset Sarah!'

'Sarah is your daughter. She's also my wife. In your present mood I can see nothing but harm from this visit. My father sent to tell you what was happening because he thought you had a right to know. But Sarah has lost our baby and that's distressing enough. If I thought you were going to add to it, Mrs Carlyon, I'd put you back in your carriage and order the coachman to return to Hayle this minute.'

Mrs Carlyon appeared to be actually swelling with rage as Jesse moved in to smooth things down.

'That's quite enough nonsense from you, Josh. Go and fetch some logs for the fire while I pour Mrs Carlyon another cup of tea. Go on, now!'

When he went, reluctantly, Jesse Retallick said, 'Josh is upset and doesn't mean anything by his bluntness. Remember he hasn't been to bed since this whole business started. He is tired. On top of that, he's had an experience to unnerve a far older man. He had to deliver his own child and it died. I think he blames himself—'

'And so he should.'

'No, he shouldn't.' Jesse Retallick silenced the other woman. 'He did as much as anyone could. Had he not kept his head you might not have a daughter now. Here's your cup of tea, Mrs Carlyon. If I seem ungracious it's because I too am tired. I'll tidy up here then go to my own cottage.'

'Leave what you have to do here,' said Molly Carlyon. 'I'll attend to everything. You go home to your husband.'

She gave a tight forced smile. 'I'm a worrier and there was little else to do in the coach on the way here.'

'You don't have to explain to me. There wasn't one of us – Josh, Ben or myself – who wasn't worried sick all night. It must have been dreadful to travel all that way not knowing what you would find when you arrived.'

'Yes, and I'm sure Sarah's father won't sleep tonight, either. I said I would send for him immediately if I felt he was needed.'

'Ben will get word to him tomorrow,' Jesse promised. 'Now I really must go. I'll be back in the morning to see how Sarah is.'

Outside, Jesse met Josh coming across the yard.

Before she allowed him past her into the house she made him promise to hold his tongue and not quarrel with Sarah's mother. Not until he gave his word did she go down the path to her cottage, satisfied that all was well in the old farmhouse, albeit temporarily.

Meanwhile, Mrs Carlyon went upstairs to Sarah's bedroom before Josh came in. She tucked in the blanket and straightened the pillows.

Josh made himself up a bed in a small bedroom before going in to see how Sarah was. She was still sleeping and looked very pale and fragile.

'Your bed has been made up in the room next to this one,' Josh said to Mrs Carlyon quietly.

'I'll stay here, thank you. In case Sarah wakes during the night.'

'If you need anything you'll find me in the end room.' Josh had the uncomfortable feeling that he was an interloper in his own home. He laid a gentle hand on Sarah's forehead, pleased to feel it cool; then he went to his own makeshift bed. He was asleep within a minute of laying his head on the pillow.

Waking in the morning light, Josh heard the murmur of voices from the bedroom along the corridor. Flinging back the bed-clothes he dressed and hurried along to Sarah's room. She was lying propped up against the pillows, her eyes dark hollows in her bloodless face.

The smile that she gave him was brief, but for a moment he felt its warmth. Then it was replaced by an expression that made him remember her last words before she had fallen asleep.

'Hello, love.' He kissed her and took her hand. 'How are you feeling this morning?'

'Much better, thank you.'

'I'll go and freshen myself up.' Mrs Carlyon had not thawed from the previous evening.

'No. Don't go!' Sarah cried, struggling to sit up. Without warning she burst into tears. Josh's arms went about her and he held her to him. But he could not stop her sobbing. It seemed that whatever he said only caused her to cry more bitterly.

Determinedly, Mrs Carlyon eased her from his arms and laid her back against the pillows. 'There! There! Don't cry like that. You're all right now.'

To Josh she said, 'Leave us now. She's too upset to reason with. She must rest.'

Bewildered, Josh left the room and readied himself for work. He could still hear her crying as he passed the room on the way out but dared not go inside again.

He worried about her all that morning and went home at lunch-time to see her, but she was asleep once more. Jesse Retallick and Mrs Carlyon were both in the house and agreed that it would be better not to disturb her again. He returned to work having caught no more than a glimpse of her through the partly open bedroom door as she lay snuggled down in bed.

That evening he rushed straight home. Finding no one downstairs in the kitchen, he went up to the bedroom where he was greatly relieved to see Sarah sitting up in bed looking far more cheerful than she had been before. But as soon as he spoke to her she began weeping uncontrollably once more.

For two days this state of affairs continued. Nothing he said or did could prevent her from crying whenever he entered the room where she was. He tried talking to her, telling her that losing the baby was not her fault, that it was nobody's fault; but she would not listen. He tried holding her and saying nothing, but the crying sounded even louder in the silence. Always in the background was the disapproving tight-lipped presence of Sarah's mother.

Sarah left her bed for the baby's funeral, the Carlyon coach brought into use to take her to the chapel. Josh hoped with the brief simple ceremony behind them Sarah would begin to improve, but nothing changed. Sarah sank into a morass of unhappiness that nothing Josh did would disperse.

After a week he dreaded returning home. He despaired of life ever returning to normal. He had a guilty feeling of relief when Mrs Carlyon announced she was taking Sarah home to Hayle for a long period of convalescence.

'What do you mean by a "long period"?' asked Josh.

'I mean for just as long as it takes her to become a healthy happy young woman again.'

'Yes. All right. Sarah will be better with someone to talk to her all the time. Here there is nobody but Jenny of her own age, and having me around doesn't seem to be helping her. I'll miss her, though.'

'If you miss her that much you can move to Hayle to be with her. Sarah's father will find a place for you in Harvey's works. Why don't you do that? I understand you're quite a clever design-engineer and could go far. Why on earth you choose to waste your life as an engineer in this God-forsaken place I don't know. It's enough to give anyone the melancholies.'

Mrs Carlyon's opinion of Sharptor had been coloured by the bank of low cloud and drizzle that had descended three days before and showed little sign of lifting.

'It's a tiny mine, Mrs Carlyon, but God probably spends more time here than he does in most other places. Sarah was happy here in the few months before the baby came. She'll be happy here again.'

I doubt that. Molly Carlyon would have said it aloud but she did not want to antagonise Josh now. She would make quite sure that Sarah never returned to this backward part of the county.

'When are you going to leave?'

'Tomorrow. We'll make an early start and take the journey slowly.'

'Tomorrow!'

'Yes. The sooner Sarah reaches home, the sooner she'll begin to mend. I'm very worried about her state of mind.'

Josh had no intention of baring his feelings to Sarah's mother but he knew Sharptor would never be a happy place again without Sarah.

'I'll go and tell Mum and Dad so they can come up and say goodbye to Sarah.'

He walked slowly down the hill, ignoring the drizzle. He was deeply unhappy. During their brief time together Josh had learned to love Sarah. It was a quieter, less devouring love than the one he had shared with Miriam, but he accepted that there were degrees of love. Now the bonds between Sarah and himself were being cut like their pathetic child's umbilical cord he feared it would shrivel into nothingness.

Later that night, when his mother and father went home and Mrs Carlyon had retired to her own bedroom, he went quietly in to Sarah.

A small oil-lamp was burning on a table across the room from her. Although she was lying quite still, her eyes were open and they followed his progress to her bedside.

'Hello, Sarah!' He smiled down at her gently, desperately eager for her to understand. 'Tomorrow you're going back to Hayle for a nice long holiday. You'll get yourself fit and well again.'

She stared up at him and said nothing. Encouraged, he went on, 'I'll miss you, Sarah. The house is going to feel very empty without you. This week has been a nightmare for both of us, but you mustn't think you are in any way to blame. You were a very brave girl. I'm proud of you.'

He choked with emotion and could not stop himself from dropping to one knee beside the bed and kissing her. He thought she yielded to him briefly, but then she flung her head to one side violently.

'No, Josh! No! I don't want to have another dead baby. No more, Josh! Please, no more!'

'Shh!' He tried to gather her into his arms, wanting desperately to hold and comfort her, but she struggled and fought him off, shouting the whole time.

'Leave me alone! Leave me alone!'

The door banged open and Sarah's mother rushed across the room to the bed, her hair tied in rag-curlers.

'What's going on? There, now! There!' She held her daughter and glared above her head at Josh. 'What do you think you're doing? Why must you upset her tonight? She has a strenuous day tomorrow and needs all the rest she can get.'

'I wanted to say a few words to her, to tell her to hurry and get well. I don't know when I'll see her again.'

'That's entirely up to you. Now leave us. I'll quieten her down. You can see her in the morning before we go.'

He would see her in the morning, but they would not be alone. Jesse and Ben Retallick would be there, and Jenny and Tom Shovell, all waving goodbye to the shell of the girl who had been his wife for such a brief time – the bright intelligent girl who had come to Sharptor as a bride and was now leaving, a near-demented woman, with only a tiny tombstone in a village graveyard to record her stay.

Chapter Twenty-Three

With Sarah gone, Josh lost all purpose in life. For the first few weeks he leaned heavily on his family and friends. He visited Jenny and Tom Shovell and spent hours playing with young Gwen. With his own family, he talked about everything except Sarah.

He called on people he had scarcely spoken to for years. When his visits were over he walked back to the old farmhouse to sit composing letters to Sarah. Most of them travelled no further than the fire in the kitchen. But he sent off three letters in the first fortnight after Sarah left and received replies to none of them.

Then, as suddenly as it had begun, his mood changed. Josh stopped calling on friends. Instead, he began to spend his evenings at the Cheesewring Inn in Henwood village.

At first he was a welcome customer. A popular figure among the miners of both Sharptor and the Wheal Caradon, he was known to the men of the Wheal Phoenix and the many other smaller mines dotted about the moor.

At the inn he could forget the lonely house on the tor and the girl who was no longer there. While he bought the drinks he was never short of ready listeners. He learned that if he drank enough alcohol it blotted out memories as thoroughly as a hill fog wiped Kit Hill from the horizon.

If the drink failed to fulfil its purpose it was possible to find other diversions – such as the night he got into an argument with two tin-miners from west Cornwall. Afterwards he had no recollection of how the argument started, or even what it was about, but it ended with Josh skinning his knuckles on the nose of one of them and banging both their heads together so hard they were unconscious for half an hour. After this incident, the crowd about him was never quite so thick.

His father sought him out at the mine and tried to talk him out of his drinking, but Josh brushed the advice aside.

He was more shame-faced about it when Jesse Retallick confronted him one Sunday morning at the old farmhouse. She interspersed her sentences with such words as 'shameful' and 'disgusting', but that same evening he stumbled his way home with the stars reeling above him and the path eluding him. He woke in the bracken below the house the next morning to the soft nuzzling of a inquisitive moorland pony.

Not until the days had lengthened into early summer did Josh's drinking come to an end.

It was late when he roared his goodbyes from the inn doorway and took an exaggerated stride across the stone step, before lurching out into the uneven village street.

For a long swaying minute he allowed his eyes to become accustomed to the gloom, then a soft voice at his elbow said, 'Hello, Josh.'

Startled, he turned towards the voice and, losing his balance, stumbled backwards. The hands that gripped his shirt-front were slim and long-fingered, but they were strong enough to halt his backward progress and jerk him upright.

'Who's that? Miriam! What are you doing here?'

Stupidly drunk as he was, he still made an effort to overcome the slur in his words.

'I've come to see you. But I'm not going to talk to you outside this place. I gave up waiting outside inns when I was a very young girl. Let's walk.'

He tried to shake her hand from his arm. 'Leave me alone. I can get home on my own.'

'That's not what I've heard. Come on, now. Don't cause a scene and embarrass me.'

'I wouldn't want to embarrass the Reverend's lady.'

It was foolish, childishly foolish. He knew it.

'Why aren't you home with your husband and Daniel? What are you doing here in Henwood?'

'At the moment I'm trying to move you in the general direction of your home. Without very much success.'

'I can get home very well without your help, thank you.'

He straightened his shoulders and stepped forward determinedly, making almost twenty yards before hooking his toe into the mud-scraper beside the door of Henwood shop and dropping to one knee.

'Damn!' If it weren't so dark he would be able to see and not make such an idiot of himself.

He imagined that Miriam was laughing at him. Shaking her hand away roughly, he got back on to his feet unaided.

'Go home,' he said. 'I don't need your help. Or anyone else's. I'm quite capable of looking after myself.'

'It would serve you right if I did walk away and leave you alone, Joshua Retallick. Do you think I enjoy seeing a man I admire fall about as though he was an imbecile child? I've memories enough of my father to last me until I go to the grave. I don't need to watch you behave like it.'

Her anger got through to him. Although he could not keep the impediment from his speech, he felt able to think sensibly.

'I'm sorry, but I honestly don't need your help. I'll get home all right.'

'Fool yourself if you want to. You're not convincing me.'

She grabbed his arm and steered him on a course forty-five degrees from the one he was pursuing. 'That ditch you were heading for is four feet deep, with enough rocks in it to damage even your head. No, don't pull your arm away. We'll get along quicker if I guide you. I have no intention of spending the night wandering in circles around Henwood village with you.'

'What are you doing here? Where's William?'

'He's at home, looking after Daniel. My mother isn't well. I'm staying with her until tomorrow.'

Josh allowed himself to be guided along the track, uphill from the village. He was all right, he told himself; but his legs seemed to be in more of a hurry than his body.

'Why aren't you with your mother now, instead of fussing with me?'

'I'm "fussing" with you because I brought something from St Cleer for you. I don't intend giving it to you until I'm quite sure you are sober and know you've received it.'

'What is it? I'm sober enough now. Give it to me and go.'

'I appreciate your gratitude, but you can keep your orders for those who have to take them. When you're safely in your house you'll get your letter. Not a minute before.'

'A letter? Where is it? What are you doing with it?'

'It arrived on today's coach. I said I would bring it with me. I thought it might be something you were waiting for.'

'I am, Miriam. It's the first one since – since Sarah went to Hayle.'

'Yes, I thought that might be the case.'

They were close to the house now and the drink and the uphill walk were causing him to breathe heavily. But he was not as drunk as he would have been had he come home alone.

Nevertheless, Miriam was hard to convince. Inside the house she kept his head beneath the kitchen pump until he felt more drowned than drunk.

Handing him a towel from the rack beside the sink, she said, 'Here. Dry your hair and I'll give you your letter.'

He rubbed vigorously until his hair was no longer dripping water before taking the sealed letter from her.

Tearing it open, he read quickly, then handed the letter back to Miriam without a word.

'I don't want to read Sarah's letter!' She thrust it back at him.

'It's not from Sarah. It's from her young sister Mary. Read it.'

Opening out the stiff sheet of paper, Miriam could see that the writing was much more childish than it was on the outside of the envelope.

'Dear Josh,' she read. 'I hope you are not too lonely living by yourself in that big house. How is Hector? I have a new pony all of my own now. I call him Bob. Sarah is looking a lot better now, but I have not been able to talk to her properly because the doctor said she must be kept very quiet. I saw her sitting in a seat by the window yesterday and I waved. I am sure she smiled so I think she will soon be all right again. I wish you could come to stay with us, but Mummy says that would upset Sarah too much. I don't know why. I am very sorry about the baby because I wanted to be an aunt. I must end now. Lots of love, Mary.'

Her signature was followed by half a line of Xs.

'Oh! I thought the letter came from Sarah. I wouldn't have made such a fuss about it had I known.'

'I'm glad you did. It might not say a lot but it contains the first news I've had of Sarah since she left here. I'll sit down and reply to Mary tonight.'

'Is that wise? I mean . . . don't you think it would be better to leave it until tomorrow when you will have a clearer mind?'

'What you really mean is "when I am sober". No, it's all right. I'm perfectly well now. Thanks to you.'

'I wish I could do something to keep you that way, Josh.' She was taken by a sudden thought. 'When did you last eat?'

'I – I don't know. I had some breakfast this morning.'

'Then I'll cook you something now, before I leave. If you told the truth I doubt whether you've eaten at all today.'

Ignoring his protests, she searched the larder, finding eggs, bread and some salt bacon.

'I'll make a start on this but the fire is getting a bit low.'

'Yes, my mother will have called in and made it up for me a lot earlier this evening. I'll put on some wood shavings. That will get it burning.'

When he came back into the house carrying wood there was a delicious smell rising from the cooking-pan. Ten minutes later he was seated at the kitchen table demolishing a meal that would have satisfied three men like William Thackeray.

Wiping the plate clean, Josh leaned back and gave Miriam a sheepish grin.

'Miriam Thackeray, you may be a hard bullying woman, but there's no disputing that you're a fine cook.'

Her answer was a loud snort. 'Huh! You had such a hunger on you it would have made no difference had I burned it black.'

Their eyes met for a warm second but Miriam dropped her gaze immediately and smoothed the waist of her dress. 'Now I've seen you safely home and fed I must go.'

He looked at the big clock on the shelf above the fire-place and started guiltily. 'I didn't realise it was so late. You'll be getting yourself gossiped about in Henwood. Even at this hour there's bound to be someone to see you coming from Sharptor. I'll put on my coat and walk down to the village with you.'

She laughed. It had been a long time since he had heard a happy sound in that room.

'You do that and the gossips of Henwood will have something to talk about. No, Josh. You stay here. I'll go on my own. There's nothing on the moor to bother me. I'm happier walking here after dark than I am in St Cleer.'

'Thank you for the meal, Miriam. And for sobering me up.'

She stopped at the door and without looking at his face said, 'You don't know what it did to me to see you in that state, Josh. It was as though a knife was going into me, cutting open the bag of bad memories I have there. When I was a very small girl my father enjoyed a drink, but it hadn't yet possessed him entirely. In those days he would know I was waiting outside the inn and wouldn't stay late. When he came out he would swing me up on his shoulder and give me a ride home. It was only as I grew older he began to stay inside longer and longer and forget I was waiting. When he did come out I sometimes ran away from him because he was shouting or swearing at the other miners. One night my mother came down for him. It was pay-day and she wanted money for food. I saw her jostled and man-handled by drunken miners before someone told my father she was there. He was angry, very angry, because she had come looking for him. He was also very drunk. When she asked him for money he hit her. She still held out her hand so he hit her again. He hit her and hit her until she fell to the ground and stayed there. Then he went back inside the inn. All this came back to me as I waited outside the Cheesewring Inn for you to come out tonight. When you came through that door reeling-drunk it was as though I'd made a journey back in time. I felt physically sick.'

'I'm sorry, Miriam.'

'Oh, you needn't be.' She shrugged. 'You're quite entitled to tell me it's none of my business. But I hate to see a good man destroying himself. You have your problems, Josh. I might be partly to blame for them. But you won't find any answers inside an inn.'

'Where do you suggest I start looking for the answers – Hayle?'

'That's up to you, Josh.'

'Yes. I know I still owe Theophilus Strike a few years here, but if I thought it would be for the best I'd leave Sharptor and go to work for Harvey's. That's what Sarah's mother wants. But it wouldn't work. Mrs Carlyon would have too much control over our lives. It's out of the question at the moment, anyway. I can't get near Sarah. She bursts into tears at the sight of me. I'll think about it and discuss it with Sarah when she's well again.'

He made a helpless gesture. 'I hope it won't take too long. There was a time when I enjoyed the thought of having Sarah for my wife because she is the daughter of William Carlyon, the manager of Harvey's. But during the last few months I became very fond of her. We were happy during the time we were waiting for the baby.'

'Poor Josh. . . .'

'No, don't pity me. I couldn't bear that coming from you. Anyway, Sarah is back with her sort of people now. She'll be visited by friends who know which tie to wear for a wedding, who can sit down at a table and know which knife, fork and spoon to use without having to wait and watch what everyone else is doing. I only wish she was well enough to enjoy it.'

'She's being looked after, Josh. But what about you? Will you cease being Josh the engineer now and become Josh the Sharptor drunk?'

'No, Miriam.' He was serious. 'This talk with you has done me good. I'll be able to manage without the aid of the Cheesewring Inn.'

'Then I don't care what the Henwood gossips have to say. I'll have done something worth while.'

When she reached the far edge of the yellow light reaching out through the open kitchen door she stopped. 'If you're feeling the same way tomorrow evening perhaps you'll walk me back to St Cleer. Have supper with William and me.'

'Yes, I'd like that.'

'Good! I'll give you time to come home and clean up from work and wait for you at the edge of the village.'

He took Hector and suggested that Miriam ride while he walked beside her, but she objected. In the end they compromised by both riding on the uncomplaining horse, Miriam occupying the saddle with Josh behind, arms about her, holding the reins.

Just before they entered St Cleer he put the horse into a trot. Jogging and bouncing they arrived at the gate of the chapel house, red-cheeked and laughing.

From the window of his study William Thackeray watched the arrival of his wife and Josh with a frown. The frown deepened as Josh swung Miriam to the ground with his hands about her waist.

But minutes later William Thackeray's smile was as welcoming as any loving husband whose wife has been away from home.

'It's nice to have you home again,' he said, kissing her. 'Daniel will be pleased. He's playing in the back garden. And Josh! How nice to see you after such a long time – an unhappy time for you, I fear.'

He grasped Josh's hand in both his own. 'I can't tell you how sorry I was to hear about the baby and poor Sarah. How is she? I heard she was very ill.'

'Yes. She's staying with her parents at Hayle.'

'For long?' The question was accompanied by a calculating look.

'For quite some time, I fear.'

'He's been on his own for too long,' said Miriam. 'I thought it was time he had a good meal. That's why I invited him here tonight.'

'I hope it wasn't only the promise of food that persuaded him to come.' He smiled at Josh. 'Mind you, I'm forced to admit you look as though you need a good meal.'

'I'll go and find Daniel. Then I'll start the cooking.' Miriam smiled at the two men as she went towards the back of the house.

'Come into the lounge, Josh,' said William Thackeray. 'We have a lot to talk about. Have you heard about the miners' benefit scheme? Sixpence a week collected from each miner guarantees him ten shillings a week if he's home because of an injury received in the mine. Think of the peace of mind that will give to an injured miner. He'll be able to give himself time to get well without his family starving.'

'Educate the miners and adventurers in the meaning of mine safety, rig a man-lift in every mine and you eliminate most accidents. That way the miner and his family stay happy and don't have to try to manage on ten shillings a week.'

'True, Josh. Quite true. But you must admit this is a start. Build up the Union, let the miner see he has a strong movement behind him and he can demand that your safety measures be implemented.'

This was what the preacher enjoyed – having someone to talk to, to argue with, shaking the argument around and looking at it from every possible angle. Josh had always been able to satisfy this need. Miriam had the intelligence to carry on a discussion with him but she was unable to see every fact as a multi-sided prism, the argument shifting with each facet. Miriam was too positive in her approach. She saw one point of view and stayed with it, unwilling to concede half a point against it.

William Thackeray and Josh discussed the Union until Miriam called them into the kitchen for the meal she had prepared. The discussion halted for a while as Daniel was to eat with them. He provided the topic for conversation until the meal was over.

Daniel was a bright attractive child in his third year. His presence both fascinated and embarrassed Josh. He became unusually tongue-tied, wanting the boy to talk to him, yet not sure of his own ability to reply to him.

At last the meal was over and Miriam led Daniel away to bed, ignoring his vigorous protests.

'That young man has a strong will,' commented Josh.

'I suspect it's an inheritance from his mother,' replied William Thackeray. 'Now, we've discussed the benefit scheme. What do you really think of it, Josh?'

'It can do nothing but good. Unless the mine-owners think because the miners are getting paid by someone else for injury time they have no need to improve mine safety. That's likely to happen on some mines.'

'Ah! Now you are coming to the second part of my scheme, Josh. After a few months we'll have a good sum of money in the fund. When we have reached that happy state we can extend it. One thought I have in mind is that if there are too many accidents at a particular mine the fund committee will ask the mine captain to improve safety measures. Should he refuse the men stop work and receive benefit as though they were off through injury.'

'The fund won't last long if you call out the work-force on a large mine,' said Josh.

'But that won't happen.' William Thackeray's face lit up with the fervour of a crusader. 'We're not likely to get trouble from the large mines. They know poor safety only leads to lower profits. It's the smaller mine that tries to cut costs. We can beat them.'

He held up a hand before Josh could speak. 'I know what you're going to say. Such a state of affairs doesn't exist at Sharptor. And you're quite right. But Sharptor is a one-man-owned mine and few mines are as efficiently run. Even so, I don't think Theophilus Strike deserves all the credit for it. It was not such a good place to work when Herman Schmidt was mine captain. The good Sharptor record is due to your efforts and those of men like your father and Captain Shovell. Nevertheless, we will need to have the Sharptor miners in the benefit scheme. To be a complete success it needs the co-operation of every miner in the district – in the whole of Cornwall if we can extend it that far.'

'I can't see anyone raising objections,' said Josh. 'Theophilus Strike is anti-Union, but he will see this is for the good of every miner and his family. The fact that it will not cost him a penny will help.'

But Theophilus Strike did not see it that way when Josh put it to him a few days later.

'We don't need such a scheme in the Wheal Sharptor!' he declared. 'Our accident rate is lower than any other mine in the county.'

'One roof-fall at the wrong time would alter that,' replied Josh. 'I thought you'd welcome the scheme.'

'Welcome it! I welcome nothing that has the smell of unionism behind it. Who thought of it? That St Cleer preacher?'

'As a matter of fact he did.'

'I thought as much. No doubt he will administer it and call the tune. Unionism is gaining more ground than is good for anyone. Don't let yourself be fooled by high ideals, Joshua. That preacher would not be pushing it so hard if anyone else controlled its affairs. He wants to become a power in this part of the county. This is his way of doing it. To me it's no more than a matter of personal annoyance. Others feel far more strongly and will stop at nothing to stamp it out. When they're ready to make a move someone will suffer. This preacher friend of yours is far too slippery for it to be him. Make sure it isn't you.'

'Then you agree to the men contributing to a benefit fund?'

'Would it make any difference if I didn't? No, Joshua. The unionism fever is gripping every miner at the moment. If I said I'd deduct the same amount from the men's wages and give them *fifteen* shillings a week injury pay I wouldn't be considered a humanitarian. The men's first thought would be "What's Theophilus Strike getting out of it for himself?"

Nobody would join. But I have no doubt they'll jump at your offer. I won't stop them. But I do have a word of warning for you. I've always tried to run a good mine and be fair with the men who work for me. Make sure they're joining a benefit scheme and not a union of miners. A Sharptor miner serves only one master – me. I'll not have any preacher coming here to tell me how to run my mine.'

'I don't think it will ever come to that, Mr Strike.'

'Think! Boy, you stop thinking when you walk away from an engine. Now, be damned to your unionism. Go find your father and tell him I want to inspect the new deep level. You can take us down in your latest toy. Come down with us. I've been getting reports about lack of air down there. If it's true you might be able to think of a way to improve it.'

Outside the mine office it was a wet and blustery day. The davits over the shafts creaked and groaned and the wind sang mournfully in the taut cables.

The man-lift had been adjusted to perfection. After travelling two hundred and forty fathoms from grass to the bottom of the shaft, Theophilus Strike had a step down of less than a foot to the damp ground below him.

The airless humidity was immediately apparent to all of them. The slow monotonous thumping of the water-pump was like the beating of a giant heart above them. But all the body heat was down here in the deep darkness at the bottom of the mine.

They ducked into the working adit which was still in a largely exploratory state. It had not been widened or heightened for easy working. Before they had gone thirty yards they were gasping for breath, the candles on their hard hats spluttering and groping for oxygen.

The three men were in the adit for less than twenty minutes but as they ascended in the lift it seemed to Josh he had been working a full shift below ground. His clothes were wet with perspiration and his head sang from the lack of oxygen he had experienced. Looking at his father and Theophilus Strike he could see they were feeling the same.

The effort of breathing oxygen back into their systems kept

them speechless until they reached the surface. It was not until they stepped on to the ground at the top, grateful for a grey overcast day with a cool miserable wind, that any of them spoke.

'The reports are not exaggerated, Ben,' said the mine-owner, running a white linen handkerchief around the neck-band of his shirt. 'Unless we can do something about it we won't be able to get anything out from that level. It looked like prize ore too.'

'The best in the mine,' agreed the shift captain. 'But a man would be overcome by foul air inside an hour, even if I could persuade him to work there.'

'Then what would you suggest? An adit through the side of the hill?'

'No.' Ben Retallick shook his head. 'We're too deep for that. Too deep even for a sloping shaft.'

'How about you, Joshua? Can you think of anything that might help?'

Josh nodded thoughtfully. 'Yes, I have a vague idea in my mind of something that might work. I'll fix up an apparatus along the lines of the water-pump. If air is pushed down through a long pipe fitted with a non-return valve it should work. It's worth a try.'

'The lad's a genius!' exclaimed the mine-owner. 'But won't it mean another engine?'

'A very small one,' replied Josh. 'There's one for sale at the West Caradon we could get for next to nothing.'

'Then buy it. Do whatever you think is necessary. Let me know when you have it working.'

He turned to Ben Retallick. 'Make him work at it, Ben. It will keep him from that so-called preacher and his radical ideas.'

Josh smiled. 'I'll have that tunnel fit for working in two weeks, Mr Strike. I don't want the men wasting their hard-earned benefit money.'

Theophilus Strike grunted as he walked away and Ben Retallick could not hide his amazement.

'I never thought I'd live to see the day when anyone would

use the word "benefit" in front of Theophilus Strike and still work for him.'

'In a few years everyone will know about "benefit", and I hope there will be far less need of it.'

Ben Retallick's expression was serious. 'Perhaps. But Strike was right about one thing. Preacher Thackeray. You'd be well off staying away from him, Josh. There's little good in anything Thackeray does, unless he benefits from it too.'

'If it wasn't for him miners in these parts would be a lot worse off than they are now,' retorted Josh. 'He's the fire behind the movement.'

'And like every fire he needs to burn fuel,' said Ben Retallick. 'Make sure you aren't thrown on the heap for burning. It's no good shaking your head at me, my lad. Preacher Thackeray may be some sort of a hero to you, but he is as human as anyone else. Staunch unionist he might be, but he has no cause to love you.'

'What do you mean by that?'

'You don't have to raise your hackles with me, Josh. I'm your father. I don't think I have to spell out anything I say to you. You were more than friendly with Preacher Thackeray's wife before they were married. I wasn't the only one who thought she'd be part of the family one day. Then she ups and marries Preacher Thackeray as sudden as any wedding I've known. Too soon after that to be decent a babe was born. Nice folks will say it was born before its time. There's others who don't. Most of them would wager that the preacher didn't have anything to do with fathering it, either.'

Josh's face paled and then the blood rushed into it angrily, but his father stopped him before he could speak. 'Just a minute. Let me finish. I'm not saying that I, or any other decent person, has taken any notice of what they say. I'm only telling you it's been said. And if I've heard it you can be sure Preacher Thackeray has too. It's the sort of thing that festers in a man's mind, Josh. And I've heard from some that the preacher isn't the most forgiving of men.'

It was quite true. Josh knew it. But it was something more than anger that burned within him.

'I've never heard anyone say it. If I did they wouldn't repeat it to anyone else!'

'I've no doubt of it. That's why the rumours have never reached your ears,' said Ben quietly. 'I only mentioned it now because I felt you ought to know and adjust your friendship with Preacher Thackeray accordingly.'

'My friendship with Preacher Thackeray will be what it's always been,' declared Josh. 'If he takes notice of rumours of that sort he's not the man I believe him to be.'

'I hope time proves you right and me wrong.'

Ben Retallick walked out of the office, leaving Josh looking after him. Josh had argued strongly for the preacher, but he knew even more than his father how dangerous the preacher could be if he chose. Soon after Harry Reeve and the other Kit Hill miners' leaders were transported there had been an ugly rumour circulating that Preacher Thackeray had arranged their arrests. It was said he was jealous of the stature they were gaining in the eyes of the Kit Hill men.

But, as quickly as he remembered, Josh shrugged it off. What he had said to his father had been the truth. Preacher Thackeray had done a great deal for the cause of the Miners' Union. To doubt him now would be totally unworthy.

It was as much a result of this guilty feeling as for any other reason that Josh rode to St Cleer that evening. He found Preacher Thackeray working in his study. The welcome he gave Josh was as warm as ever. Josh immediately resolved to put any last lingering doubt about the preacher behind him.

'It's always a pleasure to see you, Josh,' said William Thackeray as he ushered his guest into the house. 'Let me make some tea for you. I'm alone for an hour or so. Miriam is taking a class for older girls this evening.'

'I didn't realise she was a teacher these days,' said Josh.

'Oh, there isn't much that Miriam can't turn her hand to,' smiled William Thackeray. 'She's the perfect wife for a minister of the Church. She teaches, stands in for me during my absences, corrects my sermons, and can hold her own in a union meeting against any man foolish enough to doubt her capabilities. I tell you, Josh, she's one in a million.'

'Yes.'

'But, talking of wives, what am I thinking about? There's a letter here for you. It came on today's coach. Miriam asked me if I would take it over to Sharptor for you tomorrow. Now, where has she put it?'

He began searching through the compartments of his bureau. Finally he held a sealed letter up in triumph.

'Here we are! I hope it contains good news for you, Josh.'

Josh took the letter and to his surprise and delight recognized Sarah's handwriting. It looked more irregular than usual but there was no doubt about it.

Tearing it open he began to read excitedly. Gradually the expression on his face changed from delight to surprise, then through disbelief to dismay.

The preacher was watching him closely. 'Is it bad news, Josh? Is something wrong?'

'It's. . . . She. . . .' His mouth opened again but instead of speaking he handed the letter to William Thackeray.

On the opened-out page the unevenness of the writing was even more apparent than on the envelope. The scrawled words wandered untidily across the page. But their meaning was clear enough.

'My Dear Josh,' the letter began. 'Forgive me for what I have to say. I cannot tell you how much it upsets me to write so, but I feel it is the only honest thing I am able to do. You know I was never really happy at Sharptor. After all that has happened I could not bear to live in that house again. That is why I am writing now. Mother has said many times it would have been better had we never married. Although there was a time when I bitterly resented her words, I now realise it is true. I have brought only unhappiness to you, dear Josh. I was not even capable of giving you a child. This is not a part of my illness; the doctor says I am almost over that now. My tears threaten to wash away every word that I write, but it must be said. The sooner I tell you, the quicker you can begin a new life without me. I do not want to see you ever again, Josh. Whatever you decide to do with your life I wish you the happiness and success I know you can achieve. I cannot write more now. God bless you. Sarah.'

'You can't take any notice of this letter, Josh. The very writing shows that the poor girl is far from well. I'm amazed her mother allowed such a letter to be sent to you. Sarah must have worked herself up into a piteous state to have penned a letter like this. Ignore it, I implore you.'

Josh looked at the preacher with unseeing eyes. 'I wish I could. If only I could. There's too much truth in it to be ignored. I knew she wasn't happy at Sharptor, but that would have changed with time. Now, with her mother feeding her every thought, it can never be.'

Punching a fist into the palm of his left hand he spun on his heel and reached for his coat.

'Where are you going?'

'To Hayle. There's no answer to be found here, and no peace in me until I've seen for myself how well Sarah is. Whether things really are over between us.'

'Josh, is that wise? Go home and think about it. Leave a decision until tomorrow.'

'No. There are times for thinking and times for action. I've been thinking for too long.'

Without another word Josh strode from the house, and William Thackeray made no further attempt to stop him.

Josh untied Hector from the rail outside the chapel and reined the horse's head around. Then he rode out through the village at a fast canter and was soon out of sight beyond the houses.

Within an hour of leaving St Cleer it was dark and great caution was needed. The road was pot-holed and rutted for most of its length. It was impossible to distinguish road from verge. The slow journey gave Josh ample time to think of what he would do when he arrived. He had no intention of storming into the Carlyons' house like a marauder and carrying Sarah back to Sharptor by force. It was quite probable she would never return there, as she had declared. But he wanted to be sure it was her own decision, made without any interference from her mother.

He rode even more slowly as he neared Hayle. He could have arrived before dawn. Instead, he stopped, and seated on a granite milestone watched the sun rise and colour the countryside.

The day shift was settling in at the foundry when he reached the house. His unheralded appearance brought a variety of reactions from the Carlyon family, ranging from Mary's unreserved pleasure to open hostility from Mrs Carlyon. Sarah was not downstairs, and Mrs Carlyon made it clear she had no intention of allowing Josh to go up to her.

'It was that foolish letter!' she exclaimed angrily. 'I knew I should never have allowed her to send it.'

'It was a letter from Sarah to her husband,' Josh said equally angrily. 'She had every right to send it. There was no need to ask your permission.'

'Husband, indeed!' Mrs Carlyon's snort would not have been out of place in a stable. 'And where has my daughter's "husband" been these last weeks while she's been lying upstairs? Her mind has been in such a turmoil I doubted whether she would ever be sane again. And who nursed her through nightmares so frightening they brought me out in a cold sweat? Answer me that if you can, Joshua Retallick.'

'It was because I thought it would be better for Sarah that I allowed her to return here with you. At your insistence,' replied a thin-lipped Josh. 'I have no doubt she has had the best attention possible. I'm very grateful for that.'

'Gratitude has never paid bills,' snapped Mrs Carlyon. 'When a man takes a wife it's usual for him to support her.'

'You can send every bill that Sarah has incurred to me,' flared Josh. 'They'll be paid.'

'What's all this talk of payment?' William Carlyon came into the room and shook his son-in-law's hand warmly. 'What sort of greeting is this for a man who looks as though he's ridden through the night?'

'I don't care if he's ridden for a week. He has not done his duty as a husband to Sarah and I don't think it's in her interest to see him now.'

'That's a most unfair statement,' the works manager protested. 'If Josh had felt he could have helped in any way I'm sure he would have been here with Sarah. Why, it was you who said he would only hinder her recovery. Josh has shown great strength of mind to have stayed away for this long.'

'Sarah is still not well enough to see him,' Mrs Carlyon persisted.

'She's well enough to write to me,' said Josh. 'And apparently quite well enough to have her mind poisoned against me by you.'

'That's a disgraceful assertion . . . !'

At that moment the door from the hall opened and Sarah came in. She looked quite normal and healthy until she saw Josh. Then she froze, her hand flying to her mouth.

Although at first glance she appeared to be the same Sarah he had known, there was something in her eyes that disturbed him greatly. It was a lost unreal look.

'Sarah!' As he moved towards her she shrank back. 'Sarah, I won't hurt you. I've just come to see you. . . .'

She looked around, seeking some way of escape, her face twitching as though she was in physical pain.

'There! Don't you see? You're terrifying the poor girl.'

Mrs Carlyon could hardly keep the triumph from her voice.

'Sarah, it's me. Josh.'

Sarah cringed back until she was touching the wall, then she edged her way along it sideways, moving towards the door.

'Sarah, please! I came because of your letter.'

'Leave her alone. I told you this would do no good.'

'Sarah! Josh has travelled all night to see you. Don't be silly now.'

'Sarah, Josh wouldn't hurt you.'

'Leave her alone. Go away.'

'Sarah!'

'Sarah . . . !'

Everyone was talking to her, looking at her. Their words beat in upon her like waves in a storm, pounding her brain into a thousand pieces. It was more than she could endure. Her hand touched the door-handle. She turned it – and was gone.

Josh rushed to follow her, but Mrs Carlyon barred his way.

'Leave her! Haven't you done enough? I told you this would happen.'

'Now, Molly, you're not being fair to Josh. He came here to see Sarah because he is worried about her. Had anyone asked me I would have sworn that she was well enough to see him again.'

'Mummy, you said yesterday that Sarah was almost better.' This came from Mary, and Mrs Carlyon rounded on her. The argument continued bitterly until Mary burst into tears and rushed from the room.

'All right! All right!' said Josh wearily. 'You've proved your point, Mrs Carlyon. Sarah is still a sick girl. But when is she going to be better? When am I going to be able to see her and talk to her properly?'

'When I and the doctor say so,' replied Mrs Carlyon. 'Not one minute before.'

Josh's night without sleep was beginning to catch up with him fast. He felt weary and sick. Whatever he said, whatever anyone said, there could be no arguing with the look on Sarah's face when she saw him in the room, no way of explaining away her subsequent behaviour.

'You'll let me know when that time comes?'

'When she's quite well again, I will.'

'Very well. If you'll check to make sure she's all right now, I'll leave immediately and return to Sharptor.'

'Nonsense, Josh! You must stay for a meal and get some sleep.'

Josh shook his head. 'Thank you, but no. I was at St Cleer when I received Sarah's letter. I didn't stop to let anyone at the Wheal Sharptor know I was coming here.'

'Sarah isn't in her room. Mum! Dad! Sarah isn't here.'

The cry came from Mary.

Molly Carlyon ran from the room and Josh and William Carlyon followed as far as the hall.

Josh could hear the sound of doors being opened and slammed shut as Sarah's mother searched upstairs. Then she appeared at the head of the stairs, a frightened Mary beside her.

'Sarah isn't up here anywhere. Quickly now, search all the downstairs rooms. Mary, you look in the garden. Don't forget the shed.'

She advanced down the stairs. There was sheer hatred on her face as she looked at Josh. 'If anything has happened to that girl it will be all your fault.'

'That's enough, Molly,' said her husband. 'Had we not spent so much time arguing, this wouldn't have happened. I expect she's quite safe. Perhaps in the garden.'

But she was not in the garden. By now everyone was thoroughly alarmed. The search spread to the foundry where one of the apprentices said he thought he had seen her on a horse, leaving the works through the main gate.

'She turned right, as though she was going up towards the downs,' he said.

'It's a fine day. She'll come to no harm up there,' said William Carlyon.

'That's assuming she's gone to the downs,' said Mrs Carlyon. 'She hasn't been out of the house since she came home.'

It was Josh who noticed that Hector was not where he had left him near the front gate to the Carlyon house.

'The hostler might have put him in the stable,' said William Carlyon. 'I'll go and ask.'

'I hope he has,' said Josh. 'Hector doesn't get enough exercise these days. It's as much as I can do to hold him in check. Sarah would never control him.'

But Hector was not in the stables, and in the street outside Harvey's they spoke to an old man who had seen a girl with flowing golden hair galloping a horse out of Hayle along the St Ives road.

Josh and William Carlyon were the first to get mounted on horses belonging to Harvey's. Before they rode away from the works the manager left orders for every man who could ride to follow them and join in the search for Sarah.

'Have you any idea where she might be heading?' William Carlyon flung back over his shoulder as they sped along the open road. 'Was there a special place you were both fond of?'

'There were many,' Josh shouted back. 'But only one along this road, and I pray to God she hasn't gone there. It's dangerous enough for a well person.'

But his fears were soon realised. They found Hector with trailing rein and heaving sides, blowing, at the top of a steep and narrow track that clung to the sheer side of jagged cliffs. Below was a tiny patch of sand scarcely large enough for a smuggler's boat to ground on.

Twice on the way down Josh slipped. He prevented himself from falling only by clinging to the coarse grass growing in the crevices of the rock.

There was nothing to be seen at the bottom of the cliff, only the water of the high tide lapping at the rocks. Further out the swell from the Atlantic lifted over the natural breakwater and fell away again to reveal the ragged black teeth of rocks.

Josh was to remember those black rocks.

As more men arrived from Hayle the search extended for miles along the coast. But it was not until after midday, when the tide had ebbed away, that a man standing on the cliffs above called that he could see something caught in the rocks.

A fishing boat from St Ives, one of half a dozen called in by William Carlyon to join the desperate search, went perilously close to the rocks while Josh and the works manager watched helplessly from the shore, each hoping this would not be the end of the search.

They saw the boat swing broadside on to the rocks, the men at the oars straining to hold it off. Then one of the young men put down his oar, stripped off his jersey and plunged over the side. Twice he dived down into the water. The first time he came up for a moment to draw in a deep breath before diving again. The second time he was down a longer time and when he surfaced he was dragging something behind him.

The men in the boat leaned over the side to take it from him. As they pulled it from the sea those on shore could see it was the body of a girl.

Sarah Retallick had been found.

*   *   *

'You mustn't blame yourself, Josh. It was her state of mind. She didn't know what she was doing. It wasn't your fault.'

In spite of his own deep grief William Carlyon was far kinder than his wife had been. There would be nights when Josh would wake in a cold sweat hearing her voice screaming, 'Murderer!' At him.

'Whether it was my fault today or sometime in the past I'll never know,' said Josh.

He was mounted on Hector and ready to return to Sharptor. He was desperately weary with the events of the last twenty-four hours, but he could not bear to stay at Hayle for a moment longer. Sarah would be buried in the little Hayle cemetery and Josh did not want to be there. She would be buried bearing his name but that was all. Here, in this place, he was an interloper, not a part of the Carlyon family. He wanted to keep his own memories of Sarah. A beautiful girl with long fair hair who had shared a brief part of his life. He did not want to remember her as the battered disfigured body lying in the house behind him.

'Goodbye, Mr Carlyon. You've always been very kind to me. I thank you. I'm sorry to have brought such unhappiness to your family. But I grieve for Sarah too. . . .' He would not trust his voice further.

'I know you do, Josh. Don't take what Sarah's mother said to heart. She's very distressed. She doesn't really believe you are to blame. Come back and see us in a few months' time. You'll be made welcome. I promise you that.'

Josh shook his head. 'No, Mr Carlyon. I don't think we'll meet again.'

He reined the horse around and rode away from Harvey's works. Taking the road to the east, he was as tired as any man who had travelled the road before him.

Chapter Twenty-Four

The news of Sarah's death was doubly distressing for Jesse Retallick. She had been very fond of her son's wife and the suddenness and manner of her death came as a great shock. More, she dreaded what it would do to Josh. She believed he would resume the way of life he had taken up after Sarah had left Sharptor. She doubted whether her influence was sufficient to prevent him drinking himself into an early grave.

But, contrary to her expectations, Josh did not begin drinking again. Instead, he threw himself into his work with a vigour that awed those who were obliged to work alongside him.

He constructed the pump to force clean air into the newest working shaft in the Sharptor deep level, though the problems associated with it took a long time to solve. The greatest difficulty was to make the whole length of the tube airtight. But when it was completed the miners declared that the air brought in by Josh's air-pumping machine was fresher than any to be found elsewhere in the mine workings.

With this behind him, Josh set about making modifications to his man-lift. The royalties from it were beginning to come in regularly now.

There were other problems that summer. It seemed the politicians in London never learned by their mistakes.

There was a reversion to the corn policy which had resulted

in such hardship a few short years before. It meant that the bulk of the coming harvest would be sent to the towns and cities of the south-east and the new industrial centres of the Midlands. The Cornish farmer was expected to put the maximum acreage under corn, then send off his whole crop in accordance with Parliament's wishes.

This time it was not only the miners who raised their voices against the Corn Laws. The fishermen and farmworkers were also angry.

Because he had nothing to stay home for in the evenings, Josh was prepared to go anywhere to address a Miners' Union meeting. He threw himself wholeheartedly into their cause. He became a harder, more positive man. There were few hecklers at any of the meetings who would have cared to argue with him face to face.

All through that hot summer of 1845, Josh, William Thackeray and Miriam travelled around Cornwall addressing meetings. The Miners' Union was now an accomplished thing. At one evening meeting on the sands at Par, three thousand miners turned up to hear Josh and William Thackeray spell out what the corn policy would mean to the mining community.

'This has been a good harvest year,' shouted the preacher. 'The best we've seen this century. But what happens to the corn when it's harvested? Will the stomachs of our families be full? Will the miners of Cornwall go to work with enough food inside them to keep going through the long shifts ahead? No! The Cornish miner and his family will stay hungry. He'll watch the crops in the fields ripen, see them harvested and the corn gathered in; then he'll watch as it's loaded into wagons and hauled to the ports to be carried to the cities of England – and even to other countries! Are we going to stand by and allow such idiocy?'

There was a roar from the huge crowd. Cries of 'No!' 'Never!' Then a voice from their midst called, 'But what can we do about it?'

This was Josh's cue. Moving forward he towered above the small preacher.

'See your own Mine Union Committee. Join the benefit fund

so we know how many men are supporting us. If there's no committee in your own mine, start one. When the right time comes we'll tell you what to do. If we all stand together we'll succeed. There will be no corn leaving Cornwall until we're sure as much as is needed remains here.'

His words were received well. After a few more questions were answered the meeting broke up. Josh and William Thackeray left with a feeling they now had a large and organised movement behind them, one where its members were pulling in a single direction. It was no mean achievement, as any man who had ever tried to organise Cornishmen would know.

'Well, Josh,' said William Thackeray as they set their horses up the slope through Tywardreath, 'I think Parliament in London has done our task for us. The Cornish miners are united as never before. If only we can keep them together we'll be able to improve their lot a hundredfold.'

'That's if the militia doesn't interfere,' said Josh.

'What if they do?' declared William Thackeray jubilantly. 'The militia won't be able to keep the mines running if the men down tools.'

'The adventurers won't starve if the mines are closed for a while. The men will. The fund money won't last for ever, and with tempers running as hot as they are now someone will get hurt.'

'Don't be so parochial,' said William Thackeray. 'We must think of the cause as a whole. If the militia are called in and miners are hurt – or killed – public sympathy will swing to our side. Parliament and the adventurers will become so alarmed they'll have to give the men what they demand.'

'Tell that to the families of those who die,' retorted Josh.

Preacher Thackeray looked at Josh in exasperation. 'There are times when I find it difficult to understand you, Josh. You stand up in front of three thousand men and tell them what they want to hear. They roar their support for you, make it clear they would follow you if you took up arms against the Queen. Then you turn around and tell me you're concerned because a miner or two might get hurt. We're taking part in a revolution, Josh. A revolution of the workers. In revolutions men get hurt. That's accepted. These men are fighting for the future of all miners. We mustn't get squeamish now.'

'It sounds to me as though we are fighting for different causes,' said Josh. 'You're dreaming of some great movement of the future, a power to influence Parliament and change laws. That doesn't interest me. I believe in unionism for the same reason I built the man-lift. Because the lot of the miner is unnecessarily hard and dangerous. I want to see it made easier and safer.'

'Admirable sentiments, Josh. And extremely limiting to real progress.'

Josh smiled. 'Had anyone told you a few years ago that three thousand miners would attend one of your meetings, you'd have been delirious with joy. Today you've witnessed it, and you talk of "limited" progress.'

The preacher shrugged. 'When you have three hundred you dream of three thousand. When that's achieved you look for thirty thousand. That's ambition, Josh.' He kicked the horse into a canter. 'Miriam has a rabbit pie waiting for us tonight. Tomorrow will take care of itself.'

The subject came up again during the meal. Miriam agreed with Josh on the aims of the Miners' Union, but she was well aware of the ambitions of her husband and it was to him she spoke.

'What happens on the day you have your thirty thousand miners gathered together? You know well enough what they're like. If one says go north there will be three who want to go south. They will never be able to agree on a single policy.'

'Not if the matter is thrown open to discussion.' William Thackeray poured himself some more wine. 'But given the right leader they will do whatever he says is necessary.'

'And you will be that leader?' asked Josh.

'Who else? Unless yourself. Outside this room there is nobody with either the ability or the inclination to lead them.'

'For how long do you think you would be allowed to exert this power?'

'I'm sorry, Miriam. I don't understand.'

'No, because you've been too carried away by your successes to wonder where it might end. Calling meetings and discussing ways of improving the living standards of the miner is all right. It's part of a minister's work. Although there'll be a great many grumbles from the employers, nobody in authority can fault you for it. But march at the head of thirty thousand men with the intention of forcing Parliament to change the laws of the land and I think there will be a very different reaction.'

'I don't think you understand. I have no plans to put myself at the head of thirty thousand men and march anywhere.'

'No?' This from Josh. 'How else will you stop the grain from being exported from Cornwall?'

'Now you are both joining forces against me. We don't have thirty thousand men. Even if we had I've no intention of taking the miners anywhere. My plan is for the miners to blockade the ports peaceably, to prevent grain from being taken away until adequate provision is made for the Cornish miner and his family.'

'How do you propose to stop the grain from being moved? With words? Farmers are Cornishmen too, William. They can be as stubborn as miners. We don't like these corn policies, but they mean money for the farmer. He's not going to see that slip out of his hands because someone throws words at him.'

'The policy will change long before force becomes necessary,' said William Thackeray, a trifle too casually. 'Parliament is bound to see they are wrong. They won't allow women and children to starve. The united determination of the men will be sufficient.'

'That's not what you were saying when we left Par,' said Josh. 'You told me violence in revolution is acceptable. Yes, you did! And what is opposing the will of Parliament if not revolution?'

'Yes, and don't think you're going to appear at the ports of Cornwall with your miners and take everyone by surprise. It's too late for that. There has been so much talk of the miners uniting, the adventurers have become alarmed. Rumour has it the Somerset militia is being mustered for service in Cornwall. I spoke to a coachman today who saw part of a Welsh regiment passing through Bristol, heading this way.'

'Then I hope they have the sense not to interfere with any peaceable action taken by the miners,' said William Thackeray. 'That would certainly precipitate violence.'

'It would never come to that,' said Miriam. 'The Army will arrive first and arrest the men who lead the miners. That means you and Josh. I doubt whether you'll be as lucky as the leaders of the Kit Hill incident. They were only rebelling against the mine-owners. Your fight is with Parliament. They hang men for that.'

'I fail to understand you, Miriam!' Preacher Thackeray got up from the table abruptly. 'I thought you were as strong for the Union as I am. You've even spoken out for it at my meetings. What's happened to bring about this sudden change of heart?'

'I haven't changed, William. I'm as much for the Union as ever. But I think it would be better for everyone if you preached for law and order at your meetings. Made it quite clear you wouldn't condone violence under any circumstances.'

'What absolute nonsense!' Josh had seldom seen the preacher angry. 'What do you want me to do? Drop out of the movement at this critical stage? Are you telling me I should desert the miners because there might be trouble?'

'No.' Miriam was as calm as he was angry. 'I am merely saying that you should restrict what you say in public to matters affecting miners' welfare. Anything else should be discussed with a selected few of their leaders. In private.'

For a moment William Thackeray looked as though he had been struck dumb. Then he banged his fist on the table and let out a roar of approval.

'Did you hear that, Josh? Did you hear what she said? She has more brains in her head than you and I put together. She's right, of course. Absolutely right. I should have been the first to see it. If we carry on the way we are there will be a confrontation with the militia. That can have only one end for you and me. On the other hand, if we are heard to preach moderation what grounds could they possibly have for arresting us?'

'I've always favoured moderation. If a policy is bad the sooner it's abolished the better. But not at the cost of men's lives.'

'Of course, Josh. I agree with you. If the magistrates think trouble is simmering they'll order the arrest of those who are stirring it. From now on were going to do some very clever and serious planning.'

But changing the surface image of the Union was not easy. When public meetings were called, the men attending them expected to hear scathing attacks on the iniquitous corn policy. Instead, they received glowing reports of the benefits to be gained by belonging to the Miners' Union, were told of the safety measures provided in mines as a result of union representation. Questions about the Corn Laws were carefully side-stepped. If any answers were given they were variations on a theme of non-violence. For the ordinary miner it was a frustrating and baffling period. But on most nights of the week the chapel at St Cleer was occupied by groups of their leaders from mines in east and central Cornwall. And messengers galloped the roads of Cornwall with news and instructions for the masterplan that was being formulated.

What that plan was soon became clear. One farmer, more efficient than his fellows, eager to obtain a good price in the Bristol market, brought the first creaking wagon-load of corn down the steep lane to Boscastle harbour. He found the way blocked by two hundred grim-faced miners. There was no violence and little argument. But so impressed was the farmer by their determination he promptly turned around and sold the whole of his wagon-load in Camelford market, contrary to the orders of Parliament. The whole load was eagerly snapped up by buyers who paid a price equal to any he would have received elsewhere.

The news was hailed throughout the county as a miners' victory. The more naïve among them awaited the changes in the law they were sure it would bring about.

Parliament had other ideas. The rumours from Bristol had not been false. The Monmouth militia arrived. It was first billeted in Launceston, then split into smaller units to garrison other Cornish towns. The Somerset militia too moved into the county. But by far the most ominous threat to the hopes of the miners came when the 32nd Foot – Cornwall's own regular regiment – returned from overseas duty and moved into garrison at Bodmin. The men of the 32nd were disciplined battle-hardened soldiers who scorned all civilians, Cornish or not. On pay-nights they caused the citizens of Bodmin to shutter their houses and cower inside until the barrack gates closed on the last rowdy warrior.

One of these soldiers was Morwen Trago. He arrived at Preacher Thackeray's gate in St Cleer one evening as Josh was leaving.

Morwen looked very smart in the red-coated uniform with white cross-belts. The army life evidently suited him; he looked extremely fit and bronzed.

Josh expressed pleasure at meeting him and held out his hand, but Morwen Trago ignored it.

'What are you doing here, Retallick? I would have thought marriage had got you out of my sister's system. But perhaps her husband's away and you're just sniffing around.'

Josh had almost forgotten the tragic circumstances that had preceded Morwen's enlistment into the Army. He was unprepared for the sheer hatred that showed on Morwen's face.

'That uniform has done nothing to improve your manners, Morwen. Try not to disgrace Miriam when you meet her husband.'

Morwen Trago's eyes blazed angrily and Josh tensed, expecting the hot-headed Morwen to launch an attack on him. Instead, the soldier slammed the gate shut and stalked away along the path to the house. Morwen Trago was aware that his sister had achieved status in the community by marrying a preacher and he was keenly aware of his own lack of education. He had tried to make up for it by ensuring his uniform was immaculate – the white webbing cross-belts pure white, brass buckles gleaming. So determined was he to arrive in this state that he had ridden in the coach from Bodmin sitting upright, not allowing his back to rest against the seat lest his coat crease or dirt find its way on to his cross-belts.

Miriam was overjoyed to see him. William Thackeray stayed smilingly in the background while they reminisced about imagined good times in the past, intruding only to keep Morwen's tankard filled.

There was much to tell. Morwen had been away for four years and was not aware that Miriam had a baby. For her part, although she knew her soldier brother was abroad, Miriam did not know where he was serving. Morwen came into his own telling of the countries he had seen and battles he had fought and won there.

When the conversation between brother and sister showed signs of flagging Preacher Thackeray joined in.

'You've led a very interesting and active life since you left the mine, Morwen. You'll find things very much quieter in Cornwall, I'm quite sure.'

'Don't you believe it!' Ale and brandy coupled with the warmth of the room caused his cheeks to glow fiery red. 'They don't pay soldiers to sit on their backsides and play cards in the barracks, Preacher. They've got us down here for a reason.'

'A reason for the Army here in Cornwall?' Preacher Thackeray smiled.

'Ah! You'd be surprised if you only knew. We've been told this outcry against the Corn Laws is just an excuse to start a revolution, to overthrow Queen and Parliament – just as they did in France. But they'll have a surprise when they start here.'

'I'm quite sure they will.' Preacher Thackeray leaned back in his chair and looked at the half-drunken soldier. 'But I doubt whether your regiment would be sufficient to defeat the whole of the county should they choose to rise.'

'It isn't only our regiment.' Morwen waved his tankard unsteadily before his face. 'There's the militia – for what use they might be. They're coming from Wales, Somerset and Devon. Then there's the Navy.'

'The Navy!' It was difficult to see how the fleet could be used.

'Yes. The miners are trying to stop corn from leaving from the ports, aren't they? Well, they aren't going to succeed. The

Navy has its men-of-war sailing just outside the ports. At the first sign of trouble they'll come in and land their marines. With a regiment of foot soldiers and the marines against them the miners won't last a day. You can be damned sure of that!'

'Men-of-war, eh?' Preacher Thackeray mused. He looked at Morwen, who was now staring ahead of him glassy-eyed, the tankard dangling from a finger and dripping ale to the floor.

'I think I'd better help our guest up to the spare bedroom,' he said.

'No. He's my brother. I'll do it.'

'Then we'll both help him.'

Between them they got him up the stairs and laid him on a bed. Miriam removed his boots, undid his coat and covered him with a blanket.

'Poor Morwen,' she murmured when her husband had left the room. 'What a legacy our father handed on to you.'

When Miriam returned downstairs, William was pacing the floor of the lounge. 'So Parliament is expecting big trouble? Sending marines, militia and a regular regiment against us. They're taking this far more seriously than I thought they would.'

'You'll have to cancel your plans now, William. This makes things far too dangerous.'

'Cancel my plans? Nonsense! It will alter them, of course. But there's absolutely no question of cancelling anything.' He looked at her quizzically. 'Do you think Morwen could be persuaded to help us?'

'Never! You heard him yourself. He's overjoyed at the chance of fighting miners. He seems to imagine they are all responsible for the death of our father. No, he won't help us.'

'Then we'll just have to manage without him. One thing is clear. He's not aware of my involvement or he wouldn't have said as much as he did.'

'What does that mean?' Miriam gave him a curious look.

'It means that it might already be accepted my interest is purely in the welfare of the miner. Should that be the case I'll be able to lead them quite safely, in the manner suggested by yourself.'

'You can't intend opposing the export of corn now. Not after what has been said tonight? The miners will have no chance against soldiers and marines.'

'How long is Morwen staying with us?'

'Only until the morning. Then he's walking to Henwood to spend a day with Mother before returning to Bodmin.'

'Good. I'll call a meeting for tomorrow night. I have an idea.' A few days later Preacher Thackeray's plans began to take effect. A farmer loaded up two wagons of wheat for Charlestown harbour but at the end of the lane from his farm he was surrounded by forty tough and determined miners. Despite his protests he was escorted to St Austell market square where the load was disposed of for cash in a mere fifteen minutes. The farmer reported it to the magistrate only because he would otherwise have been held to account for the corn he had grown but not 'exported'. The price was a fair one and he returned home well pleased. The same thing happened to the next farmer. And the next. Then the militia was divided into even smaller detachments with orders to patrol every market town and prevent the sale of corn.

This too failed. The farmers were intercepted as they left their farms and taken to a nearby open space where buyers were waiting. The corn was auctioned off, transferred to waiting wagons, and the farmer escorted home to his farm to prevent the magistrates being alerted before the corn was spirited away to a safe hiding-place.

It was at this point that the angry military authorities brought a plan of their own into operation. The farmers were ordered to inform the nearest magistrate when corn was almost ready for delivery to the nearest port. A small party of militiamen would then accompany them to one of many large barns hired specially for the purpose throughout the county. A guard was placed on the barn until all the corn for that area was gathered in. Then, under full escort, it was taken to the nearest port. The idea worked. It was so effective that the authorities in the county told Parliament the matter was now fully under control. As a result the ships were withdrawn from around the seaports of Cornwall.

The miners too saw it as a defeat. At the open meetings where only two weeks before they had boasted of their victories they now condemned the Union for not staying one step ahead of the soldiers. There was anger and recrimination too at the secret meetings held in the chapel at St Cleer.

At first, William Thackeray shrugged off the setbacks suffered by the Union. They had achieved modest success and obtained some corn. They had stretched the resources of the military, forcing them to guard every load of corn all the way from the fields to the ports.

But this was not enough for the miners' leaders. When Thackeray saw the strength of popular feeling, he went along with it. He began to prepare for a more violent form of protest against the corn policy.

Josh was appalled. At one meeting he stood up and told the miners' representatives why.

'There is absolutely no excuse for the use of force now. Most families have corn. While it may not be as much as they might normally use, properly husbanded it will last the winter. There was corn rioting last weekend in Tavistock. Soon it will spread to other towns in Devon and Somerset and the whole of the West Country. If we remain patient we shall win. Parliament will have to change the law.'

John Kittow agreed. But miners have never been the most patient of men. Cornish miners were no different. They jeered at Josh's apparent timidity. They were not content to wait any longer. They wanted a showdown and now was a good time.

Had Preacher Thackeray sided with Josh they might have turned the tide of the argument. But recently the two men had failed to agree on many union principles. There were times when Preacher Thackeray felt jealousy at the respect the engineer commanded. He voted against Josh's moderate policy.

Perhaps there were other reasons too for the cooling-off in their relationship.

Before Morwen Trago had left the preacher's house after his first visit he had walked with William Thackeray in the garden. They spoke of many things, of the troubles in the country and the changes that had occurred in the mining industry since Morwen left it and joined the Army. When William Thackeray mentioned Josh's inventions in the field of mine safety, Morwen expressed his misgivings about the preacher becoming too friendly with the Sharptor mine-engineer. It was not wise, he said, in view of Miriam and Josh's close attachment in the past. Then he dropped his bombshell. He had heard some of his officers talking, he said. Josh's name had been mentioned in connection with the Union.

William said nothing then, but both reasons for Morwen's concern nourished seeds that were already planted in the preacher's mind.

After the latest meeting in the chapel at which much heat was generated without any firm decision being made, the miners' leaders dispersed to go their separate ways. Josh followed his established custom of going to the preacher's house for a drink and talk with William and Miriam. There the main points of the meeting were argued out again.

'Josh, I respect your reasoning and your concern for the Cornish miner, but yours is a short-term policy. You are interested only in the "todays". I am looking ahead towards the Union to which the sons of today's miners will belong. And their sons after them. Believe me, Josh, I know what I'm talking about. I've spent a lifetime dedicated to this cause. You're a mine-engineer and far too close to the men to know what might ultimately be best for them.'

'As a preacher you should be equally close to them. Promises for the future are words. Those who employ the Cornish miner have never been mean with talk. Your argument about the future is mere speculation. If we have patience we'll gain what we want. In this case sufficient corn to feed the men's families. Ordinary people all over the country are taking an example from our actions here. The corn policy will crumble and become history before the year is out. To use tactics that can only bring about a fight between the soldiers and the miners will damage your cause. They can't hope to win in a direct fight with authority. There would be bloodshed, arrests and transportations. Why, the soldiers could strike such a decisive blow it might cause resistance to the corn policy to fizzle, becoming nothing more than a bubble of angry words.'

But Thackeray had made up his mind which side he was backing. He would not be moved.

'On the contrary, if we don't take action now a stubborn Parliament could retain their policy for years to come. A direct confrontation with the soldiers and the militiamen would force their hand. Public outrage at the death of even a single miner would swing the opinion of the whole country to our side.'

'And what of the man who is dead?' asked Josh. 'He might become a symbol, a martyr. Will that help his family? And the others – those who are crippled or maimed in the fighting. Will people be so grateful they bring them a week's pay every Friday? No, William. Your ideas may help the cause of unionism. They won't help the miners of Cornwall.'

'I agree with Josh,' said Miriam, who had listened to the argument.

'Agreeing with Josh seems to be a habit with you,' snapped her husband angrily.

'I'm quite capable of forming opinions of my own,' retorted Miriam equally angrily. 'And I believe he's right. If I thought you were right I'd say – as I have so often in the past.'

'I wish I could believe that,' snorted William Thackeray. Turning, he left the room. A few seconds later Josh heard the front door slam shut. He started after the preacher, but Miriam stopped him with a hand on his arm.

'No, let him go, Josh. There'll be no reasoning with him while he's in this mood.'

'How do you know? Has he said things like that before?'

'Yes, but I say nothing and it soon passes.'

'Perhaps it would be better if I stayed away for a while. William and I no longer agree on what is best for the miners.'

'No, Josh. Don't desert me – us – now. William is ambitious to keep firm control of the Union. It's reached a point where he'll go along with whatever the majority wants. But, although you may not think so at the moment, he has great respect for your judgement. He's in need of your advice more than ever before.'

Her hands were gripping his arm tightly and she looked pleadingly up into his face.

'I *know* your way is right. I'll do my best to convince William of that. But I need your help.'

'All right.' Josh nodded his agreement. 'But it won't be for William's sake alone. The action the miners want to take would be disastrous for all of us.'

Chapter Twenty-Five

Late in August of that year Jenny Shovell gave birth to a son. News that she was in labour came to the Retallick house shortly after dusk. Jesse threw a shawl about her shoulders and gathered up a bag of all the things she considered to be necessary at a childbirth. Josh went along to the mine captain's house with her.

There was a light coming from every window. It looked for all the world as though Jenny were having a party instead of a baby. Some of the women from the village were already there, as were two shift captains and a number of the more senior Sharptor miners. Josh went in to wish Tom Shovell well and found the middle-aged mine captain as edgy and nervous as any young prospective father.

They were all talking in the kitchen when old Mary Crabbe came in. As her part in what went on upstairs was second only to that of the principal, the men stepped back respectfully to allow her through. She went to the wide iron stove and checked the water, speaking to none of the men and not looking at their faces. Satisfied that the water was sufficient she turned, making her way across the kitchen towards the door that led to the stairs. She had almost reached it when she stopped, her hand outstretched. It was as though someone had spoken to her. Turning, she looked at the faces of the men for the first time and her wild dark eyes came to rest on Josh.

Pointing a shaking bony finger at him, she shrieked, 'Out of this house, Josh Retallick. I'll deliver no baby beneath the same roof as you, or the curse on you will be laid upon the child.'

There was a horrified silence until someone at the rear of the room gave a nervous laugh. The sound enraged the old woman.

'Laugh if you will,' she screeched. 'But either Josh Retallick leaves this house or I do. And if I leave there'll be nothing to celebrate tomorrow.'

Tom Shovell looked apprehensively from the woman to Josh and back again, utterly bewildered.

'It's all right, Tom. I'm going,' said Josh.

'You'll leave because a crazy old woman says you must?' This from one of the younger miners who had no more superstition in his body than he had brains in his head. 'Ignore the old fool, Josh. It's the full moon. You know what she's like at such times.'

'Yes, there's a grown moon,' cackled Mary Crabbe, as though confirming the miner's judgement of her. 'But before there's another you'll have reason to know how crazy Mary Crabbe is.'

'Oh, come on, Mary!' This from one of the shift captains. 'Josh has had his troubles. Give the boy some luck now.'

'Troubles? They haven't begun for Josh Retallick yet.'

'You go upstairs and tend to Jenny, Mary,' said Josh. He was as superstitious as his father and his calm voice did not reflect his true feelings. 'Perhaps sometime you'll tell me what the future has in store for me.'

'If I thought it would do any good I would,' said the old crone. 'But if you mind the business of others you must expect to inherit their troubles. That's all I have to say.'

With that she shuffled from the room. When the door closed behind her everyone began talking at once.

'You don't really have to leave,' said Tom Shovell awkwardly.

'It's all right, Tom. I never intended staying. I came here with

Mother to wish you and Jenny well. I've done that. Now, since this is a night for predictions, I'll make one. I predict that you and Jenny will have a fine son who'll grow up to be a great mine captain. Like his father.'

The other men in the room chorused their agreement and Josh left the house. He waved back at them cheerfully but felt less happy inside. Mary was a true witch. He could not recall one firm forecast she had made that had not come true.

There had been too many witnesses in Tom Shovell's kitchen to keep Mary Crabbe's words secret. The following day a worried Jesse Retallick spoke to Josh about them.

'It's this stupid union business. There's been no sense in you since you finished your time at Hayle. I hoped when you married poor Sarah – God rest her soul! – you'd settle down. Instead . . . !' She made a gesture of resignation.

'I don't know what will become of you, Josh. You're a young man. Why don't you find yourself a nice girl and marry her? You could have the choice of any girl in the country. You've got a good job, money coming in from that lift-machine you made, and that fine house on the tor. I don't suppose you've been near there for more than a month – unless it's to feed and exercise that horse of yours.'

'The house was bought by William Carlyon for his daughter,' Josh replied with a scowl. 'I want no part of it. There's been little happiness there for me.'

'That's not the fault of the house. And didn't you tell me Mr Carlyon had written to say he'd bought the house for you and Sarah and it was now yours alone?'

'I don't want the house, and the last thing I want is to marry another girl and take her there. But if you want me to leave here I'll find somewhere else to live.'

'Now, what sort of a thing is that to say, Josh?' his mother flung at him. 'This has always been your home and will be for as long as you want it. I'm only thinking of you and your future. I want to see you settled and raising a family, not wasting your time with a crowd of no-good miners who are intent on stirring up trouble. These are uncertain times, Josh. We don't want any trouble with the soldiers.'

While they were talking Ben Retallick had appeared to be sleeping in his chair but now he stood up and crossed to the window.

'I thought I could hear something unusual while you two were arguing. It seems the soldiers aren't content to stay in their barracks waiting for trouble. They've come looking for it.'

Jesse hurried to join Josh and her husband at the window.

'Well I never! Now, there's an omen for you. One minute I'm talking to you about them. The next thing you know is they're outside. I can't ever remember seeing them about here before. I don't like it. It gives me a bad feeling.'

'Nonsense,' Josh laughed. 'They didn't just drop out of the sky. They've marched here from Bodmin.'

'I wonder what they're after?' frowned Ben Retallick. 'Even with the present troubles there is nothing for them about here.'

'I would say they're marching through the mining areas to remind us the Army's in Cornwall,' said Josh. 'But it's a stupid thing to do. The miners are in an ugly mood. It might well be the soldiers who are made to realise they are not fighting helpless savages.'

There were about sixty soldiers marching up the road from Henwood village. They made a smart formation, keeping time to a lone drummer. Taking the road below the cottages, they headed southwards towards the Phoenix and Caradon mines.

The steady monotonous beat of the drum travelled ahead of them, and along the way they had collected a motley following of miners' sons and farm-boys. The boys ran alongside, jeering and catcalling, or swaggered behind in ragged mimicry. There was none of the hero-worship of only a few short years before, when the army that had beaten Napoleon's soldiers was a welcome sight anywhere in the country.

'Let's take a walk up to Wheal Sharptor,' Ben Retallick said to Josh. 'I won't rest easy until I see the soldiers clear of the mine.'

But the soldiers appeared to have no designs on the Sharptor mine. As Josh and his father climbed the hill beyond Sharptor they saw the uniformed men turn down the track to the Phoenix mine, the drummer silent as the men broke step on the uneven surface.

'The fools!' exclaimed Josh. 'What do they think they're doing? They could hardly have chosen a worse time to visit a mine. If some of the Phoenix hotheads are still above ground there'll be trouble.'

'Then we'd best go down and see what we can do to stop it,' said Ben Retallick.

'No. You stay here and make sure none of the Sharptor miners go down and interfere. I'll see what's happening at the Phoenix.'

Josh set off through the ferns and heather of the steep hillside at a run. It was only a couple of hundred yards to the mine track but the soldiers reached the Phoenix before Josh.

The officer allowed the men to break ranks, and they stood around, arrogant in their smart uniforms, passing derisive comments about the state of the mine and the men and women working within their view. Some twenty surface-workers, young boys for the most part, watched them with wary curiosity.

'You there!' the officer beckoned to one of the lads. 'My men want a drink of water. Is there somewhere near at hand?'

A grizzled old miner limped from a nearby shed to give them their answer. 'We get ours from a pump outside the engine-house. But there's a horse trough along the way; that should do for you.'

There was an angry murmur from the soldiers and nervous laughs from the surface-workers. It was fortunate the mine captain arrived upon the scene at that moment. He was underground on one of the upper levels when the soldiers started down from the road. One of the young boys working on sorting ore had hurried to fetch him.

He left the officer in no doubt as to who was in charge of the Wheal Phoenix and let him know he and his soldiers were not welcome.

'What do you want here? And tell your men to stay clear of the machinery. Apart from the danger to them the crusher they are leaning against cost a lot of money and it's difficult to obtain spare parts.'

'I came here for water for my men and a place where they could rest and eat a meal,' said the officer.

'Water they are welcome to,' replied the mine captain and turned to one of the boys. 'Jimmy, go and fetch two buckets of water and a couple of mugs.'

He turned back to the officer. 'As for a rest and meal, this is a working mine; I'll not have my boys distracted while your soldiers lounge around eating. There's a whole empty moor around us. I suggest you find a place to camp and eat there.'

'That's hardly a sociable attitude to take,' said the officer. 'We are your county's own regiment just back from service abroad. We even have a man from your own village in our ranks. Indeed, I understand he worked in this very mine. And you tell us we are not to remain here for one minute longer than is necessary!'

'That's exactly what I'm telling you,' said the Phoenix captain firmly. 'And I've already seen Morwen Trago. He's welcome to come visiting at any time. But not when he's wearing the uniform of a soldier.'

'Then I think we'll go to the mine on the hill.' He nodded in the direction of Sharptor. 'Perhaps we'll receive more civility there.'

'Don't waste your time,' said Josh. 'The Wheal Sharptor is also a working mine. Soldiers would be as much in the way as here.'

'Oh!' The officer's eyes glittered angrily. 'Are the men of the Phoenix mine spokesmen for every mine in Cornwall?'

'I'm not from the Wheal Phoenix.' Josh moved to stand beside the Phoenix captain. 'My name is Retallick. I'm the engineer at Sharptor. My father is a shift captain and we both came out to make sure you didn't come visiting.'

'Retallick? I've heard that name before.'

'It's likely. Retallick's a common enough Cornish name. More Cornish, I should think, than your own.'

The officer flushed angrily. Although he had made the comment about it being a Cornish regiment, his accent placed him as coming from far to the east of the Tamar.

'Well, I have no wish to put a strain on the hospitality of such generous hosts,' said the officer. 'Fall the men in, Sergeant.'

He half-bowed towards them. 'Goodbye, gentlemen.' Looking directly at Josh, he said, 'I feel quite sure we'll meet again, Mr Retallick. I look forward to it.'

Placing himself at the head of his soldiers, he rapped out a command. The drummer started to swing his drumsticks and the soldiers marched from the Wheal Phoenix.

'I think we convinced them they aren't needed here,' said the mine captain.

'No doubt,' replied Josh. 'But they didn't tell us their reason for the visit. I'm sure they had one. Furthermore, I think they might have achieved it.'

He did not explain further but turned and made his way up the hill to Sharptor.

The harvest that had been going well was disrupted by a fortnight of heavy rain at the turn of that month. With a third of their crops still to be gathered in the farmers fumed impotently, swearing they could not remember a worse harvesting season, muttering about ruination. But it was only in the south-western counties of England. Throughout the remainder of the land the harvesting went ahead, and Parliament realised it was not only the Cornish who were upset by the unfair corn policy. Rioting took place throughout the land. What Josh had foreseen quickly came to pass. The men of the Monmouth militia were recalled to Wales. There the fiery Welsh coal-miners were showing their displeasure in a far more violent manner than the comparatively placid Cornish.

During this period the meetings held in the St Cleer chapel became even more divided about the form of their future action. A few came over to Josh's side, sensing that the increasing national unrest must mean a reversal of Parliament's policy on the corn issue. The others, following

Preacher Thackeray's lead, clamoured for more violent action to be taken in Cornwall.

The division between the two opposing groups became so deep and the arguments so bitter that, in spite of his promise to Miriam, Josh no longer visited the preacher's house. Because he missed the stimulus of conversation with William Thackeray and the pleasure of being in the same room as Miriam, he tried once to bridge the gap between them. But the preacher would not unbend. The easy comradeship that they had once known perished in the bitterness of their opposing convictions.

When the rains ceased and the muddy water-filled tracks became passable once more, the farmers resumed the harvesting of their crops and forgot their prophecies of doom.

It was now that rumours began to circulate among the miners that they had obtained far less corn than had been thought. They were told there was insufficient to keep their families fed through the winter months.

This was not true. Josh knew it and so did the miners' leaders. But still the rumours persisted. The clamour to keep the remainder of the corn harvest in Cornwall grew.

Quite how they would achieve it nobody seemed to know. Despite their reduction in numbers the soldiers were still escorting farmers' wagons and their grip on the situation was as tight as before.

Inevitably, it seemed, the scene was being set for violence. It came on a beautiful hot day in late September. There was hardly a cloud to scar the blue sky. A pair of lazy buzzards wheeled and dipped high over Twelve Men's Moor. Above the red waste of the Sharptor mine a pair of very late swifts screamed in a breakneck dive, skimming the dusty earth with their scythe-like wings, gathering insects and building up strength for the long flight south.

Josh had been helping the engine-men to renew the padding in the main piston of the whim-engine. He was cleaning his hands in the tub outside the engine-house when a convoy of coal-laden wagons creaked into the mine, returning from the canal-head at Moorswater.

'They've got themselves a parcel of trouble up at Wheal Caradon,' called old Nehemeziah Lancellis as he climbed stiffly down from the lead wagon. 'Someone along the way told me to tell you the whole blessed mine be closed.'

'Oh!' Josh was instantly interested. 'What's happened? Have the adventurers cut their pay and caused the men to walk out? They should be working extra time up there. They've a flooded shaft to clear.'

'Ain't nothing to do with the mine.' Nehemeziah spat into the dust. ''Tis this damned corn business. Whole lot of 'em downed shovels. Gone to Looe to stop a corn boat leaving. Damn fools, the lot of 'em.'

'That's ridiculous!' Josh was alarmed. 'They know the soldiers are at Looe. They would as soon shoot a miner as a rabbit.'

'Don't know about such things,' said old Nehemeziah. 'But I was to tell you where they'm heading. Spoiling for a fight, I was told.'

'The idiots! Who was leading them, do you know?'

The hostler snorted. 'No. Might just as well ask which starling leads a flock. They'd be just a-going. Shouting and calling with no leader at all.'

'I wonder whether Preacher Thackeray is with them?'

Nehemeziah's laugh was short and derisive. 'Preacher Thackeray? He won't raise his head 'bove water when trouble's around. Thought you'd a' known that. He's the spoon as does the stirring, not the pot as sits on the fire.'

'Have you any idea what time they left?' Josh's mind was racing ahead. The men were on foot. If the Army had not got wind of their approach and made moves to intercept them it might be possible to take a horse and head them off.

'Don't know. I got news of it an hour ago. They'd be well on the way now.'

The chances of preventing the miners from reaching the port were very slim indeed, but Josh would try.

'I've got to get out of these greasy clothes, Nehemeziah. Send someone to saddle Hector for me and bring him down here.'

'You're not going to Looe? 'Tis mad! If they're stupid enough to want trouble, let 'em have it. It need be none o'your business.'

'They are miners, Nehemeziah, the same as us. Go and get my horse saddled.'

Nehemeziah walked away, muttering to himself and shaking his head. There were problems enough in earning a living without getting involved with men from other mines who wanted to fight soldiers.

Josh was not the only one worried about the Caradon miners. He was a mile out from Looe, with the steep wooded slope on one side, the muddy brown tidal waters of the Looe river on the other, when he caught up with John Kittow. The Caradon miner's leader was bouncing along on a pack-horse that had seen better days.

'Fools! Bloody fools!' was all he seemed able to say when Josh reined in beside him.

'What are their plans?' asked Josh. 'What are they hoping to do?'

'Plans!' exclaimed John Kittow, sweating and angry. 'They've no plans. They're going to keep the corn from being loaded on to a ship. That's all I know. I doubt if they've thought beyond that.'

'Weren't you able to stop them? They usually listen to you.'

'They might have listened to me, had I been at the mine.' The shift captain swore. 'I was over to Callington to hire a couple of blacksmiths. When I got back it was a mine without miners. How did you find out about it?'

Josh explained. 'And I hope we'll be in time to avoid bloodshed.'

John Kittow kicked the pack-horse with renewed vigour, provoking it into an ungainly trot.

Rounding a bend down the hill into Looe town, Josh and John Kittow became aware they were already too late. The roar of a large crowd of angry men greeted them. The sounds came from the wharf just beyond the arched bridge. On the bridge itself were farmers' wagons, tailed back to the western bank of the river. The soldiers who had been acting as escorts were forming up close to them. But these were not foot-soldiers.

They were mounted, wearing the blue jackets and plumed helmets of Dragoon Guards.

Josh kneed Hector forward, passing the dragoons as the order was given for them to draw sabres. Beyond the bridge the scene at the dockside was even worse than he had feared. There must have been six or seven hundred miners, the Caradon men having received support along the way. They were packed in a tight swaying mob on the open jetty, spilling out into the narrow streets and alleys of the town.

The small harbour was crammed with shipping, and sailors swarmed the rigging of the ships the better to view the shoreside happenings.

There were fifty wagons of corn drawn up at the water's edge, white-faced farmers and farmers' men fingering the reins of their horses uncertainly. Between the wagons and the angry miners a line of red-coated soldiers stood with guns held at the ready.

An officer was arguing with a small group of miners, none of whom Josh recognised as from the Wheal Caradon. But the officer was the same one who had led his men into the Wheal Phoenix. Josh spurred his horse forward into the crowd. After offering initial resistance, the men moved aside for him and John Kittow. He heard miners call their names as they arrived at the far edge of the crowd.

Even at this late stage it might have been possible to avert bloodshed, although a magistrate had already been to the wharf and proclaimed the Riot Act to the miners, declaring them officially a 'riotous assembly'. This was sufficient in a court to justify any violence that might be used against them. It is doubtful whether any of the miners fully realised the seriousness of their position. They had no capable leader, only hotheads like those who were arguing with the officer on the quayside.

Josh and John Kittow had hoped to persuade the miners to return to their homes peaceably once they had made their protest. They never had an opportunity to try. Exactly what was said to precipitate the disastrous scenes that followed was never clear. But in the middle of the heated argument the officer grabbed the shirt-front of one of the miners. He attempted to drag him back towards the soldiers. The miner struggled and struck out wildly. At the same time, two of the men with him began raining blows upon the officer until he fell to the ground with one of the miners on top of him.

This was sufficient for the sergeant with the platoon. At a hoarse command every second man in the line dropped to one knee. Rifles aimed at the seething mass of miners. Before a horrified Josh could do or say anything, a volley of shots rang out. When the drifting acrid smoke cleared, a second volley followed.

There were alarmed shouts and screams. Half a dozen miners lay sprawled on the ground. Those immediately behind them turned and pushed away from the red-coated soldiers. Slowly, as realisation of what had happened dawned on the miners, the whole crowd began to move forward with them – only to find their retreat barred by the mounted Dragoon Guards. They had advanced from the bridge with drawn sabres and now bore down upon the totally defenceless miners.

The mounted dragoons began hacking about them as soon as their horses were among the miners, and the crowd broke, the miners trying to escape as best they could.

Josh rode at the foot soldiers, calling on them not to fire as their guns came to the aim position once again. He was too late. Another volley was fired and more miners slumped to the ground. Josh kneed Hector forward among the soldiers, bowling some over as they fired yet again. Some of the miners found an escape route through two narrow alleyways at the side of the jetty. They fought and struggled to get away from the scene of carnage behind them.

Josh turned his horse again, pleading with the soldiers not to shoot, only to find himself caught in the charge of the dragoons. Frightened by the noise, Hector reared, crashing down against the horse ridden by one of the dragoons. The soldier's mount slipped on the smooth cobblestones and crashed to the ground, carrying its rider with it.

Then Josh was in the middle of the hacking, slashing sabres

of the dragoons. A steel blade slashed across his back and a burning pain seared through the great muscles of his shoulders. Then Hector too stumbled and Josh was thrown to the ground. He clambered to his feet and in front of him, not fifteen feet away, was the officer in charge of the foot soldiers. Bloodied and bruised, he pointed in Josh's direction and called upon his men to shoot.

'Get him! Get that man! I want him!'

All was utter confusion now. Men were running in every direction. Foot soldiers, horse soldiers and miners running or fighting all over the wide jetty. There were also a great many still figures lying on the ground – not only miners but also blue-coated dragoons and hatless scarlet-coated soldiers. Josh saw an opening between the horses of the dragoons and ran for it. From somewhere close behind a gun roared and it felt as though someone had struck him a hard blow in the left arm. He spun about and a horse collided with him, knocking him to the ground again. Picking himself up, he clutched his left arm just above the elbow. Hot blood oozed between his fingers. Then, miraculously, John Kittow appeared beside him, still mounted and with Hector's reins held in his hand.

'Quick, Josh! Get up. Hurry!'

Josh swung himself into the saddle. Urging his horse forward he clattered after the Caradon miner, ducking his head low as they swung through a passageway between houses. Then they were out on a street with shuttered shops on either side and people running beside them.

Josh followed John Kittow along the road. They galloped past the bridge and out of the town, back along the road that had brought them into Looe a scant fifteen minutes earlier.

Soon they were clear of the fleeing miners but they rode hard for another mile before John Kittow pulled his horse in alongside Josh. By now the fire in Josh's back was burning fiercely, his arm throbbing alarmingly.

'My God, Josh! You're a bloody mess. Get off here. Let me have a look at those wounds. No, further down by the river. I'll need water to clean you up.'

They walked the horses down to the water's edge where Josh

swung from Hector's back, staggering as his feet touched the ground.

'Sit down while I get your shirt off.'

The miner stripped Josh's shirt from him without ceremony, ripping it away from his body; then he dipped his neckerchief into the river and began cleaning Josh's wounds. The river was tidal, the water salt. It stung. John Kittow grunted in sympathy. The wound in Josh's arm was quickly cleaned. The musket-ball had gone straight through cleanly, without touching the bone. Josh's back was a very different matter. It was laid open from the left shoulder to the right of his waist, laying bare the large muscles around his shoulder-blade.

'I don't like the looks of this, Josh. You must see a doctor as quickly as we can reach one.'

'It had better be a doctor well away from here,' said Josh, gritting his teeth against the pain of the salt water, 'or I'll have more than a wound to worry about.'

He gasped as John Kittow wrung more water into the wound.

'There was something I didn't understand back there, Josh. I heard the officer call your name just before you were shot, and I'd swear it was Morwen Trago who fired. Why?'

'That officer brought his men on a march around the mines,' explained Josh. 'I told him he wasn't welcome at Sharptor. I told him my name and he said he'd heard of me. I doubt very much if the wound in my arm was the result of a chance shot.'

'No. It was you they were after. And if they know your name they'll come for you at Sharptor.'

'We'll worry about that when we get there. The only good thing to be said for it is if they were so interested in me it might mean that you weren't recognised. Can you bind my back, John?'

John Kittow stripped off his own shirt and began tearing it into strips.

'I'll do what I can, but it won't last long, Josh. It's no more than an attempt to staunch the bleeding.'

They heard a ragged crackle of musket-fire in the distance and both men looked back towards Looe.

'God! It sounds as though the slaughter is still going on. Who were those fools arguing with the officer, John?'

'I don't know. They weren't from the Wheal Caradon. Most likely they came from the St Austell area.'

He laid a strip of damp cloth along the line of the sabre-cut, binding the remainder of the two shirts around Josh's body to hold it in place.

'That will have to do for now, Josh. Can you get back on your horse?'

Josh nodded, with more assurance than he felt. When he stood up the countryside swung about him. With John Kittow's help he managed to climb back into the saddle and cling there.

They set off again, following the line of the canal towards Moorswater. They were almost there when they heard the clatter of horses' hoofs on the road behind. Pulling their horses off the bridle path they hid in a small copse and watched six dragoons ride past at the gallop.

'Do you think they're looking for us?' asked John Kittow when the soldiers were out of sight.

'Probably. If they are they'll warn the militia at Liskeard. We'd better stay well clear of the town.'

By the time they reached the head of the canal, Josh was reeling in the saddle.

'You can't possibly ride any further, Josh. We must find somewhere for you to rest while I go on ahead and fetch a doctor.'

'No.' Josh felt sick. The blood from his back had run down inside his trousers and dried, making him stiff and uncomfortable. But he knew they had to keep moving.

Two miles further and the sun had almost disappeared over the western moor. The trees cast long shadows across the narrow lane along which they were riding. Suddenly Josh slumped over the pommel of his saddle and would have fallen had it not been for John Kittow.

'You're in no fit state to ride any further Josh. . . .'

'I'll be all right in a few minutes.' It came out as a mumble. Josh rested both hands on the horse's neck, trying to ignore the pain that burned through his arm and back.

Another mile put them on to the moor west of St Cleer and Josh could ride no further.

'We'll make those rocks up ahead,' said John Kittow. 'I'll leave you there and go on for the Caradon doctor.'

'No. Keep clear of the mine,' gasped Josh. 'There will be soldiers there by now. Go into St Cleer and fetch the doctor. The young one. I know him. Tell him what's happened.'

At the rocks he tumbled from his horse into the arms of John Kittow, who lowered him to the ground only half-conscious. John Kittow propped him up and left him with his good shoulder resting against one of the rocks. Hector's reins twisted about his wrist.

'I'll be back in half an hour,' promised the miner.

Josh could do no more than nod.

It was a clear night with a full moon balancing on the horizon when John Kittow rode off.

Hector woke Josh from an exhausted sleep by shaking his head and jerking on the reins. Looking up, Josh saw the moon high in the sky above him. It must have been well after midnight. John Kittow had been gone far too long. Something was wrong.

Then he heard the sound which had disturbed Hector. It was the jingle of harness. Painfully and stiffly he rose to his feet and held Hector's head still, relying on the shadow of the rocks to hide him as horsemen passed along the track not twenty yards away. They were troopers. He felt sure they had something to do with the non-return of John Kittow and were now searching for him.

When they disappeared from view and he could no longer hear the sound of their horses' harness he mounted Hector, the effort causing the blood to flow once more from the wound in his back. He kneed the horse forward, heading away from the track, out on to the moor. He was not familiar with this particular area and trusted to luck and the intelligence of his horse to keep them clear of moorland bogs. Luck was with him. It was not long before they arrived at a part of the moor he knew well. Now he could move forward with more confidence. Here he had no need of tracks or paths and travelled in a straight line across the moor, heading for Sharptor and the cottage of his parents.

It was fortunate he had stayed clear of the paths. As he picked his way down the last hillside close to the cottage Hector slipped, dislodging a stone. Josh heard an exclamation of surprise from someone standing in the shadows to one side of the cottage.

'Who's there?' It was the soldiers. They had been expecting him and were waiting.

Josh pulled Hector about in a tight turn, hoping they were foot soldiers. His hopes were swiftly dashed. He heard the creak of leather as the dragoons mounted hurriedly. A single shot was fired at him but the ball sped harmlessly through the undergrowth twenty feet away.

Then horses were crashing through the bracken and he coaxed Hector into a canter. The movement jarred his wounds unmercifully. He would be unable to keep going in this manner for very long. When Hector broke clear of the tangled moorland undergrowth on to a path, Josh urged the horse to move faster still.

Another shot hummed past him, closer this time. The dragoons had also found the path. He could not outrun them with a tired horse. His only chance lay in outwitting them. Crouching as low as the pain in his back would allow, he coaxed Hector into a gallop in an effort to gain some distance. In spite of its tiredness the big horse responded magnificently and Josh risked a quick glance behind him.

He could not see the dragoons but he could hear them shouting. He had to act now.

Pulling the horse to a halt he jumped awkwardly from the saddle. Slapping its haunches, he called, 'Go, Hector! Give them a run, boy.'

It was as though the big horse understood. With head high it set off at a gallop into the night, leaving Josh to sink down into the tall ferns, a few feet from the path.

The dragoons were well spread out as one by one they passed the place where Josh was hiding. When the last of them had pounded into the distance Josh stood up and weaved his way across the hillside.

He knew where he was going. He had not been there for some years but he had no trouble finding it. He was wider across the shoulders than he had been years before and the tunnel through the gorse was slightly overgrown. As he crawled through it, a stiff needle-loaded branch scraped along his back, touching a part of the wound from which the rough bandage had slipped. He almost fainted with the pain of it. But he made it to the shelter of the rock hideout safely and collapsed on to his face in relief. The soldiers would not find him here. He was safe. Here a man could live with his freedom. Or die with it.

Josh was right in assuming that something had gone seriously wrong with John Kittow's quest for a doctor.

When the miner galloped into St Cleer he became immediately aware that news of the fight at Looe had reached the village ahead of him. Few of the houses did not have lamps glowing brightly in their windows. People clustered around doorways, talking excitedly. They were mostly women, for a large percentage of the men from here were Caradon miners. Their fate would affect the community deeply.

Dismounting at the doctor's house, he tethered his horse and banged heavily on the door. It was opened by the doctor's wife. She shook her head in answer to his question.

'No, the doctor is not in. He heard about the shootings at Looe and went there in case he should be needed. He rode off almost two hours since.'

'The news must have arrived very quickly,' said John Kittow. 'Who brought it?'

'Soldiers. They were here looking for some of the miners' leaders who had escaped on horses.

As he and Josh were the only two men belonging to the mining community who had been on horseback at Looe, John Kittow knew that it meant that the soldiers were looking for them.

He thanked the doctor's wife and turned away at a loss as to his next move. Josh needed a doctor urgently but it would be difficult to find one at this time of the night – especially one he could trust. None of the mine doctors would risk incurring the wrath of the adventurers by treating anyone associated with the militants of the Miners' Union.

Leading his horse along the St Cleer road John Kittow suddenly thought of Preacher Thackeray. Even if he were unable to recommend a doctor he might take Josh into his house to await the return of the St Cleer doctor.

John Kittow was a sound reliable shift captain. He knew mining and he knew miners. But he did not have a quick enquiring mind. If he had, he might have wondered about the number of horses tethered near the preacher's house. As it was, his mind was too full of other things. He hurried to the door, banged hard upon it and when it was opened by a pale wide-eyed Miriam he immediately blurted out, 'Where's Preacher Thackeray? I must see him. Josh is badly hurt.'

When the uniformed figure of Morwen Trago stepped into the light behind Miriam, John Kittow was stunned. By the time he recovered his presence of mind it was too late. Morwen Trago pushed his sister aside and grabbed the miner, at the same time calling for assistance. Two dragoons rushed from the shadows alongside the house and John Kittow was a prisoner.

They dragged him into the house and pushed him into a chair in the kitchen. Triumphantly, Morwen Trago said, 'So my shot didn't go astray. Where did I hit Josh? Where is he now?'

'Don't tell him!' The cry came from Miriam Trago. Her brother strode across the room and bundled her into the passageway outside. Returning, he made one of the dragoons stand against the door. He continued his questioning with Miriam banging helplessly on the other side.

'I'll ask you again. Where's Josh Retallick?'

John Kittow glared at him and said nothing.

'Don't be stupid, Kittow,' said Morwen Trago. 'Trying to protect him will do no good. We'll catch him sooner or later.

It won't be well received at your own trial if it comes out that you protected him.'

'My trial for what? All Josh and I did was try to stop the miners causing trouble. We arrived too late. You and your murderous soldiers fired on them before we could speak to them.'

'That's a likely story,' grinned Morwen Trago. 'You and Josh Retallick were there leading them, inciting them to violence, causing them to attack us. If we hadn't fired when we did they would have overrun us.'

'You're a liar, Morwen Trago. A true son of your father.'

Morwen Trago's eyes blazed and he moved as though to strike the shift captain.

Instead he shrugged and said to the dragoons, 'You'd better take him off to Liskeard lock-up. We'll find Josh Retallick sooner or later. Dead or alive.'

'Wait a minute,' John Kittow shouted. 'I came here to see Preacher Thackeray. He'll know I'm telling the truth. Where is he?'

'I doubt whether my brother-in-law would prove anything of the sort,' replied Morwen Trago smugly. 'He was here when everything was happening. He heard of the troubles only when we arrived and told him. Now he's gone to see what he can do to comfort the miners you and Josh Retallick misled into such a stupid venture.'

He signalled to the dragoons. 'Take him away. Enough has been said.'

John Kittow and the dragoons were halfway along the pathway before Miriam caught up with them.

'Wait!'

The dragoons halted.

'John! Do you know where Josh is now? Is he very badly hurt? Please tell me. I want to help him.'

'As your brother helped him – with a musket-ball?' asked John Kittow, both scorn and sadness on his face. 'Or as your husband would have helped him? He knew this was going to happen, didn't he? He could have prevented it had he wanted to. But I doubt whether there'll be any sorrow in his heart when he learns Josh has landed himself in trouble. Yes, Josh is badly hurt. He's lost a lot of blood. But I don't think he'd thank me for telling you and these soldiers where he is. If he's going to die he'll die a free man. Not in some stinking prison.'

If John Kittow had seen the look of anguish on Miriam's face as she watched the dragoons ride away with him between them he might have had more sympathy.

But in the place to which he was going thoughts of self-preservation had a habit of submerging all sympathy for others.

The Reverend William Thackeray was feeling well pleased with himself and the feeling blossomed into elation before he reached St Cleer. The miners had lost a fight today, it was true. The soldiers had beaten them in a bloody one-sided battle. Miners had died.

Yet in death they had turned defeat into victory. When the bodies of the dead miners were being carried home from the port Thackeray had witnessed whole villages turning out for them. Not understanding what it was about, young children, roused from sleep, stood in their night attire. Alongside them the older members of the families stood with bowed heads, flickering candles in their hands, paying respect to the murdered men of Cornwall.

The soldiers out in strength patrolling the lanes and roads around Looe town saw it too and were uneasy.

William Thackeray's elation stepped across the threshold of his cottage with him but went no further.

'Where's Josh? What's happened to him?'

'My dear, how can I have seen Josh? I've come straight from Looe town. I did what I could to help the miners I met on the way. Josh was not among them.'

'Are you saying you had nothing to do with Josh going to Looe to try to turn back the miners?'

'If Josh went to Looe with the miners for any reason whatsoever it was foolish in the extreme. It would be difficult for a man to profess he was peaceable if he formed part of the mob that fought in Looe today!'

'And his being out there somewhere badly hurt is not a result of your scheming? You swear it?'

'*My* scheming! My dear Miriam, it was you who advised me to preach peace and not violence. You and Josh – remember? I can hardly be blamed for the outcome of Josh ignoring his own advice.'

'So you know of no reason why Morwen should come straight to this house to boast of shooting Josh himself?'

'Should I know what goes on in the mind of *your* brother? Why, I don't understand you much of the time. Now, for instance perhaps you'll explain why you accuse your husband of all manner of treacheries and work yourself up into such a state about one who should be part of your past? Do I have to remind you that you are my wife?'

'No, William. I need no reminding. But when it's my turn to compete with your ambitions I doubt I'll fare any better than your friends.'

Before William Thackeray could make a reply Miriam turned and ran upstairs to Daniel's bedroom and he heard the bolt being secured on the inside of the door. Josh slept fitfully through the night. His wounds were paining him. John Kittow had been telling Miriam the truth when he told her Josh had lost a lot of blood. Twice he heard horses passing along the path beyond the gorse-passage. The soldiers had caught Hector and were back-tracking in an attempt to find the place where he had escaped from them. But they would find nothing in the darkness. By the time the sun rose they would have so confused any tracks he might have made they would never find them. They would probably not even be sure which track they had been on. He was quite secure where he was for the moment. Later he would make his way to a place where he could obtain food and medical attention. He realised that would only be the beginning of his problems. But he was in no state to start thinking about his future.

When next he woke the sun was high in the sky above him. This time it took him a few minutes to place where he was. He felt stiff. Painfully stretching his limbs he tried to stand. But during his exhausted sleep he had moved, causing his back to bleed excessively. There was blood on the earth beneath him and he was much weaker than he wanted to believe. After much painful effort he made it to his feet. He stayed upright for a few seconds only before feeling so sick and giddy he sank to the ground again.

It was another hour before his mind cleared sufficiently for him to be aware of the sounds about him. In the distance was the steady thump-thump of the Sharptor mine-engine. Still further away the mixed noises of the Wheal Phoenix. Somewhere above him he could hear the mewing of a buzzard, and at least two larks hovered on the wing nearby.

Out there it was a normal moorland day. Life was going on without him as though nothing had ever happened. But Josh was aware his life would never be the same again. It was all a bad dream. Only the severe pain in his back and the dull throb of his arm effectively convinced him it was all very real.

He wondered what his mother was doing. She would be worried to distraction. Ben Retallick would be going about his work at the mine, replying to anyone who asked that Josh knew what he was doing, that he would be safe somewhere waiting for all the excitement to die down. But what of John Kittow? What had happened to prevent him from returning from St Cleer?

The questions went through his mind in quick succession, but of more immediate concern was what was likely to happen to himself. He hardly possessed the strength to stand, let alone leave the hideout to forage for food. But without food he would only lie here growing steadily weaker. With these thoughts in mind he tried once more to get to his feet. This time he used the rocks as support. It was easier. He shuffled the few steps necessary to see out through a small aperture between the rocks that gave him a view over the needle-spined gorse beyond.

He saw soldiers, red-coated ones, beating through the undergrowth five hundred yards distant. But they were beating up the slope, working steadily away from his position. That was hopeful. They could have no idea of his possible whereabouts, might even have already searched the area where he now was. But it did mean he could not risk leaving the hideout yet.

He looked up at the sun. It was still early afternoon. There was no hope of contacting anyone during daylight. It would be risky enough in the dark. The soldiers would be expecting him to come out of hiding then. He sank back on to the dry earth, tired and with a strong feeling of hopelessness. Tucking his good shoulder into a crevice in the rocks he rested his face against the rough granite warmed by the sun. He was in a desperate mess and could see no way out of it.

He was still crouched in that position when Miriam found him soon after sunset that evening. Word had come back to St Cleer that he had been chased into the darkness above the Retallick cottage, that the soldiers had taken his horse only a mile away. Immediately, Miriam had known where Josh was hiding.

She had brought food with her. When she saw Josh lying so still her first thought was that she was too late, that he was dead. But when she dropped to her knees and touched his face his eyelids flickered open. He looked at her with uncomprehending eyes.

When he tried to speak Miriam whispered, 'Shh! Keep your voice very low. I've got some food and some bandages. Are you badly hurt, Josh?'

'I don't know. I think my back's on fire, although my arm throbs more. But how . . . ?'

'John Kittow told me you were hurt last night before they took him away.'

'Took him away? Who? Why? He did nothing wrong. He went to Looe to try to stop the miners. We both did. . . .'

He sank back against the rock. 'But I don't expect the soldiers to believe that. I knocked a dragoon from his horse.'

'No, they don't believe it. They are saying you led the rioting. That John Kittow was with you. He's to appear before the magistrate tomorrow. He'll then go to Bodmin Jail to await trial – when they've caught you.'

'But William knows the truth of it. He knows I've always

been against any form of violence. John Kittow felt the same way. William can tell them. He will tell them.'

Miriam's expression changed. 'No, Josh. You mustn't expect William to say anything, for or against you.'

'But he must, Miriam! He knows John and I are innocent.'

'He *knows* nothing, Josh. He wasn't there when the rioting took place. You were.'

'But he can tell them what went on before. He knows the arguments I've put forward at meetings. That I've always declared against violence. He can tell them that.'

'And admit to the court that he's one of the leaders of the Union, Josh? No, expect nothing from William and you're not likely to be disappointed.'

There was bitterness in her voice which she made no attempt to hide from him. 'Besides, I don't think he'll be in Cornwall very much longer. He's been called to London to appear before the Conference. I believe the Church wants to know about his activities here.'

'Will he go?'

'To answer the charges, yes. But wherever they send him he'll always be a union man. So he intends leaving here as the leader of a successful campaign. There's already news that Parliament is so alarmed by what's happening that they've stopped the export of corn from Cornwall and other country districts.'

Josh sagged visibly. 'Then the miners were right after all. Their way was the only way to get results.'

'No!' Miriam was trying to unwind the cloth from about Josh's body. She was having difficulty in separating it from the wound where the blood had dried through it. 'No, Josh. There wouldn't have been time for news of the fight at Looe to have got to London and action to have been taken because of that. I believe you were right. That Parliament had made their decision before the miners marched on Looe. If only they had been a little more patient there wouldn't be seven of them lying dead and many more wounded. Parliament doesn't care what's going on here in Cornwall. We're so far away that by the time the news of what's happening reaches them it's no longer news. It's the general unrest throughout the land that's forcing them to change their policies. That and farmers who are refusing to grow corn again because of the danger it's put them into.'

Josh gasped in pain as Miriam pulled out a piece of cloth embedded in the wound.

'I'm sorry, Josh.'

Miriam tried to keep her feelings hidden from him. What she was looking at, in the light of a stub of candle pushed well back into a crevice in the rocks, was a terrifying wound. Across the small of his back it was little more than a scratch. But from the shoulder to the bottom of his ribs it was a wide open gash. She had brought water with her and some herbal balm which old Mary Crabbe made up as an antiseptic. She dressed the wound as best she could.

'You should really see a surgeon and have this wound drawn together. There's little I can do to help it heal. Now, let me have a look at that arm.'

She treated the bullet wound in a similar manner but this worried her even more than Josh's back. The musket-ball had passed straight through his arm, but around the hole it had left behind the flesh was puffy and inflamed.

Miriam bound him up again and gave him the food she had brought. He ate it greedily, but it tasted dry in his mouth.

Miriam sat back on her heels watching him. When he had finished she said, 'What are we going to do with you now, Josh?'

'There's no need for you to do anything more, Miriam. I'm grateful to you for coming here. Very grateful. You've probably saved my life. But you mustn't become any more involved in this. None of this trouble is of your doing. You must think of yourself and young Daniel. How were you able to get away to come to me today?'

'My mother isn't a healthy woman these days. I don't need an excuse to come to Henwood to visit her.'

It reminded him of his own mother. He asked Miriam to get word to her, telling her not to worry about him.

'Yes, Josh. But first we must get you away from here. Far away.'

'I'll be safe enough for a while. Leave me some food. When I've eaten that I'll be able to move.'

'Josh, I can't leave you here like this. You once saved my life by coming up here to find me. Remember?'

'Yes, Miriam. There was another time. A night that changed both our lives. I'll never forget that night, either. This place seems to have a special significance in our lives. All the same, I'd rather you weren't mixed up in this mess.'

'I'm already involved. Far more than I would like to be. In fact, the whole of this might be more of my doing than you realise, Josh.'

'How? You couldn't have known what was going to happen.'

She looked down at him. 'William has always known how close we were as children. I thought he'd accepted that I was still very fond of you. But in recent months he's been saying things, making nasty insinuations. He seems to have become jealous for no reason at all. Then, when you disagreed with him over the miners, he thought you were threatening his authority. And he resented the way the miners looked to you as their natural leader. He has to work hard to keep their respect. You know he's a very ambitious man. I believe he began to see you as an obstacle to his ambitions. Later, when Morwen came to see us, I believe he said something to William that gave him an idea of what to do. They've talked together a great deal. Once Morwen came to the house with his officer. I am sure they must have been talking about you but they always stopped talking whenever I got close to them. But when Morwen left I heard William mention your name to him. I couldn't hear anything else.'

She looked at him unhappily. 'I believe William has a lot to do with you being hunted now, Josh. Now do you see why I'm sure he'll do nothing to help you?'

'I can't believe it! We've been such good friends in the past. For all our differences I'm sure William would do nothing like that.'

'I wish I could find some other explanation for what's happened, Josh. But this ambition of his is so all-powerful that

I'm sure he would sacrifice anyone, including me, to achieve his ends.'

'But how could he have known I'd go to Looe and get mixed up in the fighting there? He couldn't have arranged that.'

'I don't know – unless he sent someone to tell you about the miners. Anyone who knows you could guess what your actions would be. You'd rush to stop them. Once there Morwen and his officer could pick you out. You're known to be a strong union man so you would be blamed for any trouble that started.'

'No, Miriam. I don't believe anyone would do that.'

'*You* wouldn't do it, Josh. It isn't your way. But William would.'

The candle began to flicker and splutter. Miriam pinched it out between her fingers before she stood up and brushed down her dress.

'I'm going now, Josh. You'll be safe here for tonight. I'll return tomorrow morning with more food. No, don't argue. I want to. I only wish I could pick you up and carry you to safety as you once carried me.'

She stooped, kissed his forehead and rested her hand against his cheek for a moment. 'Goodbye, Josh. Stay as still as you can. Try not to start the wound in your back bleeding again. If it's no better tomorrow I'm afraid we're going to have to find a doctor to treat it. Whatever the danger.'

'We'll worry about that tomorrow. Thank you, Miriam.' Already he was feeling tired again.

When she had gone he thought about what she had said. Although he had expressed his doubts to Miriam, William's involvement would make sense of a lot of things that did not otherwise fit together. But he did not want to believe it.

During the night, Josh had an unexpected visitor. He woke suddenly and thought a soldier had stumbled upon his refuge, but it was an old boar badger grunting and snuffling as he led his family through the gorse-tunnel. He stopped to crunch a snail he found there, then herded his family back down the tunnel, oblivious of Josh's presence.

That was the only incident in an otherwise thoroughly miserable night. Around midnight the wind rose and within an hour it began to rain – a miserable skin-soaking drizzle that the moor was able to call up at a moment's notice. Huddled in the angle between two rocks, Josh was protected from the wind but there was no way of escaping from the rain. He lay shivering until dawn arrived wrapped in a cold grey mist.

Miriam came early, worried about the effects of the night on his weakened body. She found him cold and shivering, crouching like some sick animal. She had set out from her mother's house with some hot broth in a covered bowl. It was no more than luke-warm when she fed it between his chattering teeth, but it was sufficient to stop his shivering.

'Did you manage to get news to my mother?' he asked when the broth had stilled his teeth.

'No. I would have sent Uncle John to your cottage last night but it was too dangerous. Morwen is one of the soldiers guarding your house. He would have known what it was about. But John is going to get word to your father at the mine this morning.'

'Good!'

Josh leaned his head back against the rock and closed his eyes. 'I'm not going to recover very quickly unless this weather improves, Miriam. The muscles in my legs wouldn't support me when I tried to stand earlier. Another night like last one and I'll either die of pneumonia or my coughing will be heard by the soldiers.'

'I know. I lay awake worrying about you. We must get you inside somewhere so I can get a doctor to look at your wounds. Your back has been bleeding again and the inflammation in your arm has spread beyond the bandage. We'll have to take advantage of this mist and get you beneath a roof.'

'Yes, but what roof?' asked Josh. 'Anyone who shelters me will be in trouble if the soldiers find me. I'm a fugitive.'

'I know one place where you'll be safe. In your own house. The old farmhouse up on the hill.'

'But the soldiers must know about that.'

'They've already searched it and found it to be empty, so they're not guarding it. They're expecting you to make for your parents' cottage. I came past the farmhouse on my way here this morning, so I know there are no soldiers there. Isn't there a hay-loft above the stables?'

Josh nodded.

'Then that's the place. You'll be warm and dry there. Even if the soldiers were to search the house again I doubt whether they'd go up into the hay-loft – not if I remove the ladder when I leave you there.'

Josh managed a faint smile. 'The idea is fine, Miriam. But how do I get there? You said yourself you couldn't carry me. I haven't become any lighter during the night.'

'We'll manage somehow. If you can stumble along I'll support you. It isn't far if we go straight across the moor. You've got to make the effort, Josh. If this low cloud lifts we'll not be able to do it without being seen.'

'All right. Let's start now.'

The crawl through the tunnel was not too difficult, although it pulled the edges of his wounded back apart yet again. Once outside he got to his feet with Miriam's help. He stood with her shoulder beneath his armpit, his arm draped heavily about her.

They staggered drunkenly for about twenty-five yards before he fell, dragging her down with him.

'I'm sorry,' he gasped. 'I don't think I can make it.'

'Of course you can. You've *got* to do it now we've started. The soldiers will be out searching again soon. They'll find you here if you stay.'

Painfully he regained his feet. This time he managed to cover twice the distance before tripping.

As he lay face down in the bracken she looked at the dressing on his back. The blood was coming through, but it was not as bad as she had feared it might be. Once more she helped him to his feet and they managed another fifty yards.

So it went on. Fifty yards, twenty yards, once a mere fifteen, but always onwards and upwards, through the gorse and fern. Then after what seemed an eternity they arrived at the wall behind the old farmyard. Miriam heaved Josh over and pushed him up step by step as he made heavy work of climbing the ladder to the loft.

With a groan of relief he cleared the final rung and dropped gratefully into the sweet hay. Miriam's breathing was as heavy as his own but she dropped down beside him and cradled his head to her.

'We've done it, Josh! I told you we would.'

He could only grin weakly, too exhausted to reply.

That night she brought a doctor to him. He was a drunken little mine doctor from the North Hill district who asked no questions and seemed to have very little idea where he was.

He dressed the wound, soaking it with a strong antiseptic that Josh later swore would have burned the bristles from a pig. Then he drew the edges together with rough stitches that brought the perspiration pouring from Josh. When it had just reached the point where he thought he would either scream or faint, the job was done. Then the doctor turned his attention to the wound in Josh's arm. His method of cleaning the bullet-hole involved a swab and an iron rod. This time Josh did faint with the pain. When he came to, Miriam had led the alcoholic medical man away into the night.

But the doctor's crude methods marked a turning-point in Josh's recovery. The inflammation left his arm and the following day he devoured every scrap of food that Miriam brought for him.

His mother was aware that he was safe, Miriam told him, but she had not been told his whereabouts and would not be until the soldiers had gone from the area.

But that day never came. On the third day after the doctor's visit, Miriam brought him a basket of food in the evening, pleased to see him on his feet as she came up the ladder into the hay-loft.

'You're looking like the old Josh today,' she said to him.

'I'm beginning to feel like the Josh you once knew,' he replied. 'But isn't William wondering why you are in Henwood for so long? Or is he too busy with other things?'

'No. He came to my mother's house today.'

'And?'

She shrugged her shoulders. 'My mother *is* ill. I told him I wouldn't return to St Cleer until I felt happy about leaving her.'

'Did he accept that?'

'He had to.'

Miriam broke open a loaf of bread and put a large piece of cheese with it. She was about to hand it to him when there was a sound in the yard outside. Her hand froze halfway to him.

As Josh and Miriam looked at each other apprehensively there were footsteps at the door of the stable below them. A voice called, 'We know you're up there, Josh Retallick. Come down without giving us any trouble or I'll take great delight in coming up and shooting you again.'

It was Morwen Trago.

Miriam's eyes showed disbelief that was as quickly replaced by terror.

'He must have followed me!' she whispered. 'But I was so careful!'

Josh nodded.

She looked at him tearfully. 'What are you going to do? You can't give yourself up.'

'There's nothing else I can do. Even if I managed to escape from the back of the hay-loft I couldn't run far.'

'Then let me speak to him.'

She stood up, but Josh pulled her down on the hay beside him. 'No. I don't want you involved.'

Holding her arm to prevent her from getting up, he called, 'Morwen! You know I'm here alone?'

There was silence as the implication of Josh's words sunk in.

'If you say so,' Morwen answered.

'I do say so. Because I'm alone and have no wish to see my property torn apart I'll come down and give myself up.'

'Then come down.'

'There must be some other way, Josh,' Miriam whispered.

'No. You've risked too much already. I'm going now. Stay until we're clear. Morwen won't allow any of the soldiers to come up. Thank you, Miriam. I only wish things could have been different for us. . . .'

He kissed her quickly, then walked to the ladder. 'I'm coming down now.'

Soldiers are not renowned for their gentleness and Josh's captors made no exception of a man they believed had led a mob against them. They handled him roughly as they tied his hands behind his back and pushed him out of the stable ahead of them. Fortunately, only his arm began to bleed. He managed to keep most of their blows from his back.

For all that, he was a sorry sight as they marched him past the Retallick cottage. Seeing him from the window, Jesse Retallick screamed and ran outside. The soldiers pushed her back roughly, but Ben came out behind her and his booming voice stopped them.

'Take your hands from her! That's our son you have there. If you hope to get out of mining country with your lives you'll let his mother speak to him.'

Tom Shovell and the off-duty miners from the small group of cottages had come from their homes, drawn by the commotion. They formed up behind the shift captain as though preparing to back up his words.

Before the soldiers could get assistance they would have to pass the Wheal Phoenix, Sharptor and Caradon. They realised the truth in Ben Retallick's words.

Only Morwen Trago had anything to say. 'If I thought that was a threat . . .,' he began.

'You can take it for whatever you want,' said Ben Retallick. 'But Josh's mother will speak to him before you move on.'

'Then she'll have to make it brief,' said Morwen, giving in surlily. 'We want to make St Cleer before nightfall.'

'Josh, what have they done to you? How . . . ?'

'Everything's all right. My arm is bleeding a little, that's all. It looks far worse than it really is. Don't fuss over me. Everything is going to be all right. I'm not guilty of anything. As anyone who was at Looe knows. The court will find me innocent.'

'That's what John Kittow told the magistrate,' replied Jesse. 'But he was sent to Bodmin Jail to await trial.'

'Then the truth must wait to come out at the trial,' said Josh. 'Don't upset yourself.'

The soldiers were showing signs of impatience, and Josh said, 'I must go now. Please don't worry.'

Jesse reached up to kiss him and as he brought his head down to her Josh whispered, 'I owe a great debt to Miriam. Without her I wouldn't be alive today. Remember that.'

She drew back her head to look at him and he shook his head, 'Say nothing now.'

'Come on. We've a long march ahead of us.'

One of the soldiers pushed Josh away from his mother and set off along the track. Ben Retallick called to Josh that they would obtain the best lawyers in the county for him.

By the time they arrived at St Cleer, Josh had fallen many times and had to be helped by two soldiers. It was only the jeers of Morwen Trago that had kept him on his feet. He was determined not to give Miriam's brother the satisfaction of seeing him collapse completely.

The soldiers had a van at St Cleer. Josh was thrown roughly inside. As the other soldiers stood around boasting how they had captured the ring-leader of the rioters to any villager who would listen, Morwen Trago stepped into the van to check Josh's bonds.

Breathing heavily, Josh asked, 'How did you come to find me?'

'Because of something I should have realised all along,' hissed Morwen. 'It wasn't your mother we should have been watching, but my own sister. I always suspected you'd laid her in the fern when she was running barefoot on the moor. Now I'm sure.'

His inspection ended, he jumped from the van and slammed the door behind him. As he lay in the dark, Josh heard a bolt rammed home. Then the van lurched off and rumbled its way to Liskeard and the lock-up.

Later, well into the night, Josh was awakened by the opening of the lock-up door as a noisy sour-smelling drunk was thrown inside.

He tried to ignore his new companion by pretending to be asleep but it was not long before the shouting ceased and in the quiet of the darkness Josh felt the fingers of the stranger fumbling over his body, exploring his pockets.

Josh brought his hand up in a clubbing blow that sent the man crashing against the wall of the lock-up. The drunk fell to the floor and spent what remained of the night crying softly to himself and talking to the grotesque creatures who dwelled in a mind tortured by delirium tremens.

Chapter Twenty-Six

Josh's appearance before the magistrate was the merest formality. He was asked to confirm his name, the officer in charge of Morwen's company gave a brief version of what he alleged had occurred at Looe, and Josh was remanded to Bodmin Jail to await trial.

Bodmin Jail was a comparatively modern prison, the stones having not yet acquired the smell of decay and dirt found in most other prisons of the realm. Here was only the smell of imprisoned man – his sweat, his filth, and his fear.

There were women in the prison too. Demoniac women with tangled hair who screamed and shouted at the new arrival, beckoning to Josh through crowded bars as he climbed stiffly from the hard-sprung prison van.

In the large communal cell shared by those prisoners awaiting the circuit judge, Josh was reunited with John Kittow and nine miners who had been arrested on that violent late-summer day. All the others were strangers to him and came from mines well to the west of Bodmin Moor, adding further to Josh's growing belief in what Miriam had told him – the march on Looe had been planned well in advance.

'I'm not going to say I'm pleased to see you,' said John Kittow, leading Josh into a comparatively clean corner of the huge cage, taken over by the miners for themselves. 'As each day went by my hopes rose that you'd made good your escape. Even though part of me was worried lest you'd died in the spot where I left you. How are your wounds now? And what's been happening to you?'

Josh told the Caradon shift captain of his adventures since the night of the Looe battle, leaving out reference to Miriam. But he told him he had heard a rumour that William Thackeray might have been responsible for much of the misfortune that had befallen them.

'Now you mention it,' mused John Kittow, 'the miner who told me the men were on their way to Looe said something about going on to tell you. I wondered at the time why he should be bothering. He wasn't a man I knew well. He could have been following Preacher Thackeray's orders. But why? Why would Thackeray do such a thing?'

Josh shrugged and said nothing.

'To think that I actually went to his house for help. Had I kept away I wouldn't be locked up now.' He went on to give Josh the details of his capture before repeating, 'What can Preacher Thackeray hope to gain by betraying us?'

'I think it was your misfortune that you decided to make for Looe,' replied Josh. 'Preacher Thackeray couldn't have anticipated that.'

He inclined his head towards the other miners. 'I haven't seen any of these men before and I don't recall seeing any of the men who regularly attended Preacher Thackeray's meetings among the crowd at Looe town.'

'No, not now you mention it. But don't worry, Josh. Our own miners won't allow us to rot away in here. They'll force Preacher Thackeray to take some action to get us out.'

'You're fooling yourself if you believe that, John. The miners were marching upon Looe to score a great victory for the Miners' Union. They were going to prevent the corn from leaving the harbour, to force the soldiers to back down. None of these things happened. They not only lost – they suffered a humiliating defeat. Now they'll be too busy licking their wounds to think about doing battle on our behalf – especially as we weren't even with them. Oh yes! Preacher Thackeray will call his meetings and use brave words. He might even use some of the Union's funds to secure a lawyer for us. But nothing he does is going to make any difference. I'm quite sure he's aware of that. The judge must make an example of us. It wouldn't do for miners to believe they can take the law into their own hands. No, John. The soldiers have won. Preacher Thackeray has won. Only the miners have lost.'

'The soldiers have been putting it around that some of us were armed,' said John Kittow. 'Have you heard that?'

'I've heard nothing. But such a claim is absurd. Miners don't possess guns.'

John Kittow shrugged. 'We know that. But two of the soldiers were shot. They were probably shot by other soldiers, but nobody is likely to admit to that, especially as one of them is said to be in a serious condition.'

'That makes our chance of receiving a fair trial even more remote,' agreed Josh.

The situation looked hopeless. Then, as an evil-smelling greasy meal was being distributed that evening, Josh had an unexpected visitor. It was Dr McKinley from St Cleer. He had come, he said, to check on Josh's wounds and change the dressings on them.

As he went about his work, Josh asked him who had sent him.

'Well, it wasn't the soldiers,' said the doctor. 'Let's say I'm here on behalf of some of your friends and leave it at that. There are a great many people who are worried about you.'

He eased the dressing from Josh's back and grunted. 'Did you go to a sail-maker's assistant to have these stitches put in?'

'Do they look that bad?'

'It will heal. But you'll carry a scar like a herring-bone for the rest of your life.'

He seemed more pleased with the arm. 'That's clean enough and is healing nicely.'

Binding up the wounds he stood up and looked at Josh with sympathy.

'I've been asked to check on you every other day,' he said.

'As a doctor I'm not involved with either side. Neither am I for or against the Miners' Union. But if there's anything you wish me to bring for you, or any messages to be taken to anyone, I'll be happy to be of service.'

'There's nothing I can think of at the moment,' replied Josh. 'It will suffice to tell whoever engaged you that I'm well, and that I hope certain persons can be prevailed upon to come forward at the trial to testify that John Kittow and I had nothing to do with the march on Looe.'

'I wouldn't be unduly optimistic,' said the doctor. 'But I'll certainly pass on your message.'

He also promised to convey a report on John Kittow's well-being to his family.

The prison food was every bit as unpalatable as it looked, but all that Josh spurned was grabbed and gobbled up by other inmates of the common cell.

The following day Josh's meals underwent a radical change. He was brought a meal of beef, vegetables and even ale. When he expressed his surprise he was informed by the jailer that Theophilus Strike had arranged for him to have meals brought in from outside. There was enough food for Josh to share his good fortune with John Kittow. Somehow this small privilege made them feel like individuals again, not simply part of an anonymous mass.

That same day a cheerful roly-poly little man was escorted into the jail cell and he introduced himself to Josh as Reuben Button. He was a solicitor engaged by the mine-owner to examine the question of Josh's defence.

Button oozed confidence from every pore. 'Now,' he said, seating himself on a stool that he insisted the warder bring in for him, scorning the grubby bench that was at first offered. 'Tell me exactly what happened. From the very beginning.'

Josh told him. At the end of his story the solicitor frowned, looked quizzically at his client. 'You are quite sure you are leaving nothing untold?'

'I have told you everything,' replied Josh. 'Apart from knocking the dragoon from his horse – and that was hardly a premeditated act – I did nothing. My sole object in going to

Looe was to prevent violence, to stop the miners from doing something stupid. But they never had the opportunity; the soldiers fired first.'

'I understand the Riot Act had already been read out by the magistrate prior to your arrival,' said Button. 'That makes the whole matter far more serious. You understand that, of course?'

Josh nodded.

'But one thing confounds me. If what you have told me constitutes your sole involvement in this sorry affair, why were the soldiers so anxious to apprehend you?'

'There are two possible explanations for that. The first is Morwen Trago. We were boys together and he has no reason to be fond of me or my family. He was one of the soldiers at Looe, the one who put a bullet through my arm.'

'I see.' The solicitor was busily writing. 'We must bring that out in court. And the other reason?'

'The officer in charge of the soldiers brought them around the mines recently. He took them to the Wheal Phoenix and he was told he wasn't welcome. While he was there I warned him to keep away from the Wheal Sharptor. He asked for my name and I told him.'

'Well! Well! Well! Previous bad blood between yourself and the officer in charge of the soldiers.' He spoke slowly and deliberately as he committed each word to paper. 'I'm sure we can make something of that. Now, when were you informed about the miners marching to Looe?'

Josh told him, and the solicitor wrote his reply down.

There were many such questions and answers, and Mr Button called on John Kittow to verify certain parts of Josh's statement.

Finally and cheerfully the solicitor folded the papers and tucked them away in the bag he was carrying.

'How do you think the case will go? Is there any chance we'll be set free?' Josh asked.

'I think we have a very strong case,' said Mr Button guardedly. 'But of course this *was* a riotous assembly. That is looked upon by the courts as being most serious. However, we have an interesting defence. Very interesting. Do not become too depressed. Now, before I go I have another little matter to attend to.'

He waved a scented handkerchief in front of his nose as a door leading to the main section of the prison was opened and the odour from within escaped.

'Mr Strike – who I must say I have found to be a very generous man – personally believes in your complete innocence. He wishes that you be made as comfortable as is possible during the period prior to your trial. He has authorised me to obtain a private cell. I have an appointment with the governor in a few minutes to discuss the matter.'

'I'm much obliged to him,' said Josh. 'But would it be asking too much for John Kittow to enjoy the privilege with me?'

'Provided little extra expense is involved I foresee no problem,' said Mr Button. 'I'll make the necessary arrangements for both of you.'

Before nightfall that day Josh and John Kittow were lodged in a cell on the first floor of the jail. From the tiny barred window they were able to see the moor, rising beyond the ugly granite walls.

The days passed with very little to disturb the monotony of jail life, apart from the visits of either Mr Button or the solicitor engaged by the Miners' Union to defend John Kittow and the other miners. Josh's wounds healed to the satisfaction of the St Cleer doctor and his visits soon stopped. They had one bad day when they were told that an additional charge was to be brought against them, that of being party to a conspiracy contrary to the Treasonable and Seditious Practices Act. It was on such a charge that the Kit Hill miners had been convicted and transported when the mine store was burned down. Immediately after this Mr Button brought word that one of the wounded soldiers had died. He said the soldiers in the town were in such an ugly mood that a miner dared not venture abroad after dark for fear of being murdered. Although none of the miners in Bodmin Jail was actually being charged with responsibility for the soldier's death, it would no doubt weigh heavily against them when the evidence was produced to the jury.

The day after this, Jesse and Ben Retallick came to the jail to visit their son. The meeting was a painful one for all of them. Jesse looked old and grey with grief. All her fire had drained from her. The grim prison surroundings seemed to weigh heavier upon her than they did upon Josh. Even Ben Retallick, a man by any standards, somehow shrank in stature within the prison walls. He did little more than twiddle his hat between his fingers during the whole of the uncomfortable visit.

In sharp contrast, the later visit of Theophilus Strike was a very different affair. He was escorted to the cell by the governor of the prison. When the mine-owner demanded to know whether Josh was being treated well the governor's look practically implored Josh to say that he was.

After satisfying himself that Josh was as comfortable as could reasonably be expected in the circumstances, Theophilus Strike turned his attention to the matter of Josh's arrest and impending trial.

'The whole thing is preposterous,' he fumed. 'I've warned you in the past about the stupidity of meddling in the affairs of the miners, but that doesn't make you a criminal. You're an engineer and I need you back at the Sharptor mine.'

He was so positive in his belief in Josh's innocence that for the duration of his visit even Josh could not help but believe that he would be acquitted. Only after the mine-owner had gone did Josh realise he had said nothing new. Nothing had changed.

But the visit of Theophilus Strike had brought a breath of fresh air into the fetid prison surroundings. Josh felt better for it.

The day before the trial was to commence at Bodmin Assizes, Josh had a very special visitor. This time it was Miriam and she brought Daniel with her.

At first Josh was appalled. 'You should never have come here. It's not right for Daniel to be in such surroundings.'

'I feel the same way about you,' Miriam replied with a forced smile. 'How are you, Josh, and how are your wounds?'

For a long time they spoke of nothing in particular and there were long awkward silences before John Kittow called for the jailer and asked to be taken out for exercise. Such was Theophilus Strike's influence and open-handed generosity that the two men were able to take exercise periods whenever they wished.

Josh and Miriam protested that John Kittow should stay, but their protestations were not so strong that they might have persuaded him to change his mind.

When the Caradon mine leader had gone, Josh asked, 'Does William know you're here?'

Miriam shook her head. 'No, I haven't told him, and I won't. But it would make little difference if I did. He and I have been going separate ways since your arrest.'

'You mean you've left him?'

'No, we are still living under the same roof, but that is all.'

'Miriam, you've already done a great deal more than you should for me. I won't have you ruining your whole life on my account.'

'You're not the sole reason for things being the way they are, Josh. William knew I wasn't in love with him when we married, but I liked him a great deal, and I respected him. That was very important – to be able to respect him. Respect has gone now, and without it I find our relationship well-nigh impossible.'

'I'm sorry.' It was totally inadequate.

'You needn't be. I've accepted it and William has many other things to occupy his mind at the present time. There are meetings and committees to be formed – and more meetings. All of them full of talk about the solidarity of the Union and the defence of its members who are facing trial for their ideals. The whole thing is so hypocritical, Josh. I have listened and pried and checked every detail that I could. I'm more convinced than ever that William plotted with Morwen to have you involved in the disturbances at Looe.'

'Is it possible to get any proof? Something that my solicitor would be able to use?'

'No. There can be no proof unless either William or Morwen admit it. They are hardly likely to do that.'

'I suppose not.'

'What do you think will happen at the trial, Josh?'

He shrugged his shoulders. 'My solicitor says we have a strong case on everything but the riotous-assembly charge. I hope he's right. I understand the prosecution will be asking for the death penalty if we're found guilty of all charges.'

He saw the look of horror on her face and hurriedly added, 'But he's quite sure we needn't fear that.'

'I should hope not! You're innocent. Neither you nor John had anything to do with what happened.'

'But we were there during the trouble. I have the scars for them to prove it. No, I feel sure we'll be found guilty on the riotous-assembly charge and transported for a few years.'

'Josh, I don't want you to go away. We've both wasted more than enough of our years already.'

He took her gently by the shoulders. 'Miriam, you've already done enough to find yourself in this prison, if the facts came to light. You have Daniel to think of. Yes, you may have wasted a few years of your life. Please don't throw away the rest of it.'

Daniel was engrossed in an illustrated book Theophilus Strike had sent in, and as Miriam clung to him Josh kissed her hungrily. The fire was still there between them, but a cell was no place for romance.

'Miriam, please go now. Let what's happened between us remain one of memory's secrets. Don't allow it to destroy your life.'

'But, Josh, if they acquit you we could be together, with nothing to stop us. We could go away and start a new life.'

'If only we could! I fear it's a wistful dream, Miriam. One we can't afford. I know what's going to happen when we appear in court. You must face up to it too. Go now – please! And, whatever happens, take care of yourself and Daniel. Thank you for everything.'

Tears were commonplace in Bodmin Jail, and the jailer

avoided looking at Miriam as he let her and Daniel out of the cell.

When John Kittow returned he made no comment about Miriam's visit, until Josh told him of the suspected alliance between William Thackeray and Morwen Trago.

The miner looked at Josh quizzically. 'She told you of this though one of the men involved is her husband, the other her brother?'

'We've known each other since we were children. Had it not been for the incidents that led to the death of Moses Trago we'd have been married. As it was she married William Thackeray.'

'In itself a good enough reason for Preacher Thackeray to want you out of the way.'

'Perhaps. But I doubt if a judge would accept it as evidence. I hope those speaking for us in court tomorrow will have a stronger defence to place before the jury.'

'Amen to that!' said John Kittow.

More than two months had passed since their arrest and it was a dull sullen November day when Josh, John Kittow and the other miners went on trial.

In the early morning they were hustled from the cell block and into the tiny prison van to be taken to the Assize Court. It was the busiest time in the jail calendar. Vans trundled through the great gates one after another with their cargoes of fearful prisoners *en route* for the Assize Court.

The other nine miners had not had such a privileged period of confinement as Josh Retallick and John Kittow. They looked pale-faced, tired and unkempt. They did not resent the special treatment given to the two friends. They accepted it – just as they accepted that they were on trial for something they did not look upon as a crime. It was simply part of their lot in life – the lot of a miner, to whom life was sometimes harder than at others, but always hard.

They were eager for news and pleased that Josh knew something of what was to happen in the court-room. He represented authority as the miners knew it, and they were desperate for something familiar. Their solicitor had seen them, but, as one miner put it, 'The likes of he don't understand about the likes of we.'

They were convinced they would be transported and were already talking about their prospects in Australia. Many exaggerated rumours had come back from that far continent.

Arriving at the Assize building they were hustled below and placed in a cell with the other prisoners. On the way down they noticed soldiers on guard in every part of the court-house. The authorities were taking no chances.

During the morning the judge dealt with a few of the less involved cases. It was not until after they had been given a totally unpalatable midday meal that their names were called. The eleven men were taken along a passageway to wait in line on the stairs leading to the court-room above until a red-coated sergeant signalled to their jailers. Then they were hurried up into a dark-panelled court-room with flickering lights and a packed gallery. Outside, through the leaded windows, the November sky showed a promise of rain.

They were all squeezed into the long prisoners' dock that had steel spikes adorning the rail around it. Before them was the raised bench and the deep-red padded chairs for the mayor and county dignitaries, the large central chair being reserved for the judge.

To one side of them the jurors formed a double line, uncomfortable on their hard benches. In the well of the court, between the judge's bench and the prisoners, were the tables reserved for the barristers, solcitors, clerks and others for whom a court of law was a place of employment.

Behind the dock where the light was dimmest the public benches were packed to overflowing with miners and families of the accused men. As they filed into the dock a cheer had gone up, only to be quickly stifled by the soldiers guarding the doors. It died away to be replaced by loud whispers and the coughing of jurymen.

Then a door at the rear of the judge's bench opened and a black-gowned court usher appeared. 'Silence for His Lordship Judge Denman.'

The occupants of the court-room rose with scraping of feet and chairs. A short bulbous-nosed man with flowing grey wig and red robes swept in. After glancing at the prisoners, at the blurred faces in the public gallery and the legal representatives bowing and bobbing in the well of the court, he took his seat.

'Be seated!'

The bowing ceased, the scraping was repeated and everyone sat down again. The prisoners sat down with them but were immediately prodded to their feet.

The clerk of the court cleared his throat noisily and, reading from a sheet of paper held in front of him, called out the names of the accused men. Each had to indicate acknowledgement until, satisfied they all stood before him, the clerk read out the charges.

'You stand before this court charged that on the twenty-fourth day of September you did, in the Borough of Looe, in the County of Cornwall, riotously and unlawfully assemble to the disturbance of the peace of this realm and the terror of the people, whereby divers persons were injured. This after a magistrate of that Borough had commanded you to disperse in the name of the Queen.

'You are further charged with, that on divers dates you did treasonably and seditiously conspire against the State. . . .'

The dull voice droned on, detailing in legal jargon statute and section against which they were alleged to have offended.

When he had finished he called upon each of them in turn to state whether he were 'guilty' or 'not guilty'.

One after another the men declared their innocence. On the first occasion the reply brought a small cheer from the public gallery. The judge, in a hoarse stern voice, informed the court in general that he was not conducting a public show. Unless the members of the public refrained from voicing their feelings he would have the court cleared. There was no further sound from the miners' friends while the pleas were taken.

Now the prisoners were allowed to be seated and the case against them began to unwind.

'It is', the prosecuting barrister declared, 'quite simple and straightforward! Prior to this unhappily eventful day the miners had been stirred up by men like the defendants Retallick and Kittow. Doubtless there were others who unfortunately are not in custody. They were misled into forming unconstitutional alliances, such as the Miners' Union to which all these men belong. Such a union would not be unlawful if it restricted its activities to mining matters alone. Instead, it has taken upon itself the task of changing the laws of the land. Our land. And violence is advocated as a means to obtain that unlawful end.

'They – the men in this union – disagreed with Parliament's policy on the sale of corn. They deliberately set out to use force in order to change it, were prepared to go outside the Law to achieve their selfish and dangerous aims. It is well known to all of you that the activities of these men, representing a mere handful of Cornishmen, led to the military presence in Cornwall throughout the summer months. Farmers going about their lawful business had to be protected from these unionists. The use of threats, coercion and physical assault formed part of their campaign. They deliberately set themselves above the Law—'

'My Lord, I must object!'

This was the barrister briefed by Mr Button. 'My client is not charged with leading a revolution! I submit that my learned friend is not giving evidence that will be substantiated. He is reciting a story to the jury, for pure effect.'

'My Lord, the defendants, and in particular my learned friend's client Retallick, are charged with conspiring treason and sedition. If that is not plotting revolution I do not know what is!'

'Objection overruled.' The judge appeared to be bored already. The prosecution continued.

'There have been meetings, some held in secret, others addressed openly by the prisoner Retallick. At these meetings violence was frequently suggested – I go further, *demanded*. Yes, because the military had foiled them in every other way, the Miners' Union decided to resort to violence in a bid to achieve its ends. There can be little doubt that its members were aware that by so doing they were committing treason, that their actions would lead them into direct conflict with soldiers of the Queen.

'This disgraceful day at Looe, the rioting and terrifying lawlessness – it was not a thing decided upon a few hours before the event, or even a few days. It was part of a well-thought-out plan. Only the brave determination of a handful of soldiers prevented the citizens of Looe from witnessing the destruction of honest people's property, and with it the collapse of law and order in this county. Gathered together were men from mines throughout east and central Cornwall. Caradon, Phoenix, Kit Hill, St Austell and Par. They knew exactly where to go. They knew because the plans had been prepared beforehand. Proof beyond any reasonable doubt of a treasonable conspiracy.

'As to the incidents that arose out of this conspiracy, I shall be calling only sufficient witnesses to prove the Crown's case. A similar story could be told by every inhabitant of that unfortunate town. You will hear evidence from innocent shopkeepers. They will tell you of their terror at beholding this unruly mob. You will hear from the brave magistrate, called out when the mob was seen approaching, who, in fear for his very life, stood boldly before them, calling on them to disperse in the Queen's name. He even warned them of the consequences of their actions. They paid him no heed, doubtless scornful of the few soldiers who stood between them and their unlawful intentions.

'But the soldiers who opposed them were men of the 32nd Foot Regiment, themselves loyal men of Cornwall. They took up defensive positions to protect the ships, and the grain belonging to honest Cornish farmers. To aid them they had a small troop of Dragoon Guards.

'The officer in charge of the foot soldiers tried to reason with the rioters, but they were beyond reasoning. They attacked the officer in front of his men and, fearful for his life, the soldiers were forced to open fire in order to effect a rescue. Then the miners in their overwhelming numbers attacked the soldiers. So fierce did the fighting become that the dragoons had to be called in to assist them.

'The miners standing before you in this court were – with

two exceptions – no worse and no better than any of their fellows in that riotous crowd. The two exceptions, Joshua Retallick and John Kittow, are not simple miners. They were important members of the mining community and so must accept great responsibility for what went on about them. And so they should! For, mounted and in clear view of the others, they led that cowardly unlawful mob. Retallick attacked a trooper of the dragoons. Witnesses will be called who saw him personally knock a trooper to the ground, with utter disregard for the trooper's safety beneath the hoofs of the milling horses.

'Yes, gentlemen of the jury, so close to the fighting was the prisoner Retallick that he was himself twice wounded. But with the aid of the prisoner Kittow he made his escape. Yes, these two "leaders" deserted the miners they had led into sordid battle and fled. Indeed, Retallick was not apprehended until he had been at liberty for a number of days. That is briefly the case for the prosecution. Now I will proceed to call witnesses who will prove it beyond any shadow of a doubt.'

The first few witnesses were tradesmen from Looe, required merely to say that on the day in question they feared for the safety of their property and were terrified by the miners who marched upon their town.

Next came the magistrate, pompous and eager to impress the judge with his courage in standing up before 'hundreds of miners bent upon mischief and disturbance of the Queen's peace'. He went on to tell how, disregarding all the insults hurled at him, he completed the reading of the Riot Act before hurrying away to safety.

Mr Button, seated beside the barrister defending Josh, leaned over and whispered something. The barrister stood up to cross-examine the magistrate.

'Magistrate Phipps, I am quite sure you behaved with commendable courage. Indeed, would I be right in saying that you behaved with composure? That you assessed the situation in a calm and brave manner?'

The surprised magistrate beamed. 'I did my best, sir.'

'Then no doubt you were aware of the exact composition of the crowd?'

The magistrate looked puzzled.

'Come, now, Mr Phipps. Were they all afoot or all mounted?'

'Why, they were afoot, of course.'

'All of them?'

'Yes.'

'You are quite sure?' The barrister had to speak loudly because of an interested stir in the public gallery.

'Quite sure.'

'And yet the prosecution has informed the court that my client Mr Retallick and Mr Kittow were both mounted. Am I correct in assuming that neither of these men was present when you read out the Riot Act? They were not members of this riotous assembly?'

The magistrate opened his mouth and closed it again. He appeared to think, a puzzled frown on his face. 'We-ell. . . . They might have been at the back of the crowd. There were a lot of people there.'

'But you did not see them? You cannot point a finger and say, "Yes, those two men were present on their horses"?'

The magistrate was forced to agree that he could not.

'Thank you. There would appear to be a discrepancy between the evidence of a reliable witness and the fairy story the prosecution told to the court. Far from my client standing out in his leadership, he seems to have been most noticeable by his absence!'

There were laughs from the gallery and the judge called for order.

The counsel employed by the Miners' Union used his questioning time trying to make the magistrate say that the miners were in fact behaving in a quiet and orderly manner, that at no time was there any necessity to read the Riot Act. His argument was remarkably lacking in conviction.

Next came the evidence of the soldiers. It followed more closely the story told by the prosecuting counsel. They spoke of being ordered to fire into the crowd to save their officer, of defending themselves. Some went on to describe the arrest of one or more men in the dock. Their evidence was well rehearsed. Although a couple of them were noticeably uncomfortable when being cross-examined, they could not be tricked into going back on what they had already said. They all disagreed strongly with the suggestion that their action in firing into the crowd was more offensive than defensive.

Nobody, unless it was a miner who had been at the scene, would have doubted their evidence.

The dragoons' evidence was far more damning. They told the truth as they had seen it. When they arrived on the scene, Josh and John Kittow were part of the crowd. One dragoon told of being attacked by Josh and falling beneath the feet of the horses. It was, he insisted, a deliberate and determined attack.

'Surely not,' argued the barrister representing Josh. 'Was my client armed?'

The dragoon grudgingly admitted he did not believe so.

'Then perhaps he was holding a stave – or something you thought might have been a weapon?'

'No.'

The eyebrows of the barrister were a statement in themselves.

'Yet you had a sabre drawn and were prepared to use it upon my client?'

The dragoon showed some hesitation now.

'Yes.'

There was a loud and angry murmur from the public gallery.

'Silence!' The judge emphasised his order with the aid of the wooden gavel on the bench in front of him.

'And you are telling us that Joshua Retallick – unarmed, with nothing in his hand – *attacked* you? Attacked a soldier with a sabre clear of its sheath? A sabre raised and ready for use? You are suggesting this in all seriousness?'

'Yes.'

'Come, now. Is it not more likely that my client found himself trapped in a dangerous situation not of his making. That in trying to extricate himself from it he accidentally knocked you from your horse?'

'No, sir. It was deliberate.'

'You are quite sure?'

'Yes, sir. He had his arm raised to strike me.'

'I submit it was far more likely his arm was raised to protect himself from the blow of an up-raised sabre. That had your horse not slipped you would have split his skull open?'

'No, sir. It was a deliberate attack on me.'

The barrister shook his head. 'If such an assertion were true, it would make my client a fool. I will be proving later that he is far from that.'

The next witness was the dragoon who had slashed Josh's back. He too gave evidence that Josh was 'laying about him'. He further stated that John Kittow had also struck him.

Josh's barrister commented that John Kittow had undoubtedly saved Josh's life, that there was not a scrap of evidence to suggest that John Kittow had assaulted anyone – a point which was followed up by the Miners' Union barrister.

The dragoon was followed by the officer of the company of foot soldiers. He began his evidence by making vague allusions to Josh's position in the Miners' Union, to his having preached treason and sedition.

Josh's barrister was quick to object to such evidence on the grounds that it was 'hearsay'.

This time his objection was sustained and the officer was told to restrict his evidence to that which he knew and not that which he believed to be true. The officer then spoke of Josh's 'belligerent' attitude when they had met at the Wheal Phoenix. He swore that he had seen the Sharptor engineer with the miners when they marched into Looe.

This brought forth another flurried exchange between Mr Button and the barrister and this point was taken up with the officer. He remained adamant. He *had* seen Josh arrive with the miners and, *yes*, he was quite sure. He would not admit to any possibility of being wrong.

Then it was the turn of Morwen Trago. Like his officer he swore that Josh had been with the miners at the time they entered Looe. Further, he said Josh was urging the men to attack the soldiers. He had seen him strike down one dragoon, and when Josh had been about to attack another he, Morwen Trago, had fired at him, wounding him in the arm.

Morwen told of searching the moor around Josh's home and of capturing him in the barn. Josh was greatly relieved that no one said anything that might possibly have brought Miriam into the case.

Then it was Morwen's turn to be cross-examined by Josh's barrister.

'Is it true', asked the barrister, 'that you knew Joshua Retallick as a boy?'

'Yes. We lived close to each other on the moor near Sharptor.'

'Were you friends?'

Morwen shrugged. 'I wouldn't say that. We knew each other.'

'And did you like him?'

A shrug again. 'I neither liked him nor disliked him. I knew him, that's all.'

The barrister hitched his gown up on his shoulders. 'That is not the truth, Morwen Trago. The fact is that you hate Joshua Retallick as you hate no other man – unless it be Joshua Retallick's father.'

'No.'

'No? Really, Morwen Trago? You must be a special kind of human being, someone with a remarkable talent for forgiveness. Is it not true you believe Joshua Retallick's father to be responsible for the death of your own father?'

'He *was* responsible.'

'Surely not. Didn't your father rape a girl who lived with the Retallicks? When pursued I believe he slipped and fell into a disused mine shaft and was killed?'

'No! He didn't fall. He was pushed.'

'There is proof of this allegation, of course? Your father's – er – "murderers" were tried by a jury? And found guilty?'

'No, but that's what happened.'

'That may be what you choose to believe, Morwen Trago. It is certainly not corroborated by the known facts. But, be that as it may, do you still claim that you have no hatred for anyone who bears the name Retallick?'

The court was hushed as the jury waited for Morwen Trago to reply. He said nothing.

'Never mind,' said the barrister. 'There are certain silences that shout louder than words. We will allow that matter to rest. But I put it to you that you did *not* see my client arrive with the miners. That you have concocted your own version of the day's events, carrying it off with such conviction you have persuaded others they saw it too. What is more, if you told the truth about what you saw on this fateful day – and I have not the slightest doubt that you saw exactly what did occur – I repeat, if you were to tell the truth, not only would Joshua Retallick be acquitted but he would leave this court with the praises of the learned judge ringing in his ears, for attempting to prevent the bloodshed that took place on that September day.'

'No! That's not true!'

But Morwen Trago's cries were drowned by the noise from the public gallery. This time there was no silencing them. The efforts of the court ushers brought only stamping feet and howls of support for Josh Retallick and the miners in the dock.

It was at this stage that the judge adjourned the proceedings for the day.

On the return journey to the jail the accused miners were in an optimistic mood, convinced that the mood of those in the public gallery represented the view of the jury. Even John Kittow's morale had been boosted by the final demonstration of support. Only Josh would not allow himself to be fooled.

The next day only two more soldiers were called to give evidence. Then it was time for the defence to present its case.

It soon became apparent to Josh that his pessimism had been well founded. There were few defence witnesses and their case was held together by a very frail thread.

Of those in the dock only Josh was called into the witness-box to tell his story. He told of riding to Looe, and meeting with John Kittow on the way. How both of them had ridden into Looe town in a vain attempt to head off the miners, and of the scene in the square when they arrived. He told how the soldiers had fired before they had been attacked and, when pressed by his barrister, said except for the scuffle involving the officer he had not seen the miners use violence at any time. More. Once the soldiers had opened fire on them the miners were far too busy dodging musket-balls to offer violence to anyone.

Yes, he admitted, he had knocked a dragoon from his horse. But the fault lay with the horses rather than their riders. He had not fought the soldiers, although he considered their actions to be unnecessary and cowardly. Their first volley had been sufficient to strike terror into the ranks of the miners. After that their only thought had been escape.

His manner in the witness-box was quiet and straightforward enough to impress the jury. But then it was the turn of the prosecuting barrister to cross-examine him.

'Joshua Retallick, you have told the court you were not with the miners when they marched upon Looe.'

'Yes.'

'You rode there in great haste when you were told of their action?'

'Yes.'

'I won't go into your reasons, but is it not true you set off knowing when you caught up with them you would be able to influence them?'

'I hoped they might listen to me.'

'You "hoped they might listen". No doubt you had good reason to believe they would. They had listened to you many times in the past, when you addressed their meetings?'

'I addressed very few meetings.'

'You agree there were some?'

'Yes.'

'So you are not denying that the miners regard you as, for want of a better word, a leader? A leader of this union movement?'

'It is a miners' union and I have spoken to them at meetings.'

'And they listened to you with considerable deference, no doubt?'

'They listened.'

'Thank you, I think we are in complete agreement on this point. You are a leader of this so-called "union" of miners. Now, let us pass on to some of the things you have told the court. They do not seem to agree with what has been said by the many witnesses who came before you. You say you went to Looe in a vain attempt to prevent the miners from doing something which you now agree was "stupid", something for which the laws of this country have a much stronger word?'

'Yes.'

'But when you discovered they intended to carry out their unlawful plan of attacking the soldiers and seizing the corn wagons, you decided you would join with them.'

'No.'

'Further. When you saw the dragoons moving in to quell this riot you personally led an assault on them, attempted to beat them off to allow the miners to carry out their unlawful intentions.'

'No, I have said what happened.'

'You have told us what you would dearly like this court to believe, Mr Retallick. If the jury and I choose not to believe your version of the day's happenings I trust you will forgive us.'

With this the prosecuting counsel sat down.

'There is only one further question I would like to put to my client in re-examination, My Lord,' said Josh's barrister. 'Joshua Retallick, your intention when you went to Looe was to prevent the miners from breaking the law. Had you been successful you would not be standing in the dock now. Is that not so?'

'Yes.'

'Thank you. I have no further questions.'

Curiously, the Miners' Union barrister had few questions to put to Josh. Josh was asked only to confirm that John Kittow rode into Looe with Josh and that he had struck no blows.

His questioning over, Josh was returned to the dock with the other prisoners.

Then the character witnesses were called to speak on behalf of the miners. Shift captains in the main. But two adventurers came from the Caradon mine to speak for John Kittow. They praised his diligence and reliability and spoke of him as a man of integrity and loyalty.

When it was the turn of the character witnesses to speak on Josh's behalf it was the beginning of a series of surprises for him. The first was Theophilus Strike. His commanding presence rose above the grim court-room surroundings. In his usual forthright manner the mine-owner called the charges against Josh 'preposterous!' 'Joshua Retallick,' he said 'is a brilliant engineer. His contribution to mine safety is recognised far beyond the borders of his own county as being far ahead of his time. He has patented a mine-lift to bring miners from the depths of the deepest mine to the surface that will revolutionise current safety standards.'

Theophilus Strike went on to say that in all the time he had known Josh he had heard him neither preach nor practise violence. His interest in the Miners' Union was a humanitarian one. The mine-owner said that he was well aware of Josh's passionate interest in the welfare of the miners. He had in fact discussed it with him. He was perfectly satisfied that Josh was concerned with the well-being of the miners and nothing more.

Theophilus Strike was so positive in all his utterances that the prosecuting barrister chose not to take up a single point with him.

The next witness was William Carlyon.

The Harvey works manager smiled sympathetically in Josh's direction as he took the stand. He too spoke of Josh as a brilliant engineer with a great future. Further, he said he would rate him as possessing the potential to become one of the country's greatest.

'I believe it is true to say your relationship with the prisoner is closer than that of two engineers?'

'Yes.' William Carlyon's voice was pitched low. 'He was my daughter's husband.'

'Was?'

'My daughter died as the result of childbirth. This spring.'

The statement brought Josh sympathetic glances from the jury.

'It may be painful for you to talk about it, Mr Carlyon, but I am sure you are aware of the importance of your evidence. Will you tell us the tragic circumstances leading to your daughter's death?'

'Yes.' Despite his assurance William Carlyon's face showed strain. 'Josh – Joshua Retallick – and my daughter Sarah had a baby in the spring.'

'I am sorry, Mr Carlyon. You are talking about the spring of this year?'

'Yes.'

'Please go on.'

'It was a difficult birth. Josh was alone with my daughter and had to bring the baby into the world by himself. The baby was before its time and lived for only a few hours. My daughter was also very ill.'

'What sort of illness, Mr Carlyon?'

Josh could not look at the strained face of the works manager. He stared instead at the wooden floor at his feet.

'She became mentally unbalanced as a result of having to endure prolonged pain. . . .'

'And then?'

'She returned to Hayle to stay with her mother and myself, in the hope she would make a full recovery.'

'Did she make the hoped-for recovery?'

'No. One day Josh came to visit her. While he and the rest of us were talking in the house she rode off to the cliffs not far away. Soon afterwards her body was recovered from the rocks off-shore.'

'So, in the course of a few weeks Joshua Retallick lost both his wife and his child. It left him a lonely man, I would imagine?'

'Yes.'

'It would doubtless deeply affect the most hardened man among us,' said the barrister. 'In order to overcome such desolation most intelligent men would probably devote themselves to something that would, of necessity, occupy both their time and thoughts. A cause, perhaps. Something like a miners' union?'

'I would say that was highly probable.'

'Do you think he would become involved to such an extent that he would advocate violence, Mr Carlyon?'

'No. Josh is not a violent man.'

'That is what I too believe. Thank you, Mr Carlyon.'

The prosecuting barrister asked William Carlyon a few questions in an attempt to overturn his evidence that Josh was not a violent man, but he failed to shake him.

There were no more witnesses after William Carlyon. It was time for the prosecution to conclude its case. The prosecuting counsel stood up to address the court.

'My Lord. Gentlemen of the jury. You have listened to the evidence in a case of the utmost seriousness. A case involving a section of the community placing themselves above the Law. Attempting to impose their will upon others. This has always been regarded as one of the most serious offences in the land. It is a crime aimed at the very structure upon which our way of life depends. The upholding of law, and an ordered society. You have heard the evidence of honest men. They have told you how these men in the dock, with others, marched upon Looe with the express intention of seizing corn. They knew soldiers would be guarding it. They knew they would have to fight to have their way. This did not deter them. It could be that the orders given by Parliament to send the corn to other places was not wise. We cannot be sure of that. Parliament alone is aware of the needs of the whole country. They will stand or fall by their decisions. The laws of this land are made for *all* its people. It is of the utmost importance that they are obeyed. Not undermined in any way. I repeat. They must not be undermined. This is a mining community. The wisdom of that saying should be clear to everyone.

'This attempt to impose the will of a small minority upon the majority was more than folly. The way in which these miners sought to do it was both criminal and *treasonable*.

'The men in the dock before you come from a number of mines – irrefutable evidence that this was not a sudden storm that blew up in the heat of a summer's day, the result of an explosion of anger. This was a well-thought-out and well-planned – albeit ill-executed – uprising. That it was the result of a conspiracy must surely be beyond dispute. This treasonable folly was conspired at. There was a conspiracy to commit treason.

'When this mob arrived at Looe their behaviour was such that the Riot Act was read to them by the courageous magistrate whose evidence you have heard. The very wording of the Act is calculated to bring home to such men the seriousness of the situation, to persuade them to disperse quickly and peacefully.

'They did not disperse. They had no intention of so doing. Having gone to this peaceful town for an unlawful purpose, they were determined to see it through. Furthermore, they attempted it. Because of that one soldier died and others were injured. It can only be considered fortunate that innocent citizens of Looe were not amongst those who lost their lives.

'There is no disputing that nine of the men before you formed part of that riotous crowd. They have not attempted to deny it. They could not. Instead, they have tried to escape justice by throwing the blame for the violence upon the soldiers.

'Forget such considerations. That is not a point at issue.

'From two of the accused prisoners, Retallick and Kittow, we have heard protestations of innocence, and arguments as to whether they were at Looe when the Riot Act was read. They must be allowed to plead their case. That is justice. But I would remind you that these two men have much to lose. *Everything* to lose should they be found guilty here today.

'Against them you have heard the evidence of an officer, an honourable gentleman, and the men under his command. Men who have fought nobly in foreign lands for our country, in the ranks of the regiment Cornwall is proud to call its own. They have no reason to lie. They told you what they saw, honestly and convincingly.

'From his own lips you heard Retallick admit he was in the habit of addressing meetings of miners. "Union" meetings. Those of you who know something of this movement might refer to it by another and less pleasant name. An unpatriotic name. Retallick did not admit he was responsible for conspiring that the miners march to Looe. We could not expect him to do that. After all he pleaded not guilty.

'But I am sure that you, the members of the jury, will recognise the truth and find him as guilty as he assuredly is. His companion Kittow is perhaps more misguided than evil, but he is as guilty as Retallick. You will – you must – find him and all the other prisoners guilty as charged.'

In a heavy silence the counsel for the prosecution sat down.

The miners' defence barrister made a long speech that was repetitious and dull and had the jurors fidgeting on the hard benches. He said nothing new and his speech was delivered with a faintly apologetic air. When he ended he sat down abruptly and it was the turn of Josh's counsel.

'My Lord. Gentlemen of the jury. My learned friend for the prosecution spoke at length. Some of you may feel he spoke at *great* length. This is a barrister's privilege – indeed his duty – *when he presents a weak case.*

'I have no intention of taking up so much of your time. Neither is it necessary. Allow me only to remind you of the facts that have emerged.

'There was a disorder at Looe on the twenty-fourth of September, in this year eighteen hundred and forty-five. That is beyond dispute. But the magistrate who read the Riot Act, a cool, calm, observant citizen, did not see Joshua Retallick. Of course he didn't. Joshua Retallick was not there!

'Ah! you might say, but the soldiers saw him. Of course they did. All I dispute is *when* they saw him. I am not suggesting they are lying. Simply confused. They were excited, perhaps fearful – and who can blame them? They were greatly outnumbered. But what a pity they did not allow Joshua Retallick to talk to the crowd. Had he done so there might have been no blood shed on either side.

'He was himself wounded by a ball fired from the musket of a man who had reason to hate my client's family. About that I will say no more. Intelligent men can draw their own conclusions. But imagine, if you can, Joshua Retallic. Wounded and unarmed in the middle of a terrified crowd. Fired upon by muskets on the one side and hacked at by sabre-wielding dragoons on the other. In the *mêlée* is it surprising that he knocked a dragoon from his horse? He has told you in all honesty it was an accident. I venture to suggest he could in no way be blamed were it otherwise!

'He had gone to Looe in a vain attempt to prevent the miners from behaving foolishly. It was an action in keeping with his character. His concern for the miner was well known. It was not a secretive thing. His employer knew it, and came here to inform this court in no uncertain manner that Joshua Retallick was no criminal but a man and an engineer held in high esteem by colleagues and employer alike. William Carlyon confirmed Joshua Retallick's standing in the world of engineering. He also gave us an insight into the tragedies that have overtaken my client in the recent past – gave, if any was needed, a reason for him to have thrown himself wholeheartedly into the cause of the miner. In so doing might he not dull the sorrows that have cast such a heavy shadow over his own life?

'This is the man you are asked to judge now. A brilliant engineer. A man who cares for the miner. No stranger to personal tragedy. Is it feasible that he would act in a manner so completely out of character, as the prosecution would have you believe? No, gentlemen of the jury. I ask you that justice be done this day. That you allow Joshua Retallick to leave this court as a free man.'

The deep silence that followed his speech was broken by the judge.

'Thank you. If you've finished I will sum up the case for the benefit of the jury.'

He went through the case in a somewhat haphazard manner, missing out portions of the case he felt disinclined to emphasise, then he came out with a pronouncement that was more damning to Josh's case than anything that had gone before.

'You have heard character witnesses speak for these men, especially the prisoner Retallick. They were men who are used to speaking, men used to commanding. They did their duty as they saw it. The law of the land allows them that privilege. But what they have said about the prisoners before you does not constitute evidence. You must base your verdict on evidence such as that given you by those who were present at the sad events in Looe town that day, those who were involved in the violence that took place. You have to find the prisoners "guilty" or "not guilty" on that evidence alone. Was there a riotous assembly? There would appear to be little doubt of it. Were all the prisoners in the dock present during that riot? Once again you will have heard evidence that should answer the question beyond any reasonable doubt. Was there a treasonable or seditious conspiracy? You will take into consideration all that has been put to you on this point, paying particular attention to the places at which the accused normally worked and their distances from each other. I do not think it will be difficult to arrive at a just verdict. I trust your deliberations will not be overlong. We have a long list of cases yet to be heard and I wish to conclude these Assizes this week.'

Finishing his speech the judge rose, the prisoners were prodded to their feet and the judge bowed from the court as the jury filed off to their room.

The jury stayed out for an hour, during which time the prisoners were kept in the cells beneath the Assize court building.

Then, with a flurry of excitement, they were hustled back into the court-room to stand fidgeting in the dock as the jury returned to their places.

'Gentlemen of the jury. Have you reached a verdict on each charge?'

'We have,' replied the foreman of the jury.

'And how do you find the prisoners?'

The foreman of the jury cleared his throat noisily. 'On the charge of riotously assembling, we find the prisoners Retallick and Kittow "not guilty". All the others "guilty".'

There were some gasps from the public gallery, but the ushers were quick to silence them. The judge frowned. Whether it was due to the verdict or the noise in his court it was difficult to tell.

'And on the charge of being parties to a treasonable and seditious conspiracy?'

'We find all the prisoners "guilty".'

This time there was no denying the shouts of 'No! No!' from the public gallery.

'Silence!' This from the judge.

He looked at the men standing before him in the dock.

'I shall deal first of all with those of you found guilty of being part of a riotous assembly.' He read out the names of the miners. 'This is a most serious crime. One which cannot be tolerated in any civilised country. You are all grown men and fully responsible for your own acts. I sentence you to transportation for a period of seven years.'

There were groans and cries from their relatives.

'Now I come to the other charge on which you have been found guilty. Conspiring to commit treason. This is something which is aimed at the very foundations of the land. Allowed to go unchecked such actions can have only one outcome. In the land just across the English Channel we have seen it happen. I can think of no more serious crime. Those men I have just named will serve a further fourteen years' sentence of transportation, to run concurrently with their previous sentence.'

This provoked more cries from the public gallery. When the court ushers and some of the soldiers moved in to stop it there was some scuffling at the rear of the court-room.

'Take the men I have already sentenced down,' ordered the judge. As they were being escorted below, two persons were ejected from the public part of the court.

When all was quiet again the judge looked at Josh Retallick and John Kittow and his lips drew to a tight thin line.

'Kittow. You are, I feel, a man who has allowed himself to be led by his companion. Possibly you are more sinned against than a sinner. Nevertheless, I cannot overlook your part in this grave offence. I therefore sentence you to be transported for a period of fourteen years.'

John Kittow swayed in the dock and Josh gripped his arm in sympathy. For a few minutes he had thought there might be a chance of John Kittow escaping with a light sentence. Now, after the judge's words, he had no illusions of his own fate.

'For you, Joshua Retallick, I can find little to say in your favour. I consider your part in this disgraceful affair to be a major one. It is possible you are the actual instigator of this march upon a law-abiding town. You have been found guilty of a crime which a man of your intelligence could conceivably have carried through to its logical conclusion. The complete overthrow of organised government. Such an offence carries with it the death penalty. I will tell you quite openly that it was my determined intention to pass such a sentence upon you should you be found guilty. That I do not do so may be a mistake on my part. I may be failing in my duty. But the evidence of William Carlyon moved me, for even judges have emotions. He suggested the personal tragedies that have fallen upon you during this year may have impaired your judgement, that you may have done things not normally a part of your character. For these reasons alone I will exercise my mercy. Joshua Retallick, I sentence you to be transported for life.'

'That's not justice! He's an innocent man! You're sentencing an innocent man!'

Josh recognised Miriam's voice raised in loud protest before pandemonium broke loose in the court. He turned to see her but was hustled down to the cells below the court-room as soldiers, ushers and constables moved in upon the shouting, screaming, stamping crowd in the public gallery.

As furious fighting broke out in the public gallery Judge Denman called angrily for order. When it became increasingly apparent that his authority was being totally ignored he remained only long enough to ensure the Clerk understood his demand that the court be cleared. Until order was restored he would wait in the safety of his chambers.

Outside the court building Theophilus Strike, himself angry at what he considered to be a gross miscarriage of justice, watched the more vociferous objectors to the verdict being bodily hurled into the street from the steps of the court building.

When two soldiers appeared carrying Miriam between them

and taking advantage of her struggles to indulge in crude fondling, Strike stepped forward to her rescue.

Not stopping to argue with the mine-owner, the soldiers released Miriam and hurried back inside the building.

Miriam stood on the steps dishevelled and furious. The anger had nothing to do with her rough handling. It was her inability to do anything to reverse the monstrous judgement that had been passed on Josh.

'Young lady! Aren't you the Trago girl who married Preacher Thackeray?'

In her present mood Miriam might have said much to a man whose fellow mine-owners had helped to put Josh where he was now by their hatred of the Miners' Union, but she appreciated that Theophilus Strike had personally put more into trying to prove Josh's innocence than she had herself. She managed a simple 'Yes'.

'I thought I recognised you in the court-room.' At that moment he saw William Carlyon appear from a smaller door further along the court building. 'Will you wait here for me? I would like to have a talk with you.'

Waiting only for Miriam's nod of agreement, Theophilus Strike hurried away, and he and William Carlyon went into the now quiet Assize courts.

In the cells below the court John Kittow could only keep shaking his head, unable to believe they had really been found guilty. The other miners had received the punishment they had expected. In fact, there was little effective difference in their sentences. It was doubtful whether any of them would ever return to Cornwall.

Theophilus Strike and William Carlyon came into the cell and tried to reassure Josh.

'Try not to worry too much,' said the mine-owner. 'I'll do all in my power to help you. We'll lodge an immediate appeal.'

Josh shook his head. 'It would be a waste of your time and money. The judge had to do this. You must see that. My sentence is intended as a deterrent to others. I'm sorry about it only for my mother and father's sakes. For myself it's not such a great tragedy. There's very little here for me now. Perhaps I'll be able to make use of my engineering knowledge somewhere else.'

William Carlyon took his hand and there were tears in his eyes as he spoke.

'I find it difficult to express my feelings at seeing you in this situation, Josh. If only I could have helped more. You and Sarah. . . .'

His voice failed and he turned away.

'Nobody could have been of more help to me than you were, Mr Carlyon. I repaid your kindness by bringing tragedy into your life. Now, I would be grateful if you would both go before I start feeling too sorry for myself.'

'I'll do what I can for you,' said Theophilus Strike. 'Don't abandon hope yet. I have a great many friends to call upon. There will be justice for you yet. I'll be back with good news before very long.'

When Theophilus Strike parted company with William Carlyon outside the Assize courts he looked round for Miriam and found her waiting in a nearby doorway. Her anger had boiled away, leaving her cold and dispirited. It showed in the dejected way she stood, and the mine-owner took her arm and led her away along the street. Any resentment she might have had towards him was dispelled by his first words.

'I refuse to believe I see defeat in your face. No child of Moses Trago could possibly have heard of the word. Do you have a horse or carriage to take you home?'

Miriam shook her head.

'Good! I have a carriage at the inn along here. I'll give you a ride home and on the way we'll have a nice long talk together. You can tell me why you are so sure of Josh's innocence.'

William Thackeray was writing a letter seated at the desk in his study when the carriage drew up outside the chapel cottage. He watched in amazement as Theophilus Strike stepped from it and handed Miriam out. The mine-owner chatted seriously to her for a few minutes before climbing back inside the coach and waving the coachman on.

When Miriam entered the house her husband met her at the foot of the stairs in the hallway and demanded to know why she had been travelling in a carriage with the Sharptor mineowner.

'He brought me back from Bodmin Assizes. That's where all Josh's friends have been today – together with those of his enemies with the courage so to declare themselves.'

'And who won the day? Your Josh – or his "enemies"?'

'He was sentenced to transportation for life.' In spite of her promise to Theophilus Strike not to give up all hope, Miriam choked on the words.

'How tragic.' At that moment Miriam hated him fiercely for his sardonic hypocrisy. 'The Union will miss him. Poor Josh did much for the miners.'

'Then why weren't you in court to tell that to the judge? You could have helped him without too much risk to yourself.'

'I would have been pleased to help had it been possible. But who would have taken my word against all those witnesses who actually *saw* what went on?'

'You would never have gone into that court-room. You would have been far too worried that your part in the matter might come out. The conspiracy to involve Josh that you, Morwen and his officer were part of.'

'What an incredible suggestion, my dear. But in view of your distraught state I'll ignore it. I'm sure you'll feel better in the morning.'

His calm mocking air of superiority goaded her beyond discretion.

'You ignore it if you wish. I doubt if Theophilus Strike will.'

'Strike! You told him of your wild imaginings?'

It was the first time she had ever seen genuine fear on his face and it told her as much as words might have. William had deliberately involved Josh in the Looe riot.

'Far more than that, William. I gave him facts. I told him of the meetings between you and Morwen, gave him the date the officer came here with him to meet you.'

Now she called on her most calculated bluff. 'And I told him of the conversation I overheard between you and the officer.

Strike intends seeing that justice is done, William. You'll have little cause to celebrate your success.'

Miriam watched the battle between fear and anger being fought on William's face. The victory went to anger. Without any warning the preacher's arm swung in a wide arc and his hand struck her across the face.

It was the suddenness of it as much as the power behind the blow that caused her to stagger sideways against the wall.

'You Judas harlot! This is the thanks I get for taking you into my home and giving you my name. Don't you think I knew what had gone on between you and Josh before? Oh yes, I knew – but I forgave you. I was sure you'd put your wild ways behind you when I married you and gave you a place in decent society. I was wrong. You've lusted for Josh since the day of the wedding. You don't think I've been blind all these years? I've watched the way you looked at him – and he at you. Now you would sacrifice me for the sake of it. Give up all you have here – all that's decent – for someone who would be best forgotten.'

'I gave up all that was decent years ago, William Thackeray, for something I wish I could forget.'

She fingered the side of her face where he had struck. 'I did my best to make you a good wife, William. It wasn't always easy. You knew my feelings when you married me. I told you I never loved you, but I respected you and because of that I tried to be the wife you wanted and needed. I have no respect for you now and no amount of beating will change that. As for lusting after Josh – yes! It's quite true. And like the harlot you called me Josh could have had me whenever he wanted me. Here in your house, on the moor – anywhere. If he would take me now he could have me even in the filthiest prison cell.'

William Thackeray recoiled as though she had struck him.

'I'll be leaving your house in the morning, William. Daniel will go with me.'

William Thackeray looked as though he would argue, but Miriam was in full command of the situation now.

'I'd rather you didn't make things difficult for me, William. If I were to write a detailed letter to Conference you wouldn't remain in the Church one day more. Now, if you'll stand aside, I have things to do upstairs.'

For a moment Miriam thought he would hit her again and she threw up her head, braced for the blow.

It never came. William Thackeray turned away and scurried from the house.

As the door banged behind him Miriam's knees sagged and she caught at the hand-rail on the stairs. It was done. For months she had realised that the day had to come when she would tell William Thackeray she was leaving. She had dreaded the scene it would provoke. Now it was over. Now she could look forward, to face the hardships that lay ahead. Alone.

But Miriam had one last distressing meeting with her husband to come before the break became final.

It was after he returned from London and his long-awaited appearance before the Conference. It had been a stormy and unsatisfactory meeting for Preacher Thackeray and it showed in the way he slouched in the saddle riding into Henwood village in the last light of evening.

Miriam opened the door to him herself, leaving Daniel inside with her mother and John Trago.

William Thackeray had not anticipated a doorstep confrontation but he did his best to project some of his old authority.

'I've come for you and Daniel, Miriam.'

'Then you've had a wasted journey, William. We're not leaving here.'

'You're my wife, Miriam – and Daniel is my son. If necessary I'll seek recourse to the courts to have you return to me.'

'No, you wouldn't. You fear what I might say in a court-room.'

'I fear nothing that might be said here in Cornwall. It would not follow us to London, and that's where I've been ordered.'

'What I have to say would follow you to the grave, William Thackeray, so don't make me say it.'

'He'll not make you say or do anything.' John Trago pushed

past Miriam with no apologies for eavesdropping. Glaring down at the preacher he added, 'She'll stay here as long as she's a mind to and Daniel stays with her.'

'It's all right, Uncle John. I'm going nowhere with William. Go inside and leave this to me.' As John Trago hesitated she said, 'It will be all right. I promise.'

'If you say so.' He continued to glare at the preacher for a few more seconds. 'But if you need me, then you just shout. I'll be right out.'

Miriam waited until he had gone into the house, then pulled the door closed before turning back to her husband.

'There is nothing more to be said between us, William. Too much has happened to be undone. I'm not blaming you. I married you for too many wrong reasons and I must bear the shame of that. . . .'

'Miriam, forget what's gone. Let's try to start again. I have to return to London but that's not the end of the world. We can work together for others as we did here.'

'Did we? No, William. I *thought* that was what we were doing but it was all to build your reputation. The price of it was far too high. I don't want to see you again – ever. Your going to London will help to remove many of the difficulties for both of us.'

'But you can't have really thought about this. What will you do? And Daniel? You must consider him.'

'I have. I'll work on the mine for his food and clothes and he'll get a better education from me than any other boy about here.'

'Miriam, don't let our marriage end like this. I need you both. I love you. Come with me. . . .'

'There's nothing to be gained by this discussion. It can change nothing. Go, William. Please.'

'I beg you, Miriam. Don't let it end like this. For Daniel's sake if not mine. Where is he? Let me see him. Just once. . . .'

'No!' The cry was torn from her as William Thackeray's composure disintegrated before her eyes. Turning, Miriam fled into the house.

The understanding John Trago let her run upstairs to her

bedroom before he went outside to confront the now pathetic figure of Miriam's husband.

'Preacher, you've had your say and Miriam's told you what's in the future for her and the boy. Many years ago I told Josh Retallick to leave her be to pick up the pieces of her life again. I was telling the wrong man that day and many's the time I've regretted it. But I'm telling the right one now. Go away, Preacher. I don't want to see you here again.'

Miriam watched from the window as William Thackeray rode away. She despised him for what he had done, hated him for his betrayal of Josh. She should have been able to glean some satisfaction from his abject misery. Instead, it saddened her. The candle of greatness had burned within William Thackeray but it had not been strong enough to drive away the darkness of his jealousy and ambition.

Chapter Twenty-Seven

Josh knew nothing of the things that were going on in the world he had once known, and Theophilus Strike was unable to pay him his promised visit. For Josh never returned to Bodmin Jail.

It was normal for prisoners to spend a couple of weeks in jail before being sent to one of the convict hulks anchored off various ports and dockyards around the coast of Britain. There they would be held until a transport was available to take them to Australia. But the military authorities in Cornwall believed there would be demonstrations if the prisoners sentenced for the Looe riots were held at Bodmin. So, instead of accompanying the other prisoners back to prison, all eleven of them were taken in chains from the court to the prison hulk *Captivity* lying off the naval dockyard at Devonport. The hulk was the battered shell of an old Trafalgar man-of-war.

The communal cell at Bodmin Jail had been bad. The *Captivity* was an absolute nightmare. The boat carrying them out to it approached from down-wind. When they were still fifty yards from the dark shape the stench was enough to make a weak-stomached man puke.

The boat bumped heavily against the side of the hulk and the sentenced miners made their way precariously up a slippery gangway in the darkness, clanking heavily and wearing the broad-arrowed clothing hurriedly acquired at Bodmin.

Their names were ticked off in the uncertain light from a lantern by a jailer who peered shortsightedly at a list of names. They were then split into three groups, each man fettered by chains at his ankles and attached to the others by a second chain joining them at the waist.

It was now that Josh was parted from John Kittow. It happened so quickly that he never had time to say so much as 'Goodbye'. One minute, they were being pushed around by swearing jailers fixing and checking chains. The next, the groups were being pushed along the deck in the darkness, each bound for a separate hold.

He never saw John Kittow again. Three months to the day after he climbed aboard the *Captivity*, the ex-shift captain died, the victim of a typhoid outbreak on the foul hulk.

Josh and the three men with him were pushed down a steep wooden ladder into a dark and indescribably stinking hold. Here there were no lights. But all around were the sounds of men, moaning, snoring and coughing. The hatch cover was slammed shut and the miners left to grope their way forward in the blackness, seeking space for themselves. As they trod upon protesting, squirming bodies their progress across the crowded hold was measured by curses and oaths. They finally found a small space, and by easing out other prisoners they made room to sit down.

Sleep was out of the question. They were part of a walking nightmare. Only when the grey light of dawn filtered reluctantly through cracks between the rotting boards that secured port-holes did the miners realise the darkness had been kind to them. There was filth and scattered rubbish everywhere. Convicts lay chained together like wild beasts, their faces reflecting the same desperate likeness. Red-eyed and unshaven, they put gruff questions to the newcomers, resentful of their recent freedom. They asked about the world of which they were no longer a part. The half-real world that belonged to another lifetime. Here they were chained captive creatures, something to be shouted at, abused and baited.

If a man had to stay in the hulks for a long time he looked upon death as a friend and hurried to greet him. But not all were granted this release.

Men sentenced to short terms of transportation often spent the entire period on a prison hulk. There should have been employment for them in the royal dockyards, but since the end of the war with France the fleet had been allowed to dwindle in size. There was little for prisoners to do in the dockyards. All they could do was endure the reeking, floating garbage-ship and envy the men who shared their habitat only until a transport was available to take them to a new land.

For five ghastly weeks Josh was on the *Captivity*. Many times he feared for his very sanity. He learned to fight like the worst of his fellow-prisoners for the abominable food that was lowered to them twice daily. Once he gloated for a whole day when he was able to steal two handfuls of tasteless porridge instead of the usual one.

He had to learn to accept the most base instincts of the men around him during those five weeks of abject degradation.

Then one day the hatch cover was removed at an unusual hour and one of the jailers called his name. He kept calling until Josh, dragging his chained companions with him, reached the bottom of the ladder. The warder made him climb halfway up before he would come down to loose the chain attaching him to the others. The jailers were for the most part as ignorant and brutal as the prisoners in their care. One would not dare venture alone into a hold full of vengeful men who had little to lose by murdering a jailer.

With only the chains about his ankles, Josh awkwardly climbed the rest of the way. He breathed deep of salt air as he shuffled after the jailer to the cabin that was the hulk overseer's office.

The overseer looked at Josh in distaste as he stood before him, dirty and with five weeks' beard on his face.

'Your name Joshua Retallick?'

'Yes.'

The overseer sniffed. 'You're not my idea of a brilliant engineer.'

Josh's hopes took a sudden unreasonable climb. There must be some word from the outside world. How else would anyone on this prison hulk know that he was an engineer? To them he was just an anonymous dirty prisoner in an arrowed suit of clothing.

'I was an engineer,' he said.

'There'd better be no "was" about it,' said the overseer, waving a piece of paper at Josh. 'I've a letter here which says you're to be sent to Australia, going on a regular immigrant-ship with a warder on his way to Botany Bay with his family. Seems they've found copper in Australia and need someone out there in a hurry to install some engines. It's all in this letter that you'll take with you. It's written by William Carlyon, manager of Harvey's foundry at Hayle. Some of his engines are being sent on the ship with you. There's another letter from a Theophilus Strike, promising to pay all expenses incurred in your transfer. This isn't the right way to send a prisoner to the penal colonies, and I'll complain about it in my next report, but the release order has come from London, signed personally by a Minister of the Queen. Why he needs to bother himself with a convict I don't know.' He sniffed his disapproval. 'Your ship is lying at Falmouth. You'll get cleaned up and out of those stinking rags and then be taken there under escort. But remember, Retallick. You may be travelling on a ship with free men, but you'll still be a prisoner. Whatever your warder tells you – you do. Understand?'

'Yes.'

It was unbelievable. Josh was unable to accept the truth of it – not even when he stood on a cold jetty, shivering in a chill east wind, the stinking hulk a dark smudge on the river behind him. He had wanted to ask to see John Kittow before he left, but was terrified that if he stayed on the *Captivity* any longer a letter would arrive to countermand the previous one. And after five weeks in a prison hulk one did not ask for favours.

The two escorts travelling with him said very little along the way. When they stopped at an inn he went inside with them. Although handcuffed, he ate food such as he had not seen since leaving Bodmin Jail. He even shared ale with them and wondered at their generosity, until he realised that Theophilus Strike was footing the expenses bill.

As the coach rolled along the long straight road into Liskeard he could see the rounded hill that was Caradon Tor. He strained his eyes hoping to see Sharptor, but it was hidden from view by Caradon. Even so, for as long as it was visible he watched Caradon and its gorse-covered slopes.

They spent the night at Lostwithiel, the warders putting up at the coaching inn and Josh being lodged in the town's lock-up.

They set off at dawn and arrived at Falmouth in the early afternoon. The streets of the town were crowded with people, the shops and vendors doing a busy trade. During the time he had been in the hulk time and dates had meant nothing to Josh, but when he asked his escorts they told him it was the day before Christmas Eve.

Josh had one moment of uneasiness as they set off from the jetty in a small boat, suddenly afraid that the whole thing would turn out to be a cruel hoax and the promised ship another prison hulk. His mind was put at rest when the boat was brought up alongside a sailing vessel larger than any other he had seen. It was more than twice the size of the ore carriers that put into Looe and Hayle.

Once aboard he was escorted to a windowless cabin well down in the bowels of the ship. Here his escort handed him over to the warder who was to be his jailer on the long journey to Australia.

The warder was a very different man from the jailers on the hulk, or even in Bodmin Jail. Samuel Evans was a family man. He looked the part and spoke to Josh as a man would speak to another man, not as a warder to a prisoner.

'Hello, Joshua. I've heard a great deal about you and even had Mr Carlyon journey across from Hayle to speak with me about you. I can do nothing about the fact that you're a convicted prisoner. While we're in harbour you'll be locked in this cabin. Once we put to sea you are free to wander about the ship as though you were any other passenger. I had to ask permission from the ship's captain, of course, but he agreed. However, he reminded me that I'm responsible for your good behaviour. I've learned something about your background and the crime for which you stand convicted and I'm willing to take a chance on you. But I want your word not to attempt to escape or do anything to interfere with the running of this ship while you're at large. Do I have that assurance?'

'You have it – and my deep gratitude,' said Josh.

'Good, then it's settled. Mr Carlyon brought some clothes for you to wear on the voyage, but I fear you've lost some weight since he last set eyes on you. I'll have a meal sent down to you tonight. We should sail on the morning tide, bound for the new life that lies ahead for both of us. You're fortunate to have good and wealthy friends, Joshua. But if the hulk you've left is like those I've seen you'll already appreciate that.'

When the warder left, Josh sat down on the narrow bunk. He felt like weeping. There were still many problems ahead of him but the nightmare, the dreadful nightmare of the hulk, was over.

His cabin, though narrow and with no port-holes, was as good as most of the others on board, better than the accommodation provided for the emigrants travelling steerage.

The ship did not sail on the morning tide. More cargo arrived to delay its departure. It did not leave Falmouth until the late evening.

There was a fairly strong cold north-easterly wind blowing from the land. In no time at all the vessel was well out into the Channel.

When the evening meal was brought to the cabin, Warder Evans arrived with the clothes that William Carlyon had obtained for Josh. The two men talked as Josh ate his meal and changed into his new clothes. The following day was Christmas. The warder told Josh of the toys he had brought aboard for his children. There would, he said, be a service on the after-deck. He hoped to see Josh there. Then the warder took Josh on a tour of the boat, pointing out places he would need to know. Then, aware that Josh would want to savour his new-found freedom, the warder left him alone on the deck. From now until they arrived at their far destination, Josh would be treated as a free man.

It was dark on the deck, with only a few lanterns swinging in tiny islands of light around each gangway. It was bitterly cold too. The decks were deserted.

Josh made his way to the stern of the ship. From here he could see the light of the Lizard lighthouse in the distance. Along the coast of the scarcely discernible land that was Cornwall were the lights of small cottages. Occasionally, huddled beneath towering cliff shadows, a cluster of lights showed where a fishing village prepared for Christmas.

Josh felt a deep feeling of loneliness well up inside him. He thought of his parents in the cottage on the slopes of Sharptor, getting ready for a lonely Christmas without him. There were miners too whose companionship he had taken for granted. And Miriam. . . .

He shivered. It was cold. He could have gone below but he wanted to stay here with his thoughts, looking back until the land and the life he had known disappeared for ever.

He sensed rather than saw the figure that came up to stand close to him. Close, but back from the rail. He half-turned but could make out only a pale shadow that was a face.

'Josh, is that you?'

He could not believe it! It was not possible!

'Miriam!'

'Oh, Josh!' She was in his arms, holding him as though the north-east wind might tear him away from her.

But how . . . ? What . . . ? It couldn't be true! Now he was certain the whole thing was a dream. He would wake up soon and find himself back on the *Captivity*.

'What are you doing here?' he asked at last. Suddenly he stiffened. 'William! Is he here with you?'

'No, Josh. And don't let's mention him after tonight. William is in London.'

'And Daniel . . . ?'

'He's here on the ship with me – with us. Come down to my cabin and see him. I have a lovely cabin, Josh. Theophilus Strike got it for me.'

'Strike? What has he to do with you being here? Miriam, will you please tell me what's happening?'

She laughed at his bewilderment and squeezed his hand happily. 'I'll tell you the whole story when we get below. I'm surprised you didn't know I was on board.'

'How could I?'

'Well, I came down to your cabin last night and put my hand on the door. I heard you moving inside and I wanted to touch you so much I felt sure you would have heard my heart crying out for you.'

Her cabin, though not large, was very comfortable. It had two bunks, on the smaller of which Daniel lay sleeping.

Miriam took off her cloak and began to explain her presence on the ship.

'I was at your trial,' she began.

'I know. I heard you,' Josh smiled.

'Theophilus Strike heard me too. I was thrown out on to the street by the soldiers and he came outside to find me. He'd recognised me as Morwen's sister, he said, and had heard I was Preacher Thackeray's wife. In view of this he couldn't understand why I should be standing up in court risking arrest to shout your innocence. I told him what I believed had happened – that William and Morwen had arranged for you to become involved in whatever happened at Looe. He was very interested. He said he would cause some enquiries to be made. We discussed a lot of things when he gave me a ride home to St Cleer in his own coach.

'William saw me alighting from the coach and demanded to know what I was doing with Theophilus Strike. I told him exactly what I had told Mr Strike.'

'Wasn't that a foolish thing to do?'

Miriam shrugged. 'I was so angry it didn't matter. But it

mattered to William. He was so frightened he struck me. It was the first and last time. He also called me a lot of names and said things about you and me. They were a lot of very nasty lies but I let him believe they were true. The next morning I got some clothes together and took Daniel with me to Henwood to stay with my mother.

'William came there once to try to make me return with him, but he couldn't do much with Uncle John there and I simply refused to go. It was all very upsetting.'

'But that doesn't explain how you came to be here. . . .'

'Patience, Josh. You have the whole of a very long journey to learn about it.' But she continued with her story.

'Theophilus Strike wasn't able to obtain any further evidence and asked your father to tell me. Incidentally, both your father and mother know I'm here with you.'

'And they approve?'

'I think they were deeply shocked at first, but the day before I left Henwood your mother came to see me. She asked me to give you the love and blessing of both of them. She said she'd be happy knowing you would have me to look after you.'

'Poor Mum. But. . . .'

'I know – the story of why I'm here. . . . Two weeks ago Theophilus Strike came down to the village to speak to me again. He wanted to know what I intended doing with my future. He asked me a great many very personal questions. Then he told me the great news. He said William Carlyon had received an order for mine-engines from a man who had discovered copper ore in Australia. It was a rich find and many men in London were prepared to back the scheme. Parliament too were very interested. They thought it would help open the country up to settlers. Anyway, the man who had found the ore not only wanted the engines but also wanted a good engineer to set them up and keep them running. William Carlyon and Theophilus Strike discussed it and Theophilus Strike journeyed to London. When he returned he had a letter with him which said you could go to Australia and work the engines. It was as simple as that. I think Theophilus Strike has some very important friends in London. All that had to be done was for your fare to be paid in advance. Theophilus Strike did that immediately.'

'Thank you. That explains why I'm here! I am still no wiser about you being here too.'

'Well,' said Miriam, 'among the questions that Theophilus Strike asked me was why I was so concerned about you. I told him.'

'You told him what?'

'I told him I loved you, that I'd always loved you and that I only married William because in some horribly confused way it seemed that I was being loyal to my father.

'He asked me whether I believed it possible for you and I to make a new life together if we had the opportunity. I told him "Yes". That was all. He arranged for me to come as a passenger on this ship.'

'If I live to be a thousand I'll never be able to repay Theophilus Strike for all he's done for me,' said Josh. He looked at Miriam. 'You know I love you too, don't you?'

Miriam's answer was to cling to him fiercely.

Josh shook his head. 'God! What a mess we made of our lives. If only we'd accepted that as the only really important thing from the very beginning.'

'But we can start our new lives from now, can't we, Josh? I have a lot of money here for you. Theophilus Strike gave it to me. He said it's royalties on the patent of one of your inventions.'

'He's a good man,' said Josh. He suddenly held Miriam away from him. 'But what about Daniel? What will you tell him?'

'What is there to tell him, Josh? He's still little more than a baby. *You* are his father. You've known that all along. I told Theophilus Strike about that too. It's never been an easy thing to keep locked inside me.'

She looked at him with tears of happiness on her face. 'Now there's no need to keep anything locked away inside me. My passage was booked on this ship in the name of Mrs Retallick. We have our son Daniel Retallick with us and are heading to a new life together. Far away from the troubles of the old one.'

'You mustn't forget I'm still a convict, Miriam.'

She waved his words aside. 'Only in name. When we get there you'll find that Theophilus Strike has sorted everything out for you. You'll start work on the mine as their engineer. In a short time everybody will have forgotten you were ever a convict.'

Slipping away from him she took down a small tin box from a shelf by her bunk. Opening it she took out a piece of crumpled paper which she smoothed out and laid before him.

'Do you remember the day you wrote this for me?'

Written on the paper in a childish handwriting was a single word. 'Miriam.'

He nodded. 'I remember. You made me write it so you could copy it. Then you persuaded me to teach you to read and write.'

'Write it again, Josh.'

He looked at her in surprise and she knelt down beside him and brought his hand up to her lips. 'Just write "Miriam" for me again, as you did that day on the moor.'

Still not understanding he took the paper and a pencil from her and carefully wrote 'Miriam' on the paper. Beneath the name he had written many years before. When he had finished, Miriam took the paper from him and looked at it with as much pleasure as she had shown on that moorland day when they were children.

'That's beautiful, Josh. But now you have something far more important to teach me than how to read and write. You have to teach me how to live, to give without holding back, to be a complete person again and have so much happiness inside me it bubbles over and engulfs those I love. Will you do that, Josh? If I promise to give you my love for ever in exchange will you teach me all the things I want to know.'

'I can only teach you the things I know myself, Miriam.'

He trembled a little as he drew her, soft and yielding, to him.

'We'll both have to learn about them together.'